D0957307

Also by Omar Tyree

For the Love of Money
Sweet St. Louis
Single Mom
A Do Right Man
Flyy Girl

OMAR TYREE

JUST SAY NO!

A Novel

SIMON & SCHUSTER
New York • London • Toronto • Sydney

SIMON & SCHUSTER
Rockefeller Center
1230 Avenue of the Americas
New York, NY 10020

SIMON & SCHUSTER and colophon are
registered trademarks of Simon & Schuster, Inc.

For information about discounts for bulk purchases,
please contact Simon & Schuster Special Sales:
1-800-456-6798 or business@simonandschuster.com.

Designed by Deirdre C. Amthor
Manufactured in the United States of America

10   9   8   7

Library of Congress Cataloging-in-Publication Data
Tyree, Omar.
    Just say no! : a novel / Omar Tyree.
        p. cm.
    1. African-American musicians—Fiction. 2. Rhythm and
blues music—Fiction. 3. African-American men—Fiction.
4. Celebrities—Fiction. 5. Young men—Fiction. I. Title.
PS3570.Y59 J8 2001
813'.54—dc21   2001031174
ISBN 0-684-87293-5
ISBN 0-684-87294-3 (Pbk)

For all of the people out there
who love music
and the geniuses who create it

I knew a kid
who wanted it all:
the star treatment,
with the women,
the fame,
the fortune,
and all of the perks.

Then when he actually got it,
the indulgences,
they drove him crazy.

So now he just wants
to be normal again
and eat buttered popcorn.

—Omar Tyree,
"Be Careful What You Wish For"

VERSE 28

. . . *that's when he started talking crazy* . . .

"This is it, buddy, the Maryland Adult Well House."

I stopped daydreaming about the past and looked out of my cab window at a mental hospital of red brick and gray cement that was out in the middle of nowhere within the state of Maryland. There was nothing but factory buildings, trucks, and woods out there.

I pulled out a fifty-dollar bill to pay my taxi fare.

"That'll be thirty-five dollars."

I gave my driver the fifty and told him to keep the change.

His eyes lit up when the cash hit his hands. "Hey, thanks! You need a receipt?"

I thought about it and decided that I didn't. My visit was not about business anymore. It was personal. That's why I didn't order a limo. That would have been too high profile. I didn't want to make any news or score points in the media, I just wanted to see my boy.

I told the taxi driver, "Nah, you can keep the receipt, too."

He asked, "Well, ah, will you be needing a ride back out of here?"

He looked over my tailored style of dress and was probably sizing up my income.

"What business are you in?" he asked me.

I smiled at him. Big money makes people go out of their way for you nearly every time. I had gotten used to that.

I said, "The music business."

He nodded. "Oh, yeah? It's pretty good money there, isn't it?"

I answered, "Sometimes it is. But I have no idea how long I'm going to be here," I told him.

He pulled out a taxi receipt card and wrote his name and cell phone number on the back. "My name is John Beers. You can call me when you're ready, and I'll come back to get you. Hell, I'll even take a lunch break right now to make sure I'm available."

His name was John, how ironic. I took his card and nodded back to him. "I'll call you when I'm done."

"Okay, well, good luck with everything. And I hope everything works out all right."

I said, "Yeah, me too."

He asked, "Is this a friend, or a family member?"

I stopped and thought about it. "I guess you would have to say *both*."

He nodded again. "Well, if you need to talk about it on the way out, I'll listen."

I chuckled and said, "Thanks."

When the taxi drove off, I turned to face the tall gates that surrounded the mental hospital grounds. I took a deep breath. The Maryland Adult Well House was huge! It looked more like an institution to me, a big, clean-looking jail. I guess the name was meant to trick you into believing that it would be a warm and cozy place.

Well, here we go, I told myself.

I walked inside the hospital and took off my wool coat. I was immediately run through a security station.

"Take out your keys, coins, pens, cell phones, guns, knives, and any other foreign objects," the head security guard said to me. I assumed that he was joking about the "guns, knives, and any other foreign objects." The other guards laughed at his humor, but I just did what I was told. I was too tense to laugh or even smile at them. The situation wasn't funny to me.

After I walked through the metal detector, I was asked to show some identification. Then they collected my things and put them inside a numbered box. They gave me a palm-sized plastic chip with my box number on it and told me that I would have my things returned to me when I was ready to leave.

"Mr. Darin Harmon, thank you very much for making our job easier," the head security guard said to me.

Next they sent me over to the sign-in tables. An older woman there asked me what patient I was there to see.

I answered, "John Williams."

She said, "Oh, today is his birthday."

I was finally able to smile a little. I said, "Yeah, the big two-seven."

She logged John's name in the book and asked me for mine.

"Darin Harmon."

One of the security guards looked over at me. He was a young black man around my age. I guess he had heard of me.

The woman logged my name next to John's and wrote in the time.

After that, the young security guard smiled and nodded in my direction. He said, "John's on the North Wing. I'll take him over."

The woman at the sign-in table double-checked my name and nodded to me with her own smile. I was taking everything in like it was slow motion. I had never been to a mental hospital before.

"Have a good visit," the woman told me.

I walked over to the security guard, who led me down a long, light blue painted hallway toward an elevator. I counted every blotch and blemish in the shiny black floor as we walked. I had no idea what to expect in that place, and my mind wouldn't let me rest from the anxiety that I felt.

The security guard said, "It's fucked up what happened to John, man. I *love* that boy's music! You can just tell that he sings from the heart, that old-school shit. But it just seems like a lot of good musicians are crazy in some way.

"What do you think?" he asked me. "You been around a lot of musicians, right?"

He *did* know who I was.

Instead of answering his question, I asked him, "What about athletes? Some of these young athletes are out there too." *I could have been a professional athlete*, I thought to myself.

The guy smiled it off. He said, "Yeah, some of them athletes are crazy. But not like *musicians*. We get more patients in here *hearing* shit in their heads than anything else, man. Some of these patients in here walk around all day long talking about, 'You hear that?! You hear that?!'

"Hear what? You know what I'm saying?" he asked me. "And then you get them types that's always seeing visions and shit. Talking about, 'I saw it last night. It floated up to me like an angel sent from God.'"

I began to smile. This guy was obviously making light of the situation in there.

He said, "Don't get me wrong, man, I'm not making fun of your boy, I'm just saying that musicians are out there. I mean, they make great music and all, but then they go crazy with them drugs and shit. And it's just sad, man. So I'm glad that I'm only a fan."

I admit, I didn't have much to say in defense of John, or of the many musicians I knew of. I had my own thoughts to deal with at the moment. I wasn't up for a debate.

We made it up to the fifth floor of the hospital on the elevator.

"Well, good luck with your boy John, man," the security guard told me. I said, "Thanks," and walked out.

As soon as I walked out of the elevator and into the waiting room, I heard screams and shouts coming from inside the security-glass windows.

"*NO-O-O!* No I *didn't* have it! No I *DIDN'T!*"

"Calm down, and take a seat," a nurse was telling one of the patients, who was getting out of hand. "I know you didn't have it."

That didn't set my nerves at ease in that place at *all*!

I waited there to be introduced to John's doctor. A black man who looked more like a college professor, tall, poised, and stately, walked out. He was real calm, too. Maybe mental doctors were best that way, because their patients were not calm. Not in the *least*! I was getting nervous just looking at some of the patients there. Fresh images from the movie *12 Monkeys* came to mind, along with images from every other mental hospital movie I had seen. I never imagined that I would ever have to *visit* one of them.

The doctor shook my hand and said, "Hello, Mr. Harmon. I'm Dr. Harold Benjamin, and I handle the case of your friend John Williams during his stay here."

I nodded to him and asked, "How's he doing?" I can't lie about it. I felt much more comfortable talking about John's mental state with a black doctor as opposed to a white one. Call me prejudiced, but it seemed as if many white men considered us to be a little bit crazy anyway, as if *they* were all sane. There were *plenty* of white men in that hospital. I didn't lose sight of that.

Dr. Benjamin took a breath and said, "John suffers from what's known as a bipolar disorder, or better known as manic-depression, where he fluctuates from extreme high states of energy and optimism to extreme low forms of inactive depression, and all in a rather short amount of time."

I nodded. I knew exactly what the doctor was talking about. I said, "And he makes it seem like the low stuff is more important. Or at least it seems to occupy more of his time."

The doctor nodded back to me. "Exactly. So, on this first visit I would advise you to just listen to him and hear what he has to say. And as I continue to monitor John's progress, I'll let you know what more you can do to help. But right now is not the time to go in there and offer him the world. Just remain a passive listener. Your presence alone, and a listening ear, will do wonders for him."

I said, "Yeah, because if you try to preach to him or criticize him, he'll just get mad at you."

Dr. Benjamin said, "Exactly." Then he smiled and added, "And remember to tell him happy birthday."

I said, "Oh, of course."

The doctor led me to a small private room with a large unbreakable window on the door. My lifelong boy, John "Loverboy" Williams, was waiting for me there with a big grin on his face.

When we walked in, Dr. Benjamin asked him, "John, you recognize this gentleman?"

John squinted his eyes as he looked me over.

He said, "Nah, who dat, doc? I don't know him."

Dr. Benjamin laughed and said, "Well, I guess you two need to get reacquainted then."

I finally cracked a smile, recognizing John's humorous touch. That boy knew who I was! I went to take a seat in the comfortable chair that was set for me and waited for whatever.

John looked at me as if I had pissed him off already. He said, "Come give me a damn hug, man! What's wrong with you?!"

I stood back up and walked over to hug him before I sat back down. I mean, I wasn't scared of him or anything. John couldn't hurt me. I was just apprehensive about *everything*! What would we say? How would we start? How would it go? I was just filled with questions.

As soon as the doctor left the room, I felt boxed in. I had been warning John for years that he needed to reevaluate the things that he did in his life. What more did I have to say? So I planned to do just what the doctor had told me. Listen.

I said, "Happy birthday, man," to get it out of the way up front. I didn't want to have him think that I had forgotten about it. They were all sure reminding me of that in there. As if I didn't know my boy's birthday. Or maybe John had *told them* to do that to cover his own bases. I had come to see him that day on purpose, because it *was* his birthday.

John smiled from across a small table and said, "Yeah, it's February eighth, two thousand and one, ain't it? I'm twenty-seven. But it seem like I'm *fifty*, man."

He was wearing a loose beige shirt-and-pants outfit and he needed a haircut and a shave. His hair was not that long, it just wasn't as short and groomed as he had kept it during the prime of his career. His eyes, however, were clear and steady, the best shape that I had seen them in in years. His skin looked great too, a strong bronzed brown, like he had been out in the sun eating healthy tropical fruits.

He said, "So, what up, man? How's your wife and kids? I see you looking all spiffy with the suit and tie on. I guess you're an all-the-way producer now. You got the limo waiting for you out front?"

He was full of energy. I shook my head and told him that I had no limo.

"I didn't need all of that. I just wanted to see you, man."

"Well, what's the suit and tie for then? You didn't need that to see me either. You could have worn jeans and a T-shirt."

I said, "I don't wear jeans and T-shirts like that."

He broke up laughing and said, "Aw, you big-time for real on me now. It's all about the imagery, right, D? The star representation imagery. Yeah, so how's the family, man? What's up?"

John had never been so boisterous in his life.

I remained calm and answered, "We're all fine, we're just thinking about you."

"Thinking about me as far as what?"

I said, "Just hoping to see you and tell you that we love you, man."

I wanted to be real careful with my choice of words.

John nodded, at ease with my response. "I'm doing good, man. I just made a stupid mistake, that's all."

He was referring to the assault and the dropped attempted-murder charges that he had been sentenced for. But since money can buy the best lawyers, and celebrity status tended to sway the American courtrooms, his lawyers worked out a deal for John to spend an undetermined time in a mental hospital for his manic-depressive behavior, followed by a year of drug probation and three hundred hours of community service. However, truth be told, if my boy wasn't *the* John "Loverboy" Williams, he more than likely would have landed himself in jail.

I just listened to him like the doctor told me to without passing judgment.

John said, "I'm just saying, man. I mean, what you was telling me years ago, to just say no to all of that star shit. I mean, that shit may sound easy, man, but . . . *it ain't that simple*, man," he stressed to me.

He said, "I wish it was that simple. *God*, how I wish it was! Like, a girl come up to my room with no panties or bra on, looking good and shit, and be ready to do whatever I want with her, and I just say, 'Nah, I don't want no pussy. Not tonight.'

"I mean, yeah, I was able to do that sometimes, man, but not after *every fuckin' show*! What if I wanted some real bad that night, man? What was I supposed to do, jerk myself off, while I got *thousands* of girls waiting outside for me?

"Man, go 'head with that! You was even into it when we first started touring," he said to me.

He smiled and added, "You still remember how you met your wife, right? Don't you go catching no amnesia on me, D. I mean, I know that was painful for *all* of us, man, but that's a part of your history with your wife. Don't erase a chapter. Tell the damn truth!"

I smiled back at him and shook my head as I loosened up a bit. No way in the *world* could I forget how I met my wife or the hurt that John had caused us.

I told him, "I didn't forget."

"Yeah, I *know* you didn't. It wasn't that long ago. You only twenty-six until your birthday comes up on April twenty-eighth," he reminded me. I figured that he *did* tell the hospital to remind me of his birthday, after he quoted mine. He was showing me that his memory *and* our friendship were both still tight.

He laughed and said, "You gotta be like *forty*-something before you start catching amnesia, especially since you don't smoke weed no more. And then when your kids are teenagers, you gon' start lying to them, saying that you met their mother in the church choir."

I couldn't help myself. I started laughing.

John said, "But she changed you, man. She changed you. Then you went back to church on me. And I'm saying, man, I just wish that *I* could. But like I said before, that crazy stuff be calling me. *All* of it: the weed, the girls, the limos, the Jacuzzis, all that shit, D. You was there. You was just stronger than me, man. You was *always* stronger than me."

After he said that, he began to slow down and go silent on me. I didn't know exactly what that meant, but I'd rather he kept talking.

I said, "You had the talent, man. They weren't screaming *my* name. So the temptation was never the same for me. You can't even compare the two. People don't even know who the manager is unless they read the fine print somewhere. And any manager who gets bigger than the talent he represents will end up being an ineffective manager."

I added, "*You're* the *Loverboy*, not me."

John started to smile again.

He said, "You ever think about just getting together a bunch of girls and weed, just for old times' sake, man, and just having a big party?"

Instinctively I said, "Man, that's *crazy*! I'm a happily married man now." It was too late to catch myself. I didn't want John to blow up at me, but how could I talk to him for any length of time when his mind would ramble onto craziness so often and so easily?

He nodded and said, "See, that's just what I'm talking about. It's like a drug for me, man, *all* of it, and I gotta have it. I *gotta* have it!"

He said, "Remember when I started fucking around with hookers? I was just paranoid of so many girls trying to set me up and ruin my career, man.

Then their boyfriends and shit were after me. That's how our boy got shot and killed out in L.A., man."

I nodded to him disgustedly, but it was all true.

He said, "Well, I had to stop dealing with them hookers, man, because they were so out of touch with the world that they didn't even know who the hell I was. I was used to girls screaming my name and shit when I did them. '*Loverboy!* I love you! I LOVE YOU! *LOVERBOY!*'

"But them damn hookers, man, they wasn't even saying shit."

I broke up laughing again. John was out of his mind, but he had always told the truth, and it seemed that the fame game had hooked him forever. I didn't even know if there was a cure for that.

He said, "And the weed, man. I mean, to be honest with you, D, I wish that I had never started that shit, man. Because once you really start smoking it like I was, it's like you damned if you do and you damned if you don't.

"I just needed it to feel normal after a while. Imagine that, man," he told me. "You gotta smoke fuckin' weed to feel *normal*. And then the money? Man, you know I never sweated no money. It seemed like the money just got me in trouble with people, man. I mean, you know how them rappers talk about wanting the money and not the fame. Man, fuck that! I think I want more of the *fame* and not the money. At least I'm famous for being *me*. But when you famous just for having money, they don't respect you, admire you, want to be you or *nothing*. They just want a damn payday. And that shit is the *worse*."

I sat there and listened to everything John was saying, but I still couldn't feel the pressure of walking in his shoes. It's one thing to walk *beside* a superstar, but it's entirely different to *be* the superstar. In a nutshell, that's what my boy was telling me. I would never be able to understand it. Not really. I could only imagine it.

He said, "Man, I even thought about turning that shit into a song, D. Check this out: '*Just say no-o-o, no-o-o, no-o-oh . . . no-o-o, no-o-o, no-o-oh. Just say no-o-o, no-o-o, no-o-oh . . . no-o-o, no-o-o, no-o-oh.*'"

He stopped and asked me, "You think the people would like that, man? I don't have no lyrics yet, that's just the hook. But what do you think? You think the people would like that, or what?"

When John first started with his music, he could care less about what people thought *before* he had completed it. And he never called anything a hook. He called it a chorus or the title. That was just how much the music game had changed him over the years. He went from a music purist to a music popularist. He had to struggle with what would be more popular with the fans, versus what was true to his heart.

I just smiled and nodded to him. I said, "Why don't you work on the lyrics for me, and I'll tell you once you finish with the lyrics. All right?"

He nodded back to me and said, "All right. That's on, that's *on!*" Then he started bobbing his head to an imaginary beat and yelled, "You *feel me*?! *What if I die tonight?!*"

I shook my head. John was going back into his legends-must-die mold. It was his theory that living too long after your prime only made you a mortal, and to be *immortal* you had to die in the prime time of your life and career work. The soldier of his philosophy was the one and only musical fatalist, Tupac Shakur.

I said, "John, man, don't start that stuff again. Barry White is a *legend*, and *he's* still living. Isaac Hayes. Smokey Robinson. Gamble and Huff. Stevie Wonder . . ."

John ignored me and went on quoting more of Tupac's anthems: "'*I smoke a blunt to keep the pa-a-ain out, and if I wasn't high I'd probably try to blow my bra-a-ains out!*'"

In desperation, I kicked some legendary lyrics that I knew of: "'*You got these har-r-r-rd rocks, with har-r-r-rd times, in har-r-r-rd play-ces . . . wouldn't you like to go-o-o . . . go awaaay, go AWAAAY, go awaaay!*'"

John stopped cold and smiled. "Yo, who wrote that shit right there, man?" he asked me sarcastically.

I answered, "The same bad brother who wrote: '*If we shared the moon tonight / we could talk of lessons learned / say the things we've yearned to say / and fade our pains away.*'"

John chuckled for a minute, then he turned stone serious on me.

He said, "You think that shit is something to die for, man, some love song shit? The people don't hear that shit no more, man. So if the soul of rhythm and blues is dead, then tell me this, D . . . is love something to die for in the year two thousand and one?"

He said, "They don't feel that love shit no more. They listen to your shit for a week and a half, and then they move on to the next nigga's shit."

John had me on the spot.

I said, "Love is something to *live* for, man. And if you really *love* something, then you would want to *live* to see it every day; see it grow, develop, and prosper, just like when God created the sun, the moon, the earth, and everything in it. *Us* even! Darin Harmon and John Williams, boys for life, through all of the stress and the strife, regardless of how other people feel about it, man."

John just started laughing and talking loud again. He said, "Aw, don't tell me D trying to get *po-etic* on me! What are you thinking about, writing songs, too, now? Whatchu gon' write, man, some gospel? *Sanctified* music?!"

I said, "I thought about writing a few things. Yeah."

John started laughing louder. "Aw, man, you want me to write something for you? I could write something for you. You just tell me what you want."

I said, "First, I want you to finish the lyrics to your *own* song. And then I could check that out the next time I come to see you."

He said, "When?"

He had me on the spot again.

I said, "Ah . . . I guess whenever you want me to, man. I'm your boy, right?"

He said, "Tomorrow then."

I was shocked by his decisive answer for a second, but then I smiled it off. John had always been decisive when it came to crafting his music. He just knew right off the bat what he wanted.

I nodded my head and said, "All right, then. I'll come back and see you tomorrow."

He stood up from his seat and said, "Yeah, and I'll have that song ready for you then. *Just Say No!* with an exclamation point at the end, because you gotta *mean* that shit when you say it. '*NO!* I don't want no drugs! *NO!* I don't want no pussy! *NO!* I don't want no money!' All those things will just lead you to the devil anyway. Ain't that right, D? You a church boy again, now. *I* just ain't."

How could I keep a straight face with this guy? I laughed hard even when I didn't want to.

I slipped up at the mouth again and asked him, "Have you talked to your mom lately?" It *was* his birthday.

He said, "Nah. But she knows where I am just like you do. If she wants to talk to me, she knows where to find me." With that he sat back down again.

John's relationship with his mother had never really been a good one. She suffocated him when he listened to her, and she flat out ignored him when he didn't. I still couldn't quite understand her, but I figured that their silence with each other had gone on long enough.

I asked him, "You want me to call her up?"

John looked at me with spite in his eyes. "Call her up for what, man?"

"You know, to tell her that you're all right. That I sat down and talked to you."

He stood up again and said, "Man, *fuck that!* She knows how to dial seven numbers! Or ten! Or eleven! *Whatever, man!* She knows how to get in touch with me. She don't care about me anyway. She probably the one that made all this crazy shit happen to me. She probably had a voodoo doll, sticking needles in my head just 'cause I ain't stay in the church with her.

"She a hypocrite, man! That's all!" he shouted. "She a big *hypocrite*! Acting like *she* all perfect!"

Bringing up his mother was the wrong thing to do. So I quickly changed the subject to something that I knew he would love. Music.

I asked him, "So, you really think you can have this song ready for me by tomorrow?"

He looked and studied my face for a second. *"Just Say No!?* Hell yeah! *Tomorrow!"*

I grinned and nodded to him. I said, "You know I love you, right, man? You my boy. You like a brother to me."

I just felt that it was the perfect time to say it. It felt right.

John eased up and smiled. "I love you, too, man. Now stand up and give your boy another hug before you leave."

I stood up and hugged him a second time.

He backed away and said, "All right then, I'll see you tomorrow."

I didn't know that I was ready to leave yet, but John was already walking toward the door.

I shrugged it off. "All right then, I'll see you tomorrow."

When Dr. Benjamin met back up with us, he asked John his question again.

"So, do you recognize this gentleman yet?"

John said, "Yeah! This my boy D, from back Charlotte, North Cacalack! We came up in the church together. Christ Universal on the east side. And D is a big-time producer now. He got a wife and kids, a big house, and *everything*!"

He said, "I'm proud of him, doc. *Real* proud! He's even coming back to see me tomorrow. Is that all right with you, doc?"

Dr. Benjamin nodded and grinned. "That's good."

John said, "Yeah, that's what I thought, too. So I'll see you tomorrow then, D. And I'll have that song ready for you."

John broke away from us all energized, as if he were about to start writing his new song, *Just Say No!*, immediately. In the doctor's presence, I felt kind of embarrassed by it. I didn't know if challenging John to write a new song in his present state of mind was a good thing to do.

I looked to Dr. Benjamin and said, "I kind of asked him to write the lyrics to a new song that he brought up to me. Was that a good thing to do? Or not?"

The doctor chuckled at my hesitancy.

He said, "Has John ever had problems writing music before?"

I answered, "Never. But the music itself was never a problem for him. It was all of the stuff that went on *surrounding* the music that drove him . . ." I stopped myself and said, "You know . . ."

"Crazy?" Dr. Benjamin filled in for me.

I smiled and had to look away, ashamed of myself. John was my *boy*! How could I think about him and talk about him like that?

Dr. Benjamin said, "You can say it. We're all cracked up in our own little ways. But most of us find ways to hold all of the pieces together, and that's what we're going to attempt to do with John. So a challenge of music will be good for him."

He said, "But what do you think overall about your first visit with him?"

I said, "Well, you know, he seems a little loud, but he knows what he's saying and everything. I mean, I understand him."

The doctor looked at me funny. "How did you think he would be?"

I was at a loss for words. I said, "I got no idea, doc. I mean, I've never been in . . . you know, a place like this before."

Dr. Benjamin started to laugh and tossed a reassuring arm around my shoulder. "John's in good hands here, Darin. He's not ready to jump out of any windows or anything. He's doing fine."

I said, "Well, I guess since he's not around all of the hype and the temptations out there on the street, that he's actually better off to be in here for a while. I mean, that's what I thought about it when they first sent him here."

The doctor nodded. He said, "We all need a moment of sanctuary every once in a while, don't we?"

"Yeah."

He said, "Okay. So, I guess I'll be seeing you tomorrow," and shook my hand as he walked me back to the elevator.

On my way, I asked him, "Hey, doc, does this manic depression run in the family or anything?"

He nodded and said, "Yes it does. There have been many hereditary studies done on depression. Why, is his father or mother manic?"

I said, "I don't know about his father, but *definitely* his mother. I think somebody needs to check *her* out too." I was serious!

Dr. Benjamin was willing to talk to me in detail about it, but I was anxious to get out of there and prepare myself to come back the next day. He noticed my rush and let me go.

He said, "I'll see you tomorrow."

I got on the elevator and thought, *I don't even have a change of clothes with me.* But it wasn't as if I couldn't go out and buy some. A pair of blue jeans and a T-shirt, just for John.

As soon as I made it off the elevator on the main floor, the young security guard was there to walk me back to the entrance.

He asked me, "So what happened up there?"

I tried to pull his leg. I said, "John got upset with me and slammed a chair into the window. After that they had to tie him down and restrain him."

The security guard just smiled at me.

He said, "Man, he ain't *that* damn crazy. I've been around him since he's been here. He just needs some mental rest, man, that's all. He just needs to rest his mind a minute."

I nodded. That was a good way of looking at it. John needed to rest his mind a bit. I just didn't know if him trying to rest his mind inside a mental hospital where there were many others who were *not* resting *theirs* was the right place for him to do it.

I made it back outside after retrieving my things from security. I immediately called my wife on my cell phone to tell her that I'd be staying in Maryland for at least another day with John.

"Well, how is he doing?" she asked me.

I paused and thought about it. "He's fine for now, but how about I tell you more after I see him tomorrow? And I'll just use today's visit as a breaking-the-ice meeting or something, I don't know."

I needed to see, hear, and feel more from John before I could come to any conclusions on anything. At the back of my mind, I really wanted to see if he could still write any good songs, too. I couldn't help it. I was curious about that.

My wife agreed to talk about it later, and I told her that I'd call her again later on to talk to our children. Then I called up my friendly taxi driver, John Beers. I thought that maybe he could drive me to a nice hotel. Then again, maybe I needed to stay at a *not*-so-nice hotel so that I could remember where John and I had started from. It had been a long road for us. *Real* long!

I remember when / he was just a momma's boy . . .

Churches were everywhere down south, and in Charlotte, North Carolina, the church was still the cornerstone of the community. I thought the whole world went to church every Sunday just like my family did. That was where I first laid eyes on John Williams, at Christ Universal Baptist, long before he became Loverboy. I say "laid eyes on" because I used to watch John in church before I even met him. He was a quiet and calm, well-mannered kid with a mother who was all over him. I mean, she would brush his hair, lotion his face, wipe crust out of his eyes with her fingers, fix his shirt and tie, retie his shoes. *Everything*, and right there in church in front of everybody. I had two older brothers and one younger sister, and my brothers taught me that letting your mom do too much for you was a bad thing. So it became a fight for my mother to even *touch* me, let alone do it in church in front of *hundreds* of people. And there was John, who didn't have any brothers or sisters, with a mother who practically re-dressed him right there in the pews every Sunday.

I was really disturbed by this boy's situation. Every single Sunday, I felt an urge to walk over to him and lay down the law of boyhood. "Man, don't let your mom baby you in church like that. You fix your own face and hair and clothes." But his mom guarded over him like a cop or something. She barely let him out of her sight. I always thought that she looked too *old* to be his mother. Call me mean if you want, but she looked more like his *grandmother* to me.

I couldn't concentrate on anything else in church while John's mother continued to baby him. John and I were not even in grade school at the time, but my brothers were, and they had taught me plenty about standing my ground against Mom. Against Dad? Well, we weren't that crazy. Not *yet*

anyway. I even used to wonder where John's dad was. Maybe his dad could
have saved him.

I finally got a chance to get close to John when we were both pushed
into the children's choir at age six. John had already been taking piano
lessons and whatnot, but I wanted no part of that choir, so I would act up in
rehearsal.

"Darin Harmon, I will tell your *mother* on you, young man! Do you hear
me?!" Sister Dennis, the choir director, would shout at nearly every rehearsal at me.

I mumbled, "Tell her. I don't want to be in no choir anyway." I always
made sure to do my back talk somewhere near John, so that he could see a
good example of how to be defiant. It never worked, though. That boy
would smile and go right back to doing what he was told. That only made
me more persistent in acting up, until I was finally kicked out of the choir.
That's when John's mother forbade him to play with me. I had no proof of
that at the time, but it sure seemed like it. Half of the time, he wouldn't
even look in my direction in church. Once that happened, I considered the
boy a lost cause. I began to ignore him too. He wasn't my type of kid anyway. So I moved on and started playing sports, and John continued to be a
choir-singing, piano-playing momma's boy.

Years later, we ended up in the same class in elementary school, and the
game was on again. I was pressed to turn John Williams into a rebel. Every
day there was a new kid picking on him about his neat clothes, his hair, his
quietness. *Everything!* They were all jealous of how peaceful John seemed.
Every once in a while he got frustrated about it, but he never would strike
back at anyone. So I had to bail him out of trouble nearly every day. You
would think that I was his bodyguard or something.

One day while we were out in the school yard, I just asked him, "Don't
you want to protect yourself, man? God!"

He said, "I don't know how to fight."

"Put up your hands. I'll show you."

My brothers had taught me most of *my* moves.

As soon as John put up his hands, I popped him straight in the mouth.

He said, "Ow," and grabbed his lip.

That boy had no idea how to block or to avoid a punch.

I said, "You were supposed to block it, man."

"Block it, how?"

"You smack it down with your hand." I said, "All right. You try to hit me.
I'll show you."

John swung the weakest punch in the world, and I smacked his arm so hard that he lost his balance and nearly fell to the ground.

This girl named Mary said, "I can fight better than *that*. Even my little *brother* can."

I said, "So what?" and went back to teaching John how to fight. Or trying to.

Mary said, "Let *me* fight him."

"Girl, get away from here," I told her. "This is boy stuff."

John said, "My mother told me never to hit girls anyway."

Mary said, "What if they hit *you* first?"

Come to think about it, Mary was a tomboy back then. Big-time!

"I'll just walk away," John answered her.

I frowned at him and said, "Man, you walk away too much already. You need to learn how to stand up and fight."

Mary sucked her teeth and said, "That boy can't beat a fly. Look at how skinny he is."

I said, "Aw, girl, everybody don't eat chicken and biscuits every night like you do."

Me and John started laughing, and instead of Mary going after me, she went right after him with a flurry of slaps and punches. She was all over him before I could grab her. When I finally grabbed her off of him, she punched me straight in my eye. And that did it! I don't even remember where I hit her because I could barely see, but I swung three hard punches that connected.

The next thing I knew, Mary was wailing like a big baby and holding her face in her hands. When the teachers arrived, they pulled her hands down, and Mary's face was smeared with blood from a busted nose. I knew I was in trouble then. You didn't have to tell me a *thing*. I would have a whipping coming, and all because of John.

I got suspended for three days, my dad whipped my behind that night, and *then* my parents made me sit on my sore rear at the kitchen table and explain what happened. You would think they would ask me what happened *before* they whipped me. Not in *my* household. When you cut up, you got your whipping *first, then* you could explain. I didn't understand the purpose of explaining things *after* getting a whipping already. What was the use? But that was old-school Southern discipline for you. You were *not* getting away with anything. And talking wouldn't save you.

I said, "I was just teaching John how to fight, and—"

"John who?" my mother asked me.

"John Williams from church."

My mother frowned and said, "That boy needs to learn how to handle his *own* business. What are you doing fighting for him? And fighting a *girl* at that! You want some boy to punch *your sister* in the nose?"

"No, but—"

"Then what happened?" my father asked me.

"She just jumped in and started talking about—"

"'*She*' *who?*" my mother asked me.

"Mary. She just jumped in saying how skinny John was and—"

"That's when you hauled off and punched her in the nose?" my father said.

"No, she starting hitting him and—"

"Did he hit her first?" my mother asked me.

That was the other thing I couldn't understand. My parents would ask you to explain it to them, but then they would barely let you finish a sentence.

I said, "No, he didn't hit her. She just started—"

My father raised his voice and said, "You mean to tell me that this girl just went and hit this boy for no reason?"

I nodded my head and said, "Yeah, so I just—"

"That boy need to get out the house more anyway," my mother said to my father.

"Mmm hmm, that boy need to go somewhere and do *something,*" my father responded. "But *Darin* don't need to be around that boy no more, I know *that.*"

He said, "So then what happened?"

"I tried to get Mary off of him and that's when she punched me in my eye."

"And then you went and punched Mary in her nose?" my mother asked me.

"I didn't know I had punched her in her nose."

My father raised his voice again. "You didn't *know* you punched her in the nose?"

"I had my eyes closed. I couldn't see."

My father said, "Well, you see this *belt* right here don't you?"

I looked up again at his big brown leather belt and my heart started racing. "Yes."

He asked, "Was it worth it?"

I was confused for a second. "Hunh?"

"Yes!" my mother yelled at me. "You answer your father with a yes or a no."

"Yes," I said back.

"Oh, so it *was* worth it? So you want some more then," my father said to me.

"NO! I meant yes, because I didn't understand you—"

"You didn't understand what?"

"Your question?"

I don't know what was worse sometimes, the whipping or the torture of explaining why you had gotten into trouble in the first place. First they would whip your body, and then they would whip your mind. All the while, your behind still felt as if it was on fire.

My father said, "Well, you know you ain't seeing no outside until next week, right?"

I nodded and dropped my head. "Yes."

"Boy, you look at me when I'm talking to you!"

I heard my father's belt jingle and I looked up in a hurry and said, "YES, I know!"

"You know what?"

"That I'm on punishment."

"Good. Now go to your room and finish up your homework."

That was the best part of getting punished. Freedom to go to your room. But then you had to do your homework while laying on your stomach. That was usually when my older brothers would laugh at me. It was all fair, though, because I laughed at them when they got theirs.

I cursed John Williams with every word I could think of that night. I told myself that I would leave that momma's boy alone for the rest of my life. I meant it, too. Or at least I *thought* I did.

My mom came to my room later on and told me to come with her. I stood up and wondered what else was coming to me. Hadn't I paid enough?

My mother led me to the kitchen telephone, where my father waited with the receiver in his hand.

He said, "Here he is," and handed the phone to me.

"Hello," I answered.

"Hi, Darin. This is Sister Williams, John's mother. He told me what happened to you two at school today, and I just wanted him to call you up so that he could apologize to you."

I didn't even know that they had our phone number. I guess it was pretty easy to get, though. We went to the same church, lived in the same neighborhood, knew a lot of the same people, and John and I went to the same school together.

Anyway, his mother let him on the telephone.

He said, "Sorry, Darin. I didn't mean to get you in trouble."

I nodded my head, not really wanting to say anything. "Okay." That was about it. We didn't have much else to say to each other, so I handed the phone back to my dad.

"You wait right here," he told me.

My mother talked to Sister Williams about John playing sports and becoming more active around the neighborhood, but I knew that he had his music lessons to go to, so his mother turned my mother's suggestions down. Then my mother dropped the bomb on me.

"Well, I don't see any reason why these two boys can't be friends," she said.

My father and I both looked at each other. I didn't want to be friends with that boy anymore. My mother went right ahead, talking about us hanging out and doing things together, like she was a matchmaker or something.

When she hung up, my father asked, "Do you think this is a good idea?"

My mother said, "Well, this boy obviously needs somebody to be friends with."

"Yeah, but why does it have to be with *our* boy?"

I didn't say it, but I was thinking, *Yeah, why me?*

My mother answered, "Well, Darin has already gotten into trouble with him, so he might as well get into *good* things with him too. And John's not a bad boy, he just needs someone his age to be around."

My father looked at me and said, "Yeah, well, your *friend* John told us that you called Mary fat. Now how come you didn't tell us that?"

My heart started racing again.

My mother laughed and said, "He didn't say that. He said he joked about her eating chicken and biscuits every night."

"Yeah, well how come Darin didn't tell us that?"

Because y'all didn't let me! I thought to myself in a panic while keeping one eye on my father's belt. No way did I want to be *John's* friend. That boy would tell everything. That's why my mother was trying to match us up. She wanted a stool pigeon around to keep me in check. I was reading her game plan.

I said, "I didn't get a chance to tell you."

My father gave me an evil eye. He raised his finger to me and said, "Darin, don't you ever *think*, in your *life*, that you're *ever* gonna get away with anything. You hear me? Because even if I don't find out about it *now*, it's *always* gonna come back to haunt you later."

• • •

When I saw John at school again, he had brought me some homemade cake to share at lunchtime. I didn't want to take it from him, but it smelled good. It tasted good too. His mother could really bake a good cake!

I asked him, "Your mother cooked this?"

He smiled and said, "Yeah."

I got greedy and asked him if he would bring me some more the next day. I figured that if he was going to be my friend, then he would have to pay me for it. It was wrong, but I was a kid, you know. So John promised to bring me good food whenever I wanted him to until his mother got wise to what was going on.

She called my mother again and asked her if she packed enough food and goodies for me to eat at lunch at school.

"Darin!" my mother hollered at me.

"Yes."

"Come here, boy!"

I walked up to her while she was still on the phone with Sister Williams.

"Have you been asking John to bring you extra food to school every day?"

I said, "Umm . . . well, they have homemade cake and pies and stuff."

"Boy, you need to be *ashamed* of yourself!" my mother yelled at me. "I'll make sure that he won't do it again," she told John's mother.

When I saw John at school again, I wanted to wring his neck, but I figured that he'd tell on me for that, too. So I just asked him why he told, you know, like in a regular conversation.

He said, "Well, she kept asking me if you had enough to eat at lunchtime. And, you know, I said, sometimes. But I told her that you liked her cooking. And at first she would smile about it. But then she started getting mad."

I thought about it and laughed. It wasn't John's fault. His mother had just caught on to me.

I said, "John, do you like your mother, man?" I was ready to play a game of devil's advocate.

He said, "Yeah, I love her."

"But don't she get on your nerves sometimes?"

He said, "Don't yours sometimes?"

I looked at him and broke up laughing again. John wasn't as dumb as I thought he was. In fact, John had been a straight-A student, and I wasn't. I guess I just thought that I could push him around because he wasn't rough-and-tumble like I was.

"Do you like that music stuff?" I asked him. By that time I had been in-volved in organized football, basketball, soccer, *and* baseball.

John nodded and said, "Yeah, sometimes."

"But not all the time, right?"

He smiled at me. "Do you like playing sports all the time?"

I said, "Yeah," and I meant it. I could play sports all day long, and with-out a care in the world.

John said, "Well, me too then."

"You don't even know how to play sports."

He said, "I'm talking about playing music."

"So you could play the piano all day long?" I asked him. I didn't believe that. No way! You would probably get a cramp in your hands and in your butt from sitting down for so long.

He said, "I play more than just the piano."

"What else do you play?"

"The trumpet, the clarinet, the drums, and I want to learn how to play the saxophone."

I started looking at him in awe. I had no idea he could play all of those instruments. But so what? He still couldn't play any sports. And he couldn't fight.

I said, "Yeah, that music stuff ain't gon' get you nowhere. You just gon' sing in the church choir all your life. You not gon' be no Michael Jackson or nothin'."

He said, "And you're not gonna be Dr. J."

"I don't want to be Dr. J," I told him. "I like football more anyway. I'll be like Herschel Walker."

"Well, he runs track."

I said, "So? I can run track. I'm fast."

"You're not *that* fast."

"I'm faster than *you*."

We went on and on like real friends, and people got the message not to mess with John Williams anymore, because he was my new schoolboy.

. . . and then they called him Loverboy . . .

By the time we made it to high school, John and I were both exceptional at what we liked to do. I was a lightning fast football player who made sure to take track as seriously as I did football, and John was practically a musical whiz kid.

We both went to Garinger High School, which wasn't exactly the best place in the world academically, athletically, *or* musically. Nevertheless, Garinger ended up being the *perfect* place for us. By our sophomore year, we were both on our way up. Fast!

On our sorry football team, I was already being primed as a tailback on offense and a standout cornerback on defense, and John was already one of the major players in the school band. Had we gone to more challenging high schools, neither one of us could have stepped into such prime positions so early. Many high school kids didn't receive their chance to shine until their junior or senior year, but we were shining sophomores. It was like it was meant to be, for *both* of us. And then the girls came.

It wasn't as if John and I didn't have our puppy love crushes and whatnot on certain girls before high school, but you know, high school love is the more serious stuff. *I* wasn't that serious about high school love, though. With me being a star athlete in two sports, I had plenty of girls to choose from. Too many choices can easily make a guy hesitant about getting too serious with just one, so I had several different girls, and when one got too serious I would move on to the next one. But John had a whole different approach to it. He would check out a lot of different girls that he was interested in, and then he would narrow down his choices to just one. Which, in my opinion, didn't make much sense, unless you were thinking about getting married soon. I guess my older brothers had trained me on that too. Never put all of your marbles in one jar.

John had a serious thing for this one girl named Carneta James. She was definitely a heartache. Carneta could keep a young guy up at night. Young *and* old. She had smooth, dark brown skin like mine, with big baby-doll eyes, a nice body, and she was *always* dressed to impress. When she spoke to people, she would hypnotize them with this slow delivery. "Hi . . . how are you doing? Are you going to the game . . . today?" She had a way of timing out her words that made you wait for her to finish her sentences. You felt as if you were special when she spoke to you, like her slow words were very important pieces of wisdom or something.

I had to give it to John, he sure did pick well. The only problem was, Carneta wasn't really interested in him. You know, John was the kind of guy who was every girl's best friend, but not their first date.

Anyway, John kept a crush on this girl Carneta even though she had boyfriends. They were never serious boyfriends, though, because she had high standards. It seemed that these guys were always doing something to mess it up. And there was my boy John, patiently waiting for his turn.

Midway through our junior year, I took it upon myself to ask Carneta what she thought about him.

She smiled and said, "What . . . John Williams? He's nice . . . I guess."

I said, "You *guess*. I mean, what do you think about him? Would you talk to him?"

As soon as I asked her that, I wanted to take it back. It just sounded too forward.

She said, "Would I talk to him . . . God . . . no. I don't think so. Unt unh."

Then I got desperate because I knew I had screwed things up for him.

"Why not? He's a nice guy. He looks nice. He dresses nice. Everybody knows him from the band and everything. I mean, don't you like music? John can play all kinds of music for you."

She just laughed at me and started shaking her head.

"Umm . . . you know, he's nice and all . . . but he's kind of skinny."

I got mad and said, "Is that all you think about, is muscles and stuff? It's other stuff that's important for a guy."

She started laughing more and couldn't even talk.

I said, "Well, all right then," and walked away from her.

I felt guilty for the rest of that day. I had put John on the spot with Carneta without him even knowing about it. I even went out of my way to walk him home after school to see how he was feeling about things. If the word got back around to him that I asked her about him, and that she had turned him down, I wanted to be right there to apologize. I mean, Carneta was the only girl that he wanted, and I really felt bad about that. I felt like I should have just kept my mouth closed and let John continue to dream about her.

"What's up, John?" I asked him after school. "How you feeling today, man?"

He said, "I'm all right. Why?"

"Oh, no reason. I'm just, you know, asking."

He said, "I guess track season is coming up soon, right?"

I smiled. "Yeah. I'll be faster this year. It's time to kick dust and take names, boy."

John just nodded. He didn't have much to say that day. I started feeling as if someone had told him that I talked to Carneta already, and he was just holding back on me.

I asked, "So what's up with Carneta, man? You still like her?"

My heart was racing like I was at the start blocks at a track meet. I just didn't want to be responsible for messing things up with my boy. But it was too late for that. It was only a matter of time before he knew what I did. I was even thinking about telling Carneta not to say anything, but it was too late for that too. I should have told her that immediately instead of walking away from her.

John looked me in my eyes and said, "Yeah, man. She's great."

I was thinking, *Man, this boy's in love with her.*

I said, "You don't know how great she is. You barely talk to her."

"Yeah, but when I do, I can just feel it. She's great, man."

I said, "Aw, man, she makes everybody feel that way. That's just how she talks."

"What, you talked to her?"

I said, "She's in some of my classes."

John panicked and said, "You didn't tell her that I like her, did you?"

I was stuck. Then I just decided to stop all of the mousing around.

I said, "You haven't told her yourself? You *need* to."

He said, "I want to work my way up to it. You just don't come out and go after girls like her. You have to ease your way into it. That's why she stopped going with other guys. They didn't have any finesse. But I understand where she's coming from, man. She's a winner. That's all. You just have to prepare for her."

John even had philosophies about this girl.

I shook my head and said, "You giving her *way* too much credit, man."

He said, "You don't think she deserves it?"

"I'm just saying, man, a girl is a girl. She gon' like what she likes."

John looked at me and said, "Why, you know what she likes?"

I lied and said, "No, but I don't think it's as complicated as *you* make it." Carneta had only talked to athletes from what I knew.

"What do you think, she only likes athletes?" John asked me.

I froze. He was reading my mind.

I said, "Well, what if she does?"

"She don't. She just *thinks* that she does."

I couldn't help it at that point. I started laughing. John had been shot by Cupid's arrow for real.

I said, "And what makes you so sure about that?"

"I can just tell, man. She's confused right now. Most girls are."

I said, "Oh, so now you're an expert on girls. You ain't even had none yet, but now you're an expert."

I had gotten some already. I knew too many girls not to find one or two who were ready and willing.

John said, "What does that have to do with anything? I just don't want to take advantage of someone that I may not feel for. If I'm going to do anything with a girl, then I want it to be all the way. Not like *some* people I know."

He was trying to make me feel guilty about doing girls for the heck of it. What can I say? I was an early starter. And girls liked jocks.

I said. "All right, man. Do what makes you feel good," and I left him alone about it.

On the next day of school, Carneta had a short girlfriend named Denene who walked up to me with some news to tell.

She said, "You were trying to hook your friend John up with my girl Carneta yesterday?" She was smiling as if something was funny.

I lied and said, "No," just to spite her.

"You wasn't?"

"No. I don't know what she talking about. I was just asking her questions."

Denene said, "Well, you *know* who she likes, right?"

I said, "Is it John?"

"No."

"Well, I don't care then."

I wasn't pressed for playing guessing games with Carneta and her friends.

Denene said, "Well, she told me to tell you anyway."

"Tell me what?"

"That she likes number twenty-five on the varsity football team."

Number twenty-five on varsity football was *me*! I was shocked!

I said, "Yeah, right. She don't like guys for that long anyway." I was trying to blow it off. I used John's explanation and said, "She's just confused, that's all. She don't know what she want."

Denene said, "Well, all I know is that she's been liking you for a while now."

I said, "She had boyfriends all this time. How she gon' like *me*?"

"She was just trying to make you jealous. That's why she never went with any of them for long."

I couldn't believe it! That girl was crazy. She *had* to be!

I said, "Nah, go 'head. You lyin', girl. You lyin'."

"No I'm *not* either. You can go ask her for yourself."

I had no idea what to do. I thought about just ignoring it. But I was curious. I had to at least be curious. It's only human.

I caught up with Carneta again and got nervous. I wasn't nervous with her before, but all of a sudden I was.

I said, "What's up?" to see what she had to say to me.

She said, "You tell me."

"Tell you what?"

"Well . . . I don't know. What do you want to tell me?"

I shook my head and smiled. I said, "You don't know what you want. You're confused."

She said, "No . . . I'm *not* confused."

I said, "Well, what do you want from me then?" My heart was beating as fast as I don't know what. Half of me was flattered that she liked me, but the other half was mad that she didn't like my boy John.

Carneta said, "Tell me what . . . *you* want."

Right there she had me. I was hypnotized.

I said, "Umm . . . what about my boy John?"

"What about him?"

"Umm . . . I don't know, man. This just don't feel right. That's my boy."

She said, "Well, would you rather take . . . *him* to the movies . . . and share ice cream with *him*?"

This girl had me in for it. I didn't know what to say.

I backed down and said, "You just gon' drop me like you did all the rest of 'em. Why should I talk to you?" Carneta was a virgin at that. A *hard* one!

The other guys had spread the word on it. They could barely get a good-bye peck on the lips from her.

She came back at me and said, "I know what I want . . . and when I want it."

Boy, I started feeling like jelly in her hands. I had to get away from there. I said, "Whatever," and walked away from her.

I was a wreck for the rest of that school day. I kept wondering how long it would take for John to find out. Then I wondered if Carneta and I could really be a couple. I even wondered if I was going to wake up in my bedroom and realize that I was dreaming soon. But I never did.

Instead, I had another news report from Denene.

"Carneta said for me to tell you that you can't worry about your friend, you just gotta go for you."

I said, "What? She didn't say that. Go 'head, girl."

Denene said, "Okay," and walked away from me.

When I met up with John, he nearly had tears in his eyes, but he was holding them back.

He said, "You can have her, man. Go 'head, you can have her."

"Aw, man, I don't want that girl. I don't know what's wrong with her. Like you said yesterday, John, she's confused, man. She's confused."

He said, "I talked to her."

"And what she say?" I asked him.

"She said she likes you."

It felt like a dagger went through my heart. I was Dracula, sucking John's blood out and leaving him to wander around like a loveless zombie in eternal pain.

I said, "Aw, man," and just shook my head. I didn't know what else to do or say.

He asked me, "Do you like her?"

I said, "I wasn't really paying her no attention, man. I don't know. I mean, you know . . ."

I didn't have a real answer for him.

John said, "See, you don't even like her. She's great, man. She's just great. Are you gonna go for it?" he asked me.

He was all ripped up. I could see it in his face and hear it in his voice.

He said, "She's the only girl that I want, and she likes you. You can have her, though, man. You can have her. At least it's *you* that she likes."

I said, "Nah, man. Stop it. I'm not gon' do that."

John looked at me and asked, "Why, though? Why don't she give me a chance? Doesn't she realize how much I like her? I *only* like her."

Man, he was *tripping*! I said, "John, she's not the only girl in the *world*, man. Get over it!"

That boy was taking it bad, like a Mike Tyson punch to the dome.

From that point on, John got really heavy into his music, and not just the instrumentals, but into phrasing lyrics and stuff. I mean, we were still friends and all, but when it came to his music, he would cut me and everything else out. I guess it was the only thing that made him feel in control of his life. He would get in these little mood swings, and then go right back to his private music. He even became the bandleader at school, creating new songs for them.

As far as Carneta James was concerned, I blew her off for a few days until she finally asked me what was up.

I said, "You hurt my boy's feelings, man. We tight like that. I can't do that to him."

She said, "Even . . . if I wanted to come over your house?"

"Come over my house for what?"

The joyride was over with for me. Carneta was still attractive and everything, she just seemed ugly in spirit to make my boy feel so low. I wasn't taking any part of that, especially since I wasn't feeling her in the first place.

She said, "You know . . . what do guys like to do?"

"You don't even do that," I told her. I figured that she was bluffing for effect.

"That's because . . . I didn't want to with nobody . . . yet."

I blew her off again and said, "Whatever. You can tell me anything you want. That don't mean you gon' do it." I didn't feel like playing any more games with that girl. Seeing was believing, and I couldn't see a *thing* from her! Carneta was all talk and no action.

John heard about me dissing her, and he seemed relieved by it. He wasn't really happy, but at least he wasn't sad anymore. So we went back to our business of being friends. But John began to think about his music on the next level. The falling-out over Carneta started it, because before then, he was basically doing cover tunes and not really creating his own. He started having all of these little melodies on his mind and pieces of songs that he claimed he was never finished working on.

A couple of times I asked him, "Hey, man, where did you get that from? Let me hear it."

But he would always smile and say, "It's not finished yet."

After a while, I got tired of hearing that "not finished yet" excuse, so I learned to ignore him.

• • •

Before senior year kicked in, John and I started taking SAT prep courses. I actually needed it more than he did. John was good at taking tests. He didn't have straight A's anymore, but he had enough to keep an A average. I had a low B average and I needed a high enough SAT score to qualify for the football scholarships that I began to be offered.

While studying for the SATs at John's house, I noticed that he and his mother listened to a bunch of older music over there. I guess I hadn't paid much attention to it before, because there was always music on at the Williams house. I took it all for granted. But then I noticed that John's mom was always listening to the older music from guys like Nat King Cole, Sam Cooke, Otis Redding, Marvin Gaye, and plenty of gospel. I didn't know who a lot of the women singers were, but they were mostly singing gospel, jazz, or the blues; Billie Holiday, Sarah Vaughan, Nina Simone, and Aretha Franklin types. From hanging around with John so much, I *had* to know a little something about music.

I asked John about his father before, and he always said that his mother didn't discuss it. But listening to all of that music in his house made me wonder if his father was a musician as well.

John said, "I don't know."

I said, "Do you ever wonder about it?"

He said, "Of course."

"Well, what does your mom say when you ask her about him?"

He said, "I don't ask her much."

I just shook my head. Sometimes I couldn't believe how simplistic John and his mother could be. They both seemed so lifeless. Music really filled the void for them. I decided to just let my boy be himself.

Thanks to John, I scored 980 on my SATs, which was good enough to qualify for Division 1 sports. But the school that I really wanted to go to, Florida State, had already signed all of their scholarships. I thought about going to Georgia or North Carolina, but both of those schools were only mildly interested in me. Meanwhile, John was being courted by Florida A&M and North Carolina A&T for scholarships in music and band. He had more schools looking at him, but his mother wanted him to attend a black college, and my mom got to talking about the same thing. Both of my brothers attended black schools, but neither one of them were on athletic scholarships. I wanted to play football for a big-time white school that got major television exposure, the kind of school that would give me the best opportunity to go pro, which was definitely my career goal.

However, when push came to shove, North Carolina A&T was ready for me to sign actual paperwork, where a lot of the major white schools were not. Since John was already being recruited by A&T, and my parents would not allow me to turn them down, we both signed letters of intent for the Aggies. Overall, I guess we had done all right for ourselves.

On our senior prom, we ended up going with two girls from our church. It was all nice and nothing extra. And Carneta James went on the prom with a fat stomach and a bloated face. She was five months pregnant by some football player from North Mecklenburg High School. I guess she *wasn't* bluffing me. I could have been the one to break her in.

"Do you still think she's so great?" I asked John at our senior prom.

He smiled at me and said, "We all have our moments of greatness, man. And then they fade away like smoke. And smoke rises into the wind and blows away like threads of hay."

I looked at him and started laughing. John had a way with words sometimes.

At North Carolina A&T, John had more free time than ever, and he devoted most of it to his music. I was busy trying my best to become a standout football player again. But at the college level, and on a pretty good team, there were plenty of guys who were just as fast and as good as I was. These players were older, bulkier, and had more experience in big games. During all of my years at Garinger High School, we won an average of three out of ten games a season. That was another reason why I wasn't recruited by many of the larger white colleges. My high school just wasn't competitive enough to gauge my talent.

Anyway, at A&T I stayed in the athletic dorm at Cooper Hall, right across from where John stayed, in Scott. I spent a lot of my time hanging out with the other athletes, and John spent a lot of his time at Frazier Hall, where he took his music classes. I had a run-down car to get around in, and John had a Korg keyboard machine with a stand and an amplifier. I still had my picks with a few freshmen girls who were interested, and John was still in the friend zone. Every time we talked, I discussed what was going on with the football team, and he talked about music. But it was all cool to us because we had been that way for years. We would always be involved in different things. We just accepted each other that way.

By our sophomore year in college, neither one of us was standing out like we did in high school. Even with our scholarships, I was just another football player and John was just another music major who played in the band. Not to say that we were not having a good time at A&T, we just were not as special as we were back in high school.

John came to me real excited one day and said, "Hey, D, I'm gonna perform in that talent show at Harrison Auditorium next week for homecoming."

I started laughing.

I asked him, "What are you gonna play, your keyboard? That keyboard is *phat*, man."

A Korg keyboard was top-notch equipment, and John barely let that thing out of his sight. It was his mother's graduation present to him. It cost a couple thousand dollars! But since John had gotten a scholarship to school, Sister Williams could afford to buy it for him. Brand spanking new!

John said, "I'm gonna sing with it too."

I was stunned for a second. I said, "Seriously?"

He said, "Yeah."

"So, you finally finished a song?"

He smiled at me. "Aw, man, that was back in high school. I've finished plenty of songs now."

I hadn't heard any. But I hadn't asked either. I said, "What's the name of it?"

"*May I.* It's old-school," he told me.

"Old-school, meaning what? Whose song is it?"

He said, "It's my song, it just don't have no chorus. It's all verse. Because you know, at talent shows, man, you not gon' have time to do much real singing anyway. So I got something just for this occasion."

Up to that point, John had been singing in the choir, playing music in church, in the band, and all of that, but he had never done any *solo* singing.

I said, "John, you're talking about singing *solo*, man? Where this come from all of a sudden?"

He said, "I've never been in a group."

He had a point. John was extra private with his music.

I asked him, "Are you sure about this, man?" I was curious, but I had to know that he wasn't pulling my leg or something.

He said, "Yeah, I'm serious, man. I've done a lot of thinking about this. But I need you to be up there with me."

That was the hook. I said, "Wait a minute. You need me up there to do what?"

He smiled. "I just need your support, man."

"On the *stage*? I mean, I'm not dancing or nothing, am I?"

He started laughing and said, "Nah. It's not even that kind of song. It's what they call a standard. An old-school love song. I just need you to sit with my keyboard and feel the music."

I said, "You want me to sit with the keyboard? But aren't you gonna be playing it?"

"Nah. I'm gon' program it to play itself. So all you have to do is start it for me."

I grinned and said, "Aw, go 'head, man. I'm just supposed to *sit* there? How is that gonna look?"

"You can act like you're playing it," he told me.

I looked at him and frowned. "Come on, man, everybody know I don't play no music."

"I'm saying, I just need you there for me, man. Just for this first time, D."

"First time?" He must have had plans that I didn't know of.

He said, "Yeah, 'cause I might be nervous. But after you get past the first time, you just keep singing after that."

I said, "So, where do you plan to go with this?"

John stopped for a minute. He shrugged his shoulders and said, "I don't know, man. I just want to try this out and see."

I smiled and agreed to it. "All right. I'll do it . . . just don't fuck up, though."

After I said that, jokingly, I wanted to take it back. I didn't want to make him nervous before we even got up there. But John surprised me.

He said, "Don't worry about me, man. I got this. This is music."

I couldn't wait! My boy John was going to sing solo at Harrison Auditorium at NC A&T. The talent show had ten performers lined up, and each person had four minutes to do their thing. Ironically, John was number seven at first, but then this one girl complained so bad about being number six that he swapped with her. It was the fall semester homecoming celebration, sophomore year, 1993, and John and I were both nineteen.

I asked, "Why you switch places with that girl, man? You had the lucky number."

He said, "It takes more than luck. Either you got it or you don't. It don't matter when you sing. You just have to control the crowd."

It was as if John had become superconfident overnight. I mean, he was always good at his music, he just never had that I-*know*-I'm-good attitude until that night. And this was *before* he sang his first song. I guess he had done a lot of practicing.

So I stepped back and said, "Well, go 'head wit' ya' bad self."

He smiled at me and kept his cool. John was six foot one, 165 pounds. He was dressed in a cream-and-gold shiny disco shirt with a wide collar. He wore brown slacks and shoes. His hair was cut sharp and neat at a low height, and he had trimmed his long sideburns to the same length as his hair. He looked poised and ready, so I just waited with him from backstage.

When they got to number five, John was still cool, but *I* was getting nervous. I started thinking, *What if he go out here and they don't like this old-school song?* I mean, I was used to John's classical music flavor because I was his boy, but everyone else was listening to new-school hip-hop tracks, including performer number five, a girl with a feel-good beat that had everybody bouncing.

Then it was John's turn. I carried out his keyboard and stand, and started setting things up. John walked over and got the keyboard ready for his music.

I said, "Is everything all right, man?" I was just asking to be sure.

He said, "Yeah. You just press this button after I look over at you."

I looked out from the stage and thought, *Shit!* As with most homecoming events, the auditorium was jam-packed, and a lot of my teammates from the football team were there. I felt like *I* was the one who was about to sing. I was nervous as hell, and all I had to do was press a damn button!

They introduced him: "Next up, from Charlotte, North Carolina, is John Williams. He's going to sing us a ballad called *May I.*"

When the girl said "ballad," I was ready to fall out. That word just didn't sound good with the young, restless crowd that was there. A ballad would have sounded great at a church event or at the Apollo Theater in New York, but this was *college* in the gangsta rap era. Most college students were busy rocking Dr. Dre and Snoop, Luke Campbell, Pete Rock and C. L. Smooth, and Outkast. I thought my boy John was barking up the wrong tree. But then again, Jodeci was still going strong, and they were from near us in Charlotte. Boyz II Men, from Philly, were holding it down too, and there were a few A&T graduates in the audience who could appreciate singing, so I tried to remain calm and let my boy do his thing.

John walked up to the microphone and just held it for a minute while the crowd quieted down.

I smiled a little. He wasn't going to rush. Then he looked over at me and I pressed the start button. John looked back out at the crowd with the microphone in hand and started to sing:

Ma-a-ay I-I-I hol-l-ld your-r-r han-an-an-n-nd.

The music came on from the keyboard and fell right into place with a piano:

Bloomp, bloomp, bloomp, bloomp, bloomp, bloomp, bloomp-bloomp-bloomp . . .
May I-I-I-I wal-l-lk with you-u-u-u
Bloomp, bloomp, bloomp, bloomp, bloomp, bloomp, bloomp-bloomp-bloomp . . .
May I-I-I tal-l-lk to you-uw-wu-u-u
There are so-o-o many thin-n-ngs—that—we-e-e could do.

Then the piano started changing up while John sang his second verse:

If I held your han-an-an-n-nd
Bloomp, bloomp-bloomp, bloomp-bloomp . . .
I'd take you-u-u far-r-r awa-a-ay
Bloomp, BLOOMP-BLOOMP, bloomp-bloomp . . .
So-o-o much I would sa-a-ay tooo you-u-u-u
Bloomp, bloomp-bloomp, BLOOMP BLOOMP . . .
If I-I-I could ha-a-ave your ti-i-ime.

I looked out at the audience for a minute, and John had the whole place in suspended animation. I mean, you couldn't hear *nothing* in that place! I was thinking, *Oh shit, he's doing it, with some* old-school *flavor!* I cracked a smile while John kept singing to this banging piano groove:

Ma-a-ay I-I-I kiss your lips—with mi-i-ine
Imagine how the star-r-rs would shy-i-ahine-i-ine
If we take our wal-l-lk at ni-i-ight
Where we-e-e could sha-a-are the moon.

If we-e-e sha-a-ared the moon to-ni-i-ight
We could tal-l-lk of less-sons learn-n-ned
Say the things we-e-eve yearn-n-ned to sa-a-ay
And fa-a-ade our pa-a-ains away.

May I touch your skin-n-n—with mi-i-ine
Make our bod-dies in-ter-twy-i-ahine-i-ine.

All of a sudden, Big Joe, a huge senior on the football team, yelled out from the back of the auditorium, "SING THAT SHIT, LOVER-BOOOY!

SING THAT SHIT!" People started breaking out laughing, but John kept right on going, unfazed by it:

You would be my gir-r-rl for li-i-i-ife.

Then the piano music stopped for his fade-out:

And I-I-I-I-I—would be-e-e-e-e—your ma-a-an.

I swear to *God*! They went *crazy* in that place! They gave my boy a standing ovation, even the people who just came out to laugh and bullshit. Man, I was proud as hell! That was MY BOY up there! YEEAAHH!

And Big Joe was screaming at the top of his lungs, "GIVE LOVERBOY THE TROPHY! WE DON'T EVEN NEED TO HEAR NOTHING ELSE! JUST GIVE IT TO HIM NOW!"

... *his singing filled him up with joy ...*

The last act to perform in the talent show at A&T that night was a four-member rap group from East Orange and Newark, New Jersey. They used this old-school Run-DMC beat and rocked the crowd out of this world! It was an all-out party in the aisles! And each rapper had his own tight flow to the beat:

BOOM, BOOM-TAT, BOOOM-BOOOM, TAT
BOOM, BOOM-TAT, BOOOM-BOOOM, TAT
HERE WE GO, HERE WE GO, HERE WE, HERE WE, HERE WE
    GO!

My older brothers *loved* that Run-DMC song and they had played it around me a lot. Obviously, the booming beat got the nineties crowd excited too.

Harrison Auditorium went off: "HO-O-O! HO-O-O! HO-O-O!"

I guess that's why the New Jersey group wanted to go last. They knew what that beat would do. Sure enough, the rap group edged John out with the judges and won first prize.

I didn't know how John would take it, but I was prepared to pump him up. He did a hell of a job, but whenever you have judges in the way, it's ultimately out of your hands. True art can never really be judged by a few people anyway. Each artwork needs to be judged on its own merit. It was an apples-and-oranges kind of thing that night.

Anyway, I looked at John after they announced the winner, and he wasn't fazed at all.

I said, "You think you should have won, man?" I wasn't sure myself. It was a real close call. That New Jersey group had set the place on fire!

John looked at me and said, "I *did* win. Did you see how the crowd responded when I sang up there?"

He had a point. I nodded and smiled at him.

He said, "Black people will always go off for a dance song. Every culture gets excited about dance songs. But when they respond to a love song like that, then you *know* you got something."

I was impressed! John was becoming a real performer right before my eyes. Then a bunch of people rushed him as we tried to make our way out the door with his equipment.

"Don't worry about that, Loverboy. You did good."

"Yeah, you did good, man."

"Yo, keep singing, man. Just keep singing."

"Did you write that song yourself?"

"Yeah, that song was beautiful."

"Well, you can sing that song to me *any* night, Loverboy. You da man."

They were calling him "Loverboy" as if it was his name. Big Joe had started something. It took us a while to get back to the dorms. Plenty of people had something to say. John had *never* gotten that much attention in his life! I was happy for him. To tell the truth, though, I didn't make much of it. I was actually thinking more about myself and how I needed to shine on the football field in the homecoming game that Saturday against Alcorn State. John had inspired me.

When we finally made it back to the dorms, a little after ten o'clock, John asked me what I was doing for the rest of the night. I guess he was still charged from the whole experience and the attention that he was getting.

I was already getting tired of it, so I told him that I had some homework to finish, and we went to our separate dorms.

I walked up to my room and laid out on my bed, dreaming about grabbing an interception and running it back for a touchdown against Alcorn State's famed quarterback, Steve "Air" McNair. I was five foot eleven, 190 pounds, and a solid cornerback. I just happened to have two seniors in front of me in starting positions. But I couldn't even rest in peace that night before other football players started banging on my door, talking about John.

"Yo, your boy can sing, man? Is he gonna try to get a record deal? *I* would. I mean, Loverboy can get *much* trim if he keep singing like that, D. He ain't no *bad*-looking guy either. So if *fugly* singers can get laid, you *know* your boy can."

I laughed at the idea. I said, "He ain't got laid yet. We'll see."

I even got phone calls from a couple of my lady friends that night.

"Darin, I didn't know your friend John could sing like that. How long has he been singing?"

I took a deep breath and said, "Since he was six years old in the church choir. But look, I'm trying to get some sleep tonight. I have to rest up for this game on Saturday."

"Oh, well, go ahead and get your rest then. Just tell your friend, *the Loverboy*, to keep singing."

I took my phone off the hook for the rest of the night and tried to nod off and go to sleep, but I couldn't. I was actually feeling jealous of my boy, and I couldn't help myself. In retrospect, I had to ask myself, *How long had John been jealous of me as a star athlete?* So I felt guilty about it.

Sometime after midnight my roommate came in the room. He looked at me still trying to sleep in my bed and said, "D, your boy got the girls *open* like crazy tonight. I mean, they were *wide* open for that boy! I even seen Loverboy heading back to Bennett with one."

"Heading back to Bennett with who?"

Bennett College was an all-girls school that was a good walking distance from A&T.

My roommate said, "Man, I don't know who she was. Some brown-skinned girl with a phat body. I guess your boy 'bout to get paid already. Paid in panties."

I just smiled it off. I told myself, *Yeah, she's probably just asking John a bunch of questions like they all do. He'll be walking back home alone with no action.*

That next morning, John was practically waiting for me before class. He caught up with me like eight o'clock in the morning.

He asked me, "Did you have a girl over last night? I was trying to call you. You forgot to put your phone back on the hook."

I smiled and said, "Oh, yeah. I did forget to put the phone back on the hook."

He smiled back at me and said, "It finally happened, D."

"What happened?"

"I was with a girl last night."

I said, "From Bennett College?"

"Yeah, how you know?"

"I got spies working for me," I told him.

John said, "Well, yeah, man, it finally happened for me. I got some."

I just stopped walking. I said, "Wait a minute. You mean to tell me that you can sing *one* damn song at homecoming and get some ass after going dry for *nineteen* years?"

"I guess so," he told me. He was grinning his ass off.

I never dared to ask him, but I figured that John had been jerking off or something. He talked about girls enough. He just couldn't get any.

I said, "So who was she?"

"Janese."

"That girl from South Carolina? Oh, yeah, she's nice," I told him.

He said, "Well, she's my first love now."

I looked in his face and asked, "You not in love with her or nothing, are you?"

He paused. "I can't really say. I mean, I like her and all."

He wasn't in love with her. John would have known immediately if he was. He would have known that before he even went over to her place. Instant true love was rare anyway.

I said, "So, how did it happen? Did she always want to give you some, and last night was just the night for it?"

I figured John would make me late for class, but what the hell. During homecoming, plenty of people miss class anyway unless you have a test or a big assignment to turn in, and I had neither.

John said, "Well, she asked me if I had written *May I* for her."

I said, "What? Go 'head, man. She didn't ask you that shit."

"Yes she did, too."

"So what you tell her?" I just *knew* that John didn't tell her he had unless it was true. The boy was honest like that.

"I said yeah," he told me.

I started laughing. "You wrote that song for her for real?"

John said, "Well, you know, it's for *all* women."

I said, "But she didn't ask you that. She asked you if you wrote it for *her.*"

"Well, she's a woman, ain't she?"

I broke out laughing again. John was learning how to game for some trim.

I said, "You lied to her, man."

"But I didn't."

"Yes, you did. But don't worry about it. We all lie to get it. Or *most* of us do. Unless you really like the girl."

John said, "I do like her."

"As much as you liked Carneta back in high school?"

He thought for a second. He said, "That was a different time in my life."

I cut to the chase and asked him, "Well, how was it?"

He smiled. "It felt good, man."

"Did you nut?"

He paused and went into deep thought about it.

"Umm . . . I don't know. What does it feel like?"

After he asked me that, I figured that I wouldn't even make class that morning. I couldn't stop laughing, and I *damn* sure wanted all of the details.

"What does it *feel* like? You must didn't do it right then. Did *she* like it?" I asked him. I could imagine John having no idea what he was doing.

He said, "Oh, yeah, she was moaning all loud and going crazy. I thought somebody was about to knock on her door and tell us to stop."

"Go 'head, man. You bullshittin'. And you don't even know if you nutted. How you gon' turn her out like that and you didn't even know what you were doing?"

"Well, she got on top of me, man, and she was like, doing it herself."

I said, "Oh, now *that* explains it. So Janese had a little bit of a freak in her, and she let it all out on you."

John laughed and said, "I guess so, because I didn't even have any condoms. *She* had some."

I held out my hand and said, "Well, welcome to manhood."

John smiled but he didn't give me a handshake on it.

He said, "Just because I got some, that doesn't make me a man. I have a long way to go yet."

I nodded to him and took my hand back.

"All right, well . . ." I didn't know what else to say. I said, "Well, let me get to class, man. I'll talk to you later on."

John whispered, "I didn't even take a shower yet, D."

I looked at him and frowned. "Why not?"

"Well, if you thought that I was lying to you when I told you, I wanted you to smell me for proof."

I said, "Are you fucking crazy, man?! Go take your damn shower, boy! I'm not gon' *smell* you. You crazy!"

John laughed and started walking backward to his dorm at Scott.

"All right, D. I'll see you later on, man."

That boy had to be out of his mind! I had to smile at it, though. John was like a big kid with a new trick up his sleeve. And when I made it to my first class that morning, it was basically over with. Only five students had shown up anyway.

•   •   •

On that homecoming Saturday, instead of me picking off an interception and running it back for a touchdown, I sat on the bench the whole game as both teams ran up the score. Alcorn State beat us 45–34. Steve "Air" McNair threw four touchdown passes and nearly four hundred yards against our senior cornerbacks, while I rode the pine. To top things off, my boy John had people talking about him while he performed in the school band *before, during, and after* the halftime show.

I figured I would get drunk and get laid myself that Saturday night to heal my wounded ego. Even that idea backfired on me.

"Can you sing a song to me like your friend *Loverboy*?" this girl named Tanya teased me. She was only joking, but I wasn't in the mood for that. I was just about to take her clothes off when she said it, too.

"Why don't you stop fucking asking me about him?"

She said, "What? Darin, I was only joking. You don't need to get an attitude with me."

I said, "Yeah, just shut up and take your clothes off."

It was alcohol talking. I was drunk.

Tanya said, "Oh no you *didn't!*" and pulled away from me. "You don't talk to me like that."

"Stop wasting time, then," I told her.

She said, "Oh, I won't," and headed for the door.

I don't remember all that I did that night, but I had a headache in the morning when John called me on the telephone.

He said, "I got some more last night, man."

"From Janese?" I asked him.

"Nah, from this other girl."

I shook my aching head and moaned. John had been turned out to the sex game. In *two* days!

"What's wrong?" he asked me.

"I got a hangover, man. A bad one."

He said, "Yeah, I had one last night, too."

"Had one what? A hangover?" John didn't drink. But I did.

He said, "No, not a hangover. I'm talking about when I did it last night. Man, it kind of felt like my whole insides were squeezing out of my thing."

I grabbed my head and screamed, "I got a headache, man! Don't do it to me this morning!" I wanted to laugh so bad, but my head was killing me!

John said, "My bad. I'll tell you later on then."

"Nah, you can tell me now, just don't say nothing too funny."

He said, "I'll try not to. But this girl knew what she was doing even more than Janese, man. I mean, she was on the bottom, but she was grabbing on me real good, and squeezing me real tight. And then when I did it, like, my whole body just *froze*, man. And she squeezed me real, *real* tight.

"And aw, man, that felt *great!* And I was like, *Wow!* And then we did it again."

I thought I was ready to have an aneurysm in my head or something. The thing that made it worse was that John had no idea how funny the shit was. I mean, he was only telling it like it was, but *damn!*

I said, "So how long have you known this girl, man?" I wanted to see if these girls had just opened up to John recently, or had he simply figured out how to score.

"Antoinette? For about a month now. She's a freshman."

"So, how did you get her?"

"Well, she's a music major, so she wanted me to listen to some of her stuff, and then she just came on to me, talking about how talented I was."

"*Talented?* Man, these people only heard you sing *one* song," I told him.

"Yeah, but she has her own keyboard, so I showed her a few things on it. And she knows I'm on a music scholarship. You don't get a scholarship for nothing."

John was right. I was downplaying his talent from my own jealousy, so I moved on from it.

"And then she gave you some?" I asked him.

"Yeah. Basically. And she was real passionate about it."

"So what are you going to do now? Are you going to keep *both* of these girls?"

I wanted to see if John had thought things through.

He said, "Man, I have *no* idea. I didn't even think about that. But I came up with a new song last night, though."

I said, "A new song?"

"Yeah. Because you know how we have that midnight rule for dorm room visitation. Well, I came up with a song called *At Midnight*. Me and Antoinette were talking about that, because I had to leave before she wanted me to."

"Did you take a shower this time?" I asked him with a laugh.

He laughed back and said, "Yeah, as soon as I got back in last night."

I said, "Good. And don't do that shit again, man. That ain't too healthy."

He said, "Oh, yeah, some people invited me to perform at Norfolk State's homecoming next Friday night."

I started smiling again. "And?" I asked him.

He said, "You down to go?"

I laughed. "We got a game next week, man."

"But it's a home game. Norfolk is only a couple of hours from here. We could drive up there, D, do our thing, and I'll drive back while you sleep."

I said, "Nah, man. I'm trying to rest *in a bed* before my game. My car ain't comfortable."

"We could be back before one, though. How many hours of sleep do you need? You can still get your eight hours. *Both* of us. I still have to play in the band at the game."

I wouldn't commit myself to it. I said, "Nah, man. I'm not going up there."

When we hung up that morning, I felt guilty again. Was I acting out of jealousy, or just pure laziness? I figured that if I had something up at Norfolk State that *I* wanted to do, I would have had no problem driving up there and back. So it *had* to be jealousy. I thought about that and decided to call John back.

I said, "I'll drive up there with you, man."

He said, "Hold on," and clicked over to his other line. When he came back, he said, "Thanks, D. I didn't want to go with anybody else, man, because I can't share things with people like I do with you. But if you forced me to . . ."

I said, "So you wasn't even gonna try and beg me first?"

"Nah, man. You're a Taurus. I mean, you can either be supportive or not, but begging you never made a difference."

He was right. If I made up my mind, it was made.

I asked him, "You were already making phone calls for a ride up there?"

He said, "I had to. I'm going, man. This is another opportunity for me. I'm gonna do this new song, *At Midnight*, up there, with *May I*. They asked me to do two."

"Is it another contest?"

"Yeah, for them, but they want me to sing, like, right after the intermission."

"What, like a featured singer?"

"Yeah. You believe that?" He was all excited about it.

I asked him, "Are they paying you?"

"Nah."

"Well, shit, you need to get paid if you're gonna be a featured singer after intermission, man."

"But what if they say no."

I was stuck for a minute. *What* if they say no? I thought.

I laughed and said, "Well, then you do it for free then. But you can at least ask them first."

John paused and said, "I don't really like asking for money, man. I just want to perform. How about I call them back up and let you do it, and say that you're my manager?"

I started laughing again, but John was serious.

I said, "If *I* call, I'm asking for a thousand dollars. Five hundred per song."

John put me on the spot and said, "Do it then."

At first I was ready to back down, but then I figured, *Why not do it? Let me put my actions where my mouth is.* I was never the kind of guy who would back down from anything. I had two older brothers. I was *trained* to stand up to challenges.

I said, "All right then. Give me their number."

I called the homecoming organizers up at Norfolk State University, and they were really excited about having John sing up there. That surprised me. I thought they would act as if it was no big deal.

I said, "Yeah, John Williams is my boy and everything, and we came up in church together, but he doesn't like dealing with the money aspect of performing, so I figured that I would do that for him. And I think that a thousand dollars would be fair to both parties, you know, five hundred dollars for each song."

I didn't know if I was going about it the right way with being so honest, but that was the deal.

They said, "A thousand dollars? We can do that."

I was shocked! I said, "Yeah, so that would be a deal then."

When we hung up the phone, I starting thinking that maybe I had asked for too little. After all, talent show performances were always packed during homecoming events. They would have plenty of door money. Nevertheless, I was happy to give John the news.

He said, "They agreed to it?"

"Yeah. And I'm thinking that maybe I should have asked for *five thousand* to see if they would meet us halfway."

I had learned my first big lesson of management: never ask for too little, because they will be more than happy to give it to you.

That Thursday, the organizers called John back and tried to back out of the deal.

John got me back in the conversation with them, because they were trying to run the bullshit game all through him. I had obviously told them too much information.

They said, "We looked into our budget, and we just don't have the resources to pay him anything, but we've already pumped his name up around campus, and everybody is really excited about hearing him. This could be another big opportunity for him to get his name out there."

I got real slick and said, "So you guys have already pumped everything up for *Loverboy*. And the women are all looking forward to hearing him prove it, hunh?"

"Yeah, they really are."

"And they know that he's going to perform *two* songs?"

"Well, we don't know about two songs. If time permits, you know."

John was waiting right beside me in his room.

I said, "But they know that he also writes his own music and lyrics?"

"Well, we just put the word out that he's really talented, and everybody's looking forward to seeing him."

I said, "Okay, well we'll just collect our money from the door then. After the first hundred people walk in, you should have over one thousand dollars. What is it, ten dollars a ticket? And the capacity is like what, five hundred or so?"

There was a long pause. "Well, we have other things to take care of on our end."

"And John *Loverboy* Williams is one of them."

John couldn't tell everything that was going on, but he was smiling at my demeanor, because I was not playing with those people. It pissed me off more that they tried to run through John after I told them that he didn't like to talk about money. I guess they thought that he wouldn't tell me or something. Or maybe they figured that Thursday would be too late to do anything about it.

They asked me, "Well, was he paid for the talent show at A&T last week?"

"He wasn't a featured performer last week," I responded. "But you invited him as a featured talent."

"Well, he can perform in our talent show if he wants."

I said, "You know what? If John still wants to perform after you agreed to one thing, and then tried to call back at the last minute for something else, then you find him another ride up there then, because I'm not going to be a part of this," and I handed the phone back to John. I had done my best to try and get him paid, and that was all I could do. The rest was up to him.

John looked at me with the phone to his ear and said, "Well, you made a deal with my manager, and now you're trying to change it—

"No, he *is* my manager. To manage means to basically control affairs, and if I didn't listen to what he felt was fair, then I would need to fire him.

But I have no intentions of firing a lifelong friend who is only looking out for my best interests."

John was silent for a few minutes while I waited for the outcome.

He said, "Sorry, but I can't do it then . . . I'm not interested in one song. I was told that I would be paid for two, and I'm already looking forward to singing both of them . . . Well, thanks for getting me all excited for nothing . . . That's not my problem. If you would have kept the deal that you agreed to, that wouldn't have been a problem for you either. But now it is . . . Yeah, we'll be here."

John hung up the phone and immediately started to panic.

He said, "Fuck, man. Now they may not do it at all."

"What they say?" I asked him.

"They said they'll see what they can do and call us back. But what if they *don't* call us back?"

I said, "They want you to sing just one song now?"

He said, "Yeah, but I want to sing my new one. I've been working on it all week. Now we ruined it, man. I *knew* we shouldn't have tried to get any money out of this. I just want to sing, man. I just want to *sing*."

He was already stressed out about it. That boy had found a new addiction, man. *I* panicked after that. I didn't want John feeling all down about a lost opportunity to sing because of *me*. That boy could be melodramatic about things. So I broke down and said, "I'll just call them back then and tell them that you'll do it for free."

I smiled and asked him, "Is this *At Midnight* song as good as *May I*?"

He smiled back at me. "Hopefully, you'll see for yourself tomorrow night at Norfolk."

I shook my head thinking about the homecoming organizers at Norfolk State again. I wanted to at least talk about them before I called them back.

I said, "You see how people try to do you in business, man? And all I was asking for was a fair deal. If they couldn't do it, they could have told us Monday, Tuesday, or Wednesday.

"With my father working for a housing contractor, I've heard plenty of stories about people trying to get over on business. He had a different story just about every week."

Both of my brothers were business grads because of all of my father's stories. My middle brother, Darryl, was even planning to go on to law school to further his education on contracts.

I said, "All right, well, give me the phone and let me call them back." I told him, "I ain't no damn manager, man. I couldn't even get you a thousand dollars from Norfolk."

As soon as John handed me the phone, the damn thing rang in my hand. It caught me off guard. I shook and said, "Shit."

John took it back and answered, "Hello?" That boy was *anxious*! He said, "Yeah, this is John." He nodded his head and smiled. "That's good to hear."

I assumed that Norfolk State was agreeing to something.

I said, "Tell them to put it in writing. And we want the money *before* you perform." I added in a low tone, "Because I don't trust them now."

John asked them for everything I told him to in his own patient way. Then he hung up the phone and smiled at me again.

"What was that you were saying about *not* being a manager?" he asked me. I mean, that boy was happy as hell!

I grinned and said, "Shit, man, we're just kids out here. A thousand dollars ain't nothing."

John said, "That's my point, though. Everybody starts from somewhere. This could be *your* start."

I blew him off. I said, "Yeah, whatever, man." But it was funny how that boy went from panicking to praising me in just a few minutes. That's how John was, though. Hot and cold.

We made it up to Norfolk State that Friday night, and there was another jam-packed homecoming crowd just waiting for John to do his thing. But they had screwed up his name. They had "John LOVINGBOY Williams" printed up all over campus! Can you *believe* that!

John smiled at me and said, "That ain't no big deal to me, man. My name ain't really Loverboy anyway."

I said, "Yeah, but *still*, man, they need to get the shit *right*. These assholes got this shit all over the campus. *Lov-ving-boy*," I emphasized for effect. "That shit sounds kinky, man. It's *Lov-ver-boy*. There's a *difference*."

John just started laughing at me. He was still happy to be there.

Then the organizers pulled an okie-dokie on us when we went to collect on our money. They only gave us $750.

"That's all we can afford to give you."

I was looking at the crowd up there like, *Bullshit! They're trying to play us!*

John didn't even care, though. He was like, "Okay. Let's just do it then."

I said, "Wait a minute, John. I thought we were supposed to have a thousand dollars in writing."

There wasn't no paperwork to be seen up there. But at least they gave us *most* of the money. So I just backed off and let it slide. John wasn't about to pay me no mind anyway. That boy just wanted to sing.

Norfolk had more funk in their talent show performances than we had at A&T. But no one rocked the house like the rap group from New Jersey or John did. Or at least not yet. Maybe Norfolk's best performers were waiting to perform last, too.

They introduced John correctly as the Loverboy, and the crowd started looking, but I didn't have a sense of what the vibe was, especially after they had advertised the wrong damn name up there. John even went out and bought a new brown outfit that looked pretty cool. I sat with his Korg keyboard, nervous as hell again, and ready to press that start button. It wasn't a fearful nervous, though. It was a restless nervousness. I wanted my boy to shock the house again. I wasn't jealous of him anymore either. He was my boy, and he needed my full support. So I was prepared to give it to him.

John held the microphone for a few seconds again, with no words spoken while the crowd got ready for him. Then he looked over at me. I pressed the start button, and John did that shit again:

Ma-a-ay I-I-I hol-l-ld your-r-r han-an-an-n-nd.

I laughed my ass off when Norfolk realized that my boy had them under his spell. They had a lot more hip people from up north who went to Norfolk, too. Thugs, playboys, fly girls, you name it. They were screaming and hollering all kinds of things, but it never broke his concentration. John got all of them open. Then I changed his disc for the second song, *At Midnight.*

John gave them a short introduction, telling the crowd that he had just written the song that week. They even laughed when he told them about his inspiration for the song. I guess we can all relate to running out of time in the dorm rooms. John seemed to be at ease up there on the stage, like he was *meant* to be there.

He looked over at me to press the start button again. For this *At Midnight* song, John had produced a beat, with a bass line, horns, and his piano again, all coming from the keyboard like a mini orchestra. First the piano came in playing all high notes with a slight echo. The beat followed right behind it:

*BLINK, KA-LINK-KA-LINK-KA-LINK-KA-LINK-KA-LINK-KA-
   LINK-KA-LINK*
*BLINK, KA-LINK-KA-LINK-KA-LINK-KA-LINK-KA-LINK-KA-
   LINK-KA-LINK*

The slow beat followed right behind the piano:

DOOOMP, TAT, DOOOMP-DOOM-TAT
DOOOMP, TAT, DOOOMP-DOOM-TAT

Then the bass line slid in:

DOOOOM . . . DOOOOM . . . DOOOOM
DOOM-DOOOM . . . DOOOOM . . . DOOOOM . . .

And the horns trailed John's vocals, starting off with the chorus:

At mid-ni-i-ight
BARNP-BARRN-NARRRNN
it gets so lo-o-o-ne-le-e-e with-oouut you-u-u
At mid-ni-i-ight
BARNP-BARRN-NARRRNN
it's so-o-o co-o-old up in my lonely room
At mid-ni-i-ight
BARNP-BARRN-NARRRNN
I wish I could be with you-u-u any-where
At mid-ni-i-ight
so we can get down un-der the moon-light
at mid-ni-i-i-ight.

I'm not even going to lie about it. I didn't pay close attention to the verses. I was sitting there hypnotized, thinking to myself, *This boy is* bad*! I can't* believe *this shit!* And the girls were losing their damn *minds* in that place!

"I'LL MEET YOU AT MIDNIGHT!"

"YOU DON'T NEED TO BE LONELY, BABY!"

"WE CAN GET DOWN ANYWHERE, ANYPLACE!"

"DO THAT SHIT, BABY! *SING!*"

"WHAT ARE YOU DOING LATER ON TONIGHT?!"

I started thinking that we wouldn't be able to leave that night. After the show, John's dumb ass tried to walk through the crowd instead of finding a back door somewhere. I guess he *wanted* to be mobbed.

"Can you sign *anything* for me? I just want to have your autograph before you turn famous."

"Shit, he *should* already *be* famous, singing his ass off like that."

"Who you tellin'?"

"You don't have a record deal yet? Well, somebody *needs* to sign you."

"I want an autograph, too."

"Me, too."

"To hell with an autograph, *I* want a date."

"Can you make *me* sing like that . . . at midnight?"

I was standing off to the side, watching all of these fine women mob my boy, and two weeks ago he couldn't even get laid. That shit was amazing!

This tall, light brown dude in a suit and tie stepped up out of nowhere and tried to hand John a business card.

"My name is Todd Light, with Ecstasy Records, and I'd *definitely* like to speak to your manager."

John pointed him in my direction.

I acted like I was really important and said, "Darin Harmon. I'm pleased to meet you."

He looked at me as if it was a joke.

"*You're* his manager?"

"You expected an old man?" I joked to him. "Young people are getting it done nowadays. Look at Sean 'Puff Daddy' Combs and Jermaine Dupri."

I figured that after John ripped the house like he did, I could talk all the big-time shit that I wanted.

"What are you guys, straight out of college?"

I guess this guy had been in the business for a while, but I had never heard of any Ecstasy Records.

I said, "We're still *in* college."

He said, "Oh. Well, yeah, I'd like to talk to you guys."

He finally handed me his business card. He was local, with an office in Richmond, Virginia.

I asked him, "You want a number for us?"

He seemed hesitant after he found out that I was Loverboy's manager.

He said, "Well, when you guys call I'll get it then."

I nodded to him, immediately thinking about throwing his business card away. He didn't want our business bad enough. I could feel it already.

I said, "All right then, we'll call you."

When I turned back to John, he was still glowing and signing autographs in the middle of all of the attention he was getting.

"Excuse me, but you said that you're his manager?" one girl asked me. Her girlfriends were in the background. They all looked like they were ready for excitement, too.

I said, "Yeah, I'm his manager." I was already beginning to expect things.

She said, "Well, what hotel are you staying in?"

I thought, *Damn, we don't even have a hotel.* So I told the girl the truth.

"Actually, we have to get back down to A&T tonight. We have another event tomorrow morning."

She looked disappointed. She said, "For real? Y'all going back *tonight*. Why?"

I repeated myself, having second thoughts about leaving: "We have something to do tomorrow morning."

"Well, can y'all leave later on? I mean, we trying to hang out, you know. We came all the way down here from D.C."

I guess she was the group's spokesperson. She had a *phat* body, too, with some tight black jeans on! Boy, she just didn't know how tempted I was to stay, but I figured that we would have plenty of nights to hang late when we *would* have a hotel room and no game to prepare for the next morning.

I said, "Sometimes we all can't get what we want right when we want it. But if you want to leave us a phone number, you know, we can call you up whenever we do a show or something up in your area."

I had been to Washington, D.C., only once, for a football game against Howard University. There were plenty of black people up there, too. George Clinton from the funk group Parliament called it *Chocolate City*.

The girl took a deep breath before taking out something to write on.

"Are you really gonna call? I mean, don't play with us if you're not."

I said, "Yeah, we'll call you, as soon as we have something in your area."

One of her girlfriends overheard me and said, "Well, you don't have to wait until something is going on in D.C. to come *see* somebody."

Boy, these girls were *aggressive*! I thought, *Shit!* John would need all of the management in the world to deal with girls who would be that forward with him. He had limited experience with those kind of women. They usually didn't give him any time of day. *I* even had a hard time keeping up with them. Most of the time, those in-your-face girls were just not worth the agony they would put a guy through.

I took a few of their phone numbers and tried to push John along in the direction of our car before we ended up *leaving* at one o'clock instead of arriving back at A&T at that hour. As we made our way back to the car we *still* had company.

This light brown girl stepped up and asked us, "Do you mind if we walk with you to the car and ask you a few questions about performing?"

She had a girlfriend who was as light as she was. And they both appeared high-maintenance, with fancy hairstyles and outfits, way out of John's league. Or previously at least, because his singing seemed to elevate him *ten notches*.

I said, "As long as you can keep up with us."

That damn keyboard that I was carrying wasn't paperweight. After holding on to it for nearly an hour, it was wearing me out, and I still had a game to play that next morning.

John was all ears for these girls.

He said, "What kind of questions do you have?"

"Well, you write your own songs, right?"

John smiled and said, "Yeah."

"And do you write songs for anyone else?" She stopped and said, "I'm sorry, my name is Pyra and my partner is Angie. We call ourselves Two Scoops."

I turned back and started laughing.

I said, "Two scoops of what? Vanilla?"

I was only joking with them.

Angie spoke up and said, "Yeah, but that's only for the meantime. We're still trying to decide on a new name."

Pyra said, "And we could use some good management, too."

I looked at them again and figured that they were probably older than us. They looked like they were in their early twenties and out of the teen years.

I said, "What do you think, John? Could you use some backup singers? Would you two be willing to do that?" I asked them.

They both said, "Yeah, whatever."

Angie said, "I mean, we just didn't want to push up on you while everybody else was crowding around, because we wanted to talk real business."

I was still amazed at how fast things were moving. The music industry must have been something else! It was like free food at a crowded picnic, and everybody wanted something to eat.

John said, "Yeah, I've had a couple of ideas for backup singers. All I have to do is sit down and work it all out."

Pyra said, "Well, we're not trying to be backup singers for *long*, but if it'll help us to get our start, we'll do it. But we just want you to know up front that we still want to do *our* own thing, too."

"You don't have management now?" I asked them.

They looked at each other and grinned.

Pyra answered, "Yeah, but it's not the kind of management that we *need*. You know, sometimes things get a little *too* personal."

I didn't want to get into that. They both looked good, and I could easily see how any guy in his right mind could get *personal* with them. I wanted to get personal, too, from just looking at them.

On our way back to North Carolina A&T, John was still smiling his ass off behind the wheel of my get-around car.

I asked him, "What do you think about all of this, John?"

His head was on cloud nine. I guess mine would have been, too, if I had a chance to shine in football.

John said, "It's a dream come true, man. I've been dreaming about being up on the stage for *a while* now."

I said, "Yeah, well, this is still the bottom ranks. I mean, how far do you want to go with this?"

He looked at me and asked, "What did that guy with the business card say?"

I frowned at him. "I don't know about him, man. He seemed like he didn't want to really deal with me. That gave me bad vibes. I mean, if you really want to work with somebody who is talented, you don't worry about the manager, you just try to sign the talent. And that guy acted like I was too young to even talk to him."

John nodded. He said, "Yeah, if we do a lot more shows and stuff like this, we'll get a bunch of people asking to sign us anyway."

I corrected him and said, "Sign *you*. And I know. There'll be a lot of people asking. That's why I'm not sweating that guy. But what do you think about those two backup singers?"

John smiled. "Two Scoops? I think they looked good. I wouldn't mind them singing behind me."

I laughed and said, "But what if they can't sing, and they just *look* good?"

John paused. He said, "Well . . . I can't use them then. And I don't want to write any songs for somebody who can't sing either. But I liked how they waited for everyone to fade away before they stepped up like that. That was smart."

I agreed with him. "Yeah, that *was* smart."

We continued on our way back to school and talked the whole way about the events of the night and the craziness of the music business. I mean, we weren't really even in it yet, but we could both just *imagine* how wild it could be.

. . . then we hit the long road . . .

In November, we played what became an annual rival football game, the Battle of the Border, against South Carolina State. It was the Aggies against the Bulldogs, a big game of bragging rights for North and South Carolina, and we were favored to win it, with a 6-2 record to South Carolina's 3-5. My parents, my brothers, and my sister were there, and John's mother was there to see him perform in the band. I was *dying* to get in and show off in my blue-and-gold in front of my folks. I didn't want a reccurrence of the homecoming game, where I only got dirty during the kickoff coverage. And not that I wished anyone to be injured to get my opportunity, but that's how it happened. One of our starting cornerbacks twisted his ankle on a play and had to come out.

The coaches started to look around for a replacement, and I was right there, man, ready to go in and play.

The defensive coach looked me right in my mug through my face mask and said, "Harmon! Get on in there!"

He didn't have to ask *me* twice. I ran right on field.

As soon as I reached the huddle with the starters, I heard my sister screaming from the stands like a damn maniac, "DAAAR-RINNNNN!"

She said that she was going to do it if I ever got in the game, too. She had her high school friends there to back her up on it, you know, the little-sister girlfriends who had crushes on me.

The guys in the huddle said, "Aw'ight, Darin, you in here, boy. *Act* like you can play."

I nodded my helmet and responded, "I'm ready for this, man. I'm ready."

As soon as we lined up against the Bulldogs' offense, with me on the corner, I had to match up against a speedy receiver. I can't even lie, my heart was racing like the summer Olympics. I mean, it wasn't that I couldn't play football or that I was scared or anything, I just hadn't been in the action. So I had to calm myself down.

Sure enough, they ran a crossing pattern on me, and I chased the receiver down and knocked down the pass before he could pull it in.

"*That's* how you play it, *D! That's* how you play it!" the starters were telling me. Big Joe was one of them, up on the defensive line. He seemed like he was twice my size in that huddle. But I didn't sweat it. I had a job to do.

I was hyped and ready after the first couple of hits. On the next play, I had to come up and help out on the run, and their bruising running back gave me a forearm to the chin before I could get him down with help.

"*Yeah*, Darin! You *playin' it*, boy! You *playin' it!*" Big Joe screamed at me.

My teammates were all hyping me up and all that, but I was woozy as hell. I was thinking, *Damn! He cracked the hell out of me!* But that's the game of football. So I had to suck it up and play.

I lined up again, and my sister was still yelling her lungs out, with her girlfriends instigating it, I'm *sure*.

"DAAAR-RINNNNN!"

On every defensive play for the rest of that game, I kept expecting to be pulled, so I played every snap like it was my last. But since it was a blowout, 40–17, there was really no reason to pull me. None of those points had been scored on *my* side.

After the game, the coach gave me a nod and a smile. He said, "Good game, Harmon. I guess we have something to look forward to for next year."

That was music to my ears! I had finally worked my way into playing time. Man, I had a *good* time *that* night! *Everybody* did, you know, except for the players and fans from South Carolina.

John smiled at me later on that day and said, "It looks like you're about to be the man again, D. Just like in high school. They couldn't get nothing on your side."

I said, "Thanks, man. I was nervous a little bit at first. Or not really nervous, just excited, you know. I mean, we *both* blowing up now, John. You with the music, and me with football. This feels *good*, man! *Good!*"

I still didn't consider myself to be a real manager, but after the big game, I felt more energized about helping John out in his music career. It was like we were both about to live out our dreams.

By then John had completed a new song, called *Unappreciated*, with parts for backup singers. He was writing about how he felt as a young man before he started singing. He was telling it straight up, and I liked all of his songs because you could easily relate to them. Everybody feels unappreciated sometimes. I felt unappreciated on the football team until I got my chance to play that game.

Anyway, John planned to sing the new song with Pyra and Angie singing backup. But he had also written a female response verse. That's where I saw a problem.

I asked, "John, who's gonna sing this response?"

He smiled and said, "Angie has the stronger voice."

I said, "Yeah, but Pyra has the stronger ego."

We had heard a few of their demo tapes and it turned out that they could sing. We both came to the conclusion that Angie was the better singer, though. However, Pyra did most of the leading, *and* most of the talking.

I said, "John, unless you're gonna write a response verse for both of them, then I wouldn't use that, man."

He said, "A response verse for both of them would create an imbalance. That would be like a ménage à trois or something."

I smiled and said, "Yeah. That's cool."

John shook it off. "Nah, I'll just take out the extra verse and write a bridge then."

When John got a chance to practice the new song with Two Scoops at Frazier Hall, I made sure to stop by and see how things were going.

John had penned another great slow song:

Sometimes when a man lives the right way
and he does all of the things that he's supposed to do
he feels, deep inside, like the world don't even care.
And when he decides to just walk away
that's when they want to call him and say . . .

Pyra and Angie came in with the chorus:

I miss you-u-u-u . . .
I miss you-u-u-u . . .
Don't you know how I miss you-u-u-u . . .
I miss you-u-u-u . . .
You gotta know that I miss you-u-u-u . . .
I miss you-u-u-u . . .
Oh, baby, I miss you-u-u-u . . .
I miss you-u-u-u . . .

Then John slipped back in and added, *"That's what they tell me when I'm gone,"* before singing the next verse.

I'm telling you, my boy was *BAD*!

Angie walked over to me late that night when they were finished practicing and said, "Are you *sure* he's only nineteen?! The stuff he writes about sounds like he's *forty-five* or something."

I laughed. I said, "That's because he's been listening to that at home for so long, that old-school shit. Why, you don't like it?" I asked her.

She was hesitant. She said, "I mean, it sounds good and all, but I'm just thinking about the audience. Because if he's really nineteen and he's promoted that way, and then he comes out and sings like he's forty, I just don't know how that's gonna work."

I said, "Well, what about Johnny Gill? It works for him."

"Yeah, but he has that deep, baritone voice."

I thought that John's tenor (normal male voice) was perfect. Too much bass could actually get in the way of a guy's delivery. Everybody couldn't be Barry White. John had the perfect voice for his stage name, *the Loverboy*. He had perfect harmony between his voice and his music.

I said, "We just won't talk about his age then. A lot of the songwriting comes from older guys anyway. Boyz II Men don't write their own songs."

Angie said, "And that's why I don't really follow Boyz II Men. I like Jodeci. I mean, I can relate to what they're saying more."

Angie was all about the business of music. I respected that. There was a lot that I could learn from her.

I nodded my head and said, "I see your point. Don't worry, though, he's only written a few songs. He's gon' write some younger stuff." I was going to tell him to try it myself.

Angie said, "Yeah, and some up-tempo stuff, too."

When I talked to Pyra that same night, she was a lot more personal and less business.

She said, "Darin, can I ask your opinion on something? If you had a girlfriend that you trusted, right, and she had to go out of town on business, would you be all concerned about who she's with and what she's doing *every* minute of her damn day?!"

I smiled. I said, "It would depend on how much I trusted her."

"So, if you *did* have to know everything, then that would mean you *didn't* trust her then?"

"Basically, yeah," I told her.

"Mmm hmm, that's what I thought. He doesn't trust me," Pyra responded, talking about whomever.

Pyra reminded me of a high school girl. She always needed to validate her point with someone. And she was constantly flirting, with her eyes, body language, outfits, hair, and with the questions that she asked you. I wouldn't trust her out on the road either.

When Angie and Pyra headed back home to Virginia, I asked John, "So, what do you think about how things went tonight?" It was close to midnight on a Wednesday.

John said, "It went better than I expected it to."

"Yeah, because you had everything organized for them."

He was used to being the bandleader in high school.

John nodded and didn't speak for a second.

He said, "You know what I've been thinking lately, D?"

"What?"

He looked me in my eyes and answered, "Working on my music full-time."

I started smiling. I said, "First you need to work on getting a record deal or something."

"Not really. Record deals are easier to get when you've been out there on the road already. I want to travel the country with the few songs that we have now, and build up my name. And if things work the way they should, I can get a record deal in *no* time."

I looked back into John's eyes to see if he was serious, and he was.

"So, you're talking about giving up your scholarship to sing? I mean, at least finish school first, man. You can always sing. Your mom ain't gon' let you stop going to school anyway. Have you talked to her about all of this?"

I didn't know if John had even told his mother that he had started performing. He hadn't talked about having any conversations with her about it.

He looked straight ahead like a man on a mission and said, "I'll just have to tell her then."

I started laughing, imagining his mother telling his ass off and forcing him to get back to concentrating on his schoolwork. It wasn't as if he was doing something totally unrelated. He was studying music and playing in the band.

John stopped my laughter and said, "I'm not joking, man. I'm gonna tell her this weekend. I've been thinking about it a lot lately. I mean, I know what I want to do now."

I said, "You, ah . . ." I didn't know *what* to say.

He asked me, "You still want to be my manager, right?"

I smiled again. I said, "John, I'm ready to break my way into the starting lineup now on the squad. I'm not dropping out of school with you, man. I'm no real manager. I'm just your boy."

I couldn't believe that he was even *asking* me that. He knew how much football meant to me.

John said, "Well, what we'll do is keep doing events when we can on weekends, because football season is almost over with anyway. And then when the season starts again next year, I may have a record deal."

I joked, "Yeah, and then you can get yourself a *real* manager."

John didn't think it was funny, though.

He said, "I still want you to be my manager, man. You could read up on it and learn the business. I just want to concentrate on the music, and I know that you wouldn't try to cheat me or anything. I heard that a lot of people get cheated by their managers, and I know that I could always trust you to point me in the right direction and look out for me."

He smiled and said, "You've been doing it *this* long."

"Yeah, but I can't do much else for you but watch your back."

John had a lot of confidence in me. He just smiled and said, "Not yet. But Angie and Pyra like you. They say you're easy to get along with, but you also say what you need to say."

I was flattered. "They said that?" I asked him.

"Yeah. They said that they would let you be their manager, too, if you wanted."

I actually sat there and thought about it. But still, my football career came first.

I grinned and said, "We'll just see what happens when it happens, man."

I wasn't there when John went home to Charlotte to tell his mother about his plans that Sunday morning, but he told me all of the details, and I could imagine the whole scene.

Sister Williams was all dressed up from church. She was wearing a bright dress with white gloves and a fancy church hat, and she was smiling up a storm because her baby boy was coming home to visit her from college.

John waited for his mother to get through her hugs, kisses, and I'm-so-proud-of-you talk so that he could drop his bomb on her.

He said, "Mom, I've been thinking a lot lately about what I want to do with my life."

His mom was nodding eagerly. I have no idea what she expected from him. Maybe she figured John would use all of his musical talent for gospel or classical music, I don't know.

Anyway, John said, "I want to sing."

She looked at him skeptically. "Okay. But John, you've always sang."

He said, "I'm not talking about singing in church with the choir, Mom. I want to sing for everybody."

She asked him, "What do you mean? The music of the church choir is for everybody."

John shook his head and said, "Mom, I'm tired of going to church and praying and everything. I just want to go out there and sing good music for the people. For *everybody.*"

Sister Williams frowned at him and said, "You are *not* saying this to me."

"I *am* saying it. I've been listening to you my whole life, Mom, and it's time for me to listen to my own heart now."

She got frustrated and said, "Who has put these things in your head, John? *Who?*"

He said, "Nobody did. I don't need anyone to tell me what I want to do with my own life."

"And now you want to sing *secular* music?" she asked him.

"I don't call it secular. It's just music. Is the music that we play in the band secular?"

She said, "You *mind* your manners, John! You don't *speak* to me that way!"

He said, "Well, I'm dropping out of school. I've learned enough to do what I need to do now."

Sister Williams got irate and responded, "Oh no, you're *NOT* quitting school! Satan has gotten hold of you, boy!" She raised her hands to the roof and said, "Jesus, Lord, exorcise the demons from my son's head! *Please*, God!"

She grabbed John's head to pray right there in the living room, but John backed away from her.

"John, you don't know what you're *doing!*" she screamed at him. "*Think* about this, boy! This is *insanity!* You didn't work this hard on your music to quit school and sing the songs of sin and of Satan!"

John shook his head and started to walk toward the door. He was ready to take the bus back up to Greensboro.

His mother yelled, "JOHN, don't you walk out that door! DON'T YOU WALK OUT THAT DOOR!"

John kept right on walking. His mother dashed to the door to grab him.

She hollered, "PLEASE, LORD, I'M PRAYING AND BEGGING YOU!"

John said, "Stop it, Mom. I'm just doing what I feel in my heart."

"And your heart has been *run down by the devil!* Now you're going to *stay* in school, and you're gonna *pray to God* for his forgiveness."

John dropped his head, embarrassed by his mother's reaction, and tears welled up in his eyes. But he wasn't changing his mind. He felt it. He had to do his own thing.

He said, "I'm sorry, Mom. But I have to go now."

His mom screamed, "NO, NO, *NO!* I WON'T *ALLOW* THIS! LORD, GIVE ME THE *STRENGTH* I NEED TO HOLD ON TO MY ONLY CHILD!"

John held his mother's hands and tried to peel them away from him so he could walk out the door.

She yelled, "JOHN, *DON'T DO IT!*"

He walked out of the house anyway and started running down the street with tears streaming down his face, but he wasn't turning back. When he made it to the bus station for the trip back to Greensboro, he anticipated his mother driving up and trying to jump out and grab him again. But it never happened. I guess she figured that he would come back on his own, like he had always done when they had a disagreement. His mother would always win. But this time it was different. John was finally establishing his independence. I mean, he felt bad about it, but he still wanted to do his own thing.

Once he told me all of this when he got back to school that Sunday night, I just *knew* that *my mother* would be calling me. Sure enough, when I made it back to my dorm room, my roommate told me to call home, ASAP!

As soon as I got on the phone with my mother, I said, "Mom, I had nothing to do with John making his own decisions. In fact, I told him that he should stay in school and graduate."

"Well, how did this all happen?" she asked me.

"I mean, you know, he just found out that he could sing, and that's what he wants to do now."

She said, "But he hasn't even sang a solo song in church yet."

"Well, I guess he didn't need to, because the boy can sing," I told her. "Everybody knows it up here at school. He sang during the homecoming talent show and *ripped it up.*"

My mother said, "Oh yeah? He really can sing that well, hunh?"

"Yeah!"

She said, "Well, he's breaking his mother's heart talking about this dropping out of school stuff. So you make sure that you talk to him again. And have him call home. She says that he hasn't been answering his telephone.

"That boy is just about to give his mother a nervous breakdown," my mother told me.

When I hung up the phone, I thought about how long John had been under his mother's foot, and I realized that it must have been a real shock for her to finally have him stand up for himself. Maybe they both needed to get over the shock by talking it all out. So I made a visit to John's dorm room at Scott, and his roommate told me that he had gone to Frazier Hall again with his keyboard.

I jogged over to Frazier and walked in on John in the studio. He was working on another new song. He even had a minor audience of music majors and band members. They were already starting to worship his gift.

As soon as he saw me, he went into the chorus of his new song to send me an obvious message:

I need free-dom (CLAP)
Free-dom (CLAP)
Free-dom to do my thing.

Give me free-dom (CLAP)
Free-dom (CLAP)
Free-dom and let me sing.

I need free-dom (CLAP)
Free-dom (CLAP)
Free to choose right from wrong.

Give me free-dom (CLAP)
Free-dom (CLAP)
Free-dom to write my song.

Freedom was funky as ever, and up-tempo! It even had a choirlike bounce to it, like one of those joyful songs that makes everybody get up and rejoice in church. It was one of those Holy Ghost songs that got the older women dancing. I listened to that and shook my head with a smile. I said to myself, *This boy ain't going back. The devil got him for real.*

Then I quoted James Brown, "*'Give it up / or turn it loose!'*"

My father loved him some James Brown, and when you had "it" (the talent), you had to let it loose and do something with it. John definitely had "it," so I didn't know what to say to him. I *wanted* to say, "Hey, man, just do your thing and go for it." But I had promised my mother that I would try and talk to him again about staying in school and calling his mother that night.

John read my mind before I even got close to him.

He said, "I'm not turning back, man. So don't even waste your time talking about it. I'm doing what makes me happy, and I'm gon' keep doing it."

Instead of getting into an argument, I asked him about Janese, his first love, from Bennett College. I figured I would loosen him up a bit first.

He smiled and said, "She's mad at me now, too."

"Why?"

"She says I spend too much time thinking about my music. She says I need to give it a break."

I started laughing. Girls would say the same thing about me and football. They just didn't understand. *A man's gotta do what a man's gotta do.*

I asked, "And what about the other girl?"

John said, "The way I see it is like this, D. I got *one* girlfriend. And you know who that is, man?" he asked me.

I said, "Your music."

"That's right. And I ain't breaking up with her for nobody. She was here with me in the beginning, and she'll be here with me in the end. But I can't say that for everything else. These girls' emotions change when the wind blows. And I can't take that stuff, man. I got my own problems."

I smiled and said, "Who made you an expert on girls already?" He had just recently lost his virginity. He never had that many girlfriends before that. I could only name three, all from the church and all short-lived, with barely a kiss from them.

John said, "That's just the way it is, D. You say the wrong thing to a girl and she's ready to quit you already. But if I play the wrong note with my music . . . the music don't hold no grudges."

He smiled and added, "She don't hold out on me or nothing. She gives it *all* up to me. Any time I want it."

The boy sounded outright freaky, but in a musical way.

I said, "Okay, you got one girlfriend now. But just do me a favor, man. Can you call your mom tonight and tell her that you still love her? Because if I remember correctly, she was the one who first hooked you up with your girlfriend right there," I said, referring to his expensive keyboard.

John nodded to me and chuckled. "All right, I'll call her, man. But just to say that I still love her. Because I don't have much else to say. And if she tries to talk me out of doing my music . . . I might just have to hang up on her."

I thought to myself, *Damn! This boy is dead serious! The music just created a new monster.*

John and his mother came to an agreement that he would stay in school until he could prove, with a record deal, that he could make a living from his music. I figured that his mother believed he wouldn't be able to get a deal and that she would end up having her way with him again. Obviously, she had no idea how talented her son was. And if John couldn't get a record deal with his singing, writing, music compositions, and stage performances, then *nobody* should have one!

At the end of football season, the senior cornerback in front of me was able to finish out with his starting position. We lost our last game to Howard 21–10, and we just missed the play-offs with an 8-3 record. We even lost out on the Heritage Bowl bid to Florida A&M that year. I wasn't too upset about it, though, because I knew that I would be the starter for the next two years of my college career, and we had a lot of guys to work with. I felt confident about the future.

So I traveled with John, Pyra, and Angie to a show at a Christmas Expo event in Richmond, Virginia, that was set up for us by Todd Light and Ecstasy Records. John wasn't getting paid to perform this time, but I figured it was another show for him to wet his whistle with a couple of new songs, and backup singers to boot.

As usual, John brought the house down with *May I*, and then performed his two new songs, *Unappreciated* and *Freedom*, with Pyra and Angie singing backup.

At the end of the show, Todd and his partner, Steven Huntley, an older guy with bank, were ready to sign John up for a recording contract. But no way in the *world* were we signing the first contract offered to us, unless it was coming straight from the powers at Sony or Warner Bros. or something. I didn't have to know much about the business of music to know that. I would never sign with the first sports agency who wanted to sign me for a football contract, so no way in the world was John going to sign the first record deal that was offered to him.

I said, "We're actually more interested in just doing shows and testing the market right now."

John was one hundred percent behind me. He didn't even speak on it. He just let *me* do the talking.

The older guy, Steve Huntley, said, "You could do all of the shows in the world, but the record deal is what you want, right? Don't you want to get your music on the radio and sell your tapes and CDs in the stores?"

I don't know if I was just being petty at the moment, but when he said *tapes* before he said *CDs*, I kind of figured that his record company was a little behind the times. It was nearly 1994, and CDs were the new wave in music.

I answered, "Definitely, but we want to make sure that we're still smiling and not frowning when that time comes. So we want to test all of our options first."

I guess I *was* a pretty good manager, because those guys didn't stress me at all. John wasn't signing their contract, and that was it. But I realized that my boy was right; hitting the road would have people falling out all over the country for him. It was a dynamite plan. All we had to do was keep the shows coming.

When we left, Pyra had a slight attitude problem.

She said, "I can't believe you just flat-out turned them down like that. That could have been our way in. You don't have to *stay* in a deal with them. We could have all used it as a springboard."

I still wasn't representing Two Scoops. They were just going along for the ride. And as far as I was concerned, John could pick *any* two girls out of a church choir to sing backup. It wasn't as if he *needed* Pyra and Angie. We were doing *them* a favor. But I didn't say anything about it, out of respect for Angie.

Pyra also had a pager that kept going off. Her man was definitely stressed. Or whoever it was who kept calling her.

She made a phone call and started cussing up a storm, letting *somebody* have it.

I looked at John, thinking to myself, *This girl has some major social problems.*

She hung up from her phone call and hollered, "Damn, I *hate* petty-ass niggas!"

Angie just shook her head and kept quiet.

John and I decided that we would stay in Richmond that night and drive back to school in the morning, so Todd Light put us up in two rooms in a no-thrills hotel. I thought about not taking anything from him since we weren't signing his contract, but hell, it was the least that they could do for the free performance that day. Our group had easily outdone the others who performed.

After a while, with Pyra still ranting and raving about everything, I pulled her aside and tried to calm her down.

I said, "What's wrong with you? We put on a good show tonight, right? Were you satisfied with the performance at least? I mean, you'll have more opportunities to shine. This is just one night and one show. So just calm down."

I didn't want to make any promises to the girl, but I wanted to at least give her something to look forward to.

She broke down and said, "Aw, man, it's just so much fucked-up shit going on in my life right now, that's all. I just fuckin' need a vacation or something. I need to get high right now, or *something*. Just to calm my nerves, you know."

She started looking at me all flirtatiously again, as if I had some get-high on me, which I didn't. I was a hard-core athlete, and I didn't mess with that smoking shit. I knew other guys who did, but I wasn't one of them.

I said, "Well, I don't know what to tell you. I just know that you're too good looking to be all stressed out over small stuff like you are."

I sounded much older than nineteen myself. But I did have two older brothers, so I knew immaturity when I saw it. And Pyra was definitely acting childish.

She softened up and smiled at me.

"Can I have a big hug right now?" she asked me. "I just need somebody to hold me."

I hugged the girl, but then her hands starting going up and down my back as she squeezed me, like a Loverboy song.

I had to slip out of her hold before I ended up in bed with her. I wouldn't have minded that, but I was trying to stay professional, and I didn't need any extra baggage. Pyra didn't seem too stable to me.

She sighed and said, "Thank you."

"Don't worry about it," I told her.

I had to think about everything under the sun to keep my Johnson in check that night, because I didn't want to make anything complicated by messing around with Pyra. I mean, I still didn't view myself as a real manager, but if Pyra had any illusions that sleeping with me or being with me in any way could get her closer to where she dreamed of being as a performer, I didn't want to mislead her. So instead of me just being a guy and taking advantage of an open opportunity, I decided to take the higher ground and just leave the girl alone. It could have been that she just needed a good stiff one up in her that night, but still, I didn't want to complicate my position. The fact was, I couldn't do a *thing* for the girl. She had limited talent and was a big head case, and I would much rather screw a girl who liked me for being a football star. At least I would know what I was getting into.

We all hung out and got something to eat in Richmond that night, and I fell asleep while watching some HBO movie in the hotel room.

When I woke up that morning, John was taking a shower.

He walked out with a towel wrapped around him.

I asked him, "Where did you sleep last night, man?" I had the whole bed to myself that morning. This cheap hotel didn't have any double beds.

John smiled and said, "You're not going to believe me."

I just waited for his answer.

He said, "Pyra has a lot of energy, man. A whole *lot* of energy! She just wouldn't let me sleep last night. She kept talking about 'Come on, come on.'"

I said, "You got her?"

He said, "Did I *ever*? We must have went at it for, like, four or five hours, until the sun came up."

At first I just shook my head. That boy was a damn rabbit. Then I got nervous.

I said, "Wait a minute. Did you use rubbers for all of that?"

John stopped and said, "Nah. I hope she don't have nothing. But I don't think she does. She was real clean, man."

I said, "Yeah, I would *hope* so, but she still could have gotten pregnant on you. Shit, man! That girl got problems.

"And where was Angie when all of this happened?" I asked him.

He said, "Oh, I don't know. She left and never came back. So after a while, I just figured that she wasn't. I started thinking that she came back here with you or something."

I said, "Nah, man, she wasn't with me."

Pyra had set his behind up to lay him. I didn't trust that girl at all after that. No wonder her man didn't want her out on the road.

I said, "John, what do you think about her, man?"

He said, "Pyra?"

"Yeah, who the hell else are we talking about?" I was getting irritated with him.

He said, "Well, you *know* she's fine, she just needs somebody to love her."

I shook my head and said, "Man, that girl needed some love a *long-ass* time ago. She just seems insatiable, like she could never get enough attention. And she ain't gon' get it from *you*. You got your girlfriend already, right? So now you just fucked up your backup singers. You mark my words, John. You should have just left that damn girl alone."

After dealing with Pyra and Angie, I started thinking about my own football career over the Christmas break from school. I met up with old high school friends and rivals from my football days at Garinger High School in Charlotte's Mecklenburg County Division, and we all talked about Steve "Air" McNair's chances of going pro as a great American quarterback from the black college ranks at Alcorn State. At the same time, I was still curious about the music industry and my boy John, so I went and bought a book on music management and started reading up on things.

My mother caught me reading in my room one day and asked me what it was all about.

I said, "I've been looking after John and his music, and he keeps asking me to be his manager, so I figured I would do some reading up on it."

My mother smiled and said, "I thought you didn't have anything to do with it."

I said, "Mom, he came to *me* with this. I didn't go to him."

"Mmm hmm. I knew it was more to it than what you told me over the phone."

I looked at my mother from my desk chair and said, "The boy is good, Mom. What can I say? I can't act like he's not."

"And you really think he has a chance to become a singer."

I nodded my head and said, "Yeah." If I believed that I could play pro football, then I *had* to believe that John could be a nationally known singer. It was that simple.

When I visited John over at his house for the holidays, his mother was all over me for inside information. I was nervous as it was because I knew that she would ask me things. I just had no idea how pressed she would be for the answers.

"How long has John been thinking about this music career, Darin?"

John was right there with me, but they both acted as if he wasn't even in the room. It was weird. My parents never ignored me. They just made sure that they controlled the conversation.

I looked at John, hoping that he would answer the question himself. He didn't.

Out of respect for his mother, I answered, "Ever since the homecoming talent show, I guess."

She looked at John and said, "You didn't tell me you performed at the homecoming talent show."

He said, "Yeah, I did," and that was it.

"So, where else has he performed?" his mother asked me.

I was wondering how long they were going to keep me in the middle of things. I felt that they were both acting irrational.

I said, "He did the homecoming at Norfolk State, and we did this Christmas show in Richmond, Virginia."

They had me looking like a damn stool pigeon.

She said, "So where else do you plan to perform?"

I didn't know if she was asking me or John.

I looked at John, and he didn't appear to be ready for an answer.

I said, "Well, we're planning to go to a music conference in Philadelphia coming up in January. There's a lot of connections that we need to make."

Sister Williams looked at me and said, "*We?* So, how involved are *you* in this, Darin?"

Fuck! I had put my foot in my mouth. John started smiling as if it was all fun and games.

I said, "I'm just going along for the ride."

That's when John started laughing.

His mother said, "Are you being deceitful with me, Darin? Are you two in a group, singing that godforsaken nasty music together? Does your mother know?"

Jodeci hadn't exactly created the most positive musical image for Charlotte church boys. I guess Sister Williams figured that we were following in *their* footsteps. But we weren't.

I said, "No, we're not in a group. *I* can't sing a lick."

John spoke up again and said, "Darin's just been managing me."

"*Managing?* So you *knew* about this then, Darin," his mother said to me. "You've *condoned* it."

I looked at John and frowned. Was that boy trying to put me through the wringer on purpose, or what?

I said, "Well . . . I'm just reading up on it now. I really don't know enough about the music business to be a manager. I'm just tagging along with John as his friend."

Sister Williams said, "Darin, you've *never* just *tagged along*. You've *always* been the one making the decisions for you two.

"Don't you *dare* deceive me, young man!" she yelled at me. "You show some *respect* for your elders. You're not tagging along for the ride. You're his manager. And that means that you're in this *Satan* business together!"

I said, "*You* listen to secular music. Marvin Gaye didn't sing all gospel."

Sister Williams went off and said, "DARIN, YOU GET OUT OF MY HOUSE, RIGHT NOW! You *don't* speak to me that way!"

I stood up and got to walking. John went ahead and followed me out.

"WHERE DO YOU THINK *YOU'RE* GOING, JOHN?" his mother asked him.

John didn't even answer her.

"WELL, YOU CAN *BOTH* STAY OUT THERE THEN!" she yelled at us and slammed the door.

I looked back at John and shook my head. I said, "Man, your mom is *buggin'! Seriously!*"

He said, "I know."

"Yeah, but you was sitting up in there instigating. 'He's my manager.' What did you do that for?" I asked him.

He said, "I just wanted you to see how she was, that's all."

I said, "Man, I *know* how she is already. *Both* of y'all buggin'!"

. . . where he was fresh and starry-eyed . . .

Up north at the Philadelphia Music Conference, things started to come together for me as an amateur manager. I couldn't call myself a professional but I was learning. I sat in on the panel discussions and sucked up as much information on the music business as possible. John was more interested in the music making itself, so he enjoyed the live performances that they had.

In the panel discussions, they talked about music publishing, booking agents, attorneys, signing the actual record deals, A&R departments, marketing and sales, artist royalties, road management, music trends, and a bunch of the other subjects that I had read about over the Christmas break. I asked a few questions, gathered pamphlets, took down notes, and collected a bunch of phone numbers.

We left Angie and Pyra behind on this trip. They could have come if they wanted to, but we were not willing to make it a car-pool thing. Or at least *I* wasn't. If they were not going to make it up and back on their own, then so be it. And they chose to pass, which was what I hoped for. I was trying to look out for John, and Two Scoops was just getting in the way. Not so much Angie, but since they were a package deal, I had to toss Angie in the same bag as Pyra and move on.

Anyway, when I caught back up with John at the music conference, he was sitting in on a percussion performance.

I sat down in the chair beside him and asked him about the drummer, a short, bald-headed young guy. "Who is this?"

John said, "Tony Richmond. He's good, *ain't* he?"

This guy Tony was working the drums like nobody's business! I always wondered how long it would take to get the full coordination together to play the drums well. I imagined it was like driving a stick shift car in steadily changing road traffic. You had to use all of your limbs in a definitive rhythm. But this guy Tony seemed like he was *born* for it. I especially liked how he worked the high hat:

Tic-Ticka-DOOM-TAT
Tic-Ticka-DOOM-DOOM-TAT
Tic-Ticka-DOOM-DOOM-TAT-DOOM
Tic-Ticka-DOOM-TAT . . .

Usually when most people hear that *tic, tic, tic* sound of the high hat in music, you kind of ignore it. But once you're able to see and hear percussion artists perform by themselves, you understand exactly how important that high hat is to driving the rhythm of the beat.

John smiled and said, "I want to talk to this guy. A lot of people don't use the drum like that anymore. They use drum machines and samplers in a lot of music now."

We owed that to hip-hop music. Ironically, the drummer had become null and void in an era where the beats meant everything.

After Tony was finished with his performance, he had a flood of people who wanted to ask him about drumming, so we patiently waited our turn.

John said, "He looks young, too, don't he?"

I said, "Yeah. He looks around twenty-two, like Angie and Pyra. And hopefully he acts his age," I joked.

John just chuckled at it.

When we finally got to him, Tony looked tired of talking. He seemed to be an energetic guy, though. I guess anyone would be tired after putting on a great drum performance and then answering Twenty Questions.

John stepped up and asked him, "Are you doing a show tonight?" A lot of performers were showcasing in the Philadelphia area that weekend.

He looked at John and said, "Yeah. I actually forgot about it. Thanks for reminding me. I'm going to be at Zanzibar Blue tonight with a jazz set."

"Are they having an open microphone, or do they have featured singers already?" John asked him.

Tony looked confused. "Umm . . . I don't know. Why, you wanna sing?"

John answered, "Yeah."

I smiled. John was right on his case.

Tony said, "Well, I'll ask and find out. I mean, it's not really my band or anything, they just asked me to sit in with them."

John said, "All right, well, we'll hang out with you then. You need help with your equipment?"

Tony started laughing. "Where y'all from, down south? You got an accent."

I finally spoke up and said, "Yeah. We from Charlotte."

"Charlotte. Y'all tryin' to be the next Jodeci?"

I said, "Nah. This is Loverboy, the one and only."

John said, "Yeah, and this is my manager, D Harmon."

Tony laughed and said, "We got two young bucks from down south. The Loverboy, hunh? Can you sing like that?"

We both smiled at him and laughed with confidence.

Tony read it and said, "Oh, it's like that?"

John said, "I'm pretty good," being modest about it, you know. Then he asked how old Tony was.

He answered, "I'm turning twenty-three next week."

John said, "You're an Aquarius like me then. I'm turning twenty on February eighth."

Tony smiled and nodded back to him. "All right then, Loverboy and D Harmon. I'm gon' see what y'all got tonight. I'll try to get you on."

Zanzibar Blue was a nice, low-key spot in downtown Philadelphia, and John and I were nearly the youngest people in there that night. It represented a new audience for him, older jazz enthusiasts. But it didn't matter to me. John's style seemed to transcend all ages and classifications. The boy was just creative like that.

We listened to the jazz set patiently, feeling everything out, and then they had an intermission.

Tony Richmond walked over to us and said, "They're gonna let you in on the second set. So get ready to do your thing, man. What kind of tempo do you need? I'll start it off with the beat, and the band will just follow you."

John nodded and thought to himself for a minute. I was thinking he would perform *At Midnight*. It would have been the perfect fit. He didn't have any backup singers for *Freedom* or *Unappreciated*. And *May I* didn't really need a full band, so I just figured *At Midnight* would do.

John said, "Just give me something medium tempo and sentimental."

Tony smiled and nodded back to him. He said, "All right. Sentimental it is."

When they introduced John to the stage with his Loverboy tag, from Charlotte, North Carolina, people seemed to get energized. They started twisting and turning in their seats, and anticipating something good. I mean, if you're going to call yourself a Loverboy in front of a crowd of music lovers, you were either a fool or you had better be able to back it up. It was just a perfect damn name for demanding attention.

John walked up on their small stage in front of the dining tables. He was wearing his singing uniform of slacks and shoes, with another loose-fitting, attention-getting shirt. But instead of holding on to the microphone and looking toward the back of the room like he usually did, John kept his head down and spread his arms as if he was hovering behind the microphone stand.

Tony started it off with a medium-tempo, sentimental beat, just like John had asked him:

Tic-Tic-TAT-Tic-KA-DOOM
Tic-TAT-Tic-KA-DOOM
Tic-TAT-Tic-KA-DOOM
Tic-TAT-Tic . . .

John slipped right in on beat and sang:

The sta-a-a-age
she's my lov-ver
and when we get to-ge-ther
boy do we get down.

The sta-a-a-age . . .

The brass and bass line slid in after John's lead:

BLARNP-BLARRN
BOOMP-BOOOM-BOOOM
BOOMP-BOOOM-BOOOM

. . . she's my lov-ver
and if you've hear-r-rd about us
you kno-o-ow we ro-o-ock the town.

The sta-a-a-ge . . .

John finally decided to raise his head and his arms, looking like a brown Jesus with short-cut hair and sideburns. He had them eating out of the palms of his open hands! I didn't really know if he was freestyling a new song or trying something that he had been working on. I didn't care. John was doing his thing again!

DAMN! That's my BOY *up there!* I was thinking to myself.

I looked to Tony Richmond on the drums and he was smiling his ass off as he changed up the beat to add pep to John's lyrics:

Ti-DOOM-DOOM
DOOM-TAT-DOOM
Ti-DOOM-DOOM
DOOM-TAT-DOOM

The sta-a-a-age
she's my lov-ver
she asked me for my lov-ving
so I gave her a try.

The sta-a-a-age
she's my lov-ver
and if I can't be with her
boy I think I'd die.

The jazz band lost their cool, and the band members got all excited and started going off in there, tearing the roof off the mother! Loverboy was KICKING THEIR ASS! THE BOY SIMPLY HAD IT! John started breaking it down with the band. That's when I knew that he was freestyling:

I WOULD JUST DIE WITHOUT HER
I TELL YA I'D JUST DIE
DIE
DIE AND DIE AND DIE.

THE STA-A-A-AGE
SHE'S MY LOVE, LOVE, LOV-VER
SHE OPENED HER HEART TO ME
AND I GAVE MY HEART BACK.

THE STA-A-A-AGE
SHE'S MY LOV-VER
AND NOW THAT WE'RE TO-GE-THER
YOU CAN'T PULL US A-PART . . .

There were so many people jumping up and down to get John's contact information that I felt like a stock trader on Wall Street. Everybody wanted Loverboy's Orange Juice. It got real hot in that place. John had heated things up for them. I mean, I was so overwhelmed by everything that I couldn't really put two and two together on who was important and who was not. But John made the decision for me. He didn't let Tony Richmond out of his sight. So after we had talked to plenty of people about music and our plans, we ended up with Tony Richmond, helping him to carry his drum equipment back to his old blue van.

I asked Tony sarcastically, "So, what did you think, man? Is he the Loverboy, or what?"

Tony shook his head with big eyes and said, "*Shit!* After a while I thought *I* had some panties on up in that juhn. And I don't even go that way. Y'all gon' make me get high as shit tonight! *Lifted!*"

He had this Philadelphia slang that I didn't understand sometimes, but it was all love and all real.

John said, "You had the beat, man. I was just making it up and following you."

Tony looked at John as if he was crazy. And it was cold up in Philadelphia in January. But none of us seemed to mind after the heat that was left sizzling at Zanzibar Blue.

Tony said, "Shit, you lyin' to me! If my beats could make people sing like that, I'd be rich already. I'd have fuckin' Michael Jackson money, and you two Southern niggas wouldn't be nowhere near me. I'd have *helicopters* flying my shit out of here."

He stopped laughing and said, "For real, though, we got's to stay in touch."

John said, "That's why we're still here with you. I've been in the church choir and bands all of my life, and I know a good drummer when I see one."

"Shit, I'm glad you do," Tony said. He looked at us both and asked, "Y'all get high?"

John and I hesitated. Neither one of us did.

Tony started laughing and answered his own question before we could.

"Naw, y'all don't get high. I can see it in y'all faces. Y'all two natural-born country boys. And the weed might fuck up your mind."

John said, "The rappers act like the weed helps them to write."

Tony paused for a second as if he was really thinking about it. He said, "Naw, it loosens you up, and then you start writing shit because your mind is unclouded. But you don't need that shit, John. You're already loose. Weed can do the opposite and put more on your mind sometimes than what you want up there."

He laughed and said, "You start acting paranoid and shit, like your shit ain't no good, and that people hate you. That's when you start fuckin' up."

He asked us, "Where y'all staying at up here? Y'all reserved a hotel room, or you're planning to sleep in the car?"

I said, "Nah, we got this hotel room off the road."

"Is it cheap?"

John and I both smiled and said, "Yeah."

"Well, give me y'all numbers before y'all jet."

We all traded phone numbers and said our good-byes for the night, but we *definitely* wanted to stay in touch with Tony for the future.

As soon as we hit the streets of Philadelphia in my car, a horn from a black Cadillac Seville blew at us to pull over.

I looked at John and John looked at me.

I asked, "You know who that is, man?"

John said, "Nah. You?"

"If *I* knew, what the hell would I ask you for?"

We pulled over to see what was what. This big old guy in nice clothes stepped out of the Cadillac and smiled at us.

He looked at John and said, "Boy, can you *sing*. Where you from?"

"Charlotte."

"North Carolina?"

I spoke up and said, "Yeah," just so the guy would know that we were together.

He said, "I'm Chester DeBerry," and pulled out a business card.

John handed it to me. I flipped it over and read "BMG Music." This guy was a sales rep for music distribution. But how could that help us? We didn't have our own record label or anything. Then again, if we hooked up with a small label and had our own distribution channels . . .

I couldn't help it. I was thinking fast because the music business moved fast. Or at least when people recognized that you were money in the bank. John was more than that. He was money in the *vault* as far as I was concerned.

This guy Chester asked us where we were staying again, and we told him about the cheap place that we had found off the freeway for $48 a night.

He laughed. "Well, you guys sure know how to go for it. Don't mind where you're staying, just get on out there and make it happen." He nodded his head and said, "I admire that. You guys are two young pathfinders. So, who are you, the manager?" he asked me.

I said, "Yeah, how you'd guess?"

He said, "Are you kidding me? That's the oldest partnership in the books; the talent and the business. And by the time it's over with, the business side usually ends up with most, if not *all*, of the money."

I shook my head and said, "Nah, John is my boy. We've been close since before grade school."

"I understand that. But I've been in the music business since before either of you were born." Then he smiled and said, "I'll tell you what I'll do. You always want to make new friends in this business, so even though I promised myself that I wouldn't get too involved this year, I'll offer to put you guys up for the night in the host hotel, at the Philadelphian. I want you guys to mingle a little bit with everybody else. Because if *anybody* deserves to be in the middle of the action this year, it's *you guys*."

I didn't see any bad strings attached to that deal. How could he harm us? We hadn't signed anything.

I looked at John and said, "What do you think?"

He said, "Hey, man, let's do it. I'm game. Are you giving us the penthouse?"

John was all pumped up, deservedly.

Chester laughed and warned him, "That's exactly how the *talent* gets in big trouble."

"I was only joking," John told him.

Chester stopped and said, "If it's on your mind, then it's in your heart. And you can take my advice or you can leave it, but don't ever let this superstar shit go to your head. You keep yourself a tight-knit, family-like setting, and you keep all of that other shit *outside* of your circle. You hear me? That's the only way you can survive this thing."

We nodded and followed Chester's Cadillac to this fancy downtown hotel. Aspiring musicians were everywhere, and representing every culture. You had pink-headed girl rock bands, thuggish rap groups, made-up soul singers, and the plenty of gray-haired types who were trying to hold on by finding fresh new young talent to exploit.

Chester sure was right. We were in the middle of everything!

After getting us a nice room on the eighth floor of the twenty-four-floor hotel, he told us to page him if we needed anything.

John and I sat our small bags down inside of the hotel room and looked at each other like two kids at the circus.

I said, "Do you *believe* this shit, man?! This music shit is *crazy*. It's like, anything goes in this business. And we not even really in it yet."

John smiled and said, "So, you still want to play football instead of being my manager?"

I didn't even hesitate. "Hell yeah!" I told him. That music stuff hadn't knocked me over *that* much. It still couldn't top playing football at the Super Bowl. *Nothing* topped the Super Bowl! At least not in America.

John said, "Yeah, we'll see."

"Yeah, we *will* see," I told him.

He said, "Well, let's go see who's in here."

I was all for it. We had a hotel room to ourselves, and there were plenty of girls downstairs to choose from. I had no strings attached to any of them, and I was on the hunt to get busy.

As soon as we made it down into the noisy lobby area, John actually beat me to the punch and talked to some girls. That boy was growing confidence overnight!

"Are you all singers?" he asked three dark brown sisters. They were all dressed in tight white outfits that made them stand out from the crowd.

One of them answered, "Does it *look* like it?" before they started laughing.

I thought to myself, *Actually, you look more like three skinny stage dancers to me,* as a comeback line for them dissing my boy like that. But John didn't think much of it.

He asked them, "What's your stage name?"

They answered, "Chocolate Fantasy."

I started laughing. Aspiring singers had some of the most ridiculous names that you could think of. I guess that once, or *if*, they made it to the real contract stage, people who knew better would advise them to stick to something more tame.

"You guys have, like, sexy songs then? Who writes for you?" John asked them.

One of them took offense to that. She was the shortest. She said, "Why somebody gotta *write for us?* I'm tired of hearing that. We can't write our *own* songs?"

John said, "Are they good?"

"Are *your* songs any good?"

"How do you know that I even write songs?"

"Well, you're asking all of these questions, you must do *something?*"

The first girl, who made the sarcastic comment, was ready to go, but the short girl and the third member of the group seemed ready to argue John down.

I put in my two cents and said, "What are you thinking about, writing a song for a girl group now, Loverboy?" I did it on purpose, just to have a little fun while being the devil's advocate.

The third member said, "Loverboy? That's your stage name?" I figured that would happen. It was my setup.

This third girl was the prettiest, in my eyes. I mean, they all looked good, just a little underweight for my Southern taste, but the third member's face and eyes were from heaven. She reminded me of Whitney Houston with hair and a good, deep suntan. I would take that girl home to my momma. After I put some weight on her, though.

"Where are y'all from?" I asked them.

"New Jersey."

"What part?"

"Where *y'all* from, down south somewhere?" the short writer said with a smile.

I hated that. As soon as Northerners detected the slightest accent, they started talking that "down south" stuff, as if we all lived on country farms with pigs and cattle.

I said, "We from Charlotte, like Jodeci."

That did the trick. They were all smiles after that.

"I like Jodeci," the prettiest one nodded and told me.

"I like you," I told her right back.

She said, "Plenty of guys do." But I could tell that I had caught her off guard. If she was white, she would have blushed. I could tell from how she turned away to stop herself from grinning.

"You sing, too?" the short and snappy one asked me.

I shook my head and said, "Nah, I manage, like Puffy and Jermaine Dupri." They were the hottest young names in management and production, yet they were heavy on the music end, where I was not. I started thinking that if I did become a manager, I needed to learn a lot more about *making* music.

The first girl was not impressed with us, and she was still ready to go, so they had a dilemma on their hands.

"Sidney, you need to just chill, girl. If we find him, we find him," the short girl said. She seemed to be the leader, but I didn't want to be wrong, so I just kept it to myself.

John asked her, "What's your name?"

"Oh, I'm Kellie, this is Dawn, and . . . I guess Sidney is trying her *damnedest* to leave us," she said of her group member. Sidney had slipped away.

"You're here without a manager?" I asked them.

"No, we have a manager. But we ditched him, you know, because he sweats us a little too hard," Dawn told me.

"Like how?" I asked.

Kellie said, "Just worrying too much, like we don't know how to handle ourselves. Shit, I've been handling my own business for a long time. I don't need that *baby-sitting* shit!"

I shook my head and smiled. Kellie was definitely the group leader. She *had* to be.

Dawn said, "You want me to go get her?" referring to Sidney.

Kellie said, "Hell no, girl. Let her do her own thing then, since she's so damned *pressed*."

John said, "Who is she looking for?"

"Some damn guy she met down here a few months ago," Kellie answered. "It's obvious that he's trying to ditch her now. She needs to move the hell on." She laughed and said, "We write songs about shit like this."

Dawn sang, *"It's time to move on, girl,"* and snapped her fingers.

Kellie filled in and sang, *"Move on . . ."*

John jumped right on top of that and sang, *"And find a new ma-a-an, like me."*

We all broke out laughing.

Kellie said, "Hey, that was kind of nice. You want to sing a duet?"

I said, "That's why we call him the Loverboy."

Dawn asked us, "Well, where are you two staying? Do you have a room here? We don't have a room."

That was music to my ears. I said, "Yeah, we have a room. And you know, we from down south, so we share everything. *Mi casa es su casa.*"

Kellie grinned and said, "Mmm hmm, we heard all about *Jo-deci's* house."

John said, "We're not like that. We're the good boys."

We all started laughing again.

Dawn looked at Kellie and said, "I can chill with them. You want to?"

Kellie looked back in the direction that Sidney had walked in. "Oh well, if she finally gives up her search, she knows how to page us. So let's go get room service."

I stopped and said, "Room service?"

She said, "Yeah, I heard y'all know how to *feed* a girl down south, too."

I said, "Yeah, but not at *this* hotel's prices. We're just *staying* here."

Dawn asked, "Well, what y'all gon' eat?"

I said, "Hell, we'll go out and find a McDonald's somewhere. We're not sweating this hotel food like that."

I wasn't trying to build up a tab on our gift of a room from Mr. Chester DeBerry. I guess I was just being practical.

John laughed and said, "You girls sure know how to ask for what you want up here."

By that time, we had already made it to the elevators.

Kellie said, "Don't act like girls from down south don't ask for what *they* want. If they didn't, they wouldn't be so big and healthy, with them deep, old voices."

I said, "Aw, man, wait a minute. We just like our women with a little bit of stability, that way we don't lose them when the wind blows."

Dawn said, "So, what are you trying to say?"

We jumped on the elevator with listeners all around us.

I said, "I'm just saying that it would be nice not to see a girl's ribs through her shirt, that's all."

We had a comedy skit right there on the elevator. I may have been from the South and everything, but I was *never* a pushover.

Dawn said, "You can't see my damn ribs. I am nowhere *near* that skinny." She looked at this white girl riding the elevator with us and said, "Now *she's* skinny."

John was just laughing his ass off as we made it up to the eighth floor.

When we got off of the elevator, Dawn asked me, "What is your name, anyway?"

"Darin Harmon. And I'm no country boy either. Okay? We live in houses on streets, with night lights, driveways, and everything else. Okay?"

Kellie smiled and said, "We were just joking. Don't get so offended by it."

John said, "He's not offended. D likes getting into it with girls. He's been doing that all of his life."

Dawn asked, "Getting into girls how?"

I didn't know exactly how to take that, but let's just say that I took it the nasty way. So I started laughing while John opened the room with the key card.

"You gon' answer my question?" Dawn pressed me. I guess she liked me.

I said, "Yeah, maybe a little later on."

Somehow we avoided that room service call and just had a great time talking about the North and South, black people, white people, dark skin, light skin, videos, American stardom, and a little bit of everything while we all enjoyed one another's company.

At about two in the morning, John and Kellie were in one bed talking about music, and Dawn and I were in the other bed playing footsies. We were all lying on top of the covers, and I wanted that girl Dawn some kind of bad. She *knew it*, too! She was teasing me with every look and every move she made.

Kellie was saying, "I've been singing since I was about five years old."

John asked, "And what are you, about thirty-four now?"

We all started laughing again. They were no older than we were.

Kellie said, "You better watch yourself with that. I do *not* look old." She said, "So, how long have you been singing?"

John said, "For about four months."

Dawn shouted, "Liar!"

I said, "Nah, he's serious. He's more of a musician."

Kellie said, "So, you produce and write your own music, *and* you sing?"

John said, "Yeah."

"Damn. That's some R. Kelly and Keith Sweat shit," Kellie responded to him.

"And Prince," I added. "Don't forget about Prince."

John said, "And Babyface Edmonds. But when I get up there onstage . . . it's just me and the mike. And it's like, I know that people are out there listening to me and whatnot, but I'm in a zone . . . right there onstage. And nobody can take that feeling away from me. *Nobody!*"

The room got real quiet for a minute. John had us listening to another solo of why he loved to sing. Either that or we were all falling asleep and John had simply outlasted us.

He said, "I just feel that . . . if you have a gift, then you owe it to the world to share it. You know what I mean?"

Kellie said, "Yeah, I feel the same way."

Dawn grunted, "Mmm hmm."

I said, "Yeah, me too. I feel that way about football," just so I wouldn't be left out.

Dawn gave me a love tap on my left thigh that only teased me more.

John said, "Singing onstage is like you've just stepped into another world. It's a natural high. Like you're the god of the moment . . . with the world, like, waiting for your voice to fill up the emptiness. And just to feel that kind of power up there . . . man, I would do it for nothing."

I said, "Not if *I'm* around you ain't. So you make sure you keep that singing-for-free shit to yourself."

We all shared another laugh together.

Then John asked, "What about your friend Sidney? Is she okay? Do you need to go and look for her?"

Kellie laughed and said, "Shit, at two o'clock in the morning, whatever the hell she was looking for, she must have found it. I ain't thinking about that girl. She's always running off by herself somewhere. I'm tired of chasing after her."

I said, "Damn, it's like that? What happened to sister love to the end?"

Kellie said, "We came to the end."

I kind of felt that that was fucked up. I couldn't ever see John and me coming to an end. I just figured that we'd be boys for life no matter what. But I heard of plenty of girls breaking friendships over what seemed to be pettiness. I thought that sister bonds were supposedly extra strong, but sometimes I had to wonder. Or maybe it was just that way in the music business.

Anyway, when we all got quiet again, it was obvious that we were all ready to fall asleep. That's when Dawn whispered in my ear, "You have a T-shirt or something for me to sleep in?"

That was more music to my ears.

I whispered back, "With nothing else under it?"

She grinned and said, "You wish. Maybe when we know each other better."

My Johnson was hard anyway. I figured we still had to get through the night while sleeping in the same bed together. Maybe she would change her mind.

When I got up to get her a T-shirt from my bag, I looked over at John and Kellie, and they were both sound asleep and still in their clothes, probably dreaming about singing on stage and whatnot. But me, I just wanted to sing under the sheets with Dawn. Body talk music.

VERSE 6

. . . on his way to a dream . . .

Dawn wouldn't let me bone her that night. She let me work my fingers until my right arm was sore, but every time I tried to sneak in place for the real deal, she pushed me away. Then she had the nerve to whisper, "Go downtown on me."

I was like, "Nope. Maybe when we know each other better." Afterward, I kept thinking that I could have gotten some if I did what she asked me to, but I wasn't brave enough or *fool* enough to find out.

We traded phone numbers with them that morning, and when John and I got back to school at A&T, my boy was restless as ever. His whole interest in school was gone. He didn't even feel like playing in the band at the basketball games, and he was still on scholarship. I guess that weekend treat of being so close to music stardom was too much for him to bear.

On the management end, I had about thirty phone calls to make on John's behalf, following up with all of the people that we had met at the Philadelphia Music Conference. John said that I could make all of the phone calls from his room, and that he would pay for them. This boy had no idea how many different assignments I had to work on to manage him. All his ass thought about was performing. He really *needed* a manager!

I said, "Okay, John, here's what we need to do. We need to contact a strong booking agent to get you more shows. I'm not really connected like that anyway. We also need to set up your own music publishing and copyright all of your songs, because you write and perform your own stuff, and you want to get full credit for that. Plus, you could write for other artists through your own publishing company. Then I can call my brother Darryl to talk about the whole *business* side, with accounting and everything, because I don't know that much about money to really help you when it gets thick, man.

"And eventually, we have to sit down and talk to a good attorney who knows a lot about the music business," I said. "Because when you're ready to start talking to different record labels about getting you a record deal, you're gonna need someone who knows what they're doing."

I had it all mapped out like a football game plan, because I knew that I wouldn't be there to help John with everything. I figured that I also needed to contact some real managers who could help him out full time and do more for him than I could. Outdoor track season was right around the corner. I also had to get myself ready for football's spring training. My boy was on the way to *his* dream, and I wanted to start preparing again for *mine*.

John just nodded his head and was mute about everything I had explained to him.

I asked him, "What's wrong, man? You look down."

He said, "I just want to do my thing, man. I'm tired of school. I want to teach and learn my own lessons about music. That's all these teachers are talking about anyway, man, music theories based on what other people did."

I said, "You're gonna get there, man. Just hold your horses a little bit."

I started making the phone calls, and if any contact didn't remember who John "Loverboy" Williams was, I made it a short conversation. I was interested only in people who wanted to work with John as badly as *John* wanted to perform onstage. I also wanted people who would be on the straight and narrow when it came to the business. If you couldn't help us, then I couldn't help you.

I noticed immediately that some of the stronger contacts in the music business were harder to reach. I ended up leaving a bunch of messages with their secretaries and whatnot. But the smaller people, who answered their own telephones, seemed too eager.

"Oh, yeah, Loverboy was *great!* That kid can *sing!* When can you guys sit down and talk to us?"

Maybe I was just too skeptical about things, but I didn't feel any warm response to that. I had plenty of smaller colleges who were eager to recruit me out of high school for football and track, and I just knew better than to jump at the first happy face available. I was so damn skeptical that I started playing the big man on campus by challenging some of the people to represent us with no paperwork signed.

I told this one booking agent from the Detroit, Michigan, area that we needed to see what kind of venues he could get for John before we could get serious with him. I had no idea what I was doing, I just knew that John was getting anxious, and that made *me* feel desperate to make things happen faster because I knew that I was running out of time with him. So instead of passing the torch to a more experienced manager, I made a last-ditch effort to work something out on my boy's behalf.

This guy from Detroit said, "You know what? We have a Black History Month Celebration coming up in Detroit that would be a perfect spot to see what Loverboy is made of."

He was kicking the ball right back to me. I just smiled at it.

"How much is it worth?" I asked him.

"Two plane tickets, food, and a couple of nights in a hotel."

I started laughing. This guy was straight business.

He said, "Look, I don't mind taking a chance on you if you take a chance on me. But there won't be any money involved until we sign a contract."

I thought about it, and it sounded fair. If John killed them in Detroit, like I knew he would, then only a fool would not try to sign him. In the meantime, it gave John another opportunity to do his thing in a new city and in front of a new crowd. Motown's crowd! Then I thought about including Tony Richmond as a band mate.

"We have a drummer who needs to fly in from Philadelphia," I said.

"Well, that's *your* problem. I'm signing Loverboy right now, not a whole band. He's a solo singer, right?"

I said, "Yeah, but you know you can't jam without a drummer, man." I was trying to convince him.

"We got plenty of drummers right here in Detroit. How many of them do you need?"

His point was made. He wasn't doing it.

I said, "Well, let us think about it and call you back."

"Don't make it a long wait. Time is of the essence."

I hung up with him and looked at John.

He asked me, "What's up? We got another gig?"

"Yeah, in Detroit. But I'm trying to get Tony in on it. You want him?"

John nodded and said, "Yeah. And I'll pay for it if I have to."

John always had a stash of money somewhere. He was one of those bare necessities guys.

I said, "Well, let me call him first. Ain't no sense in offering more than we need to. And he may want more than you can pay."

I called Tony Richmond in Philly and he answered on the second ring.

"Hello."

"Hey, Tony. This is Darin and Loverboy calling from North Carolina."

"Oh, what's up, man? I'm still in fuckin' bed. You lucky this long distance, or I'd hang up on your ass."

I said, "We got a gig in Detroit, man, but since we won't sign with the booking agent just yet, he's just giving us plane tickets and a hotel room. We wanted to include you, but he wouldn't do it."

Tony said, "Detroit? I got family out in Detroit, man. When y'all going?"

I said, "Next month for a Black History Month Celebration."

"Well, yo, tell that booking agent to get me plane tickets, too, and I'll just stay at my cousin's crib. Can you do that?"

I said, "So, all you need is plane tickets?" I wanted to make sure.

Tony paused for a minute. He said, "I'll put it to you like this, I like you niggas, man. I wanna see if John'll blow up like I *think* he is. And if he blows up, then I'm blowing up right with him. Is that a deal?"

I smiled at the idea. I said, "That's what I'm calling you up for, man. That's a deal."

I hung up and told John, "We just need to get him plane tickets."

John nodded and told me, "Okay. Let's find out how much the tickets cost."

I laid all of the groundwork for the trip to Detroit and John seemed a little more stable again. I mean, that boy was starting to fiend for shows like a junkie or something. I figured that hooking him up with Tony Richmond was the right thing to do, so that they could rise to the top together instead of John being all by himself when I decided to return to my own sports thing. I wanted to talk to Tony about both of them being represented by the same manager. I just trusted that Tony guy. He seemed real down-to-earth and sincere.

On John's twentieth birthday, February 8, his mom called him up to wish him a happy birthday and to check up on him.

I happened to be in his room when he received the phone call.

He said, "Thanks, Mom. I love you, too . . . Well, I feel closer to my goal now." He rolled his eyes and said, "Well, I'm still in school for now." Then there was a long pause. I figured that he was ignoring her again. It was something else to watch John and his mother in action. It was as if John had finally figured her out. He was all that she had, her son and God. Once John understood that, he began to have this power over his mother where he could basically do whatever he wanted to and dare her to do something about it. It was like having an employee who was the only man for the job, so you couldn't fire him. John began to string his mother along like a plaything, and then she would complain and bring *me* into it. I figured after all those years I spent trying to make John a rebel, when he finally decided to do it, it came back to haunt me.

John looked at me and said, "She wants to talk to you, man."

I mumbled, "Shit. I knew I should have left the room."

I answered the phone and said, "Hi, Sister Williams."

She asked me, "Is John still going to his classes?"

That mother's intuition thing is something else. I guess she could just sense that John was losing his interest in school.

I said, "Yes ma'am, as far as I know he is."

"And what's going on with this music stuff?"

I said, "Well, he's still trying to work toward getting a contract." It was no sense in lying about it just because his mother didn't want it to happen.

She said, "Well, has he sung in the school choir?"

"No ma'am."

"Why not?"

"Ahh . . . I guess he just hasn't thought about it," I answered.

"Well, tell him to try it, Darin. He listens to you. He always has."

I hated when she started talking like that. She made it seem that I was John's daddy or something, and I wasn't.

I told her that I would try anyway, just so she could sleep in peace that night. But I didn't promise her that he would agree.

When we hung up with John's mother, I said, "Have you ever thought about singing gospel, or a solo in the school choir, man?"

John started smiling. "You think the choir director hasn't asked me that already? He's called me about once a week, ever since I performed at homecoming."

"So, what do you tell him?"

"I tell him no. Every time he asks me."

I said, "But why not do it?" We were still from the church, and even though John and I no longer went every Sunday, I didn't see anything wrong with him singing in the school choir.

John said, "How many singers do you know that are famous from staying in the choir?"

I said, "Nobody told you to *stay* in the choir, I'm just asking you to sing with them. You could practice some more with your voice and all."

The telephone rang before John could answer me.

"Hello," he answered it. He looked at me in alarm and said, "I got some plans already . . . I can't do that . . . But I— But— Well . . . Yeah, all right," he said, defeated.

I asked him, "Who was that?"

"Pyra. She's on her way down here with Angie."

I started smiling. I had done my best to keep Two Scoops out of my mind. As far as I was concerned, John could grab backup singers from anywhere. He didn't need any extra stress from an unorganized and only moderately talented duo. Leaving people in the wind was part of the business. Just like I learned in track, if you can't keep up, you don't advance to the next round.

I asked John, "So what do they want to do, hang out on your birthday?"

"Yeah, but I already made plans," he told me.

"With who?"

"Janese, from Bennett."

I said, "So, she forgave you?"

"I mean, she knows that I'm busy trying to do what I need to do, but then she started talking about how I've gotten too big for her and all that kind of stuff."

I laughed and asked, "So she got you with the guilt trip?"

He said, "Yeah, I guess so."

"Well, good luck tonight, man. It sounds like you gon' need it."

I was planning to ask John all of the details that next morning, but I was pulled into it before the night could even get started.

Pyra called my room and said, "Where is John?"

"Enjoying his birthday somewhere, I guess," I told her with a grin. I had company of my own that night.

Pyra said, "Well, I *know* that, but where?" as if I was supposed to tell her.

I said, "Pyra, did John tell you he had plans?"

"Look, I told him I was on my way down here, and he said okay. Now where the fuck is he? Don't play with me, man."

I wanted to laugh at her, but I kept my composure.

I said, "I don't know what to tell you."

Pyra paused for a second. She said, "All right then, watch this," before she hung up in my ear.

My company asked me, "Who was that?" She could hear Pyra's voice over the phone.

I said, "One of John's new friends," and went on about my business.

According to what John told me over the phone that night, Pyra and Angie drove to a Bojangles' fast food joint, probably on their way back home, and they spotted John and Janese waiting in line to be served.

I broke out laughing before he could even finish. I guess it was just meant to happen to him that night.

"So what happened?" I asked him.

He said, "Man, Pyra stepped up to me talking about, 'John, didn't I tell you I was on my way down here?' So I told her again that I already had plans, you know. So she looks Janese up and down and says, 'I see.' Then she said, 'Can I speak to you for a minute?'

"So I walk over to see what she has to say, and she looks me straight in my face and says, 'Leave that bitch and come on.'"

I said, "No, she didn't say that."

John said, "Yes she did, too. So I told her I couldn't do that. And she said, 'You can do anything you fuckin' want to do. She ain't nobody. Or is she?'"

John said, "And by that time, Janese had overheard what she was saying. So Janese turns and says, 'Some people just don't know how to conduct themselves like ladies.'"

I broke in and said, "I told you that girl Pyra was crazy, man." My ribs started hurting from the laughter while John continued.

"Then Pyra said, 'Did I say anything to you? I didn't *think* so.'"

"So, who threw the first punch?" I asked him.

"Oh, they didn't fight. It was other people in there, so the manager came out and calmed everything down before it got to that."

"So where are you now, with Pyra and Angie?" I teased him. John used to be a big pushover for forceful girls. They would get over on him just like his mom used to do.

He said, "Nah, I told Pyra to go find something else to do. But I'm at a hotel with Antoinette now."

I said, "Antoinette?"

"Yeah, the freshman music major I told you about."

"Well, what happened to Janese?"

"Aw, man, when we left, right, she started talking about, 'Light-skin girls always think they *rule* the fucking world. That shit gets on my damn nerves.' Man, I didn't even know that Janese could curse like that. So I told her, 'Well, I'm still with you. The light-skin girl didn't get her way this time,' right? And Janese started talking about, 'Yeah, but you *like her*, though. Now I *see* what you were so *busy* doing.'

"So I told her, man, 'Look, this is my birthday, and I want to have a good night. I didn't invite her down here. She just came on her own. I'm with you. So let's just enjoy it.'

"Then she started grunting and acting all antisocial, man," he told me. "So I said, 'Look, if you don't want to be with me tonight, then just let me know, because the night is still young and it's still my birthday.'

"Then she got real mad after that and started talking about, 'So what are you going to do, *Loverboy*, go find somebody else to be with? You know what, you're just like all the rest of these guys out here. You don't really care about me, John. I'm just temporary enter*tainment* for you,' and all this other stuff."

He said, "So after that, man, we just went our separate ways. And then I went and called up Antoinette to see what she was doing, because I didn't feel like being alone."

I couldn't believe what I was hearing. That boy had arrived at full play-erhood. If the first girl ain't acting right, then call the next one. I broke up laughing.

I said, "Well, what did Antoinette say when you called her?"

"Oh, man, I told her straight out, you know. If you don't want to be with me tonight, then I understand. I just don't feel like sleeping alone."

I said, "Oh my God! You told her that?" Not only had John arrived, he was *bold* about it!

He said, "Yeah, man. I mean, I didn't want to mislead her. And I felt like . . . you know, doing something for my birthday."

I thought about it and realized that it would be the first time John would ever get any on his birthday. I went ahead and asked him about that just to make sure.

He said, "Yeah, man, this'll be my first time. You know, on my birthday."

I said, "Well, where is Antoinette now?"

"She's up in the room. I'm downstairs on a pay phone, man. I just had to tell you how my night was going, D. It's crazy, man. I'm gon' have to write a song about this. *Crazy Situations.*"

I started laughing again and said, "Well, go ahead and enjoy yourself, man. It's your birthday."

I hung up the phone with my boy that night and thought about it. *When John blows up with this singing thing . . . if girls have a problem with him now, they're really gon' feel the burn from him later.* I could just imagine it. Twenty thousand in dark arenas. And John was a solo act, so he wouldn't even have to share. I thought to myself, *Damn! No wonder this boy's so anxious!*

We made it out to Detroit's airport with our bags and John's keyboard, and we were ready to be picked up by the booking agent. Tony Richmond's plane from Philly was due to arrive thirty minutes after ours.

When we reached the baggage claim area, this big muscle-bound guy asked us, "Are you Darin and John?"

We nodded and said, "Yeah."

He smiled at us and stuck out his beefy hand.

He said, "My name's Daren, too."

"With an *i-n?*" I asked him.

"An *e-n.*"

"Oh. Well, this is Loverboy," I told him, introducing John.

Daren nodded and smiled at him. "You better be able to sing with a name like that."

I said, "I know, right? That name sets him up every time. And then my boy knocks them down like bowling pins."

John just sat back and smiled. He never was much of a talker when it came to his music. He would just go out there and bring the house down.

I said, "Our drummer is landing from Philly in about twenty more minutes, on Delta."

Big Daren nodded and said, "Okay, well, let's load your stuff up first and go get him."

We loaded our stuff into a fully carpeted black van.

John looked inside and nodded. "That's nice."

Daren said, "Yeah. We know how important and expensive the music equipment is, so we make sure to protect it as best we can."

I said, "That's a good idea." And so far, I liked how we were being treated.

While we waited for Tony, I asked Daren if he played any football. He had the size for it.

He smiled and said, "Yeah. Middle linebacker. I went to Michigan State. I got into the booking business after playing a couple of years in the Canadian league. You play?"

"Yeah. Cornerback. I'm at North Carolina A&T. This'll be my first year starting, coming up."

He nodded. "What division is that in? That's a black school, right?"

I said, "Yeah. We're in Division one-double-*A.*"

Daren said, "That's a long-shot division."

I asked, "You ever heard of Steve 'Air' McNair, from Alcorn State?"

He got excited and said, "Oh yeah! That boy deserves the Heisman. With all them damn yards he's passing for, if he was *white* there would be no doubts about it."

I smiled and said, "He's from my same division. A *black* school."

Daren laughed and said, "All right, young brother. You don't have to prove that you can play. I believe you."

John spoke up and said, "But still, I'm trying to convince him that managing me is a better deal for him. How come you didn't keep playing in the Canadian league?" he asked Daren.

Big Daren shook his head. "After a while, it started to take too much of a toll on my body. Taking pain medicine all the time, with the bumps and bruises. I just figured that if I couldn't make the NFL, then why bother. I just lost the love for the game. I mean, I still like to *watch* it, but plenty of us had to put the ball up and find something else to do, you know. It's plenty of other opportunities out here."

He smiled and added, "You'd be surprised how much money you can make transporting the stars and their equipment. And there's plenty of perks involved in it, too."

John looked at me and said, "You hear that? You put the ball down and make other money."

I gave John a look, but I kept my thoughts to myself. I was thinking, *What would* you *say if I told you to stop the fucking singing and become a damn game announcer?* I was a little pissed with John, but I figured I'd tell his ass a thing or two later on when we were alone. Just like music was *his* thing, football was mine. He needed to respect that.

When Tony rolled in, we loaded all of his stuff in the van and headed to the hotel. Herbert Blake was waiting for us when we arrived. He was wearing all black with no tie. He looked liked a cool hipster in his early forties.

He looked at Tony and said, "Oh, *this* is your drummer from Philly? I heard you play at the music conference."

Tony nodded and said, "Yeah, I showed them a little somethin'-somethin' over there. That was me."

Blake's familiarity with Tony was a good thing for me as well, because I wanted to push John and Tony on him as a package deal.

I spoke up and said, "Well, these two guys are qualified to make some real good music together."

Blake nodded and said, "Well, how close are you guys to signing a record deal? Maybe I could help you out with that."

Tony joked and said, "What, is Berry Gordy still here in Detroit with Motown Records?"

We all laughed.

Blake said, "He moved Motown out to L.A. a while ago. But I have a few connections of my own. You guys show *me* something, and I'll show *you* something. We could even make a live demo tape with the audience screaming in the background."

That sounded like a good idea to me, but what would Blake get out of it? I nodded and said, "Yeah, we'll have to think about that."

Blake said, "That's fair enough. Thinking ain't never cost me a dime, unless I made the wrong decision *after* thinking. Or in this case, it's if *you* make the wrong decision. Well, let's check you guys into a room."

Blake had made reservations at a Hyatt Regency in the Detroit suburb of Dearborn. If he was trying to impress us, he had succeeded. This hotel was *phat!*

Tony said, "I'm staying over my cousin's crib. I just need a ride over to Southfield."

Blake looked at him and frowned. "Is that what you want to do? I could put you up in a room. I have an account over here. I mean, since they went through the trouble of flying you out here by themselves, the least that *I* could do is give you a room. That way you guys can all travel together like you're supposed to."

Tony smiled and said, "Aw'ight. You don't have to talk me into it. I'll just call my cousin and tell him then."

Blake looked at me and John and said, "That showed me a lot of initiative, you know, that your drummer meant that much to you. Because a lot of young guys in this business will get their *own* opportunities and just break camp on their bands. You know what I mean?"

He smiled and added, "Then again, in *some* cases, they *needed* to break camp, because dead weight has been known to drown everybody."

Before he left us that night, Blake said to have a good time in Detroit but not to overdo it, because he wanted all of our energy ready for the shows on Saturday and Sunday afternoon. We would fly back to Greensboro that Monday morning, and Tony would fly back to Philly.

John and I walked into our hotel room and started acting like two kids again.

I said, "We got this room for *three nights*, John. Oh, we gon' get some girls up here, man."

John laughed and asked me, "Have you kept in touch with Dawn from New Jersey?"

"Nah, not really," I told him.

He smiled and said, "Yeah, me neither. I think I only talked to Kellie once."

That was just the nature of the business. If you really stayed in contact with every person you met, you would have a killer phone bill, and we didn't have that kind of money while in college.

It didn't take us long to hit the night life in Detroit that Friday. Tony's cousin Bean took us to this place that was jam-packed with Detroit locals. They had to tell the security there that we were performers to even get us in, because John and I were not twenty-one and we had no fake IDs. But it was all worked out and they let us in, as long as we didn't try to order any drinks from the bar.

The first thing I noticed in there was that Detroit wasn't a dress-up kind of city. There were a lot of jeans and tennis shoes in that place, like at a college party. The parties that my older brothers went to in North Carolina and around the South were a lot of dressed-to-impress spots with no jeans or tennis shoes allowed. But the beats were *booming* in Detroit!

Tony smiled at us and hollered, "YOU HEAR THAT? THE BEATS MAKE THE PARTY EVERY TIME! JOHN HAS TO WRITE SOME PARTY GROOVES TO REALLY GET THE PEOPLE JUMPIN'! *I'M TELLIN' YOU!*"

His cousin Bean agreed with him. He was a mellow, light-skin dude with light brown hair and freckles.

"YEAH, THEY LOVE BEATS UP HERE IN DETROIT!" he told us. "DETROIT AND CHICAGO BOTH LIKE THAT HOUSE MUSIC FEEL! THAT BIG KICK DRUM! BOOM! BOOM! BOOM!"

John just looked around and took it all in.

The beats in that place were so thick that it made my chest vibrate. They were playing a lot of funky oldies music, too, that classic soul sound when the bands were still big.

I said, "WHAT DO YOU THINK, JOHN?!" I could barely hear myself talk.

John said, "I just can't wait to do *my* thing, man. I just can't *wait*." That boy seemed seriously anxious. He was getting impatient with the whole process of putting in his dues. John was much more impatient than I was about playing football. I just understood that I had to wait my turn.

He said something to me about a girl, but since he wasn't talking as loudly as the rest of us, I could barely hear him.

"HUNH?"

"LOOK AT THIS GIRL OVER HERE!" he repeated.

She had to be about twenty-three, one of the younger sisters in the party. And boy did she fill out her blue jeans! An artist couldn't draw better curves than what this girl had if he used a compass. I mean, DAMN she was curved! I just started laughing and shaking my head.

"GOD *DAMN!*" Tony commented. Him and his cousin Bean saw what we saw. Bean started laughing like I was.

Tony said, "IS SHE STANDING OUT, OR *WHAT?* AND THE THING ABOUT IT, HER ASS AIN'T LIKE IT'S ALL THAT BIG, IT'S JUST . . . IT'S JUST . . . *PERFECT!*"

John nodded his head with a grin and started walking toward this girl as if he was in a hypnotic trance. I know everything he said to her because we asked his ass a hundred times afterward.

"Excuse me. You wanna dance?" he asked this girl.

She looked at him and said, "What?"

They were both talking lower than everyone else, and when she turned to face him, her titties were just as ripe as the rest of her, with a smooth brown face and empty eyes, as if nothing fazed her. Hell, with a body like hers, I guess that *nothing* did!

John spoke up louder. "I SAID, DO YOU WANT TO DANCE!?"

She began to shake her head before he was even finished with his question. After she told him no, John just stood there like he was still in a daze.

He said, "WHY NOT!?"

She didn't even acknowledge him. She just walked away.

Me, Tony, and Bean all assessed the situation and started laughing in the distance. I guess that was why no one seemed eager to speak to this girl, she was just too damn hot to handle. Her man had to be the ultimate, if she even had one. Maybe she was too much for *any* man! She had *my* knees weak from just *looking* at her. Nevertheless, John went ahead and followed the girl. That's when the shit became scary.

He walked over to her at the bar, where it was quieter.

"Do you dance at all?" he asked her where she could hear him.

She looked at him in a huff and said, "Yeah!" and turned to order her drink.

By that time, Bean looked at me and said, "AY, MAN, YOU BETTER COOL YOUR BOY OUT BEFORE HE GET HIS ASS SHOT IN HERE!"

I hurried over to John to pull him away from the girl.

He walked away with me, mumbling, "What the hell she come in here for, if she don't wanna dance?!"

John had never been much of a dancer anyway. The boy had just gone crazy for a minute. There were some rough-ass Detroit guys all staring as if John had just asked for a beat-down. That's when my heart started racing triple time.

I said, "Man, what the hell is wrong with you?! If she don't want to dance, she don't want to dance!"

I don't know if it was the singing that made John extra bold that night or what, but it scared the hell out of me. At first it was cool, but after he went overboard with it, I just wanted to get back to the hotel room, where it was safe.

We made it back to Tony and Bean, and they had already come to a quick decision. We were leaving.

Bean said, "YOU JUST PLAYED YOURSELF, BOSS! YOU SUPPOSED TO BUY A GIRL LIKE THAT A DRINK *FIRST*, AND THEN LET *HER* ASK *YOU* TO DANCE!"

Once we walked out and hit the road in Bean's car, we were all able to laugh and tease John about it.

John said, "Man, she was fine, that's all *I* know."

Tony looked back from the front seat of his cousin's Oldsmobile and said, "Boy, I can see it now. I'm gon' have a good time touring with Loverboy. This boy is *crazy!* He was gonna *force* her ass to dance. 'Get your fine ass out here and dance, girl!'"

We all started laughing again, but I had to think everything through. That was a drastic emotional swing that John had showed us. Come to think of it, he had always had these minor mood swings. I figured it was from being so damn obedient to his mother for so many years and not being able to express himself like he really needed to early on in his life, even sexually. He had all of these emotions plugged up inside him like a genie bottle, and he didn't know how to let them all out. They just tended to come from nowhere, like his stage performances. And as John was able to have more of his way from his popularity with singing, his mood swings would get worse.

. . . hearing thousands of screams . . .

I couldn't sleep that Friday night without asking John about that club incident. Tony and his cousin Bean got high and invited some girls over, but they didn't have enough girls to go around, and John just wanted to relax and prepare himself for performing the next day. So before I jumped on him about the scene he had made at the club, I watched BET videos with him.

I said, "These videos are powerful, man. A video is, like, more important than radio sometimes." They had late Friday night rap videos on from Craig Mack, Snoop Dogg, Ice Cube, the Wu-Tang Clan, Outkast, Digable Planets, and others.

I just sat there watching those videos, listening to the beats, and thinking about John's imagery as a performer. He was as clean-cut as you could get. Then it occurred to me that his mother hadn't allowed him to watch videos or listen to rap music. A lot of the New Wave culture was alien to John. He had gotten most of his references from me.

He smiled and said, "These Wu-Tang guys talk a lot about kung fu and stuff."

I laughed and said, "Yeah, that's where they get their names from."

He said, "And this guy actually calls himself the Ol' Dirty Bastard? You gotta be playin'."

I laughed and said, "Nah, he's for real."

John said, "Go 'head, man. They're just doing that for this song, right?"

I said, "Nah, that's his name, the 'Ol' Dirty Bastard.'"

John shook his head and said, "My God. No wonder my mom didn't want me listening to this. I wonder how this guy's mom feels."

"Aw, man, that's just one rap group," I told him. I asked him, "But how do you feel about that, man, to have missed out on so much? I mean, you did a little more with me around, but there's, like, so much stuff that you couldn't do that it ain't even funny."

He hunched his shoulders and said, "I don't really think about it, man. All I know is that nobody's gonna stop me from what I wanna do now."

I said, "And that reminds me. Stop talking shit about my football aspirations. I don't beat *your* shit down. I'm doing everything I can to help you."

He looked at me from his twin-sized hotel bed and said, "My bad, man. That ain't right."

"You damn right it ain't right," I snapped at him.

He smiled and said, "But you have to admit, once we get inside the music business, I don't think there's nothing like it. I can't *wait* until tomor'. I'm gon' try to rock the house."

What can I say? I couldn't stay mad at my boy for long. I decided to drop the whole issue about the girl in the club. Nobody's perfect. I guess I *was* trying to come off as John's father sometimes, and he was a few months *older* than me.

I smiled back at him and said, "We gon' have some girls of our *own* tomorrow, man. You didn't get that girl to dance with you tonight, but plenty of them will want to dance with you tomorrow. With *no* clothes on," I joked.

I went to sleep with that thought on my mind. I couldn't wait until tomorrow either. The dog in me couldn't wait.

Before we went to the Black History Month Celebration that Saturday, Tony was up early enough to go over what John wanted to perform that day.

Tony said, "I know you sing a bunch of ballads, man, but do you have any up-tempo stuff where I can really get down on my drums?"

John said, "Yeah, I got this song called *Freedom*. It's kind of funky, too."

Tony said, "How it go?"

I smiled and started clapping my hands on beat. John filled in the words:

I need free-dom (CLAP)
Free-dom (CLAP)
Free-dom to do my thing.

Give me free-dom (CLAP)
Free-dom (CLAP)
Free-dom and let me sing . . .

That was all Tony needed to hear. He nodded his head and grinned.

He said, "Yeah, we can work with that. What else you got?"

I started thinking that maybe we should have worked that all out ahead of time instead of right before the event. But knowing John and Tony, they didn't need much preparation. They had a rhythm together that fit like a glove. What they did at Zanzibar Blue up in Philly was beautiful!

I thought about that and came up with my own idea.

I said, "You can do that stage song that you sang at Zanzibar Blue up-tempo."

At first they just stared at me.

I said, "In other words, instead of singing, *'The sta-a-age . . . she's my lov-ver,'* with that pause in the middle, you just sing it straight out, *'The stage is my lov-ver-r,'* and hold the *r* at the end. Then you can do a bass line on the keyboard, like: *Da-Doom, Doom-Doom, Doom-Doooooom.*"

Tony filled in behind me, lip-syncing a drumbeat while working his hands and thigh, *Da-Doom, Tit TAT, Tit Doom, Da-Doom-Doom TAT.* He nodded and said, "Yeah, that'll work. That's funky."

John looked at me and smiled. Then he sang it the way that only *he* could:

The stage is my-y lov-ver-r-r-r-r
and when we get to-ge-ther
boy do we get down.

The stage is my-y lov-ver-r-r-r-r . . .

He looked at me again and nodded. He said, "That's pretty good, man. Good idea."

I felt like some kind of a hero.

John said, "And I'll just start it off with *May I.*"

Blake said that they would have twenty to thirty minutes to perform, and from what I was told, this event would have a young and cheap audience.

I said, "John, I wouldn't do that *May I* song, man. Save that for the album and an older audience. I would do *At Midnight.*"

John looked at me and kept smiling. He said, "Tony can get off on *At Midnight,* too. And you're right, *May I* is a classic-type song. I shouldn't even perform that one anymore until we get signed."

I knew what was coming after that. John said, "Are you sure you're not a manager?"

Tony frowned at me and said, "What, you don't wanna do this? Music is where it's at, boy! You better *recognize!*"

I shook my head and said, "If I don't make it in football, *then* I'll think about this."

Tony said, "Whatever, man. At age nineteen, if you can get into the music business with sure-shot talents like me and John, you better *think* about *taking* it. I mean, it ain't like you playing football at Penn State or some shit, where you damn near guaranteed to go pro. You're at a small black school."

John came to my defense and said, "D was one of the best football players in Charlotte, man. He knows how to play."

Tony smiled and said, "Yeah, and so do a million other motherfuckers."

I felt like saying, "A million motherfuckers play music, too," but that just would have been in spite, so I held my tongue.

Big Daren picked us up in his fully carpeted van and took us to Detroit's downtown Cobo Hall.

When we unloaded all of the equipment, I nudged John with my arm and whispered, "You moving on up, man."

He just smiled at me. Then the pampering began.

A sister in her late twenties stepped up with a big smile and said, "Hi, are you John 'Loverboy' Williams? I'm Cindy Battle, and I'm going to be your chaperone for the day. So I'd like to show you to your stage area, get you something to eat, drink, or anything else that you need. You just let me know."

John nodded to her and said, "Thanks."

Tony said, "I could use something to eat right now."

Cindy started laughing and said, "Okay, well, let me show you to your area first, and then I can go take you to get whatever you want. We also have a VIP area for performers. Their food is generally nice, but you can have anything you like. We can even order out for you."

Tony said, "Do you have any jerk chicken? They usually have jerk chicken and curry goat and whatnot at most of the other black expo events that I've been to."

She said, "I can check and see for you, but I don't remember seeing anything like that."

I thought to myself that bald-headed, weed-smoking Tony could be high maintenance compared to John. John was intensely focused. He just wanted to jump onstage and do his thing.

It was nearly three o'clock, and Blake had gotten us a prime performance time, at six. The two headliners were set to go on after John, and the event was over at eight. I couldn't even remember the names of the other acts. There was no one major there, and I was concentrating more on watching John set off another crowd and win them over. As far as I was concerned, the only acts that could top John and Tony were platinum-selling artists. And a live performance was a bit different from selling albums. You really had to know what you were doing onstage, especially when people hadn't heard of you. John was just beginning, but he was a natural. He was getting things down to a science.

Tony walked around and checked out the floor with all of the merchants selling their goods. But John and I went straight to the stage area to check out the acts who were on before him. They had a young female dance group, African drummers, a kids' fashion show, and then the music began at around five, with a gospel group, of all things.

I looked over at John and smiled at him.

John didn't even flinch. He said, "You see that not that many people ran over here to hear them. Just a few old people. But wait until they announce my name and me and Tony do *our* thing."

I said, "Are you telling me that people wouldn't recognize your talent if you sang gospel?" I knew the answer to that myself, I was just agitating John.

He grinned and said, "Nope. They would give all of the glory to the Lord."

"And you *don't?*" I asked him.

He said, "God helps those who help themselves, right?"

I said, "Right."

"And I haven't worked for it?"

I smiled. I knew about all of those hours John had spent practicing by himself and pushing his talent as far as it could go. I said, "Man, you know you worked for it."

"Well, there's nothing else to be said then," he told me. "I just thank God for giving me the talent to be who I am. But that doesn't mean that I have to sing gospel. I mean, does God bless the football players and not the basketball players?"

I got the point and smiled. Sometimes John sounded a little *too* secure. Overconfidence could be just as bad as being insecure sometimes. I think it was better to have poise right down the middle between the two, like having confidence without talking about it. Most of the time, John didn't talk about his talent, he just performed. I guess I asked for it by playing the devil's advocate again. So I just left him alone while it got closer to his performance time.

Sure enough, as soon as they announced his name, the young crowd flocked to the stage, and those who took their time hurried their step once John began to do his thing:

At mid-ni-i-ight
it gets so lo-o-o-ne-le-e-e with-oouut you-u-u
At mid-ni-i-ight . . .

Tony did his thing on the drums, following John's lead on the keyboard, and I just watched the crowd react. I won't lie either. I was trying my best to spot the phattest girls in the audience to have a good time with afterward. After doing a few shows with John and witnessing the power that his singing had on everyone, I just began to expect certain things.

When they went up-tempo with *The Stage*, the crowd started nodding their heads immediately. John and Tony made the song funkier than I imagined. Then John went ahead and used the full stage to walk from left to right and sing to girls in the audience.

The stage is my-y lov-ver-r-r-r . . .

He had never done that before. It seemed like he always had a few new tricks up his sleeve, and he was springing them without warning.

But John took the cake when they got to *Freedom*. Tony whipped up another funky beat, and as much as John said he didn't want to be a gospel singer, he damn sure seemed like a hell of a preacher when he raised his palms to the ceiling, changed the words to the song, and started chanting:

We need free-dom (CLAP)
Free-dom (CLAP)
Free-dom to be our-sel-elves.

Give us free-dom (CLAP)
Free-dom (CLAP)
Free to be no one else . . .

John had Detroit swinging, clapping their hands, and bobbing just like in church. I did my usual thing and started smiling my behind off. To cap off another excellent performance, John screamed, "I'LL SEE YOU ALL IN THE RECORD STORES WHEN THE ALBUM COMES OUT!

THEN WE CAN ALL MEET AGAIN AT THE PONTIAC SILVER-
DOME!"

I didn't even know that John knew about the Pontiac Silverdome since
he was never really a sports guy like I was. But I guess that big-time singers
performed there too.

When they got off the stage, I asked John, "What made you say that,
man?"

"Say what?"

"You know, the stuff about the record deal."

John smiled and said, "That's what we want, ain't it? I might as well let
people know."

I said, "That's a good idea, man. You need to do that at the end of every
show."

Before I could even turn around, Blake was breathing down our necks
with two friends.

He said, "You guys don't even *need* a demo tape. *Damn* that was hot!" He
turned to his two friends and said, "What do you guys think?"

One of them joked, "Let me pull my checkbook out. I'm ready to sign
him right now." Or at least I *thought* that he was joking.

At that point, I hadn't had time to set up a meeting with a lawyer yet. But
at least we had filed for John's publishing affiliation at ASCAP (American
Society of Composers, Authors and Publishers) and BMI (Broadcast Music, Inc.). We applied as JLW Music with BMI and Love Lyrics Inc. Music
with ASCAP, in case John wrote anything for someone else. I also had a
chance to talk to my brother Darryl as a business manager and consultant.
But for contract purposes, we needed a lawyer.

I got nervous and said, "Well, you know we'll need to go over any paperwork with our lawyers. John understands that."

"Yeah, well, whatever we have to do, let's do it."

These guys all looked like hustlers to me, wearing fine suits with big
hands and big gold rings, with pearly white smiles and shiny eyes. I started
thinking about the character Big Red in the movie *The Five Heartbeats*.

I said, "Well, you know, let's just all slow down a minute. We'll talk
about it." My heart was racing again, but at least I was up for the challenge.
It was the moment of truth. Or *near* the moment of truth. So I wanted to
make sure that we got things done the right way.

One of the guys asked, "Who is this, the baby genius manager or something?"

I smiled, even though the guy was trying to slight me. Being called a baby genius wasn't exactly a bad thing in *my* book. I began to look at John as a *musical* genius. Maybe we were two birds of the same feather, and I was a genius in my own right.

Anyway, when that guy called me a baby genius, that actually gave me a little bit of bravado.

I said, "Yeah, big things sometimes come in young packages. I can't change my age until I get older."

Everyone broke out laughing. But they knew that I was serious after that, so we traded phone numbers and made it urgent that we get in contact *real* soon. These guys represented ShowTime Records, another independent label that I had never heard of.

After that business was taken care of, we were able to concentrate on the other business at hand. The girls. They didn't seem to care about who else was singing that day, they were all out to get a piece of Loverboy; young, old, fat, skinny, light, dark, and all in between. And it was much different from the college arena. We had our own hotel room, no curfew, and we didn't have to worry about gossip or on-campus boyfriends to get in the way. That was *freedom* indeed!

John and Tony started signing autographs and talking about their aspirations in music, and I started scheming on dates.

"So, what does everyone do in Detroit on a cold Saturday night?" I asked this one girl. She was a knockout and as brown as I was, but she wasn't really paying attention to my question. These two yellow girls jumped in and answered me for her.

"There's lots of things to do in Detroit on a Saturday night."

They were two light-skin honeys, reminding me of Angie and Pyra from Virginia. I started thinking about John's friend Janese and her talk about light-skin girls. I hated to stereotype, but it just seemed like a lot of light girls knew how to jump right on an opportunity. I mean, it wasn't as if I was out to choose them, they had just decided to choose themselves. If you think I was ready to turn that opportunity down for some color code, you had another *think* coming. A fine sister is a fine sister in *my* book, no matter *what* shade she was. And from me not being a one-woman kind of guy, I definitely knew how to choose the girls who wanted to be down. We had no time for any hesitation.

I asked, "Do y'all have a car?"

"Yup. And we *will* travel."

Just to make sure I knew what I was getting into, I said, "So, which one of you has the crazy boyfriend who might come out looking for you?" I was thinking of Pyra again.

"What boyfriend?" they both joked.

That was the kind of response that I wanted to hear, so I kept talking to them and traded phone numbers, places, and times.

When I got a moment alone with Tony, he said, "Boy, I got me about *four* dates set up for tonight. Nine o'clock, twelve o'clock, three o'clock, and *six* in the morning."

I laughed and said, "Who agreed to six o'clock in the morning?"

"This woman with her own crib. She told me to just call before I came."

I said, "But how did you even get *in* a conversation like that?"

Tony said, "It's the game, boy. It's the game."

I said, "Yeah, go 'head, man. You makin' shit up."

Tony said, "You wanna come with me?"

I hesitated for a minute. He couldn't have been serious.

He broke out laughing the next minute and said, "Naw, I'm only bull-shittin' you, man. I ain't going nowhere at six o'clock in the morning. I'll be high as shit and knocked the fuck out by then."

I said, "Do you get high all the time, man?" I was concerned about it. I didn't want that to be a problem.

Tony said, "Naw, only when I'm awake." Then he laughed again. "Naw, I'm just fucking with you, man." He nudged me and said, "Loosen the hell up, North Carolina. I know you the big manager and everything, but *damn!* I mean, I don't get high all the time, but I like to unwind every now and then. Yeah."

When I made it to John through all of this fanfare, I asked him what he had set up for the night.

He looked at me and shook his head. He said, "Man, I had so many different people in my face saying this and that, that I couldn't even concentrate on any of that."

Tony overheard him and said, "That's what you need *Darin* to do. *He* was supposed to give out the invitations."

John laughed and said, "Invitations. I like how you put that."

Tony said, "Yeah, invitations to be with the Loverboy for a night."

I said, "Well, I gave out two."

Tony looked at me as if I had lost my mind. He said, "You gave out *two?* Man, are you *crazy!* You mean you got all of these girls out here, and you set up just *two* invitations? What if they don't show?"

He said, "Man, you supposed to give out at least *twenty.* Then you get ten of 'em to show up. But you only invite four up to the room from the lobby. Then you make the extras wait out in the hallway until you send them in for the next shift."

John and I just broke out laughing. Either Tony was a great comedian, making it all up as he went along, or he had pulling girls to the hotel room *down*.

John said, "Well, if they don't show, then we'll just take a few of *your* extras, if that's all right with you."

Tony said, "Take *my* extras. Shit, *you* the *Loverboy*. I'm just the drummer. I'm supposed to be taking *your* extras." He shook his head and said, "You Southern boys got a lot to learn, man. *A lot* to learn."

We didn't have to take Tony's leftovers that night. By the time John and I made it back to the hotel room, we had four messages from three different groups of girls who had found out where we were staying. One girl had called twice to leave three different phone numbers to reach her.

I looked at John and said, "Do you believe that? Imagine what'll it be like when you really *do* perform at the Pontiac Silverdome? You'll have to check in hotels under another name."

John just laughed it off. He asked, "So, which girls do you want to call back?"

I said, "I don't even know who these girls are. Do you know them?"

John smiled and said, "I don't know, man, I might get them all confused. I mean, it wasn't like I had time to talk to any one girl for that long."

I said, "Well, I did. I talked to these two light-skin girls with their own car. I say we just call them to be safe. Unless you don't want to deal with any more light-skin girls," I joked to him.

John grinned and asked, "Did they look good?"

I stopped and thought before I answered him.

I said, "Do you think we have a different standard of judging light-skin girls from dark-skin girls? I mean, what exactly does *looking good* mean?"

I said, "Are we talking about, like, a keen nose, a small face and lips, with curly or wavy hair? I mean, is that what makes light-skin girls look good to us?"

John caught my drift and said, "Yeah, and we judge the dark-skin girls by their body, right? She got a big behind. Or a phat-to-death body."

We both broke out laughing, but I thought it was an interesting observation.

I shook my head and said, "Nah, some brown girls got the prettiest faces in the world, though. Like that girl Stacey Briggs at school, who ran for homecoming queen, her face is pretty as I don't know what. That girl Dawn from New Jersey had the look too, but she wasn't as brown as Stacey."

John said, "But they still got white features. Stacey's nose is sharper than white people's."

I said, "Well, your nose ain't all that big either."

John said, "Yeah, my whole face is small. But I'm tall and thin, man. I mean, the more you weigh, the more your face is gonna fill out. That's just common sense."

"That ain't always true. I know a lot of big girls who have small faces," I told him.

John said, "Whatever, man. I'm tired of talking about this anyway. So what do you want to do?"

As soon as he finished his sentence, the telephone rang. I picked it up with a smile, expecting more girls. And it was, the two girls that I had met.

I said, "Hey, I was just talking about you two."

"What about us?"

"Do people in Detroit think that y'all are pretty?"

"Well, we cousins, we just *ought* to be pretty."

I said, "Oh, I didn't know you were cousins."

"Yeah, so what's up? Are you ready? Let me speak to Loverboy."

I smiled, just thinking about the forwardness of light-skin girls again. I told myself to cut it out, though, and just have a good damn time with whoever. So I passed the phone over to John.

"Hello," he answered, grinning. He said, "Yeah, well come on over then. We'll be here . . . We can go everywhere or nowhere. It's up to you two."

I looked at him and smiled. John never would have said anything like that in high school. But we weren't in high school anymore.

John hung up the phone and said, "They sound like they down for whatever."

I said, "That's what *I'm* saying."

"Well, they're on their way."

I clapped my hands and said, "Well, let's freshen up and get ready then, man." It would have been my first score on the road with John. Or at least I *hoped* that it would be.

The telephone rang again, and John answered it.

"Hello." He said, "Umm, we made plans for the night already . . . I don't know what time we'll be back."

I was listening to him from the bathroom with a smile. I wondered if he was experienced enough with multiple date situations to say the right things. *I* was experienced. But this was John's turn to find out how it was done.

He said, "You can hang out that late?"

I broke out laughing. That damn John was a *fool!* You could tell that he still had a lot of innocence about him. In a way it made him charming, as if he had no idea how powerful his voice and music were.

He said, "Well, call us up and see then. Okay? But we're about to leave out right now."

When he hung up the phone again, I said, "That wasn't bad, man."

He walked to the bathroom door while buttoning up a clean shirt and asked me, "What wasn't bad?"

"The way you handled that phone call."

He shrugged it off. "I just told her the truth, man."

"Is that how you plan to be all of the time?" I asked him. I was dying for him to say yes. It would have been real interesting to witness, because whenever you have more than a few girls calling you at once, it's almost a *necessity* to lie.

John smiled and paused before he answered. He said, "It depends on the situation."

I said, "That's what I *thought*," and started laughing again.

John said, "Man, I'm learning that sometimes it just don't pay to be too honest. It seems like it causes more pain than good sometimes. But yet, people are always saying, 'Just be honest with me. Just be honest with me.'"

"They don't mean that shit," I told him. "When most people tell you to be honest with them, what they really mean is, 'Either break it to me easy or tell me a good damn lie.'"

We broke up laughing again while getting ourselves ready to go out.

The phone rang again, and John answered it before I could tell him not to. It was getting too close to our meeting time, and unless our girls were lost, which I doubted, John didn't need to dodge any more bullets.

"Hello." He listened for a while and said, "But we're about to head out right now . . . But— Well—"

I started laughing again. It didn't sound like he was getting out of this one.

Finally, he said, "All right, if you can catch us in time."

I walked out from the bathroom after he had hung up the phone and asked him, "What did you just do now, man?"

He grinned and shook his head at me. He said, "These three girls were just pressed to come over, D. I couldn't stop them."

I shook my head and said, "Well, let's try and be gone before they all get here."

We caught the elevator down to the lobby to catch our dates. Tony was just walking out with his cousin Bean.

"Y'all all right, man?" Bean asked us. "Your boy ain't gon' grab no more girls, is he? I hear he sings so good that he shouldn't have to."

I chuckled and said, "Yeah, he's all right, man."

John just smiled it off.

Tony asked us, "Y'all all right for tonight?"

"Yeah, we're straight," I told him. I just wanted to get out of Dodge as quickly as possible.

When our girls arrived, John and I were all ready to walk back out with them and head to their car. The plan was to go out for a few hours, sneak back to the hotel with them, and make sure that we kept the phones off the hook until they had left.

Our two girls had other plans.

"Can we see y'all room?"

I spoke up and said, "Y'all can sleep in it if you want to. But we're ready to get something to eat right now."

"Let's order room service. A nice hotel like this *has* to have good room service."

I was thinking, *What the hell is up with girls and this room service shit?*

John went ahead and introduced himself. "Well, my name is John."

The girls laughed at the obvious and introduced themselves before I could.

"Well, I'm Sherry Anne, and this is my cousin Tabitha."

They looked close enough to be twins that night, but I guess that was how they planned it.

I said, "My bad. I was supposed to do that."

"Well, you were too slow on the draw, man," Tabitha told me.

"Tell me about it," I responded to her. I didn't bother to ask, but I figured they had to be straight out of high school. They still had that reckless high school energy.

Anyway, once things had slowed down from the pace that I wanted, I was able to check them out again. They were both wearing thin shirt tops that tied above the stomach, with silver rings at their navels, formfitting black pants, and black boots. Sherry Anne had on a short black coat, while Tabitha wore a matching silver one. They smelled good, too.

I started thinking with the wrong head already. My Johnson started talking to me from my pants, and these girls were practically *begging* to get up inside our room.

I said, "All right, let's go to the room then," for a quick change of plans. As soon as I had said that, the posse of three girls that John had spoken to last walked in. They were all dark brown and they were dressed more conservatively than our dates.

"So, where y'all going?" the leader of the pack asked us.

Talk about drama, I didn't even want any part of that. I just wanted to disappear.

John spoke up and said, "We were just on our way out the door."

"We see," another member of the posse said.

I could feel the tension in the air, and I was sure that John could. But John handled things a lot cooler than even I could at the time. I was too busted on the spot to even try.

John said, "Well, we'll see you around a little later," and started walking toward the rotating doors while holding on to Sherry Anne.

Somebody said, "No thanks. Y'all got what y'all want already. Ain't nobody trying to be sloppy seconds."

I couldn't believe my ears! They were telling it like it was. Maybe I just wasn't used to girls up north yet, because they were all bold as hell, just barging up in the place and making a ruckus.

When they all walked out with us, John walked over to this black stretch limo that was stationed out front and said something to the driver.

Somebody said, "Aw, they goin' in a limo. That's fucked up. That's some fucked-up shit!"

I didn't even want to look at who said it. I was too embarrassed. Sophisticated white people were all around us. We looked like a bunch of ghetto kids gathering at the wrong damn hotel!

John walked back over to us and started talking loud. "Our car is on the way."

I took his lead and said, "Yeah, but it's cold out here, so let's wait inside until it comes."

We walked right back in to escape the drama. That's when one of the doormen asked us if there was a problem.

John said, "No sir, everything is cleared up now," and started heading for the elevators.

I followed his lead again with Sherry Anne and Tabitha.

We stood and waited for the elevator.

Tabitha asked, "Who was that? They sure were *mad* at y'all. I think y'all hurt somebody's feelings."

She was rubbing it in. I didn't take too lightly to that. I was feeling guilty about the whole situation. We had chosen the light-skin girls. I mean, somebody could even argue that we were just a few shades away from choosing white girls.

John spoke up again and said, "I told them we already had plans. They did that to themselves."

I had to give one thing to John, he sure was consistent with his honesty. I mean, even when he had to lie, his lies seemed appropriate in some way.

We made it up to our room, and the two cousins took off their coats and got immediately comfortable, as if they had done it all too many times before.

I said, "How many times have y'all done something like this, you know, hung out with performers and all?" I had to make sure that I clarified everything and didn't offend them.

Sherry Anne said, "Every time somebody comes in town."

I didn't know if it was a joke or not, but everyone laughed but me, so I guess it was a joke.

Tabitha said, "No, we usually don't get this close. It's, like, *floods* of girls at some of the shows we go to."

I said, "Well, how old are you two?"

Sherry Anne said, "Well, I'm sixteen, and I'll let Tabitha lie and say whatever age she wants to tell you."

My heart started pumping. I said, "*Sixteen?* You sixteen? So, you just started driving then?"

I was totally baffled! I figured that I should have asked them that *before* I gave them an invitation, just to make sure that they were old enough.

Tabitha said, "I look grown for my age, don't I? But I'm only fifteen."

I said, "And you can both hang out like this?"

Everyone was still laughing, but I couldn't see where the damn joke was.

I looked at John and said, "What the hell are you laughing for, man?"

John said, "Chill out, man. You're acting too much like a manager. They're just playing with you."

"No we're not either," Sherry Anne told him.

John said, "Well, I guess we're about to go to jail then, because y'all look good in here."

Tabitha said, "Go to jail for what? For eating *room service?* Because I don't do nothing else."

I was about to lose my damn mind! I said, "Hold up, hold up, stop playin' for a minute. We gon' get all this shit straight. Now how old are y'all, for real?"

They started laughing at me again.

Then Sherry Anne said, "Oh, Daddy, I like it when you talk rough."

Tabitha shook her head. She said, "I can tell you from down south, because you are really slow."

At the moment, I wasn't exactly in a position to argue with her. I just waited for somebody to explain things to me, because I was left out of the joke somehow.

Tabitha said, "We may look young, but everybody is of age up in here. Okay? John got that immediately. We just played with you because you seemed to want to believe it. You must like young girls, hunh? Don't lie, Darin."

I shook my head and ignored her. I even thought about asking for a license.

I didn't regain my composure until after we had all ordered and eaten our room service. I was beginning to feel like an outsider, like John had some inside track on the speed and craziness of the music business. He was learning how to just go with the flow, and I was not in step yet. Maybe as a manager I *couldn't* be. I felt like I had to be above it all in some way, even though I wanted to be a part of it. Or did I? I still wanted to play football. I was confused as hell that night. But after I had eaten, Sherry Anne was still talking that *Daddy* shit, and my Johnson got rock hard again.

When the lights and television went off that night, it was all on in the dark. John ended up with Tabitha, and I had Sherry Anne.

At first, it was a little weird. I kept thinking I was dreaming or something. John was about to get paid right next to me with some fine-ass cousins, way the hell up in Detroit, Michigan. But once Sherry Anne slid under the sheets, slipped off her clothes, and asked me if I had any protection, I realized that everything was for real.

I got my protection out and I watched John in the dark for a minute. He was already getting busy with Tabitha, and he looked like he was moving around in circles instead of up and down and in and out.

I started laughing in the dark at my *own* joke this time. John's ass was still an amateur in the sex department. And I was planning on making them *all* pay for fucking with me earlier.

I got up inside of Sherry Anne, and I started turning that girl out like it was the last time I would have a girl in my life. She was feeling it, too.

"Oooh, oooh, oooh," she moaned.

She made a noise after every move I made until Tabitha finally said, "Shut up, girl! *God!*"

It was my turn to have some fun. I didn't mean to show my boy up like that, but I took Sherry Anne to the next level that John still had problems with. Climax. Or in a girl's case, an orgasm.

"OOOOOH, DEEEEE!"

When she started grabbing on me for dear life, I sped up the pace and did my thing.

I said, "Here it come! Here it come! You feel it?"

"YEAH, YEAH!"

And when it came, *damn* that nut was good! It was like I was popping three in one! Then I put the shoulder lock on her to push myself as far inside as I could. John couldn't match *that* shit with his singing. I had the last laugh that night. He got his thing off shortly after, but it was nothing like mine. I don't think that Tabitha was as pleased as Sherry Anne was either.

When Sherry Anne caught her breath, she said out loud, "Oooh, Darin in trouble. He just did it with a fourteen-year-old."

That time, I laughed along with them.

Then Sherry Anne kept going with it. "And I'm gon' tell the police officer downstairs on you. I'm gon' say, 'Yup, he did it to me, Officer. That boy right there from down south. And it was *gooood*. So I made him do it to me again.'"

. . . while looking sharp and dressing clean . . .

In the morning when John and I were alone again, I looked up at the hotel ceiling and started laughing out loud to myself.

John looked over at me from his bed and asked, "What's so funny, man?" He was watching more videos, this time on MTV.

I said, "Man, last night was crazy as hell. I mean, *crazy!*" I hated to admit it, but John and Tony were right. The music industry was a lot wilder than the football level that I was on. You had so many guys on the football team that by the time it got to nonstarters like myself, I had to take whoever was still willing to deal with me until I became a star on the team. Fortunately, I wasn't a bad-looking guy. Nevertheless, with John being so talented as a solo performer, there was practically no way that I could ever match him in football unless I became the next Deion Sanders. But I didn't want to admit that to John, because he was already trying his best to stop me from thinking about football.

John smiled and said, "You know they want to come back tonight."

I said, "Yeah, I know. But don't you think we might have some new girls from today's performances?"

We both laughed again. We had an open jar of sweet cookies up in Detroit, two "slow" Southern boys. I guess we weren't *that* slow. To make a long story short, we had another good time Sunday night in Detroit before flying back to Greensboro Monday morning. But during that next week at school, John went ahead and dropped a bomb on me.

I was heading to Williams Cafeteria from my dorm at Cooper Hall when John walked up to me from nowhere with a smile on his face. We had finally talked to a connected lawyer and signed with Blake as a booking agent. We were even planning to produce a quality demo tape with Tony up in Philly, so John had a lot to be happy about. Things were really coming together for him.

I smiled back at him and said, "You headin' to the caf' with me?"

He said, "Yeah, I'll go over there with you. This'll be my last week here."

I stopped and said, "What? Your last week here? What are you talking about, man?"

He shook his head and said, "I can't take it no more, D."

"Take what?"

"School, man. I can't even concentrate anymore."

I said, "But you made a deal, man."

"Come on, man," he responded to me. "That record deal is right around the corner now. We *both* know that."

"Don't count your chickens before they hatch, John," I told him. I was just stalling to come up with something to make him reconsider. "And what are you gonna tell your mother in the meantime?" I asked him.

He had a blank stare for a minute. He said, "I don't know, man. I just hope she doesn't have a heart attack or something."

He was smiling about it, all loose and silly as if it was all a big game.

I said, "This ain't no damn joke, man. You on *scholarship! Think* about that!"

"I already have. And A&T can use the money for someone else now."

"So you already did it? You dropped out of school?" My heart started racing because I knew that I would end up right in the middle of things as usual.

He said, "Yeah. I withdrew from all my classes. I'm moving in with Tony up in Philly this weekend. And I'll just stay with him until we sign our deal with whoever."

I lost my cool right there in the middle of campus and yelled, "GOD DAMN, JOHN!? How come you didn't talk to me about it first?!"

I calmed back down after noticing the minor scene that I had made.

John said, "Tell you for what? So you can try and talk me out of it?"

He was right. That's all that I would have done.

I asked him, "Why are you rushing things, man? Just graduate first." That didn't even make sense as I said it. John would have a record deal *long* before he graduated. That much I *did* know! His product was too hot to miss, and he was too hungry not to show and prove *wherever* and *whenever* he had to. Realistically, John would have to give up his scholarship anyway once he became a professional performer. I guess I was just caught off guard by the suddenness of it. I also hated the fact that I would end up having to explain things to *his* mother *and* to mine.

He said, "I gotta go after it, man. I can't wait around for it no more. You gotta get it when the gettin' is good. I'm tired of waiting. I've been waiting to do things my whole life. And I'm tired of fuckin' waiting."

John was dead serious. He was even using profanity.

He said, "Look at it this way, D. If the football coach had come to you and said that he needed you to start in the homecoming game, would you have told him no, and that you wanted to wait? For what? Because you don't think you're ready?"

My boy had a damn good point. I started smiling. Hell no, I wouldn't have told the coach I wasn't ready!

John said, "If you would have told the coach that, he probably would have cut you off the team. And just like *you're* ready to play football, *I'm* ready for this music career, man. You *know* I'm ready. *Everybody* knows it. Everybody on campus is already asking me when am I gonna record my first album."

He said, "Look, D, if you got the talent, man, like *we* do, you have to either use it or lose it. You can't keep puttin' things on hold."

One of the male students walking by overheard our discussion and said, "Yeah, that's true. Ever since homecoming, Loverboy 'bout to blow up."

I took a deep breath and accepted the inevitable. I asked him, "So, when are you leaving for Philly, man?" What else could I say?

"Saturday morning," he told me. "Tony's coming down with his van on Friday."

I felt like a big piece of me was separating at that moment. It just hit me from nowhere. I was going to miss John. I was missing him already. I was that used to being around him, and he was about to leave me behind. When you've been so close to a friend for thirteen strong years and counting, you can't even explain the friendship anymore. You just become like family. John had become my blood brother a long-ass time ago without us even thinking about it. I just cared for the boy. It was like, I was just connected to his basic goodness and his need for a friend, ever since that first moment that I saw him with his mother in church.

John snapped me out of my daze and said, "So what's up, man, you still going to eat lunch?"

"Oh, yeah," I told him. We started walking again.

He said, "Tony started talking to studio people up in Philly to see if we can cut a demo tape soon."

I didn't even feel like talking about music anymore. I felt like I was losing my boy and all he wanted to talk about was some damn career. I mean, don't get me wrong, I was happy for John and everything. I just wasn't thinking about music at that moment.

I said, "So, you'll call your mom tonight and tell her?"

John paused again. He said, "I guess I gotta tell her sometime. It might as well be tonight."

"So you and Tony are gonna sign with a manager up in Philly?" I asked him. It was my sneaky way of keeping hope alive for us in the future just in case football didn't work out.

John looked at me and said, "Nah. I was still gonna call you, man. If you don't mind."

I was pleased with that idea. I would still be connected to him. I guess it was a two-way street, and I wouldn't really be losing my boy after all.

I said, "Hey, man, call me up all you want. Especially if you're paying for it," I joked. "Just call me at night to make sure I'm there."

After John and Tony took off for Philly that weekend, things at A&T seemed boring for me. John wasn't exactly the life of the campus or anything, he just meant a lot to me. It was as if the music thing had started another level of friendship for us, and now it was gone.

I forgot all about how our parents would respond to things until John's mom called me that Sunday afternoon. I had spent the majority of the week enjoying our last few days on campus together. Part of me wanted to wait and see if John would actually do it, just up and move to Philly to chase his music aspirations in the middle of the spring semester.

Anyway, his mother called me that Sunday afternoon and said, "Darin, don't you *dare* lie to me. Is John still in school?" She sounded as if she was ready to hyperventilate, just waiting for my answer. I could even imagine the face of horror on her.

"Ahh . . ." *What the hell do I say?* I asked myself. Obviously, John had set me up again. That showed me how much of a good friend *he* was.

Sister Williams said, "I've already called his room. So you might as well just let me know."

I said, "John didn't tell you himself?"

"No he didn't!" she shouted at me. "Now what does he have to tell me? His roommate said something about Philadelphia."

Jesus! John didn't even have the sense to cover up his tracks, I thought to myself. I know that he just didn't forget about it like I had. It was *his* mother and *his* decisions, not *mine*. So why was *I* in the damn hot seat again?

She said, "Give me his phone number," with no ifs, ands, or buts about it. That's just how Sister Williams was, especially when it came to her only son. I was beginning to see exactly why John had become so stubborn. It was a direct response to his mother.

I was at a crossroads. Sure, I knew Tony's number up in Philly, but it was not my place to give it out to her.

I said, "I'll see if I can get in contact with him, and I'll tell him to call you."

"How about you give me the phone number and I'll call him myself?"

I took a deep breath and prepared to hold my ground.

I said, "With all due respect, Sister Williams . . . little John isn't a kid anymore, and it's not my place to play the middleman."

She said, "Well, what are you doing with his music?"

"I'm just giving him advice," I told her.

"Well, you give him some more advice, and you tell him to call his mother! YOU TELL HIM TO CALL HIS MOTHER, DARIN! DO YOU UNDERSTAND ME?!"

I held my ear away from the phone and shook my head.

My roommate looked over at me and said, "Damn! She *pressed!*"

I said, "Yes ma'am. I understand."

As soon as I hung up with Sister Williams, I dialed Tony's phone number up in Philly and got his answering machine: "This is Tony, the soon-to-be rich man, so leave a message and number before I blow up and need a secretary to screen my calls."

I smiled. That damn Tony was crazy. I said, "Hey, Tony, this is Darin back down in North Carolina, man, calling from A&T. Can you do me a favor, man, and tell John to call his mother? It seems he forgot to do that before he left somehow."

I hung up and waited by the phone, expecting my mother's call at any minute. When the phone rang on cue, I smiled and told my roommate, "I got it."

I answered the phone and said, "Hi, Mom."

She started laughing. She said, "I guess you know what I'm calling about."

"Yup. And I have nothing to do with it," I told her. "John just decided that it was time for him to go all out for his dream. And who am I to stop him? I wouldn't let him get in the way of *my* dream."

"But I thought he had made a deal to graduate first."

I said, "No, that was only if he didn't get a record deal."

"So he has one now?"

"Not yet, but it's on the way."

My mom paused and grunted. "That boy is gonna kill his mother yet."

I said, "But Mom, how long is he supposed to put his aspirations on hold? He has to do what he has to do and learn his own lessons. That's how *I* see it. He has to have an opportunity to fail just like everyone else."

I said, "But I don't think he's gonna fail."

She said, "I know, I know. She's been holding on to that boy for years. I wish him good luck, though. And in the meantime, you just stay in contact with him, Darin. I hear that that music business is something else."

I said, "Oh, it *is*. I *know* that already. But, you know, I'll just do what I can."

"Okay. That's all you can do is your best. And don't *you* get any ideas about dropping out of school either," my mother warned me.

I laughed at the idea. I said, "Mom, I'm just about to get my feet wet this year. I'm not going anywhere. I got big plans for *this* season, *and* for my senior year."

She said, "O-kay," as if she had some doubts. "Well, I love you, boy."

"I love you too, Mom."

I hung up and felt good about the relationship that I still had with my parents. Good old-fashioned discipline ain't that bad when it works. I mean, I wasn't perfect, but I wasn't all wild and crazy either.

It was a few days before John called me up to give me the rundown on talking to his mother.

He said, "My bad, man," referring to the heat falling on my shoulders again.

I didn't even sweat it anymore. I just wanted to stay out of their way. I had my *own* life to live. I had homework to do, and outdoor track practice had already started at school.

I changed the subject and said, "So what's been going on up there in Philly?" It was nearly March.

John said, "Well, you know, we're putting shows together locally, and we have some big stuff coming up with Blake in April, May, and June. And he's trying to hook up some big summer shows for us."

"What's UP, D?! HOW'S COLLEGE LIFE TREATING YOU?!" I heard Tony scream in the background.

I said, "Tony crazy, man. Does he smoke all the time around his house?"

"Nah. He actually smokes more after shows or whatever. He stays up late and sleeps a lot during the daytime," John said with a chuckle.

I thought about asking if the smoking and sleeping late had influenced him any. Instead, I punked out and asked him what he did for most of the day.

"Actually, I've been reading a lot of magazines and stuff on music. You know, I'm just doing research on things."

"You learn anything from it?"

He said, "Yeah, there's always room to learn different things, you know. But yo, we got some studio time set up for next week, D," he told me. He sounded excited about it.

I grinned. "So, y'all finally gon' make a demo tape?"

"Yeah."

"Using what songs?"

"*At Midnight, The Stage*, and Tony introduced me to this girl group up here in Philly who can sing pretty good, so I might do *Unappreciated* with them. I haven't done that one in a while."

I smiled. "Yeah, ever since we dropped Two Scoops," I joked. "But what about doing *Freedom?* You tore that one up in Detroit."

"Tony said that one's too preachy for a demo. We'll just put it on the album with *May I.* He said he doesn't want record labels thinking that we're gonna be a soft, preachy group."

I started laughing. I said, "Yeah, I can see that. Tony's right. Just put that one on the album after you get the deal."

He said, "But we're working on some new up-tempo stuff, too. Tony said that we need to sell a certain attitude to compete with rappers."

I thought about that and agreed with it. "Yeah, I think he might be right. That's how Jodeci is coming off, with that harder edge. But you don't want to be as hard as they are."

John said, "Nah, not *that* hard. But we don't want to come off as soft as Boyz II Men either. We want to fall somewhere in the middle like Bell Biv DeVoe and Guy."

He said, "Tony has a big collection of music, man. I listen to a lot of that, too."

It was good to hear it. My boy was doing all right. Somehow I got back to his mother before we hung up.

"So, is your mother all right with this or what, man?" I asked him.

John took a breath and said, "You know what I figured out, man. My mother overreacts to a lot of things."

I laughed and said, "Tell me something I *didn't* know."

He said, "But she's all right, man. I just figure that I'd be better off *show-*

ing her than telling her. You know what I mean? I gotta show her that I'm not going to be making 'devil' music," he joked.

I laughed my ass off before we hung up. I was noticing something new about John. His singing talent was making him a much cooler person. Because before he started singing, he could be real stuffy. But once he started to sing, *I* seemed to be the square one.

John and I talked to each other over the phone for a few weeks, staying up to date on each other's progress. John and Tony were still doing their thing and getting local recognition in the Philly and New Jersey area. And I was doing my thing on the track field. I was running all sprints; the 100, 200, and the 400. I had pretty good times, too. I had even made the 800 and the mile relay teams. The 400 relay team was where I *really* wanted to be, but we had some real horses. Two of our guys were running below-ten-second splits. I was still running above ten seconds, so I couldn't quite make the cut.

In March, I got a package in the mail from John, right before going to run in the Hampton Relays. I had talked to him on the phone that same week, and he hadn't even told me that he was sending me anything.

I opened it up and pulled out two demo tapes. I went and listened to the first tape on my portable stereo system. It was a studio production of *At Midnight* and *The Stage*, just like John had told me they would do. Then I listened to the second tape.

The first song started off with a solo drumbeat from Tony:

Tic-TAT, Tic-BOOM
Tic-TAT, BA-DOOM-BOOM
Tic-TAT, Tic-BOOM
Tic-TAT, BA-DOOM-BOOM

The beat stopped for a second before John jumped in and shouted his first lines:

HAAAY BAAABY
Tic-TAT, Tic-BOOM
IN THE BLUUUE JEAN-EAN-EANS
Tic-TAT, BA-DOOM-BOOM
YOU'RE STAN-DIN' OUT IN THE PARRR-DAY

LIKE A FLY IN THE CREAM.
Tic-TAT, BA-DOOM-BOOM

Everything sounded on point, loud and clear, and John had bass and guitar riffs lending emphasis to his lyrics:

EXCUSE ME, LAAADY
(guitar riff) I CAME TO GET DOWN
BUT MAY I HAVE THIS DAN-AN-ANCE
(deeper bass riff) TO GET DOWN
I GOT SOME NEW DAAANCE MOOOVES
THAT I'D LIKE TO USE
(guitar and bass double up) SO WE CAN GET DOWN.

They had other harmonies and instruments in there that I couldn't even
focus on. It was just so much going on all at once that you could only concentrate on a couple of things at a time. So I tried to listen to the lyrics to
see where John was going with the content of the song:

HOW 'BOUT IT, BAAABY
CAN WE GROOVE TO-NIII-I-IGHT
BUT SHE SAID THAT'S ALLL RIII-IGHT
AND SHOT MEEE DOWN.

They had a gunshot-sound effect, and then the chorus came in, the title
of the song, sung two times. Tony toned his beat down and made it simple
during the chorus to let the other instruments get off with horns and everything:

SHEEE WAS
STYLIN' AND PRO-FIL-LIN-IN-IN'
(bass, guitar, and horns) DON'T YOU KNOW WE CAME TO GET
DOWN
STYLIN' AND PRO-FIL-LIN-IN-IN-INN'
(bass and guitar) TO GET DOWN.

I went ahead and listened to the second verse, enjoying the hell out of
myself! My head was about to snap off my neck from bobbing so hard.
They were just *killing it!*

SEXY LAAADY
IF THIS GROOVE IS WRON-N-ONG
I'LL GO ASSSK THE BAAAND
TO PLAY ANOTHER SONG.

SO COME ON, BAAABY
WHAT'S THE PROB-BLEM NOW-N-OUN
I DON'T MEAN TO BE RUUUDE
I'M JUST IN THE MOOD.

AND LAAADY
I'M NOT THE MAN TO BEG-A-EGG
BUT THEN SHE LEFT ME WITHOUT A SOUN-N-OUND
AND (POW!)
SHOT MEEE DOWN.

Then the bridge came in with Tony imitating a Run-DMC beat from *Sucker M.C.'s* that my older brothers used to listen to:

DOOM-DOOM, TAT, TAT, TAT, TAT, TAT
DOOM-DOOM, TAT, TAT, TAT, TAT, TAT
DOOM-DOOM, TAT, TAT, TAT, TAT, TAT
DOOM-DOOM, TAT, TAT, TAT, TAT, DOOM-TAT . . .

John laid right on top of the beat with his lyrics, the bass, the guitar, *and* the horns:

SHE WON'T DANCE WITH ME
SHE'S TOO FINE FOR ME
SHE WON'T DANCE WITH ME
SHE'S TOO FLY FOR ME
SHE WON'T DANCE WITH ME
SHE'S TOO TOUGH FOR ME
SHE WON'T DANCE WITH ME
SHE (pause the music, and) POW!
SHOT MEEE DOWN.

They went back to the chorus for four final reps before fading out the song. I sat there and smiled so hard that my cheek muscles began to hurt.

My boy John had turned that whole Detroit club incident into a hit song! Because that wasn't a demo tape to me. That was a damn *platinum single* with a video!

The second song on the tape was another up-tempo groove. It was called *Feel Like This*. It was basically a part two to *Stylin' 'n' Profilin'*. John was saying that if the girl were to dance with him, he would make her feel the groove. And *Feel Like This* was all right, but when you hear a hit song, you *know* it's a hit! *Stylin' 'n' Profilin'* was the one! So I rewound the tape and listened to it about seven times straight, until my whole body was wet from working up a sweat to it. I mean, I could see a hot video for this song and everything. It was a monster hit!

I got on the phone immediately after I had worn myself out from listening to this hot-ass song, and I got Tony's answering service again.

I screamed, "DO *NOT* PERFORM *STYLIN' 'N' PROFILIN'* ON-STAGE BEFORE YOU GET A RECORD DEAL! THIS IS *NOT* A DEMO SONG! I REPEAT! THIS IS *NOT* A DEMO! THIS IS A DAMN *HIT SINGLE!* DO Y'ALL HEAR ME UP THERE! THIS IS DARIN! START THINKING ABOUT THE VIDEO! *GOD DAMN THIS SONG IS ROCKIN'!*"

I hung up the phone and was *pumped!* I didn't know whether I wanted to share the song with people on campus or not. I mean, I was tempted, but I decided that I just couldn't do it! People would want to make copies and could get used to hearing it. That happened all the time with good tapes. And if John and Tony performed it before they were signed, they could actually kill their hit single before they started selling records. It was like showing your best moves in a meaningless scrimmage instead of in the championship game. I mean, this song was an A+++, and you don't waste anything like that.

I hoped and prayed that John and Tony would call me back before I left for the Hampton Relays that weekend. I was panicking, thinking that they were setting up to do a show somewhere, and they were ready to try *Stylin'* on a live audience when they didn't need to. I would rather they played *old* Michael Jackson songs than kill their own before they were signed. Those were the kinds of decisions that managers were for.

When they called me back, I was just happy to talk to those guys.

John chuckled and said, "Man, we heard you. We're not crazy. We spent a lot of money to produce that song. And we're only making a few copies of it. We're sending it out through the attorney to A&R reps who are already feeling us."

I took a deep breath and said, "Thank *God!* Boy, you don't *know* how nervous I was, John. I mean, this song, man . . . this song . . ." I lost my words and just said, "DAMN! This is the *one*, man! It's record-deal *city* after this! Seriously!"

John just kept laughing. He said, "Yeah, we're in the process of setting up a few meetings now."

"With who?"

"Sony, MCA, and Virgin are all looking at us. And we got a lot of small independents, too. They call us all the time. But I wouldn't sign anything without letting you know first, man."

He said, "You helped me a lot, D. And even if you don't want to be my full-time manager, I look at you at least as a good luck charm."

I laughed. John was getting smoother every time I talked to him.

I was tempted to ask him if I could be involved in the meetings with the major record companies, but I stopped myself short of that. I felt like I could have been swallowed up by it all if I got too close again. I thought it was safer for me to help John from a healthy distance so that I could maintain my own mission to run track and play football. Because if I got too close to that music stuff . . . like I was already told, it was just too sweet of a deal to turn down.

Well, John had me inspired for the Hampton Relays that Saturday morning, and I ran the best split times that I had ever run in my life; a high twenty seconds in the 200, and a low forty-six seconds in the 400. I had decreased my 200 time by a second, and my 400 time by two seconds.

One of my teammates joked, "What the hell you eat this morning, D? *I* needed some of that shit."

During that next week, John called me back with some dates, places, and times for the record company meetings.

He asked me, "You want to be there, man, just to see everything through?"

It was another tough moment for me. My track season was going well and that would benefit me in spring football training. However, my boy was only asking for my support. How could I turn him down on that? But still, he had asked me to support him on the homecoming night and sucked me right into things then. How would I be able to back down from real money on the table?

I said, "Give me a little time to think about it, man."

"What's there to think about? I'm just asking you to be there as my boy."

John sounded like the devil asking me to play him in a friendly game of cards. He knew damn well that he wanted me to keep going with him. But I just couldn't turn the opportunity down. Not on a meeting. I mean, all I had to do was show up, express my opinions, and leave. If John signed a good deal, then I would be able to live with that and go back to what I was doing in my own life. But if I didn't go and John got jerked around like so many other musicians, then how would I live with that? I would want him to support me on an NFL draft day. So my decision was the only one that I could make.

I said, "Well, let's set up the best days and times where I can be there."

John chuckled and said, "Yeah, D. That's a bet."

Just like that, he had sucked me into thinking about the music business again. However, before I would sit down and listen to any deals being offered, I wanted to call up Mr. Chester DeBerry, who had put us up in the hotel room in Philly, just to pick his brain about the business. I just felt like the guy had reached out to us for a reason, and I wanted to tap into what he knew.

It took me a few days to finally catch up to Mr. DeBerry at his New York office, but I was determined to talk to him, even if I had to spend a little to pay for the long-distance phone calls from my dorm room.

When I finally did catch him on the line, he was very receptive to me.

"Hey, Darin. How are things going with you and John? The Loverboy."

I said, "He's ready to sign. And I just wanted to thank you again for reaching out to us that night in Philly."

He said, "You've thanked me enough already, Darin. You're not calling me just to thank me again, are you?"

I laughed and said, "No, sir. I actually wanted to ask you a few questions, if you have any time. Do I need to call you back at a better hour?"

I was just being respectful of his time. I realized that he was a busy man just from trying to catch up to him.

He said, "No, I have a few minutes for you. In fact, where are you calling from? I can call you right back and put it on my bill for you."

I gave him my phone number at the dorm and he called me right back.

He asked, "Is John still in school?"

I paused before I answered him. I guess I still felt uncertain about his decision.

I said, "No, sir, he made a decision that it was time to go for the gold."

Mr. DeBerry said, "I see. I pretty much saw that in him. John was hungry. And that can be a good thing *and* a bad thing."

I said, "I know."

"So, what labels are looking at him?" he asked me.

"He told me Virgin, Sony, MCA, and a bunch of independents."

Mr. DeBerry grunted. He said, "If you can get these guys in a bidding war, that would be the best way for you to *know* that they really want you. You hear what I'm saying? Sometimes these big labels sign people just to keep them away from the competition. It's an old-fashioned way of keeping the price of business down."

He said, "They'll sign you cheap and use you as a tax write-off. So you have to make sure that they are really committed to putting out the album and pushing it. In fact, a lot of the independent labels are doing a hell of a lot more to push new artists. I almost want to tell you to forget about the big boys unless you *know* that you'll get that bidding war."

I actually hoped that he would give me some names to drop at the major labels, but he didn't.

He said, "The key to a long career is to start out small and work your way up. You know, because some of these guys who start out at the top, they don't realize it, but the fall will kill you. And I'm not saying that Loverboy doesn't have the talent to compete up there, but if you look around at what's going on in the industry, the independents are where everything is happening. You just have to make sure you get a deal that benefits the artist more than the company."

He laughed and said, "And always keep the deal short and sweet, to let them know that they have to keep playing ball to keep you."

I asked, "What do you think about videos?" I was thinking a lot about making a good one for John. Videos seemed like the real way to go.

Mr. DeBerry said, "You gotta have 'em. Especially when you're trying to sell records to *young* people. They've grown up on videos."

I said, "Can we make that a part of the contract?"

He chuckled and said, "*Now* you're thinking. You make *everything* a part of the contract. Some people don't get shit because they don't *ask* for shit. Then they want to look around and complain about what everyone else has."

He asked, "Do you have a good attorney?"

I said, "We have a guy out of Atlanta. And he seems to know the business well enough."

"But you always want to have one waiting in the wings," Mr. DeBerry told me. "I'll give you the name and number of a young guy that I know up here in New York, just in case."

He said, "You know, I've been around in this business for a long time, Darin. And distribution has always been a killer for us. The mom-and-pop stores just can't do it on their own. So I figured that I could be of some help to a lot of these young guys out here today by getting inside on the distribution game. But many of them want to be stars without finding out how it's actually done. And they don't *ask* how. They all seem like they want to find out the hard way. So I stopped pushing myself on people. And if they want to know, I just let them initiate it. So I thank *you* for calling me up and putting me to work. Because with everything going young nowadays, many of these young folks don't figure that us *old-timers* have anything to tell them."

Mr. DeBerry told me to call him anytime, and I told him that I would.

Then he said, "If you remember nothing else that I tell you, Darin, just remember this: always try to get more than what you need, and spend less than what you want. You hear me? Just think of it like asking your mother for ten dollars to see a six-dollar movie, and then you try to get in for four dollars to have some extra popcorn money. Because more than likely, she's only gonna give you seven anyway, or eight *if* she's feeling good that day."

I laughed and thanked him again before I hung up. Then I sat down and outlined a list of needs, wants, and responses in an actual record company meeting. I didn't really know what to expect, but I wanted to be prepared for it.

I got dressed in a suit and tie and flew up to these meetings in New York on John's local show money, and I was never impressed. There was more talk going on at these meetings about the fame game and comparisons to other singers and music than real contract negotiations. The "majors" made us feel like *we* were winning the lottery instead of *them*. And there was no bidding war to be heard of. They were saying things like, "Our basic policy is" such-and-such. They were pretty much offering John take-it-or-leave-it deals with little room for negotiation.

I guess I still knew too much about the recruitment game, because if a team made you feel that you should be lucky to be there, rather than they being lucky to have you, I just didn't figure that you would get much playing time, and I expressed that to John and Tony. I felt that they still needed to look for companies who were more eager to sign them. I didn't let them sign *anything* just to be signed.

Tony said, "I think your standards may be just a little too high, D. Just a little *too* high." He told me, "We should at least get in on a deal *first*, *then* you can start asking for the star treatment."

I ignored him, because we both knew that John held the keys to the castle. They looked at Tony as minor production help. Tony was just fortunate that John was a loyal man of his word, because he could have easily dropped him. John could have dropped me as well.

I also had disputes with the attorney. This guy wanted to sign John with a contract percentage instead of being paid at an hourly rate with a retainer.

I told John not to do that, and he didn't. But at the end of it all, I looked like a nicely dressed bad guy after we had struck out with the majors.

Nevertheless, John was patient about the whole process, which surprised me. I kept thinking that he was going to just up and sign something and send me on my way back to A&T, because he was so hungry for it, but he never did.

When we had a moment alone, John said, "I feel what you're trying to do, man. I mean, they made it sound like I don't really know what I'm capable of. And it's all a game, man. I understand that. But still, we gotta sign with somebody soon anyway."

He said, "Like you said, man, this song is hot, and we want to make sure that we put it out before it gets cold on us."

Then he smiled at me and said, "Nice tie, too, man. I've been noticing that you stand out at these meetings."

John looked sharp himself. He kept a nice low haircut with long sideburns, and he continued to wear loose disco clothes as his adopted uniform. It all looked good on him, like he was natural for it, instead of looking overblown or understated.

I chuckled and said, "Yeah. I want to make sure that I look like someone who they can respect. They already think that we're slow down south. Even our lawyer thinks we don't know what's going on. And he's from the South, too. So we might have to call up a new one."

John said, "It ain't where you're from, it's where you're at, man. And I want to be at the top. So we just have to keep working to get there. And keep wearing them nice suits for me," he joked. He added, "Mr. I-Don't-Want-to-Be-No-Manager."

What can I say? I just smiled at him. John had been onto something from the start. I guess I was just manager material. A natural.

. . . *what a scene we made* . . .

In April, John's mom started tripping again. She was calling my mom nearly every day trying to get me to talk John into coming home and singing gospel songs at the church. I guess Sister Williams figured that if she couldn't stop John from pursuing a singing career, she would at least try to control what he sang *about* and who he sang *to*.

I told my mother, "John doesn't want to sing gospel. It's too limiting. He wants a much larger audience than that."

She said, "Well, how large does he want it to be?"

I thought about that for a second. "I guess as large as he can get. And you know, some people don't listen to gospel music like that. Especially young people. John's trying to compete with rap music."

My mom said, "Yuck. That ain't much to compete with."

I didn't respond to that. We were from different eras. My mother grew up in the soul and disco era with my father, aunts, and uncles. I grew up listening to hip-hop and R&B with my brothers and cousins, and the times had changed. I figured that John and Tony had it right. If you wanted an audience in the nineties, then you had to compete with the music of the day, and not of yesterday.

"Well, how close is John to signing a record deal?" my mother asked me.

I said, "He's *real* close. We have another meeting this coming Monday up in Philly. We just haven't found the right people yet."

"Well, how hard is that?"

I smiled. My mom made it sound as if getting a record deal was like finding a box of cereal at the grocery store, and it wasn't that simple. You don't just find it and grab it, you have to talk it all out. Or at least that's how I thought.

I said, "If you don't want to end up complaining about your deal like a lot of other musicians do, then it's *real* hard. But if you just want to make records and get jerked around, then John could have been signed last winter."

My mother chuckled. She said, "Well, all right then. I wish you all luck. And by the way, how's your track season going?" she asked me.

I got excited about my progress and said, "I finally made the quarter-mile relay team. And we start our spring workouts for football soon, so I'll be ready for it.

"This'll be my break-out season this year, Mom," I told her. "I can *feel* it!"

She said, "Well, all right! That's the spirit. You'll make it. You just had to be patient, that's all."

I hung up the phone with my mom and felt good about my future. John's future was another thing altogether. I was pressed to get him signed because I wanted to start getting myself mentally ready to play football. Of course, John and Tony were pressed because they wanted to be signed already and working on that first big album. They had been telling me about this independent Philadelphia label called Old School Records, who had been signing a lot of innovative rap guys, and they were now looking to compete in the market with a fresh R&B act. I liked their label name because John and Tony were definitely old-school, but everything else had to be worked out.

I flew up to Philly Sunday afternoon for our meeting at eleven o'clock that Monday morning. I was planning to hang out with John and Tony that Sunday night and just kick it like old friends. I figured we would talk about the music when it came up. We had plenty of time for that. But they picked me up from the Philadelphia airport and immediately started talking about meeting the label's A&R man and marketing director. A&Rs were the artists and repertoire people, who were *supposed* to know great acts when they heard them. They were the gatekeepers to stardom in the music industry, similar to scouts in pro sports.

"They're two cool white boys," John and Tony told me.

I looked at them and said, "Two white boys?"

We had mostly dealt with black A&Rs up to that point. I just figured that black people knew how to listen to black music. And of course, white people had the money to market it, sell it, and give out awards. But I was from the South, so what did I know about white guys up in Philly? Nothing.

Tony said, "Yeah, these white boys are cool, man. Kenny Klein and Matt Duggins. They even call them Double K and M.D."

I grinned and shook my head from the passenger seat of Tony's old van. John sat in the back on a milk crate.

I said, "I guess I'll meet these guys tomorrow then."

John just smiled at me for some reason.

Tony said, "Naw, you gon' meet 'em tonight."

"I am?"

John said, "Yeah, we all meetin' up down South Street."

"The one that Boyz II Men sang about?"

They both smiled at me and said, "Yeah."

What could I say? I shrugged my shoulders and said, "All right then."

First we dropped my things off at Tony's apartment, a large two-bedroom pad near downtown. At least John wasn't cramped there. But they had magazines and music equipment all over the place.

I said, "So what do your neighbors say when you two start blasting the music in here?"

John chuckled and answered me first.

He said, "We worked out a system of using headphones."

"But what about the drums? You can't use headphones for that."

Tony said, "I use a drum machine now. I mean, I still create off the drums, but then I copy the beats onto a drum pad. Them engineer guys said that you can do a lot more with the different levels that way. And then we just loop it and add shit while John does his thing on the keyboard."

John looked at me and nodded. He said,"We know what we doing now, D. We got a lot of different things we want to do now. The headphones let you hear it better."

Tony said, "Don't get us wrong. I mean, you still want to hear the shit pump out the speakers. But if you really want to create music that hits, you gotta do it through the headphones like them engineers do."

I said, "So you two living together was a good idea then."

Tony said, "It *had* to happen that way. You can't really keep a connection going from long distance. That's like having a long-distance girlfriend. You know you gon' fuck other girls. That shit don't work. It's torture."

We all laughed about it before we left out for South Street.

Since Tony lived so close by, we went ahead and walked down. It was pretty lively that night, even on a Sunday.

Philly's South Street reminded me of that old Whodini song, *The Freaks Come Out at Night*. It was wild down there!

We met Double K and M.D. at this steak and cheese place, and both of them wore black baseball hats with OLD SCHOOL RECORDS on them in white script with red trim.

"What's up, D? We hear that you're the man to impress. My name's Matt."

He stuck his hand out to me. I shook it and smiled.

"M.D.?" I asked him.

He said, "Yeah, ya heard about me?"

I said, "I heard *of* you."

The other guy said, "And I'm Kenny."

"Double K?" I asked.

"That's me."

I could tell that these guys had been hanging out for a while. They looked damned near like family, both with that cool, white-boy movie look. They were the kind of cool white guys who got all of the blondes. Kenny was just a little shorter than Matt. So I figured that would be how I would tell the two of them apart, short and tall, A&R and marketing, respectively.

Double K said, "So I guess you know that your boy John is very talented."

"Yeah, and with a name like Loverboy, I told him that I can't let him around *my* lady. She might start gettin' ideas," M.D. added.

I smiled and chuckled at it. John and Tony just sat back and listened.

Double K said, "He reminds me of a new-school Marvin Gaye, or Teddy Pendergrass."

"*Definitely* the passion of Teddy Pendergrass, and the creative soul of Marvin Gaye," M.D. finished.

Double K said, "This new song even has a Michael Jackson, Bobby Brown–like attitude."

"Yeah, but the tag is just so much better. *Loverboy*," M.D. said with his hands up. "I can do *lots* with that! Aw man, I'm telling *you!*"

John and Tony started laughing in the background.

I said, "What do you think about a video for the song? *Stylin' 'n' Profilin'*, right?" I was throwing my cards on the table to let those guys know that I meant real business and was not interested in all that slick talk that they were doing. But they *were* good at it. I gave them that.

M.D. spoke first this time. That was his field.

He said, "At Old School Records, we like to do things *old-school*. And we love videos like everyone else, but so much is wasted out there, man."

Double K said, "Some labels are spending close to a half a million dollars."

"And a lot of their videos don't even look like shit," Tony added from the background.

"So we want to take this thing right back to where it all begins," M.D. told me. He paused for a beat and said, "At the nightclubs. I think that a lot of people have forgotten that. So we want to produce a cheap, *quality* video with John singing at the nightclub to a hot number who keeps ignoring him. Now, what guy *can't* relate to that?

"It's a simple formula of success," he said. "Either you've got it or you don't. And we're not out to spend a couple of million dollars to find that out."

Double K added, "And we're just being honest about that. John has it. So we want to market him in the most economical way and let his talent do the rest. That's what this thing is all about. We have these major labels manufacturing stars now, and that's a trend that we're not trying to follow."

I said, "Yeah, but he still needs the money, right, to get his talent out there?" I wasn't going to let those guys tell us that John didn't need any money to market and promote, no matter how old-school they were.

M.D. said, "Yeah, we're gonna use what it takes. I mean, don't get us wrong, we're not talking about free cheese here. But we're just looking for *real* talent," he told me. "That's what being old-school means to us. And those guys who manufacture their talents—they create 'em in Franken-stein's lab, package them, sell them, and then the next year they're out looking for new toys to play with, while your guy gets tossed in the *old* toy chest."

Double K said, "And the majors *all* have those old toy chests, D. It's *out* with the old, and *in* with the new. But when you're poor like us, you really value every toy that you get."

"Yeah, but we're not *that* poor, Kenny," M.D. said and laughed. "We don't want D thinking that we don't have any money to produce these guys."

We all laughed at that.

M.D. said, "But that's what we do. We value our artists. We work the clubs. We work the streets. We get you played on the radio. We get your videos played. And we do our job one hundred and *ten* percent. And if John does his part at even *ninety* percent, then we get our two hundred percent of success."

M.D. looked me right in my eyes and said, "Now D, you tell me, and I want you to be honest about this. Does John have what it takes to be a star, or what?"

I froze and looked back at John.

He smiled and started laughing like it was all a big joke.

I turned back and said, "Hell yeah! That boy's a genius."

Double K said, "Well then, you have nothing to worry about."

"And that's exactly what we want to hear from you," M.D. finished for him.

"As long as it's the *truth*," Double K added.

"Yeah, because we're not into the gimmick music game," M.D. told me.

Double K said, "As a matter of fact, we don't even sign artists that we have to go out and find producers for. Most of our artists produce their own music. We just give them the studio time and the expertise to do it."

M.D. shook his head and said, "Outside production can be a real pain in the ass. And it's *expensive* too. Some of these producers are asking for a hundred thousand dollars a song."

"That's also how a lot of artists lose out on their royalties," Double K said. "They end up not owning anything, with plenty of bills to pay."

"That won't happen to us," Tony spoke up.

John wasn't saying much of anything.

I asked, "Well, how many points does he get on his albums?"

M.D. said, "Hey, man, we'll talk about that tomorrow. We don't rape our artists, so we won't be asking you to take your clothes off or anything. But you're going over my head on that. You'll have to ask the Big Cheese."

Double K smiled and said, "The Big Cheese is pretty reasonable."

I said, "Well, how many years do you want to sign him for? Or how many *albums*, I should say?"

"That's the Big Cheese there too," M.D. told me. "But we'd like to sign him for *twenty* years if he'll last that long."

Double K looked at John and said, "You think you'll last that long, John? That's a whole lot of lovin'. Maybe you'll go after Wilt Chamberlain's number."

We all laughed again.

John said, "That's a whole lot of years, man. I *hope* I can last that long. That's like Frank Sinatra and James Brown."

M.D. said, "Well, who does it better, baby? Old Blue Eyes, and the hardest-working man in showbiz, James Brown. Those are two great performers."

Double K said, "Nah, the Big Cheese generally tries to sign guys for three to five years. You get some labels that want to own you, but we want to make sure that you're happy with us. We don't want to be a pain in the ass to you—"

"And we don't want *you* being a pain in the ass to us," M.D. finished again. "And if it's not working, we want a fair split. But our artists are all pretty happy with us."

Tony nodded his head and said, "Yeah, they are. They all say that you're fair, and that you don't get in the way."

"Hey, in this business, that's like saying that you're a *saint*," M.D. joked.

Double K said, "But D, since you're the man to talk to, what else would you like to ask us as far as the musical and marketing direction is concerned?"

I thought about it and asked, "What do you guys think about the song *May I?*"

M.D. said, "We love it! We'd like to make that our second single, and push it for the urban classic stations and the late-night quiet storms. So we'd drop the club song first, and then push the love song. Isn't that what we all go to the clubs to do anyway, to fall in love? I mean, at least for a couple of nights or so. Then we go and try a *new* club."

We all broke out laughing again.

M.D. said, "But just don't tell my girl that I said that."

I said, "Okay, well, what about the title of this first album, and the amount of songs on it?"

I was making up anything to ask them at that point just to see how much these guys had thought about the entire package.

M.D. said, "Well, first off, we don't believe in putting twenty cuts of mostly bullshit on an album. And if you have that many songs that are bona fide hits, then we can save some of them and put a few songs on movie sound tracks to increase your exposure."

Double K nodded and said, "Yeah. It's a big waste. And by the time you even *do* twenty songs, some of them are gonna sound alike anyways. It's better to go away, experience some new things, and come back with some new sounds for the next album. That way you're always fresh without burning yourself out."

M.D. said, "Unless you're doing a sound track, a compilation album, or a greatest hits or something, twelve to fifteen songs are enough for one artist. And as far as the album title is concerned? Are you kidding me? *Loverboy: The Album.* It's just *that* simple."

Double K nodded his head and said, "Yeah. That simple."

Tony said, "*I* like it."

I looked back at John.

John smiled and nodded himself. He said, "It's like an introduction album. It builds the Loverboy name. It works, man. Then we can get creative on the next one."

"Anything else, D?" M.D. asked me. I could see by then that Matt Duggins was the more aggressive counterpuncher, as he *should be* in marketing. Kenny Klein was more reserved in the lead as the A&R.

I asked, "When would the album come out?"

M.D. answered, "This fall. We work the first single for the summer, and then drop the album in October."

"*At Midnight* would be *my* next choice for the winter season after *May I*," Double K said. "People like to get warm. Then we could drop another up-tempo song for early next year."

Those white boys meant *business! Four singles!* They had thought of everything. And I had to admit it, the two of them working together were hard to beat. I needed to rest my damn brain from them.

I finally said, "All right, well, that's enough questions for tonight. I'll save the rest for the Big Cheese."

"Well, all right!" M.D. said, celebrating. "Have you ever had a cheese steak before, Darin?"

I said, "Yeah, when we were up here in January at the Philadelphia Music Conference."

"Did you like it?"

I nodded. "Yeah."

"Well, get ready to have another one on us."

When we separated, around 1 A.M. that night, to get rest for our meeting in the morning, Tony looked at me and asked, "So what do you think?"

I joked and said, "Did you practice that whole thing with those guys before I came up here?"

Tony and John both laughed at me.

Tony said, "Naw, man, that's just the way they are. They usually talk to us for, like, three *hours* and shit. After a while I'm like, 'I wish these white boys would shut the fuck up. *God damn!*' But they just cool like that, man. And you can't manufacture cool either. They know what the fuck they talking about."

John just smiled and nodded, playing Mr. Smooth in the background. I guess he was trying not to let it all faze him.

I said, "So what do you think about it, John?"

John paused. He said, "I'm just ready to do my thing, man. And they're white, but they just seem like the right guys to do it with. This ain't about race, man. This is about *business. They're* ready to move on it right now, and *we're* ready to move on it right now."

Tony said, "Yeah, because when they first started talking that October shit to us, I was thinking, *Can they really put an album out that fast with all the marketing and stuff that we need to do?* And they basically broke it down and said that it depends on us. Could we finish an album in a month? I said, 'Damn right! I got plenty of beats. And John can write a new song in an hour.' Plus they have contacts with other musicians that we could use to collaborate on anything that we needed."

John said, "It took us a while to take them seriously, because we were thinking about getting a big money deal with the majors. But after sitting down for the deals, and all of them were talking that little-fish-in-a-big-pond shit, we decided that being a big fish in the little pond could make us expert swimmers. You know what I mean, D? Because like they said, it's all about pushing your talent, man. And me and Tony already know that we can get down. We just need an opportunity."

I nodded my head and felt pretty satisfied with things myself. Those white guys had said everything I needed to hear, and the only thing left to do was to hear the final numbers from the "Big Cheese," as they called their boss.

I said, "Well, let's sleep on it and see about it in the morning."

Tony said, "Yeah, and the lawyer said that he'd meet us there in the morning."

I frowned at that. I still didn't trust that guy from Atlanta, who was talking percentages on us. I was hoping that we could just take the contract to someone else for counsel and bring it back.

When John and I were ready to crash back at the apartment that night, he smiled at me again.

"What?" I asked him.

He said, "How is track season going?"

"My split in the four-by-one dropped below ten seconds in our home meet yesterday. And I think I might be able to run a four-four forty this year in football," I told him.

He nodded. "That's *pro* speed."

I smiled and said, "I know."

Then John started laughing, as if he had a joke in mind.

I said, "What's so damn funny, man? You've been acting silly all damn night."

He said, "Nothing. I'm just thinking about tomorrow. It's contract time."

John sounded pretty confident that this would be the one, and I couldn't find a reason to argue against it. The sooner he signed a deal, the better off we would *all* be.

I said, "All right then. Now you get to show and prove."

John couldn't stop smiling all night. He was probably smiling in his sleep. And with all of that pure talent that he had, I was just amazed that he trusted so much to me.

At our meeting that Monday morning, I was the only fool wearing a suit and a tie again. Even the Big Cheese and his black lawyer were dressed casually. And *our* lawyer hadn't made the trip up from Atlanta on time to make the meeting. But none of us were nervous without him. We just went ahead and did what we needed to do. We knew what most of the terms were by then.

We met inside of their studio building on Delaware Avenue. They may have been called *Old School Records*, but they surely had *all* new equipment. But they tried to keep an old-fashioned look to the place, leaving the studio pretty much like a big warehouse, like you would see in old movies about musicians. I guess the acoustics of the music would sound more live that way, too.

Anyway, we talked about the length of the record deal, and we decided to push for a short contract of three albums. Since it was John's first deal, I just felt that it was safer that way. If he still liked his relationship after that, he could choose to stay as long as he wanted to.

We told them that we already had our own publishing, and since they were used to dealing with artists who produced their own music, we had no problem negotiating publishing terms. They understood that John would control his own destiny. And that's the way it *should* be.

For the recording points on the album, I started off referring to some fortunate artists who get up to eighteen points for their work. Of course, I knew that those numbers were out of the question for us, but if you start at the top, you kind of erase thoughts of starting from the bottom. So we ended up hitting the middle, at fourteen points. I figured that we could ask for more in the next deal.

Then we talked about the actual album production for the fall. The Big Cheese threw out an amount of $500,000 on the table, with the single and the video production of *Stylin' 'n' Profilin'* to begin as soon as we signed. Well, it wasn't a million in production dollars or anything, but since John and Tony crafted their own music so smoothly, I didn't think that they needed that much.

John looked at me and said, "What do you think, man? You want to wait for the lawyer?"

I thought about it. We still hadn't agreed to any specific terms with this lawyer from Atlanta, and I wanted the whole process to be over and done with just like John and Tony did.

I made a decision right then and shook my head. It was pure instinct.

Everything was explained to us in plain English, and I didn't want to prolong the inevitable anymore. John had to start from *somewhere*.

I said, "Nah, man. This sounds like a good deal to me. Go ahead and sign."

Everyone got all excited but John. John kept his poise and nodded to me real slow, as if he was going over the decision in his own head. Then he picked up the pen and went for broke.

I was anxious for the entire plane ride back to Greensboro. I kept hoping that I had done the right thing. I kept rereading my copy of the contract on the plane, but nothing jumped out and alarmed me on it. If John was successful, which I had no doubts that he would be, I figured that he could ask for more points and money on his next deal.

When I got back to the dorms that Monday night, I immediately called Chester DeBerry at the home number that he had given me.

"Hello," he answered on the first ring.

I didn't want to take up too much of his time, so I just came right out with it to get it over with.

I said, "Well, Mr. DeBerry, my friend John went ahead and signed with Old School Records in Philadelphia today."

He said, "Hey, my man Darin from Greensboro. Old School Records has an account with us. They're good people."

I said, "Yeah?" and took a deep breath.

Mr. DeBerry said, "I knew those guys when they started out in music twenty years ago. Joe is a fair man."

Joe, first name only, like a real old-timer, was the "Big Cheese."

I said, "Yeah, that's what everybody says. And his A&R and marketing director convinced me."

"Who, Matt and Kenny? Those guys are real pros. We need more young *black* guys who know the ropes like they do. Young guys like *you*."

I smiled from ear to ear and said, "Thanks. But I was just trying to get back to playing football. I wanted to make sure John was all right."

He said, "That's what you're *supposed* to do. And I know you won't let John make too many mistakes, so you stay right on him."

"Oh, you know it," I told him.

I hung up with Mr. DeBerry and felt my freedom again. Not that it was all that bad working with John and the whole music business, I just wanted to concentrate on football.

John called me that same night and told me that our lawyer from Atlanta showed up pissed, saying that his flight was delayed and that he had accidentally left his cell phone at the office.

I said, "Tough cookie. I'd tell him we'll pay him for his flight, but now we don't need him." And I really didn't care. John could get a new lawyer.

. . . with pretty girls to serenade . . .

Being back at football practice was all about sweat, ambition, and raw energy. I loved it! I was in full competition mode, smashing everyone who got in my way.

One of the assistant coaches said, "Darin, I can tell that you're ready to play *this* year. Keep it up, Harmon."

I was thinking, *I've* been *ready to play!* but I kept that thought to myself. There was no sense in stirring up bad vibes right after receiving a compliment. I was much faster too. Once I got my forty speed down to that four-four level, no receiver could run away from me.

Nevertheless, for my teammates who knew, all they wanted to talk to me about was my boy John.

"I heard Loverboy got a record deal. When is his album coming out?"

I couldn't be jealous about it anymore. I had helped him to get signed. But I wanted to be known for my football skills and speed, not for my boy's singing.

I told them, "Sometime in October."

"Who he sign wit'?"

"An independent label out of Philly."

They were all like, "That's cool, man. It's gonna be good to say that we *knew* that boy when he blows up. You gon' go on tour wit' 'em, D?"

I said, "When I can, you know. He's gonna be touring this summer. They'll be dropping a single soon. But you know, I'm trying to think about practice now."

"But ain't you still his manager?"

I shook it off. "I mean, he still calls me up for advice and stuff, but I told him to go ahead and get a *real* manager now, you know, somebody who can take him further. All I really did was speak up for him when he needed me to. I didn't really hook him up with nobody. He did all the work on his own, really."

When early summer came and John's first single, *Stylin' 'n' Profilin'*, started hitting the radio waves, we were both home for a spell. We were hanging out late at the gas station on Statesville Avenue, just kicking it with old friends from Charlotte. It was your typical late-night scene with teenagers and your early-twenties crowd sitting outside their cars, blasting music, with girls flocking around. That's what you do when you don't feel like going to the clubs, don't want to pay, or can't get in.

Antoine, an old friend from Garinger High School who had never made it to college, was chilling with us and asking John if he was still into music.

John smiled slyly and said, "Yeah."

Everyone in Charlotte hadn't heard who John was yet, particularly people who hadn't gone to college with us and hadn't heard him perform. John had never done anything in Charlotte as far as singing was concerned. People still didn't pay him much mind there. The girls could tell that he had matured and dressed cooler, but that was about it.

Antoine said, "You got a music scholarship to school, didn't you?"

John said, "Yeah."

I just sat there smiling, knowing the inside joke. But John was real cool about being signed. He wasn't making a big deal about it.

Anyway, someone had their radio on when Power 98 FM started talking about the Charlotte homeboy John "Loverboy" Williams and his new song. Then they played it.

As soon as the song came on, people started turning up their car stereos and blasting it with pride. Girls were right there in the gas station parking lot, jamming! John just sat there and smiled.

All of a sudden, it just hit like a slow-motion tidal wave.

This girl walked over, staring at John, and asked him, "Ain't your name John Williams? You played in the band with my older sister at Garinger."

John nodded his head and said, "Yeah."

Antoine looked again and put two and two together.

He said, "Wait a minute. This is *you* on the radio?"

The girl started jumping up and down already.

"Oh my God! Oh my God! Ay y'all, this Loverboy right here!" she started yelling. "Can I get an autograph, man? What's up? Oh my God! Wait till I tell my sister. She had a crush on you in high school."

I was sitting there thinking, *Here we go with the craziness*. That girl knew who John was when we first drove up, but she didn't have anything to say to him until she heard that announcement on the radio. Some people are fake as hell! When you become famous it all comes out.

The girls started making their way over to my car after that. I was beginning to feel embarrassed that I wasn't driving anything sportier.

One of them said, "What are you trying to play, incognito over here?"

They were mostly the young and boisterous type who liked to do exactly what John was talking about in his song, style and profile.

Antoine was still shaking his head.

He said, "I don't believe this. *You're* Loverboy. That's *your* song."

"Hey man, you signed now? When the album droppin'?" one of the guys asked him.

Right before my eyes, everyone started to pay John attention at the gas station just like they did at A&T's homecoming. I just took in the whole scene and grinned. My boy was on his way to real stardom.

"So when you gon' start getting paid like that?" someone else asked him.

"You need some beats? I got some beats for you."

"How come you ain't got no better car than this?"

I couldn't believe my ears. John wasn't even attempting to answer them, he was just sucking it all in. The boy had this amazing calmness about everything, just like he was before he would perform.

He finally said, "It's just one song," as if he didn't have an album coming out in the fall.

Then the DJs on Power 98 FM started talking about John and his song on the radio. They went on to announce that he would be on the air that next morning. I knew that already, but the crowd didn't know until then. That pretty much intensified their frenzy.

A girl asked him, "So how come they call you *Loverboy*? Is there some inside information on that?" She was definitely flirting.

John sat up there and laughed, real mellow. "Nah, that's just my singing style," he told her.

A guy said, "Man, you 'bout to blow up *crazy* then. I like that song, man. Go 'head witcha bad self!"

John said, "Thanks, man," and nodded.

Antoine was still standing there saying, "Damn! I can't believe this! How come you didn't say nothin'?"

When we finally drove away from all of that, the first girl hollered, "I'm gon' tell my sister that I saw you, John! I mean, LOVERBOY!"

We both smiled as we drove off.

I asked John, "So how is your mom taking it now?"

He shook his head. "It's devil music, man. She hasn't changed. She's just living with it."

I frowned and said, "Aw, man, she'll come around. So what new songs have you and Tony come up with lately?"

He smiled. "We gotta few new hits. I'll let you hear 'em when we finish 'em."

I laughed and said, "The same old John. You still holding shit back on me."

"I'm sayin', man, they're not ready yet."

"What does Tony think?"

"He likes 'em."

"And *you* don't?"

"I mean, they're all right. But I'll just see how people respond when I perform onstage. It's all about making songs that move people. So, you know, I gotta wait until we start touring with the album."

I said, "What about touring this summer with Blake and them?" I still figured that John and Tony would be out there doing their thing and getting people ready for the album.

John said, "Tour with Blake and sing what? I'm not trying to sing nothing before the album comes out no more, man. We gotta start pulling back all the tapes that's out there. But when we finish with everything, we gon' flip it on 'em anyway. We got a whole live-band feel now."

I said, "Well, what did Blake say about this?" Blake was itching to make some money with them that summer.

"Old School Records worked it out with him," John told me. "So we're gonna tour with the rappers a little bit this summer to announce my name and get me out on the market with the label and stuff, and then we're gonna set up our own tour with Blake for later on this year when the album drops."

That sounded like a plan to me. I nodded my head and smiled.

I said, "So y'all gon' tour with some rappers?" That sounded interesting.

John said, "Yeah, because we're the first R&B act that Old School is puttin' out. They were involved with, like, rock and roll bands, and then they started doing rap music, and now they got us with the R&B."

I grinned and said, "It sounds to me like they're moving to where the money's moving."

John laughed and said, "Yup. That's what they're doing. That's cool with me. And they know how to create, like, an earthy feeling in the studio. I mean, we got songs that make you feel like you right in the middle of our set at a jazz club, a dance club, or at a stage performance.

"I mean, they really know what they're doing, man," he told me. "And them two white boys, Kenny and Matt, know *everybody*."

I said, "Yeah, I bet they would, the way they talked to *us*."

John said, "They gettin' us played *everywhere*. And they told us that most of their rap groups are underground, so they get most of their play from the club DJs and during certain radio shows. But we got that top forty sound, so we can get played, like, twenty times a day. But we still got that old-school soul that makes us sound different from everybody else."

He grinned and said, "They just *loving us* there, man! This is a good deal!"

I chuckled at the irony of John touring with rap groups to kick off his singing career. By that time, the Notorious B.I.G. was blowing up with that *Juicy* song from Puff Daddy's Bad Boy records. And after the Wu-Tang Clan hooked up with SWV, it seemed to me like the hybrid of rap and R&B was a sure way to going platinum.

I asked, "So are you gonna do a song singing a background chorus or something with one of these rap groups from the label?"

John just smiled and started laughing.

I said, "So, y'all must be already doing it then, since you responded that way?" I was assuming things.

"Well, they asked us to, and I just asked to hear the concept of the song first. And it was cool. They were talking about, you know, hooking up with a shorty for the weekend. And like, each rapper talked about what kind of girl he likes, and I just come in and tie it together with my singing. Tony even did the beat to it. And I added some of my keyboard playing."

I said, "Y'all get some of the song credit for that then. That's publishing rights."

I was on business alert again and couldn't help myself.

John said, "I know that, man. I ain't stupid. I'm the one who's been creating my own music all this time."

I said, "All right, as long as you know."

He said, "Everybody knows who does what. That's just what kind of label we have. We *all* get our credit."

He sounded loyal like I don't know what, and he had only been with the label for a few months.

I asked him, "So what's the title of this rap song?"

"The Weekends."

That sounded simple enough to me.

I smiled and asked him, "How does your chorus go?"

John started snapping his fingers for a medium tempo. Then he sang his chorus:

"'*Cause you're my weekend shorrr-tee / and ahhh know you like it naugh-tee /
but you never tell your momma what we do / your sweet moans are for meee and
you. And on Fridays, bay-bee / awww, girl, you reeal-lee amaze me / and I'm so
glad that you made me your friend / on Saturday nights let's meeet again.*

"*Awwww girrrl / Awwww girrrl.*"

I broke out laughing. I said, "Can these guys rap?"

John nodded his head and said, "Yeah. It's all tight. But we wanna perform it for a live audience first, so we just recorded the instrumentals on a
DAT, and we're gonna perform it live a few times before we try to put it
out."

He smiled and added, "I even get to plug my name real good on the
vamp."

I said, "Do it."

He sang: "*And if your momma has to know / where you disappear / just tell
her that you're in love / with the Lov-ver-boy.*"

I laughed again. I could imagine what that song would do to the girls,
the rough ones especially. It was freaky in a tactful way. John just knew how
to flip it, even with rap music.

I dropped him off at his mother's house that night and couldn't sleep
when I got home. My boy John was about to blow up for real, and I was still
trying to play the other side of the fence on him and not come in as his full-
fledged manager. I weighed that thing all night long. Football. Music.
Football. Music. Football. Music. And the football dream was getting its *ass*
kicked! I just kept thinking about all of them damn girls that John would
attract. Was I thinking with the wrong head?

I hadn't even seen John's video yet. I was kind of jealous that I wasn't in
it. Tony was in it. John told me that they were doing the final editing and
that it would be out real soon. Knowing John, the video was probably already in the mail to BET, MTV, and the Box. That boy loved the game of
understatement. He'd make a million dollars and tell you that he made ten
just to surprise you with it later. I laughed at that even in my sleep. That
was my boy, though. That was my boy.

I drove John down to the radio station at Power 98 early in the morning.

He shook his head in the passenger seat of my car and looked glum.

I asked him, "What's wrong, man?"

It was seven-thirty in the morning, and I hadn't gotten much sleep, but *I*
was still in good spirits. Why wasn't he?

John said, "My mom was talking about she's praying for me, man."

I chuckled. "That's good. You don't want her to?"

"Not like *she's* thinking about doing it. I'm thinking she might call the damn radio station and start apologizing to the church members on the air."

I broke out laughing. I said, "Now that would be some funny shit if she did that, man. No lie."

John said, "It ain't funny to me, man. She gon' make me block her out completely. Because I'm gonna *do* what I'm gonna do, man. I'm not trying to be just another church boy singing in the choir. It's a million of them out there. I'm trying to be the only Loverboy."

I grinned and repeated, "The only Loverboy? What do you mean by that? The rest of us ain't supposed to get no women?"

He said, "It ain't about getting women, man. Not necessarily. It's about creating emotions in people. And love is the most powerful emotion out there. But I plan to write songs that make you feel a lot of different things. I just don't want you to sing along with my music, I want you to fall in love with it and wrap yourself up in it like a warm blanket."

I just stopped all of my silly thoughts for a minute and started all over.

I said, "When you used to say shit like that when we were young, I just thought your ass was crazy from being around old people too much. Like, you didn't really get a chance to be a real kid like the rest of us. But when I hear you say stuff like that now, man, I just figure that you were just meant to do what you're doing. So, you know, I just say to keep doing it."

I joked and said, "Your mom just gon' have to call up and pray for you on the air."

All that morning on the radio, they made pun jokes about the name Loverboy.

"Will it be safe for my daughter to listen to your music? I'm trying to keep her head in her studies. Guys like you create major distractions."

"Yeah, I don't know if this is the right time in the country to be a *Loverboy*, with AIDS and whatnot going around anyway. What do you have, like, a condom in every pocket when you perform?"

I was laughing, but I don't think that was the kind of radio talk that Sister Williams wanted to hear. So every time they went to a caller, I got nervous thinking that it was her. However, most of the people calling in were proud that another Charlotte native was about to make the scene after Jodeci had done it.

John handled himself well on the show. Maybe too well. People tend to like drama, but John didn't give them any.

He said, "I look at the whole Loverboy name as me trying to make people fall in love with the music and the message. I mean, I have a lot of different thoughts that I want to write about that may not always be about love, but I still want you to feel like you're *in* love when you hear it."

That toned the jokes down immediately and gave John that same mushy, nice-guy appeal that he had growing up. He turned the Loverboy tag into what *he* wanted it to be. And the good-boy role didn't stop the attention that he received during the rest of his stay in Charlotte. I guess that folks in our Bible Belt hometown were really feeling his sincerity. I thought that his mother should have been proud. I know that *I* was. My whole family was.

After John had gone back on the summer promotions trail, my family members were all proud of what he was about to do.

My mom nodded her head at home and said, "Well, you told me he was going to do it, Darin. And he did it." We were in the kitchen as she began to prepare a big meal for four.

I said, "Yeah, but you need to talk to his mom and make *her* understand that."

My mom said the same thing that I had been saying.

"She'll come around."

My father walked into the kitchen overhearing us and said, "No she won't. She won't come around. She'll just have to live with it." He sounded like John.

My mother said, "What makes you so sure of that?"

My father looked at me with a man's insider grin and said, "I just *know* it."

He thought that Sister Williams expected to have her way with John, and she couldn't get it anymore. So instead of facing the facts, she would find a way to pout for the rest of her life. But that was my *father's* theory, not mine. I still had hope.

My mother changed the subject and said, "So, Darryl is going to help him with his accounting." She was referring to help from my older brother.

I said, "No, but he contacted an accountant who he said was good. Darryl told me he didn't want to get too involved with John that way."

My father nodded and grunted, "Mmm hmm. And what about you? Weren't you in bed with this whole thing when it first started?"

I said, "I wasn't all the way in bed with it." I smiled and added, "I was like, halfway in and halfway out."

I knew that he and my mother had talked about it several times. But my father usually only got involved when things were getting out of hand. Since I wasn't making any drastic decisions about my own schooling or career, he figured that John's problems were extra and not immediately his concern. Don't get me wrong, my father loved John like the rest of us, he just never accepted the lack of family structure in the Williams household. He also didn't want to stick his nose too far in what he figured was another father's abandoned business. I knew my father well. He wasn't perfect, but he had been a good example for all of us.

My little sister, a high school senior to be, walked in the kitchen with us, saw me, and started singing John's first two lines: *"Hay baby / in the blue jeee-eans."*

She didn't sound like John, but she was trying. She started laughing and said, "That song is a hit."

I said, "I know. I heard it a while ago. I knew it was good the first time I heard it."

My mother asked me, "So, John invited you to a performance coming up in Cleveland?"

"Yeah. It'll be the only one I can make it to this summer before football season starts up at A&T," I told her. "And this *gotta* be my year this year. I can't wait until I'm a senior to shine. I gotta do it now! *John* taught me that," I added with a grin.

"Hmmph," my father grunted.

My sister asked me, "So if I come to the homecoming this year, you'll be in the *whole* game?"

I expected to be a star on the team my junior year. I said, "You can count on that."

My mother said, "Well, we'll *all* be going."

My father looked at me and said, "When does John's album come out?"

"Sometime in October," I told him.

Something was on my father's mind, I just didn't feel like trying to read it at the time.

We all sat down, said grace, ate dinner, and then we talked about a few other subjects. When we were done and ready to go our separate ways, my father was ready to tell me what was on his mind.

He said, "Darin . . ."

"Yes."

He shook his head and changed his mind. "Ah, never mind."

I shrugged my shoulders and left it at that.

I arrived out in Cleveland, Ohio, a week later to see John and Tony perform with their label mates at this jam-packed club. The place wasn't all that big, and the hip-hop audiences were usually a little rowdier, with more males than the singing crowds John had performed for. They could wear anything they wanted to at hip-hop clubs as opposed to your dress code places. That crowd in Cleveland, although it was not the hardest that I had seen, was definitely not John's usual cup of tea. He was rarely around the rowdy types in high school *or* in college.

From the tiny backstage area, I asked John, "Have you seen that crowd out there?"

He nodded. "Yeah, Bone Thugs-N-Harmony lovers."

I had forgotten all about that group.

I said, "You've been listening to them?" I was surprised.

John said, "Not really, but everybody was talking about them when we came out here."

"Yeah, I bet they were. Those guys are like royalty out here."

John smiled and said, "Not when I get up on the mike."

We both started laughing.

Tony and the other performers were all up in the mix of the club. They were *loving it!* With hard-core acts, mixing in with the crowd is where they wanted to be.

I smiled and asked, "John, are you gonna walk through the crowd when you get up there?"

He paused and said, "Nah. I want to be untouchable."

I said, "Yeah, they'll probably want you more after that, hunh?"

"Yup. That's what I'm counting on," he told me. "That's why I'm sitting back here now. I don't want nobody to know me until after I perform."

I laughed, but it seemed to me that John was elevating the game. He was thinking things through.

I said, "Did somebody tell you to do that?" just to make sure.

He smiled again. He looked at me and said, "I can't make up my own plans, D? I've been in the marching band for years. Remember? I know how to build anticipation."

And he did. *Definitely.* So I decided to just shut my mouth and wait for him to do his thing.

When they finally got ready to call John up, he asked them to bring him a cordless microphone backstage.

"You're not coming out onstage with us?" they asked him.

John said, "Yeah, I'm coming out . . . when it's my part." And he stood his ground on that.

Tony just looked at him and chuckled, as if he knew what John was planning already.

Tony said, "Ain't no sense in *me* going out there at all. We ain't using no live drums. We using DATs."

John said, "Well, don't go out there then. I'll hold it down for *both* of us."

Sure enough, when the instrumental track started for *The Weekends*, the whole mood of the club changed. You could hear John and Tony's soulful sound immediately through the beat and the bass line:

Ba-Doom-Boomp-TAT
Boomp-Ba-Doooom-Boomp-TAT
Ba-Doom-Boomp-TAT
Boomp-Ba-Doooom-Boomp-TAT . . .

It was hard for any rapper to sound bad on *this* track. So these guys began to rip it up with smooth raps and had the crowd's undivided attention. The whole club immediately fell into sync, and started bobbing their heads up and down as if they were all riding the waves of a river. It was like a spiritual awakening of groove. No wonder music was king!

And when Loverboy finally got up to add his chorus, that was *it*. He took control of that place wearing his casual cool clothing, with his tall lean body gliding across the stage on beat, singing like a prince:

'Cause you're my weekend shorrr-tee
and ahhh know you like it naugh-tee . . .

Awwww girrrl
Awwww girrrl . . .

You could clearly see all of the girls in there beginning to jockey for position to see him up close. Tony and I just started breaking up laughing. John didn't even stop when the next verse came in. He underscored the rap with Marvin Gaye–like hums:

Mmmmm hmmm
Mmmmm hmmm . . .

As I continued to watch with a big old smile on my face, I noticed that the rappers were a little too hyper. They were dancing and bopping faster than the music. John was the only one on beat, and his slow sway began to dominate the whole performance. You didn't even want to watch those rapper guys anymore. Their clothing was too dark and drab anyway. John's cream outfit stood out in the spotlights. It was suddenly *Loverboy's stage!*

Tony leaned over to me and whispered, "John about to take *all* the girls.

He gon' need *four* limos all by himself. They are *feelin'* him up in here! And watch this," Tony hinted.

John got to the end of the song and did his vamp:

And if your momma has to know
where you disappear
just tell her that you're in love
with the Lov-ver-boy.

The music changed up to a thumping beat, and John took center stage and ran to the edge, where girls could reach up and grab him. He leaned with the microphone as if he was about to fall forward, and just did his thing:

HAAAY BAAABY
IN THE BLUUUE JEAN-EAN-EANS
YOU'RE STAN-DIN' OUT IN THE PARRR-DAY
LIKE A FLY IN THE CREAM.

Tony started jumping up and down like a lunatic. He screamed, "They gon' *rape* that boy up in here, *D*! They gon' *rape 'im!*"

Boy, when you talk about some fine black women of *all* shades, heaven came down to *us* that night! John barely had to say a word after the show. I mean, imagine being able to get girls without even *talking*. He had done all of the talking that he needed to do while up on the stage. It was like a carnival of women all around us inside the hotel lobby.

They were screaming, "Oh my God! When is your album coming out?"

"Can I be in your video?"

One girl said, "Can I be your *wife?* Your girl on the side? Your *anything?*"

I looked her right in her face, and her mug didn't match the words. You would think that this girl was ugly and desperate saying something like that, right? *Wrong!* She was so beautiful that I would drink castor oil from her toes.

John didn't even pay this girl any mind. He seemed like he was floating on air, above it all.

One of the rapper guys smiled at me and said, "This shit is ridiculous, man. I mean, we always get groupies, but *God damn!* He ain't even got no album out yet. I wish *I* could sing."

I was standing there thinking, *Me too, man. Me too.*

VERSE 11

. . . and what a high it was . . .

When I got back to football practice at A&T that summer, John's single was in steady rotation on the radio and his video was playing on the video channels. That's all that my teammates wanted to talk about after practice.

"Shit, Darin. What you still playing football for? You better get on the road wit' cha boy, man. I mean, y'all grew up together, right? And he was kind of quiet at school. He gon' need you."

I said, "No he's not. That boy knows *exactly* what he's doing."

I was starting to get edgy again. I was just tired of hearing that shit. I mean, I had my *own* life to live! Didn't I? Secretly, though, I wished that there was a way I could do both, splitting my mind and body in two, to enjoy John's ride while still pursuing my own dreams of playing football.

I got back to my dorm room and had a copy of John's songs in progress. He was even starting to update me on songs before he finished them. Along with Tony's drumbeats, they had added a live bass and guitar player, with John on his keyboard. I was afraid to listen, knowing that I would love what I heard. Or maybe not. Maybe John would slip up and miss something. So I listened to the tape anyway, still protecting my boy, looking out for him and making sure that he was heading in the right direction.

To my surprise, the first song on the tape was *May I.* They added a bass line, a wah-wah guitar, and a hypnotizing drum cadence from Tony, while keeping John's original piano chord at the heart. Usually, when producers try to remake songs, they mess it up by overdoing it or stripping away too much of the original elements. I hated remakes. But not with *May I.* They maintained John's original mood and charm, and made it more soulful.

I sat there and listened to the song as if it were the very first time:

May I-I-I tal-l-lk to you-uw-wu-u-u
There are so-o-o many thin-n-ngs—that—we-e-e could do . . .

It was amazing. Simply *amazing!* *May I* was the kind of song that was capable of putting you on cloud nine. It made me miss my boy all over again.

I listened to John's other songs labeled "In Progress" until I fell asleep that night. The next morning I woke up, got dressed, and went to football practice at Aggie Stadium. We went through our usual drills and ran offensive and defensive schemes. Then we scrimmaged the offense, and I was the first-string cover corner *at last.*

I was looking great that day, too. The funny thing about it was that I had John's songs and music on my mind the whole time. I kept bobbing my head thinking, *HAAAY BAAABY / IN THE BLUUUE JEEEANS . . . 'Cause you're my weekend shorr-tee / And I know you like it naugh-tee.*

I mean, those damn songs of his wouldn't let me *go* that practice! I started thinking, *Shit! I need* freedom *to practice and play football. May I fuckin' concentrate for a minute out here?* I should have never gone to sleep with that boy's music on.

One of my teammates even asked me, "What song are you singin', man?"

I just smiled at him and shook my head. "Nothin', man. Nothin'."

I was still able to make all of my tackles and defenses. I was even assigned to cover our fastest receiver on a fly pattern. He broke to my right and hustled up the sideline at full speed. I chased after him before I could see the ball in flight. When I spotted it, I was in perfect position to make an interception. My new track speed had paid off dividends. But in the hunt for the ball, our star receiver got desperate and tried to fight for position. And that's when it happened.

We both went airborne for the ball, and instead of making the interception, I decided to bat it away. But I came down wrong on my landing, and it felt like a gunshot had gone off in my left ankle.

"AAAHHH! SSSHHHIIITTT!"

Everybody just stopped and stared at me in silence.

"Aw, my bad, D. My bad," my teammate apologized to me.

I balled my fists up, trying to stomach the pain. I was hoping that it was an injury of the moment and not anything serious. But that was wishful thinking, so I closed my eyes and prayed to God. *Please let me walk this off, God! PLEASE!*

As soon as I tried to move, the shot of pain went off in my left ankle again.

"WHEEEW?"

I went ahead and took my helmet off to grab my naked head. You talk about *pain*! *Damn* I was feeling it!

"My bad, man. My bad," my teammate was still saying.

I didn't even feel like responding to him.

The coaches and trainers made their way over to me and started asking the usual injury questions.

"Where does it hurt?"

"My ankle."

"Can you move it any?"

I tried, and stopped trying immediately. "Nah. No way."

They took a look with my equipment, sock, and cleat in the way.

"Do you think it's broken?"

I said, "I *hope* not."

Someone said, "I doubt if it's broken. We'd be able to *see* that. He probably sprained it on the way down."

I was still hoping for the best.

"All right, let's try to get him up and ice it down," one of the coaches said.

I hoisted myself up on their shoulders, making sure not to put any pressure on my left ankle.

When they got me to the sideline and sat me down, our trainers took off my cleat to get a closer look. That was *it* after that. I *knew* I was in trouble. My ankle started vibrating and feeling hot as it swelled up.

"Get that ice on it *quick!*" I yelled to anyone who was listening.

They put the ice on it, but the ice couldn't stop the swelling. My ankle was just *dying* to get outside of that shoe and puff up on me.

One of the trainers stood up and nodded. He said, "Well, it didn't break the skin, but it looks *bad* to me. And I'm just saying that from *looking* at it."

Man, I didn't even *want* to look. I could *feel it!* Was I dreaming? Was I having a damn nightmare? Would I wake up soon in a cold sweat back in my dorm room? I closed my eyes and tried to make it all a dream. But when I opened my eyes again, all I could see were younger teammates and bench-warmers shaking their heads at me on the sideline while the first team offense and defense went right back to scrimmaging without me.

When no coaches were around to ask me how I was doing or to even talk to me, my ego went into overdrive. I wondered how they would have responded had the *quarterback* gone down to injury. Would they have left *him* on the sideline by himself with ice like they did me? I was pissed! I guess I expected practice to stop or something. But the show must go on.

Eventually the coaches made their way back over to me to see how I was doing, but by that time I had a million other thoughts on my mind.

I asked the trainers, "How long do you think it'll take for me to get back out there?"

It was early August. The collegiate season would be starting in just two weeks for some schools. Our first game was in three weeks.

One of the trainers said, "It depends on your rehab. If it's a sprain and not a break, we can tape you up real good to play by . . . mid-October. I wouldn't try it before then. But we'll need to know what we're dealing with first."

I said, "Mid-October?" I did my math and figured that I would miss five games. But if I got back by October, I could still be ready before home-coming. Then again, would the coaches let me play after missing five games? How strong would my ankle be at that time? Would I be as effective? Would I still be fast?

My situation looked glum. It looked like I would have only my senior year to shine anyway, and after all the work I had done. A standout senior year was not enough to make the pros. They needed to evaluate me ahead of time.

It's funny how slow time seems to move when you're feeling bad. That day seemed like one of the longest football practices of my life. I kept wondering if I had done something wrong that I was paying repercussions for. Was I meant to play football at all? Would I allow myself to lose hope? How much of a stretch was it for me to make the NFL from North Carolina A&T anyway? We had some guys who had made it while I was there, but those guys were stars as *freshmen*. Most of the other great players at A&T were forced to sign with the Canadian league, semipro arena football, or they took assistant coaching jobs at either their old high schools or the college level somewhere. You had to be seen and respected to even do that. So where did I stand as an injured junior who hadn't started in a game yet?

At the Greensboro hospital, I was diagnosed with a severe ankle sprain, and the doctor said the same thing as my trainer, mid-October with great rehab.

I got back to the dorms at school on crutches, and Lloyd Robertson, our starting safety, from Chattanooga, Tennessee, pulled me aside.

He shook his head and said, "This was supposed to be your season, man. We *needed* your speed this year. But now . . ."

I guess he didn't have much faith in our next guy in line, nor was he counting on me to be back in the lineup anytime soon.

I made my way back to my room and just stared up at the ceiling while elevating my ankle and icing it. Once the swelling went down, I was told to wrap it with Ace bandages. I figured that if I had to sit out for half the season, I didn't plan on telling anyone outside the team. I didn't need the pity or the added pressure on myself to make it back.

I didn't want to listen to John's music either, but it was still calling me. It really was. Was it all in the cards for me to manage him full time?

I just broke up laughing to myself, thinking about it. I also feared giving up on my own dream for his. But shit, John wasn't *dreaming* anymore. The boy was signed already, with his first album on the way!

I told myself that it was just a test to see how dedicated I was to playing football. It *had* to be a test!

"Yeah, that's what this is. A test," I mumbled to myself.

Another one of my teammates walked in on me in the room and said, "Yo, I just saw your boy Loverboy on that video he got out! Your road dawg 'bout to blow up, man!" He was real excited by it.

I smiled and said, "Yeah, tell me something I *didn't* know."

He said, "He's supposed to be performing in Jacksonville next week. That's my hometown in Florida. My little brother just told me back home."

I got curious. I said, "How he find out about it?"

"They've been talking about it on the radio down there. He's gonna be with the rap group the Executioners, Raw, and some local Florida performers."

I said, "Who? Luke?"

My teammate smiled at me. He said, "Man, Luke too *large* for that. He does his *own* shows. They get crazy at his shows, too, man, *buck naked* crazy."

I said, "I was only joking, man. I know my boy ain't doing no shows with Luke."

He said, "Yeah, your boy should have his own shows when his album comes out. He's like in that R. Kelly league. But I think your boy sings *better* than R. Kelly, man. R. Kelly sounds like his voice be breakin' up."

He started singing the first verse from R. Kelly's famous *Bump and Grind* song: "*My mind is telling me no-o-o-o . . . but my bod-dee . . . my bod-dee . . . is telling me yea-ehhh . . .*"

He sounded just like him. I broke up laughing.

I said, "I didn't know you were into songs like that, man."

He said, "Yeah. I'm into all kinds of music."

Music was universal to every player on the football team. I mean, we liked different *kinds* of music, but all of us liked music. You couldn't say that about everything else, outside of maybe movie watching. Who didn't like watching movies?

Anyway, I got to thinking about managing my boy John again, and I ended up listening to his "In Progress" tape a second time. I couldn't fight it anymore. It was only a matter of time.

I found out more about the concert in Jacksonville, Florida, and I made plans to get down there that weekend to catch John's next performance. I wanted to surprise him and just show up. I told my football coaches that I was going to a family affair back home in Charlotte. I couldn't practice, so I wasn't missing anything. So I headed right on my way to Florida to see my boy do his thing again.

I pulled up to this nice-sized arena the night of the performance in Jacksonville and checked out the sights. It was a good thing I injured my left ankle instead of my right, because I could still drive. I had my ankle wrapped and was still hobbling around with crutches when I walked up to the box office to buy a last-minute ticket for $12. The booty-shaking women were *everywhere*, wearing what I called "sex clothes." They had the sequined halter tops, tight stretch pants, and anything that fit a size too small. Then they wore heels that made long, sexy legs stand out.

If music wasn't a calling card for hotties, I don't know what was. They didn't dress like that at the football games. I mean, you always had a few hotties there, but not *eighty* percent like you had at a lot of these young concerts. I guess the young women used concerts as a time to show off.

The state of Florida allowed a lot more gold teeth, flamboyance, and teenage wildness than we were allowed in Charlotte. Charlotte was just beginning to get hip with its professional basketball and football teams coming to town. But you wouldn't know that through Jodeci's antics. I guess they used their record deal and the escape to New York as a way of exorcising their demons.

I watched with the rest of the audience to see how John looked from out at a distance instead of being on or near the stage with him like I usually was. While waiting for him to perform, I enjoyed this rapper named Raw. He stirred the crowd with his clear delivery and bouncy beats. The female dancers onstage with him were wearing hot red outfits that showed plenty of body, and they were not bad looking.

Sure enough, you never know what to expect in Florida. So when the local groups came on, shameless girls were allowed to get up onstage and act a fool, as if we were all at a nude dancing bar. I grinned and shook my head, but I never turned away. My Johnson even got hard. My ankle may have been out of commission, but the rest of me wasn't.

When the Executioners came on, who John and Tony were touring with that summer, I made sure to check the excitement level of the crowd before and after John entered the stage to see how much of an impact his singing had on the people who didn't yet know him.

From a distance, I saw why it was important for rappers to move madly about while onstage. You could barely understand a lot of their words through the energy of the crowd and the beats that they performed to. If they didn't move around like maniacs, they would be washed out as performers. Watching them and feeling the vibe was the best that you could do if they had a lot of lyrics. The Florida groups had songs with simple verses that the whole crowd could sing along with. But that didn't work too well with the real lyricists, and the Executioners were the real lyric-writing types, all four of them.

When the music to *The Weekends* came on, I started smiling for my boy like I always did. The crowd started rocking slow just like they did in Cleveland, but you could tell that they liked the faster-paced songs where they could really get raunchy in there. The Florida crowd didn't seem to have the same patience for a real groove. So by the time John slid onstage and did his chorus, I was a little bit apprehensive and no longer grinning.

John sang his part:

'Cause you're my weekend shorrr-tee
and ahhh know you like it naugh-tee . . .

Awwww girrrl
Awwww girrrl . . .

The girls who were immediately near me stopped and looked at each other. "Who's that?"

I was thinking, *Okay. So John is still human.* He hadn't knocked those girls off their feet. At least not yet.

At the front end of the stage, there was a lot more activity. Little by little, the crowd began to realize that Loverboy was up there.

"That's Loverboy? Oh *shit!* That's him!" the girls next to me realized.

I thought about that for a moment. They *definitely* had to know who he was before they got excited about him. The singing was still the same, it just made a big difference that they knew. Once that was settled, they went crazy for him in Jacksonville just like the rest of the audiences John had performed for.

I said to myself, *For larger crowds, he needs an announcement.* That Jacksonville crowd was much larger than Cleveland's. Not that Jacksonville was a bigger town, they just secured a larger arena for the performance.

By the time John performed *Stylin' 'n' Profilin'*, they were ready to give him all of the love that he wanted, and I couldn't wait to surprise him by showing up backstage afterward.

I made my way to the front of the stage and was stopped by security.

I said, "Can you send someone backstage for Tony Richmond? I'm a manager. I just got here late from my rehab appointment up in Philly."

"How come you didn't come in the backstage door then?" I was asked.

I thought fast and said, "Well, since I knew I was late, I decided to catch the performance from the crowd's viewpoint to see what we needed to work on for the next show."

The security guard nodded his head and sent someone backstage for me.

I hobbled backstage with an escort and felt special, the kind of feeling that I did *not* have once I had gotten injured on the football field.

Tony met me backstage and said, "What's up, D? What are you doing down here? Ain't you supposed to be at football practice somewhere?"

He smelled like weed and he was extra mellow. He didn't even notice my crutches.

I said, "It's a sad story, man."

He immediately looked down and said, "Oh, shit! You fucked your ankle up!"

I didn't even want to respond to that. It was obvious.

I said, "Where'd John go?"

Tony paused for a second. He smiled and answered, "He around here somewhere."

I was thinking that a fine young sister from Jacksonville had cornered him already.

I grinned and asked, "You had to wind down after the show, hunh?" referring to Tony's weed smoking.

"Always," he said, grinning back at me.

I found a seat and sat down. I figured that I'd catch up to John before the night was over. While I was waiting, the rapper Raw walked up and asked Tony about making him some new beats.

Tony said, "Hey, man, let's hook up."

Raw nodded and said, "Aw'ight. We gon' do that. And your boy can flow, man. He can hang out with me anytime."

I spoke up and said, "I like your performance, man. I could hear everything you said."

Raw looked at me and studied my face to see if he knew me before he spoke. He was the same chocolate brown as me and a little shorter, with low-cut hair. We could damn near pass for cousins. I was just a lot thicker from football.

Tony said, "This is Darin Harmon, man. This Loverboy's manager from Charlotte. They grew up together."

Raw broke a cool smile and said, "My man. I was trying to figure out if you was related."

He tossed a hand out to me.

I shook his hand and laughed. "I was thinking the same thing," I told him. "Where you from?"

He said, "Oaktown. But I ain't no M. C. Hammer. I'll let somebody else dance for me. I just want to make sure you hear my shit."

I said, "Well, it worked. You had the best performance out there. You know, outside of the girls pulling their clothes off and stuff."

He laughed and said, "You know, that's just Florida, man. They get wild like that."

I was enjoying my conversation with Raw when John walked out with dark shades on, floating on air.

Tony looked at me as if he was watching for some kind of a response.

John stopped and looked at me himself through the dark shades.

He said, "Darin, whatchu doin' here, man? I wasn't expectin' to see you here."

I studied John's posture and knew off the bat that something was going on. He looked like he was leaning a bit. So I just came right out with it.

"Are you high, man?" Although I didn't smoke or get high, I knew what people looked like when they were high, and John wearing sunshades backstage was like a murderer holding a smoking gun at a bank. The boy didn't even *wear* sunshades.

He looked at me and said, "Yeah, man. I'm high. I'm high as hell right now. But I'll be all right by the time the limos and the girls roll up."

Everyone laughed but me. I just chuckled at it. I didn't want to bust John out in front of his new friends. I figured that I'd wait to talk to him in depth about things once we were alone.

John looked down and said, "What happened to your foot, man?"

I said, "It's my ankle."

"Foot, ankle, same damn thing. What happened to it?"

He was like a comedian for his new friends as they laughed again. John had them going.

I said, "It happened at practice. A severe ankle sprain."

John just stood there for a second. He said, "So what's up now? You gon' stay on the road with us? We doin' Oaktown next. That's Raw's people."

Raw nodded with a grin and tossed his hands in the air.

"Yeah, yeah, nigga, that's *my* people. I'm gon' rock da house."

Tony said, "And then Loverboy gon' find out what Oaktown pussy smell like."

"It smell like everybody else's pussy," Raw responded.

They were getting a little *too* raw for me. Not that I never used the P-word myself, I just wasn't in the mood for it at the moment. I wanted to talk to my boy John alone.

I forced myself up and said, "Let's go talk, John."

Tony looked at us and said, "Uh oh."

I guess he knew all along that John getting high would come as a shock to me. I wasn't feeling too friendly toward Tony at that moment either. How many get-high sessions had they shared together at his apartment?

John and I found some privacy, where I asked him, "How long have you been getting high, man?"

He said, "Man, don't trip. I don't even do it that much. It's just to make it through the night every once in a while."

"Make it through the night for what? You about to get what you want, right? A singing career with your first album coming out this fall? So what's up, man?"

He said, "What's up with what?" He wasn't making the connection. John never had the need to smoke or get high before. What was he missing now?

I said, "John, you don't have to prove that you're cool with people by doing that, man. Seriously."

He looked away from me. Then he looked back and said, "Is that what you think this is, man, me being cool with people?"

"Well, what else is it then? You *want* to get high now? You never got high before."

He said, "I never got no pussy before either. I never sang like this before. Or not in front of audiences. And I never toured before."

I said, "So answer my question. How long have you been gettin' high now?"

John said, "What difference does it make, man? That's like asking a girl how long she's been boning after she's pregnant."

I lost my cool and said, "See, *this* is what your mother was talking about." I didn't mean to go there, it just came out of me.

John didn't snap. He stayed cool about it. He let out a deep breath and said, "You fuckin' up my high, man. Let's have this conversation after midnight."

Then he smiled at me and broke into song: "*At mid-ni-i-i-ight . . .*"

I was caught off guard by it and started to smile while John laughed to himself.

I said, "So I guess you don't want me to be your manager anymore, because I would fuck up your high, right?"

I was ready to play a game of reverse psychology on him.

John looked at me still with his sunshades on and said, "Nah, man. That's what managers are for, to keep you in line. But you kept turning me down."

I frowned at him and said, "Aw, nah, don't try to blame this getting high shit on *me*. You got your own mind." He was trying to twist things right back at me.

"I'm just saying, though. If everybody else is getting high, and you got nobody to stop you and say, 'Hey, man, let's do something else,' then what are you gonna do? Like I said, man, I just smoke to get me through the night every once in a while."

I said, "It sounds to me like you were doing exactly what I *said* you were doing, trying to prove that you could hang."

John had never been in the "in crowd," so I knew what I was talking about. I realized more than ever that he would need me with him to keep him in perspective about things.

Right on cue, John asked me, "So, you're finally gon' be my manager for real, man? No holding back no more, and talking about football?"

I said, "I can talk about football all I want to."

"Man, I don't mean you can't talk about it. I'm saying, you know . . ."

I cut him off and said, "I'm injured right now, so the team can't use me if they wanted to."

He looked at my heavily wrapped ankle again and asked me, "How long will it take to heal?"

"They said by mid-October."

"That's when my album is coming out."

I said, "I know."

He said, "So what are you gonna do, man?"

John was just short of begging me. I could *feel it*. He was lonely in a crowd and getting high to fit in.

I said, "I'm gon' be your boy, man, and do what I *need* to do. But if this is gonna be business, then I need my manager's fee."

John laughed out loud and dug into his pocket, pulling out loose bills. "Here you go, man. How much do you need?"

I said, "Nah, we gon' make up a simple contract. How does fifteen percent sound? That's around the going rate for fair managers."

John said, "*Twenty* percent. But if you go on the road with me, man, what are your parents gonna say about school?"

I took a deep breath myself. I smiled and said, "They gon' say the same thing *your* mom said to you, 'Stay your ass in school!'"

We both laughed and knew that it was the truth.

Finally someone broke up our privacy. "Ay, Loverboy. These hoes out here going *crazy* looking for you, man. You betta tell 'em *somethin'*."

John chuckled and said, "Where they at?" Then he looked back at me. "You don't have no problem with me gettin' busy, do you?"

I laughed. I asked him, "You got rubbers?"

The other guy said, "Shit, man, we got a whole *trunkload* of rubbers. You can't go without rubbers with these scan'lous hoes. You gon' have a *real* short career fuckin' with *that* shit. Ask Eazy-E."

I started thinking that it would be my first big move as a manager to talk John into keeping one or two main girlfriends. He could have one on the East Coast and one on the West or something. It just seemed like the logical thing to do to keep the women at bay. Not that all of them were creepin' to be sleepin', but it was better safe than sorry to have a main girl. Even though *I* didn't have one. That was the hypocrisy of it. Then again, I didn't have thousands of girls screaming my name while I performed either. Only my little sister screamed my name. And that was only because I was her big brother.

. . . to blow up a nation . . .

I sat in front of my parents at the kitchen table with a lump in my throat. I said, "Mom, Dad. This has been a tough decision for me to make because I really wanted to play football and stay in school and everything—"

"And," my father said, cutting me off already.

I calmed myself and just looked at him civilly. I didn't want the conversation to be a confrontation. I wanted us to discuss things like adults.

I said, "Please, Dad, just hear me out."

He nodded and didn't say a word, so I continued. My mother was just listening.

I said, "I've never had a serious football injury in my life. And for it to come at this time, right when I had finally made the starting lineup . . . I mean, it just felt like a sign for me to support what my friend John is doing in the music industry as his manager. I'm good at it, *and* I'm respected for it."

My mother cut in on me and said, "But what about your *own* career in something else? You don't have to play football."

I said, "I know I don't. But music management *is* a career. And there's no real classes for it. You just have to feel your way through. John has been asking me to be his manager ever since I got him his first paid performance at Norfolk State last year."

My father asked, "And how much was that for?"

I said, "A thousand dollars. But that's only ten percent *or less* than what John *could* make once he's established himself with his album coming out this year."

I was trying to make it seem more business than personal. After all, I *was* dropping out of school to manage, so I figured that I had to speak on it as a monetary career move. Of course, I couldn't admit to them that Norfolk State hadn't paid us all of the money.

My mother asked me, "And what if John just all of a sudden gets bored with it and he doesn't want to do it anymore? Then what? Do you have someone else lined up to manage?"

She had a good point. I smiled and said, "I need to make plenty of friends while I'm out there with John then. But once people know that I'm a good manager, new artists will seek me out."

My father said, "You mean you *hope* that they'll seek you out."

I thought about how easy it was for me to speak up to all of the movers and shakers in the music business, and I said, "I believe that, as your son, I can handle myself. Because you didn't raise no punks, Dad. And I don't represent myself that way."

I thought it was a good line. I had to hold in my smile. But my mother didn't hold in hers. She outright started laughing at the table.

My father snapped, "Don't you patronize me, boy," with no smile on his face. He said, "Your mother and I have already talked about all of this. We were just waiting for it to come down the pike."

I sat silently, wondering what they said in those talks.

My father went on. He said, "Your mother and I listened to those tapes that John made, and I must admit that the stuff sounds pretty good."

I cut him off and said, "Music."

"Yeah," he said to me. "So I told your mother that it wouldn't be the worst thing in the world for you to manage your friend, I was just more concerned about you finishing your education."

I cut in and said, "I can always go back to school, Dad. I'll just have to pay for it out of my own pocket this time."

He said, "You got *that* part right. So you better think about saving the money that you'll need to do it. But I told your mother that unless you can definitely make the pros in football—and there really ain't no guarantees of you doing that, son, no matter how *good* you *think* you are—I said that this music thing may not be a bad idea."

I was surprised as ever! My dad sounded like he was giving me the okay to go for it. I guess he had been waiting for me to come out with it on my own first.

He said, "I look at how my life has been, working blue-collar and killing my body on the job every day, and I figured that my boys shouldn't have to go through that same everyday shit to make a buck."

I stopped him again and said, "So, you were just waiting for me to say something about it?" I was curious.

My father looked at my mother.

My mother smiled at me and said, "As soon as I heard John's song on the radio, I told your father, 'Look, we need to talk.' And we knew that you were into football at the time and everything, but we both wondered how long it would take for you to start changing your mind. Especially since you hadn't had a chance to play like you wanted to. So we just figured that if anything went wrong *this year*, then that would be it."

I felt like jumping for joy! I had to hold myself down at the table, but that didn't stop me from smiling real wide.

My father said, "Actually, if you were the *oldest* son, or even the number *two*, I wouldn't have stood for this shit. So you get the benefit of being our last boy. I'm willing to take a chance on you to do something different. As long as you have in mind to use some of the money to go back to school and finish your education *like you said*."

My father was obviously going to hold me to my word. I started wishing that I hadn't said that. But a deal was a deal. It seemed like my heart had jumped outside of my shirt, I was so happy.

I said, "Thanks, Dad. Thanks, Mom," and took a deep breath.

My father took one too. He said, "I just hope that you don't turn this into a big mistake."

"I won't."

He said, "Well then, you go for it. But I don't want to hear none of them damn excuses from you that so many of these other people make about what didn't go right for them. Because *nothing* out here is *promised* to *any* of us. So be prepared to take the lumps just like you take the kisses."

I went back to school at NC A&T and packed up my things. The coaches acted as if they would miss me. They were trying to convince me to stay. I blew them off just like they did me when I got injured, and I kept packing.

My teammates said what I thought they would say: "So you finally gon' go ahead and manage your boy, Loverboy? Good luck, D. I hope you and your boy go right to the top."

It was all love, but they didn't really sound as if they would miss me on the football field. Even my teammates knew that I had a better opportunity of making it in the music world than in football.

The plan was for me to move up to Philadelphia with John and Tony, then John and I would look for our own apartment. I didn't want him around Tony all day with that smoking shit anyway.

The first assignment I had to deal with as a full-time manager was putting the album together and building an image for John. He may have been called Lover*boy*, but I didn't want him competing with the other young singers like Usher and Tevin Campbell. I wanted to make sure that we set ourselves apart. I wanted an audience that would take him seriously as a real crooner and not as some young wonder boy.

I said, "John, when you start getting these interviews for your music, I want you to emphasize how you always listened to the older musicians in your house and stuff, man, so that they don't start comparing you to too many young acts." We were over at Tony's place.

Tony started laughing. He said, "Yeah, we want the older bitches. None of them young girls."

I looked at Tony and said, "We want mature *listeners*, man. *Bitches* don't buy music, *young women* do."

Tony looked back at me and smirked. "Okay, *now* you want to be the big-time manager. What happened to football, Mr. *Deion Sanders?*"

I ignored him. "Whatever, man."

John smiled and added his thoughts. He said, "I got all kinds of listeners, man. I don't like how they do that old-versus-young stuff. I'm trying to write music for everybody."

Tony said, "Dig it. If the beat is bangin', the people'll feel it."

I said, "Yeah, and then they start to analyze the words and the message."

Tony said, "John has a good message. Shit, his music can speak for itself."

I shook my head. I really needed to talk to John alone. I wasn't managing Tony. He was just getting in the damn way.

I asked John, "What kind of album covers have they been discussing?" So far, they were riding with the usual dramatic facial shots. You know, photographing John's face all extra large on the single and in the promotional packages.

John smiled at me and said, "Why, you got some ideas?"

I said, "Not yet, I just wanted to see what *they* had. For instance, with this release of *May I*, I would like to see you at a piano instead of with your face all up in the frame. That's how you started out, you know, as a real musician. We want to remind people of that. You write all your own songs."

Tony said, "They'll know that by reading the credits on the releases."

I finally got irritated with Tony. I said, "So what, man? I want them to know that before they even *read* the credits. And some people *don't* read 'em. I never paid attention to that shit until John started doing his thing."

"Well that's *you*," Tony snapped back at me.

I calmed down and said, "Look, Tony, do you think that most of the people out here that listen to music are musicians themselves?"

Tony saw where I was going with it. He said, "In their own way, a lot of them are."

I said, "That's bullshit, man, and you know it. A lot of people don't read them credits."

John broke up laughing. He took my side and said, "D right though, man. If they see me at a piano, then they start thinking about me being able to *play* the piano. That's why people who can't play don't take pictures with the piano, because if someone asks them to play it, they'd be stuck."

I said, "Yeah, they would mess around and embarrass themselves."

John said, "But I would get up there and rock it for them like Herbie Hancock."

"Yeah. You want to let the fans know that you can love 'em in all kinds of ways," I added with a smile.

Even Tony chuckled.

So we took the idea to Old School Records and got the go-ahead from the art director, some sweet-feet guy named Jamie Bilford. I had nothing against gay people, but this brother was tall and all in your face with it. I guess John and Tony were used to him by then, but I had to get settled into it.

Jamie said, "Oh, I *love* that idea. That'll work. Now, you *can* play the piano, right, John?"

We all laughed again.

Tony said, "That's what we were talking about when we came up with the idea."

I looked at Tony and mocked him. "When *we* came up with the idea, Tony?"

He frowned at me and said, "I ain't meant to say that, man. I meant to say when we were *talking* about it."

I grinned and grunted, "Mmm hmm. I understand."

Tony said, "Aw, man, I know you the big-time manager now. It *took* you long enough."

Jamie asked, "So, Darin, do you have any ideas for the album cover?"

I said, "Not yet. I just figured that we need to do something different from that big-face stuff. Maybe we could put him in the middle of a crowd or something, with people grabbing at him."

Tony frowned and said, "Naw, man. That makes it sound like they can easily get him."

Jamie said, "And what's wrong with that? I'm sure that plenty of people would just *love* to have him." He gave John a look and a smile. I felt kind of queasy about that for a second, but I smiled it off.

John shook his head and said, "Nah, man, I'm untouchable. I don't want them grabbing on me. I should be onstage, and they should be trying to get onstage with me."

Tony said, "You mean how you have it in *real* life. They be trying to drag your ass *off* the stage."

"Well, can you blame them?" Jamie asked us.

I said, "Well, what do you think about that idea, Jamie? You know, this whole untouchable thing?"

John seemed to like that idea. He smiled and said, "I *am* untouchable. When I get up on that stage . . . it's *all* mine."

Jamie sized him up and said, "We may be able to work with that. We put you in the center of the frame, or maybe on a slight angle at the foot of the stage. And you're, like, leaning over with the mike to your mouth, almost like you're teasing them with your lips. And you're, like, in the middle of a performance with sweat running down your face and everything."

He stopped and said, "Oh they *love* the sweat. You *gotta* have the sweat."

I started shaking my head with a grin. Jamie was really getting into it.

He said, "And we can have you on a tall stage where they're reaching up their hands to get you, but you're not in their reach because you're untouchable."

We all started laughing, liking the idea.

John confirmed it. He said, "I like that. But I'm not trying to be sweating. I want to be dry."

Jamie asked him, "Well, you're not *dry* after the shows, are you?"

I wasn't sure how he meant that, but it didn't sound right to me.

Tony started laughing again, but John was still thinking about the album cover. I was still trying to figure Jamie out. Was he just joking, or was he serious? Did he have a crush on John?

John said, "Maybe I could go down on one knee or something, like I'm proposing." Then he smiled and said, "But I'm not."

Tony said, "Man, you better *not* do that."

Jamie said, "Oh, now *that's* wicked! That would be such a *tease!* I like that, I like that!"

I thought about it myself and figured that it would attract more-mature women, who know what that bended-knee thing is all about.

I nodded my head and spoke up on it. "That sounds like a plan. We put him on a high stage, with a bunch of hands reaching up to get him, and he's on a bended knee in the middle of a love song."

I got excited thinking about the connection to John's imagery. I said, "Yeah, that's exactly it! A Loverboy is always wanted, but hard to get. And that's what keeps the women interested. 'I *almost* had him,'" I said, imitating a girl.

We were all laughing and having a ball with it.

Jamie shook his head and said, "Oh, you guys are killing me with this. This is gonna be a *great* shoot! *Loverboy: The Album,* and he's so *un-touchable.*"

He nodded and said, "That would keep someone up at all hours of the night, plotting and things."

I still felt queasy about him, but I couldn't help but to laugh at this guy.

When we left, I had to ask John and Tony about it.

I said, "How can Jamie work at a record label that has so many hard-core rappers and stuff? I can't see them rapper guys being that comfortable around him."

Tony shook his head and said, "Don't get it confused, man. Jamie knows who to mess with and who to be straight with. He just likes fucking with John because he knows that he can do it."

John said, "Yeah, but I'm not gay, so he can say what he wants to say. But he does his job, though, and that's why he's here."

We were out in Oakland, California, at the end of the summer, hanging out with Raw and performing with the Executioners. I was making sure to get John ready for the interviews we had set up for him. The new single *May I* was just about to be shipped out to the radio stations, and it was prime time to start separating John from the other singers in his age group.

We met an older sister from the *Oakland Journal* early in the morning, and she asked John about his fast rise to stardom.

She said, "I heard that you just started singing last year." She said it as if it was unbelievable.

John answered, "Yeah, but I've been practicing for years," and smiled at her. He was being lighthearted about it. I figured that was a good way to be. Make the writers like you.

She said, "Are you prepared for this?" She sounded concerned.

John looked at her and asked, "What do you mean?" as if it was a trick question.

"Well, you just started singing last year, so I mean, who's behind your writing and producing team? Who discovered you?"

John said, "Discovered me?"

I don't think he was catching her line of questioning. Maybe it was too early in the morning for him after hanging out with Raw in Oakland. I *told* him to get to bed earlier.

I just sat back and smiled. The *Oakland Journal* was a small local newspaper, so I wasn't that concerned about it. I looked at it as a test run for when the bigger interviews came. This reporter was proving what I already knew. Many people would assume that John didn't know what he was doing and that he had a whole genius force behind him instead of him having any real talent. That's just how a lot of young singers were looked at in the nineties. That attitude from the media was exactly why I wanted to put John behind the piano for the release of *May I*.

John finally caught her drift and said, "I've been performing all year, you know, writing and producing my own stuff. I even cowrote and produced this song that I'm performing tonight with the Executioners, *Weekend Shorty*. We're gonna release that this winter for their next album.

"I mean, if you come out and listen to us tonight, that's all my sound," he told her.

I passed her a new copy of the *May I* tape so she could listen again before she wrote her story.

She took the tape and nodded.

She said, "So you *write and produce* your own music?" She sounded amazed again.

John just looked at me. It was finally hitting him.

I looked back at him and just started laughing.

John said, "Basically, I've been writing and producing music for a while. I played four different instruments and led the band for three years in high school with a lot of my own music. Then I got a music scholarship to college. I was in the church choir since age six. And you know, I just never sang anything *solo* until last year. But I was always into music and around it."

She smiled and said, "Well, so are the rest of us."

If you asked me, the sister sounded a little jealous. I started wondering if she was some kind of a singer herself who hadn't gotten her break yet. I figured she was in her early thirties.

John said, "Well, that's just how it is. Some people blow up and some people don't."

"And you're one of the lucky ones," she said to him.

John smiled and said, "Nah, I'm one of the gifted ones."

She said, "Is that right?"

John said, "Yup."

I started laughing again. She couldn't break his confidence. John was so hard to rattle that it made it impossible to try. He would just smile at you and blow it off. So she decided to change her whole line of questioning.

"Okay, well, with this whole *Loverboy* thing, how did you manage to call yourself that?"

John shook his head and said, "I didn't. Everybody else did. So I just started responding to it."

When the interview was over, John said, "She had a problem, man. You see how she kept trying to bring me down?"

I said, "Yeah, that's what I was telling you. You gotta get yourself ready for that."

John had always been the behind-the-scenes, quiet type. He wasn't used to getting daggers thrown at him. But his newfound confidence wouldn't make things any easier on him. I decided to let him know about that.

I said, "And another thing, man, some of those comments you make are a little too much. Try to be a little more modest with your answers. You know, learn to play their game, man. Don't talk yourself up, just make them like you and they'll do that on their own."

John said, "Not that woman."

I laughed and said, "Yeah, you probably right about that one. She had it in for you."

At the Oakland Theater, we had another large event. And although everyone was finding out who Loverboy was and what he looked like from his video, I told him that we needed to start announcing who he was before going out on the stage.

John didn't care one way or the other, but once the members of the Executioners heard that we wanted to announce him to the audience beforehand, some of them didn't like the idea too much.

"Wait a minute, man. This is *our* shit and we're letting John on tour with us to get him ready for his album. But he don't need no *pre*announcement. He gets announced after the song."

Luckily, the marketing director, Matt Duggins, was out there in Oakland with us to focus the argument.

He said, "Guys, we're all in this thing together. Let's show a little family love. I mean, this *Weekend Shorty* song is gonna be a hit, right? We all agree to that."

"Yeah, but this is still *our* tour, and when we agreed to let John on, he knew he wasn't getting no special shit."

All of the members of the Executioners didn't feel sour about it. They had even changed the name of the song because of John's chorus, but they didn't speak up on John's behalf. So we went back to the way they had it with John being a surprise guest.

Tony stopped me that night and said, "Well, Mr. Manager, welcome to the tour world. Ma-fuckas ain't trying to give up their stage like that. Are you *crazy?!* You better *think* before you start saying shit like that, young boah."

Tony was right for a change. I'd got a little ahead of myself. I guess I was trying too hard to be a good manager. But John just laughed at it.

He said, "They already think that I'm taking all of the best girls. They get a lot of them roughlike women, but I get the sweet ones."

I wanted to slow John down a bit with the screwing on tour too, but after the drama with the name announcement thing, I wasn't too popular with the rest of the acts on tour, so I decided to just go along with the ride for a while.

Next up was Dallas and Houston, Texas, and then we were set to go back to Philly to finish producing John's album for October.

. . . *but it was not enough* . . .

In the engineer's booth at the Old School Records studio, I had never seen so many buttons in my life! I sat there wondering how long it would take to learn what all of those damn things did. Professional music making was a lot more complicated than I thought. I figured you just went in the studio, set up your instruments and microphones, and recorded the perfect take. Boy was *I* wrong! In the studio is where you really see the magic of music taking form. There were hundreds of different effects that you could put on every voice and on every instrument to give your music that final hypnotic mix for a listening audience.

John wrote and coproduced ten of the twelve songs that made the album, and we recorded two outside songs, *What We Gonna Do?*, an up-tempo party groove, and *Special*, a ballad. *What We Gonna Do?* was needed to make sure John had enough up-tempo grooves to break the sedate harmony of the album. We didn't want people to get *too* relaxed with his first release, especially after the success of *Stylin' 'n' Profilin'*. That song made it all the way up to number four on the R&B charts and number nine on pop. From a mostly rock and hip-hop label that had never placed a song that high, that was some big news! I figured that people would be expecting more jam cuts from John. So we had a total of four party grooves. And with Tony on the beats, they were all *rocking!*

Special was a perfect complement to the rest of John's ballads. I mean, if you're gonna ask a girl *May I*, tell her that it's *Just Me and You*, and to meet you *At Midnight* for lovemaking, then she needs to be *Special*:

> . . . *and no gir-r-r-rl could take your place*
> *in my-y-y hear-r-rt*

you're that spe-cial
to me-e-e.

I thought the song was a sleeper hit because it used a lot of musical space that highlighted the words. Sometimes the music can be so tight and seductive that you ignore the words. *Special* made sure that the words stood out with its blues-sounding bass line and soft snare beat. With John's infectious singing, it turned into a beautiful song.

The rest of the album was midtempo tracks cut straight from John's soul, with *Freedom*, *The Stage*, and *Unappreciated* performed with a guest appearance from the Philly girl trio Butterscotch, and *Gifted*, where John sang:

. . . I'm just gifted with a talent
and I'm floating
on a hi-i-igh wave.

We had a great time at the album shoot with plenty of extras from the Philadelphia and South Jersey areas, and then it was mass production, packaging, and distribution time for *Loverboy: The Album*. By then, John and I had our own large apartment and a new Maxima paid for with the advance money. I sat down with John and talked about everything on Monday night, October 24, before the album release party planned on Delaware Avenue that Tuesday, October 25, 1994.

We were sitting on the sofa in front of the stereo system, listening to the album for about the tenth time, and just talking things out.

I smiled at John and said, "Well, what do you think, man? Last year this time you were just startin' out. Now you'll be doing a tour for ten thousand dollars a show." Blake had to foot the bill with John as his new headliner.

John smiled back at me and said, "Yeah, and you'll be getting two thousand of it, and Tony gets his, and the rest of the band gets theirs, and then I'm left with new stereo money."

I thought about it and laughed. I said, "Damn, I guess you're right. So you're gonna get about the same amount you got at Norfolk State last year."

John shook it off and said, "It's not a big deal, man. I just hate how people start thinking that you're gonna make automatic money. I mean, this stuff is *work*, man."

He was right about that. John had been working his ass off in the studio for a month to make everything sound just right. When the album was finished, he was still talking about lyrics he could have sung better.

I said, "You think football players sit around talking about the perfect tackles all night? When you get a good hit, it's a good hit, but you mainly want to make a solid tackle. And that's what you've done, man. You've made a solid album. People can take something from every single song on here."

I said, "You can't say that about a lot of these other new singers out here, man. You'll probably deserve the new artist of the year award or something," I added. And it was the wrong thing to say. I just didn't know it at the time.

John said, "You think so? The best new male artist?"

I said, "Yeah," like a true athlete talking about winning championships. However, judging art was a whole different ball game. It wasn't as if you just stepped onstage and sang face-to-face with your competition to see who was the best. There were all kinds of political complications involved in judging art, and national popularity had a lot to do with it. Sales figures had a lot to do with national popularity. Award winning was a conditional science.

All of a sudden, John looked at me and said, "You may not like me saying this, man, but I feel like smoking some weed tonight. I mean, I got a lot of things running through my mind right now, and I just need to relax before tomorrow."

October 25 in Philly was only the kickoff. Blake had us set up for an eleven-city tour before Christmas. Then John would take a break and go back on tour with eight more cities starting in February 1995. In every city, we were to do promotional interviews with press and radio, and then autograph signings at supportive record stores set up by Old School Records to help push John's album. I had a new calendar book just *filled* with places, dates, and times for John to do.

I can't lie. I sympathized with John's need to mellow out before the storm hit, I just didn't agree with how he wanted to do it. I joked and said, "You wanna call up some girls?"

We had plenty of phone numbers to call, I just didn't have time to zero in on which girls would be good for John to get serious about.

John smiled and said, "Nah, man. They wouldn't want to leave in time, and everything would get all complicated before tomorrow. I mean, I don't need no complications from girls, man. I just need to relax."

I asked him, "How does weed make you relax, man? I mean, what exactly does it do to you?" I had never touched weed before in my life.

John started laughing at me. He said, "Remember that time you asked me if I had bust a nut, and I asked you what it felt like?"

I chuckled and said, "Yeah."

He said, "I guess it's your turn now."

I frowned and said, "It don't make you feel like you bustin' no nut, do it?" I *refused* to believe that. *Nothing* felt like the strong pulse of ejaculation. *Nothing!* Or at least not in *my* book.

John thought to himself and answered, "It's more mental. Sex is more of a physical feeling. I mean, you *think* about sex, but you *feel it* more. But gettin' high . . . it's like . . . your mind starts to look at the same corner from a different angle. Like, instead of me thinking about all these people up in my face tomorrow for this album release party, I can relax and think about all of the fun we had to make it here."

I said, "You can think about that all you want. Nothing's stopping you from doing that. You don't need weed to reminisce. You just reminisced when I asked you that question about busting nuts. You didn't need no weed to do that."

John shook his head and grinned. "It ain't the same, man. When I'm high I ain't gotta try so hard."

I said, "Are you telling me that it's hard for you to think back to things without getting high?"

He said, "You missing the whole point, D. Weed don't always make you think back, man, it just changes your perception of the present."

I said, "Well, what the fuck you want to do that for? We got work to do tomorrow. You want to be a star, right? Well, tomorrow's the day."

I was trying to talk him out of it with force. Finally John just grinned and left it alone.

When we got up that next morning for a radio interview at eight o'clock, John had the ceiling fan on in his room, and he had lit a bunch of incense, but the room still smelled like weed.

I was not amused. I asked him, "So did you get a chance to relax last night, man?" I didn't want to feel like I was a damn baby-sitter to him, so that was all I planned to say about it. We had work to do. But I did wonder where he got it from. I suspected Tony. And when I saw Tony during our different events that day, I questioned him about it in private.

I said, "Hey, man, you think it's a good idea for John to be gettin' high now? I thought you said it wasn't good for everybody."

Tony frowned at me. He said, "Man, John ain't no damn kid. I didn't make him smoke the shit. *I* tried to stop him. But I ain't gon' sweat him about the shit either, because I smoke weed and ain't nothin' wrong wit' me."

I begged to differ on that. I asked him, "Well, how long has he been doing that shit?"

Tony said, "For a while now. He just would hide it from you."

I said, "Well, I don't understand why he did it. He don't need to get high. He got everything going for him right now."

Tony laughed and said, "So do a lot of other motherfuckers who get high. Getting high ain't got shit to do with that. You got people who are broke and get high, and you got your more successful people who get high too. John just tried it out, and he like it. It's as simple as that."

There was no sense in arguing with Tony about the weed subject, so I just planned to monitor John's smoking more closely.

John made it through the release party in one piece with all of his new fanfare, but when we hooked up with Blake again in Detroit to go over the tour, the first thing he said to me was, "That white ice is pretty cold, hunh?"

I didn't know what he was talking about. I looked at him confused and said, "Hunh?"

He said, "You signed John up with them white boys in Philly. What, you didn't trust my friends? They could have done the same thing that these white boys are doing and kept it all in the family."

I said, "Oh." I felt guilty about it. Black people up north always seemed to be a lot more in your face about white-and-black business. Down south we just accepted things and kept moving. Not to say that we didn't stand up for ourselves when we had to, we just had a less militant stance about it.

I said, "You know, man, they had the right deal at the right time. We weren't ready yet when your friends offered to sign him."

Blake said, "Yeah, because no white boys had asked you yet. Black folks seem to get *real* ready when Mr. Charlie steps in the picture."

He mocked an Uncle Tom stance and said, "'Yes sir, Mr. Charlie, sir. Where you want me to sign?'"

In the back of my mind I was cursing Blake for playing me like that, but all I could say out my mouth was, "Hey, man, we're still doing the tour with you. You still got us in the family." I even tried to smile it off.

"Yeah, as the second-generation *cousins*," he said and walked away from me.

I hoped that Blake had gotten it all out of his system, because I hated to have John touring for him if he was going to keep that attitude about us signing with Old School Records instead of with his friends. But the truth was, if I could have done it all again, I would have done the same thing. Old School Records had given us a plan and they had stuck to it. They were on the job for us, and they were getting John plenty of airplay and distribution. The album kicked off great! We had even gotten some great reviews. The critics were calling the album "soul-inspired" with a three out of four-star rating.

I couldn't say the same for Blake's tour events, though. Sure, he had made John the marquee performer, but the other acts on his list, and the arenas where John performed, were far below where I felt he should have been. John needed to be in competition with the big R&B acts like Boyz II Men, Janet Jackson, R. Kelly, Mary J. Blige, TLC, and Jodeci, not some up-and-coming acts from Blake's wanna-be star list. He was using John as a calling card to get his minor acts more play. That was all a part of the tour business, but I didn't see where John was benefiting from it. John needed to play with the big boys, not continue doing venues that he had already graduated from. It was like a college team playing a high school team. You wouldn't win any awards that way. Unless the *high school* team won. So it looked like a lose-lose deal for John.

By the time the tour picked back up in February 1995, I asked Blake about the direction of the tour, and he gave me a bunch of black-and-white bullshit as far as *I* was concerned.

"Look, you don't start at the top in this business, whether you got a hit record out or not. You work your way up. And playing with the white boys won't change that for you," he told me.

I said, "Stop blaming everything on the white boys so much. This is all about getting John the exposure he deserves in bigger arenas for more pay."

Blake got large eyes and said, "Oh, there it is. I knew *that* was coming. Here comes the money game. I'm actually *losing* money on this tour. I'm not making anything. I gots to pay for all kinds of shit to keep you on tour for a couple of months. You ain't doing *me* no favor."

I wanted to tell him that was bullshit to his face, but I was respectful of my elders, so I calmed down. Instead, I started thinking about getting John out of that damn contract with Blake.

I went to speak to John and Tony about it that night in the hotel. We had just finished doing a show in Indianapolis.

I spotted Tony in the hallway before I got to John's room.

I said, "Where's John?"

Tony smiled and said, "He's taking care of business, man. He ain't nowhere."

Tony was high. I suspected that John was too, high and with a girl. There were plenty of girls waiting around in the hallway.

I got bold and asked them, "Who are you all waiting for?"

A few of them smiled at me, but no one answered me. Some of them were in their mid-to-late twenties, and others were college girls and teenagers. Blake had all of his acts up on the same floor, and there was obviously no conduct code. They were all doing whatever they wanted.

I stepped up to John's room through the commotion and knocked hard on his door. We had business to discuss. I guess I could have waited until the morning, but I was curious to see who he had in his room. It wasn't as if he cared about any of these girls. That was the most disappointing thing about it. I thought John would at least care more about the girls that he made it with. Or maybe I was just being hypocritical now that the shoe was on the other foot. I didn't care that much about the girls I dated in my prime football years.

Anyway, I beat hard on the door again and said, "Hey, John! We need to talk, man."

I waited for a minute, and a girl actually let me into the room.

She looked and smiled, saying "Hi" before she slipped into the bathroom.

John was sitting on the edge of his bed with nothing but his underwear on. He didn't even look at me.

I dropped the whole tour conversation for a minute and whispered to him, "Do you ever think about having one special girl anymore, man?"

John started laughing and said, "Yeah. I think about having a lot of special girls now."

I can't front and say that *I* was cured from the sex jones or anything, because I was not. I just knew when to ignore my second head for business.

I took a seat next to him and said, "John, one fine-ass girl might not be a bad thing to have, man. One, *or* two, you know," I added with a chuckle.

He smiled again. He said, "I mean, I think about it, man. I just forget about it again in the heat of the moment." He shook his head and said, "This shit is amazing, man. All these girls. I ain't never had it like this before. Not even you."

On cue, the girl walked out from the bathroom, fully dressed and looking good, chocolate brown with a slim body.

She said, "Umm, I had a good time," and giggled. "Bye," she said.

John smiled at her and didn't say a word.

I shook my own head and decided to change the subject. I said, "What do you think about this tour, man? Does it seem like you're getting as much out of it as you would want?"

He grinned. Maybe I had asked the question at the wrong time.

He said, "It could be a lot better. But the album is still selling, so we're doing all right. We just have to make sure that we hook up with a better tour for this summer, that's all. Blake's contract will be up by then."

I felt relieved after John reminded me of that. We just had to be patient and ride things out.

Someone knocked on the door, and John and I just looked at each other.

I said, "You think she forgot something?"

John said, "Only one way to find out."

I said, "Well, at least put your clothes back on, man. Don't make things look so obvious."

I stood up to get the door and John began to re-dress.

When I looked through the peephole, I saw two new girls. I opened the door and waited for them to speak.

"Can we speak to Loverboy?"

I played dumb and asked them, "*Loverboy?* Who's that?" They didn't know who I was, so I could tease them that way.

"You know, the singer. This *is* his room, ain't it?"

"Well, what is his real name?" I asked them.

"Umm . . . *shit!* Loverboy."

They didn't even know his name. What did it even matter? He was the man in demand regardless. And if the girls wanted to treat it that way, where they didn't even know his real name, then it really didn't matter if he cared about them or not. It was all in their fantasies. John was just a dream man who could sing. A Loverboy indeed.

. . . he needed all the love . . .

My guess was right! Through the winter, *May I* climbed to number two on the R&B charts and number five on pop, making *Loverboy* popular enough for the momentum to push our spring release of *Special* to number one on *both* charts! We had done a video in black-and-white where John sang from a Philadelphia street corner, old-school style, wearing old-fashioned gear. We were getting so much radio airplay for *Special* from both the urban adult contemporary and the hip-hop and R&B stations that I was getting tired of hearing it. We gained plenty of crossover appeal with the MTV crowd from our up-tempo songs, and some of the pop radio stations were playing us. We even had the hard-core hip-hop crowd behind us from the release of *Weekend Shorty* with the Executioners, which was in heavy rotation with underground rap lovers. And on the club scene, *Stylin' 'n' Profilin'* and *What We Gonna Do?* kept rocking the dance floors. Before we knew it, *Loverboy: The Album* was close to going platinum. Old School Records had a new star!

M.D. was parading around at the offices talking about, "Pop the champagne, baby! Pop the champagne!"

Double K was there too, but he was more reserved with a smile.

He said, "This has all gone much better than we had planned. You haven't even started the summer tours yet. Are you going back out with Blake?"

I was happy to tell him no.

Double K nodded and said, "Good. It's time to go with a larger scale of performers. You need to get out there and really kick ass now. This album could go double platinum over the summer." He looked at John and said, "Your versatility has really paid off. We weren't expecting that."

John was up for the challenge. He looked at me and smiled. "New artist of the year, man," he told me. He seemed energized by a new goal.

I said, "Definitely." And it was *my job* as the manager to get him on that larger tour, even if we had to take less money. It was all about stealing more fans. Because the money would roll in from the album sales anyway. John had produced about seventy percent of the album. And Tony Richmond was sitting pretty from the production help that he had provided by creating most of the beats.

I got real busy and started trying to contact the tour managers for Boyz II Men. I figured that getting Loverboy on tour with them would be the perfect match for us to steal more fans. I didn't want him in the Jodeci camp, because with John and I being from Charlotte, that seemed too close to home. Jodeci didn't have the crossover appeal with their raunchy lyrics that Boyz II Men had. I also didn't need their bad influences on John. I don't think his mother would have liked that match either. Every once in a while I thought first about Sister Williams before I made a move with John's image or career.

It took a while for me to get in touch with the tour managers. They were busy, you know. That's how it went when you were successful. I was rather busy myself with John. So in the meantime, I asked the art director, Jamie Bilford, about some ideas to make John sexier with his image and tour performances.

Jamie smiled real wide and said, "I'm flattered. How did you know I was into fashion?"

I didn't, but I just figured that art directors would have ideas.

I said, "I just guessed, man." I made sure I called Jamie "man" every chance I got to make sure that he didn't toy with me the way he liked to toy with John. But business was business, and Jamie had some bright ideas.

He said, "Well, the whole *bare chest* thing with these tattoos all over the place is just getting out of hand. Especially when you don't have the body for it. And poor John doesn't have that kind of a body."

I chuckled and said, "Hey, man, we don't need it. As long as he can sing. So, what are some other ways to make him stand out?"

Jamie thought again and said, "Well, those matching prep boy outfits that Boyz II Men wear are no turn-on either. It makes it seem like they don't know what the hell they're doin' when it counts."

I started laughing again. Jamie was using it as an opportunity to cut everyone else down.

I said, "Look, man, stop worrying about everyone else for a minute and give me some ideas on how to make Loverboy drive more women crazy."

Jamie looked at me and said, "Well, why does it have to be just *women*?" I was losing my patience with him.

I said, "All right, well, never mind, man."

He said, "Hold on, hold on," and stopped me. "You're just *like* a young man. All impatient. Probably ain't even legal to drink yet."

I just shook my head and waited for his ideas. He was right about that. I wasn't legal. But it was April 1995, and I would be legal to drink later on that month when my birthday came around. John had been legal since February.

Jamie said, "Well, actually, I don't see anything wrong with John's image. That video for *Special was* special. I mean, with the black-and-white and everything, his eyes and lips just *jumped* off of the screen at you. *Mmmph!*"

I said, "Yeah. All right, man. But what about his dress style?"

Jamie said, "I've *always* liked old clothes. They're more stylish."

I looked at his contemporary style of dress and said, "Well, how come *you* don't dress in old clothes then?"

He grinned and said, "I'm not rich enough yet. But John is. And if I had the money that *that boy's* about to make, I'd hire myself a personal tailor."

I didn't like the idea of John wearing too many old-fashioned clothes. It worked for the video, but I didn't want him walking around looking like he's permanently from the 1940s. We still had a young, hip audience to attract. I didn't want to go overboard. But I did think about the tailored clothes idea. I just questioned how expensive it could be.

I got back to the apartment to go over some ideas with John, and he was checking out his new fan mail with a big grin on his face.

He got my attention and said, "Hey, D, look at this, man."

He must have had about fifteen pleasing pictures of young women, and some of them were naked pictures.

I looked and nodded. I said, "That's all you got?"

John said, "Nah, these are just the ones that I like."

I looked again, and he had picked some real standouts, all different shades of brown.

He said, "Tony told me that people who send fan mail are the crazy ones."

I said, "Why, because they took the initiative to get in contact with you? It ain't no different from the girls who break their necks to get up to your room. Tony don't call *them* crazy."

John laughed and said, "I know."

I asked him, "Hey, man, what do you think about having a tailor do your tour clothes? I mean, you *are* a singer. We need to think about that. People look for that kind of stuff."

He asked me, "Who would we get to do it?"

I frowned and said, "Do I look like I got a phone book of tailors to you?"

"Well, *you* brought it up. Get on the case then," he told me with a smile.

John may have been smiling at me, but I thought, *Shit*. I had just created more work to do. That managing shit was an *all-day-long* job!

John went right back to looking at his fan mail pictures. He said, "I think I like this one right here the best, man."

I looked at the dime piece of a sister out at the beach in a green-and-white striped bathing suit. She had the exact same penny brown tone as John, with long, shiny black hair and dark eyes.

I nodded and smiled. She was a sure beauty.

John said, "Her name is Tangela Austin, from California. She wants to be a model and an actress. She tried out for *Jet* magazine."

I said, "*Angela* with a *T*?"

He grinned and said, "Yeah. I think I might even write her back, man." He looked at her photo again and said, "*Damn!*"

It wasn't a big deal anymore to me. John had plenty of pretty girls. I even found *my* way into bed with some of them. But I was so busy trying to get John ready for the next stage of his career that I just stopped thinking about love altogether. That's how it happens. Too much shit goes on for you to think about real love in the music business. Especially when you're first getting in it.

We had gotten a call from the new Quincy Jones *Vibe* magazine for an interview on the same day that I finally talked to the tour managers about us touring with Boyz II Men that summer. I was all excited and respectful, talking as if I had to beg for it. To my surprise, they were real cool and down-to-earth about it.

"I've been listening to him. I like his music. We'll see what we can do," I was told.

I snuck an extra push in there by saying that *Vibe* had just called us for an interview.

I said, "Do you mind if John says that we're trying to get on tour with Boyz this summer?"

There was some hesitation about it. I was putting them on the spot. My heart started beating fast as if I wasn't supposed to ask that. I was even ready to say never mind and that I was joking. I didn't want to sound too much like an opportunist. We hadn't even met in person yet.

I was given a diplomatic response. "Well, it's always good to talk about your future goals. But it can be embarrassing sometimes if you don't actually reach them."

That was a good enough answer for me. I decided that John shouldn't say a word about touring with Boyz II Men until it was actually going to happen.

Before doing the *Vibe* interview, I contacted several tailors in the Philadelphia area to see about developing a stylish image for John to tour with that summer. I ended up going with a young black guy named Charles Nickels, who worked at a tuxedo rental place downtown. He had been trying to break into the fashion industry, and I liked his ideas for John. So we visited his apartment and started making plans to show something off in *Vibe* magazine. We took Tony with us to make sure he added a different view to the mix. Sometimes a little dissent was necessary to make a solid decision.

Charles had a loft apartment with not much furniture in it, but he had pieces of cloth and fresh designs all over the place. He looked like a mad scientist with fabric.

Tony smiled and said, "Well, I can see that you *live* by the fashion, man," and started laughing. We all laughed.

Charles pulled out a new book of illustrations and said, "Here's my idea. Since John is tall and rangy, I would go with designs that accentuate his height while adding highlights to the body's natural curves at the shoulders, chest, and hips."

Tony laughed and said, "John ain't got no damn chest. He needs to do some push-ups or some shit. I keep telling him that."

John said, "What do you think I'm doing when I got girls under me?"

"You ain't doing nothing but breathing hard," Tony responded.

Charles said, "But that's okay. Silk looks better on slender men anyway." He looked at Tony's bald head and said, "Bald-headed men look good in silk, too. It's all in the curves."

Tony said, "Aw, naw, we not here to dress *me* up. We're here to dress Loverboy's skinny ass."

John said, "As long as the girls still like it. And I'm not *that* damn skinny, man. So stop talking shit and respect this man's time."

Tony grinned and said, "Okay, you paying my bills. You da boss. Let me shut the fuck up then."

It was a pleasant surprise to see John assert himself like that. He was learning to use his weight.

I cut in and said, "So, you were saying, Charles?" We were getting away from the business at hand.

Charles went ahead and showed us his idea on paper.

"Well, what you do is simply round the shoulders and then taper the ribs and under the arms, which gives you a sculptured look of subtle sex appeal." He said, "It's just enough to make the women think without having to take your shirt off."

He said, "Then you want to wear straight pants that are not as baggy as before, but still loose enough to hang. Because it's still elegant and actually *more* manly to let a woman imagine than to show her too much. That's one thing that I like about the baggy look of hip-hop."

He said, "But what I would add to the pants is a tapered fit at the top." He showed us the top of the pants with two tapered lines at the hips.

He said, "That's one of the trends that I *don't* particularly like about hip-hop. I think it's *totally* uncalled for with these loose-fitting pants to show your underwear at *any* time. In fact, *I* think it's sexier not to wear any underwear at all if you can get away with it."

Before I started thinking funny about him, he said, "Just think about how great we feel as guys when we have a woman out on a date who happens to like us, and we know for a *fact* that she's not wearing any underwear."

We all broke up laughing again.

John commented first. He said, "Yeah, that's the shit right there, man. I get a lot of that now."

I said, "You won't get no disagreements from *me* on that."

Tony smiled and nodded. "Mmm hmm," he grunted.

That only made us laugh harder.

Charles went back to explaining things to us.

He said, "Then you have the jacket." He showed us the next design. There was a plain sports jacket with no pockets and four buttons for a high collar.

He said, "You only wear the jacket to walk onto the stage with. Then you take it off whenever you get ready. You might even want to give it away to someone special in the audience."

I chuckled and said, "How much are these jackets gonna cost?"

Charles nodded to me and grinned. He said, "Yeah, maybe you *wouldn't* want to give them away."

John smiled and added his opinion. He said, "Maybe we can pick out a girl to throw it to beforehand, and tell her that she has to give it back to us after the show."

I thought that was an ingenious idea, but Tony spoke up and said, "She better be able to *fight*, or have two bodyguards right next to her ass. And what if she can't even catch?"

John said, "Well, maybe we can have, like, *five* girls all in the same area, and they all know what's up."

Tony said, "Yeah, aw'ight, you keep thinking you gon' stage some shit. You gon' end up causing a riot, and your jacket'll be in ten pieces when you get it back."

I compromised the idea and said, "Well, how about we make cheap jackets for the last song, where John throws it out there to be ripped apart on purpose? That would be like a dramatic ending for us."

Charles nodded and said, "That's a good idea. We could make cheap replicas of the originals. But then again, I think Tony has a point. You're gonna cause a lot of fights out there."

I didn't really see that as a bad thing. It would get us some publicity for the tour, for sure. Especially on a *major* tour. I could see the headlines already: LOVERBOY CAUSES A RIOT AT THE SPECTRUM. But I kept that to myself.

We got an estimated price from Charles for the first suit and told him that we needed it before the *Vibe* interview in a week. We agreed to pay him $500, up front, to rush a quality job, even if he had to stay home from work to do it. The suit would cost us a grand.

He also told us that he wanted to stay within the earth tones, with off-whites, beiges, browns, yellow, and soft colors like baby blues and mint greens. He said that hard reds, dark blues, and purples could look too in-your-face or metallic. He explained that the colors of love should be fully inviting. I didn't know all that much about fashion and colors, but it sounded about right to me. Earth tone colors looked good on John's penny brown skin.

Somehow Blake found out about our plans to tour with Boyz II Men and called us up about it.

He said, "You know our contract isn't up until October, don't you?"

I said, "We signed that contract last spring." We definitely were not planning to sign on his option. And Blake knew that already.

"Yeah, but we delayed the summer tour last year to help out on this album. So, we want our summer tour back."

"Ask him how much money he wants to get out of it," John told me in the background at the apartment.

I looked at him as if he was crazy and tossed a finger to my lips for him to let me handle it.

Blake said, "I'm not lettin' you guys break out of this contract with me. I might as well let you know that right now."

The brother was really being a pain in the ass, and he knew good and well that he didn't have the connections to handle John's growing popularity. It wasn't a black or white thing, it was a *success* thing. Everyone else had been great to us.

I didn't want to say too much to Blake without having all of the facts, so I told him that I'd call him back.

When I hung up the phone with him, John said, "Look, man, we just pay his ass off, and get him up out of our face. Let me talk to him next time. I did his whole basement bargain tour with no complaints, and now he's gon' act like *this*. Man, fuck Blake! He ain't trying to play fair. He just wants to get paid."

John was acting real sour about it, and he sounded more authoritative by the day. Once he had gone platinum, that cool blue demeanor of his had turned into a red heat.

I said, "I got it, man. I got you into this with Blake, and it's *my job* to get you out."

I called up Matt and Kenny at Old School Records to find out exactly how the tour situation with Blake had been worked out.

Matt said, "Wait a minute, we didn't extend the contract in any way. We just told him that it would be worth more to him to delay his tour plans with John until the album came out in October. In the meantime, John would go on tour with our guys as prepromotion for the album. And Blake agreed to all of it. That gave him time to set up a tour with Loverboy as his marquee. It all worked toward *his* benefit."

I said, "Well, now that he found out that we're trying to hook up with a stronger tour, he's talking about he has John under contract until October of *this* year."

Matt said, "Hold on, Kenny wants to talk to you."

Kenny came on the line and asked me, "Does John have the original contract?"

He was all calm and cool about it as usual.

I told him to hold on and looked back to John. "Where did you put the original contract?"

John just stared at me. He said, "It got lost when we moved from Tony's apartment."

I said, "Are you sure?"

"You want to look for it yourself?" he asked me.

I took a deep breath. I was really running out of energy with all of the extras of managing. I said, "So, *that's* why you want to pay him off. You lost the damn contract."

John said, "That's what he wants, man. Money."

I got back on the line and told Kenny and Matt that we needed to locate the contract.

Kenny said, "Well, unless he doctored the original deal, a contract is a contract, and we signed nothing that extended it."

I hung up the phone and looked back at John.

I said, "So, hypothetically speaking, man, how much would you be willing to pay him?"

John came up with, "Twenty thousand dollars."

His royalties on a platinum album were nearly a million dollars *after* Old School Records recouped their production costs. That was not including the money John was making from the hot-selling singles. And once the radio publishing rights began to kick in, John had nothing to worry about with the money game. All he had to do was wait for it. I just didn't like the principle of paying someone who was obviously trying to get over on us.

I said, "And what if he says no and tries to take us to court?"

John said, "Let him prove it in court then."

I said, "But by us *paying him* it makes it seem as if he's right."

"Man, what difference does it make?" John asked me. "As long as we can get the hell out of the contract with him, I don't care. I just don't feel like going through this back-and-forth shit."

I didn't want to give in so fast. I told John, "I'm gonna look for that contract first."

John said, "All right, you do whatever." He was in that impatient mood of his again and snapping at me. I figured he was stressed about the moving-up process that we had to go through to climb to the top of the charts and *stay* there. But *fuck*, I was stressed about the increased workload *too*, and *I* wasn't acting up!

Anyway, Tony had moved from his old apartment near downtown into a much bigger place in West Philly, so I didn't even know where to start looking for the contract. All I was doing was wasting time and energy. I couldn't find anything. Then we finally received word that we could tour that summer with Boyz II Men.

John said, "You should have offered that twenty thousand when Blake called last time. Now he's gonna want more. *God dammit!*"

John was real pressed about it, but I ignored his ass. I had my job to do. So I took another deep breath and called Blake back.

When I got him on the line, I lied and said, "We have the contract sitting right here in front of us, and John signed nothing that says that you could extend it without us agreeing to an option."

I kept talking and said, "I also talked to Matt and Kenny at Old School Records, and they told me that you agreed to do the tour after John's album release in October to use as your marquee performer for a winter tour, and everyone has fulfilled their word.

"Now I understand that you may have some hard feelings about us going on a larger tour this summer, but we're moving up, Blake, and I think it's better to stay friends with us than to put us in a situation where we become enemies.

"I mean, *I* didn't want to do it because it doesn't seem fair to me, but John even wanted to pay you ten thousand dollars to ease this thing out. But if we have to go to court over it, then I'm prepared to do that."

I was talking a mile a minute and trying to run the game on him. I had to learn how to do that in order to stay on the job for John. Otherwise, we would be taken for plenty of rides in the music business.

All Blake had to do was ask me to read one line from the contract that I claimed was right there in front of me, and I would have been stuck. But instead of doing that, he started laughing out loud over the phone.

He said, "You a slick motherfucker, Darin. But I like that in a young brother. So I'll tell you what I'll do. You double that to twenty thousand, and I'll go ahead and wish you and John the best of luck for this summer. Unless you still want to take it to court. Because I got the *real* paperwork."

I said, "We'll put that in the mail for you then."

I got off that phone as fast as I could.

John sat there and broke up laughing at me. He asked me, "What did he say?"

"He'll take the money," I told him.

"Ten thousand dollars like *you* said?"

"Nah. He wants the twenty thousand that *you* said. And from now on, you know I'm keeping *all* of the paperwork, right?"

John smiled at me and said, "Aw'ight, Mr. Manager. Boyz II Men, here we come!" And everything seemed healed and forgiven.

The *Vibe* article with John's tailored gear was a hit! They shot him sitting in a brown leather lounge chair with his jacket laying over the arm. It was only a page long, but John got to talk about how competitive he wanted to be to keep climbing up the charts and showing that he was a real crooner. It was all good and everything, but by the time that summer tour was ready to kick off, I knew exactly what John felt like when he said that he wanted to get high. I mean, you just had to have something to balance out the stress.

Nineteen ninety-five was such a hot year for young black musicians with plenty of great music coming out that I was worn into the dirt from playing the manager game and trying to stay on top of it all. Maybe managers needed to be older than I was to handle the wear and tear. That's how I got started smoking weed with John as a stress relief. We were close to double platinum by then.

We were one week away from touring, and I had stopped sweating John about the weed smoking as long as he agreed to do it on his downtime and not when we were doing anything that needed a clear head. So during a moment of low energy on my part, I asked him again at the apartment to explain what the big deal was about getting high.

John smiled at me. He said, "I got some weed in the room."

We were just relaxing on the sofa in the living room. We were sitting behind the long wooden coffee table, watching more music videos on BET.

John was tempting me, and I was too drained to respond to him, so he went ahead and got some get-high. He brought it back out in a plastic Ziploc bag and quickly rolled the dried brown and green leaves into a fresh sheet of top paper.

I remember the last words John said to me before I tried it.

He said, "Weed ain't gon' kill you, man. It's natural. Straight from the earth."

He lit the joint with a lighter, raised it to his lips, and sucked on it hard.

I remember the crackling sound it made as it turned from red flames to bright yellow ones. Then John passed it on to me.

I took it in my fingers and raised it to my lips to suck in the smoke before I could change my mind about it. I *wanted* to get high. I wanted to see what it felt like. So I sucked in the smoke and started choking immediately. Was smoke really meant to be inhaled into the human throat?

John said, "Fight the cough, man, and just relax. When you feel that tickle in your throat, just fight it back and hold down the smoke."

I tried it again and it worked for a few seconds. Then I heard the same crackling of the flames up in my brain as I held down the smoke. When I broke up and coughed even harder, the marijuana smoke was all up in my system for the first time in my life. I had never even smoked a cigarette before. It just never appealed to me. I was an athlete, and I needed my clear lungs.

All of a sudden, with fresh weed smoke in my system, my body felt like a floating feather. The sofa felt extra plush as I leaned back into it. I was sinking deeper and deeper into the sofa. It was swallowing me.

John started laughing and finished the rest of the joint by himself. He was the pro and I was the amateur. He was the bad boy and I was the good boy being turned out. Funny how things change.

I couldn't even touch the weed anymore. I was done. I was a roasted beef patty on a hamburger bun. Someone was putting ketchup and mustard on me as I sat back on the sofa. And then came the pickles. Plop! Plop! Right on my forehead. I could feel my body rocking backward as they hit me.

John asked me, "How you feel, man?"

I heard him loud and clear. I opened my mouth real slow and said, "What?"

I could hear my own heart beating. *Thoomp, thoomp, thoomp, thoomp, thoomp, thoomp, thoomp, thoomp . . .*

John asked me, "How you feelin', D?"

I could hear him loud and clear. I opened my mouth real slow and said, "Yeah."

"Yeah, what?"

I nodded my head forward as if it weighed a ton on my neck. I finally knew what John was talking about. I could hear him loud and clear. I opened my mouth real slow and said, "Yeah, man, I see what you mean."

"You see what I mean about what?"

I said, "I understand, man. You just want to lay back and relax a minute."

John leaned over, looked into my eyes, and started laughing.

"Ha, ha, ha, ha, ha, ha."

I started laughing too. "Ha, ha . . . Ha, ha . . . Ha, ha, ha."

My laughs were all short eruptions, as if someone was pressing my stomach like the Pillsbury Doughboy.

"Ha, ha . . . Ha, ha, ha . . . Ha, ha, ha."

I couldn't seem to stop it. It was making my ribs hurt.

I said, "Stop making me laugh, man. Stop making me laugh. *Please!* My ribs are hurting!"

John only laughed harder at me. He said, "Yo, D. I think you fucked-up real good, man. My bad. You want me to get you some milk?"

"Milk? What the fuck I need milk for? Ha, ha, ha, ha!"

All of a sudden, my body started leaning and falling over. "WHOOAA! HELP ME UP, MAN! HELP ME UP!"

John barely touched me when he reached out to put his hand on my shoulder. He said, "There you go."

I started leaning to the other side.

I opened my mouth real slow and said, "It's a good thing I'm still sitting down." Then those damn painful laughs started up again. "Ha, ha, ha, ha . . ."

John said, "I'm going all out on this tour, man."

I nodded to him. "Yeah . . . you do that."

He said, "This music game is competitive as hell. I was number one for about *two weeks*. Boyz II Men were number one for *months*, man! I want to break chart records like them."

I smiled. I said, "You got your own style, Loverboy. And it's *four* of them. It's only *one* of you, man. Only *one* Loverboy. They gotta share all of their women."

John laughed again. He said, "I'm gon' try to blow them away on this tour, D. None of them can out-sing me alone. They gotta gang up on me."

I started laughing. He made it sound like a street fight.

I said, "It's all love, man. We gotta thank them for letting us on."

John stood up and walked over to the stereo system. It seemed like it took him forever to get there. He started searching for something.

I said, "Whatchu doin', man?"

He said, "You ever heard of D'Angelo?"

I shook my head from side to side real slow and said, "Nah. Who's that?"

"This guy's just coming out, man. Me and Tony been checking this out," he told me.

He turned the television down and put the CD single in for me to listen to, nice and loud. And boy, did it hit the spot! This guy D'Angelo had an easy, foot-tapping beat with a thick bass line and organs. He was singing about the love he had for a sister and her good stuff.

My body starting rowing back and forth in the sofa as if someone was pushing me in a rocking chair.

I said, "Yeeaaahh. I'm feelin' this, man! I'm *feelin'* this!"

John said, "He's from the church down south like us, man. I knew it from the first moment I heard it."

I said, "The organs, right?"

John said, "Plain as day, man. And the South got, like, a slower feel than the North. Tony pointed that out to me. It's *lots* of new music coming out. You heard Zhane, right?"

I nodded and said, "Yeah." Zhane were two harmonizing sisters right out of Philly.

John said, "Butterscotch is about to come out with their album. They're signed to Columbia now. They want me and Tony to produce a few songs for them."

I said, "Yeah, man, I know. That'll be a good move to keep pushing your sound."

John said, "This game ain't no different from football, D. You gots to be on *top*, man, or you'll get pushed out the game. It ain't all love. This is *war*."

I kept nodding my head to D'Angelo's music and began to sing along with the chorus:

I want some of your brown shuuu-gar.

John smiled and said, "I wonder what *his* mom thinks."

I said, "What? Ain't nothing wrong with this song. He singing about a girl, man. And he ain't being vulgar or nothin'.".

John looked at me and grinned. He said, "He ain't singin' 'bout no damn girl. He singin' 'bout smokin' weed."

I looked up at John and said, "Get outta here."

He said, "Look at that weed on the table. What it look like?"

I looked at the clear bag and smiled. I said, "It's brown and green."

"You better *recognize*," John told me. "*Girls* don't make your eyes turn blood burgundy. He's talking about smoking a whole lot of weed."

I started laughing again. I said, "Well, damn, that's kind of clever then."

John said, "That's what I'm saying, man. The competition is steep. He got a song on here talking about, *Shit, Damn, Motherfucker.*"

I said, "Get the hell out of here."

John went ahead and played it for me. I heard the words and went into eruptions of laughter again. I had to grab my ribs.

John said, "See what I mean, man? You can't take no prisoners out here. You gotta just do what you feel, and go for it. Ain't no holding back."

I said, "What? You wanted to write a song like this?"

"Nah. But if I ever do . . . I'm just gon' do it. You gotta be brave when you write music. Otherwise, you really don't need to be out there. So when we start putting together this next album . . . I'm gon' shock 'em all."

I started nodding and getting hyped like a trainer before a big boxing match.

I said, "Yeah, man. I hear you. Let's go get 'em!"

. . . then he was swept away . . .

Once I started getting high with him, John became a lot more talkative. We went over our game plan for the summer tour and how we would execute onstage. We agreed that I would come out onstage first to get the crowd ready for him. I hadn't done that before, but when you start getting high, you find yourself thinking about a lot of different things that may not have appealed to you in the past. You become extra brave when you're high, and it all makes sense to you for some strange reason. However, I was *not* under the influence when I walked out onto the stage at that first summer concert in Chicago.

When you stand in front of twenty thousand screaming fans of beautiful women and supercool guys at those packed concerts, you better have strong legs under you. It was like being on the football field again and waiting to receive the opening kickoff. I looked out at this massive crowd in Chicago and was nervous as hell! But it wasn't as if I hadn't felt that way before at a football game, so I just sucked it up, took a deep breath, and jumped right into it as if I was making a game-winning interception.

I grabbed the microphone out in front of the large curtains and asked the crowd, "How many women in here love to make love?"

They screamed, "WWWAAAAAAAHHH!"

They were already *pumped* out there. I guess I had asked the right question, so I got confident and kept going with it.

"Do y'all like it done the right way?"

"YEEEAAAAAAHHHHH!"

"Do y'all like to listen to music when y'all do it?"

"YEEEAAAAAAHHHHH!"

"Well, how many of y'all ever heard of John Lover—?"

They started screaming before I could even finish my sentence.

"WWWAAAAAAAHHH!"

I stopped and started laughing. I said, "I guess y'all know who he is then."

"YEEEAAAAAAHHHHH!"

This music shit is something else! I kept telling myself.

I asked them, "Y'all want him to come out . . ."

"WWWAAAAAAAAAAAAAAAHHHHHH!"

". . . and sing for y'all?"

There was a major difference in performing for a larger crowd in a much larger arena like that. I could barely hear myself. I didn't know John had love like that in Chicago. Then again, since it was R. Kelly's town, I guess they were used to soul singers. And Boyz II Men were breaking records with their sophomore album, so we were on the right damn tour to shine.

I turned around and said, "Hey, John, I think they want you to sing for 'em out here, man."

"WWWAAAAAAAAAAAAAAAAHHHHHH!"

"Where you at, Loverboy?"

"YEEEAAAAAAHHHHH!"

We pulled back the curtains to reveal the band. Tony Richmond was sitting in the center with his drums. The stage crew pushed a tall imitation light pole and a street corner sign to the front of the stage as John's props. The street sign had WILLIAMS AVENUE on one side and LOVER'S LANE on the other, both glowing under the night-light. Then John strolled out wearing his tailored outfit, and the crowd lost their minds again.

"WWWAAAAAAAAAAAAAAAAHHHHHH!"

At that point, I handed John the microphone and walked off the stage.

When the fans finally calmed down out there, John opened up on the microphone and said, "Like most sensitive men, I didn't get a lot of attention from the ladies when I was younger."

"AAAAWWWWWW!" they sympathized with him.

Then someone yelled, "DON'T WORRY ABOUT THAT, BABY!"

John responded, "Oh, I'm *not* worried about it now," and took his sports jacket off—the real one—and dropped it to the floor. They saw his tailored shirt and pants, and they lost it again.

"WWWAAAAAAAAHHH!"

"GO 'HEAD, BABY! *SING!*"

John said, "Ever since I sang my first song . . . things have changed."

"YEEEAAAAAAAHHHHH!"

Tony started the band with the soulful music of John's *May I*, and Loverboy did his thing:

Ma-a-ay I-I-I hol-l-ld your-r-r han-an-an-n-nd . . .

"WWWAAAAAAAHHH!"
"YEEEAAAAAAHHHHH!"

John, Tony, and I had worked out all of the details of the performance while we were under the influence of "brown sugar," and our plans were working like a charm!

When John got to the second song, we invited a girl onstage in blue jeans, and Tony jumped in with that beat of his:

Tic-TAT, Tic-BOOM
Tic-TAT, BA-DOOM-BOOM
Tic-TAT, Tic-BOOM
Tic-TAT, BA-DOOM-BOOM

Tony stopped the beat for John to grab the girl by the hand and scream the first verse:

HAAAY BAAABY
Tic-TAT, Tic-BOOM
IN THE BLUUUE JEAN-EAN-EANS.
Tic-TAT, BA-DOOM-BOOM

The crowd kept going crazy with everything that John did that night. He got to the last song, *Special*, where we made a switch to the cheap sports jacket, and he tossed it out into the audience. The women went crazy for it and ripped it all to pieces just like Tony said they would. But it worked for us, and we were all satisfied with the show until Boyz II Men got to that famous *End of the Road* song. That song was a *killer!*

Although we go
to the en-n-nd ahhf the ro-oad
still I ca-a-an't le-e-et go . . .

People were singing all of the words together and rocking back and forth like it was some kind of a cult going on out there. Tony and I watched from backstage and shook our heads, grinning in amazement. John was tired of looking at it.

He said, "I gotta write me a damn song like that one, man."

Tony said, "That's that harmonizing shit. You need a group to do that.

But if you asked me, our music is stronger than theirs. *Much* stronger."

I agreed with Tony on that, but it didn't matter. Boyz II Men were famous for their singing, not for their music. While on tour with them, we kept our distance. They had a squeaky-clean image, and we all wanted to get high and chill in our camp, so we stayed clear of those guys. They did their thing on tour and we did ours.

I did get John to calm down a bit with all of the groupies, though. We talked about the rape charge that Tupac Shakur had faced in New York, and the prison time that he and Mike Tyson were forced to serve from dealing with that groupie life. A guy had to be extra careful with the icon business and women. John was finally getting the message. He wanted to concentrate on his stage presence and material for his next album anyway. He started coming up with new ideas after every show.

Then at a show in Los Angeles, John finally went and did it. He hooked up with a girl that he couldn't refuse, Tangela Austin, from Manhattan Beach, California.

I went out there and warmed up the crowd as I had been doing for that summer's tour, and I noticed a sister standing out front in a full tiger-striped outfit with a matching cowboy hat. She had on a damn *tiger-striped* outfit with a matching hat! I just figured that it was California, you know. They liked to dress extra out there with their own fashion statements.

John performed his show as usual, and when Boyz II Men went on to do their thing, this girl Tangela found her way backstage with help from security.

Tony and I and the rest of the band all looked at one another. We seemed to be at a loss for words, but we all knew what we were thinking. *Who the hell is* this? I finally realized who she was from the photo that John had showed me.

I asked her, "You sent fan mail before?"

She nodded and answered "Mmm hmm" with a sly smile.

She had this cool, confident maturity about her that calmed us immediately. She was not all excited or giddy like many other women would be backstage. She wasn't anxious or pushy like some of them could be either. She acted as if she was *supposed* to be there.

Anyway, John grinned, standing at her side, and said, "I told you I was gonna meet her."

Since he hadn't said anything to me about it in a while, I had forgotten all about the girl. But I always thought that John having a girl around who he actually cared about was a good idea, so I was all smiles. He had done it on his own and before I could suggest someone to him.

Tony looked at her and said, "Well, I guess you know how to make an entrance, hunh?" He was referring to her attention-getting outfit.

She said, "I wanted to make sure that I stood out. I didn't want John to come out here and change his mind about being with me."

I found that very hard to do, myself. She was *all that*! But then again, like I said, John had plenty of knockouts by then. Tangela had the right idea. She was covering her bases with the first-impression move.

John didn't even want to stay until the end of the show that night.

He asked Tangela, "So, are you ready to show me around Los Angeles? We got the limo."

She smiled and said, "Yeah."

John looked back at us and grinned. He said, "Well, I'll see y'all later on, guys," and started walking toward the backstage exit without another word about it. I guess he had his mind made up.

Tony looked at me and said, "Damn. I guess he's out."

I chuckled and said, "Yeah, that's what I was thinkin'." I asked Tony, "What do you think about the girl, though?" She was definitely a good looker to me.

Tony nodded his head and said, "She'll do."

"She'll *do*? That's all you think?" I asked him.

He said, "Naw, I'm thinking a lot more, but that's John's piece, you know."

We broke out laughing. And with John leaving early before the groupies could start breaking their necks to get backstage with him after the show, I got more attention than I was used to.

"Aren't you Loverboy's manager?"

I said, "Yeah."

"Well, can I stay with you to get a chance to meet him later on?"

"Stay with me where?"

"At the hotel or wherever?"

There was a whole group of girls waiting for me to give them a positive answer before they would crowd me. They were not bad looking in Los Angeles either. Not at *all*! So I found myself having to swallow some of my own medicine. *Leave the groupies* alone! I stressed to myself. I hadn't always obeyed my own advice.

I said, "John's gonna be a little tied up tonight."

"Well, what about you? Don't you get a limo as his manager? Can we just chill with you?"

Tony and the rest of the band were already choosing to grab who they could grab, and it was my turn to make a move. But I was hesitant. I started thinking that maybe I needed a girl that I could settle down with myself. Managers needed love and stability too.

I managed to turn down their offers, and later on John told me all about his night out with this girl Tangela.

As soon as they got inside the white stretch limo, she relaxed as if it were hers, and as if she had known John for years.

John sat away from her in the limo on purpose and asked her, "So, how many singers or celebrities have you been out with?" He had learned to be pretty blunt with girls. I felt he overdid it sometimes.

Tangela wasn't bothered by it, though. She said, "Not one."

John smiled and said, "So, why me?"

He didn't say whether he believed her or not, he just wanted to keep the conversation going.

She grinned and took off her hat, where she had her long, black hair pinned up in a bun. She let it out to fall down over her shoulders and back before she answered him.

She said, "Everything about you was attractive to me. I mean, I like your music, the way you sing, your style of dress, your sex appeal. And then I kept thinking to myself, *Loverboy, what is* that *all about?* So I just wanted to meet you."

John said, "That's all a part of the business, though. That just the packaging," to lead her on. He liked the package himself. His whole mystique was damn good *packaging* on our part.

Tangela said, "It's not just packaging to me. I mean, I can tell what's fake and what's real. Or least I *think* I can. And if you're gonna call yourself *the Loverboy*, then you better be able to back it up."

She patted the seat next to her and said, "Come sit closer to me. Why are you all the way over there?"

John didn't budge. He said, "Because I want to figure you out."

"And you can't do that while sitting closer to me? I don't scare you, do I?"

He started laughing. He said, "Maybe three years ago."

She asked him, "Have you learned a lot in three years?"

He nodded. "Yeah."

"Really?"

"Oh yeah."

"How much?"

"What do you want to know?"

She licked her lips real easily and said, "I want to know how you kiss."

John laughed and asked her, "Just like that?"

"Just like that."

"Well, what about all of the emotions that go into love and kisses and everything?" he asked her. "Is that important to you?"

I don't think that John even viewed it as important anymore with the way women were throwing themselves at him.

Tangela said, "Is all of that important to *you?* You're the *Loverboy.* You're supposed to be the *expert.* Tell me what *you* think. That's why I asked you to begin with."

John changed the subject for a minute and asked her how old she was because she had never mentioned it to him. She *looked* our age, but you could never tell at those concerts with how girls dressed up and used makeup.

She asked him, "How old do I look?"

John swung his bat and said, "Twenty."

"Thank you," she told him. "I'm twenty-four."

That was no big deal. John had been with a few women in their thirties by then.

He said, "Okay. So, where would you like to take me? I'm hungry."

She smiled and chuckled at him. "What would you like . . . to eat?"

Damn! John thought she wanted to get to know him for real, but she was acting like a sexpot. He couldn't figure the girl out. Was she joking with that shit? She presented herself straightforward from long distance, but she was much more wicked in person. What did she want? Did she just want to screw? Did she want a relationship? Or was that all up to John?

He finally asked her, "So, what do you really want from me? You just want to hang out for the night? I thought you wanted more than that."

I think that *John* wanted more, if anything. He expected more than just another one-night hit. They had been corresponding long distance with each other.

Tangela said, "Maybe I do, maybe I don't."

My boy finally decided to play it her way and stop wasting time. He got up to sit next to her inside the limo and looked into her eyes with her sweet colored lips placed right in front of his.

He said, "So, you want to know what I kiss like?"

"Mmm hmm."

He leaned over to kiss her and she turned her head.

John had not had a girl play hard to get with him in a *while.* It was a no-win game with a newfound Loverboy. He would simply move on to the next girl.

He started laughing and shaking his head. Tangela climbed on top of him and kissed him, tickling his tongue with a French kiss twirl.

"Put your hands right here," she told him, sliding his fingers between her ribs and her breast. She started to rock with him and kissed him again.

I was getting hard just listening to John's story. Damn I wished that I was him sometimes!

He told her, "I guess you don't want to eat right now then."

She said, "I want to eat. But will the limo driver let us do that in the car?"

John started laughing, embarrassed by it. He had a hard one by then himself.

I was amazed that he could even think about what I was telling him concerning groupies, but he had the strength to stop her before they got too wild inside the limo.

He said, "You know what? I think we might be going a little too far."

She looked at him confused and said, "Why?"

He explained it to her. "I'm saying, if we really want to get to know each other, then we can't treat this like some carnival ride."

She got off of him, straightened her skirt, and sat silent. I think John had embarrassed her with his poise.

He said, "You're not mad, are you?"

She shook her head and responded, "No." What else was she going to say?

She told the driver to take them to a restaurant up on Sunset Boulevard in West Hollywood.

When they sat down to eat, she asked John, "So, how many girls do you get with when you're out on tour?"

He looked at her and frowned at the question. He shook his head and tried to ignore it while he checked out his menu. The girl seemed to be obsessed with his sexuality. What an irony. Girls usually talked about how much *guys* were obsessed with sex.

"Are you gonna answer my question?" she pressed John at the dinner table.

By that time, John started not to like her anymore. He thought that he was getting something new, and he ended up with the same old thing: skepticism, anxiety, and possession. Tangela had lost her facade of cool.

John told her, "We'll get to answer that before the night is over. But let's just eat right now."

She nodded her head as if it was all cool. Then she stood to excuse herself to the rest room.

"I'll be back," she told him.

John sat there and finished looking at his menu, no longer sweating the girl and thinking about how he would end the night with her. When the waiter came to the table and asked him for his order, since Tangela was not back from the rest room yet, John told the waiter to make another trip around. Twenty minutes later, the girl had not returned to the table with him.

The waiter asked him, "Are you sure that everything's all right?"

John said, "Let me go check."

He got up and walked to the women's rest room to look for her. He called inside and even thought about walking in. When he returned to his table, the limo driver was waiting for him there.

"Your date, Tangela Austin, said that something had come up and that she had to leave. She said you can call her on her pager later on at this number."

He gave John a piece of notebook paper with her pager number on it.

John just shook his head again. But he was still hungry, so he decided to eat there and treat the limo driver. They returned to the hotel when they had finished eating.

I looked into John's face when he told me that story that night and frowned my damn self. It was unbelievable!

I said, "What is this, some fuckin' Cinderella shit? She just up and left like that?"

John answered, "Yup." He asked me, "You think I should call her back?"

I said, "Hell no, man! That girl crazy. Tony was right about that fan mail shit."

John laughed, but he didn't toss that number away.

I said, "You're not thinking about calling that girl back, are you?"

He waited too long to answer.

I said, "Out of *all* the girls for you to try and get serious about, you went ahead and picked a nutcase. I thought this damn girl was cool. She *acted* like she was cool. We *all* liked her."

John said, "I liked her too, man. Maybe she has a good explanation."

I said, "Yeah, she's crazy."

I was being really hard on the girl, but what the hell. I didn't really know her to give her the benefit of the doubt.

In the middle of our conversation the telephone rang. We had put the hotel room under my name to keep the groupies away.

I answered it and said, "Hello."

A young woman's voiced asked me, "Is this Darin Harmon?"

I hesitated. Was some girl really calling up for me, or was she trying to get to John?

I said, "Yes, this is D Harmon," trying to sound all business.

She said, "I want to apologize to your friend. We didn't get off to a good start."

I paused. "Wait a minute. Is this Tangela?"

John looked at me surprised.

She said, "Yes, and I'm downstairs at the hotel."

I didn't know what to say to her after I had just finished bombing her out.

I said, "I'll tell him that you said sorry." I wasn't going to include the downstairs at the hotel part. I still thought that she was crazy.

John reached for the phone and said, "Let me talk to her."

I held it away from him.

She was asking me the same thing over the line. "Can I talk to him?"

There I was again in the middle of John's life.

I told Tangela to hold on. I put my hand over the receiver so she couldn't hear me. I spoke in a low, serious tone to John.

I said, "Do you really need to talk to this damn girl, man? She ain't right, John."

He said, "Well, let me hear her out. Ain't nobody perfect. She got a right to make a mistake."

I really didn't want to give that phone to him. I was tempted to hang the shit up on her, but I didn't. I conceded and passed my boy the phone.

John got on the line with her and immediately asked her where she was.

I mumbled to myself, "Damn," knowing that she would make it up into the room that night.

John hung up the phone and confirmed it.

He looked at me and said, "You didn't tell me she was right downstairs." He headed for the door to get her. Then he turned and told me, "I'm gon' need my privacy tonight, man. Aw'ight?"

I took a deep breath and said, "John—"

He cut me off and said, "I don't even feel like hearing that shit tonight, D. I just want to hear what she has to say."

He left me with that, and I walked out shortly after him to return to my own room.

Action was going on all over the hotel, and I could no longer refuse it. I figured it was better than sitting alone in my room that night and thinking about what John would be getting into. If *he* went to the devil that night, then *we* would just have to go to the devil together. So I got high and invited up the first clean-looking girl who was willing to get to know a manager who used to be a football star back in high school.

I remember the young woman asking me, "So, how often does this happen to you on tour?"

I was high and chilling, so I told her, "Never. This'll be my first time."

I remember that she laughed at my lie and asked me if I had any more weed to smoke. I guess it was obvious to her that I was high. I gave her some of my weed. We got high together. And then I made her squeal for half that night.

In the morning, John wasn't mad at me at all. He was all smiles.

He came to my room after my company had left and said, "D . . ." He shook his head and kept right on grinning. He said, "D, that girl can *fuck*, man! I'm glad as hell that she came back. She taught me *a lot* of shit last night, man!"

Then he sniffed my room and asked me, "You smoked some weed in here last night?" He looked at my bed and said, "Oh, you got busy, too. Was it somebody you cared about, D?"

He was rubbing the conversations about groupies in my face.

He started laughing out loud and said, "I ain't mad at you, man. You gotta do what you gotta do."

I was still curious. I asked him, "So, what did she say?"

He said, "Oh, she just told me the truth, man. She said she wanted to impress me because I'm, like, a star and everything, and she felt good about being with me, but she felt nervous too. And she just wanted to be close to me, but when I was distant with her, it kind of made her more nervous about being with me. Then she started saying shit that she didn't mean."

I said, "So, she didn't really want to fuck you like that? She was just acting nervous?"

John said, "Nah, she wanted to fuck me, but she didn't mean for it to come out the way it came out. She said she ended up forcing it instead of just letting it happen. She just panicked for a minute, man."

I started laughing at his candor. I said, "So, in other words, she was trying to force her fantasy on you, and it wasn't happening the way that she wanted it."

"Yeah, something like that," he told me. He said, "But D, I ain't nutted that strong in my *life*, man! And I wasn't even high last night."

He said, "She, like, told me how to take it easy and just work at one pace until she was ready to come. And she was coming all night, man. And like, whenever *I* got ready to come, D, her whole body would, like, squeeze up on me like a glove, man. Like it was made just for me.

"*Damn* that shit was good!" he told me.

I was laughing, but I still didn't trust the girl. She wasn't my choice of a main squeeze. But like Babyface once sang, she obviously had the "whip appeal."

I said, "So, how does she feel about you now?"

"Oh, she's over that nervous shit now, man," he told me.

"And is she really twenty-four acting like that?"

"Acting like what?"

"You know, like, she didn't know what she was doing?"

John frowned at me and said, "Man, she *know* what she doin'."

I said, "But can you trust her, though?"

"Trust her to do what?"

I said, "To be your girl."

John slowed down and said, "I ain't got no ropes on her or nothing, man. I told her that. I told her that it ain't no pressure on her."

I figured that John was covering bases for himself with that.

I said, "All right, we'll see." And for the moment, I left it at that.

When the royalty money started to roll in that late summer, *Loverboy: The Album* had sold close to 3 million copies. John was nearly *triple platinum!* We were all rolling in the money! John immediately started house shopping in the suburbs of Philadelphia to stay close to the recording studios at Old School Records. He bought a gold Lexus Coupe and gave me the Maxima. Then we flew back home and began looking for a house to move his mother into at Lake Norman near Charlotte. Lake Norman was *serious* property! John surprised me with that, but Sister Williams refused to take part in it.

She told John, "I will *not* have anything to do with that money. I will *not!* How *DARE YOU* come back to this house and tempt me with that? I raised you better than that. Is this all you have to show for it—money and this godforsaken music, with the talent that God gave you?"

John said, "I thought that you would leave me alone about that when I got the recording contract. I thought that was the deal."

She said, "*The deal* was for you to *stay* in school! And I don't *make* deals with the devil!"

John got wicked on her for real and said, "Well, since you so *righteous*, *Mom*, why don't you tell me the real story about my father then?"

Sister Williams still refused to talk about the man, and that only made John suspect the worst. We talked about that a few times while on tour. John thought about his father being a womanizer, an ex-convict, a married man, or *something* that his mother didn't want him to know. You bring up everything while you're high. The thoughts and words just pour out of you.

Even with all of the money and the good times that we seemed to be having from the outside, it's never "all good," as they say. There was always something in the way of true happiness. To tell you the truth, I still dreamed about playing football on occasion. I kept up on everything going on at A&T, and we were always right in the hunt of the competition. I would dream about having the courage to go for a professional tryout one day and stay in shape to do it. But who was I kidding? With as much weed as I began to smoke with John, I wouldn't be able to pass anyone's drug test, let alone perform well.

In September, John sat down with me inside an elaborate three-bedroom house that he had bought in the Philadelphia suburbs. He had given the apartment to me.

He said, "I'm thinking about moving Tangela in with me, man."

He had only known her through the summer, and he had been flying her back and forth to the concerts.

I looked at him and said, "Man, you *can't* be serious."

My own idea was now sounding like a nightmare. John didn't need to move no girl *in* with him. He needed to start thinking about the next album.

I said, "Do you think that's wise to do right now, man? I thought you told me you didn't have no ropes on her. We need to start getting ready to work on the next album anyway. You think she would be able to handle all of the time that you spend in the studio?"

He said, "Yeah. She understands where my money comes from."

I figured I had time to work on him about it, so I let it slide for the moment. I can't lie; once I started getting high, I let a lot of shit slide. I figured that I didn't need to put so much stress on my mind anymore. I needed to pace myself to last in the business, and so did John. The weed allowed us both a chance to say, "Fuck it!" and keep going.

John shook his head at his new house and said, "I'm hurtin', D. My mom still don't accept my music. And she still don't have shit to tell me about my father. How can she do that to me, man? She needs to control me that much?"

We were listening to Tupac's latest album, *Me Against the World*, extra loud and from a new stereo system. John was really relating to the material, especially *Dear Momma*, which was a hit song at the time. John called the material honest and heartfelt as compared to a lot of the other rap artists, who made up outlandish images to sell their records.

I didn't know what to say to John about his mother. He was on a low again. When he was extra cool and just getting signed, he maintained a mellow poise. But once he got excited again, it seemed to bring out the ugliness with it.

I said, "You just have to wait it out, man. Your mother'll come around." I added, "But like you told me before, to be a real artist, you have to be brave, man. You just have to keep going and feeling it. No holding back. That's why it's so painful sometimes, man. It's like doing them extra five to ten push-ups at the end of practice to be the best at what you do. And that's also why everybody can't do it. Because everybody ain't *meant* to do it."

John nodded his head real slow and smiled at me. He said, "Remember that time we were having an argument about whose dream was the best, you playing football or me doing my music?"

I smiled back at him and said, "Yeah, I remember that. I'm still trying to forget that I lost."

John said, "That seems like a long-ass time ago, man. And sometimes . . . it seems like just yesterday."

I grinned and nodded back to him. I said, "I know exactly what you're talking about, man." An old-school lyric slipped into my head right on cue: "*'Time keeps on slippin', slippin', slippin' . . . into the fu-u-u-ture.'*"

We both laughed, pushing through the pain called life and thinking about a future of our own, the good . . . and obviously all of the damn bad.

VERSE 16

. . . in a mad, mad storm . . .

Before John could get back in the studio and begin working on new songs for his sophomore album, he brought another fan mail letter to my attention. This one had no picture with it, no name, and no return address.

He handed the typed letter to me at the apartment and said, "Read this."

I looked at him and then back to the letter before I read it out loud:

"'Dear John "LOVERBOY" Williams, I am sad to inform you that I am no longer a fan of your music. When I first purchased your CD, *Loverboy: The Album*, almost a year ago, when it first came out in the stores, I thought that your music was the best thing that I had ever heard in my life. I thought that your songs were sincere, funky, and really touching. They gave me a full range of emotions, something that most other albums have not been able to do. And I was most inspired that you wrote and produced most of your songs yourself. I thought that you were a real romantic like I am. You were the kind of creative and sensitive guy that I had always dreamed about in the midst of so many sex-crazed and drugged-out knuckleheads.'"

I stopped reading and looked at John again. Was this letter for real? I started laughing and feeling guilty at the same time. I knew what was coming next before I even read it.

John said, "Go 'head, man, finish reading it."

I went back to reading the letter:

"'You probably won't remember with your busy schedule and everything, but I attended a show where you performed this year in Indianapolis. I was with a college girlfriend of mine who visited your room. I was not one of the "lucky girls" handpicked to see you that night, but my girlfriend told me all about the experience. In horror, I listened to her tell me about the hallway of young women who were waiting to see you, and how your hotel room smelled like an ounce of marijuana smoke.'"

I started laughing again, trying my best to swallow the guilt that I felt while reading.

"'I admit that it was against my friend's better judgment to sleep with you that night, or whatever you choose to call it, but I do NOT consider that to be LOVE. Is that what you write your songs for, to get all of the girls that you can get? And I would not think, through your music at least, that you would be into using drugs like so many of these terrible rappers that I refuse to listen to.

"'Needless to say, I was very disappointed to hear about your behavior that night. So I gave my used-to-be friend your album, because we are no longer associates at this point. She never even liked your music until after the concert. She was only tagging along with me that night. She was a big JODECI fan. Mr. DeVante was her "MAN." But I believe that REAL MEN don't need to sleep with every woman who is ready and willing. But I guess she got what she wanted from you, and you got what you wanted from her. And as usual, I ended up the one with the broken heart.

"'Unfortunately yours, A used-to-be BIG fan.'"

I folded that one-page letter back and didn't know what to say. It seemed like she was writing it addressed to me. I felt all hot and anxious like I did as a kid when I knew that my father would be coming home to warm my ass for something that I had done at school or in the neighborhood.

I just shook my head and said, "Damn. That's a hell of a letter, man." In the back of my mind, I hoped that John would stop reading them damn letters if they would make us feel guilty like that. I wanted to stay away from that feeling.

However, John looked strong and determined, as if the letter had energized him.

He said, "I'm thinkin' 'bout writing a song about this."

When he said that, I knew that he was serious. I figured right off the bat that it would be a good song. There were plenty of musicians who could relate to that letter, and plenty of fans out there who could relate to it too.

I nodded my head and said, "That's a good idea, man." I didn't have shit else to say. I needed to hear that song as badly as John needed to write it.

It took John exactly two days before he called me over to his house to hear it. Tangela let me in and was all bubbly at the door, looking as sexy as she always looked. But I still couldn't believe that he had just moved her in like that. I guess she had come along at the right time. Lucky her.

Anyway she said, "Hey, Darin, are you ready to hear John's new hit? It's a sing-along song."

I looked at her and said, "A *sing-along song?*" What the hell was she talking about?

She said, "You'll see what I mean," and led me to John's new production room, a large study at the back of the house. It was where he would create the initial stages of his new music. John had plenty of money to buy more expensive and updated equipment, but his Korg keyboard was still of high quality, and he found no reason to stop using it.

He smiled at me as soon as we met eyes in the room.

He said, "You ready to hear it, man?"

I said, "Yeah, let me hear it."

He took a sip of water while Tangela sat down and was all smiles. I don't know if I was player hating or what, but I didn't really want her there. The first sign of someone's talent starting to go downhill is when they get those noncritical people around them who love everything that they do. That happy-about-anything attitude doesn't help you to create good music.

John pressed the play button on his keyboard and let the song rip through the excellent speakers that he had bought. He had the speakers panned to the left and right and high on shelves in the room. He had the balanced sound that you get from the best car systems.

I translated the bass line and the string chords that John used into words after I heard his lyrics. I had taught myself to do that in order to understand the soul of the music.

The bass line kicked in first, panned slightly to the left, and sang:

I-I-I a-a-ain't per-fect
no-o-o-bod-dy's in-vin-ci-ble
I-I-I a-a-ain't per-fect
so hear my words when I sing this song.

The strings filled in, slightly panned to the right, singing:

I-I-I connn-fesss.

John kept the time with a snare drum to the right, and no kick:

One, two, three, TAT, two three, four, TAT
One, two, three, TAT, two three, four, TAT

I thought, *So far, so good.* It had a definite groove and a thoughtful mood to it. Then John dropped the lyrics straight down the middle with a centered microphone:

A girl wrote me a let-ter
and it said that I broke her heart
she said she loved the way that I soothed her
she was in love with me from the ve-ry start.

Then she heard some things about me
the kind of things we do in the dark
I can't deny the rumors about me
all I can say is I'm not invin-n-n-ci-ble.

So I wrote this song of confess-sion
I hope she hears this les-son when I say . . .

The chorus kicked in with horns and a hard drum kick that bounced along as John sang the catchy lyrics:

Ain't no-body per-fect, ba-by
Ain't no-body per-fect, unt unh
Ain't no-body per-fect, mom-ma
Ain't no-body per-fect, at all
Ain't no-body per-fect, sis-stah
Ain't no-body per-fect, no
Ain't no-body per-fect, bro-ther
Ain't no-body per-fect, naw naw.

Then the music all came together in a short climax to start the next verse:

I-I-I CONNN-FESSS.

I met a wom-man who dug me
she said she loved that I was a Lov-ver-boy
so when she took a ri-i-ide in the lim-mo
she tried to play me like I was her damn toy.

I looked over at Tangela and she was still smiling her behind off and grooving. I wonder if it was *his* idea or *hers* to add her into the song.

I had to stop all the mad-ness
I said we need-ed to just slow things down
I never thought that I could offend her
I would have liked if she could have sta-a-ayed around.

So when she called me la-ter that evening
to say she made a mistake, I ha-a-ad to tell her.

Ain't no-body per-fect, ba-by
Ain't no-body per-fect, unt unh.

Tangela stood up and started clapping her hands and was sure enough singing along:

AIN'T NO-BODY PER-FECT, MOM-MA
AIN'T NO-BODY PER-FECT, AT ALL.

I thought, *What the hell?* and decided to join in with them:

AIN'T NO-BODY PER-FECT, SIS-STAH
AIN'T NO-BODY PER-FECT, NO
AIN'T NO-BODY PER-FECT, BRO-THER
AIN'T NO-BODY PER-FECT, NAW NAW.

I broke up laughing and told Tangela, "That's what you meant by a sing-along song."

She nodded and said, "Yeah, that's a hit. People love them kind of songs."

John said, "I'm gon' hook up with Tony and let him lay down the beat before I write the bridge in."

I nodded, thinking about the content of the song. I said, "That song is *perfect* for right now. With so many people passing the buck of responsibility with their art, they will immediately jump on that song and ride it to death. '*Ain't nobody perfect,*'" I mocked. That was exactly what John was doing by writing that song, passing the buck. And it wasn't as if I didn't like the song, because I did. I was just being a thoughtful manager.

John said, "But it's true, though. Nobody's perfect out here, man."

Tangela said, "Yeah," agreeing with him.

That was exactly why I didn't want her around.

I said, "Yeah, it may be true but it's a cynical way of looking at things."

John said, "Whatever, man. That's how I'm feeling and that's what I'm writing."

When Tony heard the song later on that week to lay his beats behind it, he smiled and said, "That's them kind of songs that drive you fuckin' crazy after a while. I can tell that I'm gonna be tired of hearing that shit already."

Tangela said, "But do you like it, though?"

John had the damn girl following us everywhere.

Tony smiled and nodded. He said, "Oh, it'll work. I got a perfect beat for that."

He laid the beat down immediately, kicking it off with a cymbal:

TISSS
DOOMP-DOOMP-TAT-DOOMP
DOOMP-DOOMP, TAT
DOOMP-DOOMP-TAT-DOOMP
DOOMP-DOOMP-DOOMTAT
TISSS . . .

Oh my GOD! When Tony laid that beat down and funked it up during the chorus, it was no doubt about it, we had another number one hit on our hands!

We went into the Old School Records studio to record it with a live bass and live string and horn samples to give it a real band effect. Tony came up with using a tambourine with the drum programming instead of the high hat, for a more live appeal.

He said, "That tambourine makes it so you can't fall asleep on it."

Then it was my turn to add an idea.

I said, "John, instead of adding your bridge, how about we just get a rapper to fill in for that? I mean, those guys have plenty of stuff to confess."

Kenny, our A&R guy, heard us talking things through, and he added his opinion.

Double K said, "Yeah, as long as they don't curse. We don't want to mess this song up with a bunch of editing."

Tony asked, "Well, what about when John says damn?" He had a big old smile on his face as if he was only joking.

Double K said, "Aw, he can get away with that. It's right in the groove of the song."

John wasn't jumping up and down about the rapper idea, though. He was hesitant.

He said, "I don't know about that rap part, man. I'm trying to keep this all R&B. I was gonna add something for my mother."

Double K killed that argument immediately. He said, "We'll just record two versions then, one with the rap and one without it."

John was still hesitant, but he couldn't really argue with that.

Then Tangela spoke up, right in the middle of things. John had even let her tag along to the studio.

She said, "I think a rap is a good idea. Like Darin said, those rappers are *big* perpetrators of doing wrong, and they're always talking about it. I'm sure that plenty of them would love to get on this song. Especially if we're gonna shoot a video for it. It's more exposure for them, and everybody *knows* that it's gonna be a hit."

No one had even said anything about a video yet. I tell you I didn't trust that damn girl.

Double K looked at her and asked, "So, are you gonna be the star of the video?"

He was reading Tangela as fast as I was.

She smiled all sly and said, "Only if John wants me to be." She had a nerve to squeeze up all close to him when she said it.

Tony looked at me and started laughing. Tangela's game plan was obvious to everyone in the room but John.

Then she threw in the killer. She said, "But I want to be the girl who writes the letter."

I smiled and thought to myself, *Of course you do, because you don't want everybody to see how you* really *were.*

When I got John alone for a minute, I told him, "Can you see what this girl is doing, man? I mean, she's definitely planning to make moves off of you, John. You can't see that with your own eyes? Everybody *else* can see it."

John said, "So what, man? Everybody wants *something*. *I* want her company. I mean, you expect for her to just sit around and do nothing? Why *can't* she be in the video?"

There was a time when John would listen to me at face value. I think that time was gone. Girls could get in the way and fuck up everything. The thing that made it worse was that Tangela was always stroking my ego and telling me how great a manager I was for John, and how our loyalty as friends was so honorable. She even had John saying that she liked me. That all made it harder for me to point things out about her.

I talked to Tony alone about our little problem with the girl, and he just shrugged his shoulders.

He said, "John'll get over it. He ain't married to this girl." He stopped and looked at me in a panic. "He ain't talkin' about fuckin' marrying her or no shit, is he?" By that time, Tony had a steady girl of his own, but it wasn't as if he was faithful to her, or at least not while we were out on the road. And Tony had sense enough not to allow his girl around the business.

I said, "Nah, he's not thinking about marrying her. At least I *hope* he's not."

John and I were both only twenty-one years old.

Well, Tangela got her video wish, and she was all up in the camera, looking like some nerdy good girl writing letters and whatnot while John sang to her. Another girl played Tangela's real-life role, looking like the sleazebag. An older sister played John's mom.

I wondered if Sister Williams would bother to watch it.

John sang, *"All I can dooo is love you as your child."*

I watched the video after we had wrapped up the taping and said to myself, *Damn, that's touching.* Then I thought about Tangela's part in it again.

I shook my head and mumbled, "Ain't that a bitch."

Tangela was about to make herself into a star. That video set her up like *the bomb!* She was the pretty, smart, good girl that every brother would want to have on the passenger side of his car.

I had to give it to the girl, though, she knew exactly how to play her role. John told me all about it in spite of himself.

The same night that we finished taping the video, they went back to the house together, and she flat out told him, "You're a musical genius, John." Nobody would deny that fact, but she was telling him that as a part of her setup.

John told me that she undid his pants and went down on him right there in the hallway to the bedroom. He said that he was holding up the walls with both hands like Sampson in the Bible, while Tangela did him. Before he reached a climax, she laid him down and stripped overtop of him while they were still in the hallway. While she rode him there, she whispered to him, "This is *yours*. This is *yours*, baby. *Oh God*, this is so *yours*, John."

I'm sitting there listening to this shit and wondering if I should have somebody to knock the girl off, or try to fuck her one time myself. I had a hard-on and couldn't help it. John had been telling me about showers with her, kitchen sinks, backyards, up-against-the-walls, doggy styles, and all kinds of other shit. Since I was the closest person in the world to him, it was natural for him to tell me, but he was only increasing my love-hate relationship with the girl. I mean, I even had dreams of fucking Tangela. John didn't seem to realize that he was torturing me!

I finally told him, "LOOK, MAN, I DON'T WANNA HEAR *SHIT ELSE* ABOUT THIS GIRL! SHE'S *YOUR GIRL*, BUT I DON'T HAVE TO *LIKE HER*, AND I DON'T WANNA HEAR *SHIT ABOUT HER* NO MORE, MAN! *DAMN!*"

I had a headache from thinking about that girl!

All John did was laugh at me, while his new single, *Nobody's Perfect*, went straight to number one on the R&B *and* pop charts, including the number one requested video. He was right up there with TLC in national popularity. John even liked the rap version of the song that we planned to drop later on to give it an extended life on the charts. And that's when everything got crazy, particularly for me as John's manager.

People started calling us every single day for interviews, appearances, performances, tour invitations, magazine photo shoots, community center functions, television and radio shows, and we even had a few Hollywood people offering us movie scripts for John to play singers in, of course.

I couldn't handle all of that shit. That's when I just stopped returning phone calls. I felt like that classic scene in *Jaws* when the guy stops for a minute and says, "You're gonna need a bigger boat." Shit got really crazy in a heartbeat, and we still had a whole album to record.

John couldn't even concentrate on his music with so much going on, so we had to select a few songs from other camps to get things rolling. And John didn't really like that idea.

He said, "Look, man, a lot of this other shit is gonna have to wait so I can record some of the things that *I* want to record. I don't like this other shit."

Double K sympathized, but Old School Records also wanted to get an album ready before the year was out, and we were already into November. John was the best thing they had going for them, and they were sweating him, and sweating *me* as his manager.

Kenny said, "Look, I don't like this any more than you do, John. I *love* your music. But think about the long term. This gives you an opportunity to stretch your own music for many more years without burning yourself out so soon."

He said, "We're not gonna let you record any garbage. We want this album to do better than the first."

Tony nodded his head and said, "I can agree with that." It was all about putting out steady product and getting paid for Tony. And it sounded like they were *all* counting on John to produce at the expense of his sound.

That made me nervous. I didn't feel that the added pressure was good for *me or* John.

I listened to a few of the new songs that we picked out, and they were not bad, they just were not songs that John had created.

I told him, "You just have to find a way to make these songs your own, man. Change them the way you need to or whatever, and let's just do it. Unless you really want to put this album off."

I thought about it, stopped, and changed my tone. I didn't want to push John into recording an album that he wasn't feeling. I said, "You know what? If you want to chill for a while, then just say the word, and we'll just have to slow down the heat. We'll work on another single, and just take our time with the album."

I thought about it for another minute and said, "In fact, that's what I think we should do. We should just tell them that you like your own sound, and we'll just put out another single to hold the public off for a while until we finish the album the right way."

Meanwhile, John and Tony produced three easy songs for the Philly girl trio Butterscotch. The next thing I knew, Tangela was spending most of her time with the girl group, and she ended up in *their* video. To top *that* off, since Butterscotch were having manager problems that I didn't want to get involved in, Tangela took the things that she had learned from being around me and John, and she messed around and became their manager. I couldn't believe that shit! That girl was making moves like a hurricane!

I asked John what he thought about that.

He smiled and said, "I'm happy for her. She's making her own money now."

I couldn't argue with that, but with Tangela spending more time on the business side of things with Butterscotch, John began to stray with groupies again. He was telling me that he just used it as energy, and that it helped to keep him focused.

A lot of women wouldn't understand that sentiment from a man, particularly with the sexual prowess that John had, but I understood it. Your sexuality becomes addictive. John had learned all kinds of new sexual tricks that Tangela had showed him, and he wanted to try out his new experience with other women. My crazy behind went ahead and rationalized that maybe that would be an end to Tangela if she caught him out there and chose not to deal with it, so I didn't plan to sweat him about it.

So John went out and got busy with a heavyweight sister inside a bathroom for kicks, like some kind of a perverse porno movie, and he actually told me that he was going to write a song about it.

I stopped him and said, "John, you gettin' out of hand, man. That shit sounds crazy. Don't do that."

He chuckled at it and said, "Nah, it wouldn't be straightforward like that, though. It would be more, like, a song for all of the women out there who are not skinny. I mean, you got some sisters, man, who were never meant to be small women. *We* know that just from growing up in the South. And I'm just doing this song for them."

When John had a new song on his mind, you couldn't stop him from doing the shit, so I just waited for him to call me up and see what it sounded like.

I went over to his house filled with skepticism when he told me that he was ready with it. He let me in the door himself with Tangela out doing her manager thing, and when we strolled into his production room at the back, he had a fat blunt all rolled up and ready to smoke.

I asked him, "What are you doing with that?" I thought I was there to talk business and listen to the new song.

"I came up with this idea when I was on, man," he told me.

John had never done that before. Getting high was for the *down*time, not for the *creative* time.

He said, "Nah, I finished the song already. I'm just gon' smoke this afterward." He laughed and said, "Maybe I might hear something extra, you know."

I laughed with him even though I didn't want to. Then he pressed play on his keyboard and sat back into a black leather lounge chair. He held an organ note as the introduction to the song before the bass line and snare drum kicked in. I translated the music into words after hearing his lyrics again.

The organ note squealed:

GIR-R-R-R-R-R-R-RLLLL.

When the organ note stopped, the bass line and an extra hard drum snare jumped right in on you:

I want to rock (SMACK) your world / to- (SMACK) night
I want to rock (SMACK) your world / to- (SMACK) night . . .

John had plenty of bottom to spare in his bass line with a smacking snare drum that cut straight through it. It was as if he was trying to simulate the weight of a big woman against the force that was needed to penetrate her.

Then he dropped the organ note back in on the groove:

GIR-R-R-R-R-R-R-RLLLL
I want to rock (SMACK) your world / to- (SMACK) night
I want to rock (SMACK) your world / GIR-R-R-R-R-R-R-RLLLL
I want to rock (SMACK) your world / to- (SMACK) night . . .

John started bragging before he even sang any lyrics to it.

"Tell me this ain't jumpin', D! Go 'head, tell me it ain't jumpin'!" he said to me with a big smile on his face. He even looked a bit ragged that day, like a mad scientist who had been working on something new. He needed a fresh haircut and a shave.

I grinned back at him with my head nodding to the music. It sounded like pure hip-hop.

I said, "I thought you told me that you wanted to keep things R&B. This sounds like one of those gangsta beats from Death Row or something. Dr. Dre and Snoop. It got that gangsta bounce to it. And Tony ain't even touched it yet."

John said, "Yeah, I've been inspired, man. I've been listening to Tupac's stuff and, um, Raekwon, the Chef, from the Wu-Tang Clan. And I, like, came up with my own ideas." He shook his head and added, "That boy, the RZA, is on some *shit*, man. He produces some crazy beats."

I smiled and said, "Yeah, I can tell that you were high and hangin' out with Tony now."

As a young drummer, Tony Richmond was into all of those hip-hop producers, and he was starting to produce beats for high prices like the rest of them. He was getting musical ideas from John, and it was obvious that John was getting ideas from him.

John went ahead and admitted it. He said, "Yeah, we were hanging out with the Roots in North Philly, man, just kickin' it about different musical ideas and stuff. And it's all about the truth, man. Honesty. In fact, I'm thinking about calling that the title of this next album, because everything on it will be about plain old honest truths in life, no matter who it offends."

He said, "Big mommas need love too, man. You know what I'm saying, D?"

I blew him off and responded, "Yeah, yeah, so let me hear the lyrics."

John got serious and stopped the song to start it over again:

GIR-R-R-R-R-R-R-RLLLL
I want to rock (SMACK) your world / to- (SMACK) night . . .

John came in with his lyrics, jumping right on the beat with attitude like he did with *Stylin' 'n' Profilin'*:

I'M A SOUTHERN MAAAN
AND I'M ON THE THINN SIIIDE
SO I LIKE THE GIRLS WITH BOD-DEES
AS WIDE AS SUN-SHINE.

I DON'T DISCRIM-MI-NATE
I JUST LIKE THE PANTS TIGHT
SO DON'T WORRY 'BOUT YOUR WAY-EIGHT
AND JUST FEED YOUR AP-PE-TITE.

A drum kick started the chorus with a guitar riff and the bass line mimicking John's lyrics:

BA-DOOMP
BIG MOMMM-MA
BIG MOMMM-MAAA
TO-NIGHT IS YOURRR NIGHT.

BIG MOMMM-MA
BIG MOMMM-MAAA
I'M GONNA TREAT YOU RIGHT.

BIG MOMMM-MA
BIG MOMMM-MAAA
'CAUSE GIRL YOU'RE OUT OF SIGHT.

BIG MOMMM-MA
BIG MOMMM-MAAA
TO-NIGHT IS YOUR BIG NIGHT, BIG GIRRRL.

OH YEA-AHHH
TO-NIGHT IS YOURRR NIGHT.

That's all I stood to hear. I cut him off before the next verse. The pop music success had obviously gone to John's head. I mean, the funk was there and the groove was nice, but this song definitely sounded forced to me. And as his manager, I was pretty frank with him about it.

I said, "John, that song sounds like shit. You can't record that, man. You trying to be a comedian?"

John smiled at me, leaned back in his chair, and lit his blunt. He said, "Aw'ight. We'll see. Wait till I hook up with Tony for the beats." He took a big tote on the blunt and held the smoke down.

I looked at my boy, looking all ragged like a mad scientist, and I just shook my head. I thought to myself, *This motherfucker's about to get out of hand*. I could feel it in my *bones*.

I changed the subject for a minute and asked him about his mom.

I said, "You think she's heard *Nobody's Perfect* yet?" *My* parents had heard it.

John blew out his smoke and responded in a raspy, smoke-filled voice, "I can't worry about that right now, man. I just gotta keep doing my thing . . . and I'll just let her do hers."

. . . of broken hearts, and games of play . . .

Tony heard that *Big Momma* song that John was working on, and he laughed his ass off.

He said, "John, what are you trying to be, funny now? This shit sounds crazy. You better read another fan letter and get some new ideas."

I laughed and told Tony, "That's what I was sayin', man. This song needs to be rethought or *something*." It was a rarity for me to be in agreement with Tony. I figured that had to mean something. John was losing it.

Tony said, "But I like the bass line. That bass line is the shit."

John said, "Look, can you hook up a beat to this song, or what?" He was determined to record that thing.

Tony listened to the bass line again and nodded his head in sync with the groove. He said, "The bass line is doing all of the work. You don't need much of a beat for this one. But I see why you wanted that heavy-ass snare in there. That bass is thick as gravy."

So Tony came up with something simple, using a shaker instead of a high hat:

Chicka-DOOMP-Chicka-SMACK
Chicka-DOOMP-Chic-DOOMSMACK . . .

Tony's beat was one of the simplest that he had done in a while, but when he added it to John's bass line—

I want to rock your world / to-night
I want to rock your world / to-night . . .

—the symmetry between the two was automatic. I grinned and shook my head. I thought, *Here we go again*. It was beginning to seem as if Tony's beats could cover up any of John's faults, and I was already so tired of hearing that *Nobody's Perfect* song that I changed the radio station every time that it came on. However, the public couldn't get enough of it.

Tony even covered up the ridiculous chorus to *Big Momma* using a multiple beat that was sure to be sampled by hip-hop acts. And John went ahead and forced us to record that song in the studio anyway. I told him to at least call it *Tonight Is Yours* instead of *Big Momma*. He reluctantly agreed to the title change, and once we got band players to add all of the pieces together, it didn't sound that bad anymore. I was still hesitant to put the thing out, though. I just didn't like the direction that John was going in. I still considered him to be more of a soul artist, and although a little bit of pop was good to keep the public's attention, I felt that too much of that pop shit would destroy John's musical validity.

I had a talk with Matt, the marketing director, and he said that he would push the song on the underground DJ circuit to see what the clubs thought about it, because it definitely had a street appeal to it. I didn't want the song out there at all, to be honest about it. But it took just a few weeks for the DJs to start rocking *Tonight Is Yours* in the clubs, and the next thing we knew, we had major requests for the song in the record stores and on the radio. So Old School Records was forced to rush into mass production with push from BMG to fill the orders.

Tony laughed in my face and said, "It's the beats, man. I told y'all that a long time ago. As long as John don't fuck up the song with his singin', which is hard for that nigga to do, my beats can carry us to the charts every time. And John got momentum now with everything he puts out."

Hell, I had to believe it. Women actually liked the damn song, and I'm talking about *the words*. Even skinny women were talking about it, because they felt left out. The guys were mostly rocking to John's bass line and Tony's drum programming.

Tangela didn't like the song, though. She tried to play it off with a laugh, but I could tell from how she talked about it that she didn't like it. It was just a right-in-your-face kind of song.

"So, I need to gain some weight for you, sweetie?" Tangela joked to John. I was over at the house when it happened.

John laughed it off and said, "It's just a song."

Since I was right there when she brought it up, I instigated my point and said, "Wait a minute. I thought you told *me* that everything you record on this second album is going to be about honesty, no matter *who* it offends." I quoted him word for word.

John said, "It *is* honest. Plenty of guys out here like fat asses. You know that, man. Don't even front like that, D."

I said, "But *you're* singing the words."

"Man, I'm singing the words for everybody. It's not just about me," he told me.

Tangela said, "Oh, so you *do* like big women then?"

John was in hot-ass water. Tangela was extra easy on the eyes, but she wasn't no *body* woman. She just had the face and the hair.

John gave up his argument and said, "Aw, fuck that, y'all not gon' sweat me over some damn song. It's just one damn song."

I got in the last word and said, "It was one damn song that you were just *dying* to record for some reason."

Tangela was *pissed.* She walked away and didn't say anything else about it, or at least while *I* was still there.

When she walked off, John was pretty mad about it too. He looked at me and said, "What were you trying to do, man?"

I chuckled at it and said, "My bad, man." John didn't think it was funny.

He said, "That shit wasn't cool, man. She already been sweatin' me about who I'm wit' all the time. Every time I gotta do something, she giving me the third fuckin' degree. I don't need this extra shit, man. What's wrong with you?"

I just started laughing harder. I said, "She's been pouring the heat on you lately, hunh?" What woman wouldn't? John was in a zone, and the musical award shows were coming up, with John being invited to perform. We also expected to collect awards there. John had best new male vocalist all on his mind.

I went back home that night and didn't think much about the brief argument that I had with John. And I had to get used to Tangela being around, because she was holding her ground with him. She was starting to become what they call a common-law wife and shit.

In the middle of the night, I woke up to a continuous buzzing of my apartment intercom system. Whoever it was, they were obviously determined to wake me up, so I finally climbed out of bed to shout into my intercom.

"Who is this?" I was pissed the hell off when I said it too. I had enough damn disturbances during the daytime with people calling me about John's music career.

"Yeah, it ain't funny no more *now*, is it?"

I said, "John? What the hell is up, man? You just did this shit to get back at me?"

He said, "Let me up, man."

I buzzed him in and waited. John walked in looking as dog mad as I was.

I asked him, "What's up, man? What's up?" I didn't feel like having any conversation at three in the morning.

John took off his black leather coat and sat down, smelling like weed.

I said, "You were smoking in the car on the way over here?"

He nodded his head. He said, "Yeah, man, that stereo system is a *beast*, too."

John had recently bought himself a black 500 Series Mercedes-Benz. Tangela, of course, had taken the Lexus off his hands, and I was looking to update the Maxima with a Ford Explorer. I just hadn't bothered to buy it yet. With all of John's record points, music publishing rights, and new pop hits to boot, the money would roll in like water under a bridge. I hadn't even gotten a chance to spend much of mine. John was always treating me to shit.

I asked him again, "So, what's up, man?"

"I ain't feel like stayin' in the house tonight," he told me.

"So, you just jump up and come over to my fuckin' place in the middle of the night?" I asked him. Trust me, you need all of the sleep you can get when you manage a hot talent in the music industry.

John smiled and said, "This used to be *my* place."

"Well, it ain't your place now."

"Is my name still on the lease?"

Technically it was, because I hadn't bothered to take it off.

I said, "What are you trying to tell me? It's time for me to buy a new house somewhere like you got?"

He started laughing. He said, "Yeah, spend some money, man. Stop acting like a country boy."

I smiled and said, "Nigga, please. Don't start talking that Tony shit to me, man."

John said, "Well anyway, Tangela wouldn't let me sleep tonight because of your ass talking about that new song. She was saying, 'So, what girl *inspired* you to write *this* song, since obviously *my ass* ain't that big?'" He was emphasizing his words just like Tangela would do.

I couldn't help but laugh. I said, "That's what you get for having her around so much, man. She's all up in your head now on everything that you do."

He said, "Yeah, well, I'm up in *your* head then, because *you* started that shit tonight."

I said, "Aw'ight, well, you can go to sleep on the sofa." I wasn't planning to stay up with him over that boyfriend-girlfriend drama shit. I was going back to bed.

John said, "Where you going?"

"Where it *look* like I'm goin'? I'm goin' back to bed, man."

He stood up and started following me. He said, "No you're not, man. If *I* can't sleep, then *you're* not sleepin' either."

I said, "You can sleep. Take your ass back to the sofa." I meant that shit too!

Then the telephone rang. I stopped and asked myself, *What the hell is going on tonight?*

I went to answer the phone with John still breathing down my neck. I pushed him away, and he tried to act as if he wanted to resist me. I just looked at him as if he was crazy. I mean, John had picked up a good ten pounds or so, but I still had him by at least twenty, and he was nowhere near ready to handle me in something physical.

I said, "Man, you better cut it out and stick to that singing shit before you get body slammed in here."

He just laughed it off.

"Hello," I answered the phone.

"Darin, is John over there?" It was Tangela.

I smiled, thinking about lying to her to make her jealous. But I didn't. I had caused enough trouble as it was.

I said, "Yeah, he's here," and handed John the telephone.

He answered, "Hello."

I started walking toward my bedroom again when I heard John say, "I'm not acting like a kid."

I smiled, walked into my room, and shut my bedroom door. I climbed back in bed and could still hear John loud and clear out in the other room.

"Look, I don't ask you who *you* fuckin'. I got faith in you enough to give you that respect . . . Because I don't feel like discussing this shit at the house . . . I *do* care about it, I just don't sweat you like that. If you ask *me*, *you* the one up here acting *childish*."

I rolled over and stared up at the ceiling. They were ruining my sleep.

John said, "Aw'ight, well, look, you want me to write a fucking song about you? Would *that* make you happy? *Damn!* . . . I *know* you care about me. I care about you too. But you can't keep sweatin' me about this shit. You know how the business is. You a *manager* now, ain't you?"

I started shaking my head and mumbled, "I can't believe this shit."

When their phone call was finally over, John strolled up into my room and said, "I'm going back home, man. That girl love me, man. I gotta write a song about *her* now. She just a little bit pushy, that's all. She used to having her way, D."

I said, "That's nice to hear, now go on back home, man."

"I'm sayin', man, I'm trying to talk to you. I'm expressing myself right now."

I said, "Nah, that's the weed expressing *itself*."

John paused for a minute. He said, "You want me to go get you some so we can talk then? I got some more in the car."

I said, "John, no, man. I want you to go home to your wife."

He stopped and said, "Wife? I ain't married, man. I ain't even trying to think about that. It seem like, if I got married, I could probably only write about family stuff or something in my music. You know what I mean? I would have to, like, protect my family image."

God dammit! I thought to myself. I had just sparked a new conversation.

John went on and said, "I think that artists should stay single until they don't have it in them no more, man. And then when you finally get married and stuff, you'll be, like, tired of the single life anyway. You know what I mean, D?"

He took a seat on the edge of my bed like my mother would do.

I took a deep breath and said, "John, you determined to torture me tonight, aren't you?"

He said, "Nah. I'm not torturing you. I'm your boy. I love you, man. We from back North Cacalacki together. We went to church together, man. We know each other's families. I mean, you don't *feel* like I'm torturing you, do you? I mean, I'm just trying to express myself, man. That's what the music is all about anyway."

He said, "I think, like, if I had had a chance to express myself more when I was growing up instead of my mom sweating me all the time and shit, maybe I wouldn't have that need to express myself so much now. So, like, in a way, I owe my mom for making me as creative as I am about my music, man. Does that make any sense to you, D?"

I said, "Yeah, man, that makes sense. I thought about that a long time ago." He had me wide awake. What were best friends and managers for if I couldn't hear him out?

He said, "I wonder if my father was a musician or something, man. And like, my mom fucked him on his tour in Atlanta or something, 'cause she's from Atlanta. And then she got pregnant, and instead of her having an abortion, she moved to Charlotte to keep me, and got all religious and shit. Because I talked to my other family members, and they all tell me that my mom wasn't always religious like that."

After a while, I just listened to him as he went on.

He said, "Ain't that some wild shit, man."

"Yeah," I told him, "that is wild."

He said, "I just hear music in my mind, man. It's like, it just comes to me. And these reporters and interview people just don't get that shit. It's like, they don't understand the process of it. You know what I mean, D? I think more of these reporters need to visit recording studios so that they can understand how we put this music together, man. 'Cause some of their questions are stupid as shit. I mean, do they set out to ask you that dumb shit on purpose?"

"Dumb shit like what, John?"

He paused and thought of a question. He had been asked plenty of questions after the release of that *Tonight Is Yours* song.

He said, "Does your music intend to make a human statement?" in a reporter's voice, all crisp, clear, and direct.

I started laughing. He was making this up and overdramatizing the questions.

He responded in his own drawn voice, real calm. He said, "Well, I *am* human, and every time we open our mouths we make statements, don't we? So why wouldn't it be the same with my music?"

I started laughing again, but John had never been that sarcastic in his real responses in interviews. He was always respectful and courteous just like he was raised to be.

In the middle of my laugh, my phone rang again.

John said, "I'll get it, man."

He leaned over to my bedroom phone on the nightstand and answered it.

"Darin Harmon's residence." He said, "Oh, I'm on my way. I was just having a conversation with my manager. My boy. You understand that, don't you? I mean, *we sleep together*, so we got all day to talk."

I couldn't stop laughing. That boy was *tripping* that night.

He said, "Aw'ight, aw'ight, I'm coming right now. Damn."

He hung up the phone and smiled at me. He said, "My dick startin' to get hard already, D. I know she ain't got no clothes on waiting for me. That's how she makes up, with the pussy. She *like* to fuck, man, ever since that first night when she called me back at the hotel. And you was trying not to let her up. You could have fucked up the best pussy I ever had in my life, man. I mean, I was a phone call away from missing her that night."

I shook my head and said, "Go 'head home, man. Go 'head. You had her address and phone number anyway."

He said, "Yeah, but I didn't know that she could *fuck* like that, though. I had to find that out when I met her. And you almost messed it up."

I said, "Okay, John, but you got her now. So go on home and get her. Good night, man."

The drama with John and Tangela was far from over. He hadn't started working on a song for her fast enough, I guess, and he heard it through the grapevine that a television show wanted him on to talk about his new single, *Tonight Is Yours*, with a bunch of oversized women. I didn't take the show seriously myself, so I hadn't bothered to call the producer back.

Anyway, John accepted their invitation to a taping in New York, despite the fact that Tangela didn't want him to do it.

He said, "Look, man, I can't let her start to get in the way of my music. She just gon' have to learn to understand that." He looked at me and added, "*You* too." He seemed determined to spite us all for that song. I had another thought about it in mind. With John being bullied by his mother for so long before he finally broke away from her, he was going to make sure that Tangela and I wouldn't sink our teeth in him the same way, even if he had to spite us on purpose. And he continued to soldier his music as a scapegoat. I didn't believe he liked that one song all that much. He just wanted to be plain old hardheaded, if you asked me.

So Tony and I ended up sitting front and center in the audience in New York. We were both trying our hardest not to break up laughing at these extra large women expressing how *Tonight Is Yours* made them feel, versus the smaller women in the audience. It was all for the ratings game too, embarrassingly. Not that I was making fun of oversized women, because the women in my own family were not exactly skinny, but these people on the show were all putting shame to themselves just to get on TV for an hour. I couldn't even believe that John wanted to do that to himself, but I couldn't stop him. And Tony was enjoying the spectacle.

This one sister had an ass so fat that three guys could dance with her from the back and all get an equal serving.

She stood up in front of the host, who was holding the microphone and her name card, and said, "I like the song myself. And I'm proud of what *I* got. And I make *sure* that everybody know it, too."

With the giant caboose that she had on her, there was no way in the world that anyone could miss it. Tony couldn't stop laughing. It was all funny to him.

A second girl, who was only half the first girl's size, stood in front of the microphone and said, "The beat was nice, but I felt that the lyrics were average. I mean, the song sounded honest and all, but the lyrics weren't all that creative. I think the music made the song."

Tony was just *dying* to hear that. He smiled and started nodding his head. He said, "Yeah, the beat was bangin'."

The host responded, "But isn't Loverboy's song doing the same thing that so many other popular songs do in objectifying a woman's physical appearance? I mean, what happened to getting to know the person inside regardless of how big or how small they are?"

Of course, her audience started clapping on cue to every point the host made, right. I mean, that shit was all so damn phony. And John was sitting up on stage putting himself through that foolishness.

He said, "Everybody's objectified. You think that women's songs don't objectify the men? I used to get teased for being thin. And there weren't any women writing songs about guys like me. Nor were they writing about guys who were *short, light, and ugly.*"

The host had to laugh at that one herself.

She said, "So, John, are you trying to somehow make up for your own lack of size by now singing to full-figured women?"

Tony started laughing again.

I was thinking that Tangela would be somewhere watching the show when it aired. John had to be real careful how he answered that question. I felt nervous for him, and as if I was being asked the question myself.

John said, "I have all kinds of songs that deal with all kinds of situations and all kinds of women. I just felt that this song would include the sisters who we don't often see in the videos."

The host jumped right on him and said, "Ah, including *your* videos."

Her audience laughed, mocking him.

John took it all in stride and said, "Exactly."

Then she asked him, "So, is there going to be a video for this song too?" She had a big smile on her face, preparing for the drama.

John answered, "This song was released underground as a test to see how people would respond to it because my label didn't want it to offend people. But it ended up doing a lot better than we thought it would do. And at this point, it's too late to do a video."

Good answer, I thought to myself. John had handled himself on the show well, by telling the simple truth like he always did. Then they played different parts of the song during the television breaks as the conversations continued.

Tony said to me, "If people didn't know about the song before, it's sure gon' get enough exposure now. Or at least to the people who watch this show. And that's more money for us."

I had to agree with him on that. So John getting on that talk show wasn't a bad idea after all. Until it aired and Tangela confronted him about it. She wanted to know once and for all if he was satisfied with her. Instead of making it easy on himself and just telling the girl what she wanted to hear to keep the peace, John took the hard route.

I asked him, "So what did you tell her?"

He said, "I just told her that we're satisfying each other right now."

I said, "But she didn't ask you that. She asked you if *you* were satisfied."

He looked at me as if he didn't understand the question. "Satisfied with what?"

I said, "With her."

"How you mean? Sexually?"

"Yeah, *something.*" He was making *me* feel frustrated, so I could just imagine how *Tangela* felt. John refused to be boxed in.

I broke down and asked him, "Do you think this girl loves you, man?" I didn't think she did at first, but her act was even fooling me if she didn't love that boy by then. I mean, they had only known each other for half a year, but she was taking herself through an awful lot of turmoil for someone who *didn't* love John. She *had* to feel something.

John said, "If she does, then she has to just hang in there for me then. Because I'm not thinking about gettin' all that deep right now, man, you know . . ."

I cut him off before he could even say it. I said, "Yeah, you're all about your music right now, right?" I was tired of hearing that shit from John myself, to be frank. And I wasn't even one of his girls.

Sure enough, Tangela called me up about it and wanted to get all up inside John's head from what I knew as his lifelong friend.

I said, "Tangela, to be honest with you, John never really had a girlfriend like that."

She didn't believe me. She said, "He didn't have not *one* girlfriend *ever* in his life?"

I said, "Nah. He was always chasing girls that he couldn't get. And then when he started gettin' them, he had already discovered a *new* girlfriend."

Tangela caught on and said, "His music." *She* knew his game. She said, "Well, why he ask me to move in with him then?"

I didn't want to answer that. She had just caught John at a time of low, and she had put the whip appeal on him. She became a pleasant security blanket for him, but she just couldn't try to wrap him too tightly or he would wrestle off the sheets. I stared at the phone, not wanting to hurt her feelings with that truth. And to think that I didn't trust or like the girl at first. By then I sympathized with her, I really did. She was just barking up the wrong tree.

Out of the blue, she sighed and said, "John's birthday is February eighth. He's an Aquarius. An air sign. And that's just what he's doing, moving like the wind. He can get real hectic sometimes, too. He fuckin' snaps out on you."

I wasn't much into that astrology shit, but I said, "Yeah, he does have those mood swings. He's always been that way."

I asked her, "Well, where is he now?" He obviously wasn't with her.

She said, "With Tony. They're supposed to be working on new tracks for the album."

I smiled and chuckled. They were probably high, too. I just said, "Oh."

She said, "So he doesn't tell you everything either?"

I said, "Sometimes he does, sometimes he doesn't."

"What he tell you about me?"

I thought about all of those sexual conversations and started laughing. She didn't want to know that, and I told her so.

"You don't want to know that."

"Yes I do. Tell me."

I thought about it and shook my head. I knew better than that. Although John had a lot more women than I could ever *hope* to have with his whole Loverboy bag, I wasn't exactly an amateur with women. You just didn't tell women about male conversations. That was player rule number one.

Tangela figured that out and changed the question. She said, "Well, tell me this then, Darin, how come *you're* not attached to a woman?"

I was caught off guard with that. I laughed again, this time nervously. Was she coming on to me, or was I just reading things wrong?

I said, "Well . . . I think I've been a little caught up in this music thing, too. I mean, I'm not saying that as an excuse, I'm just saying that I guess I've been thinking more about John than about me lately. I mean, that's my job, and . . . you know, John's my boy."

My shit sounded *weak*, as weak as John's explanation. There had been plenty of women who I could have become serious about. I was a big-ass hypocrite, and Tangela was calling me out on it.

She laughed at me and said, "Mmm hmm, tell me about it. It's all the damn same." Then she leveled with me. She said, "Darin, I have a little confession to make."

My heart started beating fast. *Oh shit!* I thought to myself. What is she about to tell me?

I opened my mouth real slowly and said, "Yeah."

She said, "I've been thinking lately that . . . you know, John *is* younger than me, and maybe I need to be involved with someone who's older. I mean, he's just not ready for anything serious right now."

I breathed easy again. Because if Tangela was to tell me that she had been thinking about me . . .

Anyway, I took another breath and said, "Nah, just hang in there with him. I mean, y'all only known each other for a minute. Stick around for at least *five* and see what happens."

She started laughing. She said, "I like that. That was cute. But I just don't know anymore. I mean, with me managing Butterscotch now, I'm getting a little bit busy too. And I just need to have a clear conscience to concentrate on them the way that I need to. I can't be stressing over my own personal problems while trying to manage them."

Could you believe this shit?! The next thing I knew, I was trying to beg Tangela to *stay* after wanting her ass *out* so badly. I just didn't know how John would take it if she left him. She had *me* convinced!

I said, "Nah, just . . . you know, give him *three* minutes then. Aw'ight? Just give him three minutes." I was trying to make it all humorous, but I was really getting nervous about it.

She laughed, but the situation wasn't funny anymore.

She said, "Darin, I've already *given* him three minutes. You don't *know* how much of myself I've given to him."

I smiled and thought, *Yes I do, too,* but I still couldn't tell her what I knew.

I said, "Look, just take time out to think about things. All right? Can you do that? Because I can't get off of the phone with you like this. And as John's boy and manager, I have to look out for his best interests. And you're in his best interest right now."

Tangela paused and said, "Yeah, *right now.* And that's just what I'm having problems with. I feel, like, I'm wasting valuable time with him. And the longer I stay . . . the harder it will get for me."

SHIT! I had said the wrong FUCKING words! I was about to have a headache. That's why weed was smoked so much. It wouldn't make the stress disappear, but it let you put the shit on hold until you could figure out a logical solution for it. Which most of the time, you didn't. You just find a way to move along . . . And then you get high again.

When I hung up the phone with Tangela with no promises from her, I felt severely pained inside, and it wasn't even happening to me. I mean, if I could have written a song, I would have had a number one hit on my hands. But that was for John to do.

A week after I had talked to Tangela on the phone, my boy John brought me the bad news at the apartment. He said, "She's moving to New Jersey, man. Upstate."

I tried to act surprised and asked him, "Who?"

John said, "You know who I'm talking about, man. Tangela. She said she moving to Orange County or something."

I asked him, "Why? Does she even know anybody up there? She got family up there or something?"

He said, "Nah. Her *and* Butterscotch are moving up there. They're just trying to be closer to the studios in New York and stuff, you know. They feel like Philly got them on lockdown or something. So they all wanted to relocate to keep things rolling for them."

I said, "Oh, so they coming back then." I tried to make it seem as if it was just a quick business move for Tangela and Butterscotch that wasn't permanent.

John didn't respond to it. He said, "I gotta think about finishing my own album anyway. Me and Tony ready to lay down like three or four songs now."

I had heard a few of the things that they had been working on. Tony was starting to get more of the production credit by telling *John* things to play, while coming up with hook lines of his own that fit his beats. Tony's productions had more of a street funk edge that would attract the hip-hop lovers to John's music.

They recorded two of Tony's ideas in the same day. The first song was called *All Night Situation* that used a funky horn sample with those hypnotic beats of Tony's.

The beat rocked: *"BaDOOMP-BaDOOMP, TAT / BaDOOMP-BaDOOMP, TAT . . ."*

The horns blew: *"WE GOT ALL NIGHT! . . . WE GOT ALL NIGHT! WE GOT ALL NIGHT!"*

The bass line crooned: *"All night sit-u-a-a-a-tionnn."*

And John laced the lyrics: *"So I hope you got your rest last night / 'cause good love ain't got no stoplight."*

The second song was called *Keep It Cool*, where Tony had a funky drum solo off the hook.

John sang, *"When shit gets wa-a-ay too hot / I just keep it cool."*

Then Tony would go off on a tangent with the drums:

BaDOOMP-BOOM, BOOM-TAT-BOOM
BaDOOMP, BOOM-BOOM-TAT
BaDOOMP-BOOM, BOOM-TAT-BOOM
BaDOOMP, BOOM-BaDOOMP-TAT . . .

It sounded like a throwback to the seventies funk when the drummers just went *OFF!* And Tony was not sampling anything. He was using drum machines based off his drum set. He had, like, five different drum machines by then, collecting all of the different drum sounds that he could get. The boy was getting complicated! And PAID!

Then John just up and went AWOL on us. He lost his passion for the music and didn't feel like recording anything. I knew that Tangela leaving him like she did would have an effect on him. It was only a matter of time.

I went over to the house to talk to John about it, and he looked ragged again, uncleaned and unshaved.

He said, "What fuckin' difference does it make? I'm not taking a photo shoot. We not doing any concerts right now. I ain't got no steady woman. And my *momma* don't even love me. So what the fuck I need to look good for, man?"

He wasn't even high when he was saying this.

I shook my head and tried to take it lightly. I said, "Your momma love you, man. You *crazy!* You wanna call her up right now and ask her?"

He said, "For what? So she can tell me to go back to church and pray? Nah, I don't feel like that shit right now, man. Leave me alone about that."

I was really over there on business, to tell you the truth. We were all on the move to finish that damn album, and the heat was all coming down on me.

John caught me before I could even bring that up, though. He said, "And I don't feel like making no music right now either. So don't even talk to me about it."

Since I was his boy *before* I was his manager, I was stuck. What was more important, our friendship or the music business? . . . I chose our friendship and left John alone about it. But it wasn't an *easy* decision to make.

Tony called me up at the apartment and asked me, "What's up with John, man? You better *talk* to that boy! We got *money* on the line here. We gotta finish this fuckin' album!"

Kenny and Matt even called me up from Old School Records. "Is everything all right with John? We haven't seen him in the studio lately. What's going on?"

FUCK! John was driving *me* crazy! I started thinking that I should have forced his ass to finish that damn album the first time the issue came up, and before he recorded that damn *Big Momma* song and sent Tangela packing with Butterscotch.

You talk about having *stress*! That shit was unbearable as a manager because it wasn't anything that I could control. I couldn't *make* John sing even if I wanted to. I felt helpless, and as if I needed some outsider to help run the show, and that would mean that I wasn't a capable manager for John.

To make things worse, instead of holding it down, I fucked around and got high, invited a girl over, and took it all out on her in the bedroom.

When I finished with her, she sat up in the bed buck naked and asked me, "Is everything okay? You fucked me like you were mad at me or something."

And I *was* mad, but I wasn't mad at her. I was just mad at my situation. I was mad at John.

I said, "That motherfucker left me out to dry, man. He left me out to dry."

I was still high, so she had no idea what I was talking about. *I* didn't even realize what I was saying.

She said, "*Who* left you out to dry? What are you talking about? And why take that out on *me*?"

The girl was a prisoner of war that night. I looked at her, while still under the influence of the weed, and I got real cold on her. I said, "If you motherfuckin' girls knew how to act and understood shit, this shit never would have happened."

She looked at me and got real quiet. She stood up from the bed and nodded her head. She said, "I think it's time for me to leave now. Because somebody in here just lost their *damn mind*."

I was on a roll that night, man, talking plenty of shit. I said, "Yeah, that's what y'all do best. You know how to leave a motherfucker, you just don't know how to *stay*."

She started putting her clothes on in a hurry and said, "Because we're not *dogs!*"

I really went overboard that night, man, and I couldn't even stop myself. I said, "You could have *fooled me.* I just fucked you like one, didn't I? I called you over here, and you came right over and took your clothes off and got in the position."

That girl made it to the front door and yelled, "FUCK YOU, *AND* YOUR MOTHER! *BITCH!*" and slammed my door when she left.

I went numb after that. I sat there naked and thought to myself, *Damn! What the fuck am I doin'? This shit is crazy! Why did I just do that? WHY? Because I* could?

I was drunk with power, man. *Drunk* with it! And all I was was a manager.

I took that whole incident that night and blamed it on the weed. That was it. I wasn't going to smoke anymore. I also had some apologizing to do. But that girl didn't want to hear *shit* from me. And I couldn't blame her.

Out of the blue, John came out of his slump with a fresh haircut, a shave, and some new ideas from his production room at home. He didn't tell anyone what he had been working on either, including me. He just told us all to meet him down at the studio. We had a bass player, an electric guitar with one of those distortion machines, a second keyboard player, and John told Tony to bring his live drum set instead of using the drum machines.

Tony said, "John wants that live band effect, hunh?"

They were all excited to try it with him. They just knew that he was good. A genius. And I didn't have anything to say about it. I just wanted that whole album process to be over with before I did something *else* crazy. I had found out that *I* wasn't perfect either. How you respond to stress tells you a lot about yourself. And I didn't like what I had found out.

So John got ready at the studio with his Korg keyboard and stand and explained what he wanted from everyone. He played a string chord that I translated once I heard his lyrics:

Thaaat's whaaat sheee wannnnnn-teddd . . .

He told the other keyboard player to mimic his string chord.

He said, "You can play with it and change it up a little bit, but just don't get too far away from it." John told everyone else to follow the keyboard player's lead with plenty of space as he set up at the microphone to sing his lyrics.

So the keyboard played the string chord: *"Thaaat's whaaat sheee wannnnnn-teddd . . ."*

Tony came in with slow drums: *Tic-Doomp-Tic-TAT / Tic-Doomp-Tic-TAT . . .*

The electric guitar whined like a crybaby: *"That's what she wants to hear."*

The bass player dropped in a deep *"She wants . . . She wants . . ."*

Then John brought it all together with dramatic, rising and falling lyrics:

> *Can you IM-MAGINE ALL your dreams come true*
> *with everyTHING you ev-ver wan-ted*
> *and all the MON-NEY THAT your eyes could see*
> *well that's the KIND OF LIFE that's been revealed to me.*
>
> *But SOME OF US are satisfied with simple things*
> *and a MAN WHO LIVES his life with dignity.*
>
> *She said she wanted my HON-NEST-STEE-EEE*
> *(Thaaat's whaaat sheee wannnnnn-teddd . . .)*
> *what she wanted was HON-NEST-STEE FROM ME*
> *(Thaaat's whaaat sheee wannnnnn-teddd . . .)*
> *she wanted my HON-NEST-STEE-EEE*
> *(Thaaat's whaaat sheee wannnnnn-teddd . . .)*
> *she wanted some HON-NEST-STEE FROM ME*
> *and NOW, she's gone away . . .*

DAMN! I felt him! Everybody in the room did. That song was bad! I mean *BAD!*

They ran through a couple of practice runs, and then John said, "Okay, we sound good now." He looked to the engineer's soundproof glass with his microphone still on and said, "Okay, let's get this one and just keep going with it."

I was inside the booth with the engineer. He said, "We gotcha. All of the sound levels are right on." Then he got those million levers and buttons ready to record the first take.

John jumped into his song with full emotion while the band followed right after him. When he reached the breakdown of the song, after he had sung about all of the things that he had to offer the woman in his last verse, John went into overdrive and had a tantrum with the microphone. He actually backed up from the microphone stand and started screaming and shit:

BUT SHE DIDN'T WANT THOSE THINNNGS
NO-O-O WAAAY
SHE JUST WANTED MEEE
SHE JUST WANTED MEEE
SHE JUST WANTED MEEE
TO BE STRAIGHT WITH HER . . .

SHIT! I was thinking. *He's gonna blow motherfuckers away with this song!* And I'm sorry for all of the profanity about it, but there was just no way to explain what John was doing without having some raw expression. I couldn't say that it was just GREAT! Because it was *more* than just GREAT. It was *THE MOTHERFUCKIN' SURE-SHOT SHIT! That's* what it was. *Seriously!*

The engineer started checking the microphone levels to see if something had gone wrong. You couldn't just scream into the microphones like that without distorting something.

But the engineer checked the sound levels and said, "*Fuck!* That was some *heavy shit!*" He was a middle-aged white guy with long hair like an old-school rock band member.

He looked at me and stood up. He said, "I gotta go take a smoke."

I started laughing. I didn't know what had just happened, but I know it felt good.

When they finished that first take, the engineer told them, "I need you guys to stop and come in here to hear this."

They all walked in. We listened to the song three straight times from the engineer's booth. There was no distortion at all with John's microphone when he had his tantrum, and he had gone right to the top on the sound scale. Another eighth of an inch would have ruined it.

The engineer kept checking all of the levels to make sure. Then he shook his head and told all of us, "Guys, I'm not *touching* this. If you want to record it again, then you get another engineer in here. That was just a *perfect damn take*, with *real* emotions to it. I was not prepared for that. This is . . . this is . . ." He just stopped himself and walked out, saying, "I gotta go take another smoke."

Everybody laughed but John, happy as hell in there. We all knew that we had just recorded something special. But John was still pretty wired about taking care of business.

He said, "Well, if that's it, then that's it. But I got another song that I want to do. So nobody leave. And if you got other things you planned to do, then cancel your plans, and I'll pay you extra. And y'all *know* I got the money."

Tony said, "Shit, you da boss in here, man."

John nodded and said, "All right then. I'm gon' take me a walk outside, and then we're gonna do the second song."

When John left, Tony smiled and said, "I can't *wait* till we go on tour with *this* shit. I mean, they not gon' just throw *panties* up on stage, motherfuckers gon' get *naked* like in that movie *Caligula!*"

Everybody started laughing while Tony continued. He said, "John was home practicing that shit, man. He knew exactly how far he had to stand away from the mike for that shit to work. And he made it happen. *On the first damn take!*"

Tony started shaking his head with a big grin. He said, "Man, I gotta hurry up and have me some kids so I can tell them that I *played* with this motherfucker."

He told his own story and said, "'*Who, Loverboy?* Shit, we made *music* together. *I* broke that motherfucker in at the Zanzibar Blue, back in nineteen ninety-four. God dammit, I'm telling you the *truth, boy!* Your father ain't *drunk!* I ain't drunk at all! I *knew* that motherfucker! John *Loverboy* Williams, from Charlotte, North Carolina.'"

Tony was so excited that he didn't stop talking until John got back from his walk. By then, the engineer and the rest of the band were all ready to start the second song. *Honesty*, the title song of Loverboy's sophomore album, was a wrap.

As soon as John walked back into the studio, Tony looked at him and screamed, *"BUT SHE DIDN'T WANT THOSE THINNNGS!"*

We all laughed again before we got back to business. Even John chuckled at it. And me? I was pretty much speechless. I just wanted to hear more music, like everyone else in the room. John had blown us away!

VERSE 18

... I couldn't stop him ...

John's second song that day, *Come Back to Me*, used a musical lead-in from *Honesty*, and then they all did an instrumental track called *Space and Time*. It all felt like an old-school jam session where the music never ended, producing three great songs in one long day.

John sang real calmly on *Come Back to Me*, as if he wanted to sweet-talk the girl back into his life:

So tell me what I gotta do to make you come back to me ...

Then, on *Space and Time*, he filled in with subtle teases of passion:

It feels so good right there
don't mooove, don't move ...

After the studio session, I walked John to his car and was proud of him. He really knew what the hell he was doing with his music regardless of what was going on in his life. He obviously could handle the stress a lot better than I could. But when we arrived at his Mercedes-Benz, he had another fat blunt of weed rolled up and ready to be smoked.

I said, "John, I think we both need to cool out with the weed, man. That shit is becoming a crutch."

John flat out ignored me. He climbed into the driver's seat of his car, closed the door, and rolled down the window to look at me. He smiled and said, "It's Philly time," with the blunt and his car lighter in hand. He lit up and immediately started smoking.

What more could I say? I asked him, "You want me to drive, man?" It was close to ten o'clock at night. We had all been in the studio since early that morning, making new music, listening to it, and mixing it down for tapes to take home. Everybody wanted an original copy of the studio session as if it would be legendary. John didn't need to be driving and smoking after all of that. I wanted to be around him a little longer that night anyway. We needed to talk.

He said, "Get on in and drive then, man. I can get my smoke on better that way." He climbed over into the passenger seat, and I got behind the wheel of the Benz. But instead of talking about John's need to get high, I asked him if he had read any more of his fan letters recently. I needed to get him thinking more positively about the audience he had inspired.

He grinned, holding down the weed smoke. He let down his passenger side window to blow it out.

He said, "Man, after we put out that *Nobody's Perfect* song, I've been gettin' a thousand fuckin' letters a day. I can't even answer that shit no more. I was letting Tangela read some of them for *her* kicks."

I laughed at it. "They all want you to write songs for 'em, hunh?" I asked him.

He nodded and said, "Yeah, man. Like I'm a photographer now, and everybody wants me to snap their picture. I'd mess around and run out of film trying to do that."

I had no idea where I was driving, I was just cruising on Delaware Avenue past the clubs and the warehouses of South Philadelphia.

John asked me, "Do you ever get real horny when you high, man?"

I started laughing again. I said, "Of course. But it depends on what frame of mind I'm in."

He nodded and said, "I know. Sometimes I want to fuck, sometimes I don't." Then he smiled. He said, "Sometimes I just want my dick sucked. You ever heard that Eddie Murphy song *Put Your Mouth on Me?* Me and Tony were tripping off that song one day," he told me with a cough and a chuckle. The weed smoke was sinking deep into his lungs, and into his mind. That weed was *strong*, too! I could smell it. I was tempted to even try some of it. But I had to ignore the temptation and retain my sanity that night.

I wanted to tell John to get his act together and chill with all of his success, but the boy was still able to make *great* music! What if he was the perfect gentleman who didn't smoke or anything? Would that make him a better musician? I seriously doubted it. Most people who worked with him didn't see his smoking as a problem. He didn't seem to respond to it the way I did. Weed only made John seem more mellow and talkative.

He looked out the window and said, "You feel like picking up some girls tonight at one of these clubs, man?"

I didn't. I said, "Nah, man, let me just enjoy this ride for a while. This the first time that I've driven it." I tried to get his mind off of the girls by talking up his car, you know. I had left my car parked near the studio.

John got slick on me. He said, "I'll let you drive the girls to my crib. Then you can drive them back home." He said, "Hell, man, I'll let you *hold* the damn car. You should buy one yourself, really. They only cost sixty thousand in cash. You got the money."

I laughed it off. I sure did have the money. We weren't even twenty-two yet, and both of us could afford to buy luxury cars with all cash. Nevertheless, we were riding around talking about picking up girls at nightclubs like any other twenty-year-olds would do. The money didn't change your mentality at all. In fact, the money made us think more that we *deserved* to be treated special.

I said, "John, aren't you tired by now, man? I mean, we've been inside the studio *all damn day*."

He said, "So what? I ain't tired. Let's go get some girls."

"Come on, man, let's just chill tonight. You need to clear your mind."

"I don't feel like chillin' right now, D. I've been chillin' for *weeks* now. Fuck that chillin' shit! Let's go get some girls, man." He was persistent about it.

I found myself wishing that Tangela was back around again. *Damn!*

I took a deep breath and tried to ignore him.

John said, "Maybe I should try to fuck a white girl now. What do you think about that, D? I heard they *love* giving blow jobs. And *swallowing*, too. I want to experience that, man."

I finally got fed up and said, "John, you need to get a *grip*, man. You need to get a grip on things. *Seriously!*" I told him. We were both getting out of hand. *Way* out of hand!

John just looked at me and smiled it off. He said, "That's what I'm trying to get, man, a grip around my dick. You can't feel me on that, D? I'm horny right now, man. I'm just being honest about it."

I said, "Well, you *need* to start learning to control some of that shit, man. The smoking, too." I may as well have been talking about myself.

John put out his blunt and got mad at me. He yelled, "Well, what the fuck am I supposed to do, man? Make music and then go home and go the fuck to sleep? *You* tell *me!* *You're* the manager!"

He said, "But that don't mean I'm gon' *listen* to that shit, though."

I said, "Just learn to enjoy what you got, man. A lot of people would *love* to have the talents that you have, John. And you act like you don't even appreciate them."

I said, "You need to go back and listen to your own song."

He grinned and started singing the chorus to *Unappreciated*:

Don't you kno-o-ow how I miss you-u-u-u
I miss you . . .

Maybe that wasn't a good idea for him, to think about somebody missing love, with Tangela gone. I was hoping that he wasn't thinking about her, but I *knew* that he was. He just hadn't said it out his mouth yet. But all of his actions proved it.

I shook my head against my better judgment and said, "All right, let's go to the club then, man." I did it just so he could forget about Tangela.

John got all excited and said, "*Now* we talkin'."

I had just made a deal with the devil. I spun the car around for a U-turn and went back to the club area to park. We weren't even dressed for an outing. Or not as sharply as *I* would have liked us to be.

As soon as we approached the front door, people started to notice.

"Ay, that's Loverboy," this cool brother said.

John nodded to him and said, "Yeah, what's up, man? I'm out here to get my groove on. I'm human, too."

The brother laughed and said, "I can dig, man. Get on down."

"Yeah, that's what I plan to do up in here," John told him.

Everybody in the line started laughing. But I knew that the weed was making him talk like that. I wondered if they could smell it on him.

The guards at the door noticed John, too.

"I love your music, man," this big bouncer brother told him. He said, "Keep representing old-school love."

John smiled at him and said, "Yeah, I will."

We got in the club, and people continued to speak to us.

This girl smiled and said, "Hey, Loverboy. When you gon' write a song for me?"

"As soon as we make some sweet music together," John responded to her.

She was caught off guard by it. She came right back at him and asked, "Well, what are you doing tonight?"

She wasn't one of the finer women in the room, so I hoped that John would sidestep her, to be honest about it. She was only a five, and there were plenty of eights and nines in the room. I could have pulled a *seven* myself, so I wasn't trying to let John go out with a *five*.

I pushed John along and smiled at the girl. I told her, "We have a long day tomorrow."

She asked, "Well, who are you?" She had stars all in her eyes, as if she was waiting for me to announce myself as a famous band member or something.

I said, "I'm just the manager," and slipped away.

The next thing I knew, the DJ was giving John a shot out on the microphone before playing *Tonight Is Yours*. And that about did it. My hope of us staying incognito was gone.

People started crowding us and shit, and girls wanted to dance with him. John was loving all of the attention.

He said, "Hold on, y'all. One at a time, one at a time."

He was getting himself spun around left and right with me in the middle, trying to direct traffic away from him. Finally, some of the bouncers helped us out of the jam.

"He's a good guest, people. Let 'em breathe. Let 'em breathe," the bouncers were saying.

We hadn't hired any bodyguards or anything at that point. We were still two young country boys, believing that we could just show up and be ourselves.

Anyway, John ended up dancing with three girls, all eights and up, and he was pitching strongly to them as I stood nearby.

"What are y'all doing later on? Y'all all together?"

"Why, what's going on? Is there another party somewhere?"

John said, "Yeah, at my house. Invitation only."

"Who else gon' be there?"

John said, "*Me, us,* and whoever else y'all want."

I started smiling and shaking my head.

"I don't know," one of them responded. She was the cutest, a mid-nine with one of those shorthaired Toni Braxton looks, without the thick nose.

The other two were more mature looking and willing to go.

"You gon' offer us a couple of drinks first?"

John said, "Yeah, y'all get what y'all want."

You could see the jealousy and envy all over everyone's faces as we moved to the bar area with escorts. The two older women ordered drinks on John, as if they were only using him for his money, but the Toni Braxton girl just wanted to talk to him. I nosed in on her conversation.

She asked him, "So, where do you live?"

John said, "Up in the suburbs of Chestnut Hill."

She got excited and said, "I have friends who live up that way. Off of Stenton Avenue?"

John nodded and said, "Yeah. Why, you want to visit your friends? We could call them before we leave."

She grinned and said, "Yeah, because they would *never* believe who I was with. I can hear them now, 'Loverboy *who?* The *singer? Yeah, right!'*"

John said, "Well, we'll just pay them a visit then."

She said, "But I have to go to work tomorrow. How long do you plan on having me up?"

Oh my God! I started getting a hard rock. Girls just didn't realize what they were saying sometimes. Maybe I was taking it the wrong way.

John said, "Don't worry about that. The Benz'll take you home as soon as you're ready to leave." He looked at me and said, "This my boy Darin, my manager. I trust him with my *life*, and he'll drive you back home safely whenever you're ready."

I nodded and smiled to her. I said, "Yeah, I'd do that."

The other girls overheard it and asked, "Who's gonna drive *us* back home?"

I figured that *somebody* had a damn car there that night!

I said, "Y'all all caught taxis over here?"

"No, but we don't feel like driving either. Don't y'all have a stretch limo or something?"

I said, "Not for just going to the club. But it's enough room for everybody to fit in the Benz though."

"Well let's do that then."

When we left, it looked as if John was pairing up with the Toni Braxton girl and the other two were just tagging along for the ride. So I made sure to keep them company.

"So you're the manager?" they asked me on the way to the car.

"Yeah."

"And how much money do *you* make?"

John was with the right girl. The Toni Braxton girl wasn't asking about the money.

When we made it to the car, John sat in the back with his new friend, and I drove up front with one of the other two girls.

She took one sniff of the Benz and asked, "Do y'all get high? I wouldn't think that *y'all* would be the type of guys to get high. Maybe *drunk* but not high."

I was thinking, *John is high right now.* Way *high!*

I asked them, "Why, because John sings love songs?"

They started laughing and said, "Yeah."

The Toni Braxton girl, riding in the back with John, said, "That getting high stuff is overrated if you ask me."

"Not if you buy the right kind of weed, girl," the other girl in the back with them responded. She added, "And it *smells* like y'all had some damn *killer* in here!"

They started laughing right before a green Ford Explorer rolled up beside us and started blowing the horn loud. They were trying to run me off of the damn road. I had just started driving.

"What the fuck is *his* problem?!" the girl in the passenger seat yelled across me at the wheel.

I stopped the car to avoid an accident. One guy jumped out of the passenger seat, and another jumped out from the driver's side.

They ran up to the car as if we had done something to them.

"AYEESHA! What the fuck are you doin'?! You try'na play my boy like that?! GET THE FUCK OUT THE CAR!"

I asked, "Who is Ayeesha?" I was watching to see if any of these guys had a gun, because they were sure acting crazy like it.

The Toni Braxton girl spoke up and said, "Oh my God! They are so fuckin' *pressed!* I don't go with him no more."

Her girls asked, "That's Nick and them?"

Ayeesha said, "Nick ain't even with them. That's Mark and Craig. Nick probably out with some other girl anyway. He ain't ready to be settled down, but him and his friends are always sweatin' me and shit."

I said, "Well, tell them guys something." I didn't need John in the middle of that. He had just recorded another hit song.

John's crazy ass climbed out of the car, so I had to climb out with him.

He asked them, "What's up, man?" He wasn't asking in a fighting way, he was just asking.

The lead guy said, "That's my boy girl, man. You not taking her with you. You ain't fuckin' wit' her like that." I guess they knew who John was.

Ayeesha climbed out of the car behind John and said, "I don't fuck with Nick no more like that. I can do what I *want* to do. And y'all need to stop following me the fuck around, too."

These guys were older than us, bigger than us, and definitely badder than us. And I'm not going to lie, I wanted to jump right back in that car and drive the hell out of there, but John was outside like a damn fool already.

I lied and said, "We were just giving them all a ride home. She's not by herself. It's all love."

The lead guy looked at me and said, "Do I look like a fuckin' fool to you, man? You ain't driving them home. They got their own car."

The other girl in the backseat said, "We were having car problems," and started laughing. It was all a game to them, but John and I didn't need that kind of fun.

Ayeesha said, "Whatever," and went to get back inside of the car before one of the guys tried to grab her arm. John reacted and tried to shield her from him.

"Motherfucker, if you don't get the fuck out of my way, you gon' make the news tonight. I swear to *God!* She don't play my boy like that."

I inched up to get closer to John, and the other guy inched up to get closer to me.

At that point, I was thinking, *Fuck this girl! We need to just get the hell up out of here!*

I said real calmly, "Look, all of this is just a big misunderstanding. We just met Ayeesha, and we didn't know she had a boyfriend. So y'all can take her home."

Ayeesha said, "No they *can't* either. I'm not going anywhere with *them*. And I don't have no damn *boyfriend.*" She was really being defiant, and at *John's* expense.

I said, "Well, you're gonna have to explain that to him, because we have to go now."

Ayeesha looked at me and said, "So what are you trying to say? You don't want me to go now?"

I was on the spot. I said, "It would make things a lot less complicated if you didn't."

John said, "But she *wants* to go," still talking with his wrong head.

I said, "That ain't our problem, John. She don't belong with us."

Ayeesha got the message and climbed out of the car.

She said, "Aw'ight, well, fuck it then." But she didn't climb into their Explorer. She started walking the streets. John's crazy ass took off behind her.

"Where are you going?" he asked her.

"Yo, just leave her the fuck alone, man. Like your man said, it ain't your problem," the other guy told John.

John ignored him. He asked Ayeesha, "You need to call this guy up on the phone and talk to him about it."

The lead guy said, "She needs to get in the jeep and go the fuck back home. That's what she *needs* to do. Out here acting like a *hoe.*"

Ayeesha heard that, and it started a brand new argument. She stopped and marched right back to us in the street.

"Acting like a fuckin' *hoe?*" she repeated. "Why, Craig, because I wouldn't let *you* fuck me? Let's talk about how *you* tried to push up on me that night."

The girls in the car started laughing, and Craig backed down, looking guilty as sin.

He said, "Aw, girl, don't even try that shit. I ain't *never* try to push up on you. You out here trying to make a fuckin' scene."

She said, "Yeah, right. *We know* it's the truth."

The other guy looked at Craig and asked, "You tried to push up on her, man? That's foul."

I guess he wasn't even giving his friend the benefit of the doubt, but I didn't care. I just wanted us to be gone already.

I said, "Let them work that out, John. Let's go, man."

John said, "Nah, man, let's just drive her home like we started to do. We can work it out when she gets home. But we don't need to be all out in the street with this."

I took a deep breath and looked to see if anyone else would make a move.

Ayeesha said, "Well, *I'm* going home," and climbed back into the Benz. "Fifty-sixth and Master, Darin," she said, using my name. Hell, I didn't even *know* Philadelphia like that.

Craig said, "All right, watch what happens," and started to walk back to his driver side door.

I didn't know if he was going to get a gun or what, but I got John into the car, and jumped behind the wheel to speed off.

They sped down the street after us in the Explorer, and my heart started beating like a rabbit's. I was thinking that we would either be shot at or run off the road and into a damn pole or something. Luckily, we had green lights, so I floored that Mercedes-Benz and we took off way ahead of the Explorer with more horsepower.

The girl sitting up front with me screamed, "Damn, this shit can *go!*"

I saw a sign that said I-95 South, and I whipped a right turn, jumped dead on the highway, and I kept flooring the car until we were out of sight and flying down the road.

John was laughing his ass off. "Damn, I'm glad *you* driving, D. I couldn't have done that shit."

I was pissed off at his ass, but once we were in the clear, I started laughing nervously myself.

I asked Ayeesha, "So, where is Fifty-sixth and Master? Is that in West Philly?" I knew a little bit about Philly, I just needed help in getting there.

Ayeesha said, "I'm not going home now. I just told *them* that. They don't need to know my business. They don't tell me *his*."

I started smiling, knowing the deal. Guys were some hypocritical motherfuckers.

John asked her, "But that's where we need to drive you later on, though?"

Her girl in the back answered, "No, my car is still down at the club. You can drive us back to the car, and I'll drive her home."

She laughed and said, "Because we don't want y'all gettin' back into it with Nick and his boys."

I smiled and said, "Thanks."

We made it out to John's place in Chestnut Hill, and the other two girls were all into checking out the house. I followed them around making sure they didn't steal anything or start casing the joint for later. I just didn't trust them, and I felt *far* from sexual that night. It was too much going on in my head. But I *was* interested in what John was up to with Ayeesha when they disappeared into his master bedroom. I just couldn't help myself. I mean, in just a few years, *John* was the one with all of the stories, and *I* had become the eager listener. So I was all ears again as soon as I drove his car back to him at close to six in the morning. I had driven all three girls back to Delaware Avenue.

I woke John up and said, "So what went down in here, man?" I realized that he had boned Ayeesha already. Her girls even talked about it openly in the car on our way back. They had both fallen asleep and taken catnaps on John's leather furniture inside of the living room. I guess the alcohol that they drank had done it to them.

John just smiled at me, not even opening his eyes when I asked him. He didn't even walk out of his room to say bye when Ayeesha left that morning.

He said, "I turned her out, man. I turned her out."

"You turned her out how?" I asked him.

John was incoherent about the whole thing that night, but I pieced it all together after he told me.

Once we got inside the house, John was still feeling horny, and he wanted Ayeesha. She was still older than both of us, at twenty-three, but she could pass for eighteen, and she had this young, spirited attitude about her. And not only that, John had gone through drama out on the street that night to even get the girl home.

So he ignored the other two girls and left them up to me to entertain.

He asked Ayeesha, "You want to see my room?"

She smiled at him and said, "I don't know if I should. Is the party in there? Where are all the other people?"

She knew damn well that it wasn't that kind of a party. But she had that tease thing going on that just made a guy want to work harder for it.

John asked, "You want to stay out there with them, or do you wanna go with me?"

Ayeesha paused for a minute. Then she smiled and said, "I'll go with you."

They walked into his extra large master bedroom that had plenty of mirrors and black furniture that Tangela had picked out, including the king-size water bed.

Ayeesha smiled and said, "A water bed. I've never been on one before."

John said, "Like you said with the weed, water beds can be overrated."

"For real?"

"Yeah, they move too much," he told her. "I'm thinking about getting rid of it."

"Why?" She went right over to it, took her shoes off, and melted down into it.

John joined her there with his shoes still on.

He asked her, "Do you want it? I'll have it delivered to you."

"Yeah, right."

"Nah, I'm for real. Then you can think about me every time that you're on it."

She melted again and said, "Awww, that's so sweet. I guess you really *are* a Loverboy, hunh?"

John grinned and said, "That's what they call me."

She got curious and asked him, "So, did you get that name *before* or *after* you started singing?"

He said, "After. Nobody paid me any attention before."

John was just straight-up honest like that. And once you got to his level of popularity, girls seemed to *love* that truth serum shit. John couldn't get away with that shit when he was still a nobody at A&T. Girls were some damn hypocrites, too.

"Were you lonely?" she asked him.

He said, "That's where all of my songs come from. I'm *still* lonely. I always feel like I'm one girl away from heaven."

The thing that took me out was how girls thought John was gaming when he would say things like that, but he wasn't. That was just who he was. He was a romantic, and he never really faced that fact, he just used it. It was that innocence about him that got to people. That shit would never work for me.

Anyway, Ayeesha cuddled up all close to him on the water bed and asked him, "Why do guys smoke so much? My old boyfriend was into that smoking stuff, too."

John said, "It's hard being a guy."

She responded, "Like it ain't hard being a woman. I'm tired of hearing that shit from guys. Y'all don't even get periods."

John asked her, "Are you on it right now?"

"On what?"

"Your period?"

She laughed and said, "No, why?"

"Because periods can get in the way."

"Get in the way of what? We're not doing anything."

John said, "We're not?"

Ayeesha shook her head and said, "No, unless I *want* to. And I haven't made up my mind yet."

"But you're thinking about it, though?"

She shook her head and said, "Guys are *all* the same."

John said, "That's why they call us *guys*. But women still have babies, right? So y'all fuckin', right? We *all* fuckin'. It's just a matter of who we choose to fuck."

Ayeesha couldn't stop from laughing. "Oh my God."

"What?" John asked her.

She said, "What happened to your finesse as a Loverboy?"

He said, "I got finesse. But it's in the singing. I save my finesse for the real stuff. Unless I'm singing to you."

She said, "Well, sing to me then."

John opened his mouth real quietly and sang:

Will she let me come insi-i-ide
like raindrops falling
against the win-dow-pane.

Will she let me come insi-i-ide
and ride a wave of love
out to the o-pen seeeas.

Ayeesha laughed and said, "Is that a new song you're working on? That's nasty."

John said, "No it's not. It's creative. You want to take your clothes off as badly as I do. It's natural."

She said, "I just met you, though. I don't have feelings for you like that."

John kept his cool and said, "You got feelings for this guy who has his boys out looking for you tonight, though. Don't you? You got feelings for him." He was using a slick psychology on her.

She said, "I've known him for a while. He just . . . he just don't know how to *act* sometimes."

John said, "I know. Those kind of guys never know how to act. But that's who women love. And I try to write songs to heal everyone, but y'all keep going back to the same shit. Y'all just gon' make me a rich man, that's all."

John came back to Ayeesha and said, "But *you* need healing tonight. And you think that other guy is gonna heal you? Do you? Do you really?"

Ayeesha thought about it and said, "No. Probably not."

"That's what I'm sayin'," John told her.

Ayeesha added it up. She said, "So, you're saying that you can *heal me* tonight? Is that what you're saying?" She still had a smart grin on her face as if it were all a game.

John said, "I can tell that you need a strong orgasm. You probably haven't even felt it done to you right."

Ayeesha got serious and said, "No, I can't say that. I've had it done right. Just not in a while, because he's been getting on my nerves lately."

John said, "I can see that," and began to touch her ever so softly.

Ayeesha could feel it, and she couldn't fake it like she wasn't curious.

She said, "I don't even believe that I'm thinking about this right now."

John asked her, "What are you thinking about?"

He had been hard and soft several times that night while scheming to get laid, but when she touched him in the right spot, the response to that was immediately readable.

"You're ready, hunh?" she asked him.

"You're not?"

"I'm not gon' say."

John said, "You want me to lock the door? I don't want you to be embarrassed by anything."

She said, "Umm . . . yeah, go lock the door."

At that point in the story, my rock started to rise, too, because I knew John was about to hit it.

He walked back over to the water bed after locking the door, so that we couldn't walk in on them, and he and Ayeesha went on about their business as if we weren't even inside of the house with them that night.

She said, "You can't come inside of me like raindrops, because I'm not taking anything. And that's dangerous for you anyway. For *both* of us. So I need some protection."

John had a whole barrel of that. He got up and got some without a word. He slipped back onto the bed with her and sunk his tongue into her mouth.

"Mmm, I wasn't expecting that," she moaned to him.

He said, "You want to take my clothes off?"

She smiled and said, "That's different. All right. Hold still."

John held still as she pulled his shoes, socks, pants, and boxer drawers off. Then he closed his eyes with his hands behind his head and let her study his full rise.

John told me, "And then I felt her lips and her small tongue stroke across my dick, man. And I was like, ooh. That shit felt good, man. She had a nice, wet tongue."

I said, "For real? She went down on you like that, without you even asking her. I thought she said that wasn't safe," I reminded him.

John said, "You think I was gonna open my mouth and ruin it, man. Shit, I *wanted* my thing sucked. And she did a good job, too."

I asked, "All the way?" meaning to a climax.

John shook his head. "Nah. She wanted to make sure she got hers, you know. So when she stopped, I put the condom on, and then I just pushed all the way up inside of her and just sat on that G-spot, man. And she was going crazy. She came like four times."

He said, "If you hit that right spot with girls, man, you don't even have to do that much work. You just make sure you stay on that spot, and they'll do most of the work themselves."

I asked him, "Did she have a good one?" I still couldn't help myself.

John said, "It was all right. But I turned her out, though. That was *my* main thing. I wanted to prove that I could outfuck her old boyfriend. I even hit her from the back when she went to wash up in the bathroom. I had her up against the sink, and she was holding it all in so y'all wouldn't hear her squealing."

I said, "Man, they fell asleep after a while. But they teased her on the car ride back to Delaware Avenue, though. So you gon' keep her?" I asked him. I wanted him to find stability again instead of sleeping around.

John paused. He said, "I doubt it, man. I mean, she was all right but . . . *I* had more fun gettin' her. She going back to that dude anyway. That's why she blew me like that. She just wanted to go crazy for a minute. She know she ain't got no future with me. It was just medicine for her. I told her that. She needed a healing."

He said, "*All* girls need that healing. They need the freak to just crawl up out of them every once in a while. Tangela taught me that, man. And she's right. She said, 'Every woman wants to be unleashed, but it just takes the right guy to be able to do it.'"

I asked him, "And you think that *you're* that guy?"

He said, "That's why they call me the Loverboy."

John was more sick in his head than I was, equating sex to healing. Tangela had sunk deeper into him than what I had thought.

If *anyone* needed *healing* it was *John*. The whole thing about him being lonely was true. He had never had a real girlfriend, and Tangela Austin was in and out of his life like a dream. John had even lost his closeness to his mother. If you want to even call their relationship close. And then he had never known his father. He had never even met him or seen what he looked like. That shit *had* to be lonely. The music and the power that it gave him were the only things that John had. *That* and his friendship with me.

As for me, I had to deal with my own need to dominate. I was raw with women because I didn't know how *not* to control things. Even with John. I was losing it because I couldn't control what *he* was doing. After all, I was the manager, right? So we *both* needed healing.

Like a typical control freak, I got desperate and called Tangela in New Jersey before Christmas, trying my best to get her thinking about John again. I could never catch her at home, though, and I always got her answering machine. I left her a message telling her that John could use a telephone call from her or something, if just to say hello. And I sent her a copy of the jam session that we did in the studio. I wanted her to hear the new music that we were putting together, and the powerful songs that John had written inspired by her. I even went out on a limb and asked her if she wanted to go to the National Music Awards show with us in early March of 1996.

John was sure to be nominated for the best new male artist of the year award for 1995, and they had asked him to perform his latest pop hit, *Nobody's Perfect*. I figured that Tangela would have found at least some sentimental value in that. That song and the video had launched her career as a player in the music business.

As John, Tony, and the band finished up the final songs for the new album, to be released in February 1996, I figured we could use some downtime. After all, it was Christmas season, so I asked John at his house if he wanted to fly home to Charlotte with me and hang out with our folks before the new album release and award season rolled around.

He shook his head and said, "Nah, man. I'm staying up here."

I said, "You not gonna at least spend Christmastime with your mom, man?"

"She ain't called me about it."

I said, "Well, call *her* for a change."

"And say what?"

I said, "'Hey, Mom. This is your son, John, up in Philadelphia. I miss you. And I was wondering if you wanted anything for Christmas.'"

John started laughing. He said, "'Yeah, boy, you can take your narrow behind back to church for Christmas and ask the Lord for his forgiveness.'"

I said, "What's so wrong with the church, man? We grew up in the church, John." It was as if the church and Sister Williams were both rolled up into one, and John wanted to defy both of them. But I didn't see why it had to be that way. We *needed* the church in our lives again. *Both* of us!

John said, "The church is filled with a bunch of blind people, man. Sheep being led around by the shepherd."

I said, "And what are you doing when you take the stage with your singing?"

John smiled at me and started laughing, catching on to my point. He was a *shepherd* his damn self.

He said, "I'm not going back home, man. I don't feel like it."

"So, what are you gonna do up here in Philly then? You not gon' hang out with Tony. Tony's spending more time with his girl now, or making beats for rap acts."

John said, "Shit, I don't need Tony all the time to have me some fun, man. I know how to get around."

I didn't trust John's "getting around," but I wasn't staying up there in Philly for the holiday season, so John was just going to have to be by himself.

I said, "All right, man. Suit yourself. I'll just see you around next year then."

John said, "Try to call me on New Year's Eve, man. I want to see if I can bring the new year in right."

I asked, "Bring the new year in right how?" Was he talking about getting busy again?

"With a big house party or something," he told me. I didn't like the sound of that, but I had to let it go so that I could go home.

I got a round-trip plane ticket and flew home. My whole family met me at the airport, including both of my older brothers. They were all proud of me and of John and his music.

"So, John really decided not to come home for Christmas?" they all asked me.

I said, "Well, he's not here. So unless something changes and he shows up, he's made up his mind."

I knew my father and I would have a conversation alone before that night was out. He had that look of urgency in his eyes. I went to him at the house that night and asked him what was on his mind.

He asked me, "How are you holding up?"

I took a breath and tried to level with him. I said, "This is a hard business. It's hard trying to keep John's emotions together *and* my own. One day we're making great music and everything is going great, the next day he's miserable and everything is falling apart. And then the pressure falls right on me."

I didn't want to include anything about the girls and the drugs. I wasn't a damn fool. I kept thinking that it was just a phase that John and I were going through. Tony seemed to be coming out of that phase himself. He had a steady woman, and he was getting high less and less as he got busier with producing rap music.

My father nodded and said, "If you guys are not in school, then I understand that there's a lot of time spent doing nothing. Maybe you need to make his schedule a little more busy, and have John doing more community events that would keep his spirits up."

He smiled at me and said, "You know, like celebrity baseball games and such. Don't they have those things all the time?"

I grinned. My father was right. We weren't really in the loop with community functions. Outside of just making the music, I was busy trying to chase John around and make sure he didn't ruin himself. Getting him busy with activities outside of just making music was a good idea. It was also a good idea to keep *myself* active.

I told my father, "You know what? That's a good idea, Dad. I mean, I've always gotten those kinds of phone calls, but since John wasn't really hearing me a lot of times, I just let that kind of stuff slide. Well, now I'll just throw his name in the hat and *make him* do it."

My father grimaced and said, "He hasn't, ah, been listening to your suggestions? I mean, you're the manager, right?"

People made it seem as if I really could rule with an iron fist or something. I didn't want to say that John didn't listen to me at all, because that would have been an overstatement, but he had sure broken me as far as what I could expect from him. I had let things go once I began to get high with him. And I surely couldn't tell my father that.

I took the middle ground and said, "It comes and goes. Sometimes he does, and sometimes he just wants to make his own moves. Which is understandable, because he's the musician, and I'm not. This is *his* career."

I tried my best to give John the benefit of the doubt in my father's eyes.

He said, "Has he been in steady contact with his mother?"

I smiled. My father was asking me to share a lot of complicated truths with him.

I said, "Nah. They have something going that . . . I just can't understand it sometimes."

"She's not happy about what's going on with him?"

I said, "I don't know. I haven't spoken to her since John tried to buy her that house in Lake Norman."

My father grinned and said, "Well, you know you can't *buy* people's respect down here in the South. That bullshit with the money may work up north, but it don't work down here. If people don't like what you're doing in the South, they won't want your money. And then some of 'em will take your money, and then talk about your ass in church."

We shared a laugh. I told him, "You know that's right." I said, "But John doesn't even touch most of his money. He just wanted to buy his mother a good house, and she turned him down."

My father looked at me sideways. He said, "A 'good house'? In *Lake Norman*. Shit, that ain't no damn 'good house.' That's a mansion. She ain't wanna be up there with them folk. And I don't blame her either. The South is a hard place to change."

He said, "So, what are you doing with *your* money?"

"I barely touch mine either," I told him. "Especially since John is always treating. So I've been studying stocks and bonds and stuff for both of us to get into."

My father grinned and said, "That's good. 'Cause remember, you still owe us some schoolin' and a degree. That was our deal."

He said, "But that John sure is making some hits with his music. It seems like every time I turn around, he got a new song out. He even got *me* listening to the radio now."

My father was excited about John like everyone else was. He said, "And I'll tell you another thing, that damn *Big Momma* song had a whole lot of churchwomen talking about it."

I said, "Uht oh. I told him not to do that song. And it's called *Tonight Is Yours*."

My father said, "They call it *Big Momma*, and when people talk about something as much as these women have in church, that means that they really like it. Somebody was finally singing about *their* behinds."

I broke up laughing again. I wondered how Sister Williams was taking all of that talk.

I asked, "Does Sister Williams hear them talking about John?"

My father looked at me funny again and said, "Of course she does."

I said, "Well, what does she say about it?"

He said, "She ignores it and prays."

I just shook my head. Sometimes I really couldn't argue with John's sentiments of the church. Praying wouldn't always change things, especially things that needed immediate fixing. John needed some love, and his mother was holding out on him.

I made sure to pay John's mother a visit at her house that week to talk to her about her son. I had bought an extra large Christmas card for John, and I drove all around Charlotte getting old friends and teachers of ours to sign messages of love to him to let him know that he didn't need to feel as if he was alone in the world. Plenty of people loved him whether he made good music or not.

When I arrived at Sister Williams's house with the Christmas card in hand to show her, she opened the door and hesitated to let me in.

She said, "Yes, Darin."

She looked even older than the last time I saw her. She stood at the door with new gray hairs on her head, still strong-willed and rigid. I felt like lying and telling her that John was there with me just to see what she would do.

I said, "May I come in and talk to you. I have a Christmas card for John that we've all been signing."

She backed up and let me in. I immediately handed her the card to take a look at it.

She smiled, seeing some of the names of our teachers at Garinger High School, and some of the music teachers that John had over the years.

"I bet Mr. Haynes is praying for John, too, now," she said to herself. She wasn't really talking to me.

I followed her into the living room, where she sat down on old, well-kept furniture. She still had John's younger photos all around the room, but nothing recent.

I asked her, "Would you like me to send you some recent photos of John,

Sister Williams?" I had plenty of great photos of John from different press packets and interview shoots.

Sister Williams frowned at me and said, "I only want *pure* pictures of John."

I said, "We have plenty of those. John takes a lot of good pictures."

She ignored me and continued to read the card and the signatures.

I said, "It would be great if you could sign that for John or send a personal card of your own to him. That big gap in the middle there is for you. I wouldn't let anyone else sign there until you had signed it," I told her.

To my surprise, Sister Williams stood right up and got a pen to sign it with. I was so happy about that that I was tempted to leave without saying another word.

Then she asked me, "How is he doing?"

I stammered with the truth on my mind inside of a religious woman's house. Crosses, candles, and Bibles were everywhere! More than when John still lived there.

I said, "Ah, well, he, he's doing good. Pretty good. Yeah."

I felt like a lying fool. A sinner. And I was. I had some praying to do myself. But would I do it?

Sister Williams said, "Has he chosen a church to worship in in Philadelphia?"

I said, "Well, not yet, you know. It's a whole lot of different churches up there. Philadelphia is a big city, you know. Much bigger than Charlotte."

I was digging myself deeper into a sinful grave.

She looked at me and said, "So, you're telling me that my John hasn't gon' to church at all? In *two years*?"

What could I say? I hadn't gone to church either.

"Well, we've just been really busy with the music career and everything."

"You could *never* be too *busy* for the Lord, Darin. What kind of *foolishness* are you telling me? Don't you *come in here* and disrespect my house with this *foolishness*."

Boy, I wanted to get out of there *badly!* But I was trapped.

She asked me, "Now you tell me what kind of lifestyle he's living with all of this money and these songs with no Lord in his life, Darin. You tell me what kind of lifestyle he's living. Is he giving back to the Lord for his talent?"

She really wanted an answer, too. I sat there ready to pop like a popcorn kernel in a microwave. She was really grilling me. If John was living a good life, I could have taken it, but since I couldn't say that he was, I was in deep doo-doo. I just kept finding myself in the middle of John's life, every way that I turned.

"Ain't nobody perfect, Sister Williams," I found myself saying. I was quoting John. It was the only thing that came to mind.

At that point, she was ready to dismiss me.

She stood up with the card extended to me and said, "Nobody *said* they perfect, Darin, but we all live *each* and *every day* to get *closer* to the Lord. And I don't see John doing *anything* but getting *farther away* from his grace. And I'm not gonna *stand for it!*"

She said, "So you take this card and you give it to him."

I don't know what got into me at the moment, but out of the blue, I spoke up and said, "John just wants to know who his father is. That's all. Can the Lord tell him that?"

I didn't know how I expected her to respond, but when she took a few breaths and remained calm, I was rather surprised by it. I guess I was expecting her to go off the handle like she usually would do. In fact, I was trying to make her go there on purpose, because I was just frustrated.

She looked at me and said, "Darin, when John is ready to face the Lord, then he'll be ready to know."

I was confused. I wanted more than that, but she was so peaceful about it that I thought about leaving it alone.

I forced myself to respond anyway. I said, "Well, *I* think he needs to know right now. It's tearing him apart. How can a guy walk around all these years and not know who his father is?"

She gave me some wicked eyes and hollered, "You show some *RESPECT* in my house, YOUNG MAN! Mind your *DAMN MANNERS!*"

I didn't feel like hearing that drama, man. So I took the card and headed back for the door, ignoring the rest of Sister Williams's tirade. I felt sorry for John. I felt sorry for *both* of them. I felt sorry for *me* for being in the middle of it. It just didn't make any sense, praising the Lord while ignoring your own flesh and blood. Did I lack faith? Was I wrong? I mean, I wasn't saying that John and I were right, because we were not, and I admitted it. John even admitted it in his songs and everything. But *hell, man,* how could his mom be that unforgiving?! She wouldn't even allow an open conversation! Was *she* right to be that way?!

I opened up the card when I reached the rental car that I was driving, just to see what she had written. Right there, as large as day, Sister Williams wrote, "GET CLOSE TO THE LORD! YOU SHALL KNOW HIS NAME!"

I shook my head and couldn't believe it. She had just *ruined* a perfect idea. John wouldn't want that right in the middle of his damn card. But I was tired, man. I was *tired!* So I took that shit right to the post office to mail it to John and let him take it however he was going to take it. It was *his* crazy mother, not mine.

When I got to the post office, it was taking forever to get to the front of that line in down-home Charlotte. I kept changing my mind back and forth over whether I should mail the card off to John or just forget about it.

God dammit, I wish this line would MOVE! I was thinking to myself. I was the only one who looked concerned about the molasses-like speed in there. I guess I had gotten used to the hustle and bustle of the North, especially with all of the people in and out of the music business.

Before I could get all the way to the front of the line with the card in hand to mail off, someone yelled out, "Hey, nigga! What up, dawg?"

I was standing there embarrassed, thinking, *Damn! That's the South for you.* I didn't even turn around to see who it was.

The next thing *I* knew, the guy was all up in my face in the line, standing six feet five and as wide as the sunshine, like in Loverboy's song *Tonight Is Yours.*

It was Big Joe's country ass from North Carolina A&T's football team. He was the first person to ever call John "Loverboy," at the homecoming talent show that night *years* ago. He wasn't slow to remind me of that either.

He said, "Nigga, that Loverboy is blowing AAHHPP! I tell niggas all the time, I say, 'I *named* that nigga. He went to A&T with us, dawg. That nigga, FOLKS!'"

He grabbed my hand as proud as he could be and said, "Darin, it's good to *see you, dawg.* You motherfuckers are representin' for the dirty SOUTH like that, NIG-GA!"

I was *beyond* embarrassment! I mean, I wasn't ashamed of my Southern roots or anything. Nor was I politically correct with what I said all the time, but DAMN! Big Joe was all up in the middle of the post office with that shit.

I said, "Let me take care of this mail, man, and I'll talk to you outside. All right?"

Big Joe nodded his head and said, "Yeah, nigga, come on wit' it. We need to *talk* about thangs, dawg. I wanna be a bodyguard."

I just wanted to run the hell home and climb *under* my bed! That shit was ridiculous. You would think that a college education would *refine* that country shit. We weren't out in the damn sugarcane fields hollering profanities under the heat of the sun anymore. *SHIT!*

I mailed the Christmas card off to John, happy to leave that place, and walked outside to face Big Joe again.

Before he could even open his mouth to me, I said, "Joe, I understand that you're excited about what's going on and you're happy to see me and everything, man, but we gotta watch our language in certain arenas . . . dawg." I didn't want to put down my brother, I was just trying to bring him up a bit. Joe had always talked like that in the locker room. However, we were not in the locker room anymore.

He smiled like a giant-size teddy bear and said, "Aw, my bad, dawg. I'm just happy to see you, man. I mean, I've been thinking about y'all lately. Loverboy need a bodyguard don't he? That nigga ain't never had no weight on him."

I laughed. We could actually use a traveling bodyguard by that point in John's career. He was *definitely* at that level, and he still wanted to test the street life. But then again, Big Joe needed to calm *waaaay* down before we could hire him for that kind of a job. He still had that attack-mode football energy in him. That would get us into more trouble than *not* having a bodyguard.

I asked, "Well, what have you been doing with yourself, man?"

He said, "I was playing arena ball in Florida for a minute. But that shit wasn't paying no real money, man. So I tried to sign on with a couple of NFL practice teams or something just to get my daughter something to eat. You know what I mean? I was still trying to do the football thing. That's why I'm in Charlotte now. I was with the Panthers camp for a minute."

Obviously, Big Joe could talk straight. He was just a little excited with me, that's all. He was a defensive lineman, and they tended to *get* excited like that. I understood it. So I gave Big Joe a business card.

He said, "I'm gon' call you up, too, man. I'm serious about the body-guard thing. I mean, I *named* your boy. And now y'all using it. LOVER-BOOOY!"

I laughed and said, "Yeah, I hear you, man. We gon' talk about it."

When I hit the church that Sunday morning with my family, I was swarmed by everyone who was interested in John's music or music of their own.

"Well, when is he doing a show back home in Charlotte?"

"I got a young cousin who can sing. Can I give her your number?"

"Boy, I really have some *issues* with that *Big Momma* song. I'm not saying that I don't like it, I'm just wondering where his head was when he wrote it."

"Is John working on a new album yet?"

"Is he gonna sing any good gospel music?"

"Has he settled down with a nice girl? I got a good niece I could introduce him to up in Greensboro. She's just as *sweet* as she can be. And *smart*, too."

My older brothers were laughing their behinds off.

They said, "All of this for a momma's boy who could barely walk a girl home from school when he lived here. Funny how things change."

I said, "Yeah, tell me about it," and kept on laughing. But Sister Williams was not a part of the fun that day. She kept her distance and continued to ignore everything. I just couldn't reach her.

VERSE 19

. . . o-o-oh no-o-o- . . .

I flew back to Philly in the new year of January 1996, and I drove straight over to John's place in Chestnut Hill. I didn't even call him first. I just wanted to show up and see what he was up to. I couldn't catch him at the house on New Year's Eve like he told me to, so I left him a message, and I was nervous about not being able to reach him.

I pulled up to his driveway and was happy to see his Mercedes-Benz parked and in good shape. He hadn't gotten in any accidents while driving high or anything.

I rang the doorbell at his front door and waited.

John answered the door and was good-spirited without being high for a change. He looked fresh and energetic as if he was ready to go jogging.

He said, "Hey, what's up, D? How was Charlotte?"

I wondered if he had gotten the Christmas card that I had sent him.

I said, "Everybody wants to know when we're coming down to do a show or something."

I walked in behind him and noticed the Christmas card sitting wide open on the fireplace mantel. I was happy to see that. Sister Williams's comments hadn't turned him sour to it.

John said, "You didn't tell them when I was coming home, man? You should have told them."

I frowned and said, "Told them what?"

"That we'll be there this summer," he told me. "We got a new album dropping and a new tour coming this year, right? So let's make sure we hit Charlotte."

It was right about time to start organizing a summer tour, so I nodded my head on it.

I said, "And this is *your* tour this year, John. We don't need Boyz II Men anymore. *You* da man now. We're not signing any exclusive deals. And we're going *everywhere* this summer."

John smiled and said, "And you *know* that. This new album is gonna have all *kinds* of hits on it, D. We listened to the whole thing and had a few outsiders check it out, and they *all* knew what time it was. *Honesty* is going to be *the one!*"

He said, "I just had to go through a little turbulence to make it happen. Drama is good for creativity, man. It's almost like, if you don't have no drama in your life, then you can't really create shit."

I smiled and said, "So you gon' make up a philosophy to support everything that you do, hunh?" I was also thinking, *Wow! This boy is* jumping *with energy today.* That made me feel *real* good!

John said, "Whatever it takes to make it happen, man. Whatever it takes."

I said, "So, since we're gonna call all of the shots this summer, I'll let people know that we'll be listening out for who wants to tour with 'the Love Boat.'" I was just joking, since the energy was all lighthearted that day.

John started laughing. He said, "I like that. Yo, we can have, like, a real boat on stage, too. And I get stranded on a deserted island, right. And then we can pull a girl up onstage to be stranded with me. And I'll sing my ass off to her."

He said, "Yo, that shit would work."

I chuckled and said, "I wonder how much the expenses would be for something like that?" I was thinking as a businessperson, you know.

John said, "Man, fuck the expenses. Whatever it costs, we got it."

And we did. We had been very efficient with money, so we had plenty of it.

John said, "I told M.D. and Double K the same thing about this video we're about to shoot for *All Night Situation.* We're gonna drop *Honesty* last, when the summer kicks in, around June. I want a dope video for that single, too.

"Fuck this cheap stuff, man," he told me. "That shit is *weak!* We're established now, so we gotta go *all out* or nothing!"

John had too much running through his mind for me to handle. I had to slow him down a second to get back in the mix of things.

I smiled and asked him, "So, what did you think about that card I sent you for Christmas?"

He said, "You got Mr. Haynes to sign it, hunh?" He started laughing.

Mr. Haynes was a real character. He acted like an oversized kid sometimes. But that's why everybody loved him. He was free-spirited.

John said, "You know what I was thinking about when I saw all them old names on that card?"

I said, "Nah, what?"

He said, "What if you got Carneta James to sign it? She probably got, like, three kids now. I need to send her a New Year's card or something, saying, 'How you like me now, bitch?'"

I started laughing, but that wasn't right. John knew it , too.

He said, "Nah, if it wasn't for her I probably wouldn't have started writing songs."

I joked and said, "Nah, some other girl would have broken your heart, and you would have been writing your first songs about her."

John laughed and said, "Yeah, you probably right. I just had it in me. *Somebody* would have brought it out."

I asked him, "So, what do you think about what your mom wrote?" I *had* to ask him about it. Since he had the card all out in the open like he did, I figured it was up for conversation.

John shrugged and said, "What do you want me to say? That's just my mom, man. She got her own way about *her*, and I got my own way about *me*."

That was the end of that.

Then John had a surprise for me. He grinned and said, "Tangela going to the awards with us. I drove up there to Jersey and hung out with her and Butterscotch and them on New Year's Eve. I was telling them that maybe they should go on tour with us this year. Their album comes out right after mine."

Honesty was slated for release on February 27, 1996, and we still had to shoot the album cover. We were behind schedule on a few things, but everyone knew that a new album was coming out from the release of the hot singles *Nobody's Perfect* and *Tonight Is Yours*. And since the music awards show was in March, it served as a perfect platform to help push the album. Matt and Kenny bettered the idea by pushing the album release back to late March and using the award show as a springboard for the album release. Old School Records were masters at squeezing a dollar, and it was making us all richer from it. They had much less money to recoup from us.

I smiled from ear to ear about the news on Tangela, but I needed to hear more to be secure with what John was telling me.

I said, "So, what's up with Tangela? Y'all gettin' back together now?"

He said, "Nah, you know, we talked about it and everything, but we both know that we're busy, and we just decided to deal with each other on that level. You know, so it's, like, a friendly business kind of thing."

Whatever, I thought to myself. *As long as this boy's happy about it.*

I said, "Have you talked to Jamie about the new album cover yet?"

"Yeah, we were just gonna do something simple this time around, like me sitting on one of those leather lounge chairs that they use in the shrink offices. You know, it would be like, I'm just lettin' it all out of my system, what's going on with my life and everything. I'm just being honest with you."

I nodded and smiled. I liked the idea. That was Old School Records' whole philosophy: make it simple and make it count.

I said, "That sounds like a winner to me."

John said, "And Charles is making a lime green outfit up for me now. We could shoot the album cover next week and get it over with."

I said, "Done. Let's do it."

That's the kind of John that I looked forward to working with, clear-headed and fluent with his ideas.

We shot the photos for the new album cover with John wearing a tailored lime silk outfit, while laying horizontally on a long leather shrink's chair. Then we printed HONESTY above him, and JOHN LOVERBOY WILLIAMS below. It was easily done, and very effective.

John also wore light green at the National Music Awards out in Los Angeles, with Tangela wearing cream. We just *knew* that John would win the best new male artist of the year award. We were all counting on it. We were all dressed to impress and looking good, sitting there with the likes of Whitney Houston and Bobby Brown, Patti LaBelle and Aretha Franklin, Mariah Carey and Janet Jackson, TLC and Da Brat, Tupac Shakur, Suge Knight, and the Untouchable Death Row family, Puff Daddy Combs, the Notorious B.I.G., Faith Evans, and the Bad Boy camp, R. Kelly, Jodeci, and Mary J. Blige, Stevie Wonder and Quincy Jones, Babyface and Toni Braxton, and all of these other popular singers, musicians, producers, and managers, all under one fabulous roof. And in the middle of all those great people, Loverboy was going to perform his number one pop hit, *Nobody's Perfect.*

I wished that they would have asked him to sing something else. *Anything* else. But a hit is a hit, and that's the song that they wanted to hear. So John came out and did his thing, and everybody knew the words to it:

A girl wrote me a let-ter
and it said that I broke her heart . . .

AIN'T NO-BODY PER-FECT, BA-BY
AIN'T NO-BODY PER-FECT, UNT UNH . . .

Tony and I looked at each other and smiled, knowing full well that we were both tired of hearing that damn song. But John wasn't tired of performing it, and Tangela still loved it, too. However, when it was time for John's award nomination for best new male artist of the year, a nomination was all that he would get.

Tony frowned and said, "Motherfucker! That's a jerk, man. They jerked you! How you gon' go triple platinum with your first album, with all them hits we had on it, and they don't give you no damn awards? That's *robbery*, man! All this award shit is set up."

Everyone else played it off and clapped their hands for the eventual winner. Even John and Tangela clapped their hands graciously, but they knew that Loverboy deserved it. I ignored the shit myself and didn't budge. I was sitting there thinking, *Ain't this a bitch!* We all felt that award was in the bag.

Tony said, "Fuck it, we know we making more money, though. And we gon' blow *everybody* away with *this* album! Next year we gon' get *male artist* and *album* of the year, *period!* Fuck that new artist shit anyway!"

John only chuckled at Tony's outrage, but I could tell that he was upset. He had been upbeat all night until that happened.

At the hotel room, Tangela stayed with him. It was better her than me to give John some ego massaging that night. I was getting tired of it, and Tangela certainly had that extra physical touch.

There were lots of parties to go to, but I hung out with Tony that night with no drugs and no groupies. We just talked about things that went on in the music industry. Since we were not out in front like the big stars, no one really knew who we were, so we could just chill in the hotel lobby and watch everything going on at the ballroom afterparty.

Tony said, "Yo, D, I've been thinking about this for a while, man. John needs more of a mainstream public image. Doing that talk show last year turned me on to that. That shit was fun."

He said, "We need to get out there and let people know that we makin' money and doing things. Look at what Death Row and Bad Boy records are doing. I mean, I'm not saying that we need to get all into that whole coast drama shit, but them motherfuckers are gettin' a whole lot of media play with that shit. Every damn *day* they in the news."

I said, "But that shit ain't no *good* news."

Tony said, "Who really cares if it's good news or not? All they gotta do is do something positive, and all is forgiven. You ever notice that? So the key is just to stay out there with something."

I nodded to him. It was the same thing that my father was saying about staying busy with less downtime to worry you.

Tony said, "Look at TLC. That damn Left Eye babe burnt a fuckin' house down, and that didn't stop *them* from being popular. They sold damn near *ten million* albums. Think about it, man. As long as you out in the public eye, you can be forgiven."

I said, "Yeah, I see what you mean, man. And these award shows are all about a popularity contest."

Tony said, "Yeah, man, and we've just been chillin', and doing the music thing. You need to get John out there. You gotta stop him from chasing pussy so much, and get him in the mix of the news."

I smiled. I said, "Tell him to stop chasing *pussy*, hunh? Look who's talkin'."

Tony grinned and said, "I've cooled out with that shit. I mean, I'm on the other side of twenty-five now. I've had my fun, man. It's all about business now. We all making money, I'm just trying to make sure that John gets his just due, that's all. So we need to say fuck Old School Records with all that saving money shit and go all out on this tour, man. BMG already backing us with the marketing and distribution dollars. And this is John's year to blow the fuck up. For real!"

Tony was telling me everything that I knew already. All I could do was nod my head and agree with him.

This pretty brown sister walked up in a gold-sequined dress and said, "Excuse me, but aren't you Darin Harmon, the manager of John Loverboy Williams?"

I looked at Tony, who smiled at me before I answered her.

I said, "Yeah, I'm D. Harmon." I was thinking that she had a crush on me or something physical, you know. It was all male ego talking. I *was* looking sharp that night, and although I wasn't a musician, I was firmly in the business with handling John's career.

I was waiting for her to throw the pitch to me.

The sister said, "My name is Evelyn Harris, and I'm a staff writer for *Harmony* magazine." She extended her hand to me and added, "I've been wanting to do an interview with you and Loverboy about your long-term friendship and your relationship in the music business."

Tony nodded to me and said, "*That's* what I'm talking about. You need to get busy pushing who John is with some real feature story stuff."

I gave the sister my card and told her immediately that we would do it.

I stayed up and thought for the rest of that night about all of the ideas that I could use to keep John busy. It felt like I was a parent trying to figure out ways to keep my toddler out of nonconstructive activities, while tiring him out with things that *I* had planned for him. But so be it.

When we arrived back in Philly, I called Old School Records and informed them that we needed a larger budget for John's next video. We talked to directors about making a whole *Love Boat–Fantasy Island* kind of thing, with John and a date getting stranded on an island for a night. It reminded me of the *Gilligan's Island* setup, but in a music video format.

When I got an estimated price range, the video would *cost* as much as a low-budget movie!

Tony said, "Shit! That's gettin' close to a million dollars."

I said, "Look, y'all been telling me to go all out, and Old School Records is putting up *half* of it."

John was all for it. He said, "Let's just do it, man. I don't care about the price."

Tony said, "That's how motherfuckers end up going broke, man. And then y'all want to have a God damn *boat* on the tour, too? *Shid!*"

Tony was unbelievable!

I said, "Tony, you full of fucking mouth, man. You was telling me out in California to go for it. Now we get back home and you changing your tone and shit."

Tony said, "Man, I didn't tell you to start spending no fuckin' million dollars for no damn videos. I was just saying to live a little bit and have some fun out in the public life. That's all. I didn't say shit about no million-dollar videos."

John cut him off and said, "All right, whatever, man. We gon' do it anyway. I got the money."

Tony smiled and said, "Yup, I can see it now. You gon' pay a million dollars for this one. *Two million* for the next video. *Three million* for the one after that. And then you gon' be a broke motherfucker asking *me* for money by the time we get ready to do the third album."

Tony was exaggerating his ass off, but I laughed at it anyway.

John ignored him and said, "And we gon' do that boat thing on tour, too, D. *I'm* the captain here. *Everybody* gon' talk about *that*. Watch."

Tony kept it going like some kind of comedy routine. He said, "Yeah, and they gon' talk about how your country ass went *broke*, too. You *need* to just put a big-ass country sofa on the stage and sing from that."

John finally said, "Shut up, man. I mean, this is *your* damn song idea. Now you want me to do this for *another song* instead of this one?"

Tony changed his tune again. He said, "Ah . . . naw. *All Night Situation* is definitely the song to do it with. No doubt."

John said, "Yeah, that's what I *thought*."

We went ahead and set everything up for the video shoot on an island off the Florida coast. In the meantime, I figured that it was time for me to step up my own game plan in the music industry to add all of the necessary elements that John would need to win a best artist and a best album award for his sophomore album. *Honesty* was definitely a worthy album, so I had to go about making it happen.

First I had to have the right attitude about myself. I had to think BIG! No more *small* thinking. So I went ahead and used some of that money that I had built up with John to buy a penthouse condominium in downtown Philadelphia. I hired Big Joe from the football team as a bodyguard for all of us, and let him move into my old apartment. I also gave him the Maxima and bought myself a dark green Mercedes 500 SL.

After buying new furniture and psyching myself into thinking about earning my new living expenses, I listened to different new groups that I figured I could establish relationships with while on tour with John that summer.

Butterscotch, the girl trio from Philly that Tangela was managing, were already in our corner, and I contacted the manager for a young guy group called the Three Romeos. They had a Boyz II Men sound and could use the exposure as Loverboy's opening act, just like Boyz II Men had done for us a year earlier.

We shot the music video right before the album release. It took us three days, and John ended up having a fling with the young actress who we paid to play the stranded role with him. Tony was right, that boy was fiending for every girl who looked at him too hard.

When *Honesty* was released, it went right to number one on the R&B and pop charts. We were doing plenty of interviews, including the interview with Evelyn Harris from the R&B-music–based *Harmony* magazine. Since she wanted to add me into the mix of the questions, I even invited her over to my new condo to do it. I wanted to show off a little bit like I was a Big Willie and have her report on that. The public loved to read about famous people's money and assets, so she obliged.

Evelyn walked in wearing a dark blue pants suit and looking very businesslike, with her coat draped over her arm. As I took her coat to hang in the closet, she looked around at my skyline of Philadelphia and said, "Hmmm, pretty nice place."

I said, "Yeah, I just decided to splurge recently."

John laughed and said, "Yeah, he's making *me* want one now."

I offered Evelyn something to drink, and she asked me if I had any springwater.

"Yeah, I have springwater," I told her. I went to bring her a glass.

Evelyn took a sip, made herself comfortable in my new leather sofa, and wasted no time getting into the interview.

She set up her tape recorder and asked John the first question about his relationship with me.

John looked at me and started laughing.

He said, "I wasn't no businessperson, I just wanted to sing. But my man D always had my back like that. So he was gonna make sure that I wasn't singing for free."

She asked me where I got my business mind from.

I said, "My father works for a contractor in North Carolina, and he used to have plenty of stories to tell me and my two older brothers about people trying to get over. Then both of my brothers ended up becoming business majors in college, so I was just schooled well on talking about getting paid for your services."

"So how did you two first meet?" she asked us.

John spoke up first and said, "In church. Darin was the bad boy getting kicked out of the youth choir, and I was the good momma's boy who paid attention and did what I was supposed to do."

I laughed and said, "I was just an average boy getting into your everyday situations. John was just *extra* sheltered."

She looked and said, "Is that true, John? You had a tight leash on you?"

John said, "Was it *ever*. I was basically suffocating. And to this day, my mom is still telling me to drop all of this music stuff and find my way back to the Lord."

She said, "Have you thought about doing that?"

John said, "Yeah, I *think* about it. I just ain't doing it. I mean, I still believe in God and all, I just believe that he has another purpose for me. And he's speaking to me through my music. So like this album says, it's all about honesty. And everybody in church is always praying because they know that they're *not* always honest."

She said, "That's an interesting statement. I mean, if you look at so much of the art and culture from the black community today, most of it is coming from people under the age of twenty-five who just want to tell it like it is."

I jumped in on that and said, "Yeah, because that's where the honesty is coming from. It's like, each generation has to re-create the truth for themselves in what they're going through. And that's black kids, white kids, Hispanics, Asians, *everybody*. I mean, John's mom won't even *listen* to his music, and all he's doing is being real about the truth of our times. But when you get to a certain age, you stop wanting to deal with those truths. And it's like, the world is just supposed to stop and start with *you* just because you're older now. But it don't work that way. So each generation has to start over again with their own thing."

John smiled and looked at me. I guess he didn't expect for me to defend him and his music like that. He said, "Yup," and nodded his head. "And some people try to *hide* the truth when they get old."

I knew where he was going with that without him saying it. He was talking about his mother and the information that she refused to give him about his father again.

Evelyn said, "But we also know that young people make a lot of mistakes that they could have learned *not* to make from wiser, cooler heads. So, have there been any older men or people in the music industry who helped you along?"

I spoke up first on that, too. John just let me have the floor on the interview.

I said, "Oh, most definitely. Chester DeBerry at BMG was the greatest thing that could happen to us, and he was glad that we reached out to him. And even though Herbert Blake is no longer our booking agent, he was very instrumental in helping us to get out there. Plenty of other older people helped us out, too. And the guys at Old School Records have been *great* to us."

I said, "But I mostly have to thank my father for having faith in me and setting a good example of the inner strength and courage that I had to have to be able to do this at such a young age. Because a lot of guys my age can barely find a job or decide if they want to go to school or not, let alone manage a career worth millions of dollars. So I have to give a lot of the credit to my mother and father with just old-fashioned, you know, Southern upbringing."

She asked John, "So, who was your inspiration as a singer?"

John said, "Probably Marvin Gaye, you know. He had the same upbringing in the church, like myself and a lot of other singers have, and he wanted to do things his own way and send a message out in his music like I do. So I see a lot of similarities in that."

He said, "And you know, they called Marvin Gaye a stubborn kind of man, and I'm kind of stubborn, too when it comes to my music."

I started laughing again. I nodded my head and said, "Yeah, you got *that* right. *Stubborn*."

John smiled and said, "It works for me, though."

When we finished the interview, Evelyn stopped the tape and went off the record with us.

She said, "You know, I *really* like you guys. You have been very professional about everything, and I already liked John's music, but I had no idea that both of you would be this mature about everything."

Evelyn had to be at least in her early thirties, so I looked at her as a young elder. But she wasn't condescending toward us, and I liked that. She treated us with respect, and I could tell that it wasn't just a job to her.

I said, "Well, when we're doing this ourselves like we are, we *have* to be professional. There's nobody else that's gonna do it for us. That's just the situation that we're in."

John nodded and said, "Yup. We got no time to play. It's all about making our way in the music world and not quitting."

Evelyn nodded her head and said, "Do you guys have a strong publicist?"

I paused for a minute. I read her mind immediately. She was offering. I could see it in her face. She was reaching out to us like that. She liked us *that* much.

I asked her, "You think we need a stronger one?"

She said, "Well, your public image is about more than just taking an interview, it's about how you set it up, and what information is given and when. It's really a science to all of it. That's why some artists get more press than others when they don't really deserve it. And I think that what *you* guys are doing deserves a lot more press. You are *both* a lot more talented and hardworking than *ninety percent* of the people out here."

I smiled. Evelyn was pouring on the gravy. I would say maybe *sixty percent* than others, but not *ninety*. Ninety percent was *way* up there. But we really had no way of knowing.

I opened up the door for her and said, "Well, what would you suggest?"

She said, "I've been thinking about doing my own thing in the entertainment industry for a while now, and I just wanted to make sure that I went about it the right way. And I just feel it in my gut. You guys would be the *perfect project* to take on."

John smiled and said, "Project, hunh?"

Evelyn raised her index finger. She said, "See that? One *word* could be *that* powerful. That's just how important a publicist is today. The media," she said with a pause, "can make you or break you."

John said, "Yeah, that's why I didn't win that damn Best New Male Artist of the Year Award. I didn't have enough press on my side. We sold three million albums and people tried to act like they didn't know about it."

Evelyn said, "But yet, they had you to *perform* at the awards show. So they got what *they* wanted, and I want to help make sure that you get what *you* want."

I just smiled at her. Talk about *timing!* Things were just coming all together at another level for us.

I said, "So, how does this work?"

Evelyn broke down all of the services that she would provide for us, and her fee, and it sounded as if she would take a lot of extra stress off *my* hands. I wouldn't have to deal with the public at all if I didn't want to, and she knew a lot more media people than I did. She could set up the television and the magazine covers whenever we needed the push.

John was all for it. He said, "Let's do it, man. She likes *us*, and *I* like her."

We shared a laugh while I tried to put all of the numbers together.

I said, "So, we'll be your first clients then?"

Evelyn smiled and said, "My brand-new baby. And you'll get *all* of my attention."

I thought about whether she had set the whole thing up to take us on a business ride, but I just felt that she was being sincere with us. I felt it in *my gut* that she was a good person who cared about us. I think that our story and our dedication to what we were doing had really touched her, so I couldn't turn the idea down.

I said, "All right. We'll try this out then."

She said, "Well, what I'll do is get together a contract and a business plan proposal by next week sometime, for you guys to go over with your lawyer." Then she whispered to us and said, "And I know it's not ethical as a reporter right now, but I'll also try my best to get you the cover of *Harmony.*"

She stopped herself and said, "Now I can't *promise* you that, *yet*, but let me tell you, we're gonna work this thing to the point where you can get the cover of *everything* before I'm finished."

I don't know why I hadn't thought about hiring our own publicist before, but like I said, I was still young and still learning while on the job. Like Evelyn was saying, I had been working hard.

When she left us, John looked at me and smiled.

He said, "We making a lot of moves, man. We're already at number one, and we're still moving. Our new video ain't even out yet. I'm liking how this is feeling."

I smiled back at him. I said, "Yeah. And now I gotta get us a new lawyer before things get real wild on us."

John said, "Do what you gotta do, man."

And I planned to.

I searched for the phone number that Chester DeBerry had given me for the lawyer in New York a few years ago, and when I couldn't find it, I just decided to give Mr. DeBerry a call to thank him again for schooling us on the business, and try and see if I could get the lawyer's number from him again.

Mr. DeBerry got on the phone with me and said, "Darin, I'm *damn* proud of you guys. You boys are really doing it, from the bottom to the top, and in your *own* way."

He said, "I just listened to that new album a few days ago in my office, and that thing is gonna be *hotter* than a snowman in hell!"

I started laughing. Them damn old-timers could say the craziest things I ever heard.

I said, "That's all John, man. And the drummer, Tony Richmond. *Both* of them boys are geniuses. I'm just happy to go along for the ride."

Mr. DeBerry said, "Darin, don't you get on this phone and bullshit me. I know what's really going on." He said, "I don't care how God damn fancy the boat is, it can't make it to port without the captain. And *you're* the *captain*, Darin. There's no doubt in my mind about it. So, what are you up to now?"

I chuckled and said, "We're about to hire an outside publicist, and I wanted to get back in contact with that lawyer in New York who you were telling me about a couple of years ago."

"It's done," he told me.

He gave me the name and number and asked me, "How is John making out? Now be honest with me, Darin. Is it all going to his head yet?"

I started laughing again. I told him the truth. I said, "John is like living in a candy store right now. And I'm trying my best to keep him with just one piece."

Mr. DeBerry laughed so hard that I thought it wasn't too healthy for him.

He said, "That boy was a late bloomer wasn't he?"

I said, "Well . . . not really *that* late." I didn't want to tell *all* of John's business.

Mr. DeBerry asked me, "Well, when did *you* start, Darin? A lot earlier than *he* did, didn't you?"

We couldn't stop laughing with each other. But I didn't want to answer him, though.

I said, "John got one girl who's a little bit older than him, but she wants more than *he* wants to give right now."

Mr. DeBerry said, "It'll happen for him. He'll wake up. We *all* wake up sooner or later and find out that *ten of 'em* ain't better than *the one* who counts. And I've been married to mine for thirty-two years now."

I said, "Yeah, I *hope* so," for me *and* John.

Mr. DeBerry caught on to my doubts and said, "Well, maybe you're right. Some of these guys today just aren't feeling the love like we used to back in *my* day."

He said, "And what about you? How are *you* makin' out?"

I said, "Most of the time, I'm too busy thinking about John to get that involved. I mean, I'm a young guy out here, too."

He started laughing again, but what could I say? I wasn't connected to a woman of my own yet. I was only turning twenty-two years old. I had plenty of time to settle down. I didn't have to apologize to anyone for not having an official girlfriend. A lot of them couldn't handle the rigors of the business anyway. *I* was still having problems holding things down.

When I hung up the phone with Mr. DeBerry, I thought about my older brothers. Neither one of them was married, and they were in their mid- and late twenties, so I had no need to get serious yet. As long as I kept myself under control.

I told myself out loud, "Yeah, to hell with that. I'm all right. As long as I'm not trying to do every other girl out there like John is doing."

Sure enough, we hired Evelyn Harris as our publicist with *Honesty* as the number one R&B and pop album in the country, and we had magazine covers everywhere! We had a *USA Today* feature story, and many national newspapers were ready to line up to interview us for when the summer tour kicked off in June. The video for *All Night Situation* was released, and it quickly became a top request at every video network. We were on our way to going *double platinum* before we even *started* to tour!

Then Evelyn outdid herself with a double-edged-sword move right before the tour hit. She proposed to several magazines to have a national contest for lucky girls to have an official date with John "Loverboy" Williams in all eighteen cities where we expected to tour. Since Tangela and John were starting to get close again after the National Music Awards, that Loverboy date idea was a new explosion to set her off.

John called me up and had a mouthful to say about it.

He said, "Man, what the hell is wrong with this girl? You know what she's telling me now, man? She made a whole list of shit that I can't do if I plan to stay with her, as if I'm gonna fuck every girl that I go out on these tour dates with."

He said, "Man, I told her that this is a great idea that gets us lots of extra publicity. And now she trying to ruin the shit for me."

I said, "Yeah, well, I knew that was going to be a problem when Evelyn came up with this idea. I don't think she knew how close you and Tangela were, and I didn't really stop her because I didn't think that all of these magazines would go for this. I'm surprised at it myself. Evelyn is really *working* it, man."

John laughed and said, "I know. But why you didn't think it would work, though, man? You don't think that the women love me like that? What, I still gotta prove it to you?"

He started laughing again as if it was all a game to him. He was high. I could sense it through the looseness of his words.

I said, "All right, what I'll do is call up Tangela and tell her that we'll have an official chaperon or something to follow y'all around."

John got quiet for a minute. He said, "Wait a minute, man. We don't need no damn chaperon. We gon' have all mature women doing this. They all have to be at least twenty-one. We don't need no damn chaperon."

I said, "John, do you realize that these magazines are going to be writing stories on these dates? You gon' have to watch every step you take, man. Seriously."

John said, "And you think that some of them are not gon' lie about it and make shit up for their own popularity? Man, women love that kind of drama."

I said, "John, this shit ain't for no drama, man. This is just a good publicity idea for your name. It's a *Loverboy* thing."

John said, "That's what I'm saying. So why can't I show 'em a little love for real?"

I stopped and thought for a minute. That shit wasn't funny anymore. I was seriously thinking about calling Evelyn back up and calling the whole thing off. I didn't want to tell her, but John just wasn't in the right frame of mind to do the harmless, platonic date thing.

I said, "John, when you're not high, we're gonna have a talk in the morning at your crib, and we're gonna go over this thing. Because if you don't think you can do this without trying to stick every last girl who you go out with, then we definitely can't do it. This shit could be disastrous."

John said, "I can't believe you, man. I mean, I'm not *that* pressed. Some of these girls may be ugly anyway. I may not *want* to fuck some of them."

Unbelievable! I was thinking to myself. *This shit is ridiculous!*

I said, "Well, I'll call you up, man, and we'll talk about this in the morning."

He asked me, "Why don't you want to talk about it right now?"

"Because you're high right now, man, and you're not thinking straight."

"I'm thinking straight," he told me. "Getting high don't mess me up like that. I know what I'm saying. And I'm *not* gon' hit every girl on this tour. But I mean, come on, man. I gotta hit *some* of 'em. I mean, not *one* out of *eighteen* girls, man? That shit sounds like torture. What if they want it?"

I was convinced. Evelyn and I would have to rethink that whole Loverboy date idea to make things safer for *all* of us. I guess she figured that John was still an obedient church boy who would not fool around. She just didn't know the facts. They didn't call him *Loverboy* for nothing. And I was going to have to break the news to her.

. . . *but he could still sing . . .*

Evelyn beat me to the phone call early that next morning from her office in New York. She said, "Darin, I just had a very *heated* conversation this morning with Tangela Austin, who manages the group Butterscotch, about our publicity plan for John's tour dates this summer."

She said, "Are they a couple? I didn't know."

I took a breath and said, "It's a long story. I guess they were *trying* to get back together. Or actually, *I* tried to make that happen myself because they were going out for a while last year, and when they broke up, John didn't take it too well. That's actually what I had in mind to talk to you about myself."

Evelyn said, "Well, as his publicist, I hate to be in John's business. However, his business is now *my business*, if you can understand me. I'll need to know as much as possible about his private life, so that I'll know how to proceed with things."

I said, "Yeah, that's kind of my fault. I didn't stop you and explain the situation in time. I just figured that you had an idea to work with, but I didn't think that it would actually work this fast."

She said, "So, what all do I have to know about John that we need to have an understanding about? Because he doesn't tell you much of anything in his interviews, outside of his music. And on *one* end that's good because he's able to maintain a private life that way, but on the *other* end, if *I* don't know what his private life is like, then we *all* could end up getting burned, and you'll have me out here looking like a fool."

She said, "Now it's my *priority* this morning to find out *everything* that I need to know, even if I have to drive down there to Philly and drill John about everything myself. So let's kick it, Darin. What is John like behind closed doors? Because he doesn't seem to be the type to tell on himself."

I went ahead and told Evelyn about John's bedroom ways, and I hung up with her without ever bringing up his marijuana habit. Afterward, I felt guilty about it. I figured I would have to talk to John about *everything* so we could work on getting him the recognition that he deserved without any embarrassing setbacks. Evelyn believed that we could make John the hottest thing on the market if he didn't screw anything up on the damn tour.

I grabbed my keys and caught the elevator down to the parking garage. I called John on my car phone while on the way to his house.

I said, "I'm on my way up there, man. We need to talk about this whole tour situation."

John said, "Aw'ight, I'm here."

I made it to his house, walked in, and I remained standing. I wanted to get right into it with him.

I said, "I talked to Evelyn this morning, man, and she said that you gotta be on your best behavior during these publicity dates so that we don't ruin anything."

John just sat down and looked at me. He said, "You want something to drink, D? Some orange juice or anything, man?"

I asked him if he had heard what I just told him.

He said, "Yeah, man, I heard you. And I'm just thinking, man." He paused.

I said, "Thinking what?"

"Maybe this ain't no good idea. I mean, if I can't do shit with these girls, then they just gon' be gettin' in my damn way," he told me.

I got frustrated and said, "John, you don't need to fuck every night on tour. *Nobody* fucks that much," I told him. "Tangela's gonna be on tour with us anyway. You need to just share a room with her."

John said, "You must ain't heard it yet then."

"Heard what?"

"Tangela called me this morning and told me that Butterscotch may not be touring with us. She's trying to hook them up on tour with Janet Jackson now," he told me. "She said she got West Coast connections like that."

I frowned. Tangela hadn't called *me* with that news. I figured that she was bullshitting him.

I said, "Okay, *now* we're playing a damn game of tug-o'-war, and we don't have time for this shit. So let's call Tangela back up and let *me* hear her say that."

John said, "I'm not calling her, man. You call her your damn self."

I smiled and said, "You know you want to call her. Go 'head with that. Don't even play. Y'all both got feelings for each other and be frontin' on each other whenever times get rough."

"Whatever, man. She wearing off on me now. I gave her a song, and now I can move on from her."

I asked him, "Move on to what?"

He smiled and said, "More new pussy."

I told him, "John, you gon' fuck up this whole tour over some ass. You *need* to think about the business end of it, man. It ain't worth fuckin' up your career over some *bullshit!*"

I just shook my head. That boy was really making me work.

He stopped laughing once he read the despair on my face.

He settled down and said, "Aw'ight, man. I can be good with this tour date thing. I'll just have somebody, like, waitin' in the wings for when I get back to my room."

I said, "And no smoking weed *before or on* these dates. If you gotta do it, then do it *after* the dates are over."

John smiled and said, "What if the girl wants some? A lot of girls smoke weed, too. It's not just guys."

I said, "John, this is for your own good, man. Do you want to win them awards next year, or keep getting jerked around? Because if you go ahead and—"

He cut me off and said, "Aw'ight, man. Aw'ight. I can do the shit."

I changed the subject. I asked him, "So you're dead serious about Tangela breaking the tour? I mean, she can't do that. This would be good exposure for Butterscotch. She could fuck up *their* careers because of *you.*"

"Not if they tour with Janet Jackson," he told me. "Janet Jackson's tours are *always* rockin'."

I said, "According to Evelyn, *your tour* is gonna be the hot one this summer."

John said, "Yeah, she's *supposed* to say that. That's her *job.*"

I got back to my penthouse condo, where I had a new office area. I called Tangela on my business line to see what was going on with the tour situation.

She said, "Darin, I don't even know why I'm talking to you anymore. Why did you get me back involved with that boy? He's more out of it than he was before."

I tried to put the guilt trip on her. I said, "That's because you left him. He needs to learn how to trust again."

Tangela said, "No, he *needs* to grow the fuck up! That's what he *needs* to do! Wasting my God damn time. I *told you* about that, Darin. Now you went and got me all pissed off about it again. *I knew* I should have just stayed away from that triflin' shit. He just needs to grow up."

I paused and said, "So, you're actually planning to mess up Butterscotch's tour opportunity on account of John? I mean, as one manager to another, Tee, that's just not professional. You're gonna have to be strong enough to continue doing business."

Tangela calmed down and said, "Don't call me Tee. Okay? I'm a grown damn woman, and I don't need no nicknames right now."

I said, "Okay. My bad. But I'm just saying, you really need to think about this tour. John has all of the momentum in the world right now, and you have an inside track with me, so *use it.*"

Tangela turned me down and said, "No. I've already talked about this, and Butterscotch agrees with me to try our hardest to get on Janet Jackson's tour this summer. So I wish y'all luck. And that's the *least* that I can do. Because if he wants to fuck around with all of these little *hot dates* that he has coming up, then he can go ahead and do it until his *dick* falls off, for all *I* care."

I said, "Tangela, that's all a business thing. John's not gonna—"

She cut me off and said, "Tell it to the next one."

There wasn't another word that I could get in there before she hung up on me.

I set down the phone and mumbled, "Damn!" Now I had to look for another hot girl group to open for us.

I thought about calling Zhane, but they were a little too mature and not popular enough to get the young guys open like I knew Butterscotch would. They were *hot*, and Tangela was selling me out. Or John had sold *both* of us out by acting like an asshole. I was in another bind.

I called up Matt at Old School Records to see if he had any ideas on new upcoming girl groups who could open for us.

Matt asked me the obvious. "What happened to Butterscotch? I thought that they were the *perfect* match for you guys. They even cut a song with John, and he wrote a few for them."

I said, "Yeah, man, but they have plans now to tour with Janet Jackson this summer."

Matt said, "Oh, yeah, that'll do it. Are they really signed on with the Jackson sister? That's great."

I said, "Nah, they're just hoping for it, actually."

Matt said, "Well, maybe they'll come back in on John's tour if they can't make it on Janet's."

"Yeah, but we can't count on that," I told him. "We gotta move on and get somebody else."

He said, "Well, I'll call around and see what we can do. And yeah, I just wanted to tell you that the video for *All Night Situation* is really doing great. I mean, we *still* think you guys went way over budget on it, but at least it *looks* like it could be worth it."

I said, "Yeah, we just figured that we'd try it out to see if it would work for us, and it *is* working."

Matt said, "Yeah, well, you got *my* vote on that. And everyone knows that it looks good, we just hope that you guys find another creative idea that can go just as far with about *half* of the money next time," he said with a laugh.

That was Old School Records for you. They were always concerned about trying to keep the price of business down. But like they say, *Scared money don't make none.*

When the tour finally rolled around for us, Tony had gotten acquainted with our new traveling bodyguard, Big Joe, and he was all jokes about it over at my penthouse with John.

Tony said, "You know y'all proving that y'all still country with Big Joe around, right? I thought you was getting out of it when you bought this penthouse pad, D, but now you done brought the barn up north and shit, instead of going back to the barn."

John joked back to him and said, "Just don't let Big Joe hear you saying that shit. He might break a couple of your fingers and fuck up my beats for the tour."

Tony smiled and said, "Shid, I'd lay that motherfucker down with a pipe to his head in a *hot* minute. I make my damn *living* with these hands." He held them up as if they were golden.

I just laughed at him.

Then Tony asked me, "So, who is this new girl group, Juicy? Are they any good, man?" He looked at John and shook his head before I could answer him.

He said, "This nigga just had to go and fuck up our deal with Butterscotch. Now we got some damn new-jack chicks jacking a title from a Big Poppa song."

John laughed it off and ignored the slight to him.

I said, "They're not really new jacks, man, they're just coming up, that's all. But they *look* good, *and* they have potential. They have a lot of great dance moves for the tour, too," I added.

Tony looked at me and said, "*Dance moves?* So they can't really sing then?"

He said, "Saying that they got great dance moves is like saying that the car has air-conditioning in it. The fuck is that, man? Is that the best thing they got goin' for 'em? We need some girls who can *sing*, man, and get the people open for us. I mean, I like these Three Romeo guys, but since they black, they should have called themselves the Three Dolemites or something."

John started laughing and said, "Or the Three Superflys?"

We had all been watching the blaxploitation movies of the seventies.

I said, "Those guys were all old, man. Maybe Loverboy should do a movie and make a new playerlike hero for the nineties crowd."

John smiled and said, "Yeah, I'm wit' that. Get me a script to read."

I nodded and told him that I would, but the most important thing at that time was getting ready for our big tour.

We kicked off the Loverboy Fantasy Tour in Detroit during the last weekend in May at the Palace, where the NBA Pistons played with Grant Hill as a major basketball star. The Palace was a new place, and by the end of May, Loverboy's sophomore effort, *Honesty*, was still fluctuating between the number one and number four album on the R&B *and* pop charts in the country. *All Night Situation* was also another number one hit, mainly on the strength of the video.

We let the Three Romeos open the tour, with Juicy going on second with their dance moves, before it was Loverboy's stage. The stage crew set down a giant shiny blue tarp to look like water. Then they placed our imitation island at the front end of the stage, and got the boat ready to roll out. Could you imagine what was about to happen? We actually had an eight-feet-tall wooden boat that was sixteen feet long, with white sails on it, and a giant fan to simulate wind. The boat had hidden wheels underneath and a motor that got up to twenty-five miles an hour. It cost us close to $50,000 to make it work the way we wanted it to. And then we had travel expenses to tour with the damn thing.

Backstage, I looked at John and asked him if he was ready to take it to the next level. With all of the money we were spending, his ass had *better* be ready!

He looked at me and smiled, wearing a safari hat and an all-white tailored outfit from Charles Nickels, who was making a name for himself through John.

John said, "I'm gon' do my thing like I always do, man."

I walked out to do my introduction onstage, and Big Joe stopped me before I could get there.

He reached out his big hand to me and said, "I just want to thank you for this opportunity, D. I'll never forget this shit, dawg. You and Loverboy looked out for folks. Y'all didn't turn y'all back on nobody. And I appreciate that shit, man."

Big Joe looked sharp, wearing all black, with a fresh haircut and a shave. He made me proud of my hire.

I joked to him and said, "Yeah, because we didn't want you to beat our asses if we *didn't* hire you."

Big Joe broke up laughing and said, "Aw, go 'head, nigga. Go 'head."

I walked out onto the stage in front of the curtains and took a deep breath in front of the audience. We had it all rehearsed.

I opened up my mouth with the cordless microphone in hand and said, "Everybody, I got some bad news to report."

I paused to make sure they all passed the word around and got good and nervous, thinking the worst.

Somebody screamed out, "DON'T EVEN TRY THAT SHIT! I WANT ALL MY DAMN MONEY BACK THEN!"

I kept my poise and told them, "Loverboy has been lost at sea."

Then we turned off all of the lights inside the Palace, and boat sirens went off, with searchlights bouncing through the audience.

The crowd went off with anticipation.

I asked them, "So, who out here wants to be stranded on an island for a night with Loverboy?"

We were using the whole story line from our new video, and the crowd lost their minds like we expected them to.

"WWWAAAAAAAAAAAAAAAAHHHHHH!"

Girls started trying to crash the front as soon as we pulled the curtains back and showed them the island sitting up onstage to their right.

The security men held them all back, and then Big Joe picked out the one lucky sister to dance on the elevated island. She was actually John's date for Detroit. The local radio stations were working with us for the tour dates through call-ins, and the magazines would contact them for the story. Evelyn had masterminded the whole setup.

A second curtain pulled back to reveal Tony and the band. They were on top of an imitation mountain that stood fifteen feet tall and was placed back at center stage. It had a flat surface at the top for them to stand on and play their instruments. That mountain cost us some big cheese, too.

Then Tony kicked things off with the beat:

BaDOOMP-BaDOOMP, TAT
BaDOOMP-BaDOOMP, TAT . . .

At that point, I walked off of the stage and let John make his entrance while standing on top of his slow-moving boat with his microphone in hand.

The boat rolled in and onto a platform to the audience's left. Then Loverboy sang:

It's an all night sit-u-a-a-a-tionnn . . .

"WWWWWAAAAAAAAAAAAAAAAAAHHHHHHHHH!"
My ears started popping from the deafening screams in that place. John was about to light their fires with a *blowtorch:*

We got the ti-i-ime
we got the pla-a-ace
let's make a date
and you can have it yourrr wa-a-ay.

An all night sit-u-a-a-a-tionnn . . .

The boat made it slowly to the center of the stage, with a captain behind the wheel and his foot on the gas pedal. And the crowd continued to kill everyone's ears.

"WWWWWAAAAAAAAAAAAAAAAAAHHHHHHHHH!"
Loverboy continued to do his thing:

It's just me and you-u-u
what you wanna dooo
you gotta fan-ta-see
and that's all-l-l right with me.

An all night sit-u-a-a-a-tionnn . . .

The boat made it over to the girl on the island, where John began to climb from a ladder to join her. Once he made it onto the island with her, he laced the song's climax verse on her, with the horns from the band backing him up:

So I hope you got your rest last night
'cause good love ain't got no stoplight.

The music stopped, and John asked Miss Lucky Detroit, who was dressed in a sexy green two-piece, how she was feeling.

She said, "I'm feeling all right. I'm just happy to be here."

He said, "Are you nervous up onstage with me? You know, sometimes love can make a girl feel a little nervous."

Girls started screaming from the crowd, "I'M NOT NER-VOUS! TAKE MEEE!"

Miss Lucky Detroit said, "No. I'm not nervous."

She was dark brown and as cute as a church girl, too. A *good, clean-living* girl.

I was thinking to myself, John's definitely gonna want to do her. *Shit*, she would have been high on my *own* hit list. She just had *the look* that you wanted to know better!

John said, "Well, you know what?" He backed up from her and screamed:

HAAAY BAAABY.

Tony started the beat:

Tic-TAT, Tic-BOOM
YOU'RE LOOKIN' GOOD IN GREE-EE-EEN
Tic-TAT, BA-DOOM-BOOM . . .

They started dancing around the island, with John trying out some new dance moves that made the crowd go off again.

"WWWAAAAAAAAAAAAAAAAHHHHHH!"

Big Joe found his way back to me and yelled, "That nigga stone crazy up in here, dawg! That Loverboy nigga dun' lost his mind!"

Obviously, Big Joe was getting excited again.

I said, "Aw'ight, Joe, just keep his back, man. Watch his back."

Big Joe got big eyes and said, "Oh shit, my bad. My bad! Let me get back out there wit' 'im."

When they finished performing *Stylin' 'n' Profilin'*, Big Joe and the security guys helped Miss Lucky Detroit back down from the stage.

Then John walked to center stage on the tarp and said, "Now I want some sisters who can float on the water with me. Who large enough in here to float on the water?"

I didn't like that part so much, nor did I like the song, but John worked it anyway. So they got three big mommas up on the stage with him, and that funky-behind bass line to *Tonight Is Yours* slid in:

I want to rock your world / to-night
I want to rock your world / to-night . . .

Tony kicked off the beat right behind it:

Tit-DOOMP-Tit-SMACK
Tit-DOOMP-Tit-DOOMSMACK . . .

And the keyboard and guitar players both whined:

GIR-R-R-R-R-R-R-RLLLL.

John was up onstage dancing with these proud big sisters, and the whole place rocked when he sang his lyrics:

I'M A SOUTHERN MAAAN
AND I'M ON THE THINN SI-I-IDE
SO I LIKE THE GIRLS WITH BOD-DEES
AS WIDE AS SUN-SHIIINE . . .

John finished jamming with the sisters on that song and said, "I'm not making fun of my big sisters out here tonight. I got nothing but love for *every* sister!"

He said, "And we all got our own issues in life, right? Ain't none of us in here perfect. No matter *who you are* or *how you look.*"

He looked back toward the band on the mountain behind him and said, "Tony, let's hear it, man."

Tony did his thing with the drums again.

TISSS
DOOMP-DOOMP-TAT-DOOMP
DOOMP-DOOMP, TAT
DOOMP-DOOMP-TAT-DOOMP
DOOMP-DOOMP-DOOMTAT
TISSS . . .

The bass line kicked in with the strings, and this time *everybody* sang the lyrics:

A GIRL WROTE ME A LET-TER
AND IT SAID THAT I BROKE HER HEART . . .

AIN'T NO-BODY PER-FECT, BA-BY
AIN'T NO-BODY PER-FECT, UNT UNH . . .

Everything about John's performance, including the setup and our execution, was *smoking* that night! Evelyn was absolutely right! We were going to have one of the hottest tours that year. No question about it! John just had too many hit songs to miss. Evelyn was scheduled to join us for our second show, in Indianapolis, to see the masterpiece that we had created.

With about ten minutes left to perform for that first tour night in Detroit, John told the audience, "Some of you who haven't picked up the new album yet have not heard this song. But this one is very dear to my heart, and it expresses everything that I believe about my music."

He said, "It's the title song of the new album. *Honesty.* And that's what it's all about, being true to yourself. So if I can't *believe in it* . . . then I can't sing it. And I can't perform it."

He stood back on the imitation island and waited for the music to come in.

The keyboard player established the lead: *"Thaaat's whaaat sheee wannnnnn-teddd . . ."*

Tony came in with slow drums: *Tic-Doomp-Tic-TAT / Tic-Doomp-Tic-TAT . . .*

The electric guitar whined like a crybaby: *"That's what she wants to hear."*

The bass player dropped in a deep *"She wants . . . She wants . . ."*

Then John sang his lyrics from the deserted island onstage, his metaphor as a musical genius. He was way out there in a creative sea, and nobody could reach him there. All they could do was hear his music and attempt to *feel* what *he* felt:

Can you IM-MAGINE ALL your dreams come true
with everyTHING you ev-ver wan-ted
and all the MON-NEY THAT your eyes could see
well that's the KIND OF LIFE that's been revealed, to me.

But SOME OF US are satisfied with simple things
and a MAN WHO LIVES his life with dignity.

She said she wanted my HON-NEST-STEE-EEE
(Thaaat's whaaat sheee wannnnnn-teddd . . .)
what she wanted was HON-NEST-STEE FROM ME
(Thaaat's whaaat sheee wannnnnn-teddd . . .).

The crowd was hypnotized. Some of the people who knew the song from the album already broke down and started crying. I could see them wiping their eyes. *Thousands* of them! I teared up my damn self. My boy John was a heavy motherfucker, carrying the emotions of the world on his creative shoulders:

BUT SHE DIDN'T WANT THOSE THINNNGS
NO-O-O WAAAY
SHE JUST WANTED MEEE
SHE JUST WANTED MEEE
SHE JUST WANTED MEEE
TO BE STRAIGHT WITH HER . . .

It wasn't a part of our plan, but John brought the whole house down when *he* ended up crying as the song winded down.

John wiped his eyes, gathered himself together, and told the crowd, "I love y'all, man! Y'all just don't know! I could never do this without y'all!"

Then he broke down and cried again.

DAMN! In a minute, tears were all over my face. I couldn't stop them from rolling down. High emotions and gravity were just fucking my whole face up.

I mumbled to myself, "This motherfucker," and tried to smile and wipe my tears away.

John helped me out from the microphone when he said, "I want to ask y'all a question before I leave the stage tonight."

They started screaming, "YEEEAAAAAAHHHHH!"

"WHAT YOU WANT TO ASK US, BABY?" someone yelled.

John climbed back on his boat and paused. Then he opened his mouth and said, "May I *please* hold somebody's hand tonight?"

"WWWWWAAAAAAAAAAAAAAAAHHHHHHHHHH!"

I broke out laughing and said, "This mother*FUCKER!*"

Loverboy went ahead and closed out the night with the song that had started it all, while riding his boat back home:

Ma-a-ay I-I-I hol-l-ld your-r-r han-an-an-n-nd . . .

As the boat faded away from the stage, with John's lyrics on your ears and his music in your soul, the faces and energy of the crowd told you everything. They would have paid *twice* or *three times* to see Loverboy perform. And they were *definitely* going to talk about it.

Big Joe was the first one to say something to me as he headed backstage. His face was more messed up than mine was.

He said, "Darin, I will go to the *grave* for that nigga, man! Nobody *ever* made me feel that *touched*, man, in my *life!*"

He shook his head and wiped his face. He said, "That nigga right there, dawg. He just . . . he . . ." Big Joe couldn't even get his words out.

He said, "That boy just on some *shit*, man! *God almighty!*"

I laughed and said, "Yeah, I know. I feel the same way about him, man. The boy's a living legend. *Seriously!*"

. . . *like a king* . . .

If I ever had to put my finger on the high point of John's career, it would be that night in Detroit. That was a *hell* of a show, man! For *everybody!* That boy had us *all* open!

Evelyn made it out to the Indianapolis show, and she fell under the same protective trance that everyone else was falling under with John. As long as he could sing and perform like he did, Loverboy could do no wrong. He was becoming *untouchable* just like he had said, like Death Row records began to claim with Tupac Shakur and Snoop Dogg. And not only was John still screwing like a lion in mating season, but those magazines were not *daring* to print anything that even *hinted* what was really going on with those dates of his. It seemed as if a decision was made to push Loverboy to the top of the American music throne, and no one was trying to slow down his ascension.

By the time we reached the midway point of our tour, *Honesty* had sold more than *5 million* albums, and it was still ringing the register as a top-ten seller on the R&B *and* pop charts!

We had just completed a sold-out show in St. Louis, Missouri, when I began to realize that I was losing any semblance of control over John. The fame was really starting to go to his head.

I just happened to be headed to his suite where we were staying at the Regal Riverfront Hotel when I saw some of the band members and the Three Romeos slipping into the room right next to John's. They were all excited and laughing like kids.

I got curious and walked into the room behind them. They were all in the room listening to the activities going on inside John's suite, with drinking glasses up against the wall.

I said, "What the hell are y'all doing?"

They started breaking away from the wall, shocked that I had caught them in the act.

"Aw, you gotta hear this shit, man. John is crazy," one of the Three Romeos said to me.

I grabbed one of their glasses and listened through the wall for myself, just to see how sick they had all become.

The bed in John's suite was rocking like a ship at sea.

"Oooh, baby! Oooh, yeah!" some girl was moaning.

John was talking to her. "Is this what you want?" he asked her.

"Yesss! Yesss!"

"How bad do you want it?"

"Ooooh, baaay-beee!"

"I can't *hear* you!" John snapped at her. "How bad do you *want it?!*"

The girl squealed, "I want it *bad!* I want it *real* bad!"

I had heard enough. I broke out of the room and went to beat on John's door to stop the madness.

"HEY JOHN! IT'S DARIN, MAN! WE NEED TO TALK!"

I got no answer, so I continued to beat on the door like a police officer.

"HEY JOHN! *JOHN!* OPEN THE *FUCKING* DOOR, MAN!"

I still got no response. I was *pissed!* That motherfucker was *tripping!* And he was on the *tour* with that shit!

I walked back inside of the other room with the band members and the Three Romeos, and I proceeded to beat on the wall to stop John's crazy ass. Failing at that, I raised my voice to everyone in the room.

I said, "I want everybody to get the FUCK OUT OF HERE! This ain't some GOD DAMN PEEP SHOW! What the FUCK Y'ALL THINK THIS IS?! I will FIRE EVERY MOTHER*FUCKER* in this ROOM, and replace your ass for this *FUCKIN'* TOUR! Now try to play me!"

They all left that room in a *hurry*.

I was so hurt that night that my boy was tripping like that that I decided to take a ride around St. Louis in the limo just to think to myself, and to get away from the hotel. I was holding down *my* end of the business, but that motherfucker John was *losing it!*

I spotted Tony down in the lobby before I made it out to the car. He was with his girlfriend from Philly. Tony had finally broken down and allowed her to go on tour with him, and that represented a major statement about his commitment to her.

He said, "Hey, D, let's go in the bathroom right quick, man. I got something to talk to you about."

I said, "I don't have to go to the bathroom."

I just wanted to get the hell out of the hotel as fast as I could. I was ready to explode up in there. I was stressed again, and about to lose it my *damn self* if I didn't leave.

Tony insisted. "Come on, man, it'll only take a minute."

I took a deep breath and obliged. Tony walked in the bathroom with me and was smiling from ear to ear. He was dressed tastefully, looking good, and smelling like nice cologne.

He said, "Check this out," and pulled out a black ring box from his small brown leather carrying case. He opened the ring box, and I looked down at a huge diamond setting up on a fancy gold band.

Tony said, "I'm nervous as hell right now, man. But I'm about to take my girl out on the casino boat and do it. I'm ready to propose, man. I've had *my* fun. It's time to get real now."

I looked into Tony's face and was proud of him. He had really matured in the few years that I had known him. Our success had pretty much stabilized him, where it had done the *opposite* for John.

I smiled and said, "So, you're actually gonna pop the question tonight, hunh? That's good, man." He had loosened me up a bit.

Tony took a deep breath and smiled again. He said, "Yeah, man. What do you think? You think I should?"

I broke up laughing. I said, "You're asking *me* for advice? Get the hell out of here."

Tony said, "Yeah, man, what do you think?"

I got serious with him. I said, "I think you came a long way since I first met you, man. I wish I could say the same thing for John, right?"

Tony frowned and shook his head. He said, "I told you, man. Now you got these Three Romeo guys looking up to everything he does. And you know John's hitting *two* members of Juicy now. So he got *them* fightin' over him on the down low. But that shit gon' come to a head soon. You mark my words."

He said, "But hell, I don't want to talk about him. I want to talk about *me* now. You think I should get married?"

I thought about it for Tony. I said, "Only you can answer that. But yeah, that would be a good thing to do."

"Why?" he asked me.

I said, "Because you'll always have somebody there for you when times get rough on you." I was thinking about myself, actually. *I* needed someone for that.

Tony chuckled and said, "Yeah, but I love this girl, too, man. I mean, you make it sound like it's all business and shit, like I just need somebody to talk to. That manager stuff been going to *your* head, too. You better find your-self a steady girlfriend somewhere."

I said, "Well, if *you* know so much, then why you asking me?"

"Man, I'm just stalling for time right now," he responded and smiled at me. He said, "I know what I need to do. I'm *ready* for this."

I said, "Well, get on out of here and go do what you need to do then."

Tony laughed and slipped his ring box back into his leather carrying bag. He said, "I'll tell you how it went tomorrow sometime, man. Where were you headed to anyway?"

I said, "For a ride in the limo. I need to think."

Tony nodded to me and said, "Aw'ight then." We both walked out of the bathroom and went our separate ways.

I found one of the limo drivers stationed out front, and I walked over to the car, a black stretch limo with colored interior lighting.

The limo driver, an older white guy, was listening to John's new album, *Honesty.* I could hear it through the window.

He noticed me, hopped out of the driver's seat, and smiled. He said, "Yes, sir."

I told him that I'd like to take a ride through the city of St. Louis.

He said, "No problem," and rushed to get the door for me.

"Is there anywhere in particular you'd like to go?"

I said, "Nah, just drive me around, and I'll just look out the window at whatever strikes me."

"You got it," he told me.

As soon as we took off, he started talking about John's album.

He said, "You know, I've been listening to this album, and this music is really good. I'm glad that you guys gave me a copy. I'll have to get it signed. What was the title of his first album?"

I said, "*Loverboy: The Album.*"

He looked into the rearview mirror and smiled at me from his driver's seat.

He said, "Was it as good as this one?"

"Yeah, it was good. We're just getting more attention for this one," I told him.

He nodded and said, "Yeah, that's the way it goes sometimes. Your best album can sell the *least* amount of copies because of a lack of exposure, and then with the media attention, some people can sell *millions* of albums that are crap."

I nodded, but I really didn't feel like talking. I just wanted to relax and think.

He said, "Do you mind if I put the CD back on for ya?"

I shook my head and smiled. I told him, "You can listen to it up front for yourself if you want, but I'm a little tired of hearing it by now."

He laughed and said, "Yeah, I understand what you mean. You get to hear it nearly every night."

I added, "And if you don't mind, sir, I just want to relax right now. I don't even feel up to talking. It's just been a very long day."

Instead of saying another word, he just nodded to me in his rearview mirror. He raised the backseat window and went back to concentrating on his driving.

I rode around in the limo that night, and instead of thinking about John, I thought about Tony getting married. I smiled. *Tony* and *married* didn't sound right in the same sentence. Or at least not from when I had first met him. And he was right, too. I needed to find someone of my own before the stress of the tour began to take a toll on me. John surely wasn't helping me to remain sane. But what could I really do about it? Eventually I would have to deal with him.

I wondered what my father would say if I asked *him* about it. But I wasn't going to call him up in the middle of the night or anything. I had to become a man on my own. I was twenty-two years old and a new millionaire. John had over *five million* and counting!

I shook my head in the limo and mumbled, "Damn." *I'm actually riding around in my own limo. Is this shit really* real? I asked myself.

You never stop asking yourself that reality question, you just keep pushing for more. That's the only way that you can keep it. If you stop and start sniffing yourself, paranoia can set in and things can start smelling bad for you. That's how I began to feel in that plush limo that night. I was paranoid. If John fucked up his image with some sex scandal, we could lose everything, because the boy still had a good-guy image. A *great* image!

I got back to the hotel after three in the morning and tipped my limo driver $100. What the hell? I felt like being extra generous. Really, I was trying to trick God into being nice to me that night. Do unto others as you would have them do unto you. I didn't need the money, though. I just needed kindness. And I didn't need kindness in sex like John needed it either.

I took a deep breath while I rode the elevator back up to our floor. I planned to head to John's room again and see if things had toned down.

I walked into the hallway and spotted a woman bringing two drinks to his room, at *three o'clock* in the damn morning! I guess John wasn't finished with his entertaining yet.

I rushed in the room right behind her before she could shut the door back.

The woman turned and looked at me as if I was invading her privacy. She had this look in her eyes as if she wanted to ask me, *Who the hell are you?* It looked as if I was busting her groove, you know. But I didn't give a fuck. She was busting *my* groove. I needed to talk to my damn boy!

So I answered her question for her. I said, "I'm D Harmon. I put this shit together, and I can rip it back apart if I have to."

John just smiled at my attempt of ego tripping. He was wearing the hotel's white bathrobe and slippers, and he was walking around the room like secured royalty.

He said, "Yeah, this my man, Darin. I owe him a lot." He walked over and sat down in the lounge chair with the drink in his hand and crossed his legs.

I said, "John, we need to talk alone, man." I was going to be real cool about it, too. So I calmly took a seat in the sofa and crossed my own legs. I wasn't fucking leaving. That woman had only known John for about two hours. I knew that nigga for seventeen years. She was just at the wrong place at the wrong time.

John took a sip of his drink and nodded his head. He knew I wasn't leaving. I wasn't all into astrology or anything, but I *was* a Taurus. And if I felt serious enough about something, then I wasn't *budging*.

She would have to go, that's all there was to it. John told her what time it was.

He took another sip of his drink and said, "Umm . . . Jacqueline. I'm gon' need to talk to my man for a minute."

He barely knew the woman's damn name.

She took it all in stride, though. She said, "Okay, I'll just go wait in the other room."

She meant the bedroom. John looked at me again and started giggling. I knew he was still high that night. He had probably smoked another blunt well after midnight.

He put his hand up to her and said, "Wait a minute, wait a minute. I'm sayin' . . . we probably gon' have to take a rain check or something. Okay?"

She wasn't getting that part. And I didn't plan to explain it to her. It was John's call. He had gotten himself in it, and he needed to get himself out.

She said, "I don't have to hear what y'all saying. I'll close the door and watch the movie channel or something. You know, 'cause it's kind of late to be going back home."

I had to smile to myself after that. John had a tough one on his hands.

He said, "Come here for a minute. Come sit down," and patted his lap.

She was not a *young* woman either. She was slightly older than us, like Tangela. Nevertheless, she walked over and sat down on John's lap like a little girl who was looking up to her daddy.

I just shook my head. I couldn't believe that shit no matter how many times that I saw it.

John said, "Look, I'm gon' have to come back out here to St. Louis and make it like it's your birthday or something. Okay? But I don't know how long this gon' take. So I'm gon' give you some money to make it back home."

She said, "Just like that? But baby, I didn't even get to spend any time with you yet. I mean, all I did was bring up a damn drink."

John looked at her as if it pained him to say it.

He said, "You makin' this hard for me, Jacqueline. And if you gon' make it hard for me, then I can't make you no promises for next time."

"Are you gon' *promise* anything at all? What if something comes up *next time*, too?"

He said, "Well, then it just won't be your damn day, now will it?"

I knew the feeling. I had been ice cold to women myself. What could I say?

Jacqueline said, "So, I have to go back home then? After I stayed out here all this time just to see you."

John asked her, "Would you have rather went back home?"

She stood up from his lap and said, "Yeah, now I wish I *had* went home."

John sipped his drink real cool and said, "Well, I guess I'll stay home, too, then."

That was some slick shit that I hadn't seen from John before.

Jacqueline left the room in a huff. She said, "You can *keep* your damn money. You ain't show *me* no damn love!" and she slammed the door when she left.

John didn't even flinch. He looked straight ahead and said, "They just don't know how to leave sometimes, D." He was icier than I *ever* was. A *dry* ice. That was the worst kind. It stuck to you. At least regular ice could be thawed by heated emotions. But John seemed detached from his emotions at that point. That was some stone cold pimp shit.

I asked him, "What's your problem, man? You puttin' on freak shows now? What are you, bored or something? What the fuck is wrong with you?"

"Ain't nothing wrong with me, man."

I said, "*Something* is wrong with you. You wanna talk about it?"

"Talk about what?"

I said, "It's going to your head, man. You gots to cool that shit out."

He started laughing. "I can't get no ass, D? You used to get it when you played football and I was marching around in the damn band with a hard dick. But I'm soft now. I'm real soft, man."

I said, "Yeah, but I never put on no *freak shows* in my *life*, man. *Never!*"

He said, "Man, some of these girls want to feel like they were really here with me. You know what I'm sayin'? A lot of them sound like they dreamin'. 'Am I really here with you?'" he said, mocking a girl's voice.

I started smiling, but it wasn't funny.

John said, "I'm trying to let them know that they're really here, man. That's all. Some of them *want* you to talk to 'em."

I looked him straight in his eyes and said, "That's bullshit, John. You were showing off, man. You wanted everybody to hear your handiwork."

John shook his head and said, "You just won't let me slide, will you?"

"Am I supposed to? I mean, if I let everything slide, then what kind of manager would I be?" I said, "Just look at it this way. If your music started to slide, and you started gettin' all wild and crazy with your songs, then what kind of musician would *you* be?"

I gave him a minute to think about it, and he didn't respond, so I filled him in on what I meant. But I knew that he understood me already, he just didn't want to say it.

I said, "You would be an unstable artist, right? And Old School Records would have to make a move on you. Well, I feel the same way right now, man. You're disrespecting your opportunities."

John looked at me and asked, "So what are you saying, D? You gon' make a move on me, man? After we built this up together. Just because I like laying down with company at night."

I said, "It ain't got nothing to do with your company, man. This is a *business*. You gon' have to have some decency about what you doin'. That's all *I'm* saying. I'm not asking you to be celibate or nothing. But I *would* rather you had some stability.

"I mean, you just gotta say *no* to a lot of this shit, man, like you just did with Jacqueline," I told him.

He smiled and said, "Actually, I was a little tired. I didn't feel like fucking with her. If she would have come a little earlier, we could have did some things."

I grimaced and said, "That's what I'm talking about, man. If you gon' be in the position that you're in, you just gon' have to have some more discipline. That's just how it is."

John asked, "Well, how come these *girls* ain't gotta have no discipline? Why is it all on *me?*"

"Because *you're* the one who's special," I told him. "So you have more of a burden to carry, just like Abraham had more of a burden. And Noah. David. Saul. Moses."

John started laughing again. He said, "Man, you made it to Bible study recently, D? What's all that for, man?"

He looked over at the clock and said, "It's nearly four o'clock in the morning, man. And you up in here giving me Bible lessons."

I said, "It's actually Sunday now. And you need to *recognize* that, man. You gon' have to repent for some of this."

John looked at me and got serious. He said, "Oh yeah? Well, D, when you gon' *repent* for some of *your* shit then?"

Damn! He had me. I didn't have a thing to say.

I opened my mouth and said, "Soon," unconvincingly.

John took another sip of his drink and said, "Yeah, that's what I *thought.*"

After our talk that night, the tour moved on to Dallas and Houston, and John was doing all right. He was keeping his habits in check. Then we got a call from Evelyn from her office up in New York.

She told me, "Guess what magazine cover I got John an interview for?"

I immediately said, "*Vibe.*" With all of the East Coast–West Coast battles with Death Row and Bad Boy records, Tupac and Biggie, Suge Knight and Puffy, New York and L.A., *Vibe* magazine was a hot one to be in.

Evelyn said, "No, that's a *drama* magazine right now. I got John the cover for a real *music* magazine."

I said, "Yeah. Well, what cover is that?"

Evelyn said, "*Rolling Stone.* That's the *big time* for pop."

I didn't want to argue with her, but I still considered my boy John to be more of a soul artist than some pop singer. Nevertheless, the cover of *Rolling Stone* was BIG!

I asked, "So, when are we gonna do it?"

Evelyn said, "When the tour hits Florida next week."

I nodded. I said, "All right then. I'll let John know to get ready for it."

I told John the good news right before we went onstage to perform in Houston.

He said, "I'm getting tired of some of these damn interviews, man. All they do is ask the same damn questions over and over again. They need to change up their format and just travel on tour with us or something."

He said, "Then they can write a whole damn book about it and stop teasing people with all that minor shit. Tell them what *really* goes on," he said, grinning.

Big Joe overheard him in the background and shook his head. He smiled and said, "You don't want to do that, dawg. We'd have Christians and conscientious objectors trying to ban the tour."

I said, "Yeah, and his mom would be out in the front about to have a damn heart attack. She'd be screaming, 'That's not *my baby* doing them nasty things! GET THE DEVIL OUT OF HIM!'"

We all started laughing.

I thought for a second and said, "Shit, my mom would have a heart attack, *too*, if she knew what was going on."

Big Joe said, "Mine, too. I don't think tours and mothers can go together, if you ask me. That's like mixing ice cream with alcohol."

John laughed it off and said, "That sounds good. Maybe I need to try that one day."

I frowned and said, "John, stop whining so much about interviews, man. Last year this time we had to *beg* for interviews. So you should be *happy* that they on the wagon with you this year. They've helped us to sell over six million albums now."

Honesty continued to smoke up the charts while we toured from city to city.

We met up with the reporter from *Rolling Stone* magazine in Miami. He was an old, still-hip white guy in his forties, and he came right out and asked John how often he got stoned.

I got nervous as hell about that question. I was ready to jump in and abort the interview. John was about to get just what he had asked for. The truth.

Before I could do anything about it, John joked with the reporter and said, "I guess that's why they call y'all *Rolling Stone* magazine, hunh?"

We laughed and I loosened up.

John said, "I was *born* stoned, man. We *all* are. The most creative musicians always have a crazy way of looking at things. You haven't figured that out yet?"

The reporter smiled and said, "Yeah, I have. A long time ago." Then he went back to the normal questions. "So who was one of your first inspirations?"

John answered, "I don't know who was the first. But with me recording my music and living up in Philly and everything, I've been thinking a lot about Teddy Pendergrass and those serious one-on-one conversations that he would have with women on his albums. So, like, I'd like to create that same kind of mack music for the guys in the nineties."

I started laughing. John could be full of shit when he wanted to be.

The *Rolling Stone* reporter asked him, "Well, how much trim do you get on tour, John?"

I started laughing again. That guy was trying purposefully to mix his questions up and catch John off guard.

John answered, "A lot more than I *used* to get. It's like money in the bank, man. When you got none, you can't *get* none. But once you got some . . . *Oh boy!* Look at the line!"

I decided to finally jump in and say, "Yeah, but that don't mean that you *take* all of it. Because then you'll end up in debt. Ain't that right?" I asked our slick reporter. I had to throw him off the hunt to protect John from his own candor.

He asked John, "So, like your title song, are you honest with all of them? I mean, you're not selling the candlelight dream to them or anything."

John shook his head and said, "Nah. I don't sell no dreams, man. I don't believe in that. I mean, they get my music . . . and then they get *more* music."

He smiled and added, "My music is a beautiful thing, man."

Our reporter grinned and said, "Yeah, I bet it is. That's why they call you the Loverboy, right?"

John fell right into his hands and said, "Yeah. That's why they call me what they call me, man."

After that interview, I looked at John and said, "That guy was crafty as shit."

John said, "Yeah. And I liked him for it. That was the best interview I've had yet."

From Miami we flew up to Atlanta, where we were doing two shows before heading home for our first big performance in Charlotte. Everything was cool and had calmed down on the tour. *Honesty* was pushing 7 million albums, and John and I were back to enjoying each other's company without all of the extras. He had even spoken to his mother a few times, just long enough for her to ask us if we had found any churches to attend while on tour. Then we got into Atlanta and ran into some of John's extended-family members.

A female cousin pushed her way backstage during John's first performance in "Hotlanta," and she found her way straight to me.

Big Joe told me, "She says she's one of John's cousins."

She looked like she could be related to John, so I gave her the benefit of the doubt. She also looked like she was in her mid-twenties, but she was all excited like a teenager. I didn't pay that much mind, though. Any family member would be excited for John.

I asked her, "So you're a Williams?"

She shook her head and said, "No. *Williams* is my mother's *maiden* name. My last name is Bassett. My mother got married."

For some reason, I didn't like how that sounded. *My mother got married.* What was she trying to say?

She told me that her name was Chastity, of all things, and she knew who *I* was as John's longtime friend and manager. Then she began to ask me all kinds of questions about how he got started singing. She watched some of his performance from backstage with me and started talking about John's stage presence.

She said, "John has a lot of charisma in front of crowds, doesn't he? He's kind of like a good preacher. He just has a way of controlling them."

Red alerts were going off in my mind with this girl, but I had to wait and see where the fire was. She was definitely starting something.

I asked her, "Are you trying to say that John could be a preacher or something?"

John wasn't trying to hear anything like that, I just wanted to see what her angle was.

She looked at me and grinned. She said, "Mmmph, you don't know yet. It might just run in his genes."

I frowned at her and said, "What?"

It was just me and her in a conversation at that point. She had my full attention.

I paused before I asked her the million-dollar question. Everything that she was saying to me that night was all planned out to lead up to that anyway. It was obviously her game plan to unleash the family secret on me. She was just *dying* to do it!

I said, "So, who is John's father?"

She looked at me, still with a mischievous grin on her face. She said, "From what I *heard*, it may be a big-time preacher who has a parish in College Park."

This girl was just about ready to get on my damn nerves! I don't even know why I was even pursuing it. She wasn't up to no damn good. I decided to head off the conversation with her.

I said, "Well, John's doing fine anyway. He don't need to know that. Nor does he *want* to know it. He's doing just fine."

She said, "But I feel that everyone *should* know who their father is."

I was tempted to say, "Ain't you a little too old to be getting into the gossip game?" But obviously she *wasn't* too old, so I held my tongue and just planned to move on from it.

I said, "Umm . . . keep that kind of stuff to yourself unless we have a sure way of resolving it. Because that gossip ain't gon' do John no good at this point."

I didn't like the way that she was setting things up. It seemed like she watched too many of those talk television shows. Everything didn't need to be disclosed like that, especially if it wouldn't add up to a positive closure. John didn't need that shit on his mind. He was doing good. I figured that Sister Williams had left the Atlanta area for a good reason.

But Chastity wouldn't let sleeping dogs lie. She said, "This ain't no *gossip*. I *know* what I'm talking about."

I finally cut through the bullshit and asked her, "Is this what you came here to do tonight? Because John don't need this, man. Just keep it to yourself."

I was ready to have her escorted back the hell out! I had *enough* damn problems trying to keep John on track. He didn't need no *extra* shit in his life, because it would eventually end up on *my* damn shoulders like everything else did!

His cousin said, "Okay, you sound just like everyone else. Just keep it under the rug. But it ain't fair to John. I know he wants to know. How could he *not* want to know who his father is?"

I was unleashed at that point. I said, "Well, how much do you really know about John? Because you don't know as much as *me*. I don't care if you're his cousin or not. *I* grew up with him. And I'm saying that he doesn't need to know that shit. Or not how *you* trying to put it out there, with anonymous tips and shit. You either come correct or you don't come at all."

She looked at me and said, "You *don't* have to curse at me."

I said, "I *didn't* curse at you."

She said, "Yes you *did*. You just said *shit*. How are you gonna stand here and tell me that you didn't just say that?"

I said, "I can say *shit* without it being directed at you. I said *shit* as a part of my *fucking* sentence!" The girl had blown my cool all of the way. I mean, it was obvious that she was still immature about the world. She just wanted to find herself something to get into, and I was sorry that I even gave her my time.

I said, "HEY, JOE, come get her out of here, man!" I didn't want her around me anymore.

She said, "Well, I don't need to talk to you. Blood is thicker than water," and she marched away to rejoin the crowd before Big Joe could escort her out.

I shook my head and told myself, *This shit just don't* ever *stop. If it ain't* one *thing, it's something else.* I figured that a football career would have been more about wins and losses instead of everything else. But who was *I* kidding? Everybody had drama in their lives. It was just a part of being human.

Sure enough, Chastity found her way back to John before I could warn Big Joe to keep her away from him.

She said, "John, the family would all like for you to visit us at the house before you go back up to Charlotte."

John looked all happy about it like a damn puppy with a Milk-Bone. He said, "Okay."

I didn't want to say anything until we were alone. I just hoped to keep him away long enough where she couldn't start talking that *Your father's a preacher* stuff to him.

We got in the limo and I went right to work on him about his family.

I said, "John, how well do you know your family down here in Atlanta, man? I mean, maybe you need to visit them another time when we're not so busy with the tour."

Knowing John, once we left, it would take him a while to get back down there to see them. He had been doing his own thing without them for a while. Him *and* his mother.

John said, "Nah, man. I've been thinking about hooking up with them for a while. You know, I figure that I need to know more of my family members, man. It just seems like the right thing to do."

I said, "Yeah, but that's an awkward process right in the middle of this tour, man. And like, how come they never tried to get in contact with you before?"

John said, "They have. My mother just wasn't trying to hear it. She acted like she didn't want to be a part of the family."

I was sitting there in that limo thinking, *Yeah, I know why.* But John was determined.

He said, "Maybe hooking up with my family members will give me more of that stability that you've been talking about, man."

I couldn't believe my damn ears. I wanted to just break down and whip myself in advance. John had no idea what he was about to get himself into.

I said, "John, but what if *they're* not too stable, man? I mean, you barely know them."

"Well, I'm just gon' have to *get* to know them then."

SHIT! I was thinking. I was ready to push John's ass on the next flight back to Charlotte already. I was a nervous wreck thinking about how everything would go down.

Then John smiled at me and said, "You should be proud of me, D. I haven't smoked any weed or jumped on any girls in a few days now."

He said, "This really should have been my hometown if my mom didn't move."

"But then you wouldn't have met me," I told him.

He said, "We probably still could have met up in college if things happened the same way."

I shook my head and said, "Nah. Even if we did still end up at A&T, you wouldn't have been in my circle."

John asked, "So you're saying that if we didn't go to the same church together in Charlotte, that we probably wouldn't have been friends?"

I didn't want to go down that road just in case John still had an inferiority complex about our youth. So instead of answering that question, I just said, "John, it was *meant* for us to be friends, man. That's just all there is to it. And you wasn't *meant* to be from Atlanta. You were meant to be from Charlotte."

John smiled and said, "Yeah, you right. I guess I'm just talking to be talking."

But he still wanted to visit his family members in Atlanta, though. It was Saturday night, and our flight to Charlotte was not until Tuesday afternoon. I had set it up that way just to give us a few extra days before preparing to do our first big show at home in the Independence Arena.

However, on second thought, I wished that I *hadn't* done things that way. That long Sunday and Monday would seem like forever, particularly when you're trying to get the hell out of town to avoid family drama.

John set it up for us to visit his family after church that Sunday afternoon, and I couldn't sleep that night. I kept wondering how John would take the news about his father, whether it was true or false. He had told me about the whispers he had heard from his Atlanta relatives before. And after meeting his immature cousin Chastity, who was on a mission of her own, my stomach was in a knot.

John wanted to take Tony and Big Joe with us to meet his Atlanta family, but knowing what I knew about them, I just couldn't allow it. Everybody didn't need to know John's business like that.

Big Joe wanted to visit his daughter in Atlanta anyway. And Tony wanted the extra sleep, so it ended up being just John and me.

We drove over there in the limo to a large house in an Atlanta suburb, and it was all hugs and kisses from the family members, as if they had been around John all their lives. They were having a cookout just for him in the backyard, and new people kept on coming.

They all seemed like upscale people to me, a step up from our blue-collar families in Charlotte, but they were definitely giving John the red carpet treatment.

Chastity wasn't smiling, though. She still had her mission in mind. And I had it in *my mind* to stop her. I stood close by John and was on guard at all times.

John's aunt Bernadine, Chastity's mother, began talking about John's mother, Claudia, out back while sitting in a floral yard chair.

She said, "Your mother got pregnant with you and just broke away from everything. Didn't want to talk to anyone about it. And she *still* refuses to talk about it. In fact, your mother's *always* been extreme like that."

If you asked me, it sounded as if Bernadine was saying that Sister Williams had social problems that were still unresolved. But I didn't want to get into that during the middle of our tour.

I jumped right in and said, "Yeah, well, some things we just have to learn to deal with on our own."

John had a hamburger in his hand and was going to town on it.

He mumbled, "What was so hard about it?"

Everything got real tense for a moment. It was as if everyone knew what was coming. Or at least that was how it seemed to me.

His aunt Bernadine answered, "Well, she didn't really have anyone at the time, and she had just started going back to church after breaking up with the man who she had been dating on and off for a while. So we were just concerned about what she was going to do with you."

She didn't say it, but abortion was right there on her mind. She even looked the part of a pro-choicer with her high fashion and stately manner. *If it ain't right, then get rid of it.*

I felt helpless. It was John's family, and they were about to get into the thick of things. I sat there with my heart pounding. I wondered how many pieces I would have to pick up after the big crash. How was John going to take the news?

He asked, "So, was this man she broke off with my father, and then she went back to the church to refocus herself?"

His aunt looked at him before she answered. I took a deep breath and just waited for the bullet to hit.

She said, "Your mother still hasn't told you, has she?"

John said, "Nah."

His aunt acted as if she didn't know what to do. I was paying them so much attention that I didn't notice Chastity slip into the picture.

Chastity said, "Just tell him, Mom. Get it over with. Why is everybody keeping it away from him?"

John said, "Yeah, I can handle it."

His aunt Bernadine had a little more tact than that. She stood up from her yard chair and said, "Let's take a walk together."

I was left standing there with Chastity. She looked at me and said, "He *needs* to know."

I thought to myself, *These are some fucked-up people!* But I really couldn't blame it all on them. John's mother had put him in that awkward situation by not being honest with him on her own.

I looked at Chastity and said, "You got no idea what y'all about to do to John."

"He's gonna find out sooner or later," she told me.

When John got back, he was nodding his head real cool as if everything was okay.

He looked at me and said, "We gon' have to make another run, man."

I said, "Okay." What else could I tell him? I asked him, "To where?"

He said, "To this church in College Park."

"Ain't service over with?" I asked him. It was close to four o'clock in the afternoon.

John ignored me and said, "Come on, man, let's go right now then."

John looked at me in the back of the limo and started laughing. "Ain't this some shit?" he asked me. "My father's a big-time preacher."

I said, "You don't know that yet, man."

John said, "We'll see. We're going right over there to find out now."

I said, "Is that what your aunt told you?" I just wanted to make sure.

John ignored me and said, "No wonder my mother didn't want to talk about it. This guy has five kids, and a son and daughter who are older than me. And he's younger than my mom, too. I guess she fell for that young spirit, like a lot of these older women do with me."

He grinned and said, "Like father, like son, D." He was saying all of this before we even got a chance to meet the man.

We pulled up at this huge church, and I mean it was HUGE! It was easily five stories high and three big houses wide, surrounded by enough land for three football fields.

I stepped out of the limo and said, "Damn!" right there in front of the church.

John smiled and said, "Imagine me singing gospel in *this* church. This just might be worth it, D."

He started swaggering toward the church as if it was his. A late service was just letting out, with the big hats, suits, and dresses that John and I were raised on. With a big church like that one, plenty of bills had to be paid.

John said to himself, "Can I see Reverend Stark? *Joseph* Stark?"

The boy was acting reckless, as if he didn't know how to control his energy. He was just letting it all swing loose.

He started asking people, "Hey, is Reverend Stark still in the house?"

"Yeah, he's in there," they told him hesitantly. John wasn't exactly dressed like a member. Black churches had dress codes, and we were in *secular* clothing.

Then people began to notice John.

This fine sister in a bright yellow church dress with white gloves and her purse said, "Hey, aren't you John Williams? The Loverboy?" She was smiling and showing off the biggest dimple that you could ever imagine. She said, "I was just at your concert last night. Oh my *goodness!*"

Man, she was ready to give him some right there on the front church lawn. I could see it in her eyes. Don't you think for a *minute* that church girls didn't get turned out. She said she was just at the concert, didn't she?

John pulled her leg and said, "I'm coming to sing in your church, right now," and got her real excited.

The girl opened her mouth in shock and said, "*Stop it!* No you are *not* gonna sing in *my* church!"

By that time, other people were figuring out who he was, and I started wondering how much of a scene John was about to make by walking inside of that church to speak to Reverend Stark.

No lie, man. By the time John reached the church, he had a crowd of young people and their curious parents, all walking back inside with him to see what was going on.

I didn't know if I wanted to laugh at the scene he was making, or run up and tackle his behind to stop him from making an even larger one. But I *do* know that my heart was racing. John was *crazy!* No doubt about it. A spirit had jumped up from the earth and took control of him.

He marched through the church before I could even get near him, and he made his way down to the front to see Reverend Stark.

I heard people asking, "What's going on?"

I saw Reverend Stark at the front of the church, still shaking hands and talking to church members after the late service, and I knew off the bat that he was John's father. He had the same tall, lean body and natural sway that John had onstage, and the connection just seemed to be right.

He looked up and saw John leading a mob of his church members back toward him, and the ushers stepped up like bodyguards.

"What's the problem, son? What's going on?" they asked John.

My boy must have looked like a boxer heading through the tunnel and into the ring to get it on, while a huge entourage followed behind him.

John slid his way through the ushers in a swift shoulder move like a wide receiver and made it to the front with the reverend. I guess it was just meant to happen that way.

John looked up into his face and said, "I finally get to meet you."

Reverend Joseph Stark looked embarrassed for a minute. He was slightly taller than John, standing at around six foot three, and was all done up gorgeously in his purple-and-gold robe. I could see *many* sisters falling for Reverend Stark. Next to him, most of the men in the church looked only average, including John. And Reverend Stark had the same long sideburns as John, only he had cut his instead of letting them grow like John did. That was John's desired look.

The reverend spoke to him for the first time in their lives and said, "I'm glad that the Lord's work was able to inspire you in such a way, young man. Would you like to join our church here today? We accept new members from all walks of life here."

I guess he figured that John had been touched by the spirit and couldn't control himself.

John said, "Yeah, the Lord has done a beautiful thing with me. He's set me up as a sword of truth in the midst of so many falsehoods." He clapped his hands and said, "Ay-men."

Reverend Stark smiled and nodded his head. He said, "Is there something else that I can do for you?"

I was beginning to see where John got his smooth timing and wordplay from. Chastity was right. It was all in his genes. Reverend Stark was still calm and undisturbed by the crowd. It was as if it was just him and John there having a conversation, but it wasn't, and they *both* knew that. However, they both knew how to tune the crowd out, and work the crowd at the same time. That was surely a gift. Because many people couldn't do it.

John said, "Maybe we need to talk in your quarters for a minute in private, Reverend."

Reverend Stark looked out at his church and said, "I'm rather busy right now, young man. Maybe you can make an appointment and come back to-morrow."

John didn't budge. He said, "I'm busy, too. And tomorrow may not be here for any of us."

Reverend Stark grinned and said, "We must have faith in the Lord, my son."

John came right back at him. "And we must also ask the *father* when we are in doubt."

I started smiling my behind off as usual. Reverend Stark was trying his best to blow John off and be cool about it while they stood there in front of the congregation, but he had met his match. John "Loverboy" Williams, his estranged son, was well up to the task of keeping his attention.

The reverend nodded his head and wasted no more time in letting John through. So they went back in privacy to have their conversation.

I stood there in the church with everyone else in suspense. What was going on back there? What was being said? How would it all be resolved?

The girl in the yellow dress asked me, "Is he really gonna sing in our church?"

I didn't know what to tell her. I said, "I don't know."

She said, "Well, what is he talking to the pastor about?"

I said, "Umm . . ." This girl was all up in my face for answers that I couldn't give her. I finally said, "I'm just here with him. I don't know what's going on." But I was surely going to ask.

The youths in the church were busy talking about John singing gospel songs in there anyway, as if their parish had won him over. They had no *clue* what was going on. But I can guarantee you one thing, if I knew *anything* about the church of the South, I knew that they would all gossip about it. That was for sure! But the gossip would never stop them from coming to church, because going to church in the South was what we did. It was the strongest material of our social fabric.

When John walked out with Reverend Stark, I stopped breathing for a second. I was trying to read his emotions. They were both putting on a smile for the congregation, who were still waiting for answers.

Reverend Stark said, "You come back and see us whenever you have a tune to sing, John."

John nodded his head as he walked away. He said, "I'm gon' make sure to write one just for you."

The members started screaming "Ay-men's" all over the place, and the young people and women were asking John for his autograph as we headed back toward the front door.

John must have signed twenty autographs before I finally begged the crowd to let him go. I didn't want to keep him there any longer. I knew he was feeling *something*. He was just being strong for the public.

We climbed inside the limo together, and I just felt that it was the right thing to say at that moment. So I held John's arm and said, "You got all the love in the world from me, man. Whatever you need, man, I'm here for you."

He nodded his head and sat real quiet. He didn't have a thing to say.

I tried to leave him alone about it, but I couldn't.

I asked him, "So, what went on in there, man? What did you say to him?"

He tossed his hands in front of his face and was frustrated. He took a breath and said, "You know how lonely it feels to be an outsider looking in, man? I'm *always* looking in. It's like . . . I ain't got shit of my own, man. And it's hard, D. It's *hard*."

I said, "I know, man . . . I . . ." I got all choked up.

I started over, trying to keep my composure.

I said, "I was trying to stop it, man. But you wouldn't let me."

John shook his head and said, "You wasn't supposed to stop it. You can't stop the truth. It's gon' come out, man. It's just gon' come out. No matter what."

I asked him, "So what he say, man? If you don't wanna talk about it, I'll leave you alone."

John sat quietly for a minute. Then he let his hands down from his face.

He said, "He was up in there talking that preacher shit, man. You know how they do it. 'I'm gon' pray on this and ask the Lord for some direction.'"

Then John snapped, "That motherfucker wasn't *praying* for direction when he was *laying* up with my mom. He *knew* which way he was going."

It wasn't funny, man . . . So why was I smiling? I had to look the other way. John sounded like a preacher himself, twisting the pain of the truth into satirical humor.

I said, "So he didn't deny it?"

John said, "He tried to avoid the question, man. He was steady talkin' that preacher shit. 'I can feel your pain. You have a lot of pain in your heart. I'm gonna pray for your pain. We're gonna pray together.'

"I told his ass, man. I said, 'I ain't *here* to pray. I'm here to ask you if you know Claudia Williams. So think back to twenty-three years ago, around May in nineteen seventy-three, nine months before my birthday.'

"And he nodded his head, man, and said, 'That was a long time ago,'" John told me. "Then he asked me my name and all that, and I told him I was a singer and stuff.

"Then he started saying, 'You're a wise young man with a lot of potential. You understand a lot about the world. You're a young sage.' And all this other shit about me having an old soul and whatnot, like he was trying to read my palms with some Gypsy shit. But he wasn't really trying to *answer* my *questions*, right?"

John snapped, "He was *BULLshittin'* me in there, man! So I told him. I said, 'I just wanted to meet you. I know you got a family and a church congregation and all that. I'm not here to mess that up. I just wanted to see who you were.'

"And he made sure that he kept callin' me *young man*, D. I guess so, like, I wouldn't leave with the idea that he was admittin' to anything. Because you know how old guys call you *son* when they talk to you, man. He didn't call me *son* not *one* time. It was always *young man*. Then he just gon' reach out and hug me with that preacher shit."

His voice broke up as tears started to run down his face.

He said, "I wanted to cuss his ass out, right there in the church. But he put that *preacher touch* on me, man. And I started cryin' in there like a little *fuckin'* girl, D! I was cryin' in his arms like a *bitch* . . . Slick mother*fucker!*"

I was trying to hold back my own tears at that point. That shit was nothing to joke about.

Damn! I thought to myself. *Like father, like son.* John was getting some of his own medicine.

Tears ran down my boy's face even harder. Then he started sniffing and shit. I pulled some tissue from the limo for him to wipe his face and blow his nose. I knew exactly what he meant, too. That "preacher touch," as John called it, was unbearable for *many* people. You start catching the Holy Ghost and all *kinds* of stuff when they touch you. And in John's case, the preacher was also his *father*, who hadn't touched him since *birth*.

John looked at me with tears still running down his face and said, "He got a family, man. And a big-ass church? And what I got?"

He answered his own question before I could. He said, "I got a crazy-ass *mom*. That's what *I* got. No wonder she didn't tell me shit. He didn't even know my fuckin' name, D. He ain't even know my *name!*"

I had to grab my boy and hold him in the limo because he was breaking up *bad*. Fresh tears rolled down my own face for that boy. I felt his *pain*, man! I *felt it!*

I knew that nothing good would come out of meeting his father in Atlanta like that. I didn't like the whole setup. There was no kind of preparation for it. But realistically, how was I going to stop John from wanting to at least *meet* the man, no matter *what* the situation was? I was raised by my father, so I had never experienced the emptiness about it that John had. And it was moments like that one where fans needed to see his real life. It wasn't all about singing, getting paid, and being a celebrity. Sometimes it was just about trying to keep dancing to the music that's created around you. Even when you don't like how it sounds.

. . . *but it was too late to hide* . . .

The next thing that went through my mind with John was how he would respond to his mother up in Charlotte after meeting his father like that. Now I was glad again that we *did* have a couple of days to recuperate in Atlanta before we made it back up to Charlotte.

I asked John in the hotel suite that Sunday night, "Are you okay to do Charlotte, man, or do we need to cancel and reschedule it?"

John was in a daze. He was sitting in a lounge chair with his feet up and his shoes off. He looked exhausted.

I was ready to repeat or rephrase my question when he finally shook his head and told me, "Nah. The show must go on. I don't have a cold, and I'm not crippled, so I gotta go back to work. We haven't done a show back home *yet*. People might start to think that we don't have love for Charlotte."

Of course, I agreed with him, because fans in Charlotte had been *begging* for us to do a show there, and everything was set already. We had television, radio, and newspaper stories all lined up. I was just apprehensive about John's state of mind and how it might affect his performance. I was also concerned about him meeting up with his mother. I was afraid to bring that up, but I knew it would be next on the menu.

John looked over at me from the lounge chair and said, "I'm ready to call up my mom right now, man."

I started grinning.

He said, "What's so funny?"

I told him, "I was just thinking about that before you said anything."

John paused for a second. He wasn't smiling either. He said, "I can't believe she gon' ride me like that, man, and then I come to find out that *she* ain't perfect either. My mom fucked a married preacher. I mean, how low can you go, D?"

I tried to make the situation light. I said, "Or how *high* can you go?"

John smiled at it. He said, "Yeah, she could have did the pope, right? That would have been *real* high."

We both laughed like black people had learned to do—laugh off the pain.

John said, "Pass me the phone, man."

There was no sense in trying to delay the situation. That wouldn't have worked anyway. So I got up and gave him the cordless phone and I retook my seat on the sofa to let him get it all off his chest.

He dialed the numbers to his mother's home in Charlotte and told me, "We gon' get to the bottom of this right now."

When Sister Williams came on the line, John said, "Hi, Mom. How are you doing? I got some good news for you. I went to church today in Atlanta."

It was cruel, but I started grinning and couldn't help myself.

John said, "Yeah, it was a big church. You might even know the pastor. He was some tall handsome dude named Joseph Stark. You ever heard of him?"

I was in shock, waiting for the next line.

John said, "Mom, did you hear me? . . . Oh, okay. I was just making sure. That's Joseph *Stark*, right? Or as the congregation calls him, *Reverend Stark*."

I went from grinning to feeling sorry for Sister Williams in two seconds. My heart just dropped in my chest, man. The shit wasn't funny anymore.

John asked her, "You want to talk about it, Mom? 'Cause, see, *I* thought that you were *perfect* all of these years. Now I come to find out that I'm a real bastard. No wonder you were praying so much. What, you got a scarlet letter on your chest?"

AW, SHIT! I thought to myself. John was laying into his mother HARD! I had to stop it. I stood up from the sofa, but John stood up before I could reach him and avoided me with the phone in his hand.

He said, "You wanna talk about this, Mom? I'll be home soon. We can do it face-to-face." His voice started quavering, and the tears started running down his face again as he paced the room with the phone to his ear. His voice began to rise, too.

"Nobody said that two wrongs make a right. But I'm just trying to check out how *you* can do *your* dirt, and then turn around and get all holy, but *I'm* supposed to be a *damn saint*, right?! But I got *your* genes in me, Mom. And if *you* wasn't a saint, then how am *I* supposed to be one? 'Cause, see, MARY was a VIRGIN so JESUS could be PERFECT! She didn't FUCK no preacher!"

I hollered, "JOHN, STOP, MAN! *STOP IT!*"

I had to grab the boy and rip the damn phone from his hands! Then he pushed me and started screaming at the top of his lungs, "FUCK HER, MAN! *FUCK HER!* I'M OUT HERE HURTIN', AND SHE WON'T GIVE ME NO DAMN LOVE WHILE SHE KEEP TALKING THAT CHURCH SHIT! BUT SHE A *HYPOCRITE*, MAN! AT LEAST I TELL THE FUCKIN' *TRUTH*! IT AIN'T RIGHT FOR HER TO HOLD ME RESPONSIBLE FOR *HER SHIT! SHE* DID THAT SHIT, MAN, *I* DIDN'T! BUT *I* TELL THE FUCKIN' TRUTH, MAN!"

Sister Williams couldn't take his craziness, so she hung up. I was glad that she did. John was off his damn *ROCKER* talking to his mom like that! Then again, I didn't hear what her responses were, and I couldn't imagine Sister Williams being as calm as Reverend Stark had been with John. John and his mother had an unhealthy way of antagonizing each other.

The next thing I knew, band members were all crowded up at the door, and they were all wondering what was going on. Hotel employees were there. Stray girls. *Everybody.* I didn't even know how they got the door open. I guess one of the hotel people used a master key.

I lied to them all and said, "Everything is all right. I know it got a little loud in here, but it's a personal matter, and nobody's getting hurt."

John said, "That's a *damn* lie. Don't lie for me, man. I'm hurtin' like a motherfucka in here." Then out of the blue, he started laughing.

He said, "Who got some fuckin' weed, man? I'm all right. But now y'all know why musicians get high." He pounded his chest and said, "I'm fuckin' hurtin' in here. *That's* why! I *feel* more. Y'all other motherfuckers just ignore shit. Y'all *tone* deaf, and can't hear. But I hear shit all the time. I got *demons* on my mind! DEMONS! And my *MOMMA* told me that shit!"

John was straight up, *bugging*! He was hysterical, and it was embarrassing, but that's life. I couldn't take his words and actions back. They were out there.

It took a few minutes for everyone to clear out of the room, but when they finally did, John had what he wanted, a fresh-rolled joint in his hands.

He lit it up on the sofa and said, "Ashes to ashes," and took a toke. He held the smoke down in his throat, and concluded in a smoke-filled husk, "And dust to dust," before he blew it out.

What could I do? It had been a long-ass day for my boy *and* for me. I know I had told myself not to get high anymore on account of how I responded to it under stress the last time I tried it, but I said, "Fuck it. Pass me that shit."

I sat down in the hotel suite with John and smoked that weed.

John looked at me and began to giggle. He said, "You the best girlfriend that a guy could ever have, man. Why can't your name just be . . . *Dana?*"

I looked at him and said, "John, this weed ain't *that* damn strong, man. Stop fuckin' trippin'."

John said, "I'm sayin', though, man. You the only one who been to hell wit' me and back." He shook his head and said, "Ain't nobody else willing to go there with me."

I didn't have anything to say. I had been protecting John for most of his life. I guess I was just used to it by then.

I said, "It probably wouldn't have been this way if I didn't fuck up my ankle in football practice. I'd probably be gettin' ready for the pros right now."

John took another toke and said, "Man, that's bullshit. You probably fucked up your ankle on purpose. You know you wanted to be on tour with me, man. You wouldn't have this much clout in football. You love this managing shit. Ever since we went up to Norfolk State that time. And don't tell me that you don't, either. All of the football players are listening to our music."

I smiled and said, "*Your* music." But he was right. I loved seeing that boy turn people into screaming loonies. And I loved *my* part in it. But he wasn't right about everything.

I said, "I didn't fuck up my ankle on purpose, man. What kind of shit is that?"

I still *loved* football. I loved *both*, football *and* music.

John said, "Yeah, whatever," before he passed the weed back to me.

Before we left Atlanta for Charlotte, I tried to call Sister Williams back to apologize to her for John's behavior, but I could never catch her in. I finally decided to leave her a message on her machine, even though I would have rather talked to her.

I said, "Sister Williams, this is Darin Harmon, and I am truly sorry about what happened. You just have to understand that John has a lot going on right now, and he really needs all of the love that he can get . . . Umm . . . I don't really know what else to say. But we'll be back in Charlotte to perform for this weekend. I guess you know that already. But I'm just hoping that you and John can work out your differences, because he really needs you."

When we arrived in Charlotte, John was hot and cold the whole time. He would act wild and zany whenever we had interviews and public appearances, and then he would say shit to me in private like, "These motherfuckers don't really care about me, man. They're just into this star shit. They wanna live *through* me, so they can feel more alive and shit. I'm just like them damned TV shows to 'em. Click me on, click me off. They don't really care about my fuckin' life."

I had to keep him thinking positively.

I said, "John, do you realize that *Honesty* has sold close to *eight million* albums now?"

He said, "So what?"

I said, "So, evidently a lot of people *do* love you."

John shook his head and said, "Nah, man. They love *Loverboy*. They don't have no love for *John*. They don't even *know* John."

That's exactly how the big stars get. They start separating themselves into first and third persons and the whole thing. And it was wearing me *out*! So I started getting high again, every night, and locking myself in my room so no one would know.

I even suggested to John that we swing by my parents' house for a good old-fashioned Southern family dinner.

I thought that since John was still hesitant to see his own mother, and I was hesitant about that myself, I figured I would use the stability of *my* parents' house to allow him a chance to feel real love from people who knew him *before* he was Loverboy.

My mother went to town that night and cooked barbecue chicken and ribs, corn on the cob, vinegar and greens, mashed potatoes, cabbage, homemade stuffing, macaroni and cheese, buttered rolls, and pineapple turnover cake.

She gave John a big hug and a kiss, followed by love from my sister, while we waited for everyone else to join us for dinner.

I said, "Whoa, Mom! You went *all* out, didn't you?"

She said, "Yes, indeed," all smiling and stuff. "I just hope that your brothers can get down here. You know Darryl is seeing some new girl that he's serious about."

I said, "Nah, I didn't know that."

"Yeah, he's serious." She looked at John and asked, "And what about you two? Have you two met any girls you might want to bring back home yet? I *know* you met enough of 'em by now."

My sister smiled and said, "Mmm, hmm. You know it."

My father and brothers were not yet there to help defend us as older men who had been through the dating game, so John and I started laughing.

My mother said, "Well?" She really wanted an answer.

My little sister didn't budge either. She was ready to start her freshman year at Johnson C. Smith University in Charlotte.

I got slick and asked, "Now Mom, if we had just come out of college this year, like we were supposed to, would you still be asking me that question? I mean, give it some time."

My sister started breaking up laughing. She said, "Yeah, give them some more time to be player players. That's what they *all* say."

John said, "What do *you* know about it?" all out in front of my mom.

My sister backed down and said, "Nothin'."

We started laughing again. John was definitely craftier than when we were in high school. His brain was working on a whole other level. Good *and* bad.

My brother Darryl arrived at the house from Winston-Salem right on time and with his new girlfriend. She was a nice girl and everything. She had a sweet personality. She was charming. But on the looks chart, she was only around a six. I guess I had been spoiled. John and I got to see women at their best at every single concert. Some girls would go out and spend up to $300 just to see Loverboy sing. That shit was amazing! And a big waste of money, too. But that was black women for you. They just *had* to show up looking extra *good*!

Once we were all there, settled in, and eating at the big dining room table, my father got around to asking us how we were making out in the rich-and-famous game.

John spoke up and said, "It's rough. People forget that you put your pants on one leg at a time like they do."

My father nodded and said, "Ay-men to that. That's the truth."

My brother asked us, "Is that accountant making sure that you guys stay up on your taxes?"

We both nodded and said, "Yeah."

I said, "Thanks to you, man. But we don't spend that much money anyway."

John smiled and added, "Yeah. That penthouse you got don't cost that much."

I looked at him and shook my head. That motherfucker and his damn honesty. That shit hadn't changed since we were kids. John was *always* doing that shit. My folks didn't know about the penthouse. They just knew that I had *moved*.

My mother asked me, "You have a *penthouse* now in Philly?"

My sister grunted, "Unh, hunh, player player."

I said, "That was just to get me in the right frame of mind. You know, sometimes you gotta spend money to make money. And John just wasn't satisfied where he was. He wanted to have it *all*, you know. The whole superstar treatment. So now he's gettin' it. And I had to help him to get there."

I was trying to put it all back on John.

My father asked him, "So how much is enough, John? You know, because excess can really kill you."

That was my father for you. He was always strong and steady.

John held his fork on his plate and said, "I don't know. You just . . . you just don't know what it is that you want sometimes. You *feel it*, but you can't really explain it."

My father said, "Because it already has to be *in* you, John. You can't find it outside of yourself. So if you're not satisfied from within, then you can never be satisfied by the things that surround you. No matter *how much* they add up."

John just nodded his head and didn't say anything.

My mother asked him, "Have you visited your mother since you've been home?"

I didn't even look at him for that. John could say anything. I just had to trust him.

He opened his mouth and said, "I don't know if she wants to see me."

That was John all right. He always had to make it hard. Why couldn't the boy just say no and make it easy on himself?

My mother said, "You don't *know* if she wants to *see* you? John, what are you talking about?"

I was sitting there thinking, *Here we go again. This damn boy is an absolute* fool!

He said, "She always wants things to go *her* way. And I'm just asking her to let me be me."

My father started eating his food and stayed out of it.

My mother said, "Well, John, every mother's a little hard on her boys because you all can be so *hardheaded*." She looked at us—the Harmon boys—sitting around the table to make sure that John knew that *she knew* what she was talking about, with *three* sons.

She said, "But that don't mean that she doesn't love you. How could you say something like that?"

John didn't answer, and my mother wasn't satisfied with that.

She said, "You know what, I think I need to call her right now." She stood up from the table to get the kitchen phone.

I took a deep breath at the table and started thinking, *SHIT! John did it to himself again.* But when my mother called, she got the answering machine like I did. It seemed as if Sister Williams was screening phone calls or something.

My mother left her a message to call her without giving any details. She hung up the phone and said, "You two need to drive on over there and see her tonight. Now, do you need *me* to drive you over there?"

I shook my head and said, "No, Mom. We know how to get over there."

My mother said, "Not from what *John* just said you don't."

My father finally spoke up and said, "Give it some time. He'll see her."

I was so glad when we left my family that night that I didn't know what to do with myself. As soon as they started digging into John's personal life, I felt as if I was in a pressure cooker, because whatever John did reflected on me with them. And I knew that my father wanted to talk to me alone. I planned to dodge him for as long as I could. But my father didn't play that. He called me up as soon as I got back to my hotel room.

He said, "Darin, I'm gonna ask you one time, and I want you to be honest with me, son."

I took a breath and said, "Yeah."

My father asked me, "Is John doing drugs?"

DAMN! MOTHERFUCKER! WHY DID I BRING HIS ASS TO MY HOUSE?! I asked myself.

Under pressure from my father, I lied and said, "No, we're not into that, we're just about making good music. But John has a lot of family pain going on that's ripping him apart right now. And the best thing in the *world* that he has going for him right now is *me.*"

My father paused for a long minute. I wondered if he knew that I was lying to him. I wasn't doing a good job of it. I was giving him more information than he had asked for, and he still had that father's hold over me.

He finally said, "Son, *manhood* is a *hard* thing to explain. And some things you have to do even when you don't *want* to do it. Because you know that it's right."

I was waiting for him to make his point, because I knew that he had one.

He paused again and said, "Darin, it's time for you to be a full man. So I gotta let you go. I'm just *hoping,* son . . ." I could hear the emotions in my father's voice as he said it. "I'm just *hoping* that you'll be *man enough* to make a *decision* on what's *right.*"

When I hung up with my father that night, I felt guilty as hell. I already had a joint rolled up and ready to smoke in my room. It seemed like my father *knew* that I was lying, but he was going to allow me a chance to make my own decisions about things anyway. I was a man out on my own, and John was my responsibility like an adopted son. And I wasn't raising him right. But what if there was nothing more that I could do to help John? What if I was ready to sink as low as him myself? What if I began to lose my *own* stability? I was already smoking weed again. Would I need to be replaced by new management? Did John need a firmer hand and less cuddling? Was our friendship destructive to him? Was it destructive *to me?*

DAMN! I was *wrecked*, man! *WRECKED!* My father had put the cross on me. But like John loved to say, "It was the *truth.*" If I could no longer help John with my management, not just on the business end but in the management of his *life*, then I would have to move on. It just seemed like the right thing to do. Even though I didn't *want* to do it. Because I *loved* that boy! And I had helped to build him into what he was. But on second thought, maybe I loved that nigga *too* much, and I had compromised my position of authority as his manager, and my moral judgment as his friend.

"What's wrong with you tonight, man?" Tony asked me at our opening show in Charlotte. I wasn't as upbeat as I had been during the earlier part of that week. I had been holding it down for the better part of the tour. Fourteen cities. And we still had four more to go: Richmond, Virginia; Washington, D.C.; Philly; and Boston. Finishing the tour in Boston was Tony's idea. He was a big New Edition fan. He kept saying that, outside of the Jackson Five, New Edition were the real kings of urban soul and pop music. He said that everything that was new, hip, young, and funky in urban R&B started with New Edition.

I told Tony, "I'm just a little tired, man."

He laughed and said, "*You?* Get out of here. I thought you were the Energizer bunny."

I said, "I ain't no fuckin' bunny, man. I'm just a little tired. That's all. Can't I get tired?"

Tony nodded his head and said, "Yeah, I guess you can."

I still had to go out there and introduce the show. I walked out and immediately noticed that Independence Arena was not nearly as nice as some of the other places that we performed in. Despite the love that the home city was giving us, that place just looked old, man. It needed some new life. I started thinking that we should have booked the show at the Coliseum.

I pumped myself up on the microphone and said, "Charlotte, it's good to be back home!"

"WWWAAAAAAAAAAAAAAAHHHHHH!"

"Are y'all ready for this?!"

"YEEEAAAAAAAAAAAHHHHH!"

I finished my part and let John come out and do his thing. Even though we were back home, I couldn't wait until the concert was over that night. I just wanted to go to sleep. I was going to ignore whatever happened that night and let the pieces fall where they may. To make things a little easier for John, I separated his hotel room from everyone else's and hid him in the Hilton downtown. Everyone else, including me, was staying at the Adam's Mark.

John was as tired as I was that night and he could use the sleep without the commotion. We were *all* tired. Those tours drained the hell out of you. But every city still wanted their money's worth, and we had to give them a good show.

But even with John hiding in another hotel from us, some pressed girl found him in the hallway while he was getting ice. He told me all about it. The boy couldn't even walk out in the fucking hallway without someone bugging him! Imagine having to live like that!

The girl said, "Oh my God! I don't believe this! You're right here. Somebody said that you might be staying in the Hilton. I'm just so *glad* that I came over here and checked."

John wasn't in the mood to be charismatic. He said, "Well, somebody should have kept their damn mouth shut."

She said, "You know what, though? I think it was meant to be. Honestly. Because I just left all of my friends to find you. They won't even believe me. Oh my *God*! Are you really from Charlotte? You are, like, so *famous* for your music. You just don't *know*! I *love* your music!"

John said she looked *good*, too. But he had too much on his mind, just like I did that night. Hometown or not, he just wasn't up to entertaining. So he told her that he wasn't having company that night.

She asked him, "Well, can I just talk to you for a few minutes? I mean, it's just me and you here, right? I won't bother you. I can, like, get the ice for you. I can tuck you in, or get you the remote control for the TV? Anything you want me to do. Please, John. *Please*."

Without exaggeration, this was the kind of shit that girls would say to John on the regular, all because of his singing as Loverboy. These were the same girls who wouldn't have given *John Williams* a second *look* before he started singing. And he was never ugly. I mean, the shit was mind-boggling! I *had* to feel him on that. It just wasn't right.

John told her, "Nah, I'm going to sleep."

She said, "But I've dreamt about this. You just don't know how many *times*. It *has* to happen. You're right here in front of me. I'm *this close*. *Please*, *please*, *please* don't turn me away."

The girl was begging and touching him as if that would convince him to let her in.

John held her hands together and said, "Look, I just finished what I owed you on the stage. Okay? I just gave you your whole twenty-five or thirty dollars' worth earlier. I don't *owe* you nothing more. Now let me go to sleep in here, man."

She looked at him and said, "That's some *foul* shit to say to me. What am I supposed to do, give you *more* money just to *be* with you? Is that what you're saying? You got it all like *that?*"

She wasn't even getting what he was saying. The act was over. He wasn't Loverboy no more. He was *John!* And he just wanted to go to sleep like everyone else inside of the hotel building.

John finally snapped at her and said, "Look, get the fuck out of my face, all right?! Just leave me the fuck alone!"

She looked at him with tears in her eyes and said, "You're not *saying* this to me. This is a *nightmare*. You didn't just *say* that!"

It was obvious that this girl really believed in him. All these girls weren't low-self-esteem freaks or anything. A lot of them were just taken by the spirit of John's great presence, performance, and art. He had touched the girl that way. She just bumped into him on the wrong damn night.

She said, "You don't *ever* have to worry about me bothering you again in your *life*! I will *never* forget this night as long as I *live*! And you call yourself a *Loverboy*! No you're *not*, I'm sorry!"

She started breaking down and crying right there in the hallway. But she didn't walk away from him. She didn't budge.

She said, "I am *ashamed* that you're from Charlotte. You don't *treat* people like that. And you don't know how much I *care* about you."

John said, "Girl, you don't even *know* me. And don't sit here and act like you ain't never turned a motherfucker down. Because I *know* you have. You too damned pretty *not* to. So now you gettin' some of your own *medicine*, ain't you?"

He said, "But that's life. We *all* get a payback eventually. I got my payback last weekend."

John said he was stalling to get her to leave before he walked back into his room, because he didn't want her to know which one he was in. She could have come back with a whole crew of girls and started acting crazy. He was even thinking about swapping rooms with someone on another floor. That was just how crazy superstardom was on tour. You were *forced* to act irrational.

This girl said, "Well, you don't have to take that out on *me*. I wouldn't do *anything* to hurt you. And if I'm so *pretty*, how come I can't stay with you then?" She was *that* determined!

John shook his head and finally gave in. He didn't have the ice in his veins that night to send her away for good. He sympathized with her dream, and he had the power to make it a reality for her.

He asked her, "You *still* want to come to my room?" just to make sure.

"If you want me to," she told him.

He said, "But I *don't* want you to."

"Why? You said I was pretty?"

John looked away from her and said, "God dammit, am I talking to myself over here?" He faced her again and said, "I'm *tired*! *T-I-R*—you can spell, right—*E*-fuckin'-*D*. *Tired!*"

She looked at him and said, "I'll let you go to sleep. Honestly. I just want to be with you."

John grabbed her by the hand and said, "Come on then. Because I don't want you coming back here fucking with me with your girlfriends while I'm trying to sleep. This is why people need *bodyguards*."

He got her in the room and said, "You're not leaving until I'm finished sleeping. So if you got a curfew or a man at home, you just gon' have to make up whatever. Because I'm locking every door until I'm up and ready to leave. And you better not *touch* that shit either." John was still concerned about other people finding out where he was if the girl left and ran her mouth.

She said, "You don't have to be mad at me. I'll do whatever you want me to do."

When John finished telling me all of this the next morning, I just shook my head and said, "Damn!" And of course, before the night was all over . . . he fucked her . . . *several* times.

He told me, "It's a blessing for those who *don't* have it, and a *curse* for us who do. So sometimes I wish that I was blessed again, you know, to just *dream* about shit like this. Because now that I have it, man . . . it's like I can't even fuckin' sleep without fuckin'."

He laughed and said, "I wake up at night sometimes and say, 'Where my girl at?' And she'll be right there waiting for me . . . with her legs . . . wi-i-ide open.

"I'm a hoe, man," he told me with no smile. "I'm just a *hoe*. For everybody. So I guess my father passed down his gift to me. And now I got my own congregation." Then he smiled at me as if it was all a damn game.

I tried to impart some sanity to him. I said, "John—"

But he cut me off before I could even get started.

He shook his head and said, "Nah, man, I am what I am, D. Ain't no sense in fighting it no more, man. I'm a whore for the world. And everybody wants to fuck me."

I thought to myself right then and there, *John's mind is* gone, *man!* And there wasn't a *thing* that I could do about it.

VERSE 23

. . . from troubled seas . . .

We never did get to see Sister Williams before we left Charlotte. I wasn't pressed about it either. I was having doubts about my own future with John. Everyone just didn't know it yet. And I didn't want to bring it up if it was only jitters. My father had just caught me off guard with something to think about at the right time.

Once we made it back up to Philly, Tony and his lady had a shotgun marriage with John, of all people, as his best man. And I guess that John thought it was a joke.

At the reception, he looked at me and said, "Tony actually just got married, man," as if the whole ceremony was a dream.

I said, "Yeah, you knew about it. Why did you think you were getting dressed this morning?"

He said, "Yeah, I knew about it, but *damn*, man. He actually *did* that shit."

What could I say? Tony was serious.

Matt, Kenny, Jamie, and the Big Cheese from Old School Records showed up at the reception with good news for us.

Honesty had officially hit the 8 million sold mark, and international promoters were *begging* for John to tour in Europe and abroad.

M.D. said, "You're in the limelight now, *baby*! The whole *world* wants you!"

Kenny smiled and said, "It's all on you now, John. Can you handle it?"

I was ready to shake my head on that question, but I waited for John to answer it instead. It was Tony's wedding reception, but most of the attention that night seemed to surround John. I mean, they gave Tony pats on the back for his beats and all, but it was basically the same as when we first signed the contract. Tony was no more than a sidekick. That's just how the music business was played. The less people you give credit for the success, the less you have to worry about paying them all for the next contract. Divide and conquer was still the oldest strategy in the book.

John grinned and said, "Bring it on then. I'm *always* ready for it."

Everyone laughed but me. I wasn't planning on going to Europe. The last thing I needed to do was go on an international tour with John. From what I heard from plenty of American singers and entertainers who went abroad, the international crowd was *five times* more excitable than the crowds in the U.S. The United States was the entertainment capital of the world, so American stars became EXTRA LARGE overseas! I just didn't think that I was up to it. Especially after just winding down a summer-long American tour.

I got back to my penthouse that night to relax and rest before the next concert. We had two shows later on that week at the Philadelphia Spectrum. The Philadelphia Sixers basketball team had chosen the Georgetown Hoyas' basketball star, Allen Iverson, as the number one pick in the NBA draft, and they had big plans for the year, including filling out the brand-new CoreStates Center.

John called me up from his car phone and said, "I heard this new CoreStates Center is gonna be one of the best arenas in the country, man. *Charlotte* needs to build something like that."

I was halfway asleep. I said, "John, we'll talk about it in the morning, man."

He said, "I'm on my way over to your crib. Tony doing his own thing tonight."

"Yeah, he just got married. What did you expect him to do?" I asked him.

John said, "I'm saying, man, he didn't even have a bachelor party or anything for this."

"John, Tony has been having a bachelor party for years now," I responded. "We *all* have. I won't need a bachelor party either. And *you surely* won't."

John said, "I'm not gettin' married, man."

I didn't feel like talking about it. John was still young and in the middle of his bliss years. I just hoped that he understood it was just a stage that he was going through. He was taking the moment too seriously.

I said, "Well, I'm going back to sleep, man. I was almost there. I'm not up for company."

John paused for a minute. He said, "You gon' make me have to creep tonight, man. And I don't feel like it. That's why I'm trying to hang out with you."

I said, "Well, don't do it then."

"Man, I'm tired of being alone. I don't know *how* to be alone anymore, D. For real, man."

I said, "Well, call Tangela back and tell her that you'll give up all of your other women."

He started laughing. He said, "Man, I can't do that either. She was trying to put a ball and chain on me. You can't possess me like that. All these girls fantasize about me because I'm young and single. Me being tied down would mess up their fantasies."

John was getting to the point where he just talked in circles. He was saying the same things over and over in different ways. I was starting to only like him when he was making music, and that was definitely a bad thing from a friendship perspective.

I said, "Well . . . you just go do whatever you feel you need to do tonight, man. Because *I'm* going to sleep." And I softly hung up the phone on him.

But I *couldn't* sleep that night. I felt guilty because I knew that I felt like leaving him, after so many years of having John's back. I wanted to leave him alone, and he just didn't know it yet. Maybe me telling him or hinting at it was just what he needed to straighten himself up. However, I had done that already in St. Louis. And I understood that John had some tough things going on behind the scenes in his life, but hell, he would just have to learn how to handle them. *Everybody* had something going on in their lives. It wasn't just *him*. I couldn't keep saying that I would have to make a decision on him without proving it. My words would become just as insignificant as John's were becoming. I had to *mean* what I say and stick to my guns.

I began the process of sticking to my guns at the concert at the Spectrum.

A female reporter from the *Philadelphia Daily News* wanted to interview me about John's success. I shook my head and declined.

I said, "I have no comments right now. I think that John's music can speak for itself."

She said, "But I'm not asking about John, I'm asking about *you*, the man behind the scenes."

I still didn't have any comments for her. I didn't know if I would even be behind the scenes much longer.

I said, "Interview Tony Richmond after the concert. He's another big man behind the scenes. He deserves just as much respect for his beats as

John deserves for his songs. The two go together like cereal and milk, especially with *black* music," I joked to her. "They gotta have that beat."

I said, "And then you can interview the band members. They all have a lot of faith in letting John show them the way, and then coming through for him."

She nodded. "Okay, I'll ask them all a few questions." Then she pressed me. "Are you sure you don't have anything to say about John's success? You guys are childhood friends, right?"

Those reporters could be real pains in the ass sometimes when you didn't want to talk to them. They were also pains in the ass when they didn't want to talk to you. It was a hard job, I guess. But I was trying my best to remain civil with her, so I just said, "Nah, I don't have anything to say. That's why I'm *behind* the scenes, right?"

That next afternoon, the *Daily News* article came out in their weekend entertainment section, and the reporter gave me a write-up to be proud of. She talked about how humble and loyal I was to my childhood friend who had become a star, and how I was giving credit to everyone around him instead of trying to suck up my own limelight like so many other young managers were doing in the music industry.

Everyone started calling me up about the article and giving me props. They just didn't know. That shit was making it *worse* for me. I mean, how would I look *when* or *if* I left him after that article? I felt as if I shouldn't have said *anything* to her. And the Boston show was a week away.

I had to tell somebody how I was feeling. But it had to be someone who was not as close to the situation, or to me. It's crazy, but I felt like I needed some stranger to talk to so I could do one of those "I have a friend who has a friend" explanations. I needed someone to remain objective about the whole thing.

We got up to Boston for the last concert of the tour, and I immediately liked the city. They had houses everywhere, just like in Philadelphia. You really felt like you were a part of the city just by walking down the streets in Boston. You could just *feel* the community there. We had a lot more open land and greenery down south. Your neighbor's house was not that close to you. I still had to get used to that big city feeling, and Boston had it. I even liked all of the historical tall buildings downtown as we strolled through Washington Street with Big Joe and a security team to keep the fans from ripping John apart. Because they *surely* knew who he was in Boston.

Girls were screaming "LOVERBOY!" everywhere we went.

Michael Bivins, the group member from New Edition who had started the whole Boyz II Men fame, even met up with us in town and gave us love. Tony took pictures with him and was sweating him like a groupie.

Tony said, "Y'all started it all, man! Y'all started *all* of this young urban soul and pop music. Nobody can touch y'all but the *Jackson Five*. New Edition needs to go down in the history books, Mike. *Seriously*."

Michael Bivins grinned and said, "Yo, you did your homework, man. Thanks for the love," and he gave Tony a big pound and a hug.

Tony said, "We gon' put out a song in honor of the original New Edition on this next album, man. Straight up."

He kept Michael Bivins smiling and laughing until he left us. But he said that he would check us out again at the concert.

John asked Tony, "Who said we were putting out a song for New Edition, man?"

Tony looked at him and said, "*I* did. If we do another twelve, fifteen songs on the next album, we can dedicate *one* to the boys who started it all, man."

John shut his mouth and didn't say anything more about it. He knew how crazy Tony was about New Edition.

Anyway, we did the concert that night, and I knew that John would act crazy again with the love that he was getting there in Boston. Big Joe was even liking the city. It felt like you were a part of a movement there. So after the show, when the Boston girls started popping up at our hotel for an afterparty, I just sat outside and sucked up the fresh air from the Boston harbor.

I told myself out loud, "This is the *last one* for me." I had to make myself *sound* like I *meant* it, you know. If I ever really planned on making my own move.

I was sitting on the half wall outside of the hotel, and I looked up to see if this girl had heard me talking to myself. She looked and smiled at me. I guess she did hear me.

I asked her, "You're here to see Loverboy, too, hunh?"

She said, "Yup. So how long do I have to wait in line to see him?"

I looked at this girl, man, and she was as plain as day and beautiful. She had no makeup on and no tight, hoochie clothes. She had a regular short hairstyle and a no-nonsense attitude. She was just telling it like it was. She was there to get her piece of Loverboy, and I was actually jealous about it. That just made me feel more secure about the time being right for me to move on with my own life. Because I hadn't felt jealous of John in a while. I guess I just came to realize that he was wasting a lot of gorgeous women with his crazy attitude. Or were *they* wasting *themselves* on *him*?

I said, "Have a good time then," and left the girl alone. She would do what she wanted regardless.

She said, "I plan to," and began to walk inside.

I looked back at her, and I kept saying to myself, *She's too plain to get to John. She won't make it in there.*

I mean, it wasn't as if I didn't like the girl, she just wasn't exotic or dressed to impress or anything. Come to think of it, that wasn't really Boston's style. They *all* seemed to be a bit toned down, as if they didn't need to show off or anything. She was just wearing a nice pair of blue jeans, a black silk shirt, and matching black shoes.

I don't know how long I sat there thinking to myself, but after a while, I got curious. I wanted to see if that girl had actually gotten anywhere with her plans.

I walked back inside the hotel and searched through the crowds of people in the lobby and didn't see her. Then I decided to check John's room. I just *knew* that she hadn't made it up there. But as soon as I got off of the elevator, there she was, waiting for it to take her back down.

At first, I was startled. I didn't know what to do. I looked at her and she looked at me. Since it was *her* that I was looking for, I wondered if I should get off of the elevator or stay on it.

She looked at me again and grinned. She said, "Your *boy* is a real *trip.*"

I got stuck on my thoughts and said, "Hunh? What boy?"

She said, *"Loverboy,"* and stepped onto the elevator.

I was still hesitant to make my move. I was just holding up the elevator doors.

She asked me, "Are you staying on, or getting off?"

I said, "Ahh . . . ," and decided to stay on and ride back down with her.

When the doors closed behind me, I asked her, "What do you mean my boy's a trip?"

I wasn't even thinking about whether she knew who I was or not. I just wanted to have a conversation with her. *Any* conversation.

She looked me dead in my eyes and said, "You know good and well what I'm talking about."

Do you realize how penetrating it is to look a person in the eyes on an elevator? She had me right there, man. She had jumped into my soul right there on that elevator in Boston.

I said, "So, why did you want to see him then?"

She told me, "That's exactly what *he* asked us."

I said, *"Us?* What are you talking about?"

"He had five different girls in his room, and he was asking us all questions like we were on a game show or something."

I started laughing. That shit sounded ridiculous.

I said, "Go 'head. Get out of here. He didn't do that."

It wasn't that I didn't believe her, I just wanted to hear her talk some more.

She said, "And then he was as *high* as you could be, asking us if *we* smoked."

"And what did you say?" I asked her.

"I said no. I don't smoke. But I was the only one who left, though."

I said, "You expected to have a private party, hunh?" and I chuckled at it, making conversation.

"I just wanted to find out for myself if it was true," she told me.

"If what was true?"

She said, "You know, if singers were really whores like that."

Oh shit! I thought to myself. She caught me off guard with her candor. I just started laughing again as we reached the bottom floor of the hotel.

I got off of the elevator with her and said, "You didn't know?"

She stopped and said, "I had just heard about it. I was never the kind of person to go crazy for celebrities and stuff. So I just put it in my mind that I would do whatever I had to do to find out."

I said, "With Loverboy?"

She said, "Yeah."

"Well, how come you couldn't find that out with some other singer?" I asked her.

She said, "Are you kidding me? Loverboy is the *one* right now. *Everybody* knows that! So I wanted to find out from someone who was on the top, and not on the bottom."

I said, "But this is where New Edition started. Didn't you know about *those* guys? They weren't exactly *saints* either. Bobby Brown even sang songs about it. What he had, like, three different babies before Whitney?"

She said, "And your boy John is heading the same way if he don't get a grip on himself."

"So, you weren't attracted to him like that?"

She shook her head and said, "No sir, no sir. I just like his *music*. I mean, I don't even *know* the boy outside of that. The magazines don't really tell you anything."

We were just standing there kicking it in the middle of chaos at the hotel that night. I just blocked all of that other stuff out. Whatever went down would go down without me that night. I had found myself some company.

I said, "So, where are you going now?"

"Back home."

"Where do you live?"

She asked me, "Are you from Boston?"

"No."

"Well then, you wouldn't know if I told you."

I said, "But the limo driver would know. We could drive you home. Were you about to take a taxi, or did you *drive* down here?"

I was praying that she didn't drive. I wanted badly to take her home in the limo.

She shook her head and said, "No, I took a taxi."

"By yourself?" I asked her.

She looked around and said, "Do you see anyone with me?"

I smiled and said, "Cool, so I can get you back home in the limo then."

She said, "Okay. I never rode in a limo before."

"Well, now you will," I told her. I held out my hand to her and said, "By the way, I'm Darin Harmon, the manager."

She chuckled, holding my hand in hers. She said, "I'm Chelsea Small-wood, an intelligent fan."

I grinned and said, "*Chelsea?*"

She said, "I know, I know, it's a white girl's name, right? The president's daughter. Everybody makes jokes about it."

I said, "And Smallwood sounds like an Indian name, you know, descriptive, like Blackbird, Bluefish, Greenhouse."

She laughed and said, "Whatever. It probably is, though. I have Native American blood in me. *Lots* of it."

We started walking back toward the hotel entrance, where the limos were stationed outside.

"Okay, so where do you live?" I asked Chelsea again. I wanted to be able to tell the limo driver without her doing it. I didn't want it to be so obvious that we had just met.

She said, "In Milton. And you can tell the limo driver to take Blue Hill Road straight down."

I said, "All right." I stepped up to the limo driver to let him know.

Chelsea and I climbed inside the limo together, and I felt privileged for the first time in a while. I mean, once you get accustomed to traveling in stretch limos like I had, it's no longer a thrill for you. But if you have some-one to enjoy the ride with who *hasn't* been in limos, then you begin to en-joy it all over again.

Chelsea looked up at the alternating blue, red, and yellow lights inside the limo and said, "Wow, I feel like I'm dreaming."

I smiled and told her, "You better watch that. That's what Loverboy says about girls. Then he tries to wake them up by giving them what they *dreamt* about."

She shook her head and said, "That's a shame. Some people just take advantage of things. That's why power makes people corrupt."

"We're not supposed to have that power then?" I asked her.

"I mean, you can *have* it. You just have to know what to do with it and how to control yourself," she told me.

I chuckled and said, "Ay-men to that. You gotta *control* yourself."

She looked me in my eyes again and said, "Have *you* controlled *yourself?*"

I froze and looked away for a second. This girl had some perfect timing.

She put her hand on my chin and turned my head back to face her. "Excuse me, I'm over here."

I started laughing, a guilty man with a guilty conscience. I said, "Sometimes it just gets away from you. You get caught up in the moment, you know."

"How many times?"

"How many *times?*" I repeated, confused.

She said, "Yeah, how many times did you get *caught up in the moment*, as you call it?"

I tried to smile and look away again, but she wouldn't let me. It was as if she had known me my whole life and could sit there and pick me to pieces. I was generally in control of the situation when I dealt with most women. But not with this one.

I said, "I didn't count or anything."

She said, "Mmm." She folded her arms and looked out the window while we cruised down Blue Hill Road.

I asked her, "You never got caught up in the moment in your whole life?"

She said, "No, sir."

I said, "So, everything that you've ever done has been planned?"

She said, "Yup." Then she broke out and started laughing. "I mean, we *all* get caught up, but to *keep* getting caught is stupid," she told me. "You have to start *learning* from your mistakes."

I said, "That's easy for a person to say that's not in this business. But do you know how hard it is to just say no in the music business?" I sounded like John for a minute, rationalizing.

Chelsea said, "Well, how hard was it to get *into* the music business?"

I said, "It didn't seem that hard to us. John was just talented like that."

She said, "Well, controlling yourself comes with the territory."

She had a point, so I didn't have anything to say about it.

Then she asked me, "And what's with this *weed* smoking stuff? How come every rapper or singer or boy in the 'hood gotta get into smoking weed? And then they go ahead and *brag* about it."

I was guilty again. I had stopped smoking the stuff only to start over again, *stronger* than before. I was even using tartar control toothpaste. I was still a manager, right? I had an appearance to keep up.

Chelsea said, "Are their self-esteems that low that they have to smoke all of the time like that?"

I said, "Smoking may not necessarily be because of low self-esteem. It's like a social thing. Everybody is sitting around doing it, and then *you* start to do it, and it becomes normal to you."

"So you smoke weed too then?" she asked me.

I nodded and said, "Yeah." There was no reason to lie to her. I had to lay my own demons on the line up front.

She said, "How much?"

I said, "Does it make a difference? I mean . . . you know." I was speechless. I didn't want to tell her *that* much.

She frowned at me and said, "No, I *don't* know."

I told her, "Like I said, it's just a part of managing the business." Then I asked her, "So, if you were in the position that I'm in, where you couldn't stop a friend from doing what they wanted to do, what would *you* do? Would you just up and leave them?" It was my big question to an objective outsider.

Chelsea said, "I've *had* to do that already. That's just a part of growing up. My friends from high school, I don't talk to all of them anymore. Because some of them wanted to hang around and chase these guys out in the streets. And I said, no sir, I don't have time for that. I'm going straight to school. And that's where I'm at now."

I said, "What school do you go to?"

"Northeastern. I'll be starting my junior year."

"What are you studying?"

"Business administration."

I started laughing again.

She said, "What's so funny?"

I told her, "I'm just feeling good right now, that's all. I'm glad that I met you. And both of my older brothers were business majors at North Carolina A&T."

She smiled and said, "Country business, hunh?"

I said, "Business is business. And I'm doing well with it. I just wished that my boy was doing better with handling the fame of his music. But they don't teach classes in *fame* management."

She paused and nodded to me. She asked me, "So, what are you gonna do?"

I paused myself. I said, "I guess I gotta start making my own moves."

She shrugged her shoulders and said, "Well, there you have it then."

We pulled up to her house, a single home in a low-key community outside of Boston. She had a white fence around her house with a white Toyota parked in the driveway in front of a garage.

I said, "Whose car is that?"

"My mom's."

"What does your dad drive?" I asked her. I was just stalling to keep her there in the limo.

She said, "I don't know, and I don't care. I don't get into superficial stuff like that. And my father hasn't lived with us in twelve years."

I said, "What happened?"

She looked at me and said, "He got caught cheatin'."

It wasn't funny but I laughed anyway at how she just put it out there like that.

I said, "You have a way of just letting it all out, hunh? Whatever is on your mind?"

She said, "It doesn't help me by keeping it all inside. Secrets only hurt you in the end. So why have any?"

DAMN! This girl was *powerful!* She was powerful with her simplicity. She had nothing to hide, and I didn't want her to leave that night.

I said, "Well, I guess you have to go inside now."

She said, "Mmm, hmm. Time to go."

Man, I just *loved* her carefree attitude. It was very attractive to me.

I asked her, "Did you even know who I was when you saw me outside at the hotel?"

She grinned and said, "Yeah, I was at the concert. I knew who you were. But you looked like you didn't want to be bothered tonight."

I said, "I didn't."

"That's why you were outside sitting by yourself?"

I said, "Yeah. I'm ready to quit. I just haven't done it yet."

"Why do you want to quit?"

"Because, like you said, you gotta move on and do what you feel is right for you. And you know, I feel it's time for me to move on."

She grabbed the door handle of the limo and said, "I know what you mean. It's time for me to move on into this house."

The limo driver let her out and I climbed out with her to walk her to the front door.

She said, "Well, it's been nice talking to you, Mr. Manager." She extended her hand to me again. She made it seem like I didn't have a chance in hell of taking her out. But I wasn't going out like that.

I took her hand and said, "The name is Darin, and I want to call you whenever I need an 'intelligent fan' to talk to. In fact, I want to take you out to dinner after the show tomorrow."

She shook her head and said, "Can't do it. *This* was my concert night, and I'm behind on some things that I needed to do, so tomorrow I have to start playing catch-up."

I said, "It's the weekend. You can play catch-up *after* tomorrow."

She smiled and asked me, "Remember what we were saying about discipline? You have to have it. How else can I keep doing what I need to do?"

She said, "And if I give you my number, how do I know how far down on the list I'm gonna be? I don't want you calling here and forgetting my name."

I laughed and said, "I don't have no list. And Chelsea Smallwood is a hard name to forget."

"And you're actually gonna call me from on tour?" she asked me.

I said, "This is the last city of the tour. I can fly back up here and visit you from Philly if you want."

She smiled and said, "How many times have you done that? You got a girl in every city?"

I stopped her joking and got serious for a minute. I said, "Chelsea, my name ain't Loverboy. I'm just the manager. And I want to start living my own life now."

I said, "I haven't had someone of my own in years. And I want that."

She looked at me and read my face. I must have looked like a puppy out in the rain.

She said, "Aw, you're breaking my heart. Are you sure you're not Loverboy the Second?"

I grinned and shook my head. I said, "Nah. I'm just Darin. D Harmon."

She nodded and said, "Okay, for what it's worth. Do you have a pen?"

I pulled out my pen and asked her, "Why did you say 'for what it's worth'?"

"I just don't want to create any expectations for myself that may not be there, that's all," she leveled with me.

I said, "Okay," and I left it at that. I wanted to call her up and surprise her.

I walked back to the limo and the young white driver said, "Nice girl."

I asked him, "How you know?" just out of curiosity.

He said, "Great things come in regular packages. The ones with the fancy packages are usually a big disappointment inside."

I laughed and said, "Yeah, that's right." I climbed into the limo and took one last look at the house before we headed back in town to the hotel.

After our second concert night in Boston, I called Chelsea up and asked her if I could hang out with her at her house for a second, and John became suspicious. He caught me on my way back into the hotel that night.

He said, "Hey, D, where you been, man?"

"I got a life, too, man. I went out," I told him.

"What's her name?" he asked me, grinning.

"Why?"

He said, "You not gettin' married on me, are you? I already lost Tony. Some of the other band members are talking about marriage now. I knew that wasn't a good idea for Tony to do that."

I said, "It wasn't a good idea for *you*, but you're not the only one with a life, man."

He asked, "Have you talked to Matt and Kenny? They say this film producer in Britain wants to fly us in to record a couple of songs on a sound track for this film he's working on. It would also be a way for us to do some promotions over there."

"When did they tell you that?" I asked him. Were they cutting me out of the loop already? I was curious.

John said, "I just got off of the phone with them. They couldn't find you. That's why I went looking for you. But you were MIA yesterday, too. You didn't even have your cell phone on you."

I ignored John's suspicions about my whereabouts and said, "We're just about to finish this damn tour, man. What do they think, that we're robots? When are they talking about doing this?"

John said, "In early September."

It was already August by then. We had been touring since May. I said, "That doesn't give us *no* damn time to rest." I was just building up the information to let John see just how crazy our schedule was. We *all* needed a break. A *long* one! Or *I* sure did.

John didn't care, though. He said, "But this is *Britain*, man. And they only wanted me and Tony to do these songs anyway. They got their own band members over there. So it'll just be us three going, like when we first started out; me, you, and Tony."

I smiled and said, "So, now they're cutting off your band members?"

John said, "Nah, man, you taking it all wrong. We're just gonna go over there, do a few appearances, record a couple of songs for this film thing, and set it up for us to tour over there for real next spring. *Then* we take the whole band."

He said, "We decided that we shouldn't do another album right behind the success of *Honesty*. So what we'll do is just tour the world for next year, and then come back and start putting together our third album, for early ninety-eight."

I said, "So, Matt and Kenny told you all of this in a phone conversation tonight?"

It sounded as if I was being pushed out of the way anyhow. They should have talked to me first.

John shook his head and said, "D, man, you reading this shit all wrong, man. Ain't nobody steppin' on your toes. We were just talking, and everything just made sense to me, man."

I didn't say anything. I didn't feel I needed to.

Then John went back to probing into my business.

He smiled again and asked me, "So, what's her name, man?"

I said, "Don't worry about it. You just worry about *your* girls."

John grinned. He said, "I don't worry about them. They worry about *me*."

We flew back to Philly after the end of the summer tour in Boston, and I rested for about three straight days in my apartment. I didn't feel like doing *anything*. And while Tony spent time at his new home in New Jersey with his wife, John was out there running in the streets of Philly, South Jersey, Baltimore, and Washington, D.C., with Big Joe. Evidently, the family drama had not slowed John down a bit. It only made him more reckless. He had told himself, *Well, since I know that I'm a bastard and a whore now, I might as well act like one.*

I called up Chelsea to get away before the trip to London. I hadn't told anyone that I wasn't going yet. I just didn't feel up to it. I was running out of energy, man. *Fast!*

Chelsea said, "You're really serious about flying back up here to see me? I'm flattered."

I said, "Yeah, man. I like you."

She laughed and said, "You're all right, too. Well . . . fly back up here and see me then."

I went ahead and got the plane tickets. I had no time to waste. I met Chelsea at the airport in Boston, and we rented a Ford Explorer for my stay, with a plush hotel suite right off the harbor. My room had the most beautiful view of the water that money could buy.

Chelsea said, "You know I can't stay here at your hotel with you tonight."

I thought she was teasing. You get spoiled with the fast life. You begin to think that everyone is on the same page as you.

I said, "You're not? It's a real nice room."

She laughed and said, "I know it is. But I hope you didn't think that you could just fly up here and get some, did you?"

I said, "Nah, but that doesn't mean that you can't stay at the hotel with me. You're in college now, right? Does your mom make you come home every night? Tell her you're over at your girlfriend's."

That only made Chelsea laugh harder. I mean, I didn't fly all the way up to Boston to be by myself in an expensive hotel at night, whether we did anything or not. She *had* to be teasing!

She said, "I see. Is that how you work it? You give everybody an excuse for their parents?"

I said, "Nah. I was just joking about that, but I'm serious about not being alone in here, though. I won't touch you. I'll sleep out here on the sofa if you want me to, and you can sleep on the bed."

She said, "So, let me get this straight. You're gonna spend all of this money for this hotel room and not even sleep in your own bed?"

I looked at her and chuckled. I said, "I don't want to, but if that's what you want me to do, I'll do it." I felt like a sucker, man. But that's how girls can get when they got you. And Chelsea *had* me.

She shook her head and said, "I don't want you to do that."

I smiled and said, "So you'll stay then?"

She said, "I'll have to think about it."

We hit Boston in the Explorer, and I was loving it. That place was really alive! Or maybe it was just because I really liked Chelsea, and I had flown so far to be with her. You know, Boston was *far* north of North Carolina, and I wasn't just speaking in terms of location. There were huge culture differences from the South. It was like I was in a new country or something. And it wasn't business related for a change.

Chelsea had me drive to a soul food restaurant on the black side of town, which every American city still seemed to have, and we stuffed our faces like it was Thanksgiving.

She said, "Isn't this food good?"

I said, "Yeah," and kept on eating.

Chelsea asked me what Philadelphia was like.

I said, "You want to fly down there and visit me before school starts?"

She paused before she answered me. She said, "It must be great to be able to go where you want to go and do whatever you want to do. You're not even twenty-five yet, right?"

I said, "Nah. And we got a trip to London coming up early next month. But I don't know if I want to go."

Chelsea looked at me as if I was crazy.

She said, "You don't want to *go?* Why not?"

I just shook my head. I hadn't made it definite yet.

I said, "I'm quitting. Remember? I'm tired of it all."

She said, "Are you sure you're not just saying that in the heat of the moment? I mean, give it some time. Or quit *after* you go to London."

I started laughing. I said, "That wouldn't be right." Then I got a bright idea.

I said, "If we're over there for Labor Day, would you want to fly over there to be with me for a couple of days? I'll pay for everything."

She looked at me and froze. She said, "I couldn't do that. I wouldn't feel right. This is moving way too fast. I just can't jump up and fly around the world with you."

Without really thinking about it, I asked her, "Why not?"

She shook her head and said, "Because . . ."

She didn't really have an answer. I guess she was just hesitant. I *was* moving fast on her. I was hungry for love, I guess. I mean, I hadn't had it. Maybe John was right about Tony's wedding. It was affecting us. Or maybe it was just my time, and Chelsea was the girl.

She said, "What you need to do is, go ahead and do this last event in London, and if you still feel that you need to move on when you get back . . . then do what you have to do."

When it got after midnight, and Chelsea and I were still cruising the streets of Boston, I became anxious. She was already starting to yawn, and it was only a matter of time before we would call it a night. But I felt needy. I wanted her to stay with me so badly that I felt like begging.

I took a breath and said, "So, are you ready to crash yet?"

She looked at me and smiled. "Are you?"

I told her the truth. I said, "Not by myself."

She laughed and asked, "Well, who do you want to crash with?"

I looked over at her from the steering wheel and said, "You."

Shit got real quiet for a minute.

Chelsea looked straight ahead. She said, "Would you respect me?"

"You think that I wouldn't?" I asked her back.

She said, "I don't know. I don't know what you're gonna do. This could just be your thing."

She looked me in my eyes to see how I would respond to it.

I said, "This is *not* my thing. I have never flown to be with a girl before in my life. I just wanted to be with *you*, man."

She said, "Darin, I'm not a man."

I laughed. I said, "That's just a Southern thing, you know."

She said, "No, it's a *guy* thing. They say 'man' all the time up here, too."

We both sat quietly again.

Then Chelsea said, "Okay, make a right turn here, and go down Tremont."

I didn't say another word while she told me how to get back to the hotel. But when I parked the Explorer in the hotel's garage, and Chelsea climbed out with me, I felt like jumping for joy. I was feeling like I had never been with a girl before in my life. I kept it cool, though, on the outside. I didn't want to look like no happy fool.

We took the elevator up to the room, and Chelsea said, "Well, here we go."

We walked in, and the bedroom sheets had been pulled back by housekeeping. That was usually policy at fancy hotels, but on that night it stood out to me. It seemed symbolic.

Chelsea said, "Turn all of the lights off and let's stare out the window."

I clicked the lights off and walked over next to her at the window. They were extra long windows like a balcony door, so that you could take in the whole view of the harbor.

Chelsea reached for my hand. She said, "I'm not caught up in the moment right now, Darin. I've already made my decision. So, you don't have a special lady in your life?"

"I want one," I told her. "I want you to be that for me."

She asked, "Can I trust you? You seem nice enough. A good old Southern boy. But now you've been in the music business. Maybe being from the South doesn't mean anything anymore."

I shook my head and said, "The South ain't perfect, man. We far from it." I smiled and told her, "We just go to church all the time. But yeah, you can trust me."

Chelsea moved closer to me, close enough for a kiss. Then we went ahead and kissed each other. We were just kissing at the window, but you *know* I wanted to do more. I just didn't know how much Chelsea would allow. She didn't tell me what her decision was, and I didn't want to assume, because I didn't want to mess things up. But she stopped the intrigue.

She asked me, "Do you have anything with you? I know you do."

I said, "Yeah."

Chelsea broke away and said, "Go get it."

When I went to go get the condoms from my bag, she stripped from her clothes and I noticed that she had no panties on.

I smiled and said, "You didn't wear panties today?"

She grinned at me while she slid into the king-sized bed.

She said, "It was nothing sexual. I just don't wear 'em sometimes." She was that straightforward. That's what I liked about her. Believe me, you go on an eighteen-city tour, and girls could tell you just about anything.

I stripped my clothes and went to join her under the covers.

She looked at me and smiled.

She said, "You got a nice body."

I said, "I used to play football. I was a high school star who fell off in college. Or I got *injured*, I should say."

She said, "I used to be a cheerleader. I fell off in high school. Guys' heads got too big."

I laughed. "I know what you mean. I was one of them."

While we were in the bed with the sheets pulled over our naked bodies, I didn't know how to start.

Chelsea did it for me. For *us*. She looked at me and kissed me on the cheek.

"Thank you," she told me.

I said, "For what?"

She said, "For being yourself instead of trying to act like a superstar. That would have been a real turnoff to me."

I said, "I'm tired of all that shit. I mean, don't get me *wrong*, the money is still all good. But the *other parts* I could do without sometimes. And I just wanted to get away from that shit and come up here and see you."

She said, "I know that. I can tell. You're just a little too pressed about things. It's like you're on a girlfriend clock or something. Some girls get the same way. They decide they want a boyfriend, and they start tripping for the first nice guy that they meet."

I started laughing. I said, "That's what you think I'm doing?"

"A little bit, yeah."

She was right, too. But I still liked her. She was special to me, like on Loverboy's debut album. I had picked out the song.

She said, "If anything, I'm more worried about you getting too attached to me."

I started laughing my ass off. She was tripping with that. I wasn't *that* pressed. Or was I?

I said, "You think I'm *that* bad?"

She mocked me and said, "'I'll fly you here. I'll fly you there. I'll pay for everything.'"

She had me laughing, man. That's all I could do was laugh.

Then she laid her head on my shoulder, and that was it. I started thinking about getting busy again.

I ran my hand through her short hair. It felt extra smooth.

I said, "Man, your hair feels good."

She said, "I'm not a man, Darin."

I grinned and said, "I hope you're not."

She said, "That's foul."

"To each his own," I told her.

Chelsea slid her hand down on me and started a soft massage.

I didn't say anything. I felt good. Then she raised her head to mine and kissed my lips. While she kissed me she squeezed the back of my neck.

I said, "That feels good on my neck. I've been thinking too much lately. I've been stressed out for a while now. I would have been stressed out tonight if you left me."

She said, "I can tell."

I ran my hands over her curves and got hard. She didn't hesitate to let me turn her over. I needed to be on top. I needed to go all the way with her, and women had too much power on top. It was like I could never really get into it that way.

I slid the condom on, and Chelsea flexed her legs over mine as I went in.

She was as soft as cocoa butter, and warm. Chelsea didn't exaggerate anything. She moaned just enough to let me know that I was there, and she continued to massage my neck and shoulders. Everything she did made me slow down and take my time with her. She was putting a lot of pressure on my body with hers, and she was *strong*, too. I felt like it was hard to move. But it felt *good* that way. And extra warm!

When she started to nibble on my ear, I knew that I had her open. I even thought about John's crazy behind, and I laid there on her spot.

"Mmmm," she moaned.

I couldn't *move*, and I was an ex–football player. Boy did she put the vise grip on me. *DAMN!* I wasn't used to that.

When it started feeling extra good to me, I wanted to pick up the pace. But Chelsea wouldn't let me. She had been a cheerleader all right. Because her legs were wrapped around me like a gymnast.

And when I felt it, she held me even tighter.

Man, my toes started to curl up. My arms started locking. And then my whole body just shut down for the climax of my life!

"AAAAHHHHH!" I growled.

"Mmmm!" Chelsea moaned again.

Then she made it even sweeter when she laughed at me. Her body vibrated with her laughs, and my whole insides poured out to her right there on that king-sized bed.

I was thinking, *SHIT! Did I pick* the one, *or did I pick* THE ONE*?!*

I fell limp with heavy breathing, and Chelsea laughed again while she dug her fingers into my lower back.

I said, "What's so funny?"

"You acted surprised that I could hold you down like that," she told me.

I guess she could feel my body fighting her and losing.

I just chuckled at it.

She said, "I can't let you just run over me. That's not the way I do things."

I said, "I don't want to run over you."

"You were *trying* to."

She had me there. I wanted my way in bed, but ultimately, I didn't get it, and I was better off for it. I was not in control for a change, and I dug it. I just had to learn to let go. I had met my match in every way.

I said, "So, how do you feel? Do you feel disrespected now?"

She paused. She said, "No. I feel good. I mean, I had made my decision already."

I said, "And what decision was that?" I hadn't asked her from the first time she said that.

She said, "I decided to give you a chance. And if you mess it up . . . then that's on *you*. Because I'm not gonna allow myself to feel bad about it. As long as I know I tried."

VERSE 24

. . . I guess it was his destiny . . .

When we flew over to Britain in September, all I could think about was Chelsea. I wished that I had her there with me. So I wasn't even stirred by all of the people who greeted us at Heathrow. They were screaming, crying, falling out, and going wild! There were at least twenty cameras flashing all at the same time. It was like I was watching the international news on television, only we were right in the middle of that shit.

"AAAAAHHHHH!"

"LOVERBOOOOY!"

"WE LOVE YOU!"

"WE *LOVE YOUUUUU!*"

And I'm talking about white Britons, black Britons, *and* Middle Eastern Britons.

We had a rope for crowd control with British security lined up as if John was the president. Big Joe was there with us, too. He had become John's new sidekick, because I never was, and Tony had grown away from it.

Tony joked and said, "I thought this was supposed to be a low-key, in-and-out deal?"

The British movie producer Tom Davies, who had flown us in, said, "Ah, you jus' can't stop the paparazzi from knowing when U.S. stars come into town. And then the news spreads about and you get these bloody crowds."

Those British accents were some funny shit to listen to. It was like they had no bass in their voices, and their words all melted in a fluid chatter. *Blah blah blah blah blah blah blah.*

We climbed into our cars and sped through the tight streets of London, driving much faster than I was used to inside the city, at least.

Big Joe said, "We would all get tickets driving like this in America."

Our driver started laughing. He said, "We are not as asinine about the speed of cars here as you are in the U.S. However, I've been to New York, and I must say, they don't drive slowly there eye-ther."

They wore a lot of black clothes in Britain, too. Tom Davies was dressed in a thin black leather himself, like that chic sixties look from the Black Panthers or something. Only he was a white guy with that carefree international look. They just didn't seem to be all that concerned about every hair on their heads being in place. They just let it go.

He said, "We'll check you into your hotel rooms in downtown London, take you out for a bite to eat, and the band will meet us later on at the recording studio in South Gate. It is much less congested there."

Then he smiled at John, who was playing his cool role, just watching everything go down.

He said, "John, every member of the band is very smitten by you. They jus' can't wait to meet you. They all love your music."

John said, "They don't have no band name?"

He said, "They are all from different bands who have come together to work on this project. Once they heard that you had agreed to sing, they all wanted to be a part of it."

I didn't have much to say. I was just going along for the ride and checking everything out.

We checked into the London hotel, which had a ritzy antique look to it. Everything in London had that old, classic look. We all met up in John's room after putting our things in our own. Everything in that place looked expensive, and like it had been passed down through generations.

I joked and said, "Nobody better not break anything in here. They might take your ass to prison for it. This stuff don't look cheap."

Tony laughed and said, "Dig it. This shit looks like royalty. Fuckin' castle furniture."

John smiled and said, "We deserve it, though. *Royalty.*"

He went into his closet and pulled out the bathrobe. He tried it on and said, "Yeah, this is my outfit for tonight. I'm gon' wear a bathrobe and no drawers, with about five British girls in here. All different colors. Maybe I'll call up them Spice Girls."

Tony started laughing. He said, "Shit, I ain't never had no British girl either."

I grinned at him and said, "You're married, Tony."

Tony looked at me seriously and asked, "Who's telling? You ain't tellin', are you?"

I just shook my head. Even Big Joe was talking about getting some British girls.

He sat down on the exotic furniture and said, "Shit, they might be scared of me, though. I'm a *big black* Southern nigga."

We all laughed again, up in the hotel room acting silly.

John looked at Big Joe and said, "Nah, man, just tell 'em you used to play football and now you're thinking about boxing. Shit, they got Frank Bruno and Lennox Lewis over here, right? I know they gettin' some British pussy. Tell me they're not."

Tony laughed and said, "You *know* they are!"

Big Joe laughed along with them. Those guys couldn't wait to go out and start collecting. You could see it in their excited eyes, peeking out the window and into the streets of London. They were like kids at the mall after just getting their allowances.

I mean, there was no way in the world that I could continue to tour with them and keep any moral ground with myself. I imagined them wanting to fuck a girl from every different nation that we toured. France. Japan. Ireland. Australia. Africa. You name it!

Tom Davies called us up after a while to get ready to go out and eat.

Tony said, "Let's *go-o-o!*" and started galloping toward the door, the same Tony that *I thought* had matured.

We went to what they called a pub, with plenty of security, and we walked in as a full posse. That just drew more attention to us, if you asked me. Maybe we could have used a lot less people.

I watched while Britons started whispering back and forth and looking in our direction. The smoke was practically everywhere. Everyone looked like they were smoking in that place. There wasn't any clean air police in London.

A pair of excited white women made their way over to John before we could even place our orders.

"Are you the famous singer?"

John asked them, "What do you consider famous?"

They said, "You make good music and you make a lot of people dance and act merry."

Tony and Big Joe started laughing again. It wasn't funny anymore to me. I had seen and heard it all already.

John said, "Well, I guess I am famous then. I do make good music with people dancing and acting merry."

"Would it be a bother for us to ask you for your autograph?"

John flirted with them. He said, "Where do you want me to sign it?"

They caught on to it and started giggling.

One of them said, "My husband would murder me if you signed where I would tell you."

"No, he would lick it off with a desperate tongue," the other woman argued.

The British had a way with words, I'll tell you that. They were all tripping in that place.

When the food arrived and we started digging in, Tom Davies asked John, "Has anyone offered you any movie roles in the States as yet?"

John said, "Yeah, but we've been too busy with the tour and everything to get involved. They all had production dates and stuff, you know."

He nodded. He said, "I see." Then he asked John, "Would you be willing to make a cameo appearance in this film?"

I finally spoke up out of business instincts and asked him, "What exactly is this film about? I mean, we haven't gotten a lot of the details on this thing."

He gave me his full attention and said, "The film is called *Without Reason*. It's about a love affair of a young artist and a depressed married woman."

It sounded purely British to me. They were always making movies that dealt with intimate people as opposed to the action and drama plots that American films seemed to focus on.

Tony said, "Well, it sounds like she has *reason* to me, if she's depressed."

Tom said, "Exactly. The problem is, her *husband* doesn't realize that."

John nodded his head and said, "So this story is told from the husband's perspective?"

Tom got excited as hell. He started nodding his head over his food and said, "Yeah, yeah, you guys are very intelligent. Many Americans don't seem to understand British films."

Big Joe spoke up and said, "We understand them, they just fucking slow, man."

Tony chuckled and said, "Yeah, they are kind of slow sometimes. But they're deep, too, though. If you sit through it, you can feel them more. You get a lot more out of it."

John smiled and said, "Like my music. You feel it more. And you get a lot more out of it."

Tom said, "That's why I wanted you so badly on the sound track."

John asked him, "So, what part do you want me to play in the movie?"

"I'll have to talk to my director. He'll plug you in wherever we can use you."

I was ready to start asking about the money, but I stopped myself. Did I want to get that involved in it? I still needed to think about the direction that I was going in with John's career. But since I was still on the job, before we left that pub, I asked about the business end anyway. And it was all taken care of.

When we drove out to South Gate to start our first recording session, the studio there was jam-packed! It looked like a surprise party. There were a bunch of band members who were all excited to work with John and Tony on a project. And their enthusiasm was genuine.

They started screaming, "He's HERE! LOVERBOY WILLIAMS IS HERE!"

They had two gigantic recording rooms, and several smaller ones. They were all drinking beer, wine, and smoking up a storm of cigarettes just like at the pub where we ate earlier.

They were all giving their love to John and Tony, and I just slipped into the background to watch it all. I was wishing I had Chelsea there with me again, you know, someone to talk to and laugh with. She sure knew how to make me laugh. And it wasn't that vulgar guy humor that I had gotten so accustomed to either. Chelsea had good, spirited humor and frankness. She was just a good person. Of course, I missed her *physically*, too.

Big Joe slid over to me, grinning. He said, "John has come a long-ass way, dawg. Imagine people all over the fuckin' world listening to his music now. And just three years ago, he was a wet-behind-the-ears band member who still couldn't get no pussy."

I shook my head and said, "Ain't it wild, Joe? It's *wild*."

When they started trying to rehearse a couple of the songs and put the music together, everybody wanted to be in on it.

Tony finally said, "Fuck it, I'll sit this one out and work on the next song. Let me see what y'all can come up with."

They had a few British songwriters there who had already penned lyrics for John to croon. John shuffled through the songs and picked two that he liked, and they went right to work on them. The first one was a ballad called *In My Arms*. John sang over a whole orchestra of guitars, bass, keyboard, and horn players, all squeezing their way into the fabric of the song. I couldn't even concentrate on any instrument to explain what they were playing. All I could say is that the music wouldn't let you go, and British players were all stuck in a time warp of 1970s funk, when American bands were at their height. So the sound was just groovy, and extra loud.

Then John sang the slow chorus and made it all come together like a dream in your ears:

You-u-u can laaay in myyy ar-r-r-r-r-r-rms
when we finish the ni-i-ight away
you-u-u can laaay in myyy ar-r-r-rm-ar-r-rms
and hold me ti-i-ight-lee.

You-u-u can laaay in myyy ar-r-r-r-r-r-rms
when we finish the ni-i-ight away
you-u-u can laaay in myyy ar-r-r-rm-ar-r-rms
and never le-e-eave me . . .

That song had me thinking about Chelsea even more. John had taken me right back to that hotel room on the Boston harbor. I could see Chelsea with her arms around me in the middle of the night. I could taste her lips. I could feel her heart pounding against mine. And John made me want to cry for love, man. *CRY FOR IT!* He was a *BAD MOTHERFUCKER!* I didn't have any other words to explain it.

It was like *church* in that studio. No one made a sound until the sermon was over. Then they glorified.

"YEEAAAAHHH!"

"DAMMIT! HE'S *GREAT!*"

"EVERY SONG SOUNDS HEAVENLY WITH HIM!"

"LET'S DO AN ENTIRE ALBUM!"

I started laughing. They were ready to make a throne for John in that place.

They switched the musicians, and John did an easy up-tempo song that was swinging. Tony sat out on the second song, too, and just enjoyed the whole process while watching everyone else's excitement. He looked at me and just shook his head. He didn't have to say a word. I knew what Tony was thinking. John was above cultural differences. His soulful voice and music spoke to everyone. *Immediately!* It just grabbed your ears and held on to them.

John was tired at the end of the second song. It was late, and we had just flown in that day. I was surprised that he had gone for as long as he did without resting that first night.

There was a British magazine reporter still waiting for him to do an interview. Evidently, John had told her not to leave. She was a striking, dark-haired white woman in her early twenties like us. I even questioned if she was really a reporter. She looked more like a British model. She just stood out, man, like a white horse in the woods. I wasn't a white woman watcher, but *DAMN!* Clear eyes don't lie. This white girl was *all that!*

John walked up to her and said, "Hey, let's go. We'll do the interview back at the hotel."

She followed right behind him without a word. I knew right then and there that John would open her up that night. There was no doubt about it, unless she just wouldn't go there because he was still black. And I *seriously* doubted *that*. John had surpassed the color line.

We made it to the cars, and the reporter rode with us. I guess to make herself seem more professional, she started asking John questions in front of everyone. Big Joe and Tony were too tired to care. They were already dozing off. It had been a long day.

"So, John, who was your inspiration as a singgah?" she asked him.

John said, "Sam Cooke. You know, because Sam had a lot of spiritual things going on in his life and in his music that people didn't always pick up on. I feel that same way about my life and music. It ain't just the music that drives you all the time. Sometimes it's the chaos that inspires you, and you try to make sense of it all."

Our movie producer friend nodded his head and said, "Ah, *You Send Me*." He snapped his fingers and said, "Yeah, I can see that now. You *do* remind me of the legendary Sam Cooke."

I don't think that young reporter even knew who Sam Cooke was unless her parents listened to him. Or maybe she did know. But it seemed like John changed his answer every time someone asked him that inspiration question. He was bored with being asked that shit. To tell you the truth, I think John was inspired the most by the fans. He loved the love that they showed him, and that only made him want to do more great songs for them.

The reporter was smart, though, I give her that. She didn't want to sit there looking brainless.

She asked John, "Do you always look to oldah singgahs as your guide? No recent artists have inspired you a-tall?"

John looked away from her and smiled. He said, "Nah. A lot of these new artists aren't really deep enough. Most of them don't write, produce, or even know how to interpret their own stuff. We in competition anyway. So even if I do check them out, I'm not gon' say until my career is over."

He said, "But let's finish this later on. I want to enjoy the ride."

She nodded her head and smiled at him. She seemed satisfied with his company. John had charmed her, and he was also in charge.

When we arrived back at the hotel, we all went our separate ways. I asked the phone operators at the front desk what time it was in America. I wanted to call Chelsea.

John went up to his room with the striking reporter.

I found out that it was still too early to call Boston, so I decided to wait until next afternoon sometime. But I couldn't even get a good rest that night. Someone was beating on my door at eight in the morning.

I got up to answer the door and it was John.

He walked in wearing his white hotel robe and went to sit down.

I just stared at him. What was the news?

John smiled at me and said, "I got a new song this morning, man."

I said, "Don't tell me. It's about a white girl?"

John said, "Man, is it *ever*. She kept squealing, 'Your rhythm is *strong!* Your rhythm is *so strong*, John!'"

I rubbed my eyes and headed back to my bed. John got up and followed me.

I climbed back into bed and said, "So, you got your first white girl all the way over here in the U.K. Are you proud now? Did you know that she was gonna give it to you?"

I was tired of hearing about his scores myself, but John wasn't tired of talking about them, so I let him talk.

He said, "She wasn't trying to give it to me at first. She was just being professional. But then she said that she wondered how it would be, you know. And that was it for me. I had to find a way to let her feel it."

He grinned and said, "And then I asked her if I could write a song about it."

"And what did she say?" I asked him. The *audacity* of that boy! He had some *cojones!*

He said, "She asked me if her lovemaking had inspired me. And I said, 'Yeah.' So she told me, 'You can write the song then.' She said that she would be flattered."

I asked him, "Well, what's her name, man?"

He said, "Michelle. And her grandfather is a lord in the British Parliament or some shit." He laughed and said, "So I'm fuckin' royalty over here, D. And I'm about to write a song about it."

That boy had everything that he was doing down to a science. It was like clockwork for him.

We drove back out to South Gate to record John's new song. He asked for three good female backup singers. We ended up with six. The director from the film *Without Reason* even wanted to record the studio session to

plug it as a promotion vehicle for the movie and sound track release. We
agreed to the terms on that as well. Business was still business.

Tony was back behind the drums. John told everyone how to play their
parts. Then Loverboy laced the lyrics of this lush fantasy song called *Don't
You Ever Wonder*. His new reporter friend, Michelle, arrived just in time to
hear it, as the backup singers hummed along with him like sensual angels:

> *Gir-r-r-r-rl*
> *I read your eyes*
> *(uuuuhhhh)*
> *a thousand times*
> *(uuuuhhhh)*
> *the way you smile*
> *try'na to ho-o-old back from me.*
>
> *And now we're here*
> *(uuuuhhhh)*
> *as nighttime falls*
> *(uuuuhhhh)*
> *and passions rise*
> *don't be-e-e afraid.*
>
> *You know you want*
> *(uuuuhhhh)*
> *the same as me*
> *(uuuuhhhh)*
> *your eyes don't lie*
> *so don't let your bod-dee . . .*

Big Joe started laughing from the engineer's booth. He stood there with
me and about twenty Britons, including Michelle, who was in suspended
animation. She looked as if she was in a coma as she watched him. We were
all watching recording history in the making.

> *. . . reach out your soul*
> *(uuuuhhhh)*
> *connect with mine*
> *(uuuuhhhh)*
> *nobody knows*
> *as we sip this wine . . .*

Tony changed up the beat, with the British musicians following his lead. Then the mood of the song became more subtle as John sang:

> *Don't you ever won-der*
> *what it would feel like*
> *if I slipped in-side of you-u-u*
> *why you think they call me-e-e what*
> *they doooooo . . .*
> *(the lover-r-r-r)*
> *(the lover-r-r-r).*

Big Joe said, "That's that *Loverboy* shit right there! He on that *shit* right there, *dawg!*"

I just smiled at it. Michelle grabbed at her heart with her mouth open. I thought she was about to faint in there. And every time we got to the change-up chorus, we were pulled deeper into Loverboy's ploy, until you just gave it all up to him:

> *. . . why you think they call me-e-e what*
> *they doooooo . . .*
> *(the lover-r-r-r)*
> *(the lover-r-r-r).*

I mean, that song actually made you *feel* like a helpless woman. I could feel *exactly* how that Michelle must have felt! It was the closest thing to musical seduction that I had ever heard in my life! That damn thing turned you *out!* And I was a *guy!*

I called Chelsea as soon as I got the chance.

I said, "I'm missing you more with every song that John sings."

"Awww, that's sweet. But are you enjoying yourself?" she asked me.

I said, "You know what? I've been through this already. We all know that John can do his thing. I'm not surprised."

Chelsea said, "You're serious then. You really don't feel you have anything else to offer."

I paused and thought about it. I had been thinking about quitting for a month and couldn't bring myself to do it yet. I hadn't even told anyone but her.

I said, "Yeah, man. This is it. I don't feel like I want to be involved anymore."

Chelsea said, "Well, what are you gonna do after that? Do you have someone else to manage?" She was asking the same question my mother had asked me before I signed the contract.

I said, "I don't know yet. I figure I could always *find* somebody, you know."

Chelsea cut me short and said, "Oh, yeah. Some big news happened over here."

I said, "What news?"

"Tupac Shakur got shot up in Las Vegas."

I stopped and panicked. Then I smiled. I said, "That nigga been shot up before. He'll live."

Chelsea said, "I don't know about this time."

I said, "All right. I'll read about it when I get home. He's still alive, ain't he?"

She said, "Yeah, but he's in intensive care. They say he's gonna lose a lung."

I thought about Tupac's big-winded rap style and said, "Damn. He may not be able to rap no more."

Chelsea said, "That's what I'm saying. And it's not like I'm some big Tupac fan, but when is all this thug-life stuff gonna stop?"

I didn't have any comments for that. I was thinking, *When is all of this love life gonna stop with John?*

When I joined back up with everyone at the hotel that night, they had all heard the news. John was staring at the TV in disbelief.

He shook his head and said, "Tomorrow ain't promised, man. That's why I tell myself to live for every day now. And I can't look back. The *future* calls me."

Tony joked and said, "I guess that boah ain't untouchable, John."

John didn't respond to him.

Big Joe said, "John don't have to worry about that shit, dawg. I got his *back*."

Tony said, "Suge Knight had Tupac's back. And that boah *still* got shot. Suge was in the damn car wit' 'em."

I spoke up and said, "Ain't nobody untouchable, man. That shit is a fantasy like that song John just sang." I looked at John and said, "You ain't untouchable. You just *wondering*."

We had a promotional event at this huge London department store called Selfridges, where John autographed CDs, tapes, photos, newspaper and magazine articles, and posters for two straight hours before I told everyone that it was time for us to go.

Then we attended a party that night at this club called Handover Grand, with more British fanfare, loud dance music, cigarette smoke, and wine drinking. I was tired as hell and just going through the motions at that point. I couldn't wait for it all to be over. Everyone else was enjoying themselves, but I wanted to go back home like a big baby.

Tony came over to me from the dance floor and said, "Hey, man, I gon' fuck with this girl from Yemen tonight. She bad as shit up in here, D. *BAD!*"

I looked over at this brown-skinned, black-haired British bombshell and nodded.

I said, "Yeah, she looks good, man. She got that exotic look going on."

"And you *know that!*" Tony exclaimed to me. He had a third wine drink in his hand and was half drunk already. I was stuck on my first one.

Tony said, "They can dance in here, too. Even these white girls over here."

Speaking of white girls, John's friend Michelle wouldn't let him out of her sight. She was dressed to impress in British gear, with funky designer clothes that Americans only highlighted in magazines. You had to be pretty bold to wear some of those extra chic designs the British wore. She was wearing it and playing her role *well* as Loverboy's chosen one. But that didn't mean that others didn't want a piece of him.

Another chic-dressed white girl, with short blond hair, slid up beside me with her own wineglass in hand. She said, "Ex-cuse me. Are you Darin Har-mon?" I just couldn't get over the accent thing, so I smiled at her.

I said, "Yeah, I'm D Harmon."

She looked in John's direction with Michelle and Big Joe nearby, and made sure that I knew *exactly* what she wanted.

She said, "Do you mind a-tall if I hit 'im laytah on the dog and bone?"

I looked at her and said, "What?" I had this silly grin on my face because I had no idea what the hell she was talking about.

But she was dead serious, man. She asked me, "Would he mind if I call him laytah?"

I translated and said, "Oh, you mean, can you hook up with Loverboy later on? Is *that* what you're asking me?"

She said, "Yah," with no smile. This white girl meant *business*, man. Then she asked me, "Who is *she*? She's all ova' 'im like a *vulture*."

And I couldn't stop laughing, right? I answered, "She's just a new friend of his." Then I added, "And he *will* make room for more," just to see what she'd say.

She smiled real hard and said, "I bet 'ee will," with much confidence about it. She even squeezed my arm when she said it.

The next thing I knew, this big black Briton stepped up to us and said, "What the bloody hell is going on? You'd rather have *this* bloke than me?"

This guy was as tall as Big Joe, but he was more chiseled, like a body-builder. He was real light-skin, too, like a mixed-blood. I guess I was supposed to be afraid of him, but I thought the whole thing was a big joke, man. I just wasn't taking it all seriously. Until that motherfucker punched me dead in my mouth for laughing at him. *He* took it seriously enough.

I heard the white girl screaming, "Stop it!" while holding him back.

I thought to myself, *This motherfucker just punched me in my mouth!* Then I charged his ass without thinking. I hit him twice in the head before he lost his balance and fell backward, with his white woman falling with him.

Then somebody clocked me in the back of the head and knocked me to the floor. Before I could even get back up, Big Joe was in the middle of things, throwing punches and shit. Tony was throwing punches. Security was mixing it up. And it turned into a melee in there. I didn't even know who we all were fighting. I *assumed* that the guy was by himself in there. I guess I was wrong.

When I finally climbed to my feet and got my wits back, John was asking me, "What happened, man?"

I got into that stupid fucking fight all because of *his* ass! I felt like cursing him out about it, but his *friend* was still right there next to him, so I kept it to myself for the moment.

Once everything calmed back down, we were told that we were in a fight with a group of roughnecks from an area called Brixton.

I looked at Tony, who was smiling, and said, "Ain't this some shit? We come all the way over to London, and we end up gettin' in a fight with some brothers from the 'hood over some damn white girl."

I was embarrassed by the whole situation. But I couldn't let some moth-erfucker punch me in my mouth and just get away with it.

When we made it back to the hotel that night, I had some ice on my busted lip and on the back of my throbbing head. I hadn't been in a fight since my freshman year at North Carolina A&T, when a junior teammate was trying to disrespect me in the locker room. And before they broke it up, I was winning. But I didn't win anything that night in London.

Tony was steady making jokes about it. He laughed and said, "They got boys in the 'hood all around the world, man." He had ice on his right hand.

He said, "Now they fucked up my drummin' hand. A whole club full of niggas fightin' over some blond-headed white girl. That shit was fun though, man. Me and Big Joe had your back up in there, family."

Big Joe was like, "Yeah," with a satisfied grin on his face.

I said, "I wasn't fightin' over some damn white girl, man. That motherfucker in there punched me in my mouth. That girl must *like* startin' trouble. She knew who the hell she was with."

John slipped me a joint and said, "Get high and forget about it, man. Fuck it. That's what *I* do. I'm having a *good time* over here. Ain't nothing breaking my spirits, D. I'm enjoying this to the *fullest*."

I still was pissed off, but it wasn't anything that I could do *but* forget. It was just one of those damn nights. I couldn't control shit like that. Neither could John. Unless he just stopped going out to places.

So I said, "Fuck it!" and lit up another joint. What else could I do? I needed to get that shit out of my mind, and smoking weed was the fastest way to do it.

Before I could even get high good, and with everyone out of my room, someone tapped on my door real lightly. I had to listen to it three times to make sure I wasn't hearing things. So I put out my joint for a minute and went to look through the peephole at the door. There was a poised and sexy black woman standing out in the hallway in front of my room. She was waiting patiently for me to answer. She looked as if she was prepared to wait there forever.

I frowned and wondered what the hell was going on. But this girl looked *damned* good, so I opened the door to ask her.

I said, "Ah . . . can I help you?" I was already buzzed a bit, you know.

She grinned at me. She said, "Your friend La'erboy told me to see if you were feeling all bettah."

I thought to myself, *Do you believe this shit?* But then my dick got hard before I could send her away.

I opened the door wide and I asked her, "You wanna come in?"

She walked in without saying another word to me. I locked the door back. Then we sat down and got high together . . . And you know the rest.

. . . *to hurt so bad* . . .

By the time we made it back to Philadelphia from Britain, Tupac Shakur had passed away in a Las Vegas hospital. His family had his body cremated for the burial service. John was at my penthouse apartment staring out the window with nothing to say about it. It was as if he was in mourning. The whole hip-hop nation was in mourning. Even if you didn't like him, Tupac Shakur was the kind of American star who made your blood pump. He was just always into something that kept you awake. But he wasn't "untouchable." That whole "untouchable" shit was dead, and it died with him. Everybody could be touched. I don't care how famous and loved you are.

I hated to kick John while he was down, but I had more bad news for him.

I said, "Hey John . . . you need to get new professional management, man. I don't think there's anything else that I can do for you."

I stopped right there and just let my words settle with him.

John smiled and didn't comment.

I said, "You hear me, man?"

He nodded.

I went ahead and told him everything else that I thought about in regard to his life, because his music career was just *fine*. It was his *life* that I was concerned about. And *his life* was affecting *mine*, more than I was able to control anymore.

I said, "You need to reconcile with your mother, man. Because that conversation that y'all went through was foul. Then you need to figure out a way to deal with your father. Y'all all just need to sit down and talk about it."

I said, "You need more substance in your life, man. And all these girls and the drugs ain't gon' do it. You need to get right. *I* need to get right. And if we can't do it together, then we need to do it apart."

John finally faced me. He looked at me and asked, "What's her name, man?"

I shook my head. He wasn't hearing me.

I said, "John, this isn't about me, this is about *you*, man."

He said, "If it's so much about me, then how come you leaving me then?"

"Because it's time, man. I can't help you no more."

"You not going on the international tour with us next year?" he asked me.

I shook my head and said, "Nah, man. Have a good time with it, though. Big Joe and Tony'll be with you, right?"

He just stared at me. He said, "It ain't the same, man."

I said, "Look, you had an apartment up here with Tony for months. I wasn't with you then. You don't need me on tour. You can use somebody else to set up your stage performance."

I grinned and said, "A lot of these foreign countries won't know what I'm saying anyway. But they'll still want to hear *you*."

John asked me, "Why all of a sudden, man? Is it because of that shit that happened in Britain? Fuck it, man, get over it."

I shook my head. I answered, "It's a lot of different things, man. It's just been building up on me. And it was just a matter of time. I need to start thinking about doing my own thing." I shouldn't have added that last part, but I did.

John jumped on it and said, "Well, why don't you just *say that* then? Don't try to act like you doing me no favor by leaving. Just say you want to do your own shit from now on."

I said, "All right then. *Fine*. I want to do my own shit."

He asked me, "So what are you gonna do, man? You gon' manage somebody else?"

I said, "Maybe I'll go back to school, John. Have you ever thought about that? *I* have."

John said, "Man, ain't shit in school for you. People go to school all their lives to make money like we got and they never make it."

I said, "Well, maybe I just want to finish what I started. I made a promise to my father about that, too."

John said, "So, you just gon' *quit* on what *we* started? I mean, this is *your* life now, man. Your father wasn't paying for school. You was on *scholarship* just like *I* was."

I said, "John, you're right. This *is* my life. And I got a right to decide what I want to do with it. Now you making this harder than what it needs to be, man. We still cool and all. All you have to do is get new management. And it would be best to sign under a management *team* where different people can work with you." I was thinking about people who John could respect, to be honest about it. I didn't think I had that respect from him anymore. I really didn't.

He just stood there in my apartment and stared at me again.

He said, "You really breaking up with me, man. What do you want, more money?" and he started laughing.

John *knew* that was a joke. After the tour and record sales, I had made more than *$2 million* as his manager. I had *earned* that shit, too! And it was more than enough for me to be satisfied monetarily. Some people have to work their whole life before they see that much money. I had done it in just a few years.

So I ignored his comment. I said, "I can make a few calls for you, man, to help you out with it." I was dead serious. I wasn't changing my mind about anything.

John shook his head and said, "Nah, man, don't do me no favors."

He started walking toward the front door.

I repeated, "You need to get right, man." I felt guilty because I was also talking about myself again, and it seemed as if I was taking it out on John.

He faced me at the door and said, "What are you talking about, going to church again?"

I shrugged my shoulders and said, "Whatever, man. Whatever it takes to get back to where you need to be in your mind. And you can sing to the crowds all you want, man. But I know you hurtin' inside . . . and you need to start dealin' with that."

When John walked out, I felt crushed. I was quitting on him because I could no longer control *him or* myself. I was afraid, man. John had become too powerful for me, and now he was turning *me* out. I mean, after he gave me the weed and sent a girl to my room over in London, I figured, *What else would I succumb to if I keep dealing with him?* Basically, I was a punk. And I *felt* like it. I was running away from the fight because I was losing. I had chosen to retreat and abandon my boy on the battlefield. But I had to do it, man. I *had* to do it! I had to be free to live my own life and make my own mistakes based on what *I* was doing, and what I *could* control. I also needed a new turf to reestablish goals for myself. So I thought about relocating to Boston with Chelsea.

But how would *she* see that? She had already said that I seemed needy.

But so what? I *was* needy! And I wanted to be there. I felt as if it was *meant* for me to be there, and to be with her.

When I told Chelsea about my plans, she started laughing.

"I'm serious," I told her.

She said, "I know you are. So how long will it take for you to tell me to move in with you?"

Boy, that Boston girl had my *number!* If I couldn't have my way anymore with John, then I'd have it with her, right?

I joked and said, "I don't want you to move in with me. I'm used to having my own space. You can come over on weekends, though."

I got her there. She said, *"What? Weekends?"*

I said, "Yeah, you got school studying to do, and I don't want to get in the way of that."

She said, "Oh, okay. I'm your *Weekend Shorty* now, right?"

I laughed again. I said, "You heard that song?"

"Yeah, I heard that song. I saw the video for it, too," she told me. She chuckled and said, "I shouldn't say it because of the subject, but I liked that song."

I said, "Yeah, John and Tony made it work. Don't be ashamed of it."

She said, "So, you're actually gonna quit then?"

It was the moment of truth, man. I *had* to do it! I said, "Yeah. I'm done. I've already told John . . . I gotta start living my own life now."

Chelsea got quiet on me. I guess she was thinking it over for herself. She asked me, "So, you really want to move up here to Boston now?"

I said, "Yeah, I do. Unless you want me to stay down here in Philly and keep it long distance," I joked to her. I didn't want to stay in Philly, man. *God knows!* I wanted to be up there with her in Boston. Or *anywhere!*

She said, "No sir, no *sir!* You better *bring* your behind up here to Boston! You got me going now!"

Man, it felt *good* to hear her say that! *GOOD!* I felt so damn *relieved!*

I said, "Well, let me start making the arrangements then."

That was it for me. I was on my way to Boston. Then I started getting the disparaging phone calls about my decision to stop managing John.

Tony called me up first. He said, "Yo, man, what's up?"

I didn't feel like explaining myself to everybody, so I let him spell it out to me.

I said, "What's up with what, man?"

"You quittin'?"

I said, "It's done already. I quit."

"Why, man? That boah need you. Y'all boys."

I said, "And we're *still* boys. But I don't need to be around John like that no more, man. You got your own life now, Tony, and I'm trying to move on with mine."

He said, "You don't need to quit John to do that."

I said, "Tony, you only make music with him. I gotta make calls for him, accept calls, make sure he in the right place at the right time, nurse his ego when he's hurtin'. All kinds of shit, man! It's easy to just make fuckin' music with him. I could do that, too, if I knew how to play instruments."

Tony said, "Damn, man. It don't seem like *no* groups can stay together no more."

I said, "I'm not in a God damned *group*, Tony! Y'all music ain't gon' change without me. What are y'all so worried about?"

Tony said, "John needs close people around him, man. He needs that Southern influence that you got. I can't give him that."

I said, "Here we go with *that* shit again. John is his own person, man. Especially *now*. And Southern influences don't have shit to do with it."

Tony started laughing. He said, "Is that it, man? You jealous about the women? You get yours, man. What's wrong with you, D?"

I asked him, "So it doesn't bother you at all that you're married now, and you still need to fuck somebody every night on tour?"

Tony paused. He said, "I don't fuck every night like that. And I *told you*, man, don't be *saying* that shit. But that's a part of the business that we in. Would you rather that no women wanted us? We wouldn't *be* shit if *that* was the case. I mean, the pussy is just a measure of the success. The more successful you are, the more women wanna fuck you. So take all that shit out on *them*. Don't take that out on *John*. He ya' boy, man. Straight up."

I calmed myself down and said, "Tony . . . I want to be able to have some control over my dick, *regardless*. Okay?"

He said, "Well, that's *your* problem. Keep locking yourself in your room then and don't answer the damn door."

It was a waste of time arguing with Tony. He was calling me for one reason, to get me to come back. He wasn't trying to hear anything that I had to say.

I said, "Tony, y'all gon' be just fine. Now I got shit to do," and I hung up.

Big Joe actually came over to my damn apartment about it.

I said, "Joe, I hired you, man. You wouldn't even be involved in this shit if it wasn't for me. So don't come over here trying to talk me out of shit."

Big Joe just chilled on my leather sofa and started smiling. He said, "I understand, dawg. To each his own, man. We folks, though. So I just want you to know that I got his back."

Joe wasn't exactly the best person to be around for making good decisions, but I had to put faith in somebody, because I was not going back. So I said, "Good. Keep him in good health."

After the close people got their say, the news spread around to Old School Records, and everybody was sorry to see me go. Evelyn called from New York and thanked me for the business opportunity. I even got a call from Tangela in New Jersey.

She said, "I learned a lot from you, Darin. I'm sorry to see you break up with John like that, but everybody has to move on. That's just a part of life."

Tangela was doing a great job with Butterscotch herself. They had sold two million albums of their first LP while touring with Janet Jackson, mainly off the hits that John and Tony had worked on for them, a sultry ballad called *Tell Me What You Mean* and a club jam called *Got My Eyes on You.*

I said, "This is a hard business to be in, man. The ups are up, but the downs are *way* down."

She said, "Who you tellin'? But I'm a trouper. I didn't come all the way out here not to survive it."

I said, "You know what, you don't really seem like no California girl."

I just had images of California girls being a lot more laid-back than Tangela was. She fit right in with the hustle and bustle of the Northeast.

She laughed and said, "That's because I was born in New Jersey. I didn't move out to California until I was eight."

I continued with my plans and moved to downtown Boston. I even thought seriously about going back to school up there. Northeastern wasn't a black college like I was used to, but I went and enrolled there for the spring semester anyway.

John found himself a new management team because Old School Records feared letting him go about business as usual without me. He was just too big of a young star to be floating around by himself. They had a whole lot of money riding on his shoulders. I knew it firsthand. And I had given it all up for my sanity.

This new group called themselves Top Notch Management, and most of them were from the go-go music territory of Washington, D.C. They were used to guerrilla marketing strategies and they were a lot more aggressive about staying connected in the star community than I was. They got John involved in a lot of public appearances and celebrity events, the kind of things that I was never able to get him into. I mean, it was only *one* of me, but it was a whole *team* of those guys, all working together for John. I thought it was a good deal for my boy. He was even on cable TV playing in celebrity ball games and such.

Then Chelsea answered the phone at my apartment in November. It was around nine o'clock at night, and I was relaxing while reading a magazine article. John was still getting those great public relations stories that never tainted his image. Evelyn was working wonders for him. I mean, you would think that every mother on the planet would want their daughters to bring John home for dinner with those articles. We had a little bit of bad press in London after the fight at the club that night, but they understood that it wasn't our fault. Tom Davies, our movie producer friend, even decided to use John's ballad *Don't You Ever Wonder* as the lead song in the opening credits of their film *Without Reason*. It was to be released around Christmas. And John's reporter friend, Michelle, had become the rave in London for being the inspiration for the song. Imagine that.

I didn't think much of the phone call Chelsea had answered until she started responding to some of the questions being asked to her.

She said, "My name is Chelsea . . . Is that right? So he wouldn't tell you."

When I looked up from the lounge chair, she was smiling in my direction.

She said, "Actually, I met you before."

I got curious and asked her, "Who's that?"

Chelsea held up an index finger for me to wait a minute.

She said, "In Boston."

I asked her, "Is that John?"

She nodded to me. Then she began to frown.

She asked him, "Are you okay?"

Then I got anxious. I said, "Let me talk to him."

She handed me the phone and said, "He sounds really messed up."

I put my hand over the receiver and asked her, "What, like he's high?"

"*Very.*"

I got on the phone and said, "Hey John, what's up, man?"

He stammered and said, "I—, I—, I knew you had a girl up there, man. You tried to hide her from me. But I found out, D." I just never bothered to talk about Chelsea with John.

I said, "Are you all right, man? What's goin' on?"

He said, "Man . . . ," with a long pause, "my mom just left here."

I said, "Okay. And?"

John was slurring *big-time!* I hadn't heard him *that* damned high before. I didn't even know if weed could get him that high.

He said, "Why she, she gon' s-s-sneak up on me like that, man?"

"John, what are you talking about?" I asked him.

He said, "I called her like you told me, man. And we talked about stuff. And then she gon' come down here, un-unannounced, and sneak up on me like dat."

I said, "Your mom just did that?" I was trying to put the broken pieces together from his words.

"Yeah, man."

"Well, where is she now?" I asked him.

He said, "She went back in a taxi."

"Back to where?"

He said, "I'on know, man. I'an even know she was comin'."

Why would his mother do that? I asked myself. I just didn't understand her. They were *both* crazy! Then again, Sister Williams still didn't know how John was living, she had only been *assuming* things. Not that her assumptions were wrong, though.

I asked John, "And what were you doing when she got there?" I could just imagine.

He said, "Man, you know . . . I was just windin' down."

"Winding down, doing what?"

He said, "Man, I just had some people over here."

I shook my head with the phone to my ear and looked back at Chelsea. She said, "What?"

I put my free hand up to stop her. I needed to concentrate on that phone call.

I asked, "And what were y'all doing there, John?"

He didn't want to tell me in straight words. He said, "Man, she, she jus' wasn't sposed to do that."

I took a deep breath. John was all the way in Philly and I was up in Boston. I felt like calling his new management people, but I didn't even have their phone numbers. I was trying to force myself to stay away by any means necessary.

I said, "John, stay right there, man. Okay?"

He said, "I ain't got nowhere to go."

"Good. I'll call you right back."

I hung up the phone *praying* that Tony was at his house in New Jersey. He wasn't that far from John. His wife answered the phone.

I said, "Hi, this is D Harmon. Is Tony around? It's urgent."

She said, "Hi, Darin. Tony's down in Philly, but I can give you his cell phone number."

She gave me the number and asked me how things were going for me up in Boston.

I said, "I'm just getting used to the new life."

She said, "I'm tellin' *you*. Sometimes I wish that Tony didn't have to be so *busy* all of the time. Especially since we're expecting a new baby now."

I said, "Oh, congratulations. When is it due?"

"*She's* due on June twenty-first," she told me.

I chuckled and said, "Oh, my bad. Y'all know what it is already?"

She said, "Not yet, but I *think* it's a girl."

I could tell that Tony's new wife was getting lonely. She wanted to keep talking to me even though I said it was urgent. I felt sorry for her in every way. But that was the lifestyle of the music business, and if you wanted to be married into it, then you had to be ready to handle the time spent alone.

I called up Tony on his cell phone and caught him at a South Philadelphia studio. They had a lot of new music factories popping up.

Tony answered the phone and I told him who it was. He said, "D Harmon! What's up, man? What can I do for you?" We didn't have any grudges or anything. They all accepted the fact that I had moved on.

I said, "What's going on with John, man?"

He said, "What do you mean? John's aw'ight."

"No he's *not*," I told him. I said, "I just talked to him. And that boy sounds like he's smoking *more* than weed now, man. What's going on? What's this new management company doing? They don't have anybody with him?"

Tony said, "D, I told you before. John needs you, man. You're the only one who was close to him like that. Everybody else is in awe of that boah. You know that. I told you that already."

I said, "So they don't know that he has a problem?"

Tony took a breath. He said, "Hold on a minute. Let me talk somewhere private."

Chelsea was waiting for information at the apartment, but I was too far into things to give her a blow-by-blow until I was finished with what I was doing.

Tony reestablished our conversation and said, "Darin, when we was still in Britain, and John started hanging out with some of those rock band members, he got into some *other* shit. So I don't know *what* he into now. I think he might be mixing his shit up with something."

I said, "And you *knew* about this shit?!" I was PISSED! What kind of a fucking friend was Tony to let John do that to himself?!

Tony said, "I'm not really sure, man. I mean, that's the kind of shit that *you* could find out faster than anybody else could."

I said, "Tony, how are you gonna sit here and tell me that you don't really know after you just told me that?"

Tony didn't have an answer. He said, "Darin, if you really want to find out, then you ask John."

Boy, it felt as if I was being stabbed in the heart by three different knives.

I yelled, "DAMN! MAN! Aw'ight then! Let me call him back."

I hung up the phone with Tony, and Chelsea asked me, "What's wrong?"

I said, "I'm about to find out right now."

I was pacing the apartment like a tiger when I called John back.

I said, "John, I need you to be honest with me, man. That's the only way that I can help you."

"Help me to do what? I'm about to just lay down and relax right now, man," he told me.

Knowing John, he wouldn't be lying down by himself, especially while he was wounded. I knew his M.O. as well as I knew my own.

I tried another route and said, "Let me speak to your company."

He responded, "Hunh? You didn't let me speak to *your* girl. I had to find out about her on my own."

"John, give her the damn phone," I told him. And I waited.

"Hello," a female voice answered.

I asked her, "Do you realize that John needs help right now?"

She chuckled and said, "Yeah."

She sounded as if she was high herself. Maybe I was barking up the wrong tree by talking to John's company.

I said, "Is that the way you want him to be? What are you with him for? Do you really care about him? Because if you *did*, you wouldn't want to see him like this. John needs some help."

She said, *"Hunh?"* in a tight squeal.

I asked her, "You didn't hear what I just said?" I was nearly snapping at her.

"What?" she asked me back.

The girl was not concentrating on a damn thing that I was saying to her. I started to say something else, but then I thought about it.

She mumbled, "Mmm hmm. I heard you," all out of the blue.

I put two and two together and realized that John was taking care of his business while I was on the phone with the girl.

I said, "Tell John I'll call him back when y'all done," and I hung up on her.

I looked at Chelsea up in Boston and said, "That mother*fucker!*" and just shook my head. John had *problems*, but only insiders knew about it. That's what made it so torturing for me. If everyone knew about it, then John could start to deal with his demons. But as long as everyone kept things under wraps, he was sure to sink deeper and deeper.

I thought that night about blowing the damn whistle and informing all the right people that John "Loverboy" Williams was getting way out of hand. His behind-the-scenes actions were not cute adolescent shit anymore, and everyone needed to deal with that reality. John needed to respect himself and *others* like a responsible adult, no matter *how* great he could sing.

I planned to call his new management company, Old School Records, Evelyn Harris, Sister Williams, his cousins down in Atlanta, and even his father, Reverend Joseph Stark, if I *had* to! *Somebody* had to get through to his ass! But first I wanted to get John out of Philadelphia for a minute so I could lock him down inside a hotel room and get all of the answers that I needed from him.

I contacted Big Joe in the morning and told him that I needed a big favor from him.

"What's that, dawg?" He was just waking up with a groggy voice.

I said, "I need you to get John on a plane up here to Boston, man. So I'll buy the round-trip plane tickets for both of y'all to come see me."

Big Joe got excited and said, "Hey, man, John will like to hear that. I mean, he doesn't try to talk about you much, but I know he misses you, man. People don't understand him like you do."

I cut him off and said, "Yeah, so I'm gon' get them tickets."

Big Joe didn't need to know anything else.

I went over my whole plan of conversation with questions and answers to break John down in Boston. Chelsea even heard me talking to myself a few times at the apartment.

She smiled and said, "You are *really* thinking about this. And you *should* be. Because somebody has to do it."

I said, "I know."

She asked me, "Do you think he would remember me?"

I stopped and thought about it. Chelsea was pretty, but there were plenty of girls along the tour that would stand out a lot longer than she would. I had to be honest with myself about that. Chelsea had just gotten to *me*. But she *did* make it up into John's room. I kept trying to make myself forget that. Then again, I never did see her actually inside the room.

I said, "I can't really say," and I left it at that.

When John reluctantly arrived at the Boston international airport with Big Joe—because Big Joe had to talk him into coming—it may as well have been Alaska up there for us Southern boys. It was *real* cold, so they were both incognito in winter coats, scarves, hats, and John wore a pair of blue-lens sunglasses. I had rented another Ford Explorer for us.

I gave him a hug and asked him how the flight was.

He said, "I thought we were about to fly into the ocean for a minute, man. I ain't feel like being up here. And I'm glad I dressed warm."

That was John for you. His answers to even simple questions were liable to go anywhere.

I said, "Well, I got y'all a hotel room downtown."

He said, "Just *one* room? I don't want this big nigga sleepin' wit' me. He might scare my Boston hotties away."

Big Joe laughed and said, "Aw, go 'head, sticks and bones. You know they love me more than they love you."

John said, "Is that what you tell yourself at night, man, with ya' dick in ya' hand?"

John was not as lean as he used to be, but Big Joe had definitely become a sidekick for him. John could never really joke with me like that. But I felt that things could have gotten that way if I had stayed around him longer.

So I ignored him and I checked them both into one hotel room anyway.

John was still bitching about it when we walked into the large suite. He said, "Man, you really serious about this one-room shit. We ain't kids up in here, D. I'm gon' have to get me my *own* room then."

I got right into it and said, "John, we need to talk, man."

He stopped mouthing off and just smiled at me.

He said, "I knew you were setting me up for a damn lecture up here, man. That's why I ain't wanna come. You just called me at the wrong time, D. I told you I was about to relax, man," he told me, referring to our last brief phone conversation.

I said, "John, you called me *first*. Because you know you need help, man. And you were *not* relaxing. You were fuckin'. Understand that there's a difference between the two."

Big Joe started chuckling at it. Maybe I needed to ask him to leave the room.

I asked, "And what are you smoking now, John?"

Big Joe stopped laughing. Then I decided to put him on the spot, too. "Do *you* know, Joe?" I asked him.

He shook his head and remained mute on the subject.

I said, "John, we can all *act* like your shit is normal behavior if we *want to*, but *you* know the truth, man." I pounded my hand on my heart and said, "It's right up in here."

It wasn't a laughing matter in the room anymore.

John sat down on the sofa and tried to ignore me. He said, "This new management company is killing me, man. They got me doing all these extra appearances, and these celebrity sports functions and shit. I ain't never been no athlete like that, man. You know that shit, D."

Big Joe said, "That's good for you, though. You need to work out and stay in shape, dawg."

John said, "I *am* in shape. I do more shit than either one of y'all."

They were getting off of the subject. I said, "Look, I'm not here to talk about that."

Big Joe kept talking. He said, "I'm just saying to work out every once in a while to stay toned. Other singers work out, man."

John said, "Yeah, because they want to take their shirts all off and stick their chests out and shit. I don't *need* to do that. I can really *sing*. Them other motherfuckers are using gimmicks and shit to keep your attention. They know what they doin'."

I spoke up louder and said, "Look, y'all can talk about this other shit another time. On your *own* time. But this right here is *my time*."

John said, "Well, go 'head and use it then."

I said, "John, do you ever notice how much you complain about shit?"

He looked at me and said, "I got a lot to complain about. My stakes are high." He still had his sunglasses on, too.

I said, "Yeah, your *stakes* are so high that the sun is even in your eyes up in this room?" I was hinting for him to take his glasses off. I wanted to see the whites of his eyes.

He said, "Nah, man, but you're in my face with this bullshit."

"*Is it* bullshit?" I asked him.

"Yeah, it is, man," he told me. He said, "I'm a musician. And the shit that I get into feeds me the music that I write. I can't do the shit without it. I know what the fuck I'm doing. I understand things. *Y'all* just don't."

I asked him, "So what are you telling me, John? Are you *living* a damn song, man? Is that what you're telling me?"

Big Joe started laughing again.

John nodded his head and said, "Yeah. You got it, man. Now you understand me."

I said, "John, this is *not* a God damn song! This is *real life*, man! Stop that fuckin' stupid shit! It's *not* cute, man! *Seriously!*"

I said, "This ain't no damn interview. The cameras are off. And there's no tape recorder in here."

John finally took off his sunglasses and said, "Hey D, did God create the heaven and the earth, man, and the birds, bees, and trees?"

I stopped him short and said, "It's funny how you try and remember the Word whenever you get good and ready for it. You know the Word *five* times better than I do. I'm *sure* of it. Because you paid attention. But you don't want to *live* by it though, *do you?*"

He said, "We all play our parts, man. And ain't no part perfect. And *God* created these imperfections. He created *us*, didn't he?"

Big Joe said, "That's true, dawg."

I looked at Big Joe, grinning and shit, and I was ready to tell him to shut the fuck up, but I wasn't so sure how he would respond to that, so I kept it to myself.

I said, "Joe, do you mind if I talk to John alone for a minute? I wanna whip his ass."

Big Joe started laughing. He said, "I can't let you whip his ass, man. That's my job to protect him."

John smiled at it and said, "Yeah, aw'ight," as if he could hold his own against me. And he couldn't.

I said, "Well, let me just talk to 'im."

Big Joe nodded and started walking toward the door. "You got it," he told me.

I sat down next to John on the sofa and said, "How are you feeling, man? Are things going as planned for you? Because sometimes I think I'm dreaming with the shit you get into, just like these girls who get next to you, John. Or should I say *Loverboy?*"

John looked straight ahead and said, "It ain't no dream, man. This is how I'm living. And this is the way it was *supposed* to be."

"Who says?" I asked him.

John said, "You think we really control any of this, man? Like, you can make decisions on how your life is really gonna go down? That's always been your problem, D. You think you can *plan* everything. And you *can't*. If you *could*, you'd be playing football right now."

He had me with that. That was on point.

I said, "No, you *can't* control everything. But like I told you before, man, you just gotta say *no* to the shit that you don't want to be a part of. *I* gotta say no. We *all* do. It's as simple as that. That's why I can't be with you no more, man. Because if you can't make that decision for yourself, John, then you end up jeopardizing what *I'm* trying to do. And I'm not gon' let that happen no more."

I said, "In fact, I'm not gon' let you ruin *yourself* either. Because I love you too much for that, man. And I loved you *before* this Loverboy shit. So since you can't stop yourself, we all gon' have to make it easier for you."

As soon as I said that, my cell phone rang. I only answered it because I needed a break point from John. And it was Chelsea on the line.

She asked me, "How are things going?"

I said, "I'm cool. What's up?"

I didn't want to say too much in front of John. I didn't want to make it seem so obvious that I had made plans for him, whether he assumed that much or not.

Chelsea asked, "Are you hungry? I was about to fix something at the apartment."

I said, "Yeah, well, we'll probably go out and get something to eat."

She said, "John can just go out to eat like that, or would he rather like a home-cooked meal?"

I was trying to deal with John away from Chelsea.

I said, "Yeah, we'll be all right."

"Okay then."

When I hung up the phone, John smiled at me. He asked me, "Is she nice, man?"

I didn't want to talk about it. I said, "Are you about ready to get something to eat?"

"How come you won't talk about this girl with me, man? You not afraid of me meeting her, are you?" He grinned and said, "I wouldn't do that to you, man. I'm sure she loves only you anyway."

I said, "John, that's the *last* thing on my mind right now."

"So, how come I can't meet her then?"

That wasn't what I had John up there to do. But I had to admit, I *did* feel a bit funny about that. I was wondering if John *would* remember Chelsea, or if she would bring it back up to him if he didn't.

I said, "This ain't that kind of a visit, man." I still hadn't been able to pin John down like I wanted to. The boy was like water. And he *was* an Aquarius. A water carrier.

He said, "Well, what kind of a visit is this then? I thought we were family, man."

He had me on the guilt trip. Hell, I figured that he would meet Chelsea sooner or later. Why not just get it over with? Did I really have anything to hide?

I nodded my head and said, "Aw'ight. Let's get something to eat at my place then."

John smiled and said, "Cool."

I paged Chelsea and left her a message that we had changed our minds and that we'd be on our way over. I had given her a key to the apartment and we practically lived together by that time. I was dead serious about her.

We drove on our way to my apartment, and I was filled with apprehension, but I was trying my best to fight it off. I kept trying to ask myself why I felt so strange about it. Had Chelsea told me the truth? She *had* to. She was not in John's room but for a few minutes. Or maybe it was longer than that because I had never checked my watch. However, that was ridiculous. Chelsea wasn't that kind of a girl. But she *did* march to the hotel with the intentions of getting up in John's room. And she had *made it* there.

I tried to block all of the past out of my mind and just let them meet each other, hoping and praying that Chelsea wouldn't bring their meeting up to him and that John wouldn't remember things differently.

Suddenly, I went from apprehensive to hasty, and I just wanted to get it all over with as quickly as possible.

When we parked in the garage, John said, "D finally gon' show us the girl who made him move all the way up to Boston."

Big Joe chuckled and said, "I think about moving my baby momma up to Philly with me all the time."

I ignored their talking with a grin and led them up to my nice place. John and Big Joe walked in and they immediately liked the view that I had of Boston, and the creative architecture. I was in a brand-new building that had plenty of window space for natural light. I also had a nice-size balcony.

I called Chelsea out from the kitchen to get things over with.

I said, "Chelsea, I want you to meet my boy in person, the one and only John *Loverboy* Williams."

John had somehow escaped my plan to get him to confess his demons. Instead, he was putting *me* on the spot with my confidence in my new woman.

Chelsea walked out looking prettier than usual for some reason. Or maybe that's just how it seemed at the moment. But I was sure proud of her.

She said, "Hi," and smiled at John and Big Joe.

Big Joe nodded and said, "What's up?"

John grinned and said, "Pleased to meet you."

I watched to see what her eye contact would be like with John, and they didn't have it. John was smiling at her because she was with me, and she was smiling at him because I knew him. Or was that what I was trying to tell myself? Anyway, I didn't see anything extra going on, and neither one of them brought anything extra up.

By the end of the night, we were all well fed, and I felt relieved. It was as if Chelsea had passed a gigantic test. Then I went to drive John and Big Joe back to the hotel, and Big Joe dozed off to sleep in the back of the Explorer.

John looked at me from the passenger side and said, "She's cool, man. She likes to make jokes a lot. And she pretty, too, like in a simple way. She's the kind of girl who don't need makeup. So if she put some on, she'd probably be a knockout, man."

He grinned at me and said, "You did all right, D."

I bragged and said, "You think I would just pick anybody after all of these years? We've been around a lot of women."

John nodded his head and said, "Yeah, but I'm trying to think if I remember her from here."

I thought, *Aw shit!* First I thought about throwing him off of the trail, but then I got curious.

I asked him, "Why would you think that?"

He said, "I'on know. It just seems like . . . I met her before, man. It's just something about her smart mouth. Or maybe all girls from Boston are like that. I don't know. I mean, I was just trying to decide on who I wanted to deal with when I was here. They were just cool to fuck with, man."

I tried to laugh it off, hoping that John would decide to move on from it, but he didn't.

He started smiling as if he knew something, and I didn't like that at all.

He said, "Man, I *do* remember her," and started nodding his head.

I said, "You do?"

All I could do was just wait for the bullet to strike through my poor heart.

John looked at me and asked, "Are you real close with her, man? I mean, is she marriage material for you?"

I got irritated and said, "Why, man? You fucked her? Is that what you're about to tell me?"

I lost my cool. What could I say? I was showing my insecurity. After all, Chelsea had fucked me on that first night up in Boston after talking all of that "discipline" shit. She didn't just say *no* to me! And she probably didn't say *no* to John! She had probably fucked *Loverboy* like everyone else, another whore for the fame.

That's just how insecure I was at that moment. I felt crushed before John even said anything.

John looked into my eyes and gave me mercy. I could see him reading me. He didn't have his sunglasses on anymore. It was nighttime and the streetlights were shining into the car.

John shook his head and answered, "Nah, man. She made a couple of smart-ass comments and walked out. That's probably why I remember her."

MY GOD! I breathed a sigh of relief and just looked away.

John said, "That's what you *want* me to say, right?"

I turned back to him and asked, "What?" Was he making shit up just to protect my feelings?

I said, "John, if you fucked her, man, just tell me. All right? Just get it over with."

John looked at me and said, "Like you said, we got con-*trol* over life, right? Well . . . I'm gon' show some *control* for you. So . . . no. Okay? No . . . I didn't fuck her."

I said, "John, I didn't tell you to lie to me, man."

He said, "I'm *not* lying. And *John* didn't fuck her. But that *Loverboy* . . ." He shook his head. Then he said, "Man . . . I can't always speak for him. People just take it where they want it to go."

THAT MOTHERFUCKER WAS TOYING WITH ME! And *for what?!* To show that he had *control* over me?!

Man, I got so frustrated with that boy that I reached out and punched him dead in his fucking face with my right hand.

"NIGGA, THIS AIN'T NO FUCKIN' *GAME!*" I screamed at him.

The Ford Explorer swerved, and I rushed to double-park that motherfucker to *WHIP JOHN'S ASS!* I had enough of his bullshit! Now he was trying to ruin the beautiful relationship that I was in.

I got to grabbing that boy and trying to shove his fucking head through the passenger window while I beat his ass down before Big Joe could wake up and stop me.

"WHAT THE FUCK IS GOING ON, DARIN?"

Big Joe launched himself overtop of the seat to try and stop me.

I yelled, "I'M GON' KILL THIS MOTHERFUCKER, MAN!"

"FOR WHAT?" Big Joe hollered back at me while pressing me against the steering wheel.

I forced my way out of the Explorer and ran around to the passenger side to try and grab John's ass out, but Big Joe wouldn't let me get him.

I screamed, "LET HIM GET THE FUCK OUT, JOE! LET HIM BE A FUCKING MAN OUT HERE! I WOULDN'T LET NO MOTH-ERFUCKER PUNCH ME IN *MY* FACE!"

We were in the middle of downtown Boston making a HUGE scene, three black boys from down south. But at least it was nighttime.

Big Joe climbed out of the car and said, "Yo, dawg, calm down, man! What the hell happened?! What he do? We *folks*, man! Y'all *boys!*"

John rolled down the passenger-side window and hollered, "He crying over some fucking girl! She just a girl, man! They come a dime a dozen! You gon' break us up for that shit? You'll meet another girl tomorrow."

I said, "Fuck you, John! FUCK YOU, MAN! You think this shit is a damn game? Well, get out of the car and act like you want to defend your-self then."

John actually tried opening the door, but Big Joe wouldn't let him. He said, "Y'all not gon' fight out here, man. Y'all need to talk whatever this is out."

I was too far gone for that. I was tired of talking to him.

I said, "Fuck talking, man! He needs his *ass* kicked, *that's* what he needs! He needs to be punched in his fuckin' *mouth*, just like I just did him. Since he thinks everything is a fucking game."

John said, "Man, go 'head with that crybaby shit."

"*CRYBABY?!*" I yelled back at him. "Who the fuck are you calling a *CRYBABY*, as much as *YOU* cry about shit?! You fuckin' *GIRL!* You's a *punk*, John! A *PUNK!* That's why you need *PUSSY* so much, you don't feel like a real *man* yet! And you ain't never *gon'* be! You fuckin' *MOMMA'S BOY!*"

I walked back in the apartment. Chelsea was sitting in the living room love seat. She was watching television and eating ice cream with her feet up.

She smiled at me and said, "So, what did he say?"

"What did he say about what?" I asked her.

She said, "About me, stupid."

I said, "Oh, so I'm *stupid* now, is that it?" I was standing overtop of her, blocking her view to the television.

She said, "You know I didn't mean anything by that." She looked con-cerned and asked me, "What's wrong with you? What did he say?"

I asked her, "Why? You got a guilty conscience about something? Is there something that you want to tell me?"

She frowned and said, "Tell you about what?"

I snapped and said, "About what really fuckin' happened in John's hotel room that night I met you up here."

She shut her mouth, put down her ice cream, and tried to avoid me.

She said, "I think you have problems."

I said, "What kind of *problems* am I having, Chelsea? Do *you* know?"

She said, "Darin, what is wrong with you?"

I stopped beating around the bush and came right out with it.

I said, "Did you fuck him?"

Chelsea looked me in my hard-bitten eyes and tried to stand up.

"Did I fuck who?"

"You know who the *fuck* I'm talking about!" I snapped at her.

She said, "First of all, you don't come up in here talking to me like that."

"Did you fuck him or what, Chelsea?"

"Did *he* say that?" she asked me.

I said, "I'm asking *you*. I don't care what he said."

She said, "Obviously you *do* care what he said. Why else would you come at me like this?"

"Answer the damn question, Chelsea. Did you fuck 'im?"

She got just as pissed off at me and said, "Do you *think* I *fucked* him?!"

"I don't know, that's why I'm asking you."

She shook her head and started to walk away from me, mumbling, "I don't believe this shit."

"Just *answer* the question," I told her. "That's all you gotta do."

She had tears in her eyes. *I* was hurt, and I was hurting her.

Chelsea hollered, "You *knew* that I wasn't even in his *damn* room long enough for that shit!"

I said, "I only know what you told me. Now if you didn't fuck him, then just say no. That's all you gotta say."

She screamed, "I *shouldn't* have to say a *damn thing!* You should *know* that already! So I don't know why your *fucking friend* would lie to you like that, but I don't *appreciate* this *shit!* And I'm not gon' fuckin' sit here and *take it!*"

Her voice broke up and she started throwing shit around the apartment, having a damn fit.

I said, "Well, all you had to say is *no,* instead of bullshitting about it."

She turned to me and yelled, "You know what? Fuck you! *FUCK YOU!*"

She ran into the bedroom, locked the doors, and started throwing more shit around in there, too. It didn't sound good at all, man. That's when I finally realized how crazy I was acting. John had really set me off that night. Chelsea was the first thing that I had of my own in years, and to have John, *Loverboy,* or whoever the hell he was at that point ruin my relationship with her was the last thing that I could take. And I went right ahead and ruined it myself by acting like a damn fool.

I was numb, man. I didn't know what to do. I didn't know what to say. I didn't even know how I felt anymore. I didn't know if I wanted to kill him, hug her, cry, call my father, or *what!* I was in a state of *shock*, man. Too many different things were running through my mind. So I just sat there on the love seat and dropped my head into my hands.

I mumbled to myself, "That motherfucker." He had gotten crafty all right. And I couldn't fuck with him anymore. That boy had just played me like a grand piano. And he got a standing ovation.

. . . and make us feel the pain . . .

I *refused* to let Chelsea leave that night. I fought my own ego for her. I knew she was a good woman and I was desperate to hold on, so we cried our hearts out together and wouldn't let each other go. I explained how my whole relationship with John had gone sour through life in the music industry, and she told me that she would support me in whatever I needed to do. So I decided to finish the deal and made love to Chelsea that night in tears and sweat, and without any protection. I didn't want to be protected with her anymore. I wanted to give her my all or give her nothing. Fast living creates fast decisions like that. I was driven by the passion of the moment instead of calmer logic. So on that night, or on the nights that followed, we conceived our first child, Imani. That's a Swahili name for "faith." Because we had to have faith in each other and our future together to make it last.

I stayed up in Boston over the Christmas holiday season with Chelsea, her mother, and her little cousin Damon, instead of going back home to Charlotte. In the new year of 1997, Chelsea and I chose a large church in Boston, and I started to attend church and then school with her at Northeastern University, as what else, a business major. I was cruising in my courses, too. I was older, more mature about education, with no football dreams in my way, and I already knew enough about business not to struggle with anything. So I soon went straight to the top of my class.

Chelsea and I grew stronger together, and the church became part of our union, not because we were dragged there by our parents anymore but because we wanted to call on the strength and stability that only God could grant us. And in time, we set a date and informed everyone of our wedding. The plan was to get married in Charlotte and fly Chelsea's family in, because my family was much larger than hers. I wanted them to see and experience where I was from anyway.

I didn't talk about that singer that I *used* to know. He was finally receiving all kinds of awards and recognition for his second album, but he didn't win an invitation to my wedding. I didn't even take his phone calls. I just informed everyone that we had grown apart and I left it at that.

Sister Williams showed up at my wedding, but I didn't get a chance to talk to her. I guess we did have something in common, though; we were both exiles from her son's life. I realized how she felt. You had to show tough love in order to maintain what you believe in. So my priority became my new faith in God, myself, my wife, and in my future family. And I was not giving that up for anyone.

My father didn't have any more stern lectures for me as a married man. He just took me aside for a second and said, "I'm proud of you, son. And I guess you realize now how hard the decisions are that we need to make to become our own men in this world."

I nodded my head and said, "Yeah, I sure do. I *sure* do."

Chelsea and I took a honeymoon to the Bahamas after the spring semester at school, and then we got right back to work on finishing our degrees. Since I didn't have to work to make a living for a while, I planned to go to school all year round and double up on as many credits as I could to finish early.

Meanwhile, I had to ignore all of the tests and traps that were set for me from my past career and relationships. There was all kinds of speculation being written about why I left the business. And while the singer that I *used* to know went on a world tour to continue pushing his sophomore album, there were some shots taken at my youth and inexperience in handling a major career, and even some hints at money mismanagement, which I knew was all nonsense. I did my job well, and I was always on the up-and-up with the accounting books.

I wasn't involved in the whole day-to-day functions of music anymore, but I still knew what was going on. Plenty of reporters contacted me about our split to set the record straight, but I didn't want to come off as a scorned friend-manager, so I told them all, "No comment," and went on about my life. I was done talking about him *and* having to deal with him. I had nothing to say *to or about* him.

As you could imagine, with no tour or hustle and bustle, 1997 was one of the longest years of my life. Then R. Kelly released his hit song *I Believe I Can Fly* from the Warner Bros. and Michael Jordan movie, *Space Jam*. That song did wonders for me, expressing exactly how I felt on August 27 when my daughter, Imani Harmon, was born. Man, I can't even explain how happy I was to hold my own little girl in my arms that day. She was *beautiful*! A healthy brown baby with a head full of black hair.

"Hey, girl? Do you know who I am?" I asked her.

She moved toward my voice in my arms and had her tiny eyes opened.

Chelsea smiled from the hospital bed and said, "Yeah, she knows who you are. She just can't tell you yet."

I said, "Yes, she can. She's telling me with her body," and I bent over and kissed her little lips.

The rest of that year was all about family and school for me. I was even excited about that *Stomp* song that Charlotte gospel choir leader, Kirk Franklin, had put out. Some gospel traditionalists were complaining that *Stomp* wasn't real gospel music, but I felt that gospel had to find a way to force itself into the mainstream to relate more spiritual issues to the young music listeners out there. And my wife agreed with me on that.

I started thinking about buying a house in Boston, but Chelsea told me that she might be interested in leaving the area after we both graduated from Northeastern, so I held off from it. And I wasn't missing a thing in the music industry. Not even the money. I still had plenty of it invested and growing by the day. But I'd be lying if I said that I didn't think about how much *more* money I could have been making had my friend been able to allow me some peace of mind.

As fate would have it, in early 1998, I got a phone call from Tangela in New York. I had gone an entire year doing my own thing.

She said, "Darin, can I still consider you as, like, a business mentor?"

I hesitated. I hadn't talked to Tangela in a while, and I assumed that she would have figured out everything she needed to know in the music business by then.

I said, "Ah . . . you know, I can't really say anymore, because I haven't been around the business lately. What kind of help do you need?"

She said, "Well, do you know how to fill out these publishing forms? What's the legalities of all that?"

She was asking me something that she could have asked anyone about. Filing song publishing papers with BMI and ASCAP was a simple process. I could do it in my sleep.

I said, "You just get the paperwork, fill out the percentage shares, state who gets what, and send it in."

"And how do you know when a new kind of song is a hit? You know what

I mean? I just want to sit down and pick your brains for a while, because I'm learning new things every year, and so much is constantly changing in this industry."

She said, "A hit song for last year won't even get any airplay for this year. It's just confusing to know sometimes."

I told her, "Well, you might want to call up some of the other managers who have hit artists out right now. The older guys would know more than I would. I'm still a baby myself. It's not like I've been involved in it for ten years or anything, where I could really say what's gonna happen next. I just went by what I felt was right."

I said, "So call up some of these new management companies."

Tangela finally broke down and said, "Damn, Darin. Can I just sit down and talk business with you? I know you've been out of the loop for a while, but out of all of the people that I've been around, I still respect your approach the most. And I know you're young, but that's why I'd rather talk to you. You have a younger ear with different ideas about management. Some of these other managers can be too rigid with how they wanna do things."

I wasn't falling for whatever Tangela was trying to do, so I passed on her invitation to meet and talk about the music business. I wasn't even curious about it. I just wanted to listen to great music like your average fan. I didn't want to be involved in it anymore.

Evidently, Tangela had gotten my address, because she sent me a priority package with a demo tape in it that next week. I shook my head and put it down as soon as I opened the package. But then I thought about it. I could still *listen* to new music. There wasn't any harm in that. So I put the demo tape in my stereo player while I was at home alone for a minute, with my wife and daughter out and about.

I turned the stereo system up to try and listen for the quality of the production, and when I pressed play, the first thing I heard was a New Edition vocal sample from their first hit song, *Candy Girl*. The sample repeated itself four times: *"Cannn-dee girl . . . Cannn-dee girl . . . Cannn-dee girl . . . Cannn-dee girl."*

I smiled, thinking about Tony and his love for New Edition. Then the beat kicked in, and it *was* Tony. I could tell. He had slowed the *Candy Girl* beat down to ballad speed with his own drum set:

Ticka-Doomp, Doomp, TAT
Tic-Doomp, Da-Doomp, TAT
Ticka-Doomp, Doomp, TAT

Tic-Doomp, Da-Doomp, TAT . . .

Then a familiar voice kicked in with a guitar riff and a deep bass line:

This one's for you-u-u-u . . .

Tony and the band members started calling out names with screams in the background:

(Tamika, Diane, Shaquanna . . .)
(WAAAAAHHHHH!)

And that singer that I *used* to know was crooning:

This one's for you-u-u-u-u, baaay-beee . . .

I immediately got up and stopped the tape right there. I didn't want to go near that guy again. Listening to his music was like looking for that forbidden apple in the Garden of Eden. I just had to say no to it. It's as simple as that. So I walked over and threw that demo tape in the trash.

I thought to myself, *So he's back with Tangela again. That's why she wanted to talk to me so bad.*

I shook my head and said, "I wish her good luck," and that was that.

I was minding my own business while watching an ESPN football talk show that night. They were talking about the upcoming Super Bowl between the Denver Broncos and the Green Bay Packers when Chelsea sat down beside me with Imani. I was so much into the football talk show at the moment that I didn't notice my wife with the demo tape in her hand.

She asked me, "Darin, did you *mean* to throw this in the trash?"

I looked at the tape in her hand and didn't think a thing about it.

I answered, "Yeah, I meant to throw it away," and I went back to watching the football show.

Chelsea didn't comment, while she tried to keep the baby away from grabbing it.

I finally asked her, "Why did you take it out of the trash?"

I wasn't concerned about it, I was just asking her.

She said, "Well, I went to throw something away, and I saw it in there. I don't know why, but I wanted to pick it up for some reason. So I just did it. And then I went ahead and listened to it."

I just started laughing. I said, "It's the old apple-in-the-garden trick again." How ironic, right?

Chelsea just stared at me. I felt a need to apologize to her for my bad-seeded comment.

I put my hand on her lap and said, "Baby, I didn't mean that."

Chelsea looked at me and said, "Darin, we need to heal from this."

I didn't comment. I just let her explain herself.

She said, "Now, I'm *not* telling you to get back involved with him, or to even listen to his music if you don't want to, but I've been thinking about this now for a while. And if we're gonna consider ourselves a Christian family and everything, and *he* comes from a Christian family, then we need to forgive, heal, and move forward from this."

I didn't know what to say. I just didn't want to hear it while the football show was on.

Like a typical American husband and father, I said, "All right, well, we'll talk about this later on," just like *my* father used to do with *my* mother.

Chelsea stood up and went to turn off the TV. She faced me from in front of the television set and said, "Darin, we've put this off long enough."

I said, "Well, why do we have to talk about it right this moment, Chelsea?"

She held up the demo tape and said, "Because *obviously* somebody feels that we do. Someone who is *greater* than *you* is telling you that you need to deal with this. *Right now!*"

I said, "Okay, so what do you want me to do, Chelsea? You want me to call him up? So I call him up and say what?"

I really didn't want to deal with it until I had figured out *how*. I needed time to think about it. I had gotten used to not dealing with that boy.

Chelsea said, "Why do you have to make it so antagonistic? That's what I'm talking about. Did he send this tape to you? What did he say with it? Did a letter come with it?"

I shook my head and said, "He didn't send it to me. His old girlfriend did. I guess he got her to try and do his work for him now."

Right after I said that I knew that I was in trouble. Chelsea was right. Hadn't I been the one to call Tangela back years ago and try to get *her* to forgive him? Now, Tangela was doing the same thing to me, and my reborn Christian behind was strongly rebuffing her efforts. But she hadn't come right out and said it, though. She was trying to sneak her way into it.

Chelsea said, "Well, what did she say?"

"She wanted to meet with me and talk about the music business," I told my wife. I said, "But she didn't say it was about *him*, though."

Chelsea said, "Of course she didn't. Everyone knows how you've been acting about *John* lately. You won't even say his name. And you told her no, right?" my wife asked me.

I just started smiling. Then I tried to get serious about it.

I said, "Chelsea, it's important for me, and for *us*, to try and distance ourselves from things that we don't need to be involved with anymore, that's all."

She said, "Didn't you tell me before that John's mother uses the same approach, shutting him out, and that it *didn't* work? Now I'm not going to church to be that kind of a Christian, Darin. And *we're* not," she said, holding our daughter Imani in her arms.

I looked at my wife and growing daughter and was speechless.

Chelsea said, "You can be real stubborn sometimes, you know that?" She tossed the demo tape back into my lap and said, "Do what you want with it."

When they walked back out of the room together, I grinned and mumbled, "I *know* I can be stubborn. I'm a *Taurus*."

I sat there on the sofa and shook my head. I just could never get away from that guy, could I?

I didn't want to have Chelsea hearing me listening to the demo tape, so I got out my earphones and plugged them up. I rewound the tape back to the beginning. Chelsea had obviously listened to the whole thing. I guess she didn't hold any grudges against him. She was more forgiving than I was. *Or* his mother. When I thought about that, I *knew* that I had to see Tangela and at least talk about building some kind of a bridge. It was going to be a tough process, but a *bridge* was all that I wanted to have. Because if I didn't like what was going on, I was going right back home to where I belonged. I was a family man now.

I started the tape over with my earphones on: *"Cannn-dee girl . . . Cannn-dee girl . . . Cannn-dee girl . . . Cannn-dee girl."*

Ticka-Doomp, Doomp, TAT
Tic-Doomp, Da-Doomp, TAT . . .

This one's for you-u-u-u . . .
(Tamika, Diane, Shaquanna . . .)
(WAAAAAHHHHH!)
This one's for you-u-u-u-u, baaay-beee . . .
(Lisa, Michelle, Kimberly . . .)
(OOOOOHHHH!)
Yeaaah . . .

This one's for you-u-u-u, and you-u-u, and you-u
(Stacey, Monique, Latasha . . .)
(WAAAAAHHHHH!)
This one's for you-u-u-u-u, daaarl-linnn . . .
(Rashida, Wendy, Nicole . . .)
(YEEEAAAAAHHHH!)
Oh, o-o-oh, oh . . .

I told myself, *I guess Tony talked that boy into doing a New Edition dedication song after all.* The next thing I knew, my head was bobbing and grooving just like old times. That boy was obviously still the king, and he was out to maintain his throne on urban soul music.

In the first verse he sang:

Everywhere that my love go-o-oes . . .
Ticka-Doomp, Doomp, TAT
Tic-Doomp, Da-Doomp, TAT
the girls are always asking me . . .
Ticka-Doomp, Doomp, TAT
Tic-Doomp, Da-Doomp, TAT
do you ever think about the flow we had that ni-i-ight
'cause it was ALL ri-i-ight
and I loved you ALL ni-i-ight
yeaaah . . .

So when it's time for me to hit that ro-o-oad again
they ask me, "Lover-boooy, would you write a song for me-e-e?"
yeaaah . . .

So this one's for you-u-u-u-u . . .
(India, Bonita, Paulette . . .)
(OOH MY GOD!)
Ticka-Doomp, Doomp, TAT
Tic-Doomp, Da-Doomp, TAT . . .

It was another number one hit! No doubt about it. That groove was so tight that you would need a jar of Vaseline to pull away from it. I don't even know if *that* would have worked. That boy sang just enough words in his verses not to disturb the groove. Because the groove was *extra* strong on that song. That boy sang it like it was icing on a pound cake. *For You* would have plenty of urban American girls *dying* to have their names called out by that guy named . . . *Loverboy.* I hated to say it, but I had to admit it. When it came to the music, he was just . . . *the man!*

I listened to the second song, called *Hard Rocks.* That one was all about the message of a young woman's choice of a man, with a thought-provoking bass line that I translated: *"Why don't you thin-n-nk about this . . . Why don't you thin-n-nk about that . . . Why don't you thin-n-nk about this . . . 'Cause how he liv-v-ves is wack."*

Tony was right on it with the beat:

Doomp-Doomp, Doomp-Doomp, TAT, Tic-tic-tic-TAT
Doomp-Doomp, Doomp-Doomp, TAT, Tic-tic-tic-TAT
Doomp-Doomp, Doomp-Doomp, TAT, Tic-tic-tic-TAT
Doomp-Doomp, Doomp-Doomp, TAT, Doomp-Doomp, Doomp-Doomp,
   TAT . . .

The keyboard strings were playing a cool, bouncy melody with the guitar: *"The girls, they like those hard rocks . . . Girls, they like those hard rocks . . . The girls, they like those hard rocks . . . They can't get enough of guys."*
Then that singer came in with his lyrics:

I need you to think about how he's livin'
I need you to think about your black eyes
I need you to think of love he's not givin'
so why do you keep chasin' hard rock guys?

I need you to think of rainbows and heaven
I need you to think back to your first kiss
I need you to think of laughter and giggles
I need you to think of those days you miss . . .

Then the groove changed up with the beat, and that boy sang his chorus like he *meant it:*

You got these har-r-rd rocks
with har-r-rd times
in har-r-r-d plaaay-ces
wouldn't you like to go-o-o-o

go awaaay,
go AWAAAY
go awaaay . . .

Then they went right back to the groove:

Now girl, wouldn't you like to have some real lovin'
wouldn't you like to kill the arguments
wouldn't like for no pushin' and shovin'
and sellin' the wrong things to pay your rent . . .

WHOA! I thought to myself. That boy made me get excited enough to say his name again. "John is a *GENIUS!*" I sat there and told myself with the earphones on.

Hard Rocks sounded like another New Edition–type song. It had that swing to it, yet John was *saying something.* A lot of singers couldn't get away with something like that in the nineties. They were mostly singing that sex-you-up raunchy stuff that took you nowhere but to the bedroom. John could still outclass those guys, out-sing them, and with Tony around on the drums, their *music* was still better.

They had a song called *Good News Ain't No News,* where John sang:

It ain't new-w-ws
unless you hur-r-rt some-bod-dee
It ain't new-w-ws
unless you rob, and steal, and kill
It ain't new-w-ws
unless some-bod-dee's cry-ing
'cause good new-w-ws ain't no-o-o new-w-ws . . .

What in the *world* did Tangela need to talk to *me* about? All they needed to do is put the stuff *out!* What did she need from me? John sounded like he was still intelligent, culturally aware, and was doing just fine. He even had a duet with Aaliyah, who was really popular after her second album, *One In A Million,* did nice figures. They did a song called *Double Fantasy,* with Tony working them high hats to *death* on a slow seductive beat:

Tit-Doomp-tit-TAT
Tit-tit-Doomp-tit-TAT

Tit-tit-Doomp-tit-TAT
Tit-tit-Doomp-tit-TISSS . . .

The bass line and strings whined, *"Ca-a-a-a-an I-I-I-I ha-a-a-ave my-y-y . . ."*
Then the guitar kicked in with, *"Fan-ta-seee . . ."*
I mean, it sounded like one of those old-school sound-track beats from *Superfly,* that made you feel like you were right there in the room with them while they did whatever.
John sang:

Ooooh, girl-friend
can I tell you something
I never had a queen
an exalted queen, like you
and baby
I had a dream last night
girl, that was wild, so wild
and then I held you right
do you know what I mean . . .

And Aaliyah sang it back to him:

Ooooh, boy-friend
you ain't said a thing to me
I can see where you're coming from
and I'm not the one to run
'cause I never had a lover
no, not like you, boy
with so much flavor, let me stop
before I tell you something wrong
did you hear me . . .

I broke up laughing. John still had a way of keeping things creatively tasteful in his lyrics. That made them more powerful than that raunchy stuff. I mean, what guy in his life hadn't stopped short of telling a girl all that he wanted, and ended up saying, "You know what I mean, right?" Even mack daddies and players would use that line to get a woman's full under-standing. You wanted her to commit to you and put it all on the line. Then when Aaliyah gave it back to him, what girl hadn't ever asked a guy, "Did you hear me?" whenever they were trying to get a point across? Most of the time, guys only heard what they *wanted* to hear. So girls were always trying to make sure. As a guy you ended up saying, "Yeah, I heard you," to whatever she was talking about. Women wanted guys to put it all on the line, too. Those simple lines in John's song were subtle and more powerful than less-talented writers could ever understand.

The last song on the demo tape was a cut called *Street Life* that had a jazz-blues feel to it, with blaring horns and an upright bass.

The horns squealed, *"STRE-E-ET LIFE! . . . THAT STRE-E-ET LIFE! . . . THAT STRE-E-ET LIFE! . . . THAT STRE-E-ET LIFE!"*

The upright bass played in unison with the horns, *"Think you know that . . . You don't know that . . . You don't know that . . . Think you know that."*

Tony hit the drums with a simple beat just to keep your feet tapping:

BaDoomp, Tat
BaDoomp, Tat
BaDoomp, Tat
Doomp-Doomp, Tat . . .

Then John did his part:

Street li-i-i-ife
you betta get up outta that street li-i-ife
it's robbing your youth and makin' ya' old.

Street li-i-i-ife
you betta get up outta that street li-i-ife
it's breakin' ya' down and stealing ya' soul . . .

Musically, *Street Life* reminded me of *At Midnight*, on John's first album, but it was funkier and more up-tempo. However, the real lyrical beef of the song came from the Philadelphia poet Wadud. John just got out of the way and let him have the majority of the track. So Wadud jumped on the back end of the groove with this:

Qualifi-i-ied poets, scri-i-ibes, and grio-o-ots . . .
(Think you know that—STRE-E-ET LIFE . . .)
listen for the horror stories of urban ghetto-o-os . . .
(You don't know—THAT STRE-E-ET LIFE . . .)

narrated by bold falsetto-o-os
of Mayfields named Curtis . . .
(STRE-E-ET LIFE—Think you know that . . .)
respect due . . .
(You don't know—THAT STRE-E-ET LIFE . . .)
but there's no FLOWERS on this boat . . .
and no love, where only the STRONG will survi-i-ive
(Think you know that—STRE-E-ET LIFE . . .)
the de-humanization . . .
(You don't know—THAT STRE-E-ET LIFE . . .)
where babies cry-y-y for their young mommas
who like to disappear in the middle of the night . . .
(STRE-E-ET LIFE—Think you know that . . .)
to meet with boyfriends who are afra-a-aid
of being daddies . . .

Wadud went on and on as if the track was made in heaven just for him. I mean, it was beautiful, man. *BEAUTIFUL!* It took you places in your mind. That's what music was *supposed* to do. So I listened to Wadud's poetry on *Street Life* about three more times before I finally retired and joined my wife in bed. That football talk was long gone. I had forgotten all about it.

When I climbed into bed, I thought that Chelsea was asleep, but she wasn't.

She smiled at me in the dark and said, "It sounded like you might have heard something that you *liked* out there."

I just started laughing. She had me. And John still had the gift of music.

I told her, "I just want to make a bridge to him, that's all. I'm just gonna make a bridge."

That's all that was said that night. But I tell you *one* thing, I was inspired. John had done it to me again. I began to think of finding myself a way to be a part of making great music. Maybe not as a manager anymore, but as a producer or something. After being around John "Loverboy" Williams for hit after hit after hit, I figured that I *had* to have a good ear by then. I *had* to! So I began to look forward to finding that out.

I went ahead and flew down to New York to meet with Tangela at Sean "Puff Daddy" Combs's restaurant, called Justin's, named after his first son. It was a decent place and roomy, but nothing special.

Tangela still looked good, she was just older. You could tell that the business was wearing on her. The first thing she did after we hugged was apologize to me for setting me up like she did.

"Actually, it didn't really work," I told her. "My wife got involved and told me that I needed to stop being stubborn about it and heal from this whole thing. And then I went ahead and listened to the demo tape after that."

Tangela said, "How you like it?"

I nodded to her. I said, "It's good. Is the album titled *Street Life*?"

She answered, "Yeah. That's what *John* wants. But Old School Records wants us to call it *For You*. You know, they want to keep going with the whole Loverboy image, but John is trying to get away from that."

I raised my brow at that. I asked her, "Is he?"

Tangela looked at me and smirked. "At least in his *music*, but he's still carrying on out in the streets with that. I mean, this album is like, autobiographical. He's been out there with it."

I told her, "All of his albums are. That's how he writes. You've been around him enough to know that."

I stopped and asked her, "So he's been out in the streets a lot more then, hunh?"

We gave our orders before Tangela responded to me. But we weren't really there to eat anyway. We had a lot of catching up to do.

Tangela said, "Yeah. Once he got back from that world tour, he didn't want that experience to change his music, so he started hanging in the roughest places you could imagine. Houston; Chicago; Gary, Indiana; Paterson, New Jersey. Just *rough* places, so he could write from that."

She shook her head and said, "Him and that doggone Big Joe. What's wrong with that guy? He acts like an overgrown kid sometimes. And to be so *big* with that."

She just grimaced and shook her head again.

I smiled. I said, "Big Joe's all right. He just loves John to death, you know. He was actually the one who gave John that name *Loverboy* back at North Carolina A&T, when he first started singing."

"I know," she told me. "That boy lets *everybody* know that. 'I *named* this nigga!' she mocked him. 'We *folks*!'"

I started laughing. I said, "So, how are you able to hold up with John? You just let him do what he *wants* now? You didn't *used* to be like that."

Tangela looked at me and frowned. She said, "I'm not with John like that. I'm just managing him. He can do what he wants on his free time."

I said, "*What? Managing?*"

Tangela said, "Yeah. I got my own man and my own life now. John just asked me to manage him, I guess, because he wanted to be around someone who knew him well, and who wouldn't get in his way. That's why I called you up about it."

I said, "Well, what happened to Top Notch from D.C.?"

She answered, "John fired them as soon as their one-year contract was up. And he refused to record anything new while he was with them, because he didn't even want them involved in that. So they were trying to maintain the contract to get a piece of the action for when John started working on this third album. But since they didn't have a clause in the contract where it called for them to get their artists recording deals, it was nothing that they could do about it. You know, because John was already *under* contract."

She said, "But they took a lot of money from John through this non-profit foundation that they set up called John's Love Foundation. It was supposed to be for community purposes. It was set up kind of like Sean Combs's Daddy's House. But since John wasn't trying to record anything, Top Notch started using that Love Foundation as an extra way of getting paid."

I asked, "He didn't pay them their regular managing percentage?"

Tangela said, "Yeah, but that was mostly tour money, and not album sells, because most of the albums had already been sold. So they wanted to get involved with John's publishing. That's where the *big* money is. But he wouldn't record any new songs, and Top Notch weren't tied to any of the old ones that he recorded while he was still with you."

She said, "That's why I called and asked you about the publishing thing, because I haven't really dealt with that. I was more or less *buying* songs for my artists, where the producers and writers took care of their own publishing, or the record company did it."

I nodded. When it was all said and done, *Honesty* had sold more than *10 million* worldwide!

I said, "Yeah. Now you're finding out just how valuable John is. He knows how much power he has with his publishing. He could be like the next Kenny 'Babyface' Edmonds if he kept his conscience clear of the nonsense that he gets involved in. That's why Prince is so mad at Warner Bros. over *his* bad deal. That publishing is a lot more important than people think."

I asked her, "But how did Old School Records respond to you taking over as John's new manager?" No one had called me up about that. Or maybe everyone had been told that I didn't want to be involved, and Tangela was the only one who was still willing to try me.

She said, "You know what, at first they didn't want to deal with me that way, but then they realized that this is the last album on John's contract, so they just said, 'Whatever.' Whatever makes John happy. And John just told them to talk to me."

I said, "So you're in the hot seat now. You're actually *managing* John. Small world."

"Ain't it?" she smiled and told me.

We started digging into our food.

Tangela said, "But I'm concerned about this street stuff that he's involved in, because he's starting to deal with girls who are not all crazy about him like that. I mean, don't get me wrong, they'll all try to fuck him, but John is starting to deal with the kind of street girls now who are thinking of ways to get paid off of him. And I must admit, John has been *very* fortunate up to this point."

I nodded and let Tangela continue. I could tell that she had a lot to tell me. She wanted my ear more than anyone else because I was an insider with John.

She said, "He's been pulled over a few times for having marijuana in his car. He's been taking guys' girlfriends or whatever, and getting Big Joe to back him up on it. That's where that *Hard Rocks* song came from. John actually gets his kicks off of going after attached women. I mean, he's just been doing some foul shit lately, and I'm afraid for him. These roughneck guys aren't trying to go for that shit."

She said, "But the thing I can't figure out is how he can do all of that craziness, right, and then get in the studio and write, sing, and produce like he does. That is just *amazing* to me. You would think that his crazy living would take a toll on everything that he does, but it doesn't."

I nodded and told her, "He thinks he's *living* a song. He really *believes* that. So his attitude is that he's gonna do whatever he's driven to do, and just write about it. It's as if his whole life is meant to be an album or something. Like he was born to suffer and to tell the world about it."

Tangela said, "Do you know that he was sued for five hundred thousand dollars for this car accident in Baltimore? He had a brand new Porsche that he crashed up down there."

I just smiled. John had been fortunate over the years indeed, and his luck was finally running out on him.

Tangela said, "This guy started wearing a neck brace talking about his spine was injured and all this other kind of ridiculous stuff, just to get paid. Because he wasn't all injured like that before he found out who John was."

She frowned and said, "And what's up with John's *mother*? I mean, does she love him, or *what*? That woman treated me like I was the *Anti*christ when I called her. And I was just trying to connect with her. I told her that I was no longer involved with John, and that I'm just a business associate now, and she wasn't trying to hear it. She started talking about, 'Well, you need to tell him to handle his *business* with the Lord,' and all of this kind of stuff."

I grinned and shook my head, feeling guilty.

I said, "I know how she feels now. And it has to be even harder for her because John is her only son. She just doesn't seem to understand that she can't control him. *Nobody* can. We just have to find a way to reach him, and I don't know if that's possible anymore."

Tangela said, "You know he listens to mostly rap music now. He says that they're starting to take over. He said the art of singing is dying out unless you have a rapper on your album."

I nodded, trying to think that over. I said, "After the Fugees blew up like *they* did, and all of them are now doing their own projects, I think John may not be far off on that. But that's why he wants this next album to sound a little harder. John knows what he's doing."

I told her, "You need to be firm and just tell Old School Records to go with it. *Street Life*, the third album by John 'Loverboy' Williams." I said, "And that Wadud poem is *hot*, man! *HOT!*"

Tangela got excited. She said, "Ain't it, though? That's gonna put him on the map. Spoken word poetry is coming back strong now. Have you heard of Jessica Care Moore?"

I said, "Yeah. She was on the Apollo, right?"

Tangela nodded. She said, "I thank you so much for agreeing to talk to me about John like this. You just don't know how much has been lifted off my heart by being able to talk to you about it."

She said, "Okay, well now that we got all of that out of the way"—she stopped and took a deep breath before she continued—"can I please ask you to do me one more favor?"

I smiled. I said, "It depends on what it is."

Tangela dug into her black leather pocketbook and pulled out her cell phone. She said, "Now Darin, remember, you did this to me, *several* times. And I always respected you and gave it a shot."

I started laughing. She wanted me to make up with John. I said, "I'll talk to him, but I can't promise you much more than that."

"Okay. I understand. So I'm gonna call him right now. Okay?"

She called John, caught him at home alone, and asked him how he was doing. I started thinking that it was a setup. It just seemed too easy for some reason. But what the heck, we needed to get it over with.

Tangela said, "John, somebody *real* special wants to talk to you. I'm gonna put them on the phone, okay?" She looked at me and was as happy as a kid when she passed her cell phone across the table.

I took a deep breath and spoke into the phone. "What's going on, man?"

John heard my voice and started laughing. He said, "Yo, first of all, I'm sorry, man. We family. I should have never did that to you. But it all worked out for you. You were tempted, and you survived it. There's a lesson in everything, man."

I didn't even want to get into that. I said, "Yeah, but how are *you* doing? Tangela says that you're in the streets a lot now."

Tangela looked at me in shock and slapped my arm for bringing up bad news and telling on her. I was just being real about the conversation. I didn't have anything to hide. Tangela didn't know it, or maybe she did. But she was only being used as a pawn for John to get back to me. We had, like, a funny triangle going on between us.

John said, "Actually, I've been in the studio a lot lately, trying to finish up this third album, man. She knows that."

I joked and said, "Yeah, she loves you."

Tangela looked at me again and shook her head with a big grin on her face. I was giving it to her bad.

John asked me, "What about you, man? *You* still love me, D?"

He had me on the spot. I couldn't tell him that I didn't. I couldn't go down that same road that Sister Williams had traveled with him. I just had to forgive him and love him anyway, like God did with all of us.

I said, "Yeah, John. I still love you, man. I'll always love you. You just make it hard on people sometimes, man. You make it *real* hard."

He said, "I know, man. But I'm gon' make it up to you. You gon' be real proud of me one day."

I said, "*One day?* I've always been proud of you, man. What are you talking about?"

He said, "I got some plans, man. That boah Tupac was deeper than people think. I'm telling you. Sometimes you gotta die before people take you seriously."

I asked myself, *What?!* John was still on his own thing, talking crazy. That was enough for me. I was ready to end the conversation.

I said, "John, you know what? I think that *you're* deeper than most people think."

"Nah, man, I'm just a singer right now. But I'm gon' *be* more," he told me. "You watch."

I said, "All right, well, I'm about to get back on my way home to Boston, man. And that new album, you *know* it's hot. Just make sure they call it *Street Life* like you want them to."

He said, "You know it, man. Because this their last album."

I said, "All right then, John. Love you, man."

He paused. I knew what he was thinking. He wanted to talk to me more and I was cutting him short. But he had to understand that we had to build our friendship back up. We couldn't do it over one long-distance phone conversation from a cell phone in a restaurant.

I said, "John, we got more time together, man. I'm back in your corner. I'm just not in the ring with you. And you just have to remember to remain healthy enough to keep fighting the good fight."

John started laughing again. He said, "Aw'ight, man. Enjoy your wife and your new family. I'm proud of you, D. I'm proud of you."

When I handed Tangela back the phone, she chatted with John for a few more minutes about their business, and that was that.

She asked me, "Well, what did you think?"

I said, "It sounds like the same old John to me. He still sounds out of it. And I don't know where he's trying to go, but he needs to realize that he's there already, and just learn to enjoy it."

. . . of a wounded soul . . .

I admit, I wasn't too pleased about Tangela taking over the management responsibilities for John. I mean, she was cool with me and everything, but . . . I just didn't feel comfortable with John's decision on that, and I was almost *certain* that he had planned it that way to get me involved with him again.

Sure enough, Old School Records talked John and Tangela into releasing *For You* as the first song from the new *Street Life* album in the spring of 1998. I would have released *Hard Rocks* first myself. *Hard Rocks* had more of an up-tempo bounce to it. That song would have also been the best release to establish the album's soul, and the new direction of John's career. But Old School Records were still trying to hold on to John's image as a love singer, while leaving the street-conscious material to their camp of rappers. I thought that was a mistake right off the bat, because if people loved John for anything, they loved him for his honesty. He knew what was going on out in the streets, so why couldn't he sing about it?

After hearing the whole *Street Life* LP, *For You* should have been either a third release or just a song for the fans who bought the album. The song still went to number three on the R&B charts and number seven on the pop. However, *Hard Rocks* would have made a much stronger statement for John as a maturing musician. I thought that *Hard Rocks* also had stronger number one potential in the present marketplace for urban music. A lot of urban music listeners were no longer into the Loverboy bag. The fetish for hard rock men was becoming more of the norm. Why do you think people loved Tupac Shakur and West Coast gangsta music so much? Even Bad Boy records was making a killing off the hard rock image of Biggie, who received plenty of love before and after he was shot and killed in early 1997 at age twenty-five. The people *needed* a *Street Life* album from a young singer with a real message to heal themselves. John would have been right on time with it. He *was* on time with it. Old School Records had dropped the ball.

They made amends by releasing John's duet with Aaliyah, *Double Fantasy*, as the second single, with a hot video to boot. They were both singing from penthouse suites at night in New York. The video was very well done, and expensive, taking them straight to number one with the song. However, the song seemed to boost Aaliyah's career more than it did John's. Aaliyah was hot from singing choruses for several rappers, and she had the momentum at the time. Next thing you knew, she was getting sound tracks and star movie roles. John still needed management direction to help *him* open up those new doors. Nevertheless, I avoided getting involved again. It was *Tangela's* show.

That summer of 1998 became a tag team match between Def Jam rappers Jay-Z and DMX, with Lauryn Hill's street-savvy releases slipping in the middle like a referee. Those three artists together had as many as *ten singles* between them that were getting steady airplay on radio. And Jay-Z's song *Hard Knock Life* killed John's third release, *Hard Rocks*, altogether. The two songs were as different as you could get artistically, but with the similar titles and Jay-Z's release coming out first, John came off as nothing more than a soft player hater. Especially with Jay-Z being the man of the hour with hard-core street credentials.

John was *hot* about that. That controversy forced him to answer a bunch of questions on whether he intended to send a message out to Jay-Z or not. John got in contact with me to talk about it while he was on tour that summer in Minneapolis.

He said, "Fuck, man! If we had brought our song out in the spring like *I* wanted to, before Jay-Z got out there with *his*, then it would have looked like he was following *us* instead of us following *him*. That shit makes me look *bad*, man. They just fucked up the whole flow of my album with that Loverboy *shit*! I got shit to *say*, man!"

I tried to take things lightly. I wasn't involved in it anymore. So I told him, "I thought you liked being the Loverboy."

He said, "Come, on, man. Don't patronize me. You know how this album was supposed to go down."

I said, "They couldn't have known what Jay-Z was coming out with. He releases a new single every other month. He's not even in the R&B category."

John said, "Well, *we* need to put out a song every other month like that."

I knew what was coming next. He added, "If *you* was still managing, man, it wouldn't have gone down like this. They don't respect Tangela like they respect you."

I didn't want to comment on that. I wanted to keep our newfound bridge connected, but I was definitely staying on *my side* of the water.

I said, "The album is still doing well, though, right?"

He said, "It's doing well off of reputation alone, but I'm losing people now."

I had to be real about it. *Honesty* was a more radio-friendly album than *Street Life*. But if *Street Life* would have been promoted correctly, it still would have made a stronger artistic statement. However, how many artistic statements meant anything in the new era if you didn't sell a warehouseful of albums with it? John had already won the awards. Grammys, American Music, Billboard, Soul Train. *All* of them!

All I could say was, "Use this as fuel for your next album then. Just go back in the lab with it." I liked a hardworking John Williams in the studio more than a street-hanging Loverboy anyway. Maybe new dedication to his music was what he needed, a new challenge to climb to the top again.

John said, "Yeah, we'll see, man. But it won't be with Old School Records no more, *that's* for sure! They just *lost* their bid for the next contract. Watch!"

I didn't have any comments for that either. I had my *own* contract business to think about. With the blessings from my wife, I began looking for new talent to produce on my own. Managing was no longer something I wanted to do, but producing was different. I could work from a completed project basis, and go back home with no tour or publicity commitments.

I did miss the limelight and the challenge of climbing the music charts with John, though. I wondered if we could do it all over again if I was still with him. The thought of it crossed my mind a few times. But that thought was smashed against the concrete when I received a wake-up phone call from Evelyn Harris, who was still on board as John's publicist.

She called me just a few days after I had talked to John and gave me some disparaging news about his stay in Minneapolis.

"Darin, do you know that John and that damn boy *Big Joe* got into a street brawl with some locals at a club in downtown Minneapolis?" Evelyn was obviously irritated. She said, "He's lucky Minneapolis isn't a *media* capital of the world. But it *still* doesn't look good for *other* black performers coming into that area. They had a beautiful write-up on him before John got there. Now they're writing about the boy like he's Ol' Dirty Bastard's twin brother or something."

She said, "John has to realize that he's on a *whole* new level now, and everything he *does* is a *news* story. But he's always involved in something *stupid. My* reputation is on the line with this!"

I thought about the incident I was involved in in London and said, "Yeah, but some of that he can't really control."

Evelyn cut me short and said, "I can understand that, Darin. But John shouldn't even be *in* some of these places where he goes to hang out now. It's like he's *looking* for trouble with this *Big Joe* character who's with him all the time. And that damn Tangela; he doesn't listen to her. She's just getting a free paycheck, from what I'm seeing."

Evelyn was letting me hear it because she had no one else to talk to about it. I had hired her just like I had hired Big Joe, which had become a *big* mistake, as well as Tangela's management. Evelyn was only confirming things that I had already feared. But what could I do about it? I wasn't going *back.* I had a wife and a family who came *first!* And I had my *own* business plans to tend to. Nevertheless, I told Evelyn that I'd call John and Tangela anyway to see what I could do.

I tried to reach either John or Tangela to find out what was going on, and I ended up reaching Big Joe instead. I asked him, "Where's John?"

He said, "Oh, he's up in the room talking to Tangela about something, man. They're being real secretive about shit, so I just gave them their privacy."

I went ahead and asked Big Joe, "What's this about some club brawl y'all had in Minneapolis the other night?"

He answered, "I can't understand it sometimes, man. I mean, it's like . . . when you really get money like *John* got it, D, niggas be *hatin'* on you, man. It's like they *hate 'im.*"

He made it sound as if it was the biggest discovery of his life. He was utterly amazed by that.

I said, "Yeah, if y'all running around flauntin' it in the wrong people's faces. But what about all of the *love* he's gettin'? John just *ignores* that part. He takes it for granted now."

Big Joe said, "That's what I'm sayin'. They hate the love that he's gettin'."

I said, "Because they want that same love, man." It was all elementary to me, that's why you couldn't associate with negative people once you made the big time. John and Big Joe didn't seem to realize that. Pain and despair fed itself, just like love did. So I cut the conversation short, and I planned to pray for them. But since I couldn't get them off of my mind, I asked my wife about it.

Chelsea looked at me and took a deep breath. She said, "You want me to be honest about this, Darin?"

I said, "Yeah. That's what I want us to *always* be with each other."

She said, "Well . . . I'm starting to feel like I should have never pulled that tape out of the trash when I did, because it seems like every other *week* they're calling you about something. And I don't want you to stop helping them out or anything, but it's just *wearing* on me."

I nodded my head. I just needed to hear my wife say it.

I told her, "Okay. It's done. I'll let them handle their own problems from now on, and I'll just pray for them."

However, deep down inside, I knew that *praying* wouldn't be enough. And John knew it too, because that's all his mother *did* was pray.

Chelsea graduated on time from Northeastern that spring, and I was due to finish that fall.

In the meantime, I moved on with my new business plans and found myself in a conversation with my old nemesis from Detroit, Herbert Blake. We were discussing producing an album for a young singing group that he was dealing with who had just been signed to Sony.

Blake joked with me at his office in Southfield, Michigan, right outside of Detroit.

He grinned at me and asked, "It's a small world, ain't it, Darin? Are you feeling the withdrawal symptoms from not being with John anymore?"

He was still wearing all black clothes, and he didn't look a day older than when I had first met him years ago.

I leveled with him and answered, "Yeah, man, and they won't let me forget either. But I had to move on and do my own thing. I'm not going back. I *can't.*"

Blake looked at me and said, "You can *always* go back, Darin. Don't ever forget that. There's a *whole* lot of room for forgiving and forgettin' in this business." He smiled at me to make sure that I understood. I was back talking to *him*, wasn't I?

I smiled back at him and laughed it off.

He said, "But anyway, how old are you now, Darin? Twenty-five?"

"Twenty-four."

Blake looked at me and said, "Damn! You cats were *young* and doing it. So, how old were you guys when I first met you?"

I said, "John was twenty, and I was nineteen."

Blake shook his head and said, "What in the world are they *feedin'* you kids nowadays. *Smart!* When I was coming up, most young singers were just happy to be up on the damn *stage*, let alone sign million-dollar contracts."

I chuckled and said, "That was back then. But not all of us are that smart, man. I was just trying to protect my boy." *But I couldn't protect him from everything,* I thought to myself. *Nor could I protect myself.*

Blake said, "Well, you did a damn good job of it. A *damn* good job!"

I tried to cut the small talk and get down to business. I said, "So, how far is this group along on their album?"

"They got a few songs done," he told me. "They just need a few more *hits.*"

I nodded to him. I said, "So, if I get involved and get these guys some hit songs, what's in it for you?"

I wanted to make sure I had my bases covered, because I knew that Blake was still about the money.

Blake said, "Well, unlike with you and John, I got these boys here under a *two-album* tour, with a third-album tour as an *option*, because I got them set up for this deal at Sony. And Sony knows that they have to deal with me for the long haul, or buy me out. So now I need some damn hit songs to make this group worth something, or this whole contract is shot to hell."

He said, "Shit, all I'll end up doing is *losing* money for three albums if they don't have any hit songs on 'em. You think you can get John to write us a few?" he asked me with a laugh.

Blake was still talking that losing-money jazz. He wasn't losing any money. He just wasn't making enough to want to share it. The music business was *evil* sometimes, a bunch of slaves and slave masters, and there I was about to get involved with it again.

It was time for me to make my business pitch. I said, "I know enough people with great music and great songs to do my own thing without John at this point. I know what a hit sounds like *and* I know why it's a hit."

I said, "John actually turned *down* a lot of hit songs to do his own stuff." And it was the truth. Some great songs get turned down for a number of reasons. A lot of those reasons have more to do with money and ego than real music decisions.

I said, "So, if I get you these hit songs, I don't owe you anything? Is that what you're saying?"

Blake didn't smile at all. He said, "Darin, we know each other. And I want to *stay* in business just as bad as you want to get back *in* business. But the bottom line is this: if we're not talking about pushing hit music, then we're not really *in* business. Neither one of us. You hear me?"

He said, "So, if you can find hits for the talents that I got around, then I'll always send you new artists to make money from."

Then he smiled at me. He said, "And I *know* you know what hit songs are, Darin. You guys just sold *thirteen million albums* in *three years*! And that boy John is *still* selling albums!"

Street Life went on to sell 4 million albums worldwide as well. That wasn't bad at all for an album that was underexecuted. But it couldn't match *half* of *Honesty*'s numbers.

Blake said, "You don't have to convince me that you know what the hits are. You preachin' to the choir over here, young brother. I'm already singing for you. Just go on out there and get 'em, and I'll tell Sony that I talked to you about it to get you in the door."

I left Blake's office and thought about my full plan on the plane ride back to Boston. I wanted to set up a publishing company like they did in the old days, and manufacture hit music from talented musicians. But I didn't want to shortchange anyone. I would make everything fair and square like a straight-up-and-down music agency that sought out artists to perform our songs.

I got home all excited and told Chelsea about my plans while kissing our daughter, Imani. Chelsea jumped right on the case and came up with Harmonized Music Incorporated.

I said, "I like that. It sounds a little long, but I like how you worked the name in there."

She said, "Yeah, this is *your* baby, right? And with both of us being business majors, I can help you to run it."

I nodded my head, still thinking things through. I needed to talk to a few lawyers, get my publishing paperwork ready, protect our company name, start calling some of the musicians and songwriters that I knew, and begin searching for new talent. A whole *bunch* of things needed to be done! And I was real excited about the process.

Chelsea told me, "But don't incorporate here in Boston, because we're not staying here."

I said, "Well, you still haven't told me where you want to live yet. I need to incorporate *somewhere* if we're gonna do this."

Chelsea looked at me and said, "North Carolina."

I looked back at her and asked, "Where in North Carolina?" I didn't mind going back to my home state.

Chelsea said, "Charlotte. I liked what I saw down there during the wedding, and I read that Charlotte is one of the best up-and-coming cities in the country."

I stood there and smiled with my daughter still in my arms. Imani was playing with my new mustache.

I said, "You hear that, little girl? Mommy wants to move back to Daddy's hometown in Charlotte, North Carolina, where there's a lot of green grass and room for you to run and get lost out in the woods."

Chelsea smiled and said, "I've been talking to my mother about it, and she wants to go, too. She wants to get my little cousin out of Boston. He's starting to get to that age now where the street life that John is singing about starts calling."

Her cousin Damon had been living with them since he was seven. It was another long story of the complicated thing called life. Damon was seventeen and in his senior year of high school by then.

I said, "Well, we have the street life down in Charlotte, too. Don't think it's all happy and peaceful down there. They got hard rocks everywhere. I told you, they had hard rocks in *Britain*."

Chelsea said, "But not where *we're* gonna be living, right? We're not gonna be living in the 'hood."

I started laughing. My wife had *that* right. I still had money, and I planned on making a lot more of it. It wasn't a greed thing, it was just business, and business was our major.

I told Chelsea, "All right then. We'll fly down there and start house shopping."

She said, "No we're not. I want to *build* a house. I got my own designs and stuff that I want to do. And we can just live in a smaller house or something until it's ready."

I laughed again. That was my wife, man. She was not afraid to speak her mind on things, and it was good to know that, because I knew that Chelsea would always be ready to take care of family business *and* otherwise. As they say, birds of a feather flock together, and I couldn't have a wife who wasn't ready to take care of whatever we had to do. So Chelsea was perfect for me. *Perfect!*

In the fall of 1998, in the middle of taking care of business, preparing to graduate from Northeastern in Boston, and moving back to Charlotte for family purposes, I got another desperate phone call from Tangela.

She said, "Darin, I'm about to fly back to Boston from San Francisco to see you. I need to talk to you."

I asked her, "What's going on out in San Francisco? John toured there already, didn't he?" I said, "We can't do this over the phone? What do you need to talk about?" She caught me off guard with that.

She answered, "No, I can't do it over the phone . . . I just . . . I need to talk to you."

She sounded disturbed. I said, "What's going on? Give me some kind of heads-up on it. Is John acting crazy again?"

Tangela said, "Well . . . Darin, I just need to sit down and talk to you again. Okay? Please."

They were really trying to pull me over that bridge I had created for them. I had to let Tangela know.

I said, "Since you're already on your way, I'll do it *this time*, but I'm not trying to stay involved in this, Tangela. So next time I'm gonna have to turn you down."

She said, "I understand. And hopefully there won't *be* a next time."

When I hung up the phone with Tangela, my wife stared me right in the face. She said, "I hope she takes you *seriously* about this being the *last time*, because if you're going to be some kind of *co*manager then you need to start getting *paid* for it."

I met Tangela at the Boston airport and was prepared to give her plenty of short answers. I had to cut the umbilical cord and let her take care of John on her own. She knew what she was getting involved in when she took the job. Or maybe she really didn't. But that wasn't *my* problem, and Tangela needed to understand that fact once and for all! They *all* needed to understand that. Maybe I should have sent them all a final letter of regret.

When Tangela and I sat down to talk at an airport café, she just let me have it. She said, "John got some girl pregnant out in San Francisco. I just flew from out there with the girl to pay for her abortion. And I had to pay her a hundred thousand dollars not to have the baby."

She said, "This girl was just after a lifetime payday from John, and I couldn't let her do that."

WOW! I just sat there and took the information in. But Tangela told me that it would happen. She told me that in the beginning of that year, John was starting to deal with the *wrong* kind of women.

I said, "In *San Francisco?*" I had been to the city before, and there wasn't that many black people in the Bay Area. Most of the blacks lived in Oakland out there, and if you lived in San Francisco, chances were you had your *own* money.

Tangela said, "It doesn't matter where you're from, it's what you're about. And John is making real bad judgment calls with these girls."

I said, "Well, does *he* know about it?" I just had to make sure.

Tangela nodded her head. She said, "He gave me the money to do it." Then she dropped her head as if she was ashamed of it. She told me, "But I talked him into it," and started tearing.

I reached across the table to be closer to her and to hold her hands.

Tangela looked into my face and dropped an even bigger bomb. She said, "Darin . . . I was pregnant by John when I was living with him in Philly. And . . ." Tears just started running down her face as she told me.

She said, "I had an abortion on my own and never told him. That's why I had to leave. I couldn't take it. I mean . . ."

I just sat still and let her get it all out of her system.

She said, "I thought about . . . just having the baby to be secure with him, but I knew it was wrong. And then . . . I loved John because he was such a good person, and I didn't want to do that to him. I mean, he was so innocent and . . . *good* inside. He is really a nice person who's just caught up in it, Darin. And I feel so sorry for him because he's so talented. So when I found out that this girl was trying to do this to him, I just couldn't let that happen."

She said, "But then John started saying stuff like, 'Maybe it's time for me to have a baby. Maybe that's what I need in my life right now.' And he said, 'My boy Darin has a little girl.' And since I had never told him about my pregnancy . . . I just . . . I just got jealous, Darin. And I didn't want it to happen. So I talked John into wanting to get an abortion from this girl. And then I flew out there with the money to talk her into having it. And I know it was wrong . . ."

She lost it at that point and cried, "I'm sorry," as if she needed to apologize *to me.*

She said, "I'm so sorry. I know it was wrong. And I had sex with John again because I wanted to get pregnant by him and have the baby for him this time, but it didn't happen. And I didn't know who to talk to about it, so I just called you."

AW, GOD! Can you imagine that? Why was *I* being punished like that? I didn't need to hear that stuff! I didn't need to *know it!* I was all set to go in a new direction. But it was all tossed in my lap, so I had to deal with it.

I said, "You're not flying out tonight, are you?"

Tangela shook her head and said, "No," while still crying.

I told her, "Good, because I want you to stay at my place tonight with my wife and daughter. I don't think you need to be alone with this."

She shook her head and said, "I don't want to do that. I don't want to inconvenience you like that."

I told her, "You don't have a choice. I'm gonna *make you* do it if I have to."

She said, "Don't do that, Darin."

I said, "Tangela, I *have to.* You're staying with us tonight. That's all there is to it. You have to heal. And you can't do that alone."

I drove Tangela to the apartment in Boston with her luggage, and I pulled out the sofa bed for her to sleep on in the living room. It was late hours by then, and my wife and daughter were in bed.

Tangela said, "Thank you, Darin. Thank you for caring so much for so long. You are really an angel," and she started crying again, but not loud enough to wake anyone.

I remained there with her until she could finally relax and fall asleep.

When I made it into bed with my wife, I was wide awake and staring up at the ceiling. There was no way in the world that I could sleep that night. John's life was affecting a lot of people. Things were *definitely* out of control!

I nudged Chelsea to wake her up. "Chelsea . . . Chelsea . . ."

"Hunh? What, Darin?" she snapped at me. "I'm trying to sleep."

I said, "I let Tangela sleep on the sofa bed tonight." I knew *that* would wake Chelsea up.

She paused for a second before she responded, but I knew that she would. I just sat there and waited for it.

Chelsea finally rolled over to face me. She said, "You let her *stay* here tonight? Why, she couldn't find a hotel room?"

My wife hadn't become an evil person or anything, she just couldn't comprehend the triangle that Tangela, John, and I had. The situation was hard for Chelsea to stomach.

I said, "Chelsea, we need to pray for her."

"Pray for her for what? What happened?"

I told my wife the whole story.

Chelsea paused for a minute and said, "Oh my *God!*" She was stunned. She asked herself, "What are we *doing* to each other in this world?" Then she climbed out of bed and put her slippers and housecoat on.

I asked her, "Where are you going?"

"You said we needed to pray for her," she answered.

I said, "Yeah, we do, but she's sleeping right now."

"Well, we need to wake her up then."

I said, "Chelsea, you're making this all too obvious. We'll talk to her in the morning."

Chelsea said, "No we're *not* either. We're gonna talk to her *right now.*

You brought her here," and she started walking out toward the living room.

I got up to follow her.

Chelsea went right up to Tangela on the sofa bed and woke her up with whispers.

She said, "Tangela. Tangela, we love you. And I'm sorry for my judgments about you because none of us are perfect, and we *all* need to pray for forgiveness."

She said, "We've all been hurt in some way. We've all done things that were wrong. We've all needed to heal in our lives. And God knows our pain."

Tangela sat up and started crying again while Chelsea held her there.

Then my wife looked at me and said, "Come on, Darin. We're all going to pray together."

I walked over to the sofa bed and joined them in an embrace. By that time, Chelsea was crying, too.

She said, "Tangela, Darin and I have known this pain. We've *known it*, and we had to be strong and ask the Lord to *lead us*. To tell us what to *do*, Tangela. And the Lord told us that we needed to be a *family*. To *love* family. To be *there* for the family. And to understand how to *forgive* our loved ones."

She said, "But it *hurts*, Tangela. And we have to accept that *pain* as a part of the *healing*."

Man, my wife sounded like a minister in there, and that got *me* to crying. We were all in there crying.

Chelsea said, "Lord, our God, put your hands on us tonight, and *bless us*. Make us understand that there is something for us *to do, Lord* . . ."

She said, "Let us understand that this *pain* shall not be felt *in vain*. Teach us to have *faith* in you . . ."

My daughter, Imani, started crying from her bedroom right on cue, like a sign from God.

I stood up from the crying, wiped my eyes, and said, "Let me go get Imani, Chelsea."

Chelsea said, "Bring her." I did, and then all four of us cried in the living room that night. My wife just tore us up! She tore us *up* for the Lord as if she was *called* to do it! And I believe that she was.

With my wife's prayers, I decided that I had to sit down with John next, and talk about everything with him. John needed to heal more than any of us. But somehow he knew that it was coming. He *had* to know. Because as soon as I started trying to track him down, he got real busy on new music projects and stayed on the move without telling Tangela. He wouldn't talk to her *or* me. Something was going on with him.

Finally, I decided to try Tony. Tony was back home taking care of family and still producing hip-hop tracks with his beats. So I flew down there to see him.

I arrived at Tony's beautiful house in south New Jersey, and I asked him straight out what was going on with John.

Tony shook his head and said, "I can't call it no more, man. I just show up when he's ready to make more music."

I said, "But don't that sit on your conscience, man, that you can keep making the music with him and not have any say-so over how he lives?"

Tony said, "Darin, let me ask you a question. Since you first met me at the Philadelphia Music Conference, and John sat in with us at the Zanzibar Blue that night, did I put any words in his mouth for him to sing?"

I said, "No," to the obvious.

Tony said, "So why do you keep feeling that *you* or *I* or *anybody* has say-so over how John chooses to live his life, man? He's gonna do what he wants to do. Just like you had to do what *you* needed to do."

Tony said, "I mean, we all love that boah, man. Big Joe to a *fault*. That boah crazy for John like a woman now, man. But that's just life, D. John is on a plane, man, and he's flying where he *wants* to fly. And I just get ready for him to land again, man, so we can make some more hit music."

I got frustrated and said, "Is that all you care about, Tony, is making the music, man?"

Tony got frustrated with me and said, "Didn't I just tell you that I love that boah, man? What the fuck you want me to do, Darin?! I'm tired of talking about this shit with you!"

I said, "Well, you tell him that you won't make any more music with him until he gets a grip. *That's* what you tell him."

Tony said, "Man, *you* quit 'im. *I'm* not quittin' 'im. And if you ask *me*, he wouldn't have sunk this low if you didn't quit him like that."

I forgot that I was a Christian who didn't use profanity anymore, and I said, "That's *bullshit*, man! You know good and well that his personal life was going down the tubes whether I was managing him or not. He was trying to take *me* down with him!"

Tony screamed, "*EXACTLY!* Now what do you want *ME TO DO?* If his *MOMMA* can't stop him from doing shit, and *YOU CAN'T*, then who am *I* to say shit?!"

His wife stepped into the room and asked, "What's wrong with you two? You're waking up the baby."

Tony's wife was pregnant again, and so was Chelsea.

We calmed back down, but Tony was still defiant.

He said, "Look, man, you can say what you want to say, and you can be mad at me all you want, but if John is gon' keep makin' his music, then I'm gon' be there with my drums as a part of that history. And John is the *only* person I feel that strongly about, man. The *only* person! So you can take it or leave it."

He said, "And just like you went back to church to set your priorities straight with your life and everything. Well . . . let only *God* judge me for mine. And I can handle that."

What more could I say to Tony? I had to get back to the business of my own life. So I got my degree from Northeastern that fall, moved Chelsea and the family down to Charlotte, and I was all set to start producing soul music. I quickly found out how hard it would be, too. The experience of John "Loverboy" Williams and Tony Richmond had spoiled me. Those guys came up with near perfect music so effortlessly that everything else seemed like *years* to make.

We never had to punch in John's words or keep figuring out how to plug in Tony's beats, a nice harmony, or a bass line. So I basically had to learn how to produce music from scratch, which was hard work. Nevertheless, I had to do what I had to do to start putting out hits. I wasn't used to settling for less, and by the summer of 1999, Harmonized Music Inc. had published a few dandy tunes.

We had a hit groove called *Tell Me About It*, a party anthem called *Raise Your Hands*, a ballad, *When Sunshine Falls*, and even a gospel number, called *Speak to Me*, all placed with different artists. And I was overseeing production on different projects that were in the works with Blake and other people I had met in the music business.

I made sure that I stayed in touch with Chester DeBerry at BMG, too. He knew all about the past problems and my falling-out with John. However, Mr. DeBerry remained in support of whatever I was doing.

He said, "Just keep hanging in there, Darin. You're still young and full of energy and ideas, and you're *way* ahead of plenty of other people who would *love* to be where you are right now."

I was only twenty-five years old, but I didn't have time to sit back and think about how far I had come. I had to keep going with what I began to love, the whole process of making great music that spoke to the community. Because if a song didn't say anything or make you feel anything, then I didn't want to be a part of it. I had John to thank for that as well. His songs *always* meant something, from day *one*.

I stayed in touch with Tangela and told her to let go of John and keep herself busy with other artists. She still was good with other people, it was just John that got to her. And I was good at managing John early on, but I couldn't have gone through so much with anyone else. I had my hands full just dealing with the musicians and the artists that I had to record in our studio sessions.

I also had a dress code for myself and a conduct code for anyone who wanted to work with me. I wanted to make sure that I *looked* like I was in a respectable business. I let my dress code slide while I was managing John, and so did everything else that I should have stood for. So I began to dress the part for my new role, spotless, with a maintained groomed appearance of slacks, fine shoes, tailored clothing, and a basic look of real money. Even my T-shirts had to be cleaned, ironed, and classy. Not that it would make the music any better, I just wanted people to respect me *on sight* and treat me with respect despite my young age. I was not producing hip-hop music either, so I had no reason to dress that way.

I wanted the people who worked with me to taper their language. I didn't expect them to sound like choirboys or anything, but to be more disciplined with themselves about their choice of words. I wanted no one wasting my time with silliness or a lack of professionalism about what we were doing. And I would not tolerate the drugs or the reckless sexuality. So if you wanted to be involved in those things, you had to make sure you kept it away from me, or we wouldn't be in business together.

I just had to have peace within myself about the music that I loved, and if anyone was out to destroy that peace, then it was time for them to go. And I held no bonded contracts on anyone. I didn't want to do my business that way. I wanted people making music with me who *wanted* to be there because they loved it and they respected it, and not because it was some *job* that they were forced to do to make ends meet. I didn't want those kind of people involved with me. Enough said!

So I was well at work on building a state-of-the-art studio down in Charlotte. I had dreams of competing with the hit factories of nearby Atlanta. Then I got a phone call from Tony, who was out in L.A. He got me on my cell phone after my wife gave him the number.

He said, "Your boy didn't make it, man," all out of the blue, and as if I would know what he was talking about.

I said, "What? Who didn't make it? John? What are you talking about, Tony? What happened?" I was already thinking the worst. I still hadn't heard a peep from John in nearly a year. He was not signed to a new contract with anyone, but he was still singing hooks and producing on the side like a mercenary musician. He was enjoying his freedom, I guess. And since he seemed to be dodging me, I just stopped looking for him. God can only help those who want to *be* helped.

Tony said, "Naw, not John. Your boy Big Joe got shot up out here, man. He didn't even make it to the hospital in the ambulance. We outside the hospital right now. But John *did* put him out there in the middle of shit. He sent Big Joe out to get these damn girls while we were working on these tracks out here, and they had some jealous niggas just laying for his ass. And they ran up on 'im, thinking that John was with him, and popped him while he was waitin' in the car."

He said, "Big Joe got away after he was shot and drove far enough for people to call the police and an ambulance for him."

Tony stopped a second and said, "That's fucked up, man."

I took a breath and had a moment of silence for Big Joe. I had gotten him involved in it. But how was I to know how crazy things would get with John?

I said, "Let me speak to John." I knew he had to be around. John didn't run from Tony because Tony never sweated him and made him look hard in the mirror like I did.

John got on the phone as if we had just talked to each other yesterday. He made it seem like everything was just fine out there.

He said, "Hey D. I hear them hit songs you puttin' out now, man. What are you trying to be, a Dr. Dre on the R&B tip? A Dallas Austin or something? Terry Lewis and Jimmy Jam?"

I said, "I still don't play no instruments. I just sound stuff out and get other people to bring their ideas together."

John said, "Yeah, well, it's *workin'*, man. It's *workin'*. I'm about to ask you for a few new hits for *my* next album," he joked.

I began to wonder if he was high and still crazy. Obviously he was, on *both* counts. Hadn't Tony just told me that Big Joe was shot and killed out there on account of him?

I said, "John, what happened to Big Joe, man?" before he could keep me off the subject any longer.

John paused. He said, "Man, he took a spill for the worse. Some people just don't have no love in their hearts. Kind of like my mother. It's either life or death for some people. They just won't let things be. You know what I mean, D? Some people still try to be in control of shit. But if your girl ready to leave you, then she's just ready to *leave you*, man."

I wasn't really following him *or* trying to. I said, "John, what happened, man? A to Z."

He said, "Some people just don't like me, man. They just don't like me because their *girls* love me. But they didn't have to take that shit out on Big Joe like that, man. That shit wasn't *right*! We need to *do* something about that shit!"

He started getting excited all of a sudden.

I said, "John, don't do anything stupid out there, man."

He said, "I ain't gon' do nothing stupid. I'm just gon' relax tonight and think things through. And when I wake up, *then* I'm gon' decide what we gon' do."

I said, "Let me talk to Tony for a minute." There was no sense in talking to John at the moment.

He asked me, "You don't want to talk to me no more, man?"

I started to answer, "John, you sound really—"

He cut me off and said, "Well, *here*, talk to Tony then." I heard a loud smack on the phone.

Tony came back on the line and said, "We need to get this boy in a hospital somewhere, man. He's *trippin'*! And if he throw my damn cell phone down again, I'm gon' *hurt 'im*. I've had about *enough* of this motherfucker out here, man! That's why I'm callin' you before I kill 'im."

I didn't know if Tony was playing or serious. I said, "He's still on drugs like that, man? And is he really thinking about retaliating?"

Tony said, "Come on, man, that's every day that boy high on something. And I'm not tryin' to retaliate *shit* out here! This is *L.A.* and I'm not no fuckin' gangsta! He shouldn't have sent Big Joe out into that shit in the first place. John knew them damn girls he was tryin' to fuck with was trouble. It's like he's pickin' the worst fuckin' ones now."

He said, "That damn fight over that white girl in Britain must have turned him on to that drama shit."

I said, "And nobody tries to stop him, for drug possession or *anything*? What about getting him arrested? Aren't the cops asking him questions about the shooting?" I was trying to think of *anything* to get John off the streets for a while.

Tony said, "Yeah. And then John looks all concerned and says all the right things and gets to walk away. He's a con man, D. You should see him in action."

I didn't *need* to see that boy in action. I *knew* how convincing John could be. He used his cunning to read people's emotions as another gift. He knew just how far to take you to make you do what he wanted.

I got this crazy idea and said, "Look, Tony. You think you can hold John down for a day or two while I try to get out there? I gotta get him in rehab or something, man. Seriously."

It was terrible that Tony allowed himself to become so useless to John outside of music making. Who were they making music with in L.A., anyway?

Tony said, "I'll see what I can do, man."

I immediately called and told my wife about the emergency flight that I was about to take to L.A., and she gave me her blessings. Tony said that the authorities had already called Big Joe's family, and that arrangements would be made for his funeral in Florida, where his family was from.

I got on the first plane that I could to L.A. I thought about the guilt of getting Big Joe involved for most of the ride. He was just so excited about John, man.

I thought back to the talent show at North Carolina A&T, with Big Joe screaming, "SING THAT SHIT, LOVER-BOOOY! SING THAT SHIT!" and I started to laugh . . . But then I felt terrible that I would never speak to Big Joe again. May his soul rest in peace.

When I arrived at the airport in L.A., Tony met me there with a rental car, and we drove to a two-level apartment complex somewhere in Los Angeles.

Tony pulled into the crumbling parking lot and said, "That's where they said he was."

I asked him, "That's where *who* said he was?" I was confused.

"I had some people to follow him for you, man," Tony told me.

I said, "Tony, you mean to tell me that you couldn't hold him down for *one* day?"

Tony looked at me and said, "Look, man, we got into a fight yesterday about this shit after he slammed my damn phone down. And I was already pissed off at this whole situation. The only reason I'm still out here with him is because *you* said that you were coming."

I guess Tony *was* serious about things. *Finally!*

I said, "All right, well, let me go in here and get this boy." I was ready to take care of business.

Tony grabbed me back and said, "Wait a minute, man. This ain't that kind of neighborhood, D. You don't just walk up in there looking for people, man."

"Well, how did *John* get up in there then?"

"Because he's crazy, and people take advantage of that shit," Tony answered. "John still got money, you know. He ain't lost all of that like he lost his sense."

I stopped and wondered if I was in a movie or something. It was all ridiculous.

I said, "Well, the Lord is gonna be my shield right now, man. And if it's meant for me to get shot, then I'll just get shot then."

Tony let me go and said, "All right then."

I walked up the stairs to the second floor of this place and was actually a bit nervous. What if there *was* the wrong kind of people in there? I started thinking about my wife and family. But I couldn't stop myself from wanting to see John. It was all in *God's* hands.

I knocked on a filthy white door at apartment number 213 and waited.

Someone came to the door and looked through the peephole. I stopped breathing for a second. Then they opened the door with a chain on it and looked me over. It was a light brown woman in a housecoat who looked as if she had been up all night.

She looked me over again and asked, "Who are you?"

I said, "I'm a friend of John's. I'm here to take him home."

She grinned at me as if it were a game. She said, "John ain't here. I might know where he is, though. How bad do you want to know?"

I knew the talk of slick street women, even though I wasn't in the streets. I said, "How much do you want to open this door for me?"

She looked at me again and said, "How about two hundred dollars?"

I couldn't believe that! I was so desperate to see John that I gave it to her.

She let me in to see him. John was wide awake in the bedroom, but he was drugged up, and he was wearing nothing but boxer drawers again. He didn't look that great either.

He looked up at the woman and said, "I told you not to let him in. I'm not *here*, remember?"

She said, "Baby, I know you wasn't here at first, but then money called, and I had to answer."

It was a pitiful scene. I still couldn't believe that I was even there.

John continued to ignore me. He told her, "I would have given you *more* money to keep this motherfucker away from me."

She just looked at him and smiled.

I asked him, "Is that all I am now after trying to help you for so many years, man?"

He didn't look my way when he answered me. He said, "Things fall apart, man. THINGS FALL APART. You remember we both had to read that book by that African dude at A&T?"

I said, "Chinua Achebe."

"Yeah, him," John responded.

The woman said, "Well, John, I don't really know who you are, but you sure must be important with the way this big money spender is after you."

With that, John finally looked at me and laughed.

He said, "Yeah, he looks like a million dollars now, don't he? Mr. *Big Time* record producer. But it's all because of me. He *knows* it. It's all because of *me*."

I wanted to press a button and just zap John out of that place and out of that situation, but I couldn't. It wasn't to be that easy.

I said, "John, let's put your clothes back on and let's go, man."

I moved toward his clothes on the floor.

The woman said, "Yeah, let's go, John. I'm off the clock with you this morning," while counting her money. She must have had a thousand dollars in her hands. I had an urge to snatch it all back from her, but I didn't want to create any more drama than we were already in.

John climbed to his feet to put on his clothes and said, "I'm hungry, man. Take me to get something to eat." He could barely walk.

The woman saw us to the door and said, "Anytime, John. This here was a good night."

Tony waited for us at the car. He looked surprised that I had John with me.

I said, "Let's get him back to your hotel room, Tony."

John said, "I told you I want something to eat, man. I'm hungry."

I said, "We gon' order room service."

"Room service takes too long, man," he complained from the back of the car.

I asked him, "So, what song are you working on now, John? *Down and Out in L.A.*?"

Maybe Big Joe's death was affecting John in a way where he was becoming even more self-destructive. He had never gone *that* low.

He said, "Nah, you a producer now. Why don't *you* do it?"

I said, "I'm sorry, but I don't know what you're feeling right now, John. I don't understand this process anymore. You don't have to be in pain like this to write. You're torturing yourself for nothing. And now you're getting other people hurt because of it."

I said, "You need to come home, man. You need to just settle down, make peace with yourself, and come home."

It took us a couple of days to get John cleaned up and sober in L.A., but he seemed to cooperate with us. It was as if he was waiting for the help. Then he said, "That was fucked up what happened to Big Joe, man. All he was trying to do was look out for me. But we got all these haters out here, man. I gotta write a song for my man now."

I felt for Big Joe, too. I really did. How could I not? I had brought him into it. But John was still alive, and I still had to focus on dealing with him.

I said, "Well, who's gonna protect you from *you*, John?"

He looked at me with searching, hooded eyes. He said, "I don't know, man. You ain't here to do it no more. Right?"

He had me in a corner. What could I say? That boy needed me more than ever at that moment.

I said, "I'll see what I can do, man. But I have a son who's gonna be born in the next couple of weeks, and he's my priority right now. All I gotta do now is figure out a name for him."

John looked at me and grinned. He said, "Tony having a son this time around, too."

Tony nodded his head and said, "Yup."

John paused. Then he said, "I had a baby on the way, man. And now I don't. But maybe it was for the best. I'on know how to be no father no way." He laughed and said, "I'on even know how to be a boyfriend. Ask Tangela."

I was speechless. That boy had stuff going on in his life from every angle. *Every angle!*

John still didn't return to Charlotte with me. But he went back to New Jersey to stay with Tony's family for a while, and I promised to help them out in any way that I could. They both showed up in Florida for Big Joe's funeral, and evidently, Joe had been sending his daughter's mother plenty of money, because they looked fabulous, and they were not starving. I guess I paid that much more attention because they didn't cry at the funeral. They just stood there and took it, as if they knew it would happen. I was taking it worse than they were. I thought family *always* cried at funerals.

But in the new era of the late nineties, maybe that was no longer the case. So I apologized to his mother, who *was* crying.

John told them that he would take care of them, and he meant it. I could see it in his face. He still didn't lie to you. John told you everything you needed to know with his eyes, his body, and the soul of his music.

After staying with Tony for a while, and with me calling up there to check up on him, John started talking seriously about recording his next album, the fourth. He and Tony started working on a few new songs that they let me listen to, but most of what John was singing about was too dark for a popular album. He was really getting into the blues with his music, and I had to admit that I thought he was still too young for that full-fledged blues sound.

He recorded a song called *Why?* where he talked about his inability to maintain healthy relationships, including the one he never had with his father. He recorded another song, titled *Calling Me*, that openly expressed his drug problems.

His songs sounded good as usual, but with me being a new producer and everything instead of just John's manager, I was hesitant about the content. Did he really want to put out those kinds of songs? They just seemed way too personal. They were too damaging to his image. But before the year was out, John was ready to sign a new deal with another independent instead of going major. He just didn't trust the music executives at the major labels, and he had good reason not to.

John didn't want the added pressure of trying to keep pace with the music trends anymore. He had already done it. He just wanted to put out plain old music with any label that was willing to let him do it. The hope of a new opportunity kept him clean for the majority of the new year in 2000. I mean, he still got high when he wanted to, but he seemed to stay away from the heavier stuff, and I was always praying for him to stop all of it.

However, when the summer hits of year 2000 started to hit the airwaves, John was still unsigned—by choice—and contemplating what songs he would release on his own upcoming album. He was studying the scene to see what would work, and in the middle of it all, he called me up and gave me a piece of his mind.

He said, "Carl Thomas is singing the blues with *I Wish*. He's talking about getting involved with a married woman with kids, who leaves him to go back to her family. Now you tell me that ain't the blues?"

I said, "Yeah, but it has more of a contemporary sound to it. And it's still lightweight," I told him. "The women are *eating* that song up."

He said, "But it's still the *blues*, man. That white boy Eminem is even rapping the blues in *his* music."

I said, "And the whole country is in an uproar about the things that he's saying."

John snapped and said, "YEAH! That's when you know you did something RIGHT! Fuck what them people talking about, man! You see that white boy is selling millions of albums with that shit, ain't he?"

I said, "That's because of Dr. Dre's production. Everybody knows that. Eminem's flow is average."

"Whatever the fuck, man. I *knew* I shouldn't have listened to you about that," he told me. "You just fucked up my *next* damn album! And now you got Erykah Badu singin' the blues with that *Bag Lady* shit."

He said, "You gettin' just like all the rest of 'em, D, afraid to put out the real. You got a bunch of fuckin' *safe* hits, Darin. That's what you got. *Soft shit! Harmonized?* You need to call that shit *Punkanized* Music, man."

He said, "I told you before, if you not gon' have no heart about what you want to say, then you don't need to be involved in this shit. Mary J. Blige sings the blues in her music, and she's *always* hittin'. Mobb Deep and Nas rap the blues in theirs. And all the *real* shit is blues music, man.

"The Wu-Tang Clan always uses classic blues music for *their* shit!" he hollered at me. "They dig deep in the crates for blues. You get it? Rhythm and fuckin' *blues, Darin!*"

He was on a roll. He said, "Tupac and Biggie *lived* the fuckin' blues, just like *I'm* living it! So what the fuck am I listening to you for? You got a happy wife and family."

Then he hung up on me.

I sat there with the phone in my hand and was stunned. That boy was *forever* forcing me to think. I had to assess everything that he said. And what I hated about doing that was that John was right. I *knew* he was. I had gotten soft. Jesus Christ was persecuted for bringing the real deal to God's people, who turned away from him and had him crucified. And why were so many kids walking around in the nineties with crucifixes on their chests? The crucifix had to be the number one symbol of the year. It seemed like *everybody* was singing the blues!

The next thing I knew, I was ashamed. John was onto something again, and this time *I* had missed it.

I went to bed with his conversation on my mind that night. Chelsea was up breast-feeding our infant son, Darin Harmon Jr.

I smiled at him and said, "I wonder what the world's going to be like when you get my age."

Chelsea said, "Some things are gonna be better, some things are gonna be worse."

I nodded and played with my son's toes.

Chelsea pouted, "Can you leave him alone right now? Can't you see he's kind of busy?"

I started laughing. Breast-feeding was something else. And it was natural. They didn't have bottles in nature. *Every* baby was breast-fed.

Chelsea looked at me and asked, "What's on your mind?"

I grinned and said, "How do you know that something's on my mind?"

She said, "Because usually you would be under the covers and on your way to sleep already. So whenever you're still up like this, something's on your mind."

It was great to have a wife around who knew you and loved you like Chelsea did. A good marriage was the oldest blessing in the world for a man; a good mate and plenty of land. And I had them both. So why did I still have troubles on my mind?

I asked my wife, "Do you think that the music I'm producing is soft?"

She started to giggle. She said, "Well, you know, everybody can't have that extra deep stuff."

I said, "What does that mean? That means that our music *is* soft then?"

She squirmed to get her answer right. She said, "Darin, everybody's music has its own purpose to it. I mean, Harmonized Music produces feel-good, positive stuff. That's what you're doing. And it's good. I wouldn't feel ashamed about it. I'm proud of your music."

"But it's just not heavy stuff?" I asked her.

She looked at me and grinned. "Were you talking to John earlier?" she asked me right on cue.

I said, "Yeah. And he said that our stuff is soft."

Chelsea smiled real hard before she nodded to me. She said, "A whole lot of people's music is soft compared to John's. He's like . . . R. Kelly, Bobby Brown, and Marvin Gaye all put together. He even has that spiritual Al Green flavor to him. And, like, a Miles Davis attitude, where he's gonna do whatever he wants to do, and *when* he wants to do it."

I started chuckling. I said, "I didn't know you were paying that much attention to it."

Chelsea didn't smile at that. Did I say the wrong thing to her?

I said, "I didn't mean to insult your intelligence about it. I'm just saying, a lot of women don't really . . . well, you know . . ." I just stopped myself short. I was sounding like a chauvinistic man. A woman couldn't know deeper facts about music? I just shut my mouth.

Chelsea simply said, "I love music, Darin. You don't know that by now? And the more mature you get about it, the more you begin to understand that some music is for the moment, and other music is forever. And John . . . what he's able to do with his music . . . I mean . . . you just know that you can always listen to it and feel it. It's kind of, like, what Run-D.M.C. will be for rap music in twenty more years."

She said, "Some people don't realize it now, but they will. And everybody doesn't have the ability to produce music that's going to stick around like that. John can do it all. And he really *feels* what he's doing. A lot of other musicians just can't go there."

Mmmph! My wife was nothing short of amazing to me, man! I was very fortunate to have her.

I said, "So that's it then, hunh? John just has to do his thing regardless."

Chelsea paused and thought about it. She said, "Some people are put on this earth by God to set examples of . . . *whatever,* and John is one of them. But *everybody's* not supposed to be that way. You can't *market* that. That's where America is all screwed up. Everybody wants to be *the one,* and they're not. We just have to be smart enough to realize that. I mean, enjoy John's music, yeah, but don't get sucked all the way into it. We have to know when it's time to say, 'Wait a minute. I can't be involved in this. This is meant to be a *lesson* for me.' So we have to learn from it, and find the strength to walk away when we need to."

I said, "So, how come *I'm* having such a hard time with being able to walk away from John? It seems like every time I get away from him, something else comes up that pulls me right back in."

Chelsea said, "In the Bible, Joshua had to help carry the burden of Moses. And Joseph had to help carry the burden of Mary. That's just the way it is sometimes, Darin. You're here to help carry the burden of John Williams."

I chuckled and tried to lighten the mood of the conversation, even though I knew that there was truth to what my wife was saying. I just didn't want to hear it, and because of all the pain that John had taken us through, I'm sure that Chelsea didn't want to say it. However, we had to deal with that reality. I was a part of John's burden. That was the truth. And I didn't want to be like Judas, who turned Jesus in, or Brutus, who helped to slay Caesar.

I whined and said, "But I got my own life to live, man."

Chelsea ignored me. She went ahead and started to burp our son. She said, "I'm here to help *you* carry the burden, Darin. And it hasn't been easy on *me* either. But I'm here for you. Because I love you." She looked at our son and added, "*We* love you. And so does your daughter, Imani."

I smiled and said, "I love y'all, too." And I had to rest my mind for the night.

I realized that John was on edge after our phone conversation. I didn't have a clinical definition for it at the time, but John had been manic-depressive for *years*. He would be excited for two or three days with his new music, and then depressed for four or *five* days with whatever else was going on in his life. The drugs cut the edge and helped him to get through it all. I just wasn't around him anymore to have to deal with it every day. When I was still his manager, he was starting to make *me* manic. I didn't know if *I* was happy or sad sometimes.

Of course, I couldn't find John for a while again. He barely stayed at his house in Chestnut Hill. He had a new mansion-style home in the expensive Montgomery County of Maryland, but when I looked for him there, he wasn't there either. He was just out and about in the world, man. He had all the money that he needed to be lost for *years* if he wanted to be. I heard he had a condo in Florida and one in California. I didn't know about his spending habits since I didn't handle his accounting books anymore. And after he split up with Tangela again, he had his royalty checks coming straight to him. So I just had to wait it out for him to pop up again.

Sure enough, John popped up in an Internet article that got the whole entertainment world talking about him without him having a new album out yet. There was this aggressive Internet magazine called *TheRealReview.com* that had been posting some of the most outlandish entertainment interviews that you could imagine. As the site grew popular, more and more artists began to use it as a place to vent their frustrations with their respective industries. New Wave journalists and critics also used the site as their venting place against editors and the established publishing industries.

Most of the established magazine people ignored *TheRealReview.com*, or at least publicly, but every once in a while a hot article would make people respond to it, and John's candid "Interview with a Loverboy" was one of them.

I'm not going to get into a blow-by-blow account of the article that I was forced to read, because I already knew it. I had *lived* through those situations with John. John openly talked about the wayward sex, the easy drugs, and all of the craziness that he had been involved in in the music industry. He went as far as to call himself a sacrifice. The answers that he gave came as no shock to me or to the people who really knew John, but it was a major shock for people who still viewed "Loverboy" as the perfect love crooner for their daughters to listen to. They had read so many nice, "established" articles about John and his music for so many years that they just couldn't believe the truth. I mean, it wasn't as if John was a rapper, where their life's drama seemed to help them sell more records. John was a singer, and a real musician, one who the established media had protected.

Not that I wanted the media to do otherwise. But it was obvious that they were not the objective reporters of the news that many of them *claimed* to be. They told the stories that they *wanted* to tell in a capitalistic society. And their audience *believed* what they were sold.

Evelyn Harris called me up from her publicity office in New York and asked me, "Did you read it?" She had quit working for John shortly after the *Street Life* tour. Evelyn couldn't take the hiding of the truth anymore either.

I said, "Evelyn, it was just a matter of time before someone caught him with an article. We *all* knew that that would happen."

She changed the subject and asked me, "So how have *you* been? I heard about your beautiful family and home back in Charlotte."

I said, "Yeah, that's what it's about now. *Family.* So I'm gonna make mine and stay at home."

Evelyn said, "Darin, I think that's the smartest decision that you could make in this business. Because every time you step out your door . . . that *thing* out there can just suck you into whatever drama you don't want to be a part of."

I said, "I know it. That's why I'm back in church. And I know it ain't perfect, but at least I know *who* and *what* is in there."

Evelyn laughed and said, "Amen to that. I have some praying and some forgiving to ask for myself."

Near the end of year 2000, during the Christmas season, the official craziest time of the year in America, the big news hit that eventually landed John in the Maryland Adult Well House.

I was sitting at the dinner table with my wife and kids when my mother called the house in a frenzy.

She said, "Darin, turn the TV on to the news right now! *Right now!*"

I told Chelsea, who was closer to the TV. She clicked it on, and there was a major news story being reported on the Charlotte hometown singer John "Loverboy" Williams, who had been arrested in Maryland for drug possession, assault, and attempted manslaughter charges near his home.

Apparently, a Maryland state trooper caught John in the act of choking a woman who was sitting in his parked car with him. And they were both under the influence of drugs. They even had television footage of John being led away in handcuffs. He looked as if he was in a daze.

I looked at Chelsea and we were both speechless at the table. I was *shocked*, man! I guess that with Big Joe gone, John had decided to take the strong-arm approach into his own hands. But not even Big Joe had choked any girls.

My mother called me right back in tears over the phone. She said, "Darin, I can't believe that that boy has changed like this. Nice, quiet John who never hurt *anyone* in his life. What is going on, Darin?! What is going on?!"

My mother just had no idea, man. She had *NO I-DEA*!

. . . and of suicide . . .

That's how John ended up at the Maryland Adult Well House, a musical genius, diagnosed as a manic-depressive, with a drug addiction, a weakness for women, an assault charge, and no love or show of support from his mother or his father. I would talk crazy, too, if I was in his situation. *Anybody* would.

I fell asleep in a no-frills hotel room while reminiscing on our shared lives. I was awakened by the loud telephone ring. I jumped up and grabbed the phone before it rang a second time. Cheap phones had some loud and crude rings.

I answered it, and it was Chelsea. She said, "They're going to air a repeat of that *Chris Rock Show* on HBO where he talked about John tonight."

I had heard about the jokes, but I didn't really want to watch and listen to it. It was part of modern entertainment to make fun of American celebrities who had fallen into bad situations, but I didn't know if I was up to it that night, especially since *this* celebrity was practically family to me.

Chelsea sensed my hesitation. She said, "Well, you don't have to watch it if you don't want to. I just figured that I'd call you and let you know that it was coming on."

I didn't even know if that hotel offered HBO.

I said, "All right. I'll think about it."

When I hung up with my wife, I saw that the hotel did offer HBO. So I decided to watch *The Chris Rock Show* anyway. He came out to the applause of his hip New York audience, wearing a dark suit. He started into his opening jokes and wasted no time in getting to John.

He said, "You notice how *everybody* who has a *record deal* now wants to be *hard-core*? That's how you sell records in the 'hood. Artists walk around and say, 'Hmm. If I rob this here *liquor store* while under the *influence* of some *gan-ja*, I'll go *triple platinum.*'"

Then he did his signature chuckle. I had to smile, man. I couldn't help it. Jokes kept black folks sane. Chris knew that. Laughing at our problems became the most healthy way of dealing with them.

He said, "Now, John *Loverboy* Williams is setting up *his* next album *in advance*. Loverboy said, 'If I actually *choke* a woman *half to death*, I'll sell me another *ten million* albums.'"

He started that chuckling laughter of his again, and I began to smile even harder and chuckle at it myself while shaking my head. He wasn't finished with John yet either.

He said, "Now, when *I* was coming up and listening to music, you didn't hear about *Smokey Robinson* and *Marvin Gaye choking women*. Is that how you give a woman *love* in the *new millennium*?"

He put his hands around an imaginary neck and said, "Come here, girl! I love you! I love you! I'm the *Loverboy*! You want me to write a song for ya'?!" while shaking this imaginary woman in his hands and gritting his teeth.

I started laughing out loud and couldn't stop myself. I mean, it was plain funny, man. We all just had to deal with it, including John. He had finally gone ahead and done it to himself. And I didn't know all of the particulars about the law or how John's case went down, I just knew that if he wasn't an American celebrity with plenty of money and clout with lawyers, he would have ended up in jail instead of where he was. That was for sure! But with the probation that he had for when he came out, it would be like walking on eggshells. Maybe that was even worse than doing straight time for John.

Chris Rock ended his jokes on John by saying, "I know *one thing*, whatever *drugs Loverboy* was taking, it sure wasn't *ecstasy*. *Ecstasy* supposed to make you *nice* to people. That's what I hear, anyway. *I* don't know," before he started that chuckle laugh of his again and moved on.

When I made it back to John at the Maryland Adult Well House that next morning, *The Chris Rock Show* was the first thing that he brought up to me.

He said, "Now they making jokes about me, man. That's how it starts. That's how they start to defame you. Fuck Chris Rock! That motherfucker just mad 'cause *he* can't sing. Funny-lookin' motherfucker!"

I smiled, slightly. I said, "They let you watch that in here?"

"What, you don't think we have fuckin' televisions?" he asked me. "And even if I *didn't* watch it, they gon' talk about it in here. They know who the hell I am. Even some of these crazy motherfuckers know."

He said, "But you know the craziest thing about them jokes, man? Chris Rock was right. I mean, I wasn't trying to sell no more albums or no shit, but this girl *made* me do that shit, man. She was acting like I was soft and I wouldn't do shit to her."

I looked around as if they had cameras in the room or something. I didn't know if John was supposed to talk about his case or not. Usually the lawyers told you not to talk about it.

I asked him, "Are you supposed to talk about that?"

He said, "I'll talk about any fuckin' thing I wanna talk about, man. So anyway, this girl had read that Internet article, and I didn't know. So she came to my house, right, and got high with me. Then she started talkin' shit: 'I hope you don't think you gon' get no pussy from me now. You ain't no *Loverboy* like that to me. And I think your game is *weak*. You don't *really* know how to get no pussy.'"

He said, "It was like she wanted me to try and *take it* from her or something, man. But I wasn't trying to get no rape charge for that girl."

I put my hands up and said, "John," to try and stop him. I didn't want to hear a conversation like that, but he just kept talking rapid-fire style before I could cut him off.

He said, "So I was gon' drive the girl out in the woods somewhere and just leave her ass there. But she kept talking shit to me in the car, like I was a fuckin' sucka', Darin. Talkin' 'bout, 'You better drive me back home like you *supposed to*. I'm not *gettin' out*. You must be out your *damn mind*!' And I got tired of hearing that shit, man. So I pulled over and tried to strangle that bitch. And you should have saw her fuckin' eyes, Darin. She was *scared* den a motherfucker! Because she *knew* that I was about to *kill her ass* if that cop didn't pull over on us!"

John was in one of those crazy, hyper moods of his again. And before I could respond to him accordingly, to tone him back down, he unfolded pieces of paper on the desk in front of us and said, "Anyway, man, here's that song I promised you. *Just Say No!* But I didn't write no music to it. You a big-time producer now. Let me see what *you* can come up wit'. Just make sure whoever sings it for me does it *right*."

He grinned and said, "You know, like *I* would do it."

He changed the subject and his demeanor on me just like *that*. And who was *I* to complain? I wasn't trying to go back to that *other* conversation, so I started talking music with him instead.

I said, "John, nobody can sing it like you, man. All you have to do is clear your head."

He said, "Yeah, well, like I said, I ain't singin' no gospel."

I looked the song over, and of course I liked what I read.

When I looked up again, John was looking straight into my eyes.

He said, "What do you think?"

"You told me before that you shouldn't listen to me. Remember?" I reminded him.

"I'm *not* listening to you. The song is already done," he told me. "I'm not changin' shit on it. You gon' take it home just like that."

He pointed his finger at me and said, "And if you change my shit, man, I'm talkin' 'bout *one* fuckin' line, then don't put my name on it. And I *mean* that shit."

I nodded to him and said, "I know you do, man. I know you do."

He said, "You damn right I do. Don't fuck wit' my music, man."

I said, "Why are you in a sour mood today? You were more *up* and happy yesterday." I just wanted to try and open up the conversation with him.

John looked at me and said, "Didn't the doc tell you what was wrong wit' me, man? I'm manic-depressive. I'm *supposed* to be up and fuckin' down."

I said, "You don't have to be, John. You have to find ways to remain even about things."

He said, "Man, that's bullshit. That's like with gay people. It ain't no damn way to stay *straight*. It's their destiny. They were *meant* to be gay. And everything that happens to them leads them up to that point. They'll tell you. Ask a gay person. Matter of fact, ask *Jamie* at Old School Records. Is he still over there?"

I didn't even know. I said, "I'm not sure, man. I haven't dealt with them since I left Philly."

John nodded. He said, "So, how is it back home in Charlotte, man? You likin' it back home?"

I smiled. I told him, "A lot of new people are moving down to Charlotte, man. It's blowing up, John. You need to come back home and just . . . mellow out, man. Mellow out."

I didn't realize what I was saying. *Could* John come home and mellow out? He still hadn't talked to his mother. I guess it was all wishful thinking on my part.

John looked at me with a sly grin and said, "*Mellow out?* Listen to you, man. I'm 'bout to die in here and you talking about some *mellow out*."

I said, "John, you're not dying. You just needed time away from it all, man. You need time to rest your mind and your spirit."

He said, "Yeah. I need time to rest that shit for real, without this damn medication they givin' me."

That caught me off guard. I wasn't even thinking about medication.

I asked him, "What kind of medication are they givin' you, Prozac or something?" I didn't know.

John laughed at me. He said, "*Prozac?* Nah, man, they givin' me lithium. But that shit don't really work with me like that. I still *feel* too much for that shit, man. So they thinkin' about using other drugs on me now."

He paused and said, "Or maybe they'll just give me a fuckin' lobotomy, like they did to Jack Nicholson in *One Flew Over the Cookoo's Nest.* You ever see that movie, D?"

He laughed as if it was all a joke. He said, "But I'm gon' be dead by then anyway, man. It's *best* for me to die. It's *time* to die. I'm ready for it."

I took a deep breath and said, "I didn't come here today to hear you start talkin' about dying on me, man. I really didn't come here to hear that."

John asked me, "Well, what did you come here to hear then? I *hope* you didn't come here to hear me say that everything's gonna be all right. Because it ain't, man. I'm about to die, D. That's the way it's *supposed* to be, man. We *all* die. We do what we're supposed to do while we're here, and then we die."

I said, "And who told you this, man?"

"Nobody had to tell me shit, man. If I don't die, they just gon' make a fool out of me. Nobody will be jokin' no more when I'm dead," he told me.

I said, "Man, that Chris Rock thing *did* get to you." I was starting to get concerned.

John said, "Chris Rock ain't got that much to do with it. He's just doing what *he's* supposed to do, make jokes. But I'm tellin' you, man. The *real* legends die. It's easier that way. Look how Richard Pryor livin' right now. He'd rather be dead. *Ask him.* And Michael Jackson and Prince. Man, Prince don't even got a damn name no more. And Michael Jackson don't have no color. If they would have died already, they both would be all right. We'd all be celebrating their shit instead of callin' them weird."

I said, "John . . ." I couldn't even get my words together. I wanted to just call him crazy, but then again I didn't. I didn't want to send him into another tantrum in there.

John kept going with it and said, "I'm just being real, man. Tupac and Biggie knew it. *Death* is the only way to go out, man. *Cowards* are *afraid* to die. Dying is for the *strong.*"

He said, "Biggie kicked it, like, '*You're no-o-o-bod-de-e-e till some-bod-de-e-e-e / kills you-u-u-u.*'"

I said, "John, cut it out, man, or I'm leaving. Dying is for the *stupid.* You got a *lot* to live for, man. You just gotta get your head back together."

He shook his head and said, "I'm just being real, D. My time is over with, man. It's *over*! I gotta step aside and make way for the next mother-fucker."

"And you can't do that while you're still *alive*?" I asked him.

He said, "And do what, lose *my* place in history while I grow old and feeble? Nah, fuck that, man! I'm ready to die when I'm s'posed to. *Right now!*"

"So, you gon' *choose* to lay down and die like a *punk*?" He had gotten under my skin like always. I said, "You said it already, John. *Dying* is the *easy* way out. *Living* is for the strong!" He was forcing me to keep repeating things.

He said, "Well, be strong for *both of us* then, man. *You* be strong! You was always the strong one anyway. You had a father."

He caught me off guard again. I said, "Man . . . ," and ran out of words. I started thinking about meeting with Reverend Stark in Atlanta and seeing if he would come to visit John, his estranged son. He *had* to know what was going on with John by then. Did he keep his eyes and heart closed after meeting him. *A reverend?* I could only wonder about it until I talked to him.

John looked at me real calm and said, "I just figured it all out, man. That's all, D. I mean, I know you love me, man. But I'm *supposed* to die. That's how my song ends, man. That's just how it ends. You can't change it. And you can't control it."

I nodded my head and said, "Well, there's no sense in me workin' on this new song then." I held *Just Say No!* up in my hands as if I was ready to rip it in half.

I said, "You not gon' be around to even hear it when it's done anyway. Is that what you're telling me?" I didn't want to say it out loud, but I realized at that point that John was willing to take his own life if he had to. He really *was* sick. He *needed* to be in that place.

He smiled and said, "Go ahead and rip it in half then, D. Go ahead and rip up my heart."

I stood up and yelled, "*You* rippin' up *my* damn heart, man, talking this *dyin'* stuff! I didn't come in here to *hear that*, John!"

He just kept smiling at me like a sin, slipping deep into my soul. His eyes were wide open, staring at me.

He said, "You actin' childish, man. We both know what this reality is. But look here, man. If you wanna keep me alive so much, then keep making my music for me. All right? Go ahead and do that song for me. I ain't goin' nowhere."

Did I believe him? No. Of course not. But what choice did I have?

I warned him. I said, "John, God is my witness, and if you do *anything* stupid in here, I'm gon' stop this song in *mid*production. And I *mean it*, too, man! I'm *serious!*" What else could I threaten him with? His music and his legacy were all that he cared about.

John said, "I ain't goin' nowhere. I'm just talkin' crazy right now," and he started giggling.

A cold chill came over me before I left the room with him. I walked out of there with the craziest feeling in the world that day. All I could see in my mind was that sick smile on John's face.

I asked Dr. Benjamin before I left, "Is it normal for a manic-depressive to talk about suicide?"

He looked into my face and answered me real calmly, "Yes, it is. That's why we have to continue monitoring him real closely."

I said, "You do that, doc. And make sure that you remind him that we have a new song to work on. That's one of the few things that he actually cares about in this world. That's his strongest medicine."

. . . *Just Say No!* . . .

When I made it back home to Charlotte that evening, Chelsea met me at the door with the kids and asked me about the experience with John. I kissed her and both of the kids and said, "I have a song to produce."

"One of *John's* songs?" she asked me.

I said, "Yeah."

She put down Darin Jr., who was walking by then, on our hardwood floors and said, "Let me see it. He wrote some lyrics while in there?"

I said, "Yeah, last night while Chris Rock jumped all over him."

Chelsea smiled at me. She said, "So, you *did* watch it then?"

"Yeah, I watched it," I told her as I pulled John's lyric sheets out of my bag. "John didn't like that so much either."

"They let him watch that in there?" she asked me.

My daughter, Imani, who was three years old, looked up and asked me, "Is Uncle John all better now?" She could *talk* like her mother, too, with off-of-the-charts chatter.

I said, "Yeah, Uncle John is getting better. But it'll take a while longer, baby."

Chelsea had started referring to John as our kids' uncle, along with my two older brothers, and I didn't object to it. And of course, even though Imani had only met John once in person, during Big Joe's funeral in Florida, with her hearing some of the songs that he sang and seeing the videos that he was in, John quickly became her *favorite* uncle.

She said, "Well, I hope he's all better to sing more songs."

I picked her up, kissed her on the lips, smiled at her, and said, "Me, too, baby. Me, too."

Chelsea was still waiting for me to answer *her* question. She even repeated it to me. "So they let him watch *The Chris Rock Show* in there? Was that a *safe* thing for them to do? Or maybe they didn't know what he was going to talk about."

I smiled and said, "That's what *I* asked. And John basically said that the news was going to get back to him regardless. I mean, he's not in a coma in there. And they all know what's going on. Or at least *some* of them do."

Chelsea took the lyric sheets from me as if they were ancient Bible scriptures.

I said, "I didn't know that you were *anticipating* it so much."

"I wasn't," she told me. "But I *am* curious to see it."

She looked at me a few seconds later with a raised brow, after picking Darin Jr. back up. That boy was already spoiled. I figured I had to break him out of that *real* soon.

Chelsea asked me, "Is this a *gospel* song?" She was frowning.

I smiled and responded, "What does it read like?"

"It *reads* like a gospel song, but how are you gonna produce it?"

I smiled and said, "Like a very *good* gospel song."

"And John wrote this? I thought that he wasn't gonna do gospel," she commented.

I said, "He's not. But evidently, that doesn't mean that he can't *write it.*"

Imani looked toward the lyric sheets in her mother's hand and asked, "Is Uncle John gonna sing that song?"

I answered, "No, Uncle John is not going to sing it, but he did write it for someone *else* to sing, baby. And Daddy's gonna do the music."

The first thing I did was call Tony up and tell him what I was up to.

He said, "Aw'ight. When do you want to do it?"

For some reason, I didn't think it would be that easy. I was expecting to have to twist Tony's arm to play for me.

I said, "So, you don't have any problem with doing gospel music then?"

Tony said, "Wait a minute. You said that *John* wrote this, right?"

I said, "Yeah, John wrote it, but he didn't do any music for it."

"Well, if this is *John's song*, it don't *matter* if it's gospel. We gon' add the funk to it, and make Kirk Franklin and them jealous down there," Tony told me with a laugh. "He from Charlotte, too, ain't he?"

I chuckled and said, "Yeah, he's from Charlotte."

He said, "Well, I'm just gon' ask you this, man. While we in production, I want to bring my whole family with me while I'm down there. I'm getting tired of leaving them behind all the time, and my wife be bitching up a storm now with the kids. So maybe they could all hang out for a minute at *your* big crib and get to know each other or something, man."

I grinned real wide. I said, "Tony, that's the best idea that I've heard from you in *years*, man. *In years!*"

Tony said, "Yeah, and you're *paying* for it, right?"

I laughed and told him, "Yeah, I got it. But it's not like you can't afford it on your *own*, *Mr. Beatmaker.*"

Tony laughed it off. That boy had to have *three* or *four times* more money than I did. Great beat making paid the bills *real well* in the nineties. I understood about his family situation, too. My wife Chelsea was pregnant again herself. What could I say, we could afford the extra love.

I got a whole group of musicians together with Tony on the drums, a bass player, a lead guitar, an organist, and a keyboard player, and we laid the track down in a couple of days, and mixed it for two more, so that everyone could listen to it several times with rested ears before we set the track in stone.

The basic groove was led by the bass, the drums, and the piano. Everything else slipped in and out for effects. I listened to the track over and over again with the engineers to mix it just right, while the bass, drums, and piano complemented each other in a bouncy groove:

Just . . . say no, just . . . say no
Just . . . , just . . . say no . . .

Tony did his thing on the drums with plenty of effects in the background:

Da-Doomp . . . Doomp-TAT
Doomp . . . Doomp-TAT
Doomp . . . Doomp-TAT
Doomp . . . Doomp-TAT . . .

When we settled on the final mix, Tony listened to it a few more times and nodded his head.

He said, "The mood is set, D. The levels are right on, and now whoever you got in mind to sing this thing, man, they gotta be able to bring *the noise. For real!* 'Cause I can hear John's *voice* on this thing right now, man. *Right now!*"

Everyone else agreed with him. It was John's kind of song. The final mix was great music and all, but you had to really sing the lyrics well to make it work. The track *begged* for you to sing it well.

I brought a tape home and let Chelsea listen to it after we knew that we had what we wanted.

Chelsea listened to it a few times in our bedroom and asked me with a smile, "So . . . who are you gonna get to sing the lyrics?"

I was already on it. I smiled back at her and said, "It's this trio out of Atlanta called the Midnights. They got their name straight from John's second song. I was with him when he first performed it back at Norfolk State."

I laughed, reminiscing, and said, "They stiffed us on some of the money and got his name wrong on the posters. That's when I first started managing John."

Chelsea frowned and asked, "This group calls themselves *The Midnights?* That's like some old-school stuff."

I laughed and said, "Yeah, they *sing* old-school, too. That's why I like them. They just haven't had any big breaks yet."

Chelsea still couldn't get past the name. She repeated, *"The Midnights?"*

"Chelsea, look," I told her, "they're three *dark brown brothers* like me. Okay? So I *like* what they're doing. They gon' bring dark skin back in," I said with a chuckle.

Chelsea looked at me and grinned. She said, "I don't know what *you're* talking about, but dark skin never *left* in *my* book. You just have to be able to *sing* with it."

I said, "Well, I've already called their manager. I'm gon' fly down to Atlanta to meet up with these guys."

Chelsea asked me, "Do they sing gospel?"

I started to chuckle. I said, "I don't know yet. I didn't ask them that."

"You didn't send them a copy of the song?" she asked me.

I grinned and said, "Nah. You know, some people start turning gospel music down before they even try it. That's the same thing John did. And we *know good* and *well* that most black musicians come *straight* from the church. Then they start singing secular music and front."

My wife laughed at me and said, "You better get down off of that *high horse, Mr. Gospel.* Because *you* haven't done much gospel music up to this point either."

I said, "Yeah, but I was always open to it. *Always!* Even when John first started out."

Chelsea said, "We'll see," and we left it at that.

• • • •

I flew down to Atlanta to meet with the Midnights and their manager, and I let them listen to the track a few times before I showed them any lyrics. You know, I had to play my cards right.

They said, "Yeah, this music sounds like Loverboy. That's his style. So what do we sing with it?" They were all excited about it.

I said, "All right, this song has a blues, gospel feel to it."

They took one look at the lyrics and looked back at me.

They asked me, "This is gospel . . . ?"

Like the classic Slick Rick song that my older brothers used to listen to, *it was the moment I feared.* I said, "This is a John 'Loverboy' *Williams* song, and he was always one to take chances. And I mean, I want to get someone to try and perform this thing live at the National Music Awards coming up. But you know, if y'all don't want to do it, I understand."

Their manager said, "Wait a minute. You have a spot at the National Music Awards to perform this?"

I said, "That's what I'm trying to do, have it performed on a main stage. I want everyone to hear it. I mean, are your guys even up for that?"

I was trying reverse psychology and everything. These guys really had the confident sound that I needed. So I threw in a knockout punch and went for the kill.

I said, "I could always ask Boyz II Men to go out there and perform it. They let John on his first big tour with them years ago. But I just wanted to give some new blood a chance to shine. I mean, I thought that y'all were *looking* for that opportunity."

Honestly, I didn't know if Boyz II Men wanted to sing any gospel either. Gospel music really seemed taboo for secular singers. I was being forced to jump through all kinds of hoops over it. The Midnights were still hesitant.

The lead singer, Sam Clean, stepped up and said, "I'm sayin', man, if we go gospel on our first big song like this, some people won't really try to listen out for anything else that we do."

I tried to play hardball from a manager perspective at that point. I said, "I managed John to success for years. And sometimes you just have to put yourself in a position to pass or fail. You can't keep playing the safe route thinking that something lucky is gonna happen for you. I mean, the main thing that you want to do is perform a good show, and let everybody know that you can follow in John's footsteps. Unless you don't think that John's music is a good enough example for you to follow. Because if *that's* the case, then I understand."

They *knew* that wasn't the case. Loverboy was *the bomb!* They had named themselves after one of his early songs in their college years. They were the same age as me, and they were running out of time to be stars. The new millennium would not *wait* for it to happen for you.

To make a long story short, I convinced the Midnights to try it, and I had to keep telling them to slow their vocals down and feel the power of each word like John would. It had to be done perfectly to have an opportunity with the selection process for the National Music Awards show.

I got back home and told my wife about my sins, because I really wasn't frank with those guys in Atlanta. Chelsea had another good laugh at me.

She said, "So, now you have to call up and beg someone at the National Music Awards to allow you to do this. What were you *thinking?*"

I said, "I don't know, man. Something just came over me. I felt desperate to get this thing done. And performing it at the National Music Awards is a good idea. You have to admit that."

Chelsea said, "Well, at least they *sound* good on the song."

I said, "Yeah, with a lot of hard work. John was just"—I caught myself speaking in the past tense and said—"that boy is just a genius, man. He goes in the studio and lays a song down in a couple *takes*. It took the Midnights a couple of *days*. But they finally got it right, though."

"Yeah, well, John was also doing his own *music and* his own *lyrics*, so he knew exactly what he was supposed to do," she reminded me.

I nodded to her and said, "Yeah, you're right."

Next I flew out to Los Angeles to talk to the award show organizers, and they liked the song idea, they were just hesitant like everyone else to do it.

I said, "Now, John performed for you guys when he didn't get any awards that first year, and you *know* he deserved it. Then he came right back and worked with you again the year after that. And he can't get no love now? I mean, this song could really affect some people in a positive way. We're all from the church deep down inside. Think about it. This song is what we could *use* at the awards ceremony this year to send out a strong message to new artists *and* to the community."

They heard me out and told me that they would have to think it over. Man, I felt like I was right back in the game of managing for John again. I was doing all I could to keep his spirits up and keep him alive. It was as if I was trying to save my boy's life single-handedly. I called to check up on him and to let him listen to what we were doing over the phone.

He said, "That sounds good, D. You say that these guys are from Atlanta? Did you see my father while you were down there?"

WOW! That boy was still *killing me*, man! If it wasn't one thing it was another.

I said, "John, to be honest with you, the thought crossed my mind a while ago, man. But then I got wrapped up into doing this music project for you. But I'll go back down there and tell the reverend to think about visiting you. In fact, I'll drive my whole family to the church if I have to."

I added, "Chelsea is starting to show now."

John said, "That's beautiful, man. Is this one gonna be a girl, or a boy?"

I answered, "We don't know yet."

He said, "Well, thanks, man. I was just thinking about my father lately."

He sounded real poised, not extra excited or down. I guess that whatever new medicine they were using on him was working a little better.

I hung up the phone with John and shook my head. Now I had to see about Reverend Joseph Stark for him. My wife was right. I was carrying John's burden for real. I was running around for him even more than when I was managing. He had turned me into a desperate man.

I drove my whole family down to College Park to Reverend Stark's huge church, and we waited patiently before I had a moment to meet and talk to him. When I finally received the opportunity, I made sure that Chelsea and the kids were right there with me. I wanted to put Reverend Stark on the spot and make him respond to us in all earnestness. I knew he understood how important family was. How could he not understand? The Southern church was all about family.

Reverend Stark looked us over and said, "Welcome. Have you decided on joining our parish here today?"

I shook my head and said, "No, we haven't decided on that at all, Reverend."

He asked us, "Well, how may we help you make that all-important decision. In other words, how may I *serve* you today?"

I was not planning on biting my tongue anymore. I wanted to take a page out of John's book and just tell it like it was.

I looked into Reverend Stark's handsome face and said, "You can serve us by visiting our sick loved one, John 'Loverboy' Williams, your *son*, up in the state of Maryland."

The reverend didn't flinch an inch. He was still extra cool under pressure, just like his son was while up onstage.

He said, "I'm aware of that situation. I pray for him every night."

I said, "Well, with all due respect, *Reverend*, John could use *more* than praying right now. He could use some real physical presence and love."

Chelsea said, "Amen to that."

The reverend looked at my whole family and nodded to us. He paid no one else any mind. I guess he planned to defuse things after we were gone.

He asked me, "How is he doing?"

I answered, "Not as good as he *could* be."

"Well, allow me to give you my personal office number to call," the reverend offered to us.

Chelsea spoke up and said, "We're not interested in your personal *office number*, we're interested in you *serving* love and responsibility to your estranged *son*."

Chelsea got under his armor of cool much faster than I could because he began to squirm with her words.

I backed my wife and said, "Amen. A *real* father should *be* a father, not only to his *parish* but to his *seed*."

My daughter, Imani, said, "Amen." Even she caught on to our urgency that morning. We wanted *results* and not the empty promises.

Reverend Stark nodded and said, "I thank you all for coming out and informing me on this matter. And as I said, this situation will be taken care of in *God's speed*."

With that, his helpers stepped up to lead him away from us.

When we walked back out to the car, Chelsea was *hot* under the collar!

She said, "He's lucky I'm not *ghetto*, because he *surely* needs to be *told* about himself. See, that's why I'm not a *blind* Christian. The *Word* is being interpreted and preached by *imperfect humans*. And that Reverend Stark is a perfect example of why we need to *keep* our eyes *open*. They need to call his butt *Reverend Slick*."

Imani started giggling, and that made Darin Jr. laugh, when he had no idea what was going on. He just knew that his mother was *hot* at the moment!

I grinned and said, "That's what John called him."

"That's what he *is*," my wife told me. She said, "And I'm not trying to make a blanket statement about pastors and the church, as if they're all bad, because they're not. But we *all* have to know what's *right* and what's *wrong* in our *own hearts* inside *and* outside of the church. And that goes across the board, because some of these *white* Southern pastors even had *slaves* at one time. And they didn't see a *thing* wrong with that. They worked and whipped their slaves Monday through Saturday, and then *rested* on Sundays."

I smiled. I said, "I don't even think they rested then. They probably had their whole plantations helping out at the church on Sundays, fanning the congregation and such."

I was just trying to lighten the mood a bit, you know. It was Sunday and we were all dressed to a tee. We had accomplished what we came to do, and the rest was out of our hands.

Chelsea said, "Well, I don't even wanna talk about it anymore. Put on that *Just Say No!* tape from the the Midnights."

I put the tape on for her, and as soon as the song kicked in, Imani started humming along with the groove. I took that as a good sign.

I got a call later on that week from the organizers of the National Music Awards show about the Midnights performing John's new song. I was excited to hear back from them, but they wanted to use a more well known group to sing it. Ironically, they came up with Boyz II Men and Take 6, the creative gospel group. However, I stuck to my guns. The Midnights had done it the way it was supposed to be done, and I didn't want any last-minute changes, nor an artistic license battle. A more established group would more than likely want to change the song to fit their own style, and that was *definitely* not what I wanted. So I had to fight to keep the Midnights involved. John would have been proud of me.

The show organizers called me back and hinted that they might use the song performed by the Midnights, but their performance might not make the airtime show.

I said, "Absolutely not. We can't do this song for only the people in the audience. No way! You wouldn't do Boyz II Men like that!" I was upset that they even tried to play me like that. They knew how good that song was. Gospel or not, *Just Say No!* was a hit that the people would feel, and it would no doubt increase the show's ratings. Nevertheless, they were adamant about increasing the ratings *more* by giving the song and performance to someone more established.

I told Chelsea about it, and she was pretty calm for a change.

She said, "That's the way it goes sometimes, but that just means that they *know* it's a hit. So stick it out and tell them what you want. You'll get it. They already want to use it, they just want to see if you'll bend first."

I took my wife's advice with some hesitation, but sure enough, we got the okay for the Midnights to perform John's song at the new millennium's first National Music Awards show.

I was *pumped!* The first thing I did was get in contact with John to give him the good news.

They got him on the phone at the Maryland Adult Well House, and I ran down the good news to him.

He said, "That's good. I gotta get me a haircut and a shave now before the media starts trying to come in here and do interviews with me. And I won't say nothin' bad, man. I promise you, D."

I told myself, *Yeah*, sure *you won't*. But I was too excited to sour the mood with that. I asked John to give me any words of wisdom to pass on to the Midnights before the big performance.

John said, "Yeah. You tell them niggas to *own* the stage. The stage is *theirs* when they're up there, D. And if you ain't gon' *own it*, then it ain't no sense in you being up there. And you don't *share it* with *nobody*. You tell 'em I said that."

I passed the message on to the Midnights over the phone in Atlanta, and they were jumping for joy.

"He told us to do that? He told us to *own* the stage, Darin?"

I said, "Yeah." It sounded like simple advice to me, you know. But coming from John "Loverboy" Williams, I guess it meant a lot more.

Man, when we got to the National Music Awards show out in California, I was nervous as I don't know what. I felt that way every time John stepped up to the next level, but he had always produced and set me back at ease. But now I was counting on the Midnights, and I was extra nervous again, as if I was starting all over in the music business.

The big names and new names that year were Sisqo, the return of Boyz II Men, Philadelphia's Jill Scott and No Question, Donell Jones, Next, Joe, Erykah Badu, Destiny's Child, Mya, Carl Thomas, Eric Benet. R. Kelly was back, as well as was Toni Braxton, and of course, Mary J. Blige was *always* there. Outside of that, you had a ton of rappers, led by the new-schooler Nelly, the overhype of Lil' Kim, the underhype of Mos Def and Common Sense, the West Coast Dr. Dre camp, the East Coast Def Jam camp, and the swarm from the Dirty South with Mystikal, the Big Tymers, the 504 Boys, the Three 6 Mafia, Scarface, Outkast . . . John had it right, rap music was taking *over!*

In fact, since there was so much presence from the hard-core rap acts at the awards show, I really began to worry about a gospel song being sandwiched right in the middle of all of that. But Chelsea reminded me that most of the rappers were wearing platinum crosses around their necks, so how could they front on gospel? I was still nervous, though. Everybody was hypocritical, and just because the rap crowd wore crucifixes around their necks, it didn't mean that they wanted to listen to any preaching. They did their *own* preaching, the gospel of the streets: pimping, drinking, smoking, murder, and self-destruction.

I made my way backstage before the big moment and reminded the Midnights what John had told me: *Own the stage* while you're up there!

I said, "I hate to put the heat on y'all like this, but this is a one-shot deal. You either live or you die out there. So you may as well go out there and go for broke."

The lead singer, Sam Clean, took a breath and said, "I got you, man. Just remember to breathe, and take every note slow."

I nodded to him and said, "Yeah. And just do your thing."

Their manager looked more nervous than I was back there. I guess he had never been at that level before. However, if our song went over like it was supposed to, he had better get *used* to the pressure. *And fast!*

I took my seat between my wife and Tony's wife, and we held hands before the announcement.

To my surprise, they had Quincy Jones to come out and read it. Man, I nearly stopped *breathing!* QUINCY JONES WAS GOING TO AN-NOUNCE JOHN'S SONG! I couldn't believe it! It was like a script written in heaven!

Chelsea nudged me and said, "Well, look at *that*. I told you everything would be all right."

I didn't say a word. I was too much in shock.

Quincy Jones stood at the podium in an electric blue suit with a matching tie and said, "The field of music has historically produced some of the most heartfelt artists and creators in the African-American community, and those artists and their creations have gained worldwide recognition for their rhythm and soul."

He said, "And as each generation produces its own legendary figures, we must not forget to honor the blues, the work songs, and the Negro spiritu-als from which our music has its roots. So without further ado, I present to you *Just Say No!*, a song written and arranged by *this* generation's John *Loverboy* Williams, performed by the Midnights."

I leaned back and took one last deep breath. The curtains slid open to reveal the Midnights, dressed in all white, with the band behind them. The spotlight lit them up like black angels, and then Tony kicked off the song with his drums. Sam rolled in right behind him with the lyrics, and the band followed Sam's lead with his backup singers:

Da-Doomp . . . Doomp-TAT
Doomp . . . Doomp-TAT . . .

God, how I wish it was sim-ple (SIMPLE)
how I live my li-i-i-fe
God, how I wish it was sim-ple (SIMPLE)

the way I sleep my ni-i-ights
God, how I wish it was sim-ple (SIMPLE)
to stay away from this wor-r-rld that calls me
And God, how I wish it was simple (SIMPLE)
so simple
(GIVE ME THE STREN-N-NGTH)
I need to
(PRA-A-AY)
and jus-s-st sa-a-ay (NO-O-OH).

JUST SAY NO-O-O, NO-O-O, NO-O-OH
Doomp-TAT
NO-O-O, NO-O-O, NO-O-OH
JUST SAY NO-O-O, NO-O-O, NO-O-OH
Doomp-TAT
NO-O-O, NO-O-O, NO-O-OH . . .

I took a look around the place after the first verse and chorus, and they were *eating it up* in there! They were *feeling it!* It was *working!* Their hushed silence allowed Sam Clean to open up with more confidence and volume for the second verse:

God, how I wish it was sim-ple (SIMPLE)
when I'M OUT WITH MY frien-n-nds
GOD, how I wish it was sim-ple (SIMPLE)
to change the 'hood and the STREETS THAT SURROUND ME
AND GOD, HOW I WISH IT WAS sim-ple (SIMPLE)
to build a fortress for me to hi-i-ide
(GIVE ME THE STREN-N-NGTH)
I need to
(PRA-A-AY)
and jus-s-st sa-a-ay (NO-O-OH).

JUST SAY NO-O-O, NO-O-O, NO-O-OH
Doomp-TAT
NO-O-O, NO-O-O, NO-O-OH . . .

I took another look around, and we *HAD THEM!* The whole place was in *SHOCK!* All the wanna-be thugs and everyone else in there was nodding their heads like we were ALL in church! I looked at Chelsea and just started smiling. John had done it again, with a *GOSPEL SONG!* I even wondered if Sister Williams was watching from home that night.

By the time the Midnights reached the last verse and the vamp, lead singer Sam Clean appeared possessed by the spirit of *Loverboy*. Sam looked like he was ready to go *solo* up there. He came to the edge of the stage like John loved to do, and that's when I noticed the gold cross around *his* neck.

Perfect! Bring it on home! I thought to myself.

Sam went ahead to tear down the rest of the song, and everybody in that place:

GOD, HOW I WISH IT WAS sim-ple (SIMPLE)
to have you by my si-i-ide
GOD, HOW I WISH IT WAS sim-ple (SIMPLE)
to see the li-i-ight in-SI-I-IDE OF THE DARK-NESS
AND GOD, HOW I WISH IT WAS sim-ple (SIMPLE)
to love you
to LOVE YOU-U-U-U
(GIVE ME THE STREN-N-NGTH)
I NEED TO
(PRA-A-AY)
AND JUS-S-ST LET GO-O-OH.

JUST SAY NO-O-O, NO-O-O, NO-O-OH
TO THIS WOR-R-RLD AROUND ME-E-E
NO-O-O, NO-O-O, NO-O-OH
BREAKING ME DOWN
NO-O-O, NO-O-O, NO-O-OH
TO THE WOR-R-RLD AROUND ME-E-E
NO-O-O, NO-O-O, NO-O-OH
AND JUST LET GO
NO-O-O, NO-O-O, NO-O-OH
AND JUST LET GO-O-O-O
NO-O-O, NO-O-O, NO-O-OH
LET ME GO-O-O . . .

Tears came down *TO GOSPEL MUSIC* in a *SECULAR PLACE!* The Midnights got a standing ovation for their excellent performance of John's song, and then a giant-sized screen came down with John's *Street Life* album, where he posed with dark shades and a walking stick as if he was blind. There wasn't a hater in that place! They all knew that John's music was special, and I was sure that the new song would only add to his legacy.

I couldn't *wait* to call John back up in Maryland! I had my cell phone ready.

I told Chelsea, "Let me go make this call," and I wiped my eyes on the way out through the crowd. I was *elated!* But I had a hard time finding a spot that was quiet where I could talk. That place was rocking for like *five minutes!*

This one thugged-out-looking brother wearing a 504 Boys bandanna on his head came out wiping his eyes and just looked at me and shook his head. He said, "Damn, dawg. That shit was . . . *damn!* But that's the way it is, though. You wish you *could* get rid of all this shit. You know, just say no to the motherfucker and it go away. You wish the shit *was* that simple. But it *ain't*, dawg. That shit just ain't *simple* like that."

I laughed because I was happy that everyone felt it. I didn't even care how you chose to live your life at that moment, as long as you felt John's message. And I was sure that Big Joe was feeling it in his grave, too, laughing his behind off. *That's that* Loverboy *shit right there, dawg!*

After the crowd calmed down a bit, I was able to make my phone call to Maryland. It was a good thing they gave John special privileges there to keep his spirits up, because I could basically call there and get to talk to him any time that he was up and about.

John came to the phone in a hot minute and said, "I knew you'd be calling me, man. They did it up, D. They gave 'em a standing ovation. They had it on TV for like *a minute*."

I said, "They were giving *you* a standing ovation, man. They know who wrote this song. You saw your giant screen go up there, didn't you? How many people get honored like this at your age? You're only twenty-seven. They know this is your era. You da man, John! You da *man!*"

He chuckled and said, "That's good, D. Now I can rest in peace. You went out there and did it." He sounded pleased but uncertain.

I said, "What, you were worried that the song wouldn't hit like this? Man, I don't think you know your own power out here, John. I *still* don't think you know it. So when you want me to visit you again?"

He paused. He said, "Umm . . . whenever you want to, man. That's up to you."

I said, "I'm coming to see you as soon as we get back from Cali then."

He said, "Aw'ight. Come on wit' it. *You* da man, D! None of this would have happened without you," he told me.

I couldn't wait to see him. I wanted to challenge him to write another song. I was so happy, man, that I felt like dancing back down the aisles.

I made it back to my wife and said, "John saw it! He saw it, and he's happy about it!"

Chelsea wiped her eyes for about the fourth time after the performance that night and said, "Good! And he *deserves* to feel happy."

... *then I cried for a hero* ...

Just Say No! was never thought out as a business proposition initially, but after the Midnights' performance at the awards show that night, everyone wanted a copy of the song to play on their local radio stations, which led to record stores wanting copies to sell to their customer base. I hadn't even decided on a label for the song yet. I was just trying to produce it for John and have it performed where he could see the impact that he still had on people through his music.

I did plenty of interviews for a change, though. Since I didn't really want reporters trying to bombard John at the Maryland Adult Well House, I agreed to more than half of the stories and interviews that I was asked to do.

I was mainly telling them that the song represented all of the things that we struggle with as young people on a day-to-day basis in America. There were just so many things going on in America to get caught up in in the new millennium that it took extra discipline to make the right decisions sometimes. And even though a lot of people didn't want to hear the preaching, we all needed more help to do what's right.

I also had to defuse an argument about *Just Say No!* not being a "traditional gospel" song. I mean, just because the song had a little more pizzazz and swing to it than gospel folks were used to, that didn't change what it was. We were trying to attract a young, secular audience to the song. I thought that people had gotten past that traditional gospel bag after Kirk Franklin's music, but I guess they hadn't.

Some reporters asked about the breakup that John and I had a few years back, and I just responded that people have to grow apart sometimes in order to grow together.

I said, "I think John and I needed space from each other to grow."

I was told, however, that it *looked* as if *I* was the only who had benefited from our breakup. My new career and personal life as a producer were on the way up, and John's career and personal life were on the way down. I resented that, and that insinuation made me want to stop doing the interviews. They didn't know how much I loved John. They didn't know how hard I was working on his behalf, when I *could have been* doing my *own* stuff.

Tony added his usual cynical view on it. He said, "Man, Nancy Reagan came out with that 'Just say no' to drugs campaign back in the eighties, but people still gon' do what they want to do in America, man. I mean, at least she *said* something about it. And now we make a positive song about the struggle to do the right thing, and all they want to do is argue about whether it's real gospel or not, and why y'all broke up in the first place."

He shook his head at me and said, "That's why I just do the music, man, and let people take it how they gon' take it. That's all you can really do, Darin. Because they're gonna do what they want to do with it regardless."

It was Wednesday, March 21, 2001, and I was in bed with my wife. It had been a long week and a long day.

Chelsea said, "So, you have your plane tickets all ready to fly back up there to see John tomorrow?"

I said, "Yeah." I was leaving out for BWI airport the next morning.

Chelsea nodded and said, "We *all* want to go with you next time," and put my hand on her pregnant belly. She added, "We might have a surprise for him."

I said, "He already knows that you're pregnant. I told him that."

"Did you tell him what the name is?"

I frowned at her. I said, "We don't have no name yet. Or *do we*? You picked one out?"

She said, "No, not yet. I still don't know the sex. But I've been thinking about it."

I said, "And you've been thinking about it without me?"

Chelsea smiled and said, "I'm always thinking."

Before I could say another word about it the telephone rang. It was my mother again, and she was crying. *Again.*

She said, "Oh, *Darin!*"

I asked her, "What is it, Mom? What's going on now?"

On instincts, Chelsea turned the TV on in our bedroom. We didn't watch TV much because most of the programs the networks aired weren't desirable to us. So I watched mostly sports events, and my wife watched the news, the weather, and special programs.

My mother said, "It's John. They say he was hit out there in the street." She was still piecing the information together as she spoke.

Chelsea had the story on the local news channel as my mother spoke about it. They were reporting an accident just a few miles outside the Maryland Adult Well House with a cargo truck.

I sat up to pay attention to my mother while watching the story unfold on the television.

My mother shouted, "How did they let him get out?!" She was all hysterical.

I was trying to block her out and concentrate on the news report for a minute to get more facts. The reporters were saying that John had apparently made an escape from the Maryland Adult Well House with guards in pursuit, who were not able to catch him before he ran right into the lane of a fast approaching truck.

My mother wailed, "OH, MY GOD! THAT BOY . . ."

I could hear my father in the background trying to calm her down.

Chelsea said, "Well, why didn't they try to shoot him in the leg or something?"

I was still trying to get more facts. Then they finally made the announcement: "John Williams was pronounced dead at the Montgomery County Hospital in Maryland tonight at nine-oh-eight P.M."

My mother wailed, "OH, MY *GOD!*" over the telephone.

Chelsea began to tear up and grabbed for me in bed. And me? I was just numb. I didn't know how to feel. Was it all a *joke?* Was I having a *nightmare?*

Then I thought about something John had said in my last conversation with him, from the awards show. He said, "That's good, D. Now I can rest in peace."

His words replayed in my mind over and over again: *"That's good, D. Now I can rest in peace."*

I shook my head. Everything else seemed to be spinning around me. I said, "That *mother*—," and I caught myself. I couldn't *believe* that I let that comment slip past me! I was too happy that night at the awards to realize what he was saying. I thought he meant to get a good night's sleep, not that he was talking about resting in peace *forever!* I thought he was coming out of it. I thought he was okay that night.

I had to break away from my wife in bed, and from my mother over the phone. I had to stand up and collect my thoughts for a moment.

"That's good, D. Now I can rest in peace."

John's words were haunting me, man. *Haunting me!*

I gritted my teeth and screamed, "GOD—GOD—DAMMIT!"

I didn't know what else to do, man. But I didn't feel like crying. I felt angry. I was angry at John. I just *knew* in my heart that that accident wasn't really an accident. I wondered who else John had spoken to about dying.

Chelsea was still crying and talking to my mother over the telephone, but I needed to take a walk out of the room.

Chelsea called, "Darin? . . . DARIN?"

I just shook my head and kept walking out of the room. Like I said, I didn't *feel* like crying. I felt *mad*! I felt *cheated*! That mother . . . *fucker* had done it to me again, and I wanted to bring his ass back to life and kill him my *damn self! All that shit for* nothing! I thought to myself. *He set my ass up again!*

I walked down into my music office next to the garage and called Tony up on my business line.

Tony's wife answered the telephone and told him that I was calling.

She cried and said, "I'm so sorry to hear about John. How's Chelsea taking it?"

I mumbled, "She's all right. Everybody's hurtin', you know."

Tony came on the line and said, "Man, out of all the different ways to go out in this world, that motherfucker gets hit by a damn *truck*. A damn *truck*, Darin!"

I asked Tony one time, "Did John ever talk to you about dying or committin' suicide, man?" I didn't have time for a conversation about it. I just wanted my answer.

Tony paused. He said, "Man, we all knew that John was dying. *You* knew it, too. It was like that boy was dying of a broken heart, man, with all them damn girls he had. I mean, he still felt alone for some damn reason. Even when he was with Tangela . . . I can't call it, man. That boy was just . . . Man, I can't call it. I mean . . ."

Tony went speechless on me, and I didn't really have much to say that night. I didn't have words for anyone. In fact, I just felt like staying in my office and ignoring *everything*. And I did. I took the phone off the hook, and ignored my pager, my wife, and my kids. I'm not saying that it was right, but that was just how I felt. I didn't want to be bothered. I had been bothered enough by John's life. And I just needed some time alone in his death.

When I talked to Dr. Benjamin at the Maryland Adult Well House, he was taking a lot of flak, and he expected me to join in with the bandwagon of accusers who held him and the facility responsible. But I knew better than that. Where there was a will, there was a way. John had great willpower when he focused. He could do anything he put his mind to. He had focused on his death . . . and he had done it.

At the funeral that next Wednesday, March 28, I still hadn't shed a tear. I didn't have it in me anymore to cry for John. I was all cried out. I had been crying for that boy for *years*. But there were thousands of people there at the funeral who *did* have more tears for John, enough to fill a swimming pool. Some fans had come long ways to see his remains, and our Christ Universal Baptist Church became a long line of people flowing in and out and breaking into tears over John's peaceful face.

When I got a chance to view the body with Tony and the rest of the close family, I was honestly tripping. I mean, I didn't show it, but I kept thinking that John was going to smile, or wink at me, or say something: *"I set it up good,' didn't I, D? Go 'head and admit it, man. Go 'head and admit it."*

But it never happened. It was just unreal. I kept thinking to myself, *Is this really real? Is my boy gone? Or am I dreaming this all up?*

Just like John had promised before the awards show, he had gotten a clean haircut and a shave, with his long sideburns neatly trimmed. His mom had him dressed in an all-white tuxedo, so his penny brown face and hands stood out and looked real calm in the white casket. In the accident, John had suffered a crushed rib cage and two punctured lungs, as if he stuck his chest out to take the hit. And the boy didn't have a big chest to begin with. But I had to move on, man. He wasn't getting back up. And he wasn't going to speak to me.

Tangela walked up and did her crying, and I felt her. She had carried John's seed.

Then Sister Williams stood there and started crying. But I didn't have many words for her. What positive comments could I have made to her? To be honest about it, I had been doing most of the work to try and keep John out of trouble over the years, not her. She hadn't helped that boy a bit with all of her damnation. It had only made his situation *worse* in *my* view. Sister Williams needed to check *herself* out. But since I still had my respect for her, I just decided to keep the peace.

I did hear her comments, though, and she sounded defensive in her tears. She was saying things like, "I did the best that I could do in this world

with what the *Lord* gave me. Everybody wants you *measuring up* to something. *I* measure up! I'm a *good, God-fearing* woman!"

I was concerned for her welfare. I had come to terms with Sister
Williams being manic-depressive just like her son was. Like Dr. Benjamin
had told me, it was hereditary. I wondered if Sister Williams had thought of
suicide herself on occasion.

The big surprise came when Reverend Joseph Stark showed up with his
entire "legitimate family" in tow and said a long, holding-hands prayer
over John's body.

Chelsea and I just looked at each other with our own family from the
front pews.

Sister Williams snapped out in the middle of church and said, "It's a little too LATE for that, JOSEPH! IT'S TOO *LATE* FOR THAT!"

Her family from Atlanta had to restrain her as Reverend Stark made his
way back up the aisle with his family.

I looked at Chelsea again and said, "I can't even believe she said that."

Tangela and Tony couldn't believe it either. They were right there with
us. And they both knew how John's mother had been. So I had to restrain
Tangela.

Tangela broke down and started saying, "She don't even *know* her son.
She don't even *know him! Damn hypocrite!*"

I mean, the whole funeral was a big emotional circus. But I continued to
hold my peace in there like a bystander. I just couldn't wait to get the thing
over with. Every step of it was torture, all the way up to lowering John's
body into the ground.

Sister Williams started hollering, "OH, TAKE ME WITH YOU!
TAKE ME WITH YOU! *OH, LORD, JESUS!*" and they had to restrain
her again.

I don't even want to get into how many different outbursts went on. It
was just embarrassing. I felt that if *anyone* needed to act crazy there, it was
me. Outside of maybe Tangela, no one there had been closer to John than I
was. And I still hadn't shed a tear.

"Darin, are you okay, baby?" Chelsea asked me in the car on the way
back to the house. She had her hand on my knee.

I took a deep breath and nodded to her. I said, "Yeah. This has just been
another long day." I felt like I was forty years old already. I hadn't even
turned twenty-seven yet.

Shortly after the funeral, John's new lawyer contacted me and his few
loved ones to be present at the reading of the will, including Tony and Tan-

gela. I didn't even want to be a part of that, and a whole lot of money was at stake. *Several millions!*

John had still not had a chance to spend as much money as other high-priced entertainers were spending. He was still pretty simplistic about his monetary needs. But I told Chelsea that I didn't want to be involved in the reading of the will.

She said, "No sir, no *sir*! You *have* to be involved. Nobody knows more about John's business estate than *you* do. Not even Tangela. I mean, *you* helped to *build* most of it."

I shook my head and said, "I'm not concerned about that, Chelsea, and I'm *not* going. And that's *final.*"

I had to put my foot down about it. Enough was enough.

I contacted the lawyer and told him that I didn't want to attend the reading, and that I was not really interested in John's estate. The lawyer was a laid-back brother from Alexandria, Virginia.

He said, "I understand that this is an emotional time for you, Mr. Harmon, but I think you *do* need to be a part of this."

He sounded like he was giving me inside information. I didn't know what to say to him. I didn't know if I could turn down a will statement or not. Was it legally binding? Could I sign my share over to someone else? I had to think it all through.

Before I got a chance to decide on it, I received a package at the studio in Charlotte. It was signed "from John Loverboy Williams," with his Maryland address on it.

I opened the package out of curiosity. I found several digital master recording tapes and high-bias audiotapes inside with no letter. I was on my way back to the house at the moment, so I took the tapes with me.

I asked myself in the car, *Now, do I want to do this to myself again?* I assumed that John had recorded some new songs that I hadn't heard yet, and he had set it up for me to have them, particularly with my new producer status. I wondered if his lawyer had sent them to me on the sly, but the postage stamp on the package was from Maryland, and it had John's zip code on it. Maybe he had given the package to a neighbor to mail off after his death, I don't know. I mean, John *wasn't* still alive, was he? We had just *buried* him.

The thought of John faking me out again made me want to listen to the new tape just to find out what was going on.

I slid in the first tape, marked "Loverboys," in plural, in my car system, and gave it a listen.

I turned the car system up nice and loud. John's voice came pouring out and rising up the scales with a cover of Sam Cooke's classic, *You Send Me:*

Dar-ling you-ou-ou-ou-OU-OU-OUU-ou-ou-ou-ou-ouu
se-n-nd me-e-e, you sen-n-nd m-e-e-e . . .

The first thing I thought was, *Man, John is* working *them scales*! That was
something contemporary singers didn't seem to care for, or couldn't *do*, go
up and up and *up* off of the just *one* breath. And it was nice to see John go
back to the roots of real crooning.

On the second song, the bass line rushed out at me, followed by the
opening line:

Doom, Doom-Doom, Doom, Doom, Doom . . .
Dis-stant lover-r-r-r
so many mi-i-iles away . . .

I said, "Oh, sweat, John's singing Marvin Gaye, too!" John had never
covered *anyone's* song from what I knew of, not even in practice. He always
wanted to sing his own stuff. But there he was, singing Sam Cooke's *You
Send Me*, followed by Marvin Gaye's *Distant Lover,* and he was *killing* both
of them with a full band and Tony's drums backing him up!

Man, I had to pull my car over and stop to listen to it. And John wasn't
finished yet. As soon as the Marvin Gaye cover faded out, he came back
with a cover of *Hey Love*, from the Delfonics:

Hey love, turn your head 'round
take off that frown, we're in love . . .

Not only was he singing it, but John was outdoing the original song, and
Hey Love was another *classic*! I sat there and started shaking my head with a
smile. The boy had me with the music again. What could I say?

After the Delfonics cover, John went after James Brown, *This Is a Man's
World*, going scream for scream, while adapting his own lyrics:

BUT IT DON'T MEAN A THIN-N-NG
A DAM-M-M-MN THING
without a woman who cares . . .

After that, he went right into Bill Withers's *Ain't No Sunshine:*

'Cause ain't no sunshi-i-ine when she-e-e's gone . . .

Then he covered Philadelphia International Records hits with the O'Jays' *Forever Mine*, and Teddy Pendergrass's *Love T.K.O.* I mean, the boy was on a roll with the hits! I started wondering when he had done it all. Tony had to know about it, too, because he was there on the drums, but I wanted to hear the whole tape before I called him up about it.

The next thing I knew, I was listening to that sultry opening line from Smokey Robinson's song *Ooh, Baby, Baby* that was made classic in the party scene from the movie *Cooley High:*

Ooooooh, la, la, la, lah . . .

I had never heard John sing falsetto in his *life*, but there he was doing it Smokey Robinson style:

You make mi-stakes, toooo
I'm cry-y-ying . . .

I broke out laughing like a lunatic, parked on the side of the road. I said, "This boy has lost his damn mind!" as if he was still alive with us. And he *was*! He was alive in his love for the music.

He covered Al Green's midtempo classic, *I'm So Tired of Being Alone*, and then Norman Conners's beautiful hit *You Are My Starship*. And no way in the *world* was I ready for him to do a duet with Atlanta's Monica, covering Rick James and Teena Marie's *Fire and Desire*. No *way* was I ready for that! Monica held her water to John, too, singing her heart out:

. . . it was pa-a-a-a-ain before pleasur-r-re
that was my claim to fame . . .

The last song on John's tape of covers was Lenny Williams's long and dramatic *'Cause I Love You*, which was a *perfect* match for John, singing it *his* way. John sang it with less crying and more sensuality that made the song feel more as if he was reminiscing on *lovemaking* than *losing* love:

Baby, I'm thinking of you
trying to be more of a man for you . . .

The song made me think back to John's early days with Tangela.

I finally drove home and tracked Tony down on his cell phone. I asked him about the cover songs and he just started laughing.

He said, "Yeah, man, John was trippin' off that shit. He had the Rhino CDs and some other old-school shit."

I asked Tony, "How long did it take y'all to record all that?" I was feeling energized again and out of my glum mood. Good music was something *else*! It could change your whole state of mind around!

Tony said, "I wasn't on all them songs, man. John was doing that shit for *months*. And he was paying musicians like *ten G's* a song to play for him in real time. And I kept asking him what he was gonna use it for, you know? But he kept talking about, 'This is for my personal collection, man. This is for my personal collection.'

"So, you know, I told him, 'I don't *need* the money, man. You call *me* when you ready to do your own songs.' And then he started doing all this old black-and-blue soul shit. And some of them were hittin', you know? But after a while, I said, 'John, nobody wanna listen to a whole album of this sad shit, man. Throw some real jams up in there.'"

I listened to Tony and said, "Black-and-blue soul, hunh? That sounds all right."

I don't know, it just had a ring to it. Black-and-blue soul.

Tony said, "Yeah, it's all in there. He was recording all kinds of stuff, but he didn't want to put it out. And I said, 'Man, you gon' get like Prince with a whole lot of shit that you can't use if you don't put another album out soon.' I mean, you know how fast songs can get old sometimes, D. You gotta throw 'em out there in the time that's hot."

I hung up the phone with Tony and pulled out another one of John's tapes. This one was labeled "John Williams." So I went to listen to that one. The first two songs, *Why?* and *Calling Me*, I had heard already. They were the diary songs of John's last years. They represented just what Tony was talking about with his black-and-blue soul comment.

John also had written a midtempo song for Big Joe called *Gunshots*, where he sang:

> . . . *and I heard gun-shots*
> *over yon-der*
> *I heard gun-shots*
> *and my nig-ga-a-a was gone* . . .

It reminded me of the blues all right, and it was *funky*, man. John *worked it*! And I couldn't complain about the N-word too much, because people were still using it, *especially* down in the South. John was just being real about it.

He had another funky jam called *Like Jesus*, using loud hand claps and a swinging bass groove:

> *They got me on the cross like Je-e-e-sus*
> *They got me on the cross like Je-e-e-sus . . .*

I mean, the song had my head bobbing and all, but I still didn't know how it would go over on an R&B album in the year 2001. Tony had a point: who would really want to listen to that? I just wasn't sure.

John stole another chapter from James Brown's book with a wild groove of temptation and indulgence called *Gots ta Have It*. Tony was heavy on the drums, with a driving bass line, guitar, and horn riffs backing him up, while John sang:

> *I GOTS TA HA-A-AVE IT*
> *TAT, Ba-Doomp, Boomp-TAT*
> *GI'ME THE HONEY, THE MONEY, AND DRUG-G-GS*
> *I GOTS TA HA-A-AVE IT*
> *TAT, Ba-Doomp, Boomp-TAT*
> *GI'ME THE HONEY, THE MONEY, AND DRUG-G-GS*
> *AND YOU CAN GE-E-ET IT*
> *TAT, Ba-Doomp . . .*
> *JUS' OPEN ON UP-P-P, AND GI'ME YOUR SOUL . . .*

I laughed, man, even though the song wasn't anything to laugh about. It reminded me of a psychedelic seventies song from Jimi Hendrix or Sly and the Family Stone or something. It was just *wild*, man! But it surely made you want to keep listening to it over and over again, just like a good temptation was supposed to do. That John was *crafty*.

Of course, he *had* to have a few love songs in the mix, and this one song called *Hold Me Down* was a real *baby maker*. I mean, *seriously*!

John got into this thing, man, and started yelling and sweet-talking at the same time:

> *HOLD ME DOWN*
> *don't let me le-e-eave you, baby*
> *HOLD ME DOWN*
> *don't let me LE-E-EAVE TO-NIGHT . . .*
>
> *Jus' HOLD ME DOWN*

don't let me be-e-e mean, baby
HOLD ME DOWN
with your swe-e-e-et, sweet, sweet-sweet-sweet . . .

I started laughing so hard that my rib cage began to hurt. I mean, I knew *exactly* what he was talking about. When you have a woman with that "swe-e-e-et, sweet, sweet-sweet-sweet," boy, you don't have to *say* nothing else! The lyrics were under*stood*!

John had a mellow blues song that even played with that third-person-narration stuff that so many stars get wrapped up into, called *Blame It on the Loverboy.* It was as if *John Williams* was not to blame for the problems. I didn't laugh at that one, though. That song opened up some old wounds of mine. I mean, it sounded like he was singing it just for me:

I was not the one
you had so much fun with
and I was not the one
who turned you out.
Girl, I was not the one
your man was gunnin' for.
No, I was not the one
who made you wet.
Just blame it on the Lover-boy . . .

I wasn't laughing at that one. Not at all. And the serious mood of that song set me up for what was coming next. Tony kicked it off with the drums, followed by John's slow lyrics, an upright blues bass, a piano, soft horns, and doo-wop backup singers:

Tit-tit-TAT-tit-tit-tit-TAT-tit . . .
Dooo you-u-u kno-o-o-ow
(DOOO YOU-U-U KNO-O-OH-OH)
how I fe-e-e-el
(HOW I FEEL-E-EEL)
You-u-u don-n-n't kno-o-oh-oh
(YOU-U-U DON-N-N'T KNO-O-OW).

Then the music stopped for John's solo:

'Cause what I fe-e-e-el is too re-e-e-eal for tho-o-o-ose

who don't know the so-o-o-oul . . .

The bass followed John right back into the song, with the soft horns, the piano, Tony's drums, and an added touch of conga drums that John rarely used. He got into the first verse and broke things down with one of the deepest grooves that I had heard in *years!* I mean, when you hear a song that got *it*, you *know it!* And *Do You Know* was the *ONE!*

John sang:

I've been around the world
cruisin' fancy cars with pretty girls
and I've screamed from the mountains high
and drank from the coldest fountains
but you don't know my pain
and the things that make me in-sane.

The conga drums made you think back to the roots and souls of all black people:

Ba-Doop-Doop-Doop-Doop-Doop-Doop . . .

The upright bass made you think of the Southern blues:

You-u-u don-n-n't kno-o-ow . . .

The piano and horns made you think about the days of Harlem's jazz:

Do you know my pa-a-ain . . .

Tony's drums brought it all home and kept the pace for the hip-hop generation:

Tit, Doomp-Doomp, TAT
Doomp-Doomp
Tit, Doomp-Doomp, TAT
Doomp-Doomp . . .

And then John laced the lyrics with that vocal drug of his:

And all you seem to know

is what you heard about me
on some show, or seen on the tube
but you don't know the things
that I've been goin' through
only She knows, my Merciful Lor-r-rd . . .

Ba-Doop-Doop-Doop-Doop-Doop-Doop . . .
Tit-TAT
Dooo you-u-u kno-o-o-ow
(DOOO YOU-U-U KNO-O-OH-OH)
how I fe-e-e-el
(HOOW I FEEL-E-EEL)
You-u-u don-n-n't kno-o-oh-oh
(YOU-U-U DON-N-N'T KNO-O-OW)
'cause what I fe-e-e-el is too re-e-e-eal . . .

And if ya' THINK ya' kno-o-ow
how I-I-I feel
then PRAY FOR ME-E-E
'cause She kno-o-o-o-ows . . .

Ba-Doop-Doop-Doop-Doop-Doop-Doop . . .

It finally hit me, man. While I listened to *Do You Know?* alone in my North Carolina house, my eyes started to get wet. John was *SINGING TO ME, MAN!* He was singing a folk-gospel-blues song with a sixties doo-wop and hip-hop swing all wrapped up in one. That boy was plain *genius!*

O-o-oh, my Merciful Lor-r-rd
I KNOW I'VE SINNED
AGAIN AND AGAIN
WILL YOU FORGIVE ME
I'M COMIN' HOME
PLEASE MEET ME AT THE GATES
'cause You kno-o-o-o-o-ow . . .

Ba-Doop-Doop-Doop-Doop-Doop-Doop . . .

Aw, man, I broke down and cried like a big *punk*. I even had snot coming out of my nose I was crying so badly. Then I started talking to myself and sounding crazy: "I'LL DO IT, MAN! I'LL PUT IT OUT! *BLACK AND BLUE SOUL!* I'LL DO WHATEVER YOU WANT ME TO DO, BOY! *AWWW, MANNN! I MISS YOU, BOY! I MISS YOU, MANNN!*"

I don't know when Chelsea and the kids walked in on me, but they caught me crying all over the place and talking to myself like that.

Imani cried, "DADDY! DADDY!" I must have scared the life out of her. Chelsea just grabbed on to me and held on with Darin Jr. at her side.

I said almost in a whisper, "I miss that boy, Chelsea. I just miss him, man."

She said, "I know, baby. We *all* miss him. We *all* do! And we're gonna name our second son John L. Harmon. We're gonna name him after John. We love him, too, baby. We *all* love him. And we *forgive him.* He's a part of us now."

She held my head up and looked into my face with her own tears falling. She said, "John brought us together, Darin. And he made us *strong.* And we thank him. We *thank him!*"

. . . who turned us black and blue.

My boy John was gone in the body, but not in the spirit. His spirit was still alive and thriving, inspiring thousands of new fans to rush out to record stores and buy up his backlist from Old School Records.

John had done it! He had set everything up to secure his position as a legendary musician. But I still didn't believe that he had to *die* to do it. He had cheated us all out of much more that he could have written and performed.

I went ahead and attended the reading of his will, and John had named me as the sole authority over all of his music publishing rights. Man, that was a BIG responsibility! John had written, produced, and recorded close to a hundred songs, and nearly *half* of them were still unreleased! But he knew that I could handle it, and I could. So I just had to prepare myself for the extra workload.

John split the bulk of his money between his mother and Tangela, but after taxes, his estate was not worth as much as I thought it was. I guess John had been spending more money than I thought with his habits, but he was still valued in the low millions. He gave his Korg keyboard not to his mother, who had bought it for him, but to Tony, who had helped him to produce seven number-one hits and four top-ten hits in only three albums. And with the new interest in John's backlist, they had sold close to *20 million* albums together worldwide, and the sales were *still coming*! Of course, they could have done even more, and I planned on making it happen with the many unreleased songs that I had in my possession.

In his will, John also wanted us to set up music scholarship programs to be honored in his name at Garinger High School in Charlotte and at North Carolina A&T in Greensboro. That was very positive of him. But on the negative side, we had at least five civil lawsuits filed against John and his estate, including one from the girl who he had choked. And they were all asking for more money than John actually had.

"He did this and that to me, and I want *fifty million*."

It was ridiculous!

So I had to suck it up and get busy for my boy again, just like old times. I decided to turn down a new deal with Old School Records and sign with the parent company at BMG for John's unreleased songs, mainly because of all of the help and early advice that Chester DeBerry had given us. I mean, it only seemed right for me to sign there. So we rushed a million singles of what I decided would be the first release of John's *Black and Blue Soul* LP, *Just Say No!* from the Midnights. The radio stations and record stores were already begging us for it.

I sent a copy of John's *Loverboys* covers to Sister Williams, in the hope that it would soothe her spirits to hear her son singing the classics that she had listened to. But I couldn't really count on it. It was just wishful thinking. My mother made a stronger effort to comfort Sister Williams in her loss, though, and that was a good thing, because I had my own family and business to think about.

Tony and Tangela still planned to play an active part in the music industry, and we vowed to help each other out whenever possible. The industry just seemed too addictive to try to get away from. Music making was universal, man. It was *universal*!

Over the next few weeks, I went about organizing the entire *Black and Blue Soul* album, beginning with the CD design. I took the best recent photo that John had taken while at the Maryland Adult Well House before he died, and we transposed it against a shadowy black-and-blue background. Then we printed the title in white script, BLACK AND BLUE SOUL, with JOHN "LOVERBOY" WILLIAMS in plain bold text.

The plan was to release a total of six singles from the twelve-song LP. That was a lot of releases, but I wanted to expand John's music to several markets. *Just Say No!* was set for gospel and R&B charts, then I planned to release *Do You Know?*, the soulful blues song, on the smooth groove adult stations. *Hold Me Down*, the baby maker, would go to R&B and pop top forty. *Blame It on the Loverboy*, the blues-folk song, would go to blues stations and possibly some country-folk stations. Then we would release *Gots ta Have It* to the underground hip-hop clubs for its big beat and wild energy. I was sure that hip-hoppers would want to sample it in some way. I even thought about taking that one to some rock stations, for a hip-rock crossover. Then we would wrap the album up by placing a final up-tempo song called *Sweat It Up* on the R&B

and pop charts around the Christmas and New Year's season to close out the year. We were just going to flood the airwaves with John's versatile genius, Jay-Z style, and see how many more believers we could convert.

In the news, John had plenty of stories that were coming out that talked about his life and times as a musician, love crooner, writer, producer, and of course as a ladies' man and drug user. I tried to ignore the negative stuff, but I did read a few of the more positive stories. I even wanted to use a quote from the Boston-bred rapper, Guru, that I read in a *Boston Globe* newspaper article that Chelsea had brought to my attention.

Guru was the vocal half of the hip-hop group Gang Starr. He had performed a song with John a year ago called *Late Night Serenade* that was nothing but more genius. In the newspaper article, Guru commented that John was a much deeper cat than most singers and musicians are allowed to be nowadays.

He said, "The industry has watered down a lot of the heavier music of this era to make chart music. So everybody's swimming in shallow waters. And then a cat like Loverboy comes along with *his* music, and he just *drowns* you in it. The only thing is, most of the listeners have gotten so used to the shallow stuff that they don't even know when they're drowning."

I wanted to use a piece of Guru's quote inside of the CD copy for the album. So we printed, "A cat like Loverboy comes along with *his* music, and he just *drowns* you in it."

We also got permission to use Quincy Jones's words at the awards show: "Each generation produces their own legendary figures" . . . John Loverboy Williams is *this* generation's legend.

We set the album release date for Tuesday, September 4, 2001. We were all ready to go by that summer, releasing John's songs for different charts. My third child and second son was also due that summer, on Thursday, July 26. Chelsea and I had agreed on naming him John L. Harmon after my lifelong boy.

The week before my second son was born, to be named after John, I planned to visit John's grave site in Charlotte, with a bottle of expensive wine. It couldn't have been a better day when I decided to do it either. It was bright, hot, and sunny. So I waited until early afternoon when it was a little cooler. I wore a white T-shirt and blue jeans, down-to-earth gear, just for my boy.

I poured out a spill of the wine on John's grave and said, "Here's for my brother who ain't here. Or at least not here in the body."

Then I smiled and took a drink straight from the bottle. It would have been corny if I had brought glasses. What *real* boys drink out of glasses?

I said, "John, we got the album all ready for you, man. *Black and Blue Soul.* I got that idea from Tony. I knew he was good for something."

I started laughing and stopped myself.

I said, "Oh, you want some more wine. Aw'ight." I poured some more wine on his grave and said, "Don't get drunk on me, boy. And don't get *me* drunk. I gotta drive back home to the family in one piece. We got little John L. coming next week."

I said, "Yeah, man, and the L. in his name just stands for L. It's just an initial. Because ah . . . we don't mean no offense, man, but Chelsea and I decided that there's only *one* Loverboy, and that's *you.* So our boy is just L, like L.L. Cool J."

I thought about that and said, "Well . . . maybe I want to take that back. Because L.L. ain't been known for turning down the *ladies* either."

I started laughing again. I didn't feel silly, though. I was talking to my boy, man. I felt good that day.

I said, "Your mom called me up recently, man, and thanked me. I mean, I don't know if you would have wanted me to or not, but I sent her a copy of them oldies jams that you recorded just to see if she would respond to it. And you know, she didn't say much, man, but a thank-you was good enough for me. That makes me know that she acknowledges that you were a tight singer . . . whether she agreed with your lifestyle or not."

I drank a sip and shrugged my shoulders. I said, "I can't explain your mother, man, no more than *you* can. She's just . . . she's just hard to crack, man. I mean, my kids might feel the same way about me and Chelsea one day, thinkin' that *we* don't make any sense."

I poured some more of the wine on his grave and said, "Yeah, and your *pop* is a trip, too, man. He almost caused a *riot* at the funeral. Then I hear he went back home and came clean to his congregation in Atlanta about being your father. And they messed around and *forgave* him for it. In fact, the younger congregation members think that Reverend Stark is cooler now because he *is* your father. Ain't that crazy, man? If he really deserved forgiveness, then he should have come clean while you were still alive."

I shook my head and said, "Stuff like that can only happen in the black church, man. You know them white churches ain't going for that. But you know, they ain't perfect either. They sweep their dirt under the rug just like any other church. They say a few Hail Mary's and Our Father's and it's all forgotten. So Chelsea tells us to keep all of our eyes open when we go, man. She said we not gon' be *deaf, dumb,* and *blind* Christians. We gon' keep our eyes *open.*"

I said, "You feel me, man?" and I took another drink.

I started reminiscing on our college years and North Carolina A&T, and I broke out laughing.

I said, "Remember that morning, man, when you first got laid at A&T? And I asked you if . . . you know, if you had bust one? And you told me, 'I don't know. What it feel like?'"

I laughed hard and said, "You was *crazy*, boy! What it *feel* like? And then when it happened for you, you told me, 'It felt like my whole *insides* was squeezing out of my thing.'"

Tears started running out of my eyes, I was laughing so hard.

I said, "And then you ain't take no shower that first time, thinking that I was gon' *smell you*. But you learned how to do your thing, man."

I stopped myself and said, "Maybe you learned *too* well." Then I poured him another spill before I took another drink for myself.

I said, "Yeah, we need to drink to that. We need to drink to . . . overdoing it. Because you just can't have too much of a good thing, man. That just ruins it. And it makes you forget about the more *important* stuff in life. Like having a real family. What I got now . . . You know what I mean?"

I said, "I guess now you do." I shrugged my shoulders and said, "I'm just being real, man. I'm just being real."

I said, "But brothers gonna work it out, John. Remember that song from the *Mack* sound track, man, Willie Hutch and them? And you had the same name as in the movie, right? We were trippin' off of that: '*Brothers gonna work it out. Brothers gonna work it out.*'

"I know, I know, I can't sing like you, man . . . '*BIG MOM-MA! BIG MOM-MAAA . . . TO-NIGHT IS YOURRR NIGHT!*'"

I laughed and said, "Boy, I thought you were *crazy* when you made up that song. But they still rock it in the clubs, so I guess you knew what you were doin', hunh? But we gon' work it out though, John. We gon' get this new album out with BMG, man, and we just gon' work it out."

Before I knew it, something took over me. I didn't feel good about being there anymore. I felt empty, man, all in one quick motion. Was I drunk with no food in my stomach? I didn't know. I just felt sick and alone, all out of nowhere. Then the tears started running from my eyes again while I tried to hold myself together.

I took a deep breath and said, "Nah, I'm gon' hold it together, man. What kind of a man keeps crying all of the time anyway? That ain't no real man. I got kids to raise. I mean, I just . . ."

I started rocking and swaying, hearing John's song in my head:

Dooo you-u-u kno-o-o-ow
(DOOO YOU-U-U KNO-O-OH-OH)
how I fe-e-e-el
(HOW I FEEL-E-EEL) . . .

I broke down and said, "Aw, man, you *killin' me*, man! You *killin' me*, JOHN! I'm hearing music melodies, and seeing visions, and videos. But I *love you*, boy!"

I looked down at his grave and repeated myself louder. "I said, *I LOVE YOU, BOY!*"

Then I calmed down. And I told him on a more thoughtful note, "I gotta tell my son how he got his name now. I gotta tell him about your legacy, man. And hope that he can put all of the pieces together . . . you know, about the *lessons* in life. 'Cause we all gotta pick that road to travel, man. And can't nobody pick it for you. Can't *nobody* pick it for you."

Then I just . . . started shaking the wine overtop of John's grave as if we had just won the Super Bowl together. I mean, he had become a *legend*, man! A *soul* singer! *MY BOY!*

Ma-a-ay I-I-I hol-l-ld your-r-r han-an-an-n-nd
Bloomp, bloomp, bloomp, bloomp, bloomp, bloomp, bloomp-bloomp-bloomp . . .

Acknowledgments

First and foremost, I'd like to thank Mr. Eric Monte for writing the screenplay for the classic urban American film, *Cooley High*. Much respect, big brother. I'll make sure that they know your name. ERIC MONTE!
I'd like to thank my initial readers, Pamela Artis—as always—and Corey B. King for your advice and guidance on the text. I'd like to thank Vance De-Bose, Bill Jolly, Johnny Chrome, and my new right-hand-man attorney, Keino Campbell, for your valuable information on the music industry.

I'd like to thank my great editors, Geoffrey Kloske and Cherise Grant, my top-notch artist Christopher B. Clarke, my visionary art department Jackie Seow and Rochelle Jackson, my out-of-the-box publicity department Aileen Boyle and Rebecca Davis, my make-noise-at-all-costs advertising with Mark Speer, the keep-pushing-me-to-the-top sales department, and to all of the people who I don't get a chance to talk to every day—I still love you guys. I'd also like to thank the two big chiefs who push all of the buttons that allow me to keep doing what I'm doing at Simon & Schuster, Carolyn Reidy and David Rosenthal. You guys have given me a fair deal. Even-steven. Nicole Graev for making sure that I receive all of my important mail and faxes on time. And copy editor Isolde C. Sauer.

I'd like to thank the magazines, newspapers, and radio stations who were kind enough to give me any itty-bitty piece of your space or time. I know how you guys like to only give it up to the "important people." Hopefully, I'll be there one day. And to all of the distributors, retail stores, and book vendors who continue to stock, push, and report my book sales each new year. Now you guys just have to order more, *more*, and MORE!

I'd like to give a big shout out to all of my family members and good friends, who have remained in my corner—and me in yours. And last but not least, I'd like to thank all of the passionate *readers* out there who continue to support my work. For the record, I want to let you guys know that I *do not* plan to merely entertain you with my hard work and toil. I plan to enlighten, inspire, educate, and wake up all of the sleepers out there to the true realities of our cultural world. Nor do I plan to be just "one of" the many writers who you support. I plan to be "one of *the best.*" And with your continued support and word of mouth, we want to push the folks in Hollywood to start paying serious attention to us for future films.

And it don't stop. And it *won't* stop. So I'll see you at the book stores and libraries at the same place, same time next year, for the publication of *Leslie*, an urban horror story, by yours truly—Omar Tyree.

P.S.: I'm still doin' it, Mom! I'm still doin' it! All the way to the top!

About the Author

Omar Tyree is an author, journalist, lecturer, and poet. His books include *Flyy Girl*, *For the Love of Money*, *A Do Right Man*, *Sweet St. Louis*, *Single Mom*, *Capital City*, and *BattleZone*. He lives in Charlotte, North Carolina.

To learn more about Omar Tyree, visit his Web site at www.OmarTyree.com.

More powerful fiction available in paperback from *Essence* bestselling author Omar Tyree

Just Say No!
0-684-87294-3

For the Love of Money
0-684-87292-7

Sweet St. Louis
0-684-85611-5

Single Mom
0-684-85593-3

A Do Right Man
0-684-84803-1

Flyy Girl
0-684-83566-5

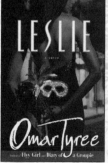

Leslie
0-7432-2870-7

Diary of a Groupie
0-7432-2871-5

SIMON & SCHUSTER
PAPERBACKS
A VIACOM COMPANY